T0354030

THE
JEEVES OMNIBUS
Volume 2

Books by P. G. Wodehouse

THE
JEEVES OMNIBUS
Volume 2

P. G. Wodehouse

Hutchinson
London

First published in this collection 1990
© in this collection the Trustees of the P.G. Wodehouse Estate 1989
Carry on Jeeves © P.G. Wodehouse 1925
Right Ho, Jeeves © P.G. Wodehouse 1934
Joy in the Morning © P.G. Wodehouse 1947

All rights reserved

41

This book is sold subject to the condition that it shall not, by way of trade
or otherwise, be lent, resold, hired out, or otherwise circulated without
the publisher's prior consent in any form of binding or cover other
than that in which it is published and without a similar condition
including this condition being imposed on the subsequent purchaser

The Random House Group Limited
20 Vauxhall Bridge Road, London SW1V 2SA

Random House Australia (Pty) Limited
20 Alfred Street, Milsons Point, Sydney
New South Wales 2061, Australia

Random House New Zealand Limited
18 Poland Road, Glenfield
Auckland 10, New Zealand

Random House (Pty) Limited
Isle of Houghton, Corner of Boundary Road & Carse O'Gowrie,
Houghton 2198, South Africa

Random House Publishers India Private Limited
301 World Trade Tower, Hotel Intercontinental Grand Complex,
Barakhamba Lane, New Delhi 110 001, India

Reprinted 1991, 1992 (twice), 1999, 2006 (twice)

The Random House Group Limited Reg. No. 954009

www.randomhouse.co.uk

A CIP catalogue record for this book is available
from the British Library
Penguin Random House is committed to a sustainable future for
our business, our readers and our planet. This book is made from
Forest Stewardship Council® certified paper.

Printed and bound in Great Britain by Clays Ltd, Elcograf S.p.A.

ISBN 9780091745745
Typeset by Pure Tech Corporation, Pondicherry, Indi

Contents

RIGHT HO, JEEVES

To
Raymond Needham, K.C.
With Affection and Admiration

1

'Jeeves,' I said, 'may I speak frankly?'

'Certainly, sir.'

'What I have to say may wound you.'

'Not at all, sir.'

'Well, then – '

No – wait. Hold the line a minute. I've gone off the rails.

I don't know if you have had the same experience, but the snag I always come up against when I'm telling a story is this dashed difficult problem of where to begin it. It's a thing you don't want to go wrong over, because one false step and you're sunk. I mean, if you fool about too long at the start, trying to establish atmosphere, as they call it, and all that sort of rot, you fail to grip and the customers walk out on you.

Get off the mark, on the other hand, like a scalded cat, and your public is at a loss. It simply raises its eyebrows, and can't make out what you're talking about.

And in opening my report of the complex case of Gussie Fink-Nottle, Madeline Bassett, my cousin Angela, my Aunt Dahlia, my Uncle Thomas, young Tuppy Glossop and the cook, Anatole, with the above spot of dialogue, I see that I have made the second of these two floaters.

I shall have to hark back a bit. And taking it for all in all and weighing this against that, I suppose the affair may be said to have had its inception, if inception is the word I want, with that visit of mine to Cannes. If I hadn't gone to Cannes, I shouldn't have met the Bassett or bought that white mess jacket, and Angela wouldn't have met her shark, and Aunt Dahlia wouldn't have played baccarat.

Yes, most decidedly, Cannes was the *point d'appui*.

Right ho, then. Let me marshal my facts.

I went to Cannes – leaving Jeeves behind, he having intimated that he did not wish to miss Ascot – round about the beginning of June. With me travelled my Aunt Dahlia and her daughter Angela. Tuppy

Glossop, Angela's betrothed, was to have been of the party, but at the last moment couldn't get away. Uncle Tom, Aunt Dahlia's husband, remained at home, because he can't stick the South of France at any price.

So there you have the layout – Aunt Dahlia, Cousin Angela and self off to Cannes round about the beginning of June.

All pretty clear so far, what?

We stayed at Cannes about two months, and except for the fact that Aunt Dahlia lost her shirt at baccarat and Angela nearly got inhaled by a shark while aquaplaning, a pleasant time was had by all.

On July twenty-fifth, looking bronzed and fit, I accompanied aunt and child back to London. At seven p.m. on July twenty-sixth we alighted at Victoria. And at seven-twenty or thereabouts we parted with mutual expressions of esteem – they to shove off in Aunt Dahlia's car to Brinkley Court, her place in Worcestershire, where they were expecting to entertain Tuppy in a day or two; I to go to the flat, drop my luggage, clean up a bit, and put on the soup and fish preparatory to pushing round to the Drones for a bite of dinner.

And it was while I was at the flat, towelling the torso after a much-needed rinse, that Jeeves, as we chatted of this and that – picking up the threads, as it were – suddenly brought the name of Gussie Fink-Nottle into the conversation.

As I recall it, the dialogue ran something as follows:

SELF: Well, Jeeves, here we are, what?
JEEVES: Yes, sir.
SELF: I mean to say, home again.
JEEVES: Precisely, sir.
SELF: Seems ages since I went away.
JEEVES: Yes, sir.
SELF: Have a good time at Ascot?
JEEVES: Most agreeable, sir.
SELF: Win anything?
JEEVES: Quite a satisfactory sum, thank you, sir.
SELF: Good. Well, Jeeves, what news on the Rialto? Anybody been phoning
         or calling or anything during my abs.?
JEEVES: Mr Fink-Nottle, sir, has been a frequent caller.

I stared. Indeed, it would not be too much to say that I gaped.
'Mr Fink-Nottle?'
'Yes, sir.'
'You don't mean Mr Fink-Nottle?'
'Yes, sir.'

'But Mr Fink-Nottle's not in London?'

'Yes, sir.'

'Well, I'm blowed.'

And I'll tell you why I was blowed. I found it scarcely possible to give credence to his statement. This Fink-Nottle, you see, was one of those freaks you come across from time to time during life's journey who can't stand London. He lived year in and year out, covered with moss, in a remote village down in Lincolnshire, never coming up even for the Eton and Harrow match. And when I asked him once if he didn't find the time hung a bit heavy on his hands, he said, no, because he had a pond in his garden and studied the habits of newts.

I couldn't imagine what could have brought the chap up to the great city. I would have been prepared to bet that as long as the supply of newts didn't give out, nothing could have shifted him from that village of his.

'Are you sure?'

'Yes, sir.'

'You got the name correctly? Fink-Nottle?'

'Yes, sir.'

'Well, it's the most extraordinary thing. It must be five years since he was in London. He makes no secret of the fact that the place gives him the pip. Until now, he has always stayed glued to the country, completely surrounded by newts.'

'Sir?'

'Newts, Jeeves. Mr Fink-Nottle has a strong newt complex. You must have heard of newts. Those little sort of lizard things that charge about in ponds.'

'Oh, yes, sir. The aquatic members of the family *Salamandridae* which constitute the genus *Molge*.'

'That's right. Well, Gussie has always been a slave to them. He used to keep them at school.'

'I believe young gentlemen frequently do, sir.'

'He kept them in his study in a kind of glass-tank arrangement, and pretty niffy the whole thing was, I recall. I suppose one ought to have been able to see what the end would be even then, but you know what boys are. Careless, heedless, busy about our own affairs, we scarcely gave this kink in Gussie's character a thought. We may have exchanged an occasional remark about it taking all sorts to make a world, but nothing more. You can guess the sequel. The trouble spread.'

'Indeed, sir?'

'Absolutely, Jeeves. The craving grew upon him. The newts got him. Arrived at man's estate, he retired to the depths of the country and gave his life up to these dumb chums. I suppose he used to tell himself that he could take them or leave them alone, and then found – too late – that he couldn't.'

'It is often the way, sir.'

'Too true, Jeeves. At any rate, for the last five years he has been living at this place of his down in Lincolnshire, as confirmed a species-shunning hermit as ever put fresh water in the tank every second day and refused to see a soul. That's why I was so amazed when you told me he had suddenly risen to the surface like this. I still can't believe it. I am inclined to think that there must be some mistake, and that this bird who has been calling here is some different variety of Fink-Nottle. The chap I know wears horn-rimmed spectacles and has a face like a fish. How does that check up with your data?'

'The gentleman who came to the flat wore horn-rimmed spectacles, sir.'

'And looked like something on a slab?'

'Possibly there was a certain suggestion of the piscine, sir.'

'Then it must be Gussie, I suppose. But what on earth can have brought him up to London?'

'I am in a position to explain that, sir. Mr Fink-Nottle confided to me his motive in visiting the metropolis. He came because the young lady is here.'

'Young lady?'

'Yes, sir.'

'You don't mean he's in love?'

'Yes, sir.'

'Well, I'm dashed. I'm really dashed. I positively am dashed, Jeeves.'

And I was too. I mean to say, a joke's a joke, but there are limits.

Then I found my mind turning to another aspect of this rummy affair. Conceding the fact that Gussie Fink-Nottle, against all the ruling of the form book, might have fallen in love, why should he have been haunting my flat like this? No doubt the occasion was one of those when a fellow needs a friend, but I couldn't see what had made him pick on me.

It wasn't as if he and I were in any way bosom. We had seen a lot of each other at one time, of course, but in the last two years I hadn't had so much as a postcard from him.

I put all this to Jeeves:

'Odd, his coming to me. Still, if he did, he did. No argument about that. It must have been a nasty jar for the poor perisher when he found I wasn't here.'

'No, sir. Mr Fink-Nottle did not call to see you, sir.'

'Pull yourself together, Jeeves. You've just told me that this is what he has been doing, and assiduously, at that.'

'It was I with whom he was desirous of establishing communication, sir.'

'You? But I didn't know you had ever met him.'

'I had not had that pleasure until he called here, sir. But it appears that Mr Sipperley, a fellow student with whom Mr Fink-Nottle had been at the university, recommended him to place his affairs in my hands.'

The mystery had conked. I saw all. As I dare say you know, Jeeves's reputation as a counsellor has long been established among the cognoscenti, and the first move of any of my little circle on discovering themselves in any form of soup is always to roll round and put the thing up to him. And when he's got A out of a bad spot, A puts B on to him. And then, when he has fixed up B, B sends C along. And so on, if you get my drift, and so forth.

That's how these big consulting practices like Jeeves's grow. Old Sippy, I knew, had been deeply impressed by the man's efforts on his behalf at the time when he was trying to get engaged to Elizabeth Moon, so it was not to be wondered at that he should have advised Gussie to apply. Pure routine, you might say.

'Oh, you're acting for him, are you?'

'Yes, sir.'

'Now I follow. Now I understand. And what is Gussie's trouble?'

'Oddly enough, sir, precisely the same as that of Mr Sipperley when I was enabled to be of assistance to him. No doubt you recall Mr Sipperley's predicament, sir. Deeply attached to Miss Moon, he suffered from a rooted diffidence which made it impossible for him to speak.'

I nodded.

'I remember. Yes, I recall the Sipperley case. He couldn't bring himself to the scratch. A marked coldness of the feet, was there not? I recollect you saying he was letting – what was it? – letting something do something. Cats entered into it, if I am not mistaken.'

'Letting "I dare not" wait upon "I would", sir.'

'That's right. But how about the cats?'

'Like the poor cat i' the adage, sir.'

'Exactly. It beats me how you think up these things. And Gussie, you say, is in the same posish?'

'Yes, sir. Each time he endeavours to formulate a proposal of marriage, his courage fails him.'

'And yet, if he wants this female to be his wife, he's got to say so, what? I mean, only civil to mention it.'

'Precisely, sir.'

I mused.

'Well, I suppose this was inevitable, Jeeves. I wouldn't have thought that this Fink-Nottle would ever have fallen a victim to the divine p., but, if he has, no wonder he finds the going sticky.'

'Yes, sir.'

'Look at the life he's led.'

'Yes, sir.'

'I don't suppose he has spoken to a girl for years. What a lesson this is to us, Jeeves, not to shut ourselves up in country houses and stare into glass tanks. You can't be the dominant male if you do that sort of thing. In this life, you can choose between two courses. You can either shut yourself up in a country house and stare into tanks, or you can be a dasher with the sex. You can't do both.'

'No, sir.'

I mused once more. Gussie and I, as I say, had rather lost touch, but all the same I was exercised about the poor fish, as I am about all my pals, close or distant, who find themselves treading upon Life's banana skins. It seemed to me that he was up against it.

I threw my mind back to the last time I had seen him. About two years ago, it had been. I had looked in at his place while on a motor trip, and he had put me right off my feed by bringing a couple of green things with legs to the luncheon table, crooning over them like a young mother and eventually losing one of them in the salad. That picture, rising before my eyes, didn't give me much confidence in the unfortunate goof's ability to woo and win, I must say. Especially if the girl he had earmarked was one of these tough modern thugs, all lipstick and cool, hard, sardonic eyes, as she probably was.

'Tell me, Jeeves,' I said, wishing to know the worst, 'what sort of a girl is this girl of Gussie's?'

'I have not met the young lady, sir. Mr Fink-Nottle speaks highly of her attractions.'

'Seemed to like her, did he?'

'Yes, sir.'

'Did he mention her name? Perhaps I know her.'

'She is a Miss Bassett, sir. Miss Madeline Bassett.'

'What?'

'Yes, sir.'

I was deeply intrigued.

'Egad, Jeeves! Fancy that. It's a small world, isn't it, what?'

'The young lady is an acquaintance of yours, sir?'

'I know her well. Your news has relieved my mind, Jeeves. It makes the whole thing begin to seem far more like a practical working proposition.'

'Indeed, sir?'

'Absolutely. I confess that until you supplied this information I was feeling profoundly dubious about poor old Gussie's chances of inducing any spinster of any parish to join him in the saunter down the aisle. You will agree with me that he is not everybody's money.'

'There may be something in what you say, sir.'

'Cleopatra wouldn't have liked him.'

'Possibly not, sir.'

'And I doubt if he would go any too well with Tallulah Bankhead.'

'No, sir.'

'But when you tell me that the object of his affections is Miss Bassett, why, then, Jeeves, hope begins to dawn a bit. He's just the sort of chap a girl like Madeline Bassett might scoop in with relish.'

This Bassett, I must explain, had been a fellow visitor of ours at Cannes; and as she and Angela had struck up one of those effervescent friendships which girls do strike up, I had seen quite a bit of her. Indeed, in my moodier moments it sometimes seemed to me that I could not move a step without stubbing my toe on the woman.

And what made it all so painful and distressing was that the more we met, the less did I seem able to find to say to her.

You know how it is with some girls. They seem to take the stuffing right out of you. I mean to say, there is something about their personality that paralyses the vocal cords and reduces the contents of the brain to cauliflower. It was like that with this Bassett and me; so much so that I have known occasions when for minutes at a stretch Bertram Wooster might have been observed fumbling with the tie, shuffling the feet, and behaving in all other respects in her presence like the complete dumb brick. When, therefore, she took her departure some two weeks before we did, you may readily imagine that, in Bertram's opinion, it was not a day too soon.

It was not her beauty, mark you, that thus numbed me. She was a pretty enough girl in a droopy, blonde, saucer-eyed way, but not the sort of breath-taker that takes the breath.

No, what caused this disintegration in a usually fairly fluent prattler with the sex was her whole mental attitude. I don't want to wrong anybody, so I won't go so far as to say that she actually wrote poetry, but her conversation, to my mind, was of a nature calculated to excite the liveliest suspicions. Well, I mean to say, when a girl suddenly asks you out of a blue sky if you don't sometimes feel that the stars are God's daisy chain, you begin to think a bit.

As regards the fusing of her soul and mine, therefore, there was nothing doing. But with Gussie, the posish was entirely different. The thing that had stymied me – viz. that this girl was obviously all loaded down with ideals and sentiment and what not – was quite in order as far as he was concerned.

Gussie had always been one of those dreamy, soulful birds – you can't shut yourself up in the country and live only for newts, if you're not – and I could see no reason why, if he could somehow be induced to get the low, burning words off his chest, he and the Bassett shouldn't hit it off like ham and eggs.

'She's just the type for him,' I said.

'I am most gratified to hear it, sir.'

'And he's just the type for her. In fine, a good thing and one to be pushed along with the utmost energy. Strain every nerve, Jeeves.'

'Very good, sir,' replied the honest fellow. 'I will attend to the matter at once.'

Now up to this point, as you will doubtless agree, what you might call a perfect harmony had prevailed. Friendly gossip between employer and employed, and everything as sweet as a nut. But at this juncture, I regret to say, there was an unpleasant switch. The atmosphere suddenly changed, the storm clouds began to gather, and before we knew where we were, the jarring note had come bounding on the scene. I have known this to happen before in the Wooster home.

The first intimation I had that things were about to hot up was a pained and disapproving cough from the neighbourhood of the carpet. For, during the above exchanges, I should explain, while I, having dried the frame, had been dressing in a leisurely manner, donning here a sock, there a shoe, and gradually climbing into the vest, the shirt, the tie, and the knee-length, Jeeves had been down on the lower level, unpacking my effects.

He now rose, holding a white object. And at the sight of it, I realized that another of our domestic crises had arrived, another of those unfortunate clashes of will between two strong men, and that Bertram, unless he remembered his fighting ancestors and stood up for his rights, was about to be put upon.

I don't know if you were at Cannes this summer. If you were, you will recall that anybody with any pretensions to being the life and soul of the party was accustomed to attend binges at the Casino in the ordinary evening-wear trouserings topped to the north by a white mess jacket with brass buttons. And ever since I had stepped aboard the Blue Train at Cannes station, I had been wondering on and off how mine would go with Jeeves.

In the matter of evening costume, you see, Jeeves is hidebound and reactionary. I had had trouble with him before about soft-bosomed shirts. And while these mess jackets had, as I say, been all the rage – *tout ce qu'il y a de chic* – on the Côte d'Azur, I had never concealed it from myself, even when treading the measure at the Palm Beach Casino in the one I had hastened to buy, that there might be something of an upheaval about it on my return.

I prepared to be firm.

'Yes, Jeeves?' I said. And though my voice was suave, a close observer in a position to watch my eyes would have noticed a steely glint. Nobody has a greater respect for Jeeves's intellect than I have, but this disposition of his to dictate to the hand that fed him had got, I felt, to be checked. This mess jacket was very near to my heart, and I jolly well intended to fight for it with all the vim of grand old Sieur de Wooster at the Battle of Agincourt.

'Yes, Jeeves?' I said. 'Something on your mind, Jeeves?'

'I fear that you inadvertently left Cannes in the possession of a coat belonging to some other gentleman, sir.'

I switched on the steely a bit more.

'No, Jeeves,' I said, in a level tone, 'the object under advisement is mine. I bought it out there.'

'You wore it, sir?'

'Every night.'

'But surely you are not proposing to wear it in England, sir?'

I saw that we had arrived at the nub.

'Yes, Jeeves.'

'But, sir – '

'You were saying, Jeeves?'

'It is quite unsuitable, sir.'

'I do not agree with you, Jeeves. I anticipate a great popular success for this jacket. It is my intention to spring it on the public tomorrow at Pongo Twistleton's birthday party, where I confidently expect it to be one long scream from start to finish. No argument, Jeeves. No discussion. Whatever fantastic objection you may have taken to it, I wear this jacket.'

'Very good, sir.'

He went on with his unpacking. I said no more on the subject. I had won the victory, and we Woosters do not triumph over a beaten foe. Presently, having completed my toilet, I bade the man a cheery farewell and in generous mood suggested that, as I was dining out, why didn't he take the evening off and go to some improving picture or something. Sort of olive branch, if you see what I mean.

He didn't seem to think much of it.

'Thank you, sir, I will remain in.'

I surveyed him narrowly.

'Is this dudgeon, Jeeves?'

'No, sir, I am obliged to remain on the premises. Mr Fink-Nottle informed me he would be calling to see me this evening.'

'Oh, Gussie's coming, is he? Well, give him my love.'

'Very good, sir.'

'And a whisky and soda, and so forth.'

'Very good, sir.'

'Right ho, Jeeves.'

I then set off for the Drones.

At the Drones I ran into Pongo Twistleton, and he talked so much about this forthcoming merry-making of his, of which good reports had already reached me through my correspondents, that it was nearing eleven when I got home again.

And scarcely had I opened the door when I heard voices in the sitting-room, and scarcely had I entered the sitting-room when I found that these proceeded from Jeeves and what appeared at first sight to be the Devil.

A closer scrutiny informed me that it was Gussie Fink-Nottle, dressed as Mephistopheles.

2

'What ho, Gussie,' I said.

You couldn't have told it from my manner, but I was feeling more than a bit nonplussed. The spectacle before me was enough to nonplus anyone. I mean to say, this Fink-Nottle, as I remembered him, was the sort of shy, shrinking goop who might have been expected to shake like an aspen if invited to so much as a social Saturday afternoon at the vicarage. And yet here he was, if one could credit one's senses, about to take part in a fancy-dress ball, a form of entertainment notoriously a testing experience for the toughest.

And he was attending that fancy-dress ball, mark you – not, like every other well-bred Englishman, as a Pierrot, but as Mephistopheles – this involving, as I need scarcely stress, not only scarlet tights but a pretty frightful false beard.

Rummy, you'll admit. However, one masks one's feelings. I betrayed no vulgar astonishment, but, as I say, what-hoed with civil nonchalance.

He grinned through the fungus – rather sheepishly, I thought.

'Oh, hullo, Bertie.'

'Long time since I saw you. Have a spot?'

'No, thanks. I must be off in a minute. I just came round to ask Jeeves how he thought I looked. How do you think I look, Bertie?'

Well, the answer to that, of course, was 'perfectly foul'. But we Woosters are men of tact and have a nice sense of the obligations of a host. We do not tell old friends beneath our roof-tree that they are an offence to the eyesight. I evaded the question.

'I hear you're in London,' I said carelessly.

'Oh, yes.'

'Must be years since you came up.'

'Oh, yes.'

'And now you're off for an evening's pleasure.'

He shuddered a bit. He had, I noticed, a hunted air.

'Pleasure!'

'Aren't you looking forward to this rout or revel?'

'Oh, I suppose it'll be all right,' he said, in a toneless voice. 'Anyway, I ought to be off, I suppose. The thing starts round about eleven. I told my cab to wait . . . Will you see if it's there, Jeeves?'

'Very good, sir.'

There was something of a pause after the door had closed. A certain constraint. I mixed myself a beaker, while Gussie, a glutton for punishment, stared at himself in the mirror. Finally I decided that it would be best to let him know that I was abreast of his affairs. It might be that it would ease his mind to confide in a sympathetic man of experience. I have generally found, with those under the influence, that what they want more than anything is the listening ear.

'Well, Gussie, old leper,' I said, 'I've been hearing all about you.'

'Eh?'

'This little trouble of yours. Jeeves has told me everything.'

He didn't seem any too braced. It's always difficult to be sure, of course, when a chap has dug himself in behind a Mephistopheles beard, but I fancy he flushed a trifle.

'I wish Jeeves wouldn't go gassing all over the place. It was supposed to be confidential.'

I could not permit this tone.

'Dishing up the dirt to the young master can scarcely be described as gassing all over the place,' I said, with a touch of rebuke. 'Anyway, there it is. I know all. And I should like to begin,' I said, sinking my personal opinion that the female in question was a sloppy pest in my desire to buck and encourage, 'by saying that Madeline Bassett is a charming girl. A winner, and just the sort for you.'

'You don't know her?'

'Certainly I know her. What beats me is how you ever got in touch. Where did you meet?'

'She was staying at a place near mine in Lincolnshire the week before last.'

'Yes, but even so. I didn't know you called on the neighbours.'

'I don't. I met her out for a walk with her dog. The dog had got a thorn in its foot, and when she tried to take it out, it snapped at her. So, of course, I had to rally round.'

'You extracted the thorn?'

'Yes.'

'And fell in love at first sight?'

'Yes.'

'Well, dash it, with a thing like that to give you a send-off, why didn't you cash in immediately?'

'I hadn't the nerve.'

'What happened?'

'We talked for a bit.'

'What about?'

'Oh, birds.'

'Birds? What birds?'

'The birds that happened to be hanging round. And the scenery, and all that sort of thing. And she said she was going to London, and asked me to look her up if I was ever there.'

'And even after that you didn't so much as press her hand?'

'Of course not.'

Well, I mean, it looked as though there was no more to be said. If a chap is such a rabbit that he can't get action when he's handed the thing on a plate, his case would appear to be pretty hopeless. Nevertheless, I reminded myself that this non-starter and I had been at school together. One must make an effort for an old school friend.

'Ah, well,' I said, 'we must see what can be done. Things may brighten. At any rate, you will be glad to learn that I am behind you in this enterprise. You have Bertram Wooster in your corner, Gussie.'

'Thanks, old man. And Jeeves, of course, which is the thing that really matters.'

I don't mind admitting that I winced. He meant no harm, I suppose, but I'm bound to say that this tactless speech nettled me not a little. People are always nettling me like that. Giving me to understand, I mean to say, that in their opinion Bertram Wooster is a mere cipher and that the only member of the household with brains and resources is Jeeves.

It jars on me.

And tonight it jarred on me more than usual, because I was feeling pretty dashed fed with Jeeves. Over that matter of the mess jacket, I mean. True, I had forced him to climb down, quelling him, as described, with the quiet strength of my personality, but I was still a trifle shirty at his having brought the thing up at all. It seemed to me that what Jeeves wanted was the iron hand.

'And what is he doing about it?' I inquired stiffly.

'He's been giving the position of affairs a lot of thought.'

'He has, has he?'

'It's on his advice that I'm going to this dance.'

'Why?'

'She is going to be there. In fact, it was she who sent me the ticket of invitation. And Jeeves considered – '

'And why not as a Pierrot?' I said, taking up the point which had struck me before. 'Why this break with a grand old tradition?'

'He particularly wanted me to go as Mephistopheles.'

I started.

'He did, did he? He specifically recommended that definite costume?'

'Yes.'

'Ha!'

'Eh?'

'Nothing. Just "Ha!"'

And I'll tell you why I said 'Ha!' Here was Jeeves making heavy weather about me wearing a perfectly ordinary white mess jacket, a garment not only *tout ce qu'il y a de chic*, but absolutely *de rigueur*, and in the same breath, as you might say, inciting Gussie Fink-Nottle to be a blot on the London scene in scarlet tights. Ironical, what? One looks askance at this sort of in-and-out running.

'What has he got against Pierrots?'

'I don't think he objects to Pierrots as Pierrots. But in my case he thought a Pierrot wouldn't be adequate.'

'I don't follow that.'

'He said that the costume of Pierrot, while pleasing to the eye, lacked the authority of the Mephistopheles costume.'

'I still don't get it.'

'Well, it's a matter of psychology, he said.'

There was a time when a remark like that would have had me snookered. But long association with Jeeves has developed the Wooster vocabulary considerably. Jeeves has always been a whale for the psychology of the individual, and I now follow him like a bloodhound when he snaps it out of the bag.

'Oh, psychology?'

'Yes. Jeeves is a great believer in the moral effect of clothes. He thinks I might be emboldened in a striking costume like this. He said a Pirate Chief would be just as good. In fact, a Pirate Chief was his first suggestion, but I objected to the boots.'

I saw his point. There is enough sadness in life without having fellows like Gussie Fink-Nottle going about in sea boots.

'And are you emboldened?'

'Well, to be absolutely accurate, Bertie, old man, no.'

A gust of compassion shook me. After all, though we had lost touch a bit of recent years, this man and I had once thrown inked darts at each other.

'Gussie,' I said, 'take an old friend's advice, and don't go within a mile of this binge.'

'But it's my last chance of seeing her. She's off tomorrow to stay with some people in the country. Besides, you don't know.'

'Don't know what?'

'That this idea of Jeeves's won't work. I feel a most frightful chump now, yes, but who can say whether that will not pass off when I get into a mob of other people in fancy dress. I had the same experience as a child, one year during the Christmas festivities. They dressed me up as a rabbit, and the shame was indescribable. Yet when I got to the party and found myself surrounded by scores of other children, many in costumes even ghastlier than my own, I perked up amazingly, joined freely in the revels, and was able to eat so hearty a supper that I was sick twice in the cab coming home. What I mean is, you can't tell in cold blood.'

I weighed this. It was specious, of course.

'And you can't get away from it that, fundamentally, Jeeves's idea is sound. In a striking costume like Mephistopheles, I might quite easily pull off something pretty impressive. Colour does make a difference. Look at newts. During the courting season the male newt is brilliantly coloured. It helps him a lot.'

'But you aren't a male newt.'

'I wish I were. Do you know how a male newt proposes, Bertie? He just stands in front of the female newt vibrating his tail and bending his body in a semicircle. I could do that on my head. No, you wouldn't find me grousing if I were a male newt.'

'But if you were a male newt, Madeline Bassett wouldn't look at you. Not with the eye of love, I mean.'

'She would, if she were a female newt.'

'But she isn't a female newt.'

'No, but suppose she was.'

'Well, if she was, you wouldn't be in love with her.'

'Yes, I would, if I were a male newt.'

A slight throbbing about the temples told me that this discussion had reached saturation point.

'Well, anyway,' I said, 'coming down to hard facts and cutting out all this visionary stuff about vibrating tails and what not, the salient point that emerges is that you are booked to appear at a fancy-dress ball. And I tell you out of my riper knowledge of fancy-dress balls, Gussie, that you won't enjoy yourself.'

'It isn't a question of enjoying yourself.'

'I wouldn't go.'

'I must go. I keep telling you she's off to the country tomorrow.'

I gave it up.

'So be it,' I said. 'Have it your own way . . . Yes, Jeeves?'

'Mr Fink-Nottle's cab, sir.'

'Ah? The cab, eh? . . . Your cab, Gussie.'

'Oh, the cab? Oh, right. Of course, yes, rather . . . Thanks, Jeeves . . . Well, so long, Bertie.'

And giving me the sort of weak smile Roman gladiators used to give the Emperor before entering the arena, Gussie trickled off. And I turned to Jeeves. The moment had arrived for putting him in his place, and I was all for it.

It was a little difficult to know how to begin, of course. I mean to say, while firmly resolved to tick him off, I didn't want to gash his feelings too deeply. Even when displaying the iron hand, we Woosters like to keep the thing fairly matey.

However, on consideration, I saw that there was nothing to be gained by trying to lead up to it gently. It is never any use beating about the b.

'Jeeves,' I said, 'may I speak frankly?'

'Certainly, sir.'

'What I have to say may wound you.'

'Not at all, sir.'

'Well, then, I have been having a chat with Mr Fink-Nottle, and he has been telling me about this Mephistopheles scheme of yours.'

'Yes, sir?'

'Now let me get it straight. If I follow your reasoning correctly, you think that, stimulated by being upholstered throughout in scarlet tights, Mr Fink-Nottle, on encountering the adored object, will vibrate his tail and generally let himself go with a whoop.'

'I am of the opinion that he will lose much of his normal diffidence, sir.'

'I don't agree with you, Jeeves.'

'No, sir?'

'No. In fact, not to put too fine a point upon it, I consider that of all the dashed silly, drivelling ideas I ever heard in my puff this is the most blithering and futile. It won't work. Not a chance. All you have done is to subject Mr Fink-Nottle to the nameless horrors of a fancy-dress ball for nothing. And this is not the first time this sort of thing has happened. To be quite candid, Jeeves, I have frequently noticed before now a tendency or disposition on your part to become – what's the word?'

'I could not say, sir.'

'Eloquent? No, it's not eloquent. Elusive? No, it's not elusive. It's on the tip of my tongue. Begins with an "e" and means being a jolly sight too clever.'

'Elaborate, sir?'

'That is the exact word I was after. Too elaborate, Jeeves – that is what you are frequently prone to become. Your methods are not simple, not straightforward. You cloud the issue with a lot of fancy stuff that is not of the essence. All that Gussie needs is the older-brotherly advice of a seasoned man of the world. So what I suggest is that from now onward you leave this case to me.'

'Very good, sir.'

'You lay off and devote yourself to your duties about the home.'

'Very good, sir.'

'I shall no doubt think of something quite simple and straightforward yet perfectly effective ere long. I will make a point of seeing Gussie tomorrow.'

'Very good, sir.'

'Right ho, Jeeves.'

But on the morrow all those telegrams started coming in, and I confess that for twenty-four hours I didn't give the poor chap a thought, having problems of my own to contend with.

The first of the telegrams arrived shortly after noon, and Jeeves brought it in with the before-luncheon snifter. It was from my Aunt Dahlia, operating from Market Snodsbury, a small town of sorts a mile or two along the main road as you leave her country seat.

It ran as follows:

Come at once. Travers.

And when I say it puzzled me like the dickens, I am understating it, if anything. As mysterious a communication, I considered, as was ever flashed over the wires. I studied it in a profound reverie for the best part of two dry Martinis and a dividend. I read it backwards. I read it forwards. As a matter of fact, I have a sort of recollection of even smelling it. But it still baffled me.

Consider the facts, I mean. It was only a few hours since this aunt and I had parted, after being in constant association for nearly two months. And yet here she was – with my farewell kiss still lingering on her cheek, so to speak – pleading for another reunion. Bertram Wooster is not accustomed to this gluttonous appetite for his society. Ask anyone who knows me, and they will tell you that after two months of my company, what the normal person feels is that that will about do for the present. Indeed, I have known people who couldn't stick it out for more than a few days.

Before sitting down to the well-cooked, therefore, I sent this reply:

Perplexed. Explain. Bertie.

To this I received an answer during the after-luncheon sleep:

What on earth is there to be perplexed about, ass? Come at once. Travers.

*

Three cigarettes and a couple of turns about the room, and I had my response ready:

How do you mean come at once? Regards. Bertie.

I append the comeback:

I mean come at once, you maddening halfwit. What did you think I meant? Come at once or expect an aunt's curse first post tomorrow. Love. Travers.

I then dispatched the following message, wishing to get everything quite clear:

When you say 'Come' do you mean 'Come to Brinkley Court'? And when you say 'At once' do you mean 'At once'? Fogged. At a loss. All the best. Bertie.

I sent this one off on my way to the Drones, where I spent a restful afternoon throwing cards into a top hat with some of the better element. Returning in the evening hush, I found the answer waiting for me:

Yes, yes, yes, yes, yes, yes, yes. It doesn't matter whether you understand or not. You just come at once, as I tell you, and for heaven's sake stop this back-chat. Do you think I am made of money that I can afford to send you telegrams every ten minutes. Stop being a fathead and come immediately. Love. Travers.

It was at this point that I felt the need of getting a second opinion. I pressed the bell.

'Jeeves,' I said, 'a V-shaped rumminess has manifested itself from the direction of Worcestershire. Read these,' I said, handing him the papers in the case.

He scanned them.

'What do you make of it, Jeeves?'

'I think Mrs Travers wishes you to come at once, sir.'

'You gather that too, do you?'

'Yes, sir.'

'I put the same construction on the thing. But why, Jeeves? Dash it all, she's just had nearly two months of me.'

'Yes, sir.'

'And many people consider the medium dose for an adult two days.'

'Yes, sir. I appreciate the point you raise. Nevertheless, Mrs Travers appears very insistent. I think it would be well to acquiesce in her wishes.'

'Pop down, you mean?'

'Yes, sir.'

'Well, I certainly can't go at once. I've an important conference on at the Drones tonight. Pongo Twistleton's birthday party, you remember.'

'Yes, sir.'

There was a slight pause. We were both recalling the little unpleasantness that had arisen. I felt obliged to allude to it.

'You're all wrong about that mess jacket, Jeeves.'

'These things are matters of opinion, sir.'

'When I wore it at the Casino at Cannes, beautiful women nudged one another and whispered: "Who is he?"'

'The code at Continental casinos is notoriously lax, sir.'

'And when I described it to Pongo last night, he was fascinated.'

'Indeed, sir?'

'So were all the rest of those present. One and all admitted that I had got hold of a good thing. Not a dissentient voice.'

'Indeed, sir?'

'I am convinced that you will eventually learn to love this mess jacket, Jeeves.'

'I fear not, sir.'

I gave it up. It is never any use trying to reason with Jeeves on these occasions. 'Pig-headed' is the word that springs to the lips. One sighs and passes on.

'Well, anyway, returning to the agenda, I can't go down to Brinkley Court or anywhere else yet awhile. That's final. I'll tell you what, Jeeves. Give me form and pencil, and I'll wire her that I'll be with her some time next week or the week after. Dash it all, she ought to be able to hold out without me for a few days. It only requires will-power.'

'Yes, sir.'

'Right ho, then. I'll wire "Expect me tomorrow fortnight" or words to some such effect. That ought to meet the case. Then if you will toddle round the corner and send it off, that will be that.'

'Very good, sir.'

And so the long day wore on till it was time for me to dress for Pongo's party.

Pongo had assured me, while chatting of the affair on the previous night, that this birthday binge of his was to be on a scale calculated to stagger humanity, and I must say I have participated in less fruity functions. It was well after four when I got home, and by that time I was about ready to turn in. I can just remember groping for the bed and crawling into it, and it seemed to me that the lemon had scarcely touched the pillow before I was aroused by the sound of the door opening.

I was barely ticking over, but I contrived to raise an eyelid.

'Is that my tea, Jeeves?'

'No, sir. It's Mrs Travers.'

And a moment later there was a sound like a mighty rushing wind, and the relative had crossed the threshold at fifty m.p.h. under her own steam.

4

It has been well said of Bertram Wooster that, while no-one views his flesh and blood with a keener and more remorselessly critical eye, he is nevertheless a man who delights in giving credit where credit is due. And if you have followed these memoirs of mine with the proper care, you will be aware that I have frequently had occasion to emphasize the fact that Aunt Dahlia is all right.

She is the one, if you remember, who married old Tom Travers *en secondes noces*, as I believe the expression is, the year Bluebottle won the Cambridgeshire, and once induced me to write an article on What the Well-Dressed Man is Wearing for that paper she runs – *Milady's Boudoir*. She is a large, genial soul, with whom it is a pleasure to hob-nob. In her spiritual make-up there is none of that subtle gosh-awfulness which renders such an exhibit as, say, my Aunt Agatha the curse of the Home Counties and a menace to one and all. I have the highest esteem for Aunt Dahlia, and have never wavered in my cordial appreciation of her humanity, sporting qualities and general good-eggishness.

This being so, you may conceive of my astonishment at finding her at my bedside at such an hour. I mean to say, I've stayed at her place many a time and oft, and she knows my habits. She is well aware that until I have had my cup of tea in the morning, I do not receive. This crashing in at a moment when she knew that solitude and repose were of the essence was scarcely, I could not but feel, the good old form.

Besides, what business had she being in London at all? That was what I asked myself. When a conscientious housewife has returned to her home after an absence of seven weeks, one does not expect her to start racing off again the day after her arrival. One feels that she ought to be sticking round, ministering to her husband, conferring with the cook, feeding the cat, combing and brushing the Pomeranian – in a word, staying put. I was more than a little bleary-eyed, but I endeavoured, as far as the fact that my eyelids were more or less glued together would permit, to give her an austere and censorious look.

She didn't seem to get it.

'Wake up, Bertie, you old ass!' she cried, in a voice that hit me between the eyebrows and went out at the back of my head.

If Aunt Dahlia has a fault, it is that she is apt to address a *vis-à-vis* as if he were somebody half a mile away whom she had observed riding over hounds. A throwback, no doubt, to the time when she counted the day lost that was not spent in chivvying some unfortunate fox over the countryside.

I gave her another of the austere and censorious, and this time it registered. All the effect it had, however, was to cause her to descend to personalities.

'Don't blink at me in that obscene way,' she said. 'I wonder, Bertie,' she proceeded, gazing at me as I should imagine Gussie would have gazed at some newt that was not up to sample, 'if you have the faintest conception how perfectly loathsome you look? A cross between an orgy scene in the movies and some low form of pond life. I suppose you were out on the tiles last night?'

'I attended a social function, yes,' I said coldly. 'Pongo Twistleton's birthday party. I couldn't let Pongo down. *Noblesse oblige.*'

'Well, get up and dress.'

I felt I could not have heard her aright.

'Get up and dress?'

'Yes.'

I turned on the pillow with a little moan, and at this juncture Jeeves entered with the vital oolong. I clutched at it like a drowning man at a straw hat. A deep sip or two, and I felt – I won't say restored, because a birthday party like Pongo Twistleton's isn't a thing you get restored after with a mere mouthful of tea, but sufficiently the old Bertram to be able to bend the mind on this awful thing which had come upon me.

And the more I bent same, the less could I grasp the trend of the scenario.

'What is this, Aunt Dahlia?' I inquired.

'It looks to me like tea,' was her response. 'But you know best. You're drinking it.'

If I hadn't been afraid of spilling the healing brew, I have little doubt that I should have given an impatient gesture. I know I felt like it.

'Not the contents of this cup. All this. Your barging in and telling me to get up and dress, and all that rot.'

'I've barged in, as you call it, because my telegrams seemed to produce no effect. And I told you to get up and dress because I want you to get up and dress. I've come to take you back with me.

I like your crust, wiring that you would come next year or whenever it was. You're coming now. I've got a job for you.'

'But I don't want a job.'

'What you want, my lad, and what you're going to get are two very different things. There is man's work for you to do at Brinkley Court. Be ready to the last button in twenty minutes.'

'But I can't possibly be ready to any buttons in twenty minutes. I'm feeling awful.'

She seemed to consider.

'Yes,' she said. 'I suppose it's only humane to give you a day or two to recover. All right, then, I shall expect you on the thirtieth at the latest.'

'But, dash it, what is all this? How do you mean, a job? Why a job? What sort of a job?'

'I'll tell you if you'll only stop talking for a minute. It's quite an easy, pleasant job. You will enjoy it. Have you ever heard of Market Snodsbury Grammar School?'

'Never.'

'It's a grammar school at Market Snodsbury.'

I told her a little frigidly that I had divined as much.

'Well, how was I to know that a man with a mind like yours would grasp it so quickly?' she protested. 'All right, then. Market Snodsbury Grammar School is, as you have guessed, the grammar school at Market Snodsbury. I'm one of the governors.'

'You mean one of the governesses.'

'I don't mean one of the governesses. Listen, ass. There was a board of governors at Eton, wasn't there? Very well. So there is at Market Snodsbury Grammar School, and I'm a member of it. And they left the arrangements for the summer prize giving to me. This prize giving takes place on the last – or thirty-first – day of this month. Have you got that clear?'

I took another oz. of the life-saving and inclined my head. Even after a Pongo Twistleton birthday party, I was capable of grasping simple facts like these.

'I follow you, yes. I see the point you are trying to make, certainly. Market . . . Snodsbury . . . Grammar School . . . Board of governors . . . Prize giving . . . Quite. But what's it got to do with me?'

'You're going to give away the prizes.'

I goggled. Her words did not appear to make sense. They seemed the mere aimless vapouring of an aunt who has been sitting out in the sun without a hat.

'Me?'

'You.'

I goggled again.

'You don't mean me?'

'I mean you in person.'

I goggled a third time.

'You're pulling my leg.'

'I am not pulling your leg. Nothing would induce me to touch your beastly leg. The vicar was to have officiated, but when I got home I found a letter from him saying that he had strained a fetlock and must scratch his nomination. You can imagine the state I was in. I telephoned all over the place. Nobody would take it on. And then suddenly I thought of you.'

I decided to check all this rot at the outset. Nobody is more eager to oblige deserving aunts than Bertram Wooster, but there are limits, and sharply defined limits, at that.

'So you think I'm going to strew prizes at this bally Dotheboys Hall of yours?'

'I do.'

'And make a speech?'

'Exactly.'

I laughed derisively.

'For goodness' sake, don't start gargling now. This is serious.'

'I was laughing.'

'Oh, were you? Well, I'm glad to see you taking it in this merry spirit.'

'Derisively,' I explained. 'I won't do it. That's final. I simply will not do it.'

'You will do it, young Bertie, or never darken my doors again. And you know what that means. No more of Anatole's dinners for you.'

A strong shudder shook me. She was alluding to her *chef,* that superb artist. A monarch of his profession, unsurpassed – nay, unequalled – at dishing up the raw material so that it melted in the mouth of the ultimate consumer, Anatole had always been a magnet that drew me to Brinkley Court with my tongue hanging out. Many of my happiest moments had been those which I had spent champing this great man's roasts and ragouts, and the prospect of being barred from digging into them in the future was a numbing one.

'No, I say, dash it!'

'I thought that would rattle you. Greedy young pig.'

'Greedy young pigs have nothing to do with it,' I said with a touch of hauteur. 'One is not a greedy young pig because one appreciates the cooking of a genius.'

'Well, I will say I like it myself,' conceded the relative. 'But not another bite of it do you get, if you refuse to do this simple, easy, pleasant job. No, not so much as another sniff. So put that in your twelve-inch cigarette holder and smoke it.'

I began to feel like some wild thing caught in a snare.

'But why do you want me? I mean, what am I? Ask yourself that.'

'I often have.'

'I mean to say, I'm not the type. You have to have some terrific nib to give away prizes. I seem to remember, when I was at school, it was generally a prime minister or somebody.'

'Ah, but that was at Eton. At Market Snodsbury we aren't nearly so choosy. Anybody in spats impresses us.'

'Why don't you get Uncle Tom?'

'Uncle Tom!'

'Well, why not? He's got spats.'

'Bertie,' she said, 'I will tell you why not Uncle Tom. You remember me losing all that money at baccarat at Cannes? Well, very shortly I shall have to sidle up to Tom and break the news to him. If, right after that, I ask him to put on lavender gloves and a topper and distribute the prizes at Market Snodsbury Grammar School, there will be a divorce in the family. He would pin a note to the pincushion and be off like a rabbit. No, my lad, you're for it, so you may as well make the best of it.'

'But, Aunt Dahlia, listen to reason. I assure you, you've got hold of the wrong man. I'm hopeless at a game like that. Ask Jeeves about the time I got lugged in to address a girls' school. I made the most colossal ass of myself.'

'And I confidently anticipate that you will make an equally colossal ass of yourself on the thirty-first of this month. That's why I want you. The way I look at it is that, as the thing is bound to be a frost, anyway, one may as well get a hearty laugh out of it. I shall enjoy seeing you distribute those prizes, Bertie. Well, I won't keep you, as, no doubt, you want to do your Swedish exercises. I shall expect you in a day or two.'

And with these heartless words she beetled off, leaving me a prey to the gloomiest emotions. What with the natural reaction after Pongo's party and this stunning blow, it is not too much to say that the soul was seared.

And I was still writhing in the depths, when the door opened and Jeeves appeared.

'Mr Fink-Nottle to see you, sir,' he announced.

5

I gave him one of my looks.

'Jeeves,' I said, 'I had scarcely expected this of you. You are aware that I was up to an advanced hour last night. You know that I have barely had my tea. You cannot be ignorant of the effect of that hearty voice of Aunt Dahlia's on a man with a headache. And yet you come bringing me Fink-Nottles. Is this a time for Fink or any other kind of Nottle?'

'But did you not give me to understand, sir, that you wished to see Mr Fink-Nottle to advise him on his affairs?'

This, I admit, opened up a new line of thought. In the stress of my emotions, I had clean forgotten about having taken Gussie's interests in hand. It altered things. One can't give the raspberry to a client. I mean, you didn't find Sherlock Holmes refusing to see clients just because he had been out late the night before at Doctor Watson's birthday party. I could have wished that the man had selected some more suitable hour for approaching me, but as he appeared to be a sort of human lark, leaving his watery nest at daybreak, I supposed I had better give him an audience.

'True,' I said. 'All right. Bung him in.'

'Very good, sir.'

'But before doing so, bring me one of those pick-me-ups of yours.'

'Very good, sir.'

And presently he returned with the vital essence.

I have had occasion, I fancy, to speak before now of these pick-me-ups of Jeeves's and their effect on a fellow who is hanging to life by a thread on the morning after. What they consist of, I couldn't tell you. He says some kind of sauce, the yolk of a raw egg and a dash of red pepper, but nothing will convince me that the thing doesn't go much deeper than that. Be that as it may, however, the results of swallowing one are amazing.

For perhaps the split part of a second nothing happens. It is as though all Nature waited breathless. Then, suddenly, it is as if the

Last Trump had sounded and Judgment Day set in with unusual severity.

Bonfires burst out in all parts of the frame. The abdomen becomes heavily charged with molten lava. A great wind seems to blow through the world, and the subject is aware of something resembling a steam hammer striking the back of the head. During this phase, the ears ring loudly, the eyeballs rotate and there is a tingling about the brow.

And then, just as you are feeling that you ought to ring up your lawyer and see that your affairs are in order before it is too late, the whole situation seems to clarify. The wind drops. The ears cease to ring. Birds twitter. Brass bands start playing. The sun comes up over the horizon with a jerk.

And a moment later all you are conscious of is a great peace.

As I drained the glass now, new life seemed to burgeon within me. I remember Jeeves, who, however much he may go off the rails at times in the matter of dress clothes and in his advice to those in love, has always had a neat turn of phrase, once speaking of someone rising on stepping-stones of his dead self to higher things. It was that way with me now. I felt that the Bertram Wooster who lay propped up against the pillows had become a better, stronger, finer Bertram.

'Thank you, Jeeves,' I said.

'Not at all, sir.'

'That touched the exact spot. I am now able to cope with life's problems.'

'I am gratified to hear it, sir.'

'What madness not to have had one of those before tackling Aunt Dahlia! However, too late to worry about that now. Tell me of Gussie. How did he make out at the fancy-dress ball?'

'He did not arrive at the fancy-dress ball, sir.'

I looked at him a bit austerely.

'Jeeves,' I said, 'I admit that after that pick-me-up of yours I feel better, but don't try me too high. Don't stand by my sick bed talking absolute rot. We shot Gussie into a cab and he started forth, headed for wherever this fancy-dress ball was. He must have arrived.'

'No, sir. As I gather from Mr Fink-Nottle, he entered the cab convinced in his mind that the entertainment to which he had been invited was to be held at No. 17, Suffolk Square, whereas the actual rendezvous was No. 71, Norfolk Terrace. These aberrations of memory are not uncommon with those who, like Mr Fink-Nottle, belong essentially to what one might call the dreamer type.'

'One might also call it the fatheaded type.'

'Yes, sir.'

'Well?'

'On reaching No. 17, Suffolk Square, Mr Fink-Nottle endeavoured to produce money to pay the fare.'

'What stopped him?'

'The fact that he had no money, sir. He discovered that he had left it, together with his ticket of invitation, on the mantelpiece of his bedchamber in the house of his uncle, where he was residing. Bidding the cabman to wait, accordingly, he rang the doorbell, and when the butler appeared, requested him to pay the cab, adding that it was all right, as he was one of the guests invited to the dance. The butler then disclaimed all knowledge of a dance on the premises.'

'And declined to unbelt?'

'Yes, sir.'

'Upon which – '

'Mr Fink-Nottle directed the cabman to drive him back to his uncle's residence.'

'Well, why wasn't that the happy ending? All he had to do was go in, collect cash and ticket, and there he would have been, on velvet.'

'I should have mentioned, sir, that Mr Fink-Nottle had also left his latchkey on the mantelpiece of his bed-chamber.'

'He could have rung the bell.'

'He did ring the bell, sir, for some fifteen minutes. At the expiration of that period he recalled that he had given permission to the caretaker – the house was officially closed and all the staff on holiday – to visit his sailor son at Portsmouth.'

'Golly, Jeeves!'

'Yes, sir.'

'These dreamer types do live, don't they?'

'Yes, sir.'

'What happened then?'

'Mr Fink-Nottle appears to have realized at this point that his position as regards the cabman had become equivocal. The figures on the clock had already reached a substantial sum, and he was not in a position to meet his obligations.'

'He could have explained.'

'You cannot explain to cabmen, sir. On endeavouring to do so, he found the fellow sceptical of his bona fides.'

'I should have legged it.'

'That is the policy which appears to have commended itself to Mr Fink-Nottle. He darted rapidly away, and the cabman, endeavouring to detain him, snatched at his overcoat. Mr Fink-Nottle contrived to extricate himself from the coat, and it would seem that his appearance in the masquerade costume beneath it came as something of a shock to the cabman. Mr Fink-Nottle informs me that he heard a species of whistling gasp, and, looking round, observed the man crouching against the railings with his hands over his face. Mr Fink-Nottle thinks he was praying. No doubt an uneducated, superstitious fellow, sir. Possibly a drinker.'

'Well, if he hadn't been one before, I'll bet he started being one shortly afterwards. I expect he could scarcely wait for the pubs to open.'

'Very possibly, in the circumstances he might have found a restorative agreeable, sir.'

'And so, in the circumstances, might Gussie too, I should think. What on earth did he do after that? London late at night – or even in the daytime, for that matter – is no place for a man in scarlet tights.'

'No, sir.'

'He invites comment.'

'Yes, sir.'

'I can see the poor old bird ducking down side streets, skulking in alleyways, diving into dustbins.'

'I gathered from Mr Fink-Nottle's remarks, sir, that something very much on those lines was what occurred. Eventually, after a trying night, he found his way to Mr Sipperley's residence, where he was able to secure lodging and a change of costume in the morning.'

I nestled against the pillows, the brow a bit drawn. It is all very well to try to do old school friends a spot of good, but I could not but feel that in espousing the cause of a lunkhead capable of mucking things up as Gussie had done, I had taken on a contract almost too big for human consumption. It seemed to me that what Gussie needed was not so much the advice of a seasoned man of the world as a padded cell in Colney Hatch and a couple of good keepers to see that he did not set the place on fire.

Indeed, for an instant I had half a mind to withdraw from the case and hand it back to Jeeves. But the pride of the Woosters restrained me. When we Woosters put our hands to the plough, we do not readily sheathe the sword. Besides, after that business of the mess jacket, anything resembling weakness would have been fatal.

'I suppose you realize, Jeeves,' I said, for though one dislikes to rub it in, these things have to be pointed out, 'that all this was your fault?'

'Sir?'

'It's no good saying "Sir?" You know it was. If you had not insisted on his going to that dance – a mad project, as I spotted from the first – this would not have happened.'

'Yes, sir, but I confess I did not anticipate – '

'Always anticipate everything, Jeeves,' I said, a little sternly. 'It is the only way. Even if you had allowed him to wear a Pierrot costume, things would not have panned out as they did. A Pierrot costume has pockets. However,' I went on more kindly, 'we need not go into that now. If all this has shown you what comes of going about the place in scarlet tights, that is something gained. Gussie waits without, you say?'

'Yes, sir.'

'Then shoot him in, and I will see what I can do for him.'

6

Gussie, on arrival, proved to be still showing traces of his grim experience. The face was pale, the eyes gooseberry-like, the ears drooping, and the whole aspect that of a man who has passed through the furnace and been caught in the machinery. I hitched myself up a bit higher on the pillows and gazed at him narrowly. It was a moment, I could see, when first aid was required, and I prepared to get down to cases.

'Well, Gussie.'

'Hullo, Bertie.'

'What ho.'

'What ho.'

These civilities concluded, I felt that the moment had come to touch delicately on the past.

'I hear you've been through it a bit.'

'Yes.'

'Thanks to Jeeves.'

'It wasn't Jeeves's fault.'

'Entirely Jeeves's fault.'

'I don't see that. I forgot my money and latchkey – '

'And now you'd better forget Jeeves. For you will be interested to hear, Gussie,' I said, deeming it best to put him in touch with the position of affairs right away, 'that he is no longer handling your little problem.'

This seemed to slip it across him properly. The jaws fell, the ears drooped more limply. He had been looking like a dead fish. He now looked like a deader fish, one of last year's, cast up on some lonely beach and left there at the mercy of the wind and tides.

'What!'

'Yes.'

'You don't mean that Jeeves isn't going to – '

'No.'

'But, dash it– '

I was kind, but firm.

'You will be much better off without him. Surely your terrible experiences of that awful night have told you that Jeeves needs a rest. The keenest of thinkers strikes a bad patch occasionally. That is what has happened to Jeeves. I have seen it coming on for some time. He has lost his form. He wants his plugs decarbonized. No doubt this is a shock to you. I suppose you came here this morning to seek his advice?'

'Of course I did.'

'On what point?'

'Madeline Bassett has gone to stay with these people in the country, and I want to know what he thinks I ought to do.'

'Well, as I say, Jeeves is off the case.'

'But, Bertie, dash it – '

'Jeeves,' I said with a certain asperity, 'is no longer on the case. I am now in sole charge.'

'But what on earth can you do?'

I curbed my resentment. We Woosters are fair-minded. We can make allowances for men who have been parading London all night in scarlet tights.

'That,' I said quietly, 'we shall see. Sit down and let us confer. I am bound to say the thing seems quite simple to me. You say this girl has gone to visit friends in the country. It would appear obvious that you must go there too, and flock round her like a poultice. Elementary.'

'But I can't plant myself on a lot of perfect strangers.'

'Don't you know these people?'

'Of course I don't. I don't know anybody.'

I pursed the lips. This did seem to complicate matters somewhat.

'All that I know is that their name is Travers, and it's a place called Brinkley Court down in Worcestershire.'

I unpursed my lips.

'Gussie,' I said, smiling paternally, 'it was a lucky day for you when Bertram Wooster interested himself in your affairs. As I foresaw from the start, I can fix everything. This afternoon you shall go to Brinkley Court, an honoured guest.'

He quivered like a mousse. I suppose it must always be rather a thrilling experience for the novice to watch me taking hold.

'But, Bertie, you don't mean you know these Traverses?'

'They are my Aunt Dahlia.'

'My gosh!'

'You see now,' I pointed out, 'how lucky you were to get me behind you. You go to Jeeves, and what does he do? He dresses you up in scarlet tights and one of the foulest false beards of my experience, and sends you off to fancy-dress balls. Result, agony of spirit and no progress. I then take over and put you on the right lines. Could Jeeves have got you into Brinkley Court? Not a chance. Aunt Dahlia isn't his aunt. I merely mention these things.'

'By Jove, Bertie, I don't know how to thank you.'

'My dear chap!'

'But, I say.'

'Now what?'

'What do I do when I get there?'

'If you knew Brinkley Court, you would not ask that question. In those romantic surroundings you can't miss. Great lovers through the ages have fixed up the preliminary formalities at Brinkley. The place is simply ill with atmosphere. You will stroll with the girl in the shady walks. You will sit with her on the shady lawns. You will row on the lake with her. And gradually you will find yourself working up to a point where – '

'By Jove, I believe you're right.'

'Of course, I'm right. I've got engaged three times at Brinkley. No business resulted, but the fact remains. And I went there without the foggiest idea of indulging in the tender pash. I hadn't the slightest intention of proposing to anybody. Yet no sooner had I entered those romantic grounds than I found myself reaching out for the nearest girl in sight and slapping my soul down in front of her. It's something in the air.'

'I see exactly what you mean. That's just what I want to be able to do – work up to it. And in London – curse the place – everything's in such a rush that you don't get a chance.'

'Quite. You see a girl alone for about five minutes a day, and if you want to ask her to be your wife, you've got to charge into it as if you were trying to grab the gold ring on a merry-go-round.'

'That's right. London rattles one. I shall be a different man altogether in the country. What a bit of luck this Travers woman turning out to be your aunt.'

'I don't know what you mean, turning out to be my aunt. She has been my aunt all along.'

'I mean, how extraordinary that it should be your aunt that Madeline's going to stay with.'

'Not at all. She and my cousin Angela are close friends. At Cannes she was with us all the time.'

'Oh, you met Madeline at Cannes, did you? By Jove, Bertie,' said the poor lizard devoutly, 'I wish I could have seen her at

Cannes. How wonderful she must have looked in beach pyjamas! Oh, Bertie – '

'Quite,' I said, a little distantly. Even when restored by one of Jeeves's depth bombs, one doesn't want this sort of thing after a hard night. I touched the bell and, when Jeeves appeared, requested him to bring me telegraph form and pencil. I then wrote a well-worded communication to Aunt Dahlia, informing her that I was sending my friend, Augustus Fink-Nottle, down to Brinkley today to enjoy her hospitality, and handed it to Gussie.

'Push that in at the first post office you pass,' I said. 'She will find it waiting for her on her return.'

Gussie popped along, flapping the telegram and looking like a close-up of Joan Crawford, and I turned to Jeeves and gave him a precis of my operations.

'Simple, you observe, Jeeves. Nothing elaborate.'

'No, sir.'

'Nothing far-fetched. Nothing strained or bizarre. Just Nature's remedy.'

'Yes, sir.'

'This is the attack as it should have been delivered. What do you call it when two people of opposite sexes are bunged together in close association in a secluded spot, meeting each other every day and seeing a lot of each other?'

'Is "propinquity" the word you wish, sir?'

'It is. I stake everything on propinquity, Jeeves. Propinquity, in my opinion, is what will do the trick. At the moment, as you are aware, Gussie is a mere jelly when in the presence. But ask yourself how he will feel in a week or so, after he and she have been helping themselves to sausages out of the same dish day after day at the breakfast sideboard. Cutting the same ham, ladling out communal kidneys and bacon – why – '

I broke off abruptly. I had had one of my ideas.

'Golly, Jeeves!'

'Sir?'

'Here's an instance of how you have to think of everything. You heard me mention sausages, kidneys and bacon and ham.'

'Yes, sir.'

'Well, there must be nothing of that. Fatal. The wrong note entirely. Give me that telegraph form and pencil. I must warn Gussie without delay. What he's got to do is to create in this girl's mind the impression that he is pining away for love of her. This cannot be done by wolfing sausages.'

'No, sir.'

'Very well, then.'

And, taking form and p., I drafted the following:

Fink-Nottle
   Brinkley Court,
      Market Snodsbury
         Worcestershire
Lay off the sausages. Avoid the ham. Bertie.

'Send that off, Jeeves, instanter.'

'Very good, sir.'

I sank back on the pillows.

'Well, Jeeves,' I said, 'you see how I am taking hold. You notice the grip I am getting on this case. No doubt you realize now that it would pay you to study my methods.'

'No doubt, sir.'

'And even now you aren't on to the full depths of the extraordinary sagacity I've shown. Do you know what brought Aunt Dahlia up here this morning? She came to tell me I'd got to distribute the prizes at some beastly seminary she's a governor of down at Market Snodsbury.'

'Indeed, sir? I fear you will scarcely find that a congenial task.'

'Ah, but I'm not going to do it. I'm going to shove it off on to Gussie.'

'Sir?'

'I propose, Jeeves, to wire to Aunt Dahlia saying that I can't get down, and suggesting that she unleashes him on these young Borstal inmates of hers in my stead.'

'But if Mr Fink-Nottle should decline, sir?'

'Decline? Can you see him declining? Just conjure up the picture in your mind, Jeeves. Scene, the drawing-room at Brinkley; Gussie wedged into a corner, with Aunt Dahlia standing over him making hunting noises. I put it to you, Jeeves, can you see him declining?'

'Not readily, sir, I agree. Mrs Travers is a forceful personality.'

'He won't have a hope of declining. His only way out would be to slide off. And he can't slide off, because he wants to be with Miss Bassett. No, Gussie will have to toe the line, and I shall be saved from a job at which I confess the soul shuddered. Getting up on a platform and delivering a short, manly speech to a lot of foul schoolkids! Golly, Jeeves. I've been through that sort of thing once, what? You remember that time at the girls' school?'

'Very vividly, sir.'

'What an ass I made of myself!'

'Certainly I have seen you to better advantage, sir.'

'I think you might bring me just one more of those dynamite specials of yours, Jeeves. This narrow squeak has made me come over all faint.'

I suppose it must have taken Aunt Dahlia three hours or so to get back to Brinkley, because it wasn't till well after lunch that her telegram arrived. It read like a telegram that had been dispatched in white-hot surge of emotion some two minutes after she had read mine.

As follows:

Am taking legal advice to ascertain whether strangling an idiot nephew counts as murder. If it doesn't look out for yourself. Consider your conduct frozen limit. What do you mean by planting your loathsome friends on me like this? Do you think Brinkley Court is a leper colony or what is it? Who is this Spink-Bottle? Love. Travers.

I had expected some such initial reaction. I replied in temperate vein:

Not Bottle. Nottle. Regards. Bertie.

Almost immediately after she had dispatched the above heart cry, Gussie must have arrived, for it wasn't twenty minutes later when I received the following:

Cipher telegram signed by you has reached me here. Runs 'Lay off the sausages. Avoid the ham.' Wire key immediately. Fink-Nottle.

I replied:

Also kidneys. Cheerio. Bertie.

I had staked all on Gussie making a favourable impression on his hostess, basing my confidence on the fact that he was one of those timid, obsequious, teacup-passing, thin-bread-and-butter-offering yes-men whom women of my Aunt Dahlia's type nearly always like at first sight. That I had not overrated my acumen was proved by her next in order, which, I was pleased to note, assayed a markedly larger percentage of the milk of human kindness.

As follows:

Well, this friend of yours has got here, and I must say that for a friend of yours he seems less sub-human than I had expected. A bit of a pop-eyed bleater, but on the whole clean and civil, and certainly most informative about newts. Am considering arranging series of lectures for him in neighbourhood. All the same I like your nerve using my house as a summer-hotel resort and shall have much to say to you on subject when you come down. Expect you thirtieth. Bring spats. Love. Travers.

To this I riposted:

On consulting engagement book find impossible come Brinkley Court. Deeply regret. Toodle-oo. Bertie.

Hers in reply struck a sinister note:

Oh, so it's like that, is it? You and your engagement book, indeed. Deeply regret my foot. Let me tell you, my lad, that you will regret it a jolly sight more deeply if you don't come down. If you imagine for one moment that you are going to get out of distributing those prizes, you are very much mistaken. Deeply regret Brinkley Court hundred miles from London, as unable hit you with a brick. Love. Travers.

I then put my fortune to the test, to win or lose it all. It was not a moment for petty economies. I let myself go regardless of expense:

No, but dash it, listen. Honestly, you don't want me. Get Fink-Nottle distribute prizes. A born distributor, who will do you credit. Confidently anticipate Augustus Fink-Nottle as Master of Revels on thirty-first inst. would make genuine sensation. Do not miss this great chance, which may never occur again. Tinkerty-tonk. Bertie.

There was an hour of breathless suspense, and then the joyful tidings arrived:

Well, all right. Something in what you say, I suppose. Consider you treacherous worm and contemptible, spineless cowardy custard, but have booked Spink-Bottle. Stay where you are, then, and I hope you get run over by an omnibus. Love. Travers.

The relief, as you may well imagine, was stupendous. A great weight seemed to have rolled off my mind. It was as if somebody had been pouring Jeeves's pick-me-ups into me through a funnel. I sang as I dressed for dinner that night. At the Drones I was so gay and cheery that there were several complaints. And when I got home and turned into the old bed, I fell asleep like a little child within five minutes of inserting the person between the sheets. It seemed to me that the whole distressing affair might now be considered definitely closed.

Conceive my astonishment, therefore, when waking on the morrow and sitting up to dig into the morning tea cup, I beheld on the tray another telegram.

My heart sank. Could Aunt Dahlia have slept on it and changed her mind? Could Gussie, unable to face the ordeal confronting him, have legged it during the night down a water-pipe? With these speculations racing through the bean, I tore open the envelope and as I noted contents I uttered a startled yip.

'Sir?' said Jeeves, pausing at the door.

I read the thing again. Yes, I had got the gist all right. No, I had not been deceived in the substance.

'Jeeves,' I said, 'do you know what?'

'No, sir.'

'You know my cousin Angela?'

'Yes, sir.'

'You know young Tuppy Glossop?'

'Yes, sir.'

'They've broken off their engagement.'

'I am sorry to hear that, sir.'

'I have here a communication from Aunt Dahlia, specifically stating this. I wonder what the row was about.'

'I could not say, sir.'

'Of course you couldn't. Don't be an ass, Jeeves.'

'No, sir.'

I brooded. I was deeply moved.

'Well, this means that we shall have to go down to Brinkley today. Aunt Dahlia is obviously all of a twitter, and my place is by her side. You had better pack this morning, and catch that 12.45 train with the luggage. I have a lunch engagement, so will follow in the car.'

'Very good, sir.'

I brooded some more.

'I must say this has come as a great shock to me, Jeeves.'

'No doubt, sir.'

'A very great shock. Angela and Tuppy . . . Tut, tut! Why, they seemed like the paper on the wall. Life is full of sadness, Jeeves.'

'Yes, sir.'
'Still, there it is.'
'Undoubtedly, sir.'
'Right ho, then. Switch on the bath.'
'Very good, sir.'

7

I meditated pretty freely as I drove down to Brinkley in the old two-seater that afternoon. The news of this rift or rupture of Angela's and Tuppy's had disturbed me greatly.

The projected match, you see, was one on which I had always looked with kindly approval. Too often, when a chap of your acquaintance is planning to marry a girl you know, you find yourself knitting the brow a bit and chewing the lower lip dubiously, feeling that he or she, or both, should be warned while there is yet time.

But I have never felt anything of this nature about Tuppy and Angela. Tuppy, when not making an ass of himself, is a soundish sort of egg. So is Angela a soundish sort of egg. And, as far as being in love was concerned, it had always seemed to me that you wouldn't have been far out in describing them as two hearts that beat as one.

True, they had had their little tiffs, notably on the occasion when Tuppy – with what he said was fearless honesty and I considered thorough goofiness – had told Angela that her new hat made her look like a Pekingese. But in every romance you have to budget for the occasional dust-up, and after that incident I had supposed that he had learned his lesson and that from then on life would be one grand, sweet song.

And now this wholly unforeseen severing of diplomatic relations had popped up through a trap.

I gave the thing the cream of the Wooster brain all the way down, but it continued to beat me what could have caused the outbreak of hostilities, and I bunged my foot sedulously on the accelerator in order to get to Aunt Dahlia with the greatest possible speed and learn the inside history straight from the horse's mouth. And what with all six cylinders hitting nicely, I made good time and found myself closeted with the relative shortly before the hour of the evening cocktail.

She seemed glad to see me. In fact, she actually said she was glad to see me – a statement no other aunt on the list would have committed herself to, the customary reaction of these near and dear ones to the spectacle of Bertram arriving for a visit being a sort of sick horror.

'Decent of you to rally round, Bertie,' she said.

'My place was by your side, Aunt Dahlia,' I responded.

I could see at a g. that the unfortunate affair had got in amongst her in no uncertain manner. Her usually cheerful map was clouded, and the genial smile conspic. by its a. I pressed her hand sympathetically, to indicate that my heart bled for her.

'Bad show this, my dear old flesh and blood,' I said. 'I'm afraid you've been having a sticky time. You must be worried.'

She snorted emotionally. She looked like an aunt who has just bitten into a bad oyster.

'Worried is right. I haven't had a peaceful moment since I got back from Cannes. Ever since I put my foot across this blasted threshold,' said Aunt Dahlia, returning for the nonce to the hearty *argot* of the hunting field, 'everything's been at sixes and sevens. First there was that mix up about the prize giving.'

She paused at this point and gave me a look. 'I had been meaning to speak freely to you about your behaviour in that matter, Bertie,' she said. 'I had some good things all stored up. But, as you've rallied round like this, I suppose I shall have to let you off. And, anyway, it is probably all for the best that you evaded your obligations in that sickeningly craven way. I have an idea that this Spink-Bottle of yours is going to be good. If only he can keep off newts.'

'Has he been talking about newts?'

'He has. Fixing me with a glittering eye, like the Ancient Mariner. But if that was the worst I had to bear, I wouldn't mind. What I'm worrying about is what Tom says when he starts talking.'

'Uncle Tom?'

'I wish there was something else you could call him except "Uncle Tom",' said Aunt Dahlia a little testily. 'Every time you do it, I expect to see him turn black and start playing the banjo. Yes, Uncle Tom, if you must have it. I shall have to tell him soon about losing all that money at baccarat, and, when I do, he will go up like a rocket.'

'Still, no doubt Time, the great healer – '

'Time, the great healer, be blowed. I've got to get a cheque for five hundred pounds out of him for *Milady's Boudoir* by August the third at the latest.'

I was concerned. Apart from a nephew's natural interest in an aunt's refined weekly paper, I had always had a soft spot in my heart for *Milady's Boudoir* ever since I contributed that article to it on What the Well-Dressed Man is Wearing. Sentimental, possibly, but we old journalists do have these feelings.

'Is the *Boudoir* on the rocks?'

'It will be if Tom doesn't cough up. It needs help till it has turned the corner.'

'But wasn't it turning the corner two years ago?'

'It was. And it's still at it. Till you've run a weekly paper for women, you don't know what corners are.'

'And you think the chances of getting into Uncle – into my uncle by marriage's ribs are slight?'

'I'll tell you, Bertie. Up till now, when these subsidies were required, I have always been able to come to Tom in the gay, confident spirit of an only child touching an indulgent father for chocolate cream. But he's just had a demand from the income-tax people for an additional fifty-eight pounds, one and threepence, and all he's been talking about since I got back has been ruin and the sinister trend of socialistic legislation and what will become of us all.'

I could readily believe it. This Tom has a peculiarity I've noticed in other very oofy men. Nick him for the paltriest sum, and he lets out a squawk you can hear at Land's End. He has the stuff in gobs, but he hates giving up.

'If it wasn't for Anatole's cooking, I doubt if he would bother to carry on. Thank God for Anatole, I say.'

I bowed my head reverently.

'Good old Anatole,' I said.

'Amen,' said Aunt Dahlia.

Then the look of holy ecstasy, which is always the result of letting the mind dwell, however briefly, on Anatole's cooking, died out of her face.

'But don't let me wander from the subject,' she resumed. 'I was telling you of the way hell's foundations have been quivering since I got home. First the prize giving, then Tom, and now, on top of everything else, this infernal quarrel between Angela and young Glossop.'

I nodded gravely. 'I was frightfully sorry to hear of that. Terrible shock. What was the row about?'

'Sharks.'

'Eh?'

'Sharks. Or, rather, one individual shark. The brute that went for the poor child when she was aquaplaning at Cannes. You remember Angela's shark?'

Certainly I remembered Angela's shark. A man of sensibility does not forget about a cousin nearly being chewed by monsters of the deep. The episode was still green in my memory.

In a nutshell, what had occurred was this: You know how you aquaplane. A motorboat nips on ahead, trailing a rope. You stand on a board, holding the rope, and the boat tows you along. And every now and then you lose your grip on the rope and plunge into the sea and have to swim to your board again.

A silly process it has always seemed to me, though many find it diverting.

Well, on the occasion referred to, Angela had just regained her board after taking a toss, when a great beastly shark came along and cannoned into it, flinging her into the salty once more. It took her quite a bit of time to get on again and make the motorboat chap realize what was up and haul her to safety, and during that interval you can readily picture her embarrassment.

According to Angela, the finny denizen kept snapping at her ankles virtually without cessation, so that by the time help arrived, she was feeling more like a salted almond at a public dinner than anything human. Very shaken the poor child had been, I recall, and had talked of nothing else for weeks.

'I remember the whole incident vividly,' I said. 'But how did that start the trouble?'

'She was telling him the story last night.'

'Well?'

'Her eyes shining and her little hands clasped in girlish excitement.'

'No doubt.'

'And instead of giving her the understanding and sympathy to which she was entitled, what do you think this blasted Glossop did? He sat listening like a lump of dough, as if she had been talking about the weather, and when she had finished, he took his cigarette holder out of his mouth and said, "I expect it was only a floating log"!'

'He didn't!'

'He did. And when Angela described how the thing had jumped and snapped at her, he took his cigarette holder out of his mouth again, and said, "Ah! Probably a flat fish. Quite harmless. No doubt it was just trying to play." Well, I mean! What would you have done if you had been Angela? She has pride, sensibility, all the natural feelings of a good woman. She told him he was an ass and a fool and an idiot, and didn't know what he was talking about.'

I must say I saw the girl's viewpoint. It's only about once in a lifetime that anything sensational ever happens to one, and when it does, you don't want people taking all the colour out of it. I remember at school having to read that stuff where that chap, Othello, tells the girl what a hell of a time he'd been having among the cannibals and what not. Well, imagine his feelings if, after he had described some particularly sticky passage with a cannibal chief and was waiting for the awestruck 'Oh-h! Not really?', she had said that the whole thing had no doubt been greatly exaggerated and that the man had probably really been a prominent local vegetarian.

Yes, I saw Angela's point of view.

'But don't tell me that when he saw how shirty she was about it, the chump didn't back down?'

'He didn't. He argued. And one thing led to another until, by easy stages, they had arrived at the point where she was saying that she didn't know if he was aware of it, but if he didn't knock off starchy foods and do exercises every morning, he would be getting as fat as a pig, and he was talking about this modern habit of girls putting make-up on their faces, of which he had always disapproved. This continued for a while, and then there was a loud pop and the air was full of mangled fragments of their engagement. I'm distracted about it. Thank goodness you've come, Bertie.'

'Nothing could have kept me away,' I replied, touched. 'I felt you needed me.'

'Yes.'

'Quite.'

'Or, rather,' she said, 'not you, of course, but Jeeves. The minute all this happened, I thought of him. The situation obviously cries out for Jeeves. If ever in the whole history of human affairs there was a moment when that lofty brain was required about the home, this is it.'

I think, if I had been standing up, I would have staggered. In fact, I'm pretty sure I would. But it isn't so dashed easy to stagger when you're sitting in an armchair. Only my face, therefore, showed how deeply I had been stung by these words.

Until she spoke them, I had been all sweetness and light – the sympathetic nephew prepared to strain every nerve to do his bit. I now froze, and the face became hard and set.

'Jeeves!' I said, between clenched teeth.

'Oom beroofen,' said Aunt Dahlia.

I saw that she had got the wrong angle.

'I was not sneezing. I was saying "Jeeves!"'

'And well you may. What a man! I'm going to put the whole thing up to him. There's nobody like Jeeves.'

My frigidity became more marked.

'I venture to take issue with you, Aunt Dahlia.'

'You take what?'

'Issue.'

'You do, do you?'

'I emphatically do. Jeeves is hopeless.'

'What?'

'Quite hopeless. He has lost his grip completely. Only a couple of days ago I was compelled to take him off a case because his handling of it was so footling. And, anyway, I resent this assumption, if assumption is the word I want, that Jeeves is the only fellow with brain. I object to the way everybody puts things up to him without consulting me and letting me have a stab at them first.'

She seemed about to speak, but I checked her with a gesture.

'It is true that in the past I have sometimes seen fit to seek Jeeves's advice. It is possible that in the future I may seek it again. But I claim the right to have a pop at these problems, as they arise, in person, without having everybody behave as if Jeeves was the only onion in the hash. I sometimes feel that Jeeves, though admittedly not unsuccessful in the past, has been lucky rather than gifted.'

'Have you and Jeeves had a row?'

'Nothing of the kind.'

'You seem to have it in for him.'

'Not at all.'

And yet I must admit that there was a modicum of truth in what she said. I had been feeling pretty austere about the man all day, and I'll tell you why.

You remember that he caught that 12.45 train with the luggage, while I remained on in order to keep a luncheon engagement. Well, just before I started out to the tryst, I was pottering about the flat, and suddenly – I don't know what put the suspicion into my head, possibly the fellow's manner had been furtive – something seemed to whisper to me to go and have a look in the wardrobe.

And it was as I had suspected. There was the mess jacket still on its hanger. The hound hadn't packed it.

Well, as anybody at the Drones will tell you, Bertram Wooster is a pretty hard chap to outgeneral. I shoved the thing in a brown-paper parcel and put it in the back of the car, and it was on a chair in the hall now. But that didn't alter the fact that Jeeves had attempted to do the dirty on me, and I suppose a certain what-d'you-call-it had crept into my manner during the above remarks.

'There has been no breach,' I said. 'You might describe it as a passing coolness, but no more. We did not happen to see eye to eye with regard to my white mess jacket with the brass buttons and I was compelled to assert my personality. But – '

'Well, it doesn't matter, anyway. The thing that matters is that you are talking piffle, you poor fish. Jeeves lost his grip? Absurd. Why, I saw him for a moment when he arrived, and his eyes were absolutely glittering with intelligence. I said to myself "Trust Jeeves," and I intend to.'

'You would be far better advised to let me see what I can accomplish, Aunt Dahlia.'

'For heaven's sake, don't you start butting in. You'll only make matters worse.'

'On the contrary, it may interest you to know that while driving here I concentrated deeply on this trouble of Angela's and was successful in formulating a plan, based on the psychology of the individual, which I am proposing to put into effect at an early moment.'

'Oh, my God!'

'My knowledge of human nature tells me it will work.'

'Bertie,' said Aunt Dahlia, and her manner struck me as febrile, 'lay off, lay off! For pity's sake, lay off. I know these plans of yours. I suppose you want to shove Angela into the lake and push young Glossop in after her to save her life, or something like that.'

'Nothing of the kind.'

'It's the sort of thing you would do.'

'My scheme is far more subtle. Let me outline it for you.'

'No thanks.'

'I say to myself – '

'But not to me.'

'Do listen for a second.'

'I won't.'

'Right ho, then. I am dumb.'

'And have been from a child.'

I perceived that little good could result from continuing the discussion. I waved a hand and shrugged a shoulder.

'Very well, Aunt Dahlia,' I said, with dignity, 'if you don't want to be in on the ground floor, that is your affair. But you are missing an intellectual treat. And, anyway, no matter how much you may behave like the deaf adder of Scripture which, as you are doubtless aware, the more one piped, the less it danced, or words to that effect, I shall carry on as planned. I am extremely fond of Angela, and I shall spare no effort to bring the sunshine back into her heart.'

'Bertie, you abysmal chump, I appeal to you once more. Will you please lay off? You'll only make things ten times as bad as they are already.'

I remember reading in one of those historical novels once about a chap – a buck he would have been, no doubt, or a macaroni or some such bird as that – who, when people said the wrong thing, merely laughed down from lazy eyelids and flicked a speck of dust from the irreproachable Mechlin lace at his wrists. This was practically what I did now. At least, I straightened my tie and smiled one of those inscrutable smiles of mine. I then withdrew and went out for a saunter in the garden.

And the first chap I ran into was young Tuppy. His brow was furrowed, and he was moodily bunging stones at a flowerpot.

8

I think I have told you before about young Tuppy Glossop. He was the fellow, if you remember, who, callously ignoring the fact that we had been friends since boyhood, betted me one night at the Drones that I could swing myself across the swimming bath by the rings – a childish feat for one of my lissomness – and then, having seen me well on the way, looped back the last ring, thus rendering it necessary for me to drop into the deep end in formal evening costume.

To say that I had not resented this foul deed, which seemed to me deserving of the title of the crime of the century, would be paltering with the truth. I had resented it profoundly, chafing not a little at the time and continuing to chafe for some weeks.

But you know how it is with these things. The wound heals. The agony abates.

I am not saying, mind you, that had the opportunity presented itself of dropping a wet sponge on Tuppy from some high spot or of putting an eel in his bed or finding some other form of self-expression of a like nature, I would not have embraced it eagerly; but that let me out. I mean to say, grievously injured though I had been, it gave me no pleasure to feel that the fellow's bally life was being ruined by the loss of a girl whom, despite all that had passed, I was convinced he still loved like the dickens.

On the contrary, I was heart and soul in favour of healing the breach and rendering everything hotsy-totsy once more between these two young sundered blighters. You will have gleaned that from my remarks to Aunt Dahlia, and if you had been present at this moment and had seen the kindly commiserating look I gave Tuppy, you would have gleaned it still more.

It was one of those searching, melting looks, and was accompanied by the hearty clasp of the right hand and the gentle laying of the left on the collarbone.

'Well, Tuppy, old man,' I said. 'How are you, old man?'

My commiseration deepened as I spoke the words, for there had been no lighting up of the eye, no answering pressure of the palm, no sign whatever, in short, of any disposition on his part to do spring dances at the sight of an old friend. The man seemed sandbagged. Melancholy, as I remember Jeeves saying once about Pongo Twistleton when he was trying to knock off smoking, had marked him for her own. Not that I was surprised, of course. In the circs, no doubt, a certain moodiness was only natural.

I released the hand, ceased to knead the shoulder, and, producing the old case, offered him a cigarette.

He took it dully.

'Are you here, Bertie?' he asked.

'Yes, I'm here.'

'Just passing through, or come to stay?'

I thought for a moment. I might have told him that I had arrived at Brinkley Court with the express intention of bringing Angela and himself together once more, of knitting up the severed threads, and so on and so forth; and for perhaps half the time required for the lighting of a gasper I had almost decided to do so. Then, I reflected, better, on the whole, perhaps not. To broadcast the fact that I proposed to take him and Angela and play on them as on a couple of stringed instruments might have been injudicious. Chaps don't always like being played on as on a stringed instrument.

'It all depends,' I said. 'I may remain. I may push on. My plans are uncertain.'

He nodded listlessly, rather in the manner of a man who did not give a damn what I did, and stood gazing out over the sunlit garden. In build and appearance, Tuppy somewhat resembles a bulldog, and his aspect now was that of one of these fine animals who has just been refused a slice of cake. It was not difficult for a man of my discernment to read what was in his mind, and it occasioned me no surprise, therefore, when his next words had to do with the subject marked with a cross on the agenda paper.

'You've heard of this business of mine, I suppose? Me and Angela?'

'I have, indeed, Tuppy, old man.'

'We've bust up.'

'I know. Some little friction, I gather, *in re* Angela's shark.'

'Yes. I said it must have been a flatfish.'

'So my informant told me.'

'Who did you hear it from?'

'Aunt Dahlia.'

'I suppose she cursed me properly?'

'Oh, no. Beyond referring to you in one passage as "this blasted

Glossop", she was, I thought, singularly temperate in her language for a woman who at one time hunted regularly with the Quorn. All the same, I could see, if you don't mind me saying so, old man, that she felt you might have behaved with a little more tact.'

'Tact!'

'And I must admit I rather agreed with her. Was it nice, Tuppy, was it quite kind to take the bloom off Angela's shark like that? You must remember that Angela's shark is very dear to her. Could you not see what a sock on the jaw it would be for the poor child to hear it described by the man to whom she had given her heart as a flatfish?'

I saw that he was struggling with some powerful emotion.

'And what about my side of the thing?' he demanded, in a voice choked with feeling.

'Your side?'

'You don't suppose,' said Tuppy, with rising vehemence, 'that I would have exposed this dashed synthetic shark for the flatfish it undoubtedly was if there had not been causes that led up to it. What induced me to speak as I did was the fact that Angela, the little squirt, had just been most offensive, and I seized the opportunity to get a bit of my own back.'

'Offensive?'

'Exceedingly offensive. Purely on the strength of my having let fall some casual remark – simply by way of saying something and keeping the conversation going – to the effect that I wondered what Anatole was going to give us for dinner, she said that I was too material and ought not always to be thinking of food. Material, my elbow! As a matter of fact, I'm particularly spiritual.'

'Quite.'

'I don't see any harm in wondering what Anatole was going to give us for dinner. Do you?'

'Of course not. A mere ordinary tribute of respect to a great artist.'

'Exactly.'

'All the same – '

'Well?'

'I was only going to say that it seems a pity that the frail craft of love should come a stinker like this when a few manly words of contrition – '

He stared at me.

'You aren't suggesting that I should climb down?'

'It would be the fine, big thing, old egg.'

'I wouldn't dream of climbing down.'

'But, Tuppy – '

'No. I wouldn't do it.'

'But you love her, don't you?'

This touched the spot. He quivered noticeably, and his mouth twisted. Quite the tortured soul.

'I'm not saying I don't love the little blighter,' he said, obviously moved. 'I love her passionately. But that doesn't alter the fact that I consider that what she needs most in this world is a swift kick in the pants.'

A Wooster could scarcely pass this. 'Tuppy, old man!'

'It's no good saying "Tuppy, old man".'

'Well, I do say "Tuppy, old man". Your tone shocks me. One raises the eyebrows. Where is the fine, old, chivalrous spirit of the Glossops?'

'That's all right about the fine, old, chivalrous spirit of the Glossops. Where is the sweet, gentle, womanly spirit of the Angelas? Telling a fellow he was getting a double chin!'

'Did she do that?'

'She did.'

'Oh, well, girls will be girls. Forget it, Tuppy. Go to her and make it up.'

He shook his head.

'No. It is too late. Remarks have been passed about my tummy which it is impossible to overlook.'

'But, Tummy – Tuppy, I mean – be fair. You once told her her new hat made her look like a Pekingese.'

'It did make her look like a Pekingese. That was not vulgar abuse. It was sound, constructive criticism, with no motive behind it but the kindly desire to keep her from making an exhibition of herself in public. Wantonly to accuse a man of puffing when he goes up a flight of stairs is something very different.'

I began to see that the situation would require all my address and ingenuity. If the wedding bells were ever to ring out in the little church of Market Snodsbury, Bertram had plainly got to put in some shrewdish work. I had gathered, during my conversation with Aunt Dahlia, that there had been a certain amount of frank speech between the two contracting parties, but I had not realized till now that matters had gone so far.

The pathos of the thing gave me the pip. Tuppy had admitted in so many words that love still animated the Glossop bosom, and I was convinced that, even after all that had occurred, Angela had not ceased to love him. At the moment, no doubt, she might be wishing that she could hit him with a bottle, but deep down in her I was prepared to bet that there still lingered all the old affection and tenderness. Only injured pride was keeping these two apart, and I felt that if Tuppy would make the first move, all would be well.

I had another whack at it.

'She's broken-hearted about this rift, Tuppy.'

'How do you know? Have you seen her?'

'No, but I'll bet she is.'

'She doesn't look it.'

'Wearing the mask, no doubt. Jeeves does that when I assert my authority.'

'She wrinkles her nose at me as if I were a drain that had got out of order.'

'Merely the mask. I feel convinced she loves you still, and that a kindly word from you is all that is required.'

I could see that this had moved him. He plainly wavered. He did a sort of twiddly on the turf with his foot. And, when he spoke, one spotted the tremolo in the voice:

'You really think that?'

'Absolutely.'

'H'm.'

'If you were to go to her – '

He shook his head.

'I can't do that. It would be fatal. Bing, instantly, would go my prestige. I know girls. Grovel, and the best of them get uppish.' He mused. 'The only way to work the thing would be by tipping her off in some indirect way that I am prepared to open negotiations. Should I sigh a bit when we meet, do you think?'

'She would think you were puffing.'

'That's true.'

I lit another cigarette and gave my mind to the matter. And first crack out of the box, as is so often the way with the Woosters, I got an idea. I remembered the counsel I had given Gussie in the matter of the sausages and ham.

'I've got it, Tuppy. There is one infallible method of indicating to a girl that you love her, and it works just as well when you've had a row and want to make it up. Don't eat any dinner tonight. You can see how impressive that would be. She knows how devoted you are to food.'

He started violently.

'I am not devoted to food!'

'No, no.'

'I am not devoted to food at all.'

'Quite. All I meant – '

'This rot about me being devoted to food,' said Tuppy warmly, 'has got to stop. I am young and healthy and have a good appetite, but that's not the same as being devoted to food. I admire Anatole as a master of his craft, and am always willing to consider anything he may put before me, but when you say I am devoted to food – '

'Quite, quite. All I meant was that if she sees you push away your dinner untasted, she will realize that your heart is aching, and will probably be the first to suggest blowing the all clear.'

Tuppy was frowning thoughtfully.

'Push my dinner away, eh?'

'Yes.'

'Push away a dinner cooked by Anatole?'

'Yes.'

'Push it away untasted?'

'Yes.'

'Let us get this straight. Tonight, at dinner, when the butler offers me a *ris de veau à la financière*, or whatever it may be, hot from Anatole's hands, you wish me to push it away untasted?'

'Yes.'

He chewed his lip. One could sense the struggle going on within. And then suddenly a sort of glow came into his face. The old martyrs probably used to look like that.

'All right.'

'You'll do it?'

'I will.'

'Fine.'

'Of course, it will be agony.'

I pointed out the silver lining.

'Only for the moment. You could slip down tonight, after everyone is in bed, and raid the larder.'

He brightened.

'That's right. I could, couldn't I?'

'I expect there would be something cold there.'

'There is something cold there,' said Tuppy, with growing cheerfulness. 'A steak-and-kidney pie. We had it for lunch today. One of Anatole's ripest. The thing I admire about that man,' said Tuppy reverently, 'the thing that I admire so enormously about Anatole is that, though a Frenchman, he does not, like so many of these chefs, confine himself exclusively to French dishes, but is always willing and ready to weigh in with some good old simple English fare such as this steak-and-kidney pie to which I have alluded. A masterly pie, Bertie, and it wasn't more than half finished. It will do me nicely.'

'And at dinner you will push, as arranged?'

'Absolutely as arranged.'

'Fine.'

'It's an excellent idea. One of Jeeves's best. You can tell him from me, when you see him, that I'm much obliged.'

The cigarette fell from my fingers. It was as though somebody had slapped Bertram Wooster across the face with a wet dishrag.

'You aren't suggesting that you think this scheme I have been sketching out is Jeeves's?'

'Of course it is. It's no good trying to kid me, Bertie. You wouldn't have thought of a wheeze like that in a million years.'

There was a pause. I drew myself up to my full height; then, seeing that he wasn't looking at me, lowered myself again.

'Come, Glossop,' I said coldly, 'we had better be going. It is time we were dressing for dinner.'

9

Tuppy's fatheaded words were still rankling in my bosom as I went up to my room. They continued rankling as I shed the form-fitting, and had not ceased to rankle when, clad in the old dressing-gown, I made my way along the corridor to the *salle de bain*.

It is not too much to say that I was piqued to the tonsils.

I mean to say, one does not court praise. The adulation of the multitude means very little to one. But, all the same, when one has taken the trouble to whack out a highly juicy scheme to benefit an in-the-soup friend in his hour of travail, it's pretty foul to find him giving the credit to one's personal attendant, particularly if that personal attendant is a man who goes about the place not packing mess jackets.

But after I had been splashing about in the porcelain for a bit, composure began to return. I have always found that in moments of heart-bowed-downness there is nothing that calms the bruised spirit like a good go at the soap and water. I don't say I actually sang in the tub, but there were times when it was a mere spin of the coin whether I would do so or not.

The spiritual anguish induced by that tactless speech had become noticeably lessened.

The discovery of a toy duck in the soap dish, presumably the property of some former juvenile visitor, contributed not a little to this new and happier frame of mind. What with one thing and another, I hadn't played with toy ducks in my bath for years, and I found the novel experience most invigorating. For the benefit of those interested, I may mention that if you shove the thing under the surface with the sponge and then let it go, it shoots out of the water in a manner calculated to divert the most careworn. Ten minutes of this and I was enabled to return to the bed-chamber much more the old merry Bertram.

Jeeves was there, laying out the dinner disguise. He greeted the young master with his customary suavity.

'Good evening, sir.'

I responded in the same affable key.

'Good evening, Jeeves.'

'I trust you had a pleasant drive, sir.'

'Very pleasant, thank you, Jeeves. Hand me a sock or two, will you?'

He did so, and I commenced to don.

'Well, Jeeves,' I said, reaching for the underlinen, 'here we are again at Brinkley Court in the county of Worcestershire.'

'Yes, sir.'

'A nice mess things seem to have gone and got themselves into in this rustic joint.'

'Yes, sir.'

'The rift between Tuppy Glossop and my cousin Angela would appear to be serious.'

'Yes, sir. Opinion in the servants' hall is inclined to take a grave view of the situation.'

'And the thought that springs to your mind, no doubt, is that I shall have my work cut out to fix things up?'

'Yes, sir.'

'You are wrong, Jeeves. I have the thing well in hand.'

'You surprise me, sir.'

'I thought I should. Yes, Jeeves, I pondered on the matter most of the way down here, and with the happiest results. I have just been in conference with Mr Glossop, and everything is taped out.'

'Indeed, sir? Might I inquire – '

'You know my methods, Jeeves. Apply them. Have you,' I asked, slipping into the shirt and starting to adjust the cravat, 'been gnawing on the thing at all?'

'Oh, yes, sir. I have always been much attached to Miss Angela, and I felt that it would afford me great pleasure were I to be able to be of service to her.'

'A laudable sentiment. But I suppose you drew blank?'

'No, sir. I was rewarded with an idea.'

'What was it?'

'It occurred to me that a reconciliation might be effected between Mr Glossop and Miss Angela by appealing to that instinct which prompts gentlemen in time of peril to hasten to the rescue of – '

I had to let go of the cravat in order to raise a hand. I was shocked.

'Don't tell me you were contemplating descending to that old he-saved-her-from-drowning gag? I am surprised, Jeeves. Surprised and pained. When I was discussing the matter with Aunt Dahlia on my arrival, she said in a sniffy sort of way that she supposed I was going to shove my cousin Angela into the lake and push Tuppy in to haul her out, and I let her see pretty clearly that I considered the suggestion an insult to my intelligence. And now, if your words have the meaning I read into them, you are mooting precisely the same drivelling scheme. Really, Jeeves!'

'No, sir. Not that. But the thought did cross my mind, as I walked in the grounds and passed the building where the fire bell hangs, that a sudden alarm of fire in the night might result in Mr Glossop endeavouring to assist Miss Angela to safety.'

I shivered.

'Rotten, Jeeves.'

'Well, sir – '

'No good. Not a bit like it.'

'I fancy, sir – '

'No, Jeeves. No more. Enough has been said. Let us drop the subj.'

I finished tying the tie in silence. My emotions were too deep for speech. I knew, of course, that this man had for the time being lost his grip, but I had never suspected that he had gone absolutely to pieces like this. Remembering some of the swift ones he had pulled in the past, I shrank with horror from the spectacle of his present ineptitude. Or is it ineptness? I mean this frightful disposition of his to stick straws in his hair and talk like a perfect ass. It was the old, old story, I supposed. A man's brain whizzes along for years exceeding the speed limit, and something suddenly goes wrong with the steering gear and it skids and comes a smeller in the ditch.

'A bit elaborate,' I said, trying to put the thing in as kindly a light as possible. 'Your old failing. You can see that it's a bit elaborate?'

'Possibly the plan I suggested might be considered open to that criticism, sir, but *faute de mieux* – '

'I don't get you, Jeeves.'

'A French expression, sir, signifying "for want of anything better".'

A moment before, I had been feeling for this wreck of a once fine thinker nothing but a gentle pity. These words jarred the Wooster pride, inducing asperity.

'I understand perfectly well what *faute de mieux* means, Jeeves. I did not recently spend two months among our Gallic neighbours for nothing. Besides, I remember that one from school. What caused my bewilderment was that you should be employing the expression, well knowing that there is no bally *faute de mieux* about it at all. Where do you get that *faute-de-mieux* stuff? Didn't I tell you I had everything taped out?'

'Yes, sir, but – '

'What do you mean – but?'

'Well, sir – '

'Push on, Jeeves. I am ready, even anxious, to hear your views.'

'Well, sir, if I may take the liberty of reminding you of it, your plans in the past have not always been uniformly successful.'

There was a silence – rather a throbbing one – during which I put on my waistcoat in a marked manner. Not till I had got the buckle at the back satisfactorily adjusted did I speak.

'It is true, Jeeves,' I said formally, 'that once or twice in the past I may have missed the bus. This, however, I attribute purely to bad luck.'

'Indeed, sir?'

'On the present occasion I shall not fail, and I'll tell you why I shall not fail. Because my scheme is rooted in human nature.'

'Indeed, sir?'

'It is simple. Not elaborate. And, furthermore, based on the psychology of the individual.'

'Indeed, sir?'

'Jeeves,' I said, 'don't keep saying "Indeed, sir?" No doubt nothing is further from your mind than to convey such a suggestion, but you have a way of stressing the "in" and then coming down with a thud on the "deed" which makes it virtually tantamount to "Oh, yeah?" Correct this, Jeeves.'

'Very good, sir.'

'I tell you I have everything nicely lined up. Would you care to hear what steps I have taken?'

'Very much, sir.'

'Then listen. Tonight at dinner I have recommended Tuppy to lay off the food.'

'Sir?'

'Tut, Jeeves, surely you can follow the idea, even though it is one that would never have occurred to yourself. Have you forgotten that telegram I sent to Gussie Fink-Nottle, steering him away from the sausages and ham? This is the same thing. Pushing the food away untasted is a universally recognized sign of love. It cannot fail to bring home the gravy. You must see that?'

'Well, sir – '

I frowned.

'I don't want to seem always to be criticizing your methods of voice production, Jeeves,' I said, 'but I must inform you that that "Well, sir" of yours is in many respects fully as unpleasant as your "Indeed, sir?" Like the latter, it seems to be tinged with a definite scepticism. It suggests a lack of faith in my vision. The impression I retain after hearing you shoot it at me a couple of times is that you consider me to be talking through the back of my neck, and that only a feudal sense of what is fitting restrains you from substituting for it the words "Says you!"'

'Oh, no, sir.'

'Well, that's what it sounds like. Why don't you think this scheme will work?'

'I fear Miss Angela will merely attribute Mr Glossop's abstinence to indigestion, sir.'

I hadn't thought of that, and I must confess it shook me for a moment. Then I recovered myself. I saw what was at the bottom of all this. Mortified by the consciousness of his own ineptness – or ineptitude – the fellow was simply trying to hamper and obstruct. I decided to knock the stuffing out of him without further preamble.

'Oh?' I said. 'You do, do you? Well, be that as it may, it doesn't alter the fact that you've put out the wrong coat. Be so good, Jeeves,' I said, indicating with a gesture the gent's ordinary dinner jacket, or *smoking*, as we call it on the Côte d'Azur, which was suspended from the hanger on the knob of the wardrobe, 'as to shove that bally black thing in the cupboard and bring out my white mess jacket with the brass buttons.'

He looked at me in a meaning manner. And when I say a meaning manner, I mean there was a respectful but at the same time uppish glint in his eye and a sort of muscular spasm flickered across his face which wasn't quite a quiet smile and yet wasn't quite not a quiet smile. Also the soft cough.

'I regret to say, sir, that I inadvertently omitted to pack the garment to which you refer.'

The vision of that parcel in the hall seemed to rise before my eyes, and I exchanged a merry wink with it. I may even have hummed a bar or two. I'm not quite sure.

'I know you did, Jeeves,' I said, laughing down from lazy eyelids and flicking a speck of dust from the irreproachable Mechlin lace at my wrists. 'But I didn't. You will find it on a chair in the hall in a brown-paper parcel.'

The information that his low manœuvres had been rendered null and void and that the thing was on the strength after all, must have been the nastiest of jars, but there was no play of expression on his finely chiselled to indicate it. There very seldom is on Jeeves's f-c. In moments of discomfort, as I had told Tuppy, he wears a mask, preserving throughout the quiet stolidity of a stuffed moose.

'You might just slide down and fetch it, will you?'

'Very good, sir.'

'Right ho, Jeeves.'

And presently I was sauntering towards the drawing-room with the good old j. nestling snugly abaft the shoulder blades.

Aunt Dahlia was in the drawing-room. She glanced up at my entrance.

'Hullo, eyesore,' she said. 'What do you think you're made up as?'

I did not get the purport.

'The jacket, you mean?' I queried, groping.

'I do. You look like one of the chorus of male guests at Abernethy Towers in Act 2 of a touring musical comedy.'

'You do not admire this jacket?'

'I do not.'

'You did at Cannes.'

'Well, this isn't Cannes.'

'But, dash it – '

'Oh, never mind. Let it go. If you want to give my butler a laugh, what does it matter? What does anything matter now?'

There was a death-where-is-thy-sting-fullness about her manner which I found distasteful. It isn't often that I score off Jeeves in the devastating fashion just described, and when I do I like to see happy, smiling faces about me.

'Tails up, Aunt Dahlia,' I urged buoyantly.

'Tails up be dashed,' was her sombre response. 'I've just been talking to Tom.'

'Telling him?'

'No, listening to him. I haven't had the nerve to tell him yet.'

'Is he still upset about that income-tax money?'

'Upset is right. He says that civilization is in the melting-pot and that all thinking men can read the writing on the wall.'

'What wall?'

'Old Testament, ass. Belshazzar's feast.'

'Oh, that, yes. I've often wondered how that gag was worked. With mirrors, I expect.'

'I wish I could use mirrors to break it to Tom about this baccarat business.'

I had a word of comfort to offer here. I had been turning the thing over in my mind since our last meeting, and I thought I saw where she had got twisted. Where she made her error, it seemed to me, was in feeling she had got to tell Uncle Tom. To my way of thinking, the matter was one on which it would be better to continue to exercise a quiet reserve.

'I don't see why you need mention that you lost that money at baccarat.'

'What do you suggest, then? Letting *Milady's Boudoir* join Civilization in the melting-pot? Because that is what it will infallibly do unless I get a cheque by next week. The printers have been showing a nasty spirit for months.'

'You don't follow. Listen. It's an understood thing, I take it, that Uncle Tom foots the *Boudoir* bills. If the bally sheet has been turning the corner for two years, he must have got used to forking out by this time. Well, simply ask him for the money to pay the printers.'

'I did. Just before I went to Cannes.'

'Wouldn't he give it to you?'

'Certainly he gave it to me. He brassed up like an officer and a gentleman. That was the money I lost at baccarat.'

'Oh? I didn't know that.'

'There isn't much you do know.'

A nephew's love made me overlook the slur.

'Tut!' I said.

'What did you say?'

'I said, "Tut!"'

'Say it once again, and I'll biff you where you stand. I've enough to endure without being tutted at.'

'Quite.'

'Any tutting that's required, I'll attend to myself. And the same applies to clicking the tongue, if you were thinking of doing that.'

'Far from it.'

'Good.'

I stood awhile in thought. I was concerned to the core. My heart, if you remember, had already bled once for Aunt Dahlia this evening. It now bled again. I knew how deeply attached she was to this paper of hers. Seeing it go down the drain would be for her like watching a loved child sink for the third time in some pond or mere.

And there was no question that, unless carefully prepared for the touch, Uncle Tom would see a hundred *Milady's Boudoirs* go phut rather than take the rap.

Then I saw how the thing could be handled. This aunt, I perceived, must fall into line with my other clients. Tuppy Glossop was knocking off dinner to melt Angela. Gussie Fink-Nottle was knocking off dinner to impress the Bassett. Aunt Dahlia must knock off dinner to soften Uncle Tom. For the beauty of this scheme of mine was that there was no limit to the number of entrants. Come one, come all, the more the merrier, and satisfaction guaranteed in every case.

'I've got it,' I said. 'There is only one course to pursue. Eat less meat.'

She looked at me in a pleading sort of way. I wouldn't swear that her eyes were wet with unshed tears, but I rather think they were. Certainly she clasped her hands in piteous appeal.

'Must you drivel, Bertie? Won't you stop it just this once? Just for tonight, to please Aunt Dahlia?'

'I'm not drivelling.'

'I dare say that to a man of your high standards it doesn't come under the head of drivel, but – '

I saw what had happened. I hadn't made myself quite clear.

'It's all right,' I said. 'Have no misgivings. This is the real Tabasco. When I said "Eat less meat", what I meant was that you must refuse your oats at dinner tonight. Just sit there, looking blistered, and wave away each course as it comes with a weary gesture of resignation. You see what will happen. Uncle Tom will notice your loss of appetite, and I am prepared to bet that at the conclusion of the meal he will come to you and say "Dahlia, darling" – I take it he calls you "Dahlia" – "Dahlia darling," he will say, "I noticed at dinner tonight that you were a bit off your feed. Is anything the matter, Dahlia, darling?" "Why, yes, Tom, darling," you will reply. "It is kind of you to ask, darling. The fact is, darling, I am terribly worried." "My darling," he will say – '

Aunt Dahlia interrupted at this point to observe that these Traverses seemed to be a pretty soppy couple of blighters, to judge by their dialogue. She also wished to know when I was going to get to the point.

I gave her a look.

'"My darling," he will say tenderly, "is there anything I can do?" To which your reply will be that there jolly well is – viz. reach for his cheque book and start writing.'

I was watching her closely as I spoke, and was pleased to note respect suddenly dawn in her eyes.

'But, Bertie, this is positively bright.'

'I told you Jeeves wasn't the only fellow with brain.'

'I believe it would work.'

'It's bound to work. I've recommended it to Tuppy.'

'Young Glossop?'

'In order to soften Angela.'

'Splendid!'

'And to Gussie Fink-Nottle, who wants to make a hit with the Bassett.'

'Well, well, well! What a busy little brain it is.'

'Always working, Aunt Dahlia, always working.'

'You're not the chump I took you for, Bertie.'

'When did you ever take me for a chump?'

'Oh, some time last summer. I forget what gave me the idea. Yes, Bertie, this scheme is bright. I suppose, as a matter of fact, Jeeves suggested it.'

'Jeeves did not suggest it. I resent these implications. Jeeves had nothing to do with it whatsoever.'

'Well, all right, no need to get excited about it. Yes, I think it will work. Tom's devoted to me.'

'Who wouldn't be?'

'I'll do it.'

And then the rest of the party trickled in, and we toddled down to dinner.

Conditions being as they were at Brinkley Court – I mean to say, the place being loaded down above the plimsoll mark with aching hearts and standing room only as regarded tortured souls – I hadn't expected the evening meal to be particularly effervescent. Nor was it. Silent. Sombre. The whole thing more than a bit like Christmas dinner on Devil's Island.

I was glad when it was over.

What with having, on top of her other troubles, to rein herself back from the trough, Aunt Dahlia was a total loss as far as anything in the shape of brilliant badinage was concerned. The fact that he was fifty quid in the red and expecting Civilization to take a toss at any moment had caused Uncle Tom, who always looked a bit like a pterodactyl with a secret sorrow, to take on a deeper melancholy. The Bassett was a silent bread crumbler. Angela might have been hewn from the living rock. Tuppy had the air of a condemned murderer refusing to make the usual hearty breakfast before tooling off to the execution shed.

And as for Gussie Fink-Nottle, many an experienced undertaker would have been deceived by his appearance and started embalming him on sight.

This was the first glimpse I had had of Gussie since we parted at my flat, and I must say his demeanour disappointed me. I had been expecting something a great deal more sparkling.

At my flat, on the occasion alluded to, he had, if you recall, practically given me a signed guarantee that all he needed to touch him off was a rural setting. Yet in this aspect now I could detect no indication whatsoever that he was about to round into mid-season form. He still looked like a cat in an adage, and it did not take me long to realize that my very first act on escaping from this morgue must be to draw him aside and give him a pep talk.

If ever a chap wanted the clarion note, it looked as if it was this Fink-Nottle.

In the general exodus of mourners, however, I lost sight of him, and, owing to the fact that Aunt Dahlia roped me in for a game of backgammon, it was not immediately that I was able to institute a search. But after we had been playing for a while, the butler came in and asked her if she would speak to Anatole, so I managed to get away. And some ten minutes later, having failed to find scent in the house, I started to throw out the dragnet through the grounds, and flushed him in the rose garden.

He was smelling a rose at the moment in a limp sort of way, but removed the beak as I approached.

'Well, Gussie,' I said.

I had beamed genially upon him as I spoke, such being my customary policy on meeting an old pal; but instead of beaming back genially, he gave me a most unpleasant look. His attitude perplexed me. It was as if he were not glad to see Bertram. For a moment he stood letting this unpleasant look play upon me, as it were, and then he spoke.

'You and your "Well, Gussie"!'

He said this between clenched teeth, always an unmatey thing to do, and I found myself more fogged than ever.

'How do you mean – me and my "Well, Gussie"?'

'I like your nerve, coming bounding about the place, saying "Well, Gussie." That's about all the "Well, Gussie" I shall require from you, Wooster. And it's no good looking like that. You know what I mean. That damned prize giving! It was a dastardly act to crawl out as you did and shove it off on to me. I will not mince my words. It was the act of a hound and a stinker.'

Now, though, as I have shown, I had devoted most of the time on the journey down to meditating upon the case of Angela and Tuppy, I had not neglected to give a thought or two to what I was going to say when I encountered Gussie. I had foreseen that there might be some little temporary unpleasantness when we met, and when a difficult interview is in the offing Bertram Wooster likes to have his story ready.

So now I was able to reply with a manly, disarming frankness. The sudden introduction of the topic had given me a bit of a jolt, it is true, for in the stress of recent happenings I had rather let that prize-giving business slide to the back of my mind; but I had speedily recovered and, as I say, was able to reply with a manly d.f.

'But, my dear chap,' I said, 'I took it for granted that you would understand that that was all part of my schemes.'

He said something about my schemes which I did not catch.

'Absolutely. "Crawling out" is entirely the wrong way to put it. You don't suppose I didn't want to distribute those prizes, do you? Left to myself, there is nothing I would find a greater treat. But I saw that the square, generous thing to do was to step aside and let you take it on, so I did so. I felt that your need was greater than mine. You don't mean to say you aren't looking forward to it?'

He uttered a coarse expression which I wouldn't have thought he would have known. It just shows that you can bury yourself in the country and still somehow acquire a vocabulary. No doubt one picks up things from the neighbours – the vicar, the local doctor, the man who brings the milk, and so on.

'But, dash it,' I said, 'can't you see what this is going to do for you? It will send your stock up with a jump. There you will be, up on that platform, a romantic, impressive figure, the star of the whole proceedings, the what-d'you-call-it of all eyes. Madeline Bassett will be all over you. She will see you in a totally new light.'

'She will, will she?'

'Certainly she will. Augustus Fink-Nottle, the newts' friend, she knows. She is acquainted with Augustus Fink-Nottle, the dogs' chiropodist. But Augustus Fink-Nottle, the orator – that'll knock her sideways, or I know nothing of the female heart. Girls go potty over a public man. If ever anyone did anyone else a kindness, it was I when I gave this extraordinarily attractive assignment to you.'

He seemed impressed by my eloquence. Couldn't have helped himself, of course. The fire faded from behind his horn-rimmed spectacles, and in its place appeared the old fish-like goggle.

'M' yes,' he said meditatively. 'Have you ever made a speech, Bertie?'

'Dozens of times. It's pie. Nothing to it. Why, I once addressed a girls' school.'

'You weren't nervous?'

'Not a bit.'

'How did you go?'

'They hung on my lips. I held them in the hollow of my hand.'

'They didn't throw eggs, or anything?'

'Not a thing.'

He expelled a deep breath, and for a space stood staring in silence at a passing slug.

'Well,' he said, at length, 'it may be all right. Possibly I am letting the thing prey on my mind too much. I may be wrong in supposing it the fate that is worse than death. But I'll tell you this much: The prospect of that prize giving on the thirty-first of this month has been turning my existence into a nightmare. I haven't been able to sleep or think or eat . . . By the way, that reminds me. You never explained that cipher telegram about the sausages and ham.'

'It wasn't a cipher telegram. I wanted you to go light on the food, so that she would realize you were in love.'

He laughed hollowly.

'I see. Well, I've been doing that, all right.'

'Yes, I was noticing at dinner. Splendid.'

'I don't see what's splendid about it, it's not going to get me anywhere. I shall never be able to ask her to marry me. I couldn't find nerve to do that if I lived on wafer biscuits for the rest of my life.'

'But, dash it, Gussie. In these romantic surroundings. I should have thought the whispering trees alone – '

'I don't care what you would have thought. I can't do it.'

'Oh, come!'

'I can't. She seems so aloof, so remote.'

'She doesn't.'

'Yes, she does. Especially when you see her sideways. Have you seen her sideways, Bertie? That cold, pure profile. It just takes all the heart out of one.'

'It doesn't.'

'I tell you it does. I catch sight of it, and the words freeze on my lips.'

He spoke with a sort of dull despair, and so manifest was his lack of ginger and the spirit that wins to success that for an instant, I confess, I felt a bit stymied. It seemed hopeless to go on trying to steam up such a human jellyfish. Then I saw the way. With that extraordinary quickness of mine, I realized exactly what must be done if this Fink-Nottle was to be enabled to push his nose past the judges' box.

'She must be softened up,' I said.

'Be what?'

'Softened up. Sweetened. Worked on. Preliminary spadework must be put in. Here, Gussie, is the procedure I propose to adopt: I shall now return to the house and lug this Bassett out for a stroll. I shall talk to her of hearts that yearn, intimating that there is one actually on the premises. I shall pitch it strong, sparing no effort. You, meanwhile, will lurk on the outskirts, and in about a quarter of an hour you will come along and carry on from there. By that time, her emotions having been stirred, you ought to be able to do the rest on your head. It will be like leaping on to a moving bus.'

I remember when I was a kid at school having to learn a poem of sorts about a fellow named Pig-something – a sculptor he would have been, no doubt – who made a statue of a girl, and what should happen one morning but that the bally thing suddenly came to life. A pretty nasty shock for the chap, of course, but the point I'm working round to is that there were a couple of lines that went, if I remember correctly:

She starts. She moves. She seems to feel
The stir of life along her keel.

And what I'm driving at is that you couldn't get a better description of what happened to Gussie as I spoke these heartening words. His brow cleared, his eyes brightened, he lost that fishy look, and he gazed at the slug, which was still on the long, long trail, with something approaching bonhomie. A marked improvement.

'I see what you mean. You will sort of pave the way, as it were.'

'That's right. Spadework.'

'It's a terrific idea, Bertie. It will make all the difference.'

'Quite. But don't forget that after that it will be up to you. You will have to haul up your slacks and give her the old oil, or my efforts will have been in vain.'

Something of his former Gawd-help-us-ness seemed to return to him. He gasped a bit.

'That's true. What the dickens shall I say?'

I restrained my impatience with an effort. The man had been at school with me.

'Dash it, there are hundreds of things you can say. Talk about the sunset.'

'The sunset?'

'Certainly. Half the married men you meet began by talking about the sunset.'

'But what can I say about the sunset?'

'Well, Jeeves got off a good one the other day. I met him airing the dog in the park one evening, and he said, "Now fades the glimmering landscape on the sight, sir, and all the air a solemn stillness holds." You might use that.'

'What sort of landscape?'

'Glimmering. *G* for "gastritis", *l* for "lizard" – '

'Oh, glimmering? Yes, that's not bad. Glimmering landscape . . . solemn stillness . . . Yes, I call that pretty good.'

'You could then say that you have often thought that the stars are God's daisy chain.'

'But I haven't.'

'I dare say not. But she has. Hand her that one, and I don't see how she can help feeling that you're a twin soul.'

'God's daisy chain?'

'God's daisy chain. And then you go on about how twilight always makes you sad. I know you're going to say it doesn't, but on this occasion it has jolly well got to.'

'Why?'

'That's just what she will ask, and you will then have got her going. Because you will reply that it is because yours is such a lonely life. It wouldn't be a bad idea to gave her a brief description of a typical home evening at your Lincolnshire residence, showing how you pace the meadows with a heavy tread.'

'I generally sit indoors and listen to the wireless.'

'No, you don't. You pace the meadows with a heavy tread, wishing that you had someone to love you. And then you speak of the day when she came into your life.'

'Like a fairy princess.'

'Absolutely,' I said with approval. I hadn't expected such a hot one from such a quarter. 'Like a fairy princess. Nice work, Gussie.'

'And then?'

'Well, after that it's easy. You say you have something you want to say to her, and then you snap into it. I don't see how it can fail. If I were you, I should do it in this rose garden. It is well established that there is no sounder move than to steer the adored object into rose gardens in the gloaming. And you had better have a couple of quick ones first.'

'Quick ones?'

'Snifters.'

'Drinks, do you mean? But I don't drink.'

'What?'

'I've never touched a drop in my life.'

This made me a bit dubious, I must confess. On these occasions it is generally conceded that a moderate skinful is of the essence.

However, if the facts were as he had stated, I supposed there was nothing to be done about it.

'Well, you'll have to make out as best you can on ginger pop.'

'I always drink orange juice.'

'Orange juice, then. Tell me, Gussie, to settle a bet, do you really like that muck?'

'Very much.'

'Then there is no more to be said. Now, let's just have a run through, to see that you've got the layout straight. Start off with the glimmering landscape.'

'Stars God's daisy chain.'

'Twilight makes you feel sad.'

'Because mine is a lonely life.'

'Describe life.'

'Talk about the day I met her.'

'Add fairy-princess gag. Say there's something you want to say to her. Heave a couple of sighs. Grab her hand. And give her the works. Right.'

And confident that he had grasped the scenario and that everything might now be expected to proceed through the proper channels, I picked up the feet and hastened back to the house.

It was not until I had reached the drawing-room and was enabled to take a square look at the Bassett that I found the debonair gaiety with which I had embarked on this affair beginning to wane a trifle. Beholding her at close range like this, I suddenly became cognisant of what I was in for. The thought of strolling with this rummy specimen undeniably gave me a most unpleasant sinking feeling. I could not but remember how often, when in her company at Cannes, I had gazed dumbly at her, wishing that some kindly motorist in a racing car would ease the situation by coming along and ramming her amidships. As I have already made abundantly clear, this girl was not one of my most congenial buddies.

However, a Wooster's word is his bond. Woosters may quail, but they do not edge out. Only the keenest ear could have detected the tremor in the voice as I asked her if she would care to come out for half an hour.

'Lovely evening,' I said.

'Yes, lovely, isn't it?'

'Lovely. Reminds me of Cannes.'

'How lovely the evenings were there!'

'Lovely,' I said.

'Lovely,' said the Bassett.

'Lovely,' I agreed.

That completed the weather and news bulletin for the French Riviera. Another minute, and we were out in the great open spaces, she cooing a bit about the scenery, and self replying, 'Oh, rather, quite,' and wondering how best to approach the matter in hand.

10

How different it all would have been, I could not but reflect, if this girl had been the sort of girl one chirrups cheerily to over the telephone and takes for spins in the old two-seater. In that case, I would simply have said, 'Listen,' and she would have said, 'What?' and I would have said, 'You know Gussie Fink-Nottle,' and she would have said, 'Yes,' and I would have said, 'He loves you,' and she would have said either, 'What, that mutt? Well, thank heaven for one good laugh today,' or else, in more passionate vein, 'Hot dog! Tell me more.'

I mean to say, in either event the whole thing would have been over and done with in under a minute.

But with the Bassett something less snappy and a good deal more glutinous was obviously indicated. What with all this daylight-saving stuff, we had hit the great open spaces at a moment when twilight had not yet begun to cheese it in favour of the shades of night. There was a fag-end of sunset still functioning. Stars were beginning to peep out, bats were fooling round, the garden was full of the aroma of those niffy white flowers which only start to put in their heavy work at the end of the day – in short, the glimmering landscape was fading on the sight and all the air held a solemn stillness, and it was plain that this was having the worst effect on her. Her eyes were enlarged, and her whole map a good deal too suggestive of the soul's awakening for comfort.

Her aspect was that of a girl who was expecting something fairly fruity from Bertram.

In these circs, conversation inevitably flagged a bit. I am never at my best when the situation seems to call for a certain soupiness, and I've heard other members of the Drones say the same thing about themselves. I remember Pongo Twistleton telling me that he was out in a gondola with a girl by moonlight once, and the only time he spoke was to tell her that old story about the chap who was so good at swimming that they made him a traffic cop in Venice.

Fell rather flat, he assured me, and it wasn't much later when the girl said she thought it was getting a little chilly and how about pushing back to the hotel.

So now, as I say, the talk rather hung fire. It had been all very well for me to promise Gussie that I would cut loose to this girl about aching hearts, but you want a cue for that sort of thing. And when, toddling along, we reached the edge of the lake and she finally spoke, conceive my chagrin when I discovered that what she was talking about was stars.

Not a bit of good to me.

'Oh, look,' she said. She was a confirmed Oh-looker. I had noticed this at Cannes, where she had drawn my attention in this manner on various occasions to such diverse objects as a French actress, a Provençal filling station, the sunset over the Estorels, Michael Arlen, a man selling coloured spectacles, the deep velvet blue of the Mediterranean, and the late mayor of New York in a striped one-piece bathing suit. 'Oh, look at that sweet little star up there all by itself.'

I saw the one she meant, a little chap operating in a detached sort of way above a spinney.

'Yes,' I said.

'I wonder if it feels lonely.'

'Oh, I shouldn't think so.'

'A fairy must have been crying.'

'Eh?'

'Don't you remember? "Every time a fairy sheds a tear, a wee bit star is born in the Milky Way." Have you ever thought that, Mr Wooster?'

I never had. Most improbable, I considered, and it didn't seem to me to check up with her statement that the stars were God's daisy chain. I mean, you can't have it both ways.

However, I was in no mood to dissect and criticize. I saw that I had been wrong in supposing that the stars were not germane to the issue. Quite a decent cue they had provided, and I leaped on it promptly: 'Talking of shedding tears – '

But she was now on the subject of rabbits, several of which were messing about in the park to our right.

'Oh, look. The little bunnies!'

'Talking of shedding tears – '

'Don't you love this time of the evening, Mr Wooster, when the sun has gone to bed and all the bunnies come out to have their little suppers? When I was a child, I used to think that rabbits were gnomes, and that if I held my breath and stayed quite still, I should see the fairy queen.'

Indicating with a reserved gesture that this was just the sort of loony thing I should have expected her to think as a child, I returned to the point.

'Talking of shedding tears,' I said firmly, 'it may interest you to know that there is an aching heart in Brinkley Court.'

This held her. She cheesed the rabbit theme. Her face, which had been aglow with what I supposed was a pretty animation, clouded. She unshipped a sigh that sounded like the wind going out of a rubber duck.

'Ah, yes. Life is very sad, isn't it?'

'It is for some people. This aching heart, for instance.'

'Those wistful eyes of hers! Drenched irises. And they used to dance like elves of delight. And all through a foolish misunderstanding about a shark. What a tragedy misunderstandings are. That pretty romance broken and over just because Mr Glossop would insist that it was a flatfish.'

I saw that she had got the wires crossed.

'I'm not talking about Angela.'

'But her heart is aching.'

'I know it's aching. But so is somebody else's.'

She looked at me, perplexed.

'Somebody else? Mr Glossop's, you mean?'

'No, I don't.'

'Mrs Travers's?'

The exquisite code of politeness of the Woosters prevented me clipping her one on the earhole, but I would have given a shilling to be able to do it. There seemed to me something deliberately fatheaded in the way she persisted in missing the gist.

'No, not Aunt Dahlia's, either.'

'I'm sure she is dreadfully upset.'

'Quite. But this heart I'm talking about isn't aching because of Tuppy's row with Angela. It's aching for a different reason altogether. I mean to say – dash it, you know why hearts ache!'

She seemed to shimmy a bit. Her voice, when she spoke, was whispery: 'You mean – for love?'

'Absolutely. Right on the bull's-eye. For love.'

'Oh, Mr Wooster!'

'I take it you believe in love at first sight?'

'I do, indeed.'

'Well, that's what happened to this aching heart. It fell in love at first sight, and ever since it's been eating itself out, as I believe the expression is.'

There was a silence. She had turned away and was watching a duck out on the lake. It was tucking into weeds, a thing I've never been able to understand anyone wanting to do. Though I suppose, if you face it squarely, they're no worse than spinach. She stood drinking it in for a bit, and then it suddenly stood on its head and disappeared, and this seemed to break the spell.

'Oh, Mr Wooster!' she said again, and from the tone of her voice, I could see that I had got her going.

'For you, I mean to say,' I proceeded, starting to put in the fancy touches. I dare say you have noticed on these occasions that the difficulty is to plant the main idea, to get the general outline of the thing well fixed. The rest is mere detail work. I don't say I became glib at this juncture, but I certainly became a dashed glibber than I had been.

'It's having the dickens of a time. Can't eat, can't sleep – all for love of you. And what makes it all so particularly rotten is that it – this aching heart – can't bring itself up to the scratch and tell you the position of affairs, because your profile has gone and given it cold feet. Just as it is about to speak, it catches sight of you sideways, and words fail it. Silly, of course, but there it is.'

I heard her give a gulp, and I saw that her eyes had become moistish. Drenched irises, if you care to put it that way.

'Lend you a handkerchief?'

'No, thank you. I'm quite all right.'

It was more than I could say for myself. My efforts had left me weak. I don't know if you suffer in the same way, but with me the act of talking anything in the nature of real mashed potatoes always induces a sort of prickly sensation and a hideous feeling of shame, together with a marked starting of the pores.

I remember at my Aunt Agatha's place in Hertfordshire once being put on the spot and forced to enact the rôle of King Edward III saying goodbye to that girl of his, Fair Rosamund, at some sort of pageant in aid of the Distressed Daughters of the Clergy. It involved some rather warmish mediaeval dialogue, I recall, racy of the days when they called a spade a spade, and by the time the whistle blew, I'll bet no Daughter of the Clergy was half as distressed as I was. Not a dry stitch.

My reaction now was very similar. It was a highly liquid Bertram who, hearing his *vis-à-vis* give a couple of hiccups and start to speak bent an attentive ear.

'Please don't say any more, Mr Wooster.'

Well, I wasn't going to, of course.

'I understand.'

I was glad to hear this.

'Yes, I understand. I won't be so silly as to pretend not to know what you mean. I suspected this at Cannes, when you used to stand and stare at me without speaking a word, but with whole volumes in your eyes.'

If Angela's shark had bitten me in the leg, I couldn't have leaped more convulsively. So tensely had I been concentrating on Gussie's interests that it hadn't so much as crossed my mind that another and an unfortunate construction could be placed on those words of mine. The persp., already bedewing my brow, became a regular Niagara.

My whole fate hung upon a woman's word. I mean to say, I couldn't back out. If a girl thinks a man is proposing to her, and on that understanding books him up, he can't explain to her that she has got hold of entirely the wrong end of the stick and that he hadn't the smallest intention of suggesting anything of the kind. He must simply let it ride. And the thought of being engaged to a girl who talked openly about fairies being born because stars blew their noses, or whatever it was, frankly appalled me.

She was carrying on with her remarks, and as I listened I clenched my fists till I shouldn't wonder if the knuckles didn't stand out white under the strain. It seemed as if she would never get to the nub.

'Yes, all through those days at Cannes I could see what you were trying to say. A girl always knows. And then you followed me down here, and there was that same dumb, yearning look in your eyes when we met this evening. And then you were so insistent that I should come out and walk with you in the twilight. And now you stammer out those halting words. No, this does not come as a surprise. But I am sorry – '

The word was like one of Jeeves's pick-me-ups. Just as if a glassful of meat sauce, red pepper, and the yolk of an egg – though, as I say, I am convinced that these are not the sole ingredients – had been shot into me, I expanded like some lovely flower blossoming in the sunshine. It was all right, after all. My guardian angel had not been asleep at the switch.

'– but I am afraid it is impossible.'

She paused.

'Impossible,' she repeated.

I had been so busy feeling saved from the scaffold that I didn't get on to it for a moment that an early reply was desired.

'Oh, right ho,' I said hastily.

'I'm sorry.'

'Quite all right.'

'Sorrier than I can say.'

'Don't give it another thought.'

'We can still be friends.'

'Oh, rather.'

'Then shall we just say no more about it; keep what has happened as a tender little secret between ourselves?'

'Absolutely.'

'We will. Like something lovely and fragrant laid away in lavender.'

'In lavender – right.'

There was a longish pause. She was gazing at me in a divinely pitying sort of way, much as if I had been a snail she had happened accidentally to bring her short French vamp down on, and I longed to tell her that it was all right, and that Bertram, so far from being the victim of despair, had never felt fizzier in his life. But, of course, one can't do that sort of thing. I simply said nothing, and stood there looking brave.

'I wish I could,' she murmured.

'Could?' I said, for my attensh had been wandering.

'Feel towards you as you would like me to feel.'

'Oh, ah.'

'But I can't. I'm sorry.'

'Absolutely OK. Faults on both sides, no doubt.'

'Because I am fond of you, Mr – no, I think I must call you Bertie. May I?'

'Oh, rather.'

'Because we are real friends.'

'Quite.'

'I do like you, Bertie. And if things were different – I wonder – '

'Eh?'

'After all, we are real friends ... We have this common memory ... You have a right to know ... I don't want you to think – Life is such a muddle, isn't it?'

To many men, no doubt, these broken utterances would have appeared mere drooling and would have been dismissed as such. But the Woosters are quicker-witted than the ordinary and can read between the lines. I suddenly divined what it was that she was trying to get off the chest.

'You mean there's someone else?'

She nodded.

'You're in love with some other bloke?'

She nodded.

'Engaged, what?'

This time she shook the pumpkin.

'No, not engaged.'

Well, that was something, of course. Nevertheless, from the way she spoke, it certainly looked as if poor old Gussie might as well scratch his name off the entry list, and I didn't at all like the prospect of having to break the bad news to him. I had studied the man closely, and it was my conviction that this would about be his finish.

Gussie, you see, wasn't like some of my pals – the name of Bingo Little is one that springs to the lips – who, if turned down by a girl, would simply say, 'Well, bung-oh!' and toddle off quite happily to find another. He was so manifestly a bird who, having failed to score in the first chukker, would turn the thing up and spend the rest of his life brooding over his newts and growing long grey whiskers, like one of those chaps you read about in novels, who live in the great white house you can just see over there through the trees and shut themselves off from the world and have pained faces.

'I'm afraid he doesn't care for me in that way. At least, he has said nothing. You understand that I am only telling you this because – '

'Oh, rather.'

'It's odd that you should have asked me if I believed in love at first sight.' She half closed her eyes. '"Who ever loved that loved not at first sight?"' she said in a rummy voice that brought back to me – I don't know why – the picture of my Aunt Agatha, as Boadicea, reciting at that pageant I was speaking of. 'It's a silly little story. I was staying with some friends in the country, and I had gone for a walk with my dog, and the poor wee mite got a nasty thorn in his little foot and I didn't know what to do. And then suddenly this man came along – '

Harking back once again to that pageant, in sketching out for you my emotions on that occasion, I showed you only the darker side of the picture. There was, I should now mention, a splendid aftermath when, having climbed out of my suit of chain mail and sneaked off to the local pub, I entered the saloon bar and requested mine host to start pouring. A moment later, a tankard of their special home-brewed was in my hand, and the ecstasy of that first gollup is still green in my memory. The recollection of the agony through which I had passed was just what was needed to make it perfect.

It was the same now. When I realized, listening to her words, that she must be referring to Gussie – I mean to say, there couldn't have been a whole platoon of men taking thorns out of her dog that day; the animal wasn't a pin-cushion – and became aware that Gussie, who an instant before had, to all appearances, gone so far back in the betting as not to be worth a quotation, was the big winner after all, a positive thrill permeated the frame and there escaped my lips a 'Wow!' so crisp and hearty that the Bassett leaped a liberal inch and a half from terra firma.

'I beg your pardon?' she said.

I waved a jaunty hand.

'Nothing,' I said. 'Nothing. Just remembered there's a letter I have to write tonight without fail. If you don't mind, I think I'll be going in. Here,' I said, 'comes Gussie Fink-Nottle. He will look after you.'

And, as I spoke, Gussie came sidling out from behind a tree.

I passed away and left them to it. As regards these two, everything was beyond a question absolutely in order. All Gussie had to do was keep his head down and not press. Already, I felt, as I legged it back to the house, the happy ending must have begun to function. I mean to say, when you leave a girl and a man, each of whom has admitted in set terms that she and he loves him and her, in close juxtaposition in the twilight, there doesn't seem much more to do but start pricing fish slices.

Something attempted, something done, seemed to me to have earned two-penn'orth of wassail in the smoking-room.

I proceeded thither.

11

The makings were neatly laid out on a side table, and to pour into a glass an inch or so of the raw spirit and shoosh some soda water on top of it was with me the work of a moment. This done, I retired to an armchair and put my feet up, sipping the mixture with carefree enjoyment, rather like Caesar having one in his tent the day he overcame the Nervii.

As I let the mind dwell on what must even now be taking place in that peaceful garden, I felt bucked and uplifted. Though never for an instant faltering in my opinion that Augustus Fink-Nottle was Nature's final word in cloth-headed guffins, I liked the man, wished him well, and could not have felt more deeply involved in the success of his wooing if I, and not he, had been under the ether.

The thought that by this time he might quite easily have completed the preliminary *pourparlers* and be deep in an informal discussion of honeymoon plans was very pleasant to me.

Of course, considering the sort of girl Madeline Bassett was – stars and rabbits and all that, I mean – you might say that a sober sadness would have been more fitting. But in these matters you have got to realize that tastes differ. The impulse of right-thinking men might be to run a mile when they saw the Bassett, but for some reason she appealed to the deeps in Gussie, so that was that.

I had reached this point in my meditations, when I was aroused by the sound of the door opening. Somebody came in and started moving like a leopard toward the side table and, lowering the feet, I perceived that it was Tuppy Glossop.

The sight of him gave me a momentary twinge of remorse, reminding me, as it did, that in the excitement of getting Gussie fixed up I had rather forgotten about this other client. It is often that way when you're trying to run two cases at once.

However, Gussie now being off my mind, I was prepared to devote my whole attention to the Glossop problem.

I had been much pleased by the way he had carried out the task assigned him at the dinner-table. No easy one, I can assure you, for the browsing and sluicing had been of the highest quality, and there had been one dish in particular – I allude to the *nonnettes de poulet Agnès Sorel* – which might well have broken down the most iron resolution. But he had passed it up like a professional fasting man, and I was proud of him.

'Oh, hallo, Tuppy,' I said, 'I wanted to see you.'

He turned, snifter in hand, and it was easy to see that his privations had tried him sorely. He was looking like a wolf on the steppes of Russia which has seen its peasant shin up a high tree.

'Yes?' he said, rather unpleasantly. 'Well, here I am.'

'Well?'

'How do you mean – well?'

'Make your report.'

'What report?'

'Have you nothing to tell me about Angela?'

'Only that she's a blister.'

I was concerned.

'Hasn't she come clustering round you yet?'

'She has not.'

'Very odd.'

'Why odd?'

'She must have noted your lack of appetite.'

He barked raspingly, as if he were having trouble with the tonsils of the soul.

'Lack of appetite! I'm as hollow as the Grand Canyon.'

'Courage, Tuppy! Think of Gandhi.'

'What about Gandhi?'

'He hasn't had a square meal for years.'

'Nor have I. Or I could swear I hadn't. Gandhi, my left foot.'

I saw that it might be best to let the Gandhi *motif* slide. I went back to where we had started.

'She's probably looking for you now.'

'Who is? Angela?'

'Yes. She must have noticed your supreme sacrifice.'

'I don't suppose she noticed it at all, the little fathead. I'll bet it didn't register in any way whatsoever.'

'Come, Tuppy,' I urged, 'this is morbid. Don't take this gloomy view. She must at least have spotted that you refused those *nonnettes de poulet Agnès Sorel*. It was a sensational renunciation and stuck out like a sore thumb. And the *crêpes à la Rossini* – '

A hoarse cry broke from his twisted lips:

'Will you stop it, Bertie! Do you think I am made of marble? Isn't it bad enough to have sat watching one of Anatole's supremest dinners flit by, course after course, without having you making a song about it? Don't remind me of those *nonnettes*. I can't stand it.'

I endeavoured to hearten and console.

'Be brave, Tuppy. Fix your thoughts on that cold steak-and-kidney pie in the larder. As the Good Book says, it cometh in the morning.'

'Yes, in the morning. And it's now about half-past nine at night. You would bring that pie up, wouldn't you? Just when I was trying to keep my mind off it.'

I saw what he meant. Hours must pass before he could dig into that pie. I dropped the subject, and we sat for a pretty good time in silence. Then he rose and began to pace the room in an overwrought sort of way, like a zoo lion who has heard the dinner gong go and is hoping the keeper won't forget him in the general distribution. I averted my gaze tactfully, but I could hear him kicking chairs and things. It was plain that the man's soul was in travail and his blood pressure high.

Presently he returned to his seat, and I saw that he was looking at me intently. There was that about his demeanour that led me to think that he had something to communicate.

Nor was I wrong. He tapped me significantly on the knee and spoke:

'Bertie.'

'Hullo?'

'Shall I tell you something?'

'Certainly, old bird,' I said cordially. 'I was just beginning to feel that the scene could do with a bit more dialogue.'

'This business of Angela and me.'

'Yes?'

'I've been putting in a lot of solid thinking about it.'

'Oh, yes?'

'I have analysed the situation pitilessly, and one thing stands out as clear as dammit. There has been dirty work afoot.'

'I don't get you.'

'All right. Let me review the facts. Up to the time she went to Cannes Angela loved me. She was all over me. I was the blue-eyed boy in every sense of the term. You'll admit that?'

'Indisputably.'

'And directly she came back we had this bust-up.'

'Quite.'

'About nothing.'

'Oh, dash it, old man, nothing? You were a bit tactless, what, about her shark.'

'I was frank and candid about her shark. And that's my point. Do you seriously believe that a trifling disagreement about sharks would make a girl hand a man his hat, if her heart were really his?'

'Certainly.'

It beats me why he couldn't see it. But then poor old Tuppy has never been very hot on the finer shades. He's one of those large, tough, football-playing blokes who lack the more delicate sensibilities, as I've heard Jeeves call them. Excellent at blocking a punt or walking across an opponent's face in cleated boots, but not so good when it comes to understanding the highly-strung female temperament. It simply wouldn't occur to him that a girl might be prepared to give up her life's happiness rather than waive her shark.

'Rot! It was just a pretext.'

'What was?'

'This shark business. She wanted to get rid of me, and grabbed at the first excuse.'

'No, no.'

'I tell you she did.'

'But what on earth would she want to get rid of you for?'

'Exactly. That's the very question I asked myself. And here's the answer: Because she has fallen in love with somebody else. It sticks out a mile. There's no other possible solution. She goes to Cannes all for me, she comes back all off me. Obviously during those two months, she must have transferred her affections to some foul blister she met out there.'

'No, no.'

'Don't keep saying "No, no". She must have done. Well, I'll tell you one thing, and you can take this as official. If ever I find this slimy, slithery snake in the grass, he had better make all the necessary arrangements at his favourite nursing-home without delay, because I am going to be very rough with him. I propose, if and when found, to take him by his beastly neck, shake him till he froths, and pull him inside out and make him swallow himself.'

With which words he biffed off; and I, having given him a minute or two to get out of the way, rose and made for the drawing-room. The tendency of females to roost in drawing-rooms after dinner being well marked, I expected to find Angela there. It was my intention to have a word with Angela.

To Tuppy's theory that some insinuating bird had stolen the girl's heart from him at Cannes I had given, as I have indicated, little credence, considering it the mere unbalanced apple sauce of a bereaved man. It was, of course, the shark, and nothing but the shark, that had caused love's young dream to go temporarily off the boil, and I was convinced that a word or two with the cousin at this juncture would set everything right.

For, frankly, I thought it incredible that a girl of her natural sweetness and tender-heartedness should not have been moved to her foundations by what she had seen at dinner that night. Even Seppings, Aunt Dahlia's butler, a cold, unemotional man, had gasped and practically reeled when Tuppy waved aside those *nonnettes de poulet Agnès Sorel*, while the footman, standing by with the potatoes, had stared like one seeing a vision. I simply refused to consider the possibility of the significance of the thing having been lost on a nice girl like Angela. I fully expected to find her in the drawing-room with her heart bleeding freely, all ripe for an immediate reconciliation.

In the drawing-room, however, when I entered, only Aunt Dahlia met the eye. It seemed to me that she gave me rather a jaundiced look as I hove in sight, but this, having so recently beheld Tuppy in his agony, I attributed to the fact that she, like him, had been going light on the menu. You can't expect an empty aunt to beam like a full aunt.

'Oh, it's you, is it?' she said.

Well, it was, of course.

'Where's Angela?' I asked.

'Gone to bed.'

'Already?'

'She said she had a headache.'

'H'm.'

I wasn't so sure that I liked the sound of that so much. A girl who has observed the sundered lover sensationally off his feed does not go to bed with headaches if love has been reborn in her heart. She sticks around and gives him the swift, remorseful glance from beneath the drooping eyelashes and generally endeavours to convey to him that, if he wants to get together across a round table and try to find a formula, she is all for it too. Yes, I am bound to say I found that going-to-bed stuff a bit disquieting.

'Gone to bed, eh?' I murmured musingly.

'What did you want her for?'

'I thought she might like a stroll and a chat.'

'Are you going for a stroll?' said Aunt Dahlia, with a sudden show of interest. 'Where?'

'Oh, hither and thither.'

'Then I wonder if you would mind doing something for me.'

'Give it a name.'

'It won't take you long. You know that path that runs past the greenhouses into the kitchen garden. If you go along it, you come to a pond.'

'That's right.'

'Well, will you get a good, stout piece of rope or cord and go down that path till you come to the pond – '

'To the pond. Right.'

'– and look about you till you find a nice, heavy stone. Or a fairly large brick would do.'

'I see,' I said, though I didn't, being still fogged. 'Stone or brick. Yes. And then?'

'Then,' said the relative, 'I want you, like a good boy, to fasten the rope to the brick and tie it around your damned neck and jump into the pond and drown yourself. In a few days I will send and have you fished up and buried because I shall need to dance on your grave.'

I was more fogged than ever. And not only fogged – wounded and resentful. I remember reading a book where a girl 'suddenly fled from the room, afraid to stay for fear dreadful things would come tumbling from her lips; determined that she would not remain another day in this house to be insulted and misunderstood.' I felt much about the same.

Then I reminded myself that one has got to make allowances for a woman with only about half a spoonful of soup inside her, and I checked the red-hot crack that rose to the lips.

'What,' I said gently, 'is this all about? You seem pipped with Bertram.'

'Pipped!'

'Noticeably pipped. Why this ill-concealed animus?'

A sudden flame shot from her eyes, singeing my hair.

'Who was the ass, who was the chump, who was the dithering idiot who talked me, against my better judgment, into going without my dinner? I might have guessed – '

I saw that I had divined correctly the cause of her strange mood.

'It's all right, Aunt Dahlia. I know just how you're feeling. A bit on the hollow side, what? But the agony will pass. If I were you, I'd sneak down and raid the larder after the household have gone to bed. I am told there's a pretty good steak-and-kidney pie there which will repay inspection. Have faith, Aunt Dahlia,' I urged. 'Pretty soon Uncle Tom will be along, full of sympathy and anxious inquiries.'

'Will he? Do you know where he is now?'

'I haven't seen him.'

'He is in the study with his face buried in his hands, muttering about civilization and melting-pots.'

'Eh? Why?'

'Because it has just been my painful duty to inform him that Anatole has given notice.'

I own that I reeled.

'What?'

'Given notice. As the result of that drivelling scheme of yours. What did you expect a sensitive, temperamental French cook to do, if you went about urging everybody to refuse all food? I hear that when the first two courses came back to the kitchen practically untouched, his feelings were so hurt that he cried like a child. And when the rest of the dinner followed, he came to the conclusion that the whole thing was a studied and calculated insult, and decided to hand in his portfolio.'

'Golly!'

'You may well say "Golly!" Anatole, God's gift to the gastric juices, gone like the dew off the petal of a rose, all through your idiocy. Perhaps you understand now why I want you to go and jump in that pond. I might have known that some hideous disaster would strike this house like a thunderbolt if once you wriggled your way into it and started trying to be clever.'

Harsh words, of course, as from aunt to nephew, but I bore her no resentment. No doubt, if you looked at it from a certain angle, Bertram might be considered to have made something of a floater.

'I am sorry.'

'What's the good of being sorry?'

'I acted for what I deemed the best.'

'Another time try acting for the worst. Then we may possibly escape with a mere flesh wound.'

'Uncle Tom's not feeling too bucked about it all, you say?'

'He's groaning like a lost soul. And any chance I ever had of getting that money out of him has gone.'

I stroked the chin thoughtfully. There was, I had to admit, reason in what she said. None knew better than I how terrible a blow the passing of Anatole would be to Uncle Tom.

I have stated earlier in this chronicle that this curious object of the seashore with whom Aunt Dahlia has linked her lot is a bloke who habitually looks like a pterodactyl that has suffered, and the reason he does so is that all those years he spent in making millions in the Far East put his digestion on the blink, and the only cook that has ever been discovered capable of pushing food into him without starting something like Old Home Week in Moscow under the third waistcoat button is this uniquely gifted Anatole. Deprived of Anatole's services, all he was likely to give the wife of his b. was a dirty look. Yes, unquestionably, things seemed to have struck a somewhat rocky patch, and I must admit that I found myself, at moment of going to press, a little destitute of constructive ideas.

Confident, however, that these would come ere long, I kept the stiff upper lip.

'Bad,' I conceded. 'Quite bad, beyond a doubt. Certainly a nasty jar for one and all. But have no fear, Aunt Dahlia, I will fix everything.'

I have alluded earlier to the difficulty of staggering when you're sitting down, showing that it is a feat of which I, personally, am not capable. Aunt Dahlia, to my amazement, now did it apparently without an effort. She was well wedged into a deep armchair, but, nevertheless, she staggered like billy-o. A sort of spasm of horror and apprehension contorted her face.

'If you dare to try any more of your lunatic schemes – '

I saw that it would be fruitless to try to reason with her. Quite plainly, she was not in the vein. Contenting myself, accordingly, with a gesture of loving sympathy, I left the room. Whether she did or did not throw a handsomely bound volume of the *Works of Alfred, Lord Tennyson*, at me, I am not in a position to say. I had seen it lying on the table beside her, and as I closed the door I remember receiving the impression that some blunt instrument had crashed against the woodwork, but I was feeling too preoccupied to note and observe.

I blame myself for not having taken into consideration the possible effect of a sudden abstinence on the part of virtually the whole strength of the company on one of Anatole's impulsive Provençal temperament. These Gauls, I should have remembered, can't take it. Their tendency to fly off the handle at the slightest provocation is well known. No doubt the man had put his whole soul into those *nonnettes de poulet*, and to see them come homing back to him must have gashed him like a knife.

However, spilt milk blows nobody any good, and it is useless to dwell upon it. The task now confronting Bertram was to put matters right, and I was pacing the lawn, pondering to this end, when I suddenly heard a groan so lost-soulish that I thought it must have proceeded from Uncle Tom, escaped from captivity and come to groan in the garden.

Looking about me, however, I could discern no uncles. Puzzled, I was about to resume my meditations, when the sound came again. And peering into the shadows I observed a dim form seated on one of the rustic benches which so liberally dotted this pleasance and another dim form standing beside same. A second and more penetrating glance and I had assembled the facts.

These dim forms were, in the order named, Gussie Fink-Nottle and Jeeves. And what Gussie was doing, groaning all over the place like this, was more than I could understand.

Because, I mean to say, there was no possibility of error. He wasn't singing. As I approached, he gave an encore, and it was beyond question a groan. Moreover, I could now see him clearly, and his whole aspect was definitely sandbagged.

'Good evening, sir,' said Jeeves. 'Mr Fink-Nottle is not feeling well.'

Nor was I. Gussie had begun to make a low, bubbling noise, and I could no longer disguise it from myself that something must have gone seriously wrong with the works. I mean, I know marriage is a pretty solemn business and the realization that he is in for it frequently churns a chap up a bit, but I had never come across a case of a newly engaged man taking it on the chin so completely as this.

Gussie looked up. His eye was dull. He clutched the thatch.

'Goodbye, Bertie,' he said, rising.

I seemed to spot an error.

'You mean "Hallo", don't you?'

'No, I don't. I mean goodbye. I'm off.'

'Off where?'

'To the kitchen garden. To drown myself.'

'Don't be an ass.'

'I'm not an ass . . . Am I an ass, Jeeves?'

'Possibly a little injudicious, sir.'

'Drowning myself, you mean?'

'Yes, sir.'

'You think, on the whole, not drown myself?'

'I should not advocate it, sir.'

'Very well, Jeeves. I accept your ruling. After all, it would be unpleasant for Mrs Travers to find a swollen body floating in her pond.'

'Yes, sir.'

'And she has been very kind to me.'

'Yes, sir.'

'And you have been very kind to me, Jeeves.'

'Thank you, sir.'

'So have you, Bertie. Very kind. Everybody has been very kind to me. Very, very kind. Very kind indeed. I have no complaints to make. All right, I'll go for a walk instead.'

I followed him with bulging eyes as he tottered off into the dark.

'Jeeves,' I said, and I am free to admit that in my emotion I bleated like a lamb drawing itself to the attention of the parent sheep, 'what the dickens is all this?'

'Mr Fink-Nottle is not quite himself, sir. He has passed through a trying experience.'

I endeavoured to put together a brief synopsis of previous events.

'I left him out here with Miss Bassett.'

'Yes, sir.'

'I had softened her up.'

'Yes, sir.'

'He knew exactly what he had to do. I had coached him thoroughly in lines and business.'

'Yes, sir. So Mr Fink-Nottle informed me.'

'Well, then – '

'I regret to say, sir, that there was a slight hitch.'

'You mean, something went wrong?'

'Yes, sir.'

I could not fathom. The brain seemed to be tottering on its throne.

'But how could anything go wrong? She loves him, Jeeves.'

'Indeed, sir?'

'She definitely told me so. All he had to do was propose.'

'Yes, sir.'

'Well, didn't he?'

'No, sir.'

'Then what the dickens did he talk about?'

'Newts, sir.'

'Newts?'

'Yes, sir.'

'Newts?'

'Yes, sir.'

'But why did he want to talk about newts?'

'He did not want to talk about newts, sir. As I gather from Mr Fink-Nottle, nothing could have been more alien to his plans.'

I simply couldn't grasp the trend.

'But you can't force a man to talk about newts.'

'Mr Fink-Nottle was the victim of a sudden unfortunate spasm of nervousness, sir. Upon finding himself alone with the young lady, he admits to having lost his morale. In such circumstances, gentlemen frequently talk at random, saying the first thing that chances to enter their heads. This, in Mr Fink-Nottle's case, would seem to have been the newt, its treatment in sickness and in health.'

The scales fell from my eyes. I understood. I had had the same sort of thing happen to me in moments of crisis. I remember once detaining a dentist with the drill at one of my lower bicuspids and holding him up for nearly ten minutes with a story about a Scotsman, an Irishman, and a Jew. Purely automatic. The more he tried to jab, the more I said 'Hoots, mon', 'Begorrah', and 'Oy, oy'. When one loses one's nerve, one simply babbles.

I could put myself in Gussie's place. I could envisage the scene. There he and the Bassett were, alone together in the evening stillness. No doubt, as I had advised, he had shot the works about sunsets and fairy princesses, and so forth, and then had arrived at the point where he had to say that bit about having something to say to her. At this, I take it, she lowered her eyes and said, 'Oh, yes?'

He then, I should imagine, said it was something very important; to which her response would, one assumes, have been something on the lines of 'Really?' or 'Indeed?' or possibly just the sharp intake of the breath. And then their eyes met, just as mine met the dentist's, and something suddenly seemed to catch him in the pit of the stomach and everything went black and he heard his voice starting to drool about newts. Yes, I could follow the psychology.

Nevertheless, I found myself blaming Gussie. On discovering that he was stressing the newt note in this manner, he ought, of course, to have tuned out, even if it had meant sitting there saying nothing. No matter how much of a twitter he was in, he should have had sense enough to see that he was throwing a spanner into the works. No girl, when she has been led to expect that a man is about to pour forth his soul in a fervour of passion, likes to find him suddenly shelving the whole topic in favour of an address on aquatic *Salamandridae*.

'Bad, Jeeves.'

'Yes, sir.'

'And how long did this nuisance continue?'

'For some not inconsiderable time, I gather, sir. According to Mr Fink-Nottle, he supplied Miss Bassett with very full and complete information not only with respect to the common newt, but also the crested and palmated varieties. He described to her how newts, during the breeding season, live in the water, subsisting upon tadpoles, insect larvae, and crustaceans; how, later, they make their way to the land and eat slugs and worms; and how the newly born newt has three pairs of long, plumelike external gills. And he was just observing that newts differ from salamanders in the shape of the tail, which is compressed, and that a marked sexual dimorphism prevails in most species, when the young lady rose and said that she thought she would go back to the house.'

'And then – '

'She went, sir.'

I stood musing. More and more, it was beginning to be borne in upon me what a particularly difficult chap Gussie was to help. He seemed to so marked an extent to lack snap and finish. With infinite toil, you manoeuvred him into a position where all he had to do was charge ahead, and he didn't charge ahead, but went off sideways, missing the objective completely.

'Difficult, Jeeves.'

'Yes, sir.'

In happier circs, of course, I would have canvassed his views on the matter. But after what had occurred in connexion with that mess jacket, my lips were sealed.

'Well, I must think it over.'

'Yes, sir.'

'Burnish the brain a bit and endeavour to find the way out.'

'Yes, sir.'

'Well, good night, Jeeves.'

'Good night, sir.'

He shimmered off, leaving a pensive Bertram Wooster standing motionless in the shadows. It seemed to me that it was hard to know what to do for the best.

12

I don't know if it has happened to you at all, but a thing I've noticed with myself is that, when I'm confronted by a problem which seems for the moment to stump and baffle, a good sleep will often bring the solution in the morning.

It was so on the present occasion.

The nibs who study these matters claim, I believe, that this has got something to do with the subconscious mind, and very possibly they may be right. I wouldn't have said off-hand that I had a subconscious mind, but I suppose I must without knowing it, and no doubt it was there, sweating away diligently at the old stand, all the while the corporeal Wooster was getting his eight hours.

For directly I opened my eyes on the morrow, I saw daylight. Well, I don't mean that exactly, because naturally I did. What I mean is that I found I had the thing all mapped out. The good old subconscious m. had delivered the goods, and I perceived exactly what steps must be taken in order to put Augustus Fink-Nottle among the practising Romeos.

I should like you, if you can spare me a moment of your valuable time, to throw your mind back to that conversation he and I had had in the garden on the previous evening. Not the glimmering landscape bit, I don't mean that, but the concluding passages of it. Having done so, you will recall that when he informed me that he never touched alcoholic liquor, I shook the head a bit, feeling that this must inevitably weaken him as a force where proposing to girls was concerned.

And events had shown that my fears were well founded.

Put to the test, with nothing but orange juice inside him, he had proved a complete bust. In a situation calling for words of molten passion of a nature calculated to go through Madeline Basset like a red-hot gimlet through half a pound of butter, he had said not a syllable that could bring a blush to the cheek of modesty, merely delivering a well-phrased but, in the circumstances, quite misplaced lecture on newts.

A romantic girl is not to be won by such tactics. Obviously, before attempting to proceed further, Augustus Fink-Nottle must be induced to throw off the shackling inhibitions of the past and fuel up. It must be a primed, confident Fink-Nottle who squared up to the Bassett for Round No. 2.

Only so could the *Morning Post* make its ten bob, or whatever it is, for printing the announcement of the forthcoming nuptials.

Having arrived at this conclusion I found the rest easy, and by the time Jeeves brought me my tea I had evolved a plan complete in every detail. This I was about to place before him – indeed, I had got as far as the preliminary 'I say, Jeeves' – when we were interrupted by the arrival of Tuppy.

He came listlessly into the room, and I was pained to observe that a night's rest had effected no improvement in the unhappy wreck's appearance. Indeed, I should have said, if anything, that he was looking rather more moth-eaten than when I had seen him last. If you can visualize a bulldog which has just been kicked in the ribs and had its dinner sneaked by the cat, you will have Hildebrand Glossop as he now stood before me.

'Stap my vitals, Tuppy, old corpse,' I said, concerned, 'you're looking pretty blue round the rims.'

Jeeves slid from the presence in that tactful, eel-like way of his, and I motioned the remains to take a seat.

'What's the matter?' I said.

He came to anchor on the bed, and for a while sat picking at the coverlet in silence.

'I've been through hell, Bertie.'

'Through where?'

'Hell.'

'Oh, hell? And what took you there?'

Once more he became silent, staring before him with sombre eyes. Following his gaze, I saw that he was looking at an enlarged photograph of my Uncle Tom in some sort of Masonic uniform which stood on the mantelpiece. I've tried to reason with Aunt Dahlia about this photograph for years, placing before her two alternative suggestions: (*a*) To burn the beastly thing; or (*b*) if she must preserve it, to shove me in another room when I come to stay. But she declines to accede. She says it's good for me. A useful discipline, she maintains, teaching me that there is a darker side to life and that we were not put into this world for pleasure only.

'Turn it to the wall, if it hurts you, Tuppy,' I said gently.

'Eh?'

'That photograph of Uncle Tom as the bandmaster.'

'I didn't come here to talk about photographs. I came for sympathy.'

'And you shall have it. What's the trouble? Worrying about Angela, I suppose? Well, have no fear. I have another well-laid plan for encompassing that young shrimp. I'll guarantee that she will be weeping on your neck before yonder sun has set.'

He barked sharply.

'A fat chance!'

'Tup, Tushy!'

'Eh?'

'I mean "Tush, Tuppy." I tell you I will do it. I was just going to describe this plan of mine to Jeeves when you came in. Care to hear it?'

'I don't want to hear any of your beastly plans. Plans are no good. She's gone and fallen in love with this other bloke, and now hates my gizzard.'

'Rot.'

'It isn't rot.'

'I tell you, Tuppy, as one who can read the female heart, that this Angela loves you still.'

'Well, it didn't look much like it in the larder last night.'

'Oh, you went to the larder last night?'

'I did.'

'And Angela was there?'

'She was. And your aunt. Also your uncle.'

I saw that I should require footnotes. All this was new stuff to me. I had stayed at Brinkley Court quite a lot in my time, but I had no idea the larder was such a social vortex. More like a snack bar on a racecourse than anything else, it seemed to have become.

'Tell me the whole story in your own words,' I said, 'omitting no detail, however apparently slight, for one never knows how important the most trivial detail may be.'

He inspected the photograph for a moment with growing gloom.

'All right,' he said. 'This is what happened. You know my views about that steak-and-kidney pie.'

'Quite.'

'Well, round about one a.m. I thought the time was ripe. I stole from my room and went downstairs. The pie seemed to beckon me.'

I nodded. I knew how pies do.

'I got to the larder. I fished it out. I set it on the table. I found knife and fork. I collected salt, mustard, and pepper. There were some cold potatoes. I added those. And I was about to pitch in when I heard a sound behind me, and there was your aunt at the door. In a blue-and-yellow dressing gown.'

'Embarrassing.'

'Most.'

'I suppose you didn't know where to look.'

'I looked at Angela.'

'She came in with my aunt?'

'No. With your uncle, a minute or two later. He was wearing mauve pyjamas and carried a pistol. Have you ever seen your uncle in pyjamas and a pistol?'

'Never.'

'You haven't missed much.'

'Tell me, Tuppy,' I asked, for I was anxious to ascertain this, 'about Angela. Was there any momentary softening in her gaze as she fixed it on you?'

'She didn't fix it on me. She fixed it on the pie.'

'Did she say anything?'

'Not right away. Your uncle was the first to speak. He said to your aunt, "God bless my soul, Dahlia, what are you doing here?" To which she replied, "Well, if it comes to that, my merry somnambulist, what are you?" Your uncle then said that he thought there must be burglars in the house, as he had heard noises.'

I nodded again. I could follow the trend. Ever since the scullery window was found open the year Shining Light was disqualified in the Cesarewitch for boring, Uncle Tom has had a marked complex about burglars. I can still recall my emotions when, paying my first visit after he had bars put on all windows and attempting to thrust the head out in order to get a sniff of country air, I nearly fractured my skull on a sort of iron grille, as worn by the tougher kinds of mediaeval prison.

'"What sort of noises?" said your aunt. "Funny noises," said your uncle. Whereupon Angela – with a nasty, steely tinkle in her voice, the little buzzard – observed, "I expect it was Mr Glossop eating." And then she did give me a look. It was the sort of wondering, revolted look a very spiritual woman would give a fat man gulping soup in a restaurant. The kind of look that makes a fellow feel he's forty-six round the waist and has great rolls of superfluous flesh pouring down over the back of his collar. And, still speaking in the same unpleasant tone, she added, "I ought to have told you, Father, that Mr Glossop always likes to have a good meal three or four times during the night. It helps to keep him going till breakfast. He has the most amazing appetite. See, he has practically finished a large steak-and-kidney pie already".'

As he spoke these words, a feverish animation swept over Tuppy. His eyes glittered with a strange light, and he thumped the bed violently with his fist, nearly catching me a juicy one on the leg.

'That was what hurt, Bertie. That was what stung. I hadn't so much as started on that pie. But that's a woman all over.'

'The eternal feminine.'

'She continued her remarks. "You've no idea," she said, "how Mr Glossop loves food. He just lives for it. He always eats six or seven meals a day, and then starts in again after bedtime. I think it's rather wonderful." Your aunt seemed interested, and said it reminded her of a boa constrictor. Angela said, didn't she mean a python? And then they argued as to which of the two it was. Your uncle, meanwhile, poking about with that damned pistol of his till human life wasn't safe in the vicinity. And the pie lying there on the table, and me unable to touch it. You begin to understand why I said I had been through hell.'

'Quite. Can't have been at all pleasant.'

'Presently your aunt and Angela settled their discussion, deciding that Angela was right and that it was a python that I reminded them of. And shortly after that we all pushed back to bed, Angela warning me in a motherly voice not to take the stairs too quickly. After seven or eight solid meals, she said, a man of my build ought to be very careful, because of the danger of apoplectic fits. She said it was the same with dogs. When they became very fat and overfed, you had to see that they didn't hurry upstairs, as it made them puff and pant, and that was bad for their hearts. She asked your aunt if she remembered the late spaniel, Ambrose; and your aunt said, "Poor old Ambrose, you couldn't keep him away from the garbage pail"; and Angela said, "Exactly, so do please be careful, Mr Glossop." And you tell me she loves me still!'

I did my best to encourage.

'Girlish banter, what?'

'Girlish banter be dashed. She's right off me. Once her ideal, I am now less than the dust beneath her chariot wheels. She became infatuated with this chap, whoever he was, at Cannes, and now she can't stand the sight of me.'

I raised my eyebrows.

'My dear Tuppy, you are not showing your usual good sense in this Angela-chap-at-Cannes matter. If you will forgive me saying so, you have got an *idée fixe*.'

'A what?'

'An *idée fixe*. You know. One of those things fellows get. Like Uncle Tom's delusion that everybody who is known even slightly to the police is lurking in the garden, waiting for a chance to break into the house. You keep talking about this chap at Cannes, and there never was a chap at Cannes, and I'll tell you why I'm so sure about this. During those two months on the Riviera, it so happens that Angela and I were practically inseparable. If there had been somebody nosing round her, I should have spotted it in a second.'

He started. I could see that this had impressed him.

'Oh, she was with you all the time at Cannes, was she?'

'I don't suppose she said two words to anybody else, except, of course, idle conv. at the crowded dinner table or a chance remark in a throng at the Casino.'

'I see. You mean that anything in the shape of mixed bathing and moonlight strolls she conducted solely in your company?'

'That's right. It was quite a joke in the hotel.'

'You must have enjoyed that.'

'Oh, rather. I've always been devoted to Angela.'

'Oh, yes?'

'When we were kids, she used to call herself my little sweetheart.'

'She did?'

'Absolutely.'

'I see.'

He sat plunged in thought, while I, glad to have set his mind at rest, proceeded with my tea. And presently there came the banging of a gong from the hall below, and he started like a war horse at the sound of the bugle.

'Breakfast!' he said, and was off to a flying start, leaving me to brood and ponder. And the more I brooded and pondered, the more did it seem to me that everything now looked pretty smooth. Tuppy, I could see, despite that painful scene in the larder, still loved Angela with all the old fervour.

This meant that I could rely on that plan to which I had referred to bring home the bacon. And as I had found the way to straighten out the Gussie-Bassett difficulty, there seemed nothing more to worry about.

It was with an uplifted heart that I addressed Jeeves as he came in to remove the tea tray.

13

'Jeeves,' I said.

'Sir?'

'I've just been having a chat with young Tuppy, Jeeves. Did you happen to notice that he wasn't looking very roguish this morning?'

'Yes, sir. It seemed to me that Mr Glossop's face was sicklied o'er with the pale cast of thought.'

'Quite. He met my cousin Angela in the larder last night, and a rather painful interview ensued.'

'I am sorry, sir.'

'Not half so sorry as he was. She found him closeted with a steak-and-kidney pie, and appears to have been a bit caustic about fat men who lived for food alone.'

'Most disturbing, sir.'

'Very. In fact, many people would say that things had gone so far between these two nothing now could bridge the chasm. A girl who could make cracks about human pythons who ate nine or ten meals a day and ought to be careful not to hurry upstairs because of the danger of apoplectic fits is a girl, many people would say, in whose heart love is dead. Wouldn't people say that, Jeeves?'

'Undeniably, sir.'

'They would be wrong.'

'You think so, sir?'

'I am convinced of it. I know these females. You can't go by what they say.'

'You feel that Miss Angela's strictures should not be taken too much *au pied de la lettre*, sir?'

'Eh?'

'In English, we should say "literally".'

'Literally. That's exactly what I mean. You know what girls are. A tiff occurs, and they shoot their heads off. But underneath it all the old love still remains. Am I correct?'

'Quite correct, sir. The poet Scott – '

'Right ho, Jeeves.'

'Very good, sir.'

'And in order to bring that old love whizzing to the surface once more, all that is required is the proper treatment.'

'By "proper treatment", sir, you mean – '

'Clever handling, Jeeves. A spot of the good old snaky work. I see what must be done to jerk my cousin Angela back to normalcy. I'll tell you, shall I?'

'If you would be so kind, sir.'

I lit a cigarette, and eyed him keenly through the smoke. He waited respectfully for me to unleash the words of wisdom. I must say for Jeeves that – till, as he is so apt to do, he starts shoving his oar in and cavilling and obstructing – he makes a very good audience. I don't know if he is actually agog, but he looks agog, and that's the great thing.

'Suppose you were strolling through the illimitable jungle, Jeeves, and happened to meet a tiger cub.'

'The contingency is a remote one, sir.'

'Never mind. Let us suppose it.'

'Very good, sir.'

'Let us now suppose that you sloshed that tiger cub, and let us suppose further that word reached its mother that it was being put upon. What would you expect the attitude of that mother to be? In what frame of mind do you consider that that tigress would approach you?'

'I should anticipate a certain show of annoyance, sir.'

'And rightly. Due to what is known as the maternal instinct, what?'

'Yes, sir.'

'Very good, Jeeves. We will now suppose that there has recently been some little coolness between this tiger cub and this tigress. For some days, let us say, they have not been on speaking terms. Do you think that that would make any difference to the vim with which the latter would leap to the former's aid?'

'No, sir.'

'Exactly. Here, then, in brief, is my plan, Jeeves. I am going to draw my cousin Angela aside to a secluded spot and roast Tuppy properly.'

'Roast, sir?'

'Knock. Slam. Tick off. Abuse. Denounce. I shall be very terse about Tuppy, giving it as my opinion that in all essentials he is more like a wart hog than an ex-member of a fine old English public school.

What will ensue? Hearing him attacked, my cousin Angela's womanly heart will be as sick as mud. The maternal tigress in her will awake. No matter what differences they may have had, she will remember only that he is the man she loves, and will leap to his defence. And from that to falling into his arms and burying the dead past will be but a step. How do you react to that?'

'The idea is an ingenious one, sir.'

'We Woosters are ingenious, Jeeves, exceedingly ingenious.'

'Yes, sir.'

'As a matter of fact, I am not speaking without a knowledge of the form book. I have tested this theory.'

'Indeed, sir?'

'Yes, in person. And it works. I was standing on the Eden rock at Antibes last month, idly watching the bathers disport themselves in the water, and a girl I knew slightly pointed at a male diver and asked me if I didn't think his legs were about the silliest-looking pair of props ever issued to human being. I replied that I did, indeed, and for the space of perhaps two minutes was extraordinarily witty and satirical about this bird's underpinning. At the end of that period, I suddenly felt as if I had been caught up in the tail of a cyclone.

'Beginning with a *critique* of my own limbs, which she said, justly enough, were nothing to write home about, this girl went on to dissect my manners, morals, intellect, general physique, and method of eating asparagus with such acerbity that by the time she had finished the best you could say of Bertram was that, so far as was known, he had never actually committed murder or set fire to an orphan asylum. Subsequent investigation proved that she was engaged to the fellow with the legs and had had a slight disagreement with him the evening before on the subject of whether she should or should not have made an original call of two spades, having seven, but without the ace. That night I saw them dining together with every indication of relish, their differences made up and the love-light once more in their eyes. That shows you, Jeeves.'

'Yes, sir.'

'I expect precisely similar results from my cousin Angela when I start roasting Tuppy. By lunchtime, I should imagine, the engagement will be on again and the diamond-and-platinum ring glittering as of yore on her third finger. Or is it the fourth?'

'Scarcely by luncheon time, sir. Miss Angela's maid informs me that Miss Angela drove off in her car early this morning with the intention of spending the day with friends in the vicinity.'

'Well, within half an hour of whatever time she comes back, then. These are mere straws, Jeeves. Do not let us chop them.'

'No, sir.'

'The point is that, as far as Tuppy and Angela are concerned, we may say with confidence that everything will shortly be hotsy-totsy once more. And what an agreeable thought that is, Jeeves.'

'Very true, sir.'

'If there is one thing that gives me the pip, it is two loving hearts being estranged.'

'I can readily appreciate the fact, sir.'

I placed the stub of my gasper in the ash tray and lit another, to indicate that that completed Chap. I.

'Right ho, then. So much for the western front. We now turn to the eastern.'

'Sir?'

'I speak in parables, Jeeves. What I mean is, we now approach the matter of Gussie and Miss Bassett.'

'Yes, sir.'

'Here, Jeeves, more direct methods are required. In handling the case of Augustus Fink-Nottle, we must keep always in mind the fact that we are dealing with a poop.'

'A sensitive plant would, perhaps, be a kinder expression, sir.'

'No, Jeeves, a poop. And with poops one has to employ the strong, forceful, straightforward policy. Psychology doesn't get you anywhere. You, if I may remind you without wounding your feelings, fell into the error of mucking about with psychology in connection with this Fink-Nottle, and the result was a wash-out. You attempted to push him over the line by rigging him out in a Mephistopheles costume and sending him off to a fancy-dress ball, your view being that scarlet tights would embolden him. Futile.'

'The matter was never actually put to the test, sir.'

'No. Because he didn't get to the ball. And that strengthens my argument. A man who can set out in a cab for a fancy-dress ball and not get there is manifestly a poop of no common order. I don't think I have ever known anybody else who was such a dashed silly ass that he couldn't even get to a fancy-dress ball. Have you, Jeeves?'

'No, sir.'

'But don't forget this, because it is the point I wish, above all, to make: even if Gussie had got to that ball; even if those scarlet tights, taken in conjunction with his horn-rimmed spectacles, hadn't given the girl a fit of some kind; even if she had rallied from the shock and he had been able to dance and generally hobnob with her; even then your efforts would have been fruitless, because, Mephistopheles costume or no Mephistopheles costume, Augustus Fink-Nottle would never have been able to summon up the courage to ask her to be his. All that would have resulted would have been that she would have got that lecture on newts a few days earlier. And why, Jeeves? Shall I tell you why?'

'Yes, sir.'

'Because he would have been attempting the hopeless task of trying to do the thing on orange juice.'

'Sir?'

'Gussie is an orange-juice addict. He drinks nothing else.'

'I was not aware of that, sir.'

'I have it from his own lips. Whether from some hereditary taint, or because he promised his mother he wouldn't, or simply because he doesn't like the taste of the stuff, Gussie Fink-Nottle has never in the whole course of his career pushed so much as the simplest gin and tonic over the larynx. And he expects – this poop expects, Jeeves – this babbling, shrinking, diffident rabbit in human shape expects under these conditions to propose to the girl he loves. One hardly knows whether to smile or weep, what?'

'You consider total abstinence a handicap to a gentleman who wishes to make a proposal of marriage, sir?'

The question amazed me.

'Why, dash it,' I said, astounded, 'you must know it is. Use your intelligence, Jeeves. Reflect what proposing means. It means that a decent, self-respecting chap has got to listen to himself saying things which, if spoken on the silver screen, would cause him to dash to the box office and demand his money back. Let him attempt to do it on orange juice, and what ensues? Shame seals his lips, or, if it doesn't do that, makes him lose his morale and start to babble. Gussie, for example, as we have seen, babbles of syncopated newts.'

'Palmated newts, sir.'

'Palmated or syncopated, it doesn't matter which. The point is that he babbles and is going to babble again, if he has another try at it. Unless – and this is where I want you to follow me very closely, Jeeves – unless steps are taken at once through the proper channels. Only active measures, promptly applied, can provide this poor, pusillanimous poop with the proper pep. And that is why, Jeeves, I intend tomorrow to secure a bottle of gin and lace his luncheon orange juice with it liberally.'

'Sir?'

I clicked the tongue.

'I have already had occasion, Jeeves,' I said rebukingly, 'to comment on the way you say "Well, sir" and "Indeed, sir?" I take this opportunity of informing you that I object equally strongly to your "Sir?" pure and simple. The word seems to suggest that in your opinion I have made a statement or mooted a scheme so bizarre that your brain reels at it. In the present instance, there is absolutely nothing to say "Sir?" about. The plan I have put forward is entirely reasonable and icily logical, and should excite no sirring whatsoever. Or don't you think so?'

'Well, sir – '

'Jeeves!'

'I beg your pardon, sir. The expression escaped me inadvertently. What I intended to say, since you press me, was that the action which you propose does seem to me somewhat injudicious.'

'Injudicious? I don't follow you, Jeeves.'

'A certain amount of risk would enter into it, in my opinion, sir. It is not always a simple matter to gauge the effect of alcohol on a subject unaccustomed to such stimulant. I have known it to have distressing results in the case of parrots.'

'Parrots?'

'I was thinking of an incident of my earlier life, sir, before I entered your employment. I was in the service of the late Lord Brancaster at the time, a gentleman who owned a parrot to which he was greatly devoted, and one day the bird chanced to be lethargic, and His Lordship, with the kindly intention of restoring it to its customary animation, offered it a portion of seed cake steeped in the '84 port. The bird accepted the morsel gratefully and consumed it with every indication of satisfaction. Almost immediately afterwards, however, its manner became markedly feverish. Having bitten His Lordship in the thumb and sung part of a sea shanty, it fell to the bottom of the cage and remained there for a considerable period of time with its legs in the air, unable to move. I merely mention this, sir, in order to – '

I put my finger on the flaw. I had spotted it all along.

'But Gussie isn't a parrot.'

'No, sir, but – '

'It is high time, in my opinion, that this question of what young Gussie really is was threshed out and cleared up. He seems to think he is a male newt, and you now appear to suggest that he is a parrot. The truth of the matter being that he is just a plain, ordinary poop and needs a snootful as badly as ever man did. So no more discussion, Jeeves. My mind is made up. There is only one way of handling this difficult case, and that is the way I have outlined.'

'Very good, sir.'

'Right ho, Jeeves. So much for that, then. Now here's something else: You noticed that I said I was going to put this project through tomorrow, and no doubt you wondered why I said tomorrow. Why did I, Jeeves?'

'Because you feel that if it were done when 'tis done, then 'twere well it were done quickly, sir?'

'Partly, Jeeves, but not altogether. My chief reason for fixing the date as specified is that tomorrow, though you have doubtless forgotten, is the day of the distribution of prizes at Market Snodsbury Grammar School, at which, as you know, Gussie is to be the male star and master of the revels. So you see we shall, by lacing that juice, not only embolden him to propose to Miss Bassett, but also put him so into shape that he will hold that Market Snodsbury audience spellbound.'

'In fact, you will be killing two birds with one stone, sir.'

'Exactly. A very neat way of putting it. And now here is a minor point. On second thoughts, I think the best plan will be for you, not me, to lace the juice.'

'Sir?'

'Jeeves!'

'I beg your pardon, sir.'

'And I'll tell you why that will be the best plan. Because you are in a position to obtain ready access to the stuff. It is served to Gussie daily, I have noticed, in an individual jug. This jug will presumably be lying about the kitchen or somewhere before lunch tomorrow. It will be the simplest of tasks for you to slip a few fingers of gin in it.'

'No doubt, sir, but – '

'Don't say "but", Jeeves.'

'I fear, sir – '

'"I fear, sir" is just as bad.'

'What I am endeavouring to say, sir, is that I am sorry, but I am afraid I must enter an unequivocal *nolle prosequi*.'

'Do what?'

'The expression is a legal one, sir, signifying the resolve not to proceed with a matter. In other words, eager though I am to carry out your instructions, sir, as a general rule, on this occasion I must respectfully decline to co-operate.'

'You won't do it, you mean?'

'Precisely, sir.'

I was stunned. I began to understand how a general must feel when he has ordered a regiment to charge and has been told that it isn't in the mood.

'Jeeves,' I said, 'I had not expected this of you.'

'No, sir?'

'No, indeed. Naturally, I realize that lacing Gussie's orange juice is not one of those regular duties for which you receive the monthly stipend, and if you care to stand on the strict letter of the contract, I suppose there is nothing to be done about it. But you will permit me to observe that this is scarcely the feudal spirit.'

'I am sorry, sir.'

'It is quite all right, Jeeves, quite all right. I am not angry, only a little hurt.'

'Very good, sir.'

'Right ho, Jeeves.'

14

Investigation proved that the friends Angela had gone to spend the day with were some stately-home owners of the name of Stretchley-Budd, hanging out in a joint called Kingham Manor, about eight miles distant in the direction of Pershore. I didn't know these birds, but their fascination must have been considerable, for she tore herself away from them only just in time to get back and dress for dinner. It was, accordingly, not until coffee had been consumed that I was able to get matters moving. I found her in the drawing-room and at once proceeded to put things in train.

It was with very different feelings from those which had animated the bosom when approaching the Bassett twenty-four hours before in the same manner in this same drawing-room that I headed for where she sat. As I had told Tuppy, I have always been devoted to Angela, and there is nothing I like better than a ramble in her company.

And I could see by the look of her now how sorely in need she was of my aid and comfort.

Frankly, I was shocked by the unfortunate young prune's appearance. At Cannes she had been a happy, smiling English girl of the best type, full of beans and buck. Her face now was pale and drawn, like that of a hockey centre-forward at a girls' school who, in addition to getting a fruity one on the shin, has just been penalized for 'sticks'. In any normal gathering, her demeanour would have excited instant remark, but the standard of gloom at Brinkley Court had become so high that it passed unnoticed. Indeed, I shouldn't wonder if Uncle Tom, crouched in his corner waiting for the end, didn't think she was looking indecently cheerful.

I got down to the agenda in my debonair way.

'What ho, Angela, old girl.'

'Hullo, Bertie, darling.'

'Glad you're back at last. I missed you.'

'Did you, darling?'

'I did, indeed. Care to come for a saunter?'

'I'd love it.'

'Fine. I have much to say to you that is not for the public ear.'

I think at this moment poor old Tuppy must have got a sudden touch of cramp. He had been sitting hard by, staring at the ceiling, and he now gave a sharp leap like a gaffed salmon and upset a small table containing a vase, a bowl of pot-pourri, two china dogs, and a copy of Omar Khayyam bound in limp leather.

Aunt Dahlia uttered a startled hunting cry. Uncle Tom, who probably imagined from the noise that this was civilization crashing at last, helped things along by breaking a coffee cup.

Tuppy said he was sorry. Aunt Dahlia, with a deathbed groan, said it didn't matter. And Angela, having stared haughtily for a moment like a princess of the old régime confronted by some notable example of gaucherie on the part of some particularly foul member of the underworld, accompanied me across the threshold. And presently I had deposited her and self on one of the rustic benches in the garden, and was ready to snap into the business of the evening.

I considered it best, however, before doing so, to ease things along with a little informal chitchat. You don't want to rush a delicate job like the one I had in hand. And so for a while we spoke of neutral topics. She said that what had kept her so long at the Stretchley-Budds was that Hilda Stretchley-Budd had made her stop on and help with the arrangements for their servants' ball tomorrow night, a task which she couldn't very well decline, as all the Brinkley Court domestic staff were to be present. I said that a jolly night's revelry might be just what was needed to cheer Anatole up and take his mind off things. To which she replied that Anatole wasn't going. On being urged to do so by Aunt Dahlia, she said, he had merely shaken his head sadly and gone on talking of returning to Provence, where he was appreciated.

It was after the sombre silence induced by this statement that Angela said the grass was wet and she thought she would go in.

This, of course, was entirely foreign to my policy.

'No, don't do that. I haven't had a chance to talk to you since you arrived.'

'I shall ruin my shoes.'

'Put your feet up on my lap.'

'All right. And you can tickle my ankles.'

'Quite.'

Matters were accordingly arranged on these lines, and for some minutes we continued chatting in desultory fashion. Then the conversation petered out. I made a few observations *in re* the scenic effects, featuring the twilight hush, the peeping stars, and the soft glimmer of the waters of the lake, and she said yes. Something rustled in the bushes in front of us, and I advanced the theory that it was possibly a weasel, and she said it might be. But it was plain that the girl was distrait, and I considered it best to waste no more time.

'Well, old thing,' I said, 'I've heard all about your little dust-up. So those wedding bells are not going to ring out, what?'

'No.'

'Definitely over, is it?'

'Yes.'

'Well, if you want my opinion, I think that's a bit of goose for you, Angela, old girl. I think you're extremely well out of it. It's a mystery to me how you stood this Glossop so long. Take him for all in all, he ranks very low down among the wines and spirits. A wash-out, I should describe him as. A frightful oik, and a mass of side to boot. I'd pity the girl who was linked for life to a bargee like Tuppy Glossop.'

And I emitted a hard laugh – one of the sneering kind.

'I always thought you were such friends,' said Angela.

I let go another hard one, with a bit more top spin on it than the first time:

'Friends? Absolutely not. One was civil, of course, when one met the fellow, but it would be absurd to say one was a friend of his. A club acquaintance, and a mere one at that. And then one was at school with the man.'

'At Eton?'

'Good heavens, no. We wouldn't have a fellow like that at Eton. At a kid's school before I went there. A grubby little brute he was, I recollect. Covered with ink and mire generally, washing only on alternate Thursdays. In short, a notable outsider, shunned by all.'

I paused. I was more than a bit perturbed. Apart from the agony of having to talk in this fashion of one who, except when he was looping back rings and causing me to plunge into swimming baths in correct evening costume, had always been a very dear and esteemed crony, I didn't seem to be getting anywhere. Business was not resulting. Staring into the bushes without a yip, she appeared to be bearing these slurs and innuendos of mine with an easy calm.

I had another pop at it:

'"Uncouth" about sums it up. I doubt if I've ever seen an uncouther kid than this Glossop. Ask anyone who knew him in those days to describe him in a word, and the word they will use is "uncouth". And he's just the same today. It's the old story. The boy is the father of the man.'

She appeared not to have heard.

'The boy,' I repeated, not wishing her to miss that one, 'is the father of the man.'

'What are you talking about?'

'I'm talking about this Glossop.'

'I thought you said something about somebody's father.'

'I said the boy was the father of the man.'

'What boy?'

'The boy Glossop.'

'He hasn't got a father.'

'I never said he had. I said he was the father of the boy – or, rather, of the man.'

'What man?'

I saw that the conversation had reached a point where, unless care was taken, we should be muddled.

'The point I am trying to make,' I said, 'is that the boy Glossop is the father of the man Glossop. In other words, each loathsome fault and blemish that led the boy Glossop to be frowned upon by his fellows is present in the man Glossop, and causes him – I am speaking now of the man Glossop – to be a hissing and a byword at places like the Drones, where a certain standard of decency is demanded from the inmates. Ask anyone at the Drones, and they will tell you that it was a black day for the dear old club when this chap Glossop somehow wriggled into the list of members. Here you will find a man who dislikes his face; there one who could stand his face if it wasn't for his habits. But the universal consensus of opinion is that the fellow is a bounder and a tick, and that the moment he showed signs of wanting to get into the place he should have been met with a firm *nolle prosequi* and heartily blackballed.'

I had to pause again here, partly in order to take in a spot of breath, and partly to wrestle with the almost physical torture of saying these frightful things about poor old Tuppy.

'There are some chaps,' I resumed, forcing myself once more to the nauseous task, 'who, in spite of looking as if they had slept in their clothes, can get by quite nicely because they are amiable and suave. There are others who, for all that they excite adverse comment by being fat and uncouth, find themselves on the credit side of the ledger owing to their wit and sparkling humour. But this Glossop, I regret to say, falls into neither class. In addition to looking like one of those things that come out of hollow trees, he is universally admitted to be a dumb brick of the first water. No soul. No conversation. In short, any girl who, having been rash enough to get engaged to him, has managed at the eleventh hour to slide out is justly entitled to consider herself dashed lucky.'

I paused once more, and cocked an eye at Angela to see how the treatment was taking. All the while I had been speaking, she had sat gazing silently into the bushes, but it seemed to me incredible that she should not now turn on me like a tigress, according to specifications. It beat me why she hadn't done it already. It seemed to me that a mere tithe of what I had said, if said to a tigress about a tiger of which she was fond, would have made her – the tigress, I mean – hit the ceiling.

And the next moment you could have knocked me down with a toothpick.

'Yes,' she said, nodding thoughtfully, 'you're quite right.'

'Eh?'

'That's exactly what I've been thinking myself.'

'What!'

'"Dumb brick". It just describes him. One of the six silliest asses in England, I should think he must be.'

I did not speak. I was endeavouring to adjust the faculties, which were in urgent need of a bit of first-aid treatment.

I mean to say, all this had come as a complete surprise. In formulating the well-laid plan which I had just been putting into effect, the one contingency I had not budgeted for was that she might adhere to the sentiments which I expressed. I had braced myself for a gush of stormy emotion. I was expecting the tearful ticking off, the girlish recriminations and all the rest of the bag of tricks along those lines.

But this cordial agreement with my remarks I had not foreseen, and it gave me what you might call pause for thought.

She proceeded to develop her theme, speaking in ringing, enthusiastic tones, as if she loved the topic. Jeeves could tell you the word I want. I think it's 'ecstatic', unless that's the sort of rash you get on your face and have to use ointment for. But if that is the right word, then that's what her manner was as she ventilated the subject of poor old Tuppy. If you had been able to go simply by the sound of her voice, she might have been a court poet cutting loose about an Oriental monarch, or Gussie Fink-Nottle describing his last consignment of newts.

'It's so nice, Bertie, talking to somebody who really takes a sensible view about this man Glossop. Mother says he's a good chap, which is simply absurd. Anybody can see that he's absolutely impossible. He's conceited and opinionative and argues all the time, even when he knows perfectly well that he's talking through his hat, and he smokes too much and eats too much and drinks too much, and I don't like the colour of his hair. Not that he'll have any hair in a year or two, because he's pretty thin on the top already, and before he knows where he is he'll be as bald as an egg, and he's the last man who can afford to go bald. And I think it's simply disgusting, the way he gorges all the time. Do you know, I found him in the larder at one o'clock this morning, absolutely wallowing in a steak-and-kidney pie? There was hardly any of it left. And you remember what an enormous dinner he had. Quite disgusting, I call it. But I can't stop out here all night, talking about men who aren't worth wasting a word on and haven't even enough sense to tell sharks from flatfish. I'm going in.'

And gathering about her slim shoulders the shawl which she had put on as a protection against the evening dew, she buzzed off, leaving me alone in the silent night.

Well, as a matter of fact, not absolutely alone, because a few moments later there was a sort of upheaval in the bushes in front of me, and Tuppy emerged.

15

I gave him the eye. The evening had begun to draw in a bit by now and the visibility, in consequence, was not so hot, but there still remained ample light to enable me to see him clearly. And what I saw convinced me that I should be a lot easier in my mind with a stout rustic bench between us. I rose, accordingly, modelling my style on that of a rocketing pheasant, and proceeded to deposit myself on the other side of the object named.

My prompt agility was not without its effect. He seemed somewhat taken aback. He came to a halt, and, for about the space of time required to allow a bead of persp. to trickle from the top of the brow to the tip of the nose, stood gazing at me in silence.

'So!' he said at length, and it came as a complete surprise to me that fellows ever really do say 'So!' I had always thought it was just a thing you read in books. Like 'Quotha!' I mean to say, or 'Odds bodikins!' or even 'Eh, ba goom!'

Still, there it was. Quaint or not quaint, bizarre or not bizarre, he had said 'So!' and it was up to me to cope with the situation on those lines.

It would have been a duller man than Bertram Wooster who had failed to note that the dear old chap was a bit steamed up. Whether his eyes were actually shooting forth flame, I couldn't tell you, but there appeared to me to be a distinct incandescence. For the rest, his fists were clenched, his ears quivering, and the muscles of his jaw rotating rhythmically, as if he were making an early supper off something.

His hair was full of twigs, and there was a beetle hanging to the side of his head which would have interested Gussie Fink-Nottle. To this, however, I paid scant attention. There is a time for studying beetles and a time for not studying beetles.

'So!' he said again.

Now, those who know Bertram Wooster best will tell you that he is always at his shrewdest and most level-headed in moments of peril. Who was it who, when gripped by the arm of law on Boat-Race

Night not so many years ago and hauled off to Vine Street police station, assumed in a flash the identity of Eustace H. Plimsoll, of The Laburnums, Alleyn Road, West Dulwich, thus saving the grand old name of Wooster from being dragged in the mire and avoiding wide publicity of the wrong sort? Who was it . . .

But I need not labour the point. My record speaks for itself. Three times pinched, but never once sentenced under the correct label. Ask anyone at the Drones about this.

So now, in a situation threatening to become every moment more scaly, I did not lose my head. I preserved the old sang-froid. Smiling a genial and affectionate smile, and hoping that it wasn't too dark for it to register, I spoke with a jolly cordiality:

'Why, hallo, Tuppy. You here?'

He said, yes, he was here.

'Been here long?'

'I have.'

'Fine. I wanted to see you.'

'Well, here I am. Come out from behind that bench.'

'No, thanks, old man. I like leaning on it. It seems to rest the spine.'

'In about two seconds,' said Tuppy, 'I'm going to kick your spine up through the top of your head.'

I raised the eyebrows. Not much good, of course, in that light, but it seemed to help the general composition.

'Is this Hildebrand Glossop speaking?' I said.

He replied that it was, adding that if I wanted to make sure I might move a few feet over in his direction. He also called me an opprobrious name.

I raised the eyebrows again.

'Come, come, Tuppy, don't let us let this little chat become acrid. Is "acrid" the word I want?'

'I couldn't say,' he replied, beginning to sidle round the bench.

I saw that anything I might wish to say must be said quickly. Already he had sidled some six feet. And though, by dint of sidling, too, I had managed to keep the bench between us, who could predict how long this happy state of affairs would last?

I came to the point, therefore.

'I think I know what's on your mind, Tuppy,' I said. 'If you were in those bushes during my conversation with the recent Angela, I dare say you heard what I was saying about you.'

'I did.'

'I see. Well, we won't go into the ethics of the thing. Eaves-dropping, some people might call it, and I can imagine stern critics drawing in the breath to some extent. Considering it – I don't want to hurt your feelings, Tuppy – but considering it un-English. A bit un-English, Tuppy, old man, you must admit.'

'I'm Scottish.'

'Really?' I said. 'I never knew that before. Rummy how you don't suspect a man of being Scottish unless he's Mac-something and says "Och, aye" and things like that. I wonder,' I went on, feeling that an academic discussion on some neutral topic might ease the tension, 'if you can tell me something that has puzzled me a good deal. What exactly is it that they put into haggis? I've often wondered about that.'

From the fact that his only response to the question was to leap over the bench and make a grab at me, I gathered that his mind was not on haggis.

'However,' I said, leaping over the bench in my turn, 'that is a side issue. If, to come back to it, you were in those bushes and heard what I was saying about you – '

He began to move round the bench in a nor'-nor'-easterly direction. I followed his example, setting a course sou'-sou'-west.

'No doubt you were surprised at the way I was talking.'

'Not a bit.'

'What? Did nothing strike you as odd in the tone of my remarks?'

'It was just the sort of stuff I should have expected a treacherous, sneaking hound like you to say.'

'My dear chap,' I protested, 'this is not your usual form. A bit slow in the uptake, surely? I should have thought you would have spotted right away that it was all part of a well-laid plan.'

'I'll get you in a jiffy,' said Tuppy, recovering his balance after a swift clutch at my neck. And so probable did this seem that I delayed no longer, but hastened to place all the facts before him.

Speaking rapidly and keeping moving, I related my emotions on receipt of Aunt Dahlia's telegram, my instant rush to the scene of the disaster, my meditations in the car, and the eventual framing of this well-laid plan of mine. I spoke clearly and well, and it was with considerable concern, consequently, that I heard him observe – between clenched teeth, which made it worse – that he didn't believe a damned word of it.

'But, Tuppy,' I said, 'why not? To me the thing rings true to the last drop. What makes you sceptical? Confide in me, Tuppy.'

He halted and stood taking a breather. Tuppy, pungently though Angela might have argued to the contrary, isn't really fat. During the winter months you will find him constantly booting the football with merry shouts, and in the summer the tennis racket is seldom out of his hand.

But at the recently concluded evening meal, feeling, no doubt, that after that painful scene in the larder there was nothing to be gained by further abstinence, he had rather let himself go and, as it were, made up leeway; and after really immersing himself in one of Anatole's dinners, a man of his sturdy build tends to lose elasticity a bit. During the exposition of my plans for his happiness a certain animation had crept into this round-and-round-the-mulberry-bush jamboree of ours – so much so, indeed, that for the last few minutes we might have been a rather oversized greyhound and a somewhat slimmer electric hare doing their stuff on a circular track for the entertainment of the many-headed.

This, it appeared, had taken it out of him a bit, and I was not displeased. I was feeling the strain myself, and welcomed a lull.

'It absolutely beats me why you don't believe it,' I said. 'You know we've been pals for years. You must be aware that, except at the moment when you caused me to do a nose dive into the Drones's swimming bath, an incident which I long since decided to put out of my mind and let the dead past bury its dead about, if you follow what I mean – except on that one occasion, as I say, I have always regarded you with the utmost esteem. Why, then, if not for the motives I have outlined, should I knock you to Angela? Answer me that. Be very careful.'

'What do you mean, be very careful?'

Well, as a matter of fact, I didn't quite know myself. It was what the magistrate had said to me on the occasion when I stood in the dock as Eustace Plimsoll, of The Laburnums: and as it had impressed me a good deal at the time, I just bunged it in now by way of giving the conversation a tone.

'All right. Never mind about being careful, then. Just answer me that question. Why, if I had not your interests sincerely at heart, should I have ticked you off, as stated?'

A sharp spasm shook him from base to apex. The beetle, which, during the recent exchanges, had been clinging to his head, hoping for the best, gave it up at this and resigned office. It shot off and was swallowed in the night.

'Ah!' I said. 'Your beetle,' I explained. 'No doubt you were unaware of it, but all this while there has been a beetle of sorts parked on the side of your head. You have now dislodged it.'

He snorted.

'Beetles!'

'Not beetles. One beetle only.'

'I like your crust!' cried Tuppy, vibrating like one of Gussie's newts during the courting season. 'Talking of beetles, when all the time you know you're a treacherous, sneaking hound.'

It was a debatable point, of course, why treacherous, sneaking hounds should be considered ineligible to talk about beetles, and I dare say a good cross-examining counsel would have made quite a lot of it.

But I let it go.

'That's the second time you've called me that. And,' I said firmly, 'I insist on an explanation. I have told you that I acted throughout from the best and kindliest motives in roasting you to Angela. It cut me to the quick to have to speak like that, and only the recollection of our lifelong friendship would have made me do it. And now you say you don't believe me and call me names for which I am not sure I couldn't have you up before a beak and jury and mulct you in very substantial damages. I should have to consult my solicitor, of course, but it would surprise me very much if an action did not lie. Be reasonable, Tuppy. Suggest another motive I could have had. Just one.'

'I will. Do you think I don't know? You're in love with Angela yourself.'

'What?'

'And you knocked me in order to poison her mind against me and finally remove me from your path.'

I had never heard anything so absolutely loopy in my life. Why, dash it, I've known Angela since she was so high. You don't fall in love with close relations you've known since they were so high. Besides, isn't there something in the book of rules about a man may not marry his cousin? Or am I thinking of grandmothers?

'Tuppy, my dear old ass,' I cried, 'this is pure banana oil! You've come unscrewed.'

'Oh, yes?'

'Me in love with Angela? Ha-ha!'

'You can't get out of it with ha-has. She called you "darling".'

'I know. And I disapproved. This habit of the younger g. of scattering "darlings" about like birdseed is one that I deprecate. Lax, is how I should describe it.'

'You tickled her ankles.'

'In a purely cousinly spirit. It didn't mean a thing. Why, dash it, you must know that in the deeper and truer sense I wouldn't touch Angela with a barge pole.'

'Oh? And why not? Not good enough for you?'

'You misunderstand me,' I hastened to reply. 'When I say I wouldn't touch Angela with a barge pole, I intend merely to convey that my feelings towards her are those of distant, though cordial, esteem. In other words, you may rest assured that between this young prune and myself there never has been and never could be any sentiment warmer and stronger than that of ordinary friendship.'

'I believe it was you who tipped her off that I was in the larder last night, so that she could find me there with that pie, thus damaging my prestige.'

'My dear Tuppy! A Wooster?' I was shocked. 'You think a Wooster would do that?'

He breathed heavily.

'Listen,' he said. 'It's no good your standing there arguing. You can't get away from the facts. Somebody stole her from me at Cannes. You told me yourself that she was with you all the time at Cannes and hardly saw anybody else. You gloated over the mixed bathing, and those moonlight walks you had together – '

'Not gloated. Just mentioned them.'

'So now you understand why, as soon as I can get you clear of this damned bench, I am going to tear you limb from limb. Why they have these bally benches in gardens,' said Tuppy discontentedly, 'is more than I can see. They only get in the way.'

He ceased, and, grabbing out, missed me by a hair's breadth.

It was a moment for swift thinking, and it is at such moments, as I have already indicated, that Bertram Wooster is at his best. I suddenly remembered the recent misunderstanding with the Bassett, and with a flash of clear vision saw that this was where it was going to come in handy.

'You've got it all wrong, Tuppy,' I said, moving to the left. 'True, I saw a lot of Angela, but my dealings with her were on a basis from start to finish of the purest and most wholesome camaraderie. I can prove it. During that sojourn in Cannes my affections were engaged elsewhere.'

'What?'

'Engaged elsewhere. My affections. During that sojourn.'

I had struck the right note. He stopped sidling. His clutching hand fell to his side.

'Is that true?'

'Quite official.'

'Who was she?'

'My dear Tuppy, does one bandy a woman's name?'

'One does if one doesn't want one's ruddy head pulled off.'

I saw that it was a special case.

'Madeline Bassett,' I said.

'Who?'

'Madeline Bassett.'

He seemed stunned.

'You stand there and tell me you were in love with that Bassett disaster?'

'I wouldn't call her "that Bassett disaster", Tuppy. Not respectful.'

'Dash being respectful. I want the facts. You deliberately assert that you loved that weird Gawd-help-us?'

'I don't see why you should call her a weird Gawd-help-us, either. A very charming and beautiful girl. Odd in some of her views perhaps – one does not quite see eye to eye with her in the matter of stars and rabbits – but not a weird Gawd-help-us.'

'Anyway, you stick to it that you were in love with her?'

'I do.'

'It sounds thin to me, Wooster, very thin.'

I saw that it would be necessary to apply the finishing touch.

'I must ask you to treat this as entirely confidential, Glossop, but I may as well inform you that it is not twenty-four hours since she turned me down.'

'Turned you down?'

'Like a bedspread. In this very garden.'

'Twenty-four hours?'

'Call it twenty-five. So you will readily see that I can't be the chap, if any, who stole Angela from you at Cannes.'

And I was on the brink of adding that I wouldn't touch Angela with a barge pole, when I remembered I had said it already and it hadn't gone frightfully well. I desisted, therefore.

My manly frankness seemed to be producing good results. The homicidal glare was dying out of Tuppy's eyes. He had the aspect of a hired assassin who had paused to think things over.

'I see,' he said, at length. 'All right, then. Sorry you were troubled.'

'Don't mention it, old man,' I responded courteously.

For the first time since the bushes had begun to pour forth

Glossops, Bertram Wooster could be said to have breathed freely. I don't say I actually came out from behind the bench, but I did let go of it, and with something of the relief which those three chaps in the Old Testament must have experienced after sliding out of the burning fiery furnace, I even groped tentatively for my cigarette case.

The next moment a sudden snort made me take my fingers off it as if it had bitten me. I was distressed to note in the old friend a return of the recent frenzy.

'What the hell did you mean by telling her that I used to be covered with ink when I was a kid?'

'My dear Tuppy – '

'I was almost finickingly careful about my personal cleanliness as a boy. You could have eaten your dinner off me.'

'Quite. But – '

'And all that stuff about having no soul. I'm crawling with soul. And being looked on as an outsider at the Drones – '

'But, my dear old chap, I explained that. It was all part of my ruse or scheme.'

'It was, was it? Well, in future do me a favour and leave me out of your foul ruses.'

'Just as you say, old boy.'

'All right, then. That's understood.'

He relapsed into silence, standing with folded arms, staring before him rather like a strong, silent man in a novel when he's just been given the bird by the girl and is thinking of looking in at the Rocky Mountains and bumping off a few bears. His manifest pippedness excited my compash, and I ventured a kindly word.

'I don't suppose you know what *au pied de la lettre* means, Tuppy, but that's how I don't think you ought to take all that stuff Angela was saying just now too much.'

He seemed interested.

'What the devil,' he asked, 'are you talking about?'

I saw that I should have to make myself clearer.

'Don't take all that guff of hers too literally, old man. You know what girls are like.'

'I do,' he said, with another snort that came straight up from his insteps. 'And I wish I'd never met one.'

'I mean to say, it's obvious that she must have spotted you in those bushes and was simply talking to score off you. There you were, I mean, if you follow the psychology, and she saw you, and in that impulsive way girls have, she seized the opportunity of ribbing you a bit – just told you a few home truths, I mean to say.'

'Home truths?'

'That's right.'

He snorted once more, causing me to feel rather like royalty receiving a twenty-one gun salute from the fleet. I can't remember ever having met a better right-and-left-hand snorter.

'What do you mean, "home truths"? I'm not fat.'

'No, no.'

'And what's wrong with the colour of my hair?'

'Quite in order, Tuppy, old man. The hair, I mean.'

'And I'm not a bit thin on the top . . . What the dickens are you grinning about?'

'Not grinning. Just smiling slightly. I was conjuring up a sort of vision, if you know what I mean, of you as seen through Angela's eyes. Fat in the middle and thin on the top. Rather funny.'

'You think it funny, do you?'

'Not a bit.'

'You'd better not.'

'Quite.'

It seemed to me that the conversation was becoming difficult again. I wished it could be terminated. And so it was. For at this moment something came shimmering through the laurels in the quiet evenfall, and I perceived that it was Angela.

She was looking sweet and saintlike, and she had a plate of sandwiches in her hand. Ham, I was to discover later.

'If you see Mr Glossop anywhere, Bertie,' she said, her eyes resting dreamily on Tuppy's façade, 'I wish you would give him these. I'm so afraid he may be hungry, poor fellow. It's nearly ten o'clock, and he hasn't eaten a morsel since dinner. I'll just leave them on this bench.'

She pushed off, and it seemed to me that I might as well go with her. Nothing to keep me here, I mean. We moved towards the house, and presently from behind us there sounded in the night the splintering crash of a well-kicked plate of ham sandwiches, accompanied by the muffled oaths of a strong man in his wrath.

'How still and peaceful everything is,' said Angela.

16

Sunshine was gilding the grounds of Brinkley Court and the ear detected a marked twittering of birds in the ivy outside the window when I woke next morning to a new day. But there was no corresponding sunshine in Bertram Wooster's soul and no answering twitter in his heart as he sat up in bed, sipping his cup of strengthening tea. It could not be denied that to Bertram, reviewing the happenings of the previous night, the Tuppy-Angela situation seemed more or less to have slipped a cog. With every desire to look for the silver lining, I could not but feel that the rift between these two haughty spirits had now reached such impressive proportions that the task of bridging same would be beyond even my powers.

I am a shrewd observer, and there had been something in Tuppy's manner as he booted that plate of ham sandwiches that seemed to tell me that he would not lightly forgive.

In these circs, I deemed it best to shelve their problem for the nonce and turn the mind to the matter of Gussie, which presented a brighter picture.

With regard to Gussie, everything was in train. Jeeves's morbid scruples about lacing the chap's orange juice had put me to a good deal of trouble, but I had surmounted every obstacle in the old Wooster way. I had secured an abundance of the necessary spirit, and it was now lying in its flask in the drawer of the dressing table. I had also ascertained that the jug, duly filled, would be standing on a shelf in the butler's pantry round about the hour of one. To remove it from that shelf, sneak it up to my room, and return it, laced, in good time for the midday meal would be a task calling, no doubt, for address, but in no sense an exacting one.

It was with something of the emotions of one preparing a treat for a deserving child that I finished my tea and rolled over for that extra spot of sleep which just makes all the difference when there is man's work to be done and the brain must be kept clear for it.

And when I came downstairs an hour or so later, I knew how right

I had been to formulate this scheme for Gussie's bucking up. I ran into him on the lawn, and I could see at a glance that if ever there was a man who needed a snappy stimulant, it was he. All nature, as I have indicated, was smiling, but not Augustus Fink-Nottle. He was walking round in circles, muttering something about not proposing to detain us long, but on this auspicious occasion feeling compelled to say a few words.

'Ah, Gussie,' I said, arresting him as he was about to start another lap. 'A lovely morning, is it not?'

Even if I had not been aware of it already, I could have divined from the abruptness with which he damned the lovely morning that he was not in merry mood. I addressed myself to the task of bringing the roses back to his cheeks.

'I've got good news for you, Gussie.'

He looked at me with a sudden sharp interest.

'Has Market Snodsbury Grammar School burned down?'

'Not that I know of.'

'Have mumps broken out? Is the place closed on account of measles?'

'No, no.'

'Then what do you mean you've got good news?'

I endeavoured to soothe.

'You mustn't take it so hard, Gussie. Why worry about a laughably simple job like distributing prizes at a school?'

'Laughably simple, eh? Do you realize I've been sweating for days and haven't been able to think of a thing to say yet, except that I won't detain them long. You bet I won't detain them long. I've been timing my speech, and it lasts five seconds. What the devil am I to say, Bertie? What do you say when you're distributing prizes?'

I considered. Once, at my private school, I had won a prize for Scripture knowledge, so I suppose I ought to have been full of inside stuff. But memory eluded me.

Then something emerged from the mists.

'You say the race is not always to the swift.'

'Why?'

'Well, it's a good gag. It generally gets a hand.'

'I mean, why isn't it? Why isn't the race to the swift?'

'Ah, there you have me. But the nibs say it isn't.'

'But what does it mean?'

'I take it it's supposed to console the chaps who haven't won prizes.'

'What's the good of that to me? I'm not worrying about them. It's the ones that have won prizes that I'm worrying about, the little blighters who will come up on the platform. Suppose they make faces at me.'

'They won't.'

'How do you know they won't? It's probably the first thing they'll think of. And even if they don't – Bertie, shall I tell you something?'

'What?'

'I've a good mind to take that tip of yours and have a drink.'

I smiled. He little knew, about summed up what I was thinking.

'Oh, you'll be all right,' I said.

He became fevered again.

'How do you know I'll be all right? I'm sure to blow up in my lines.'

'Tush!'

'Or drop a prize.'

'Tut!'

'Or something. I can feel it in my bones. As sure as I'm standing here, something is going to happen this afternoon which will make everybody laugh themselves sick at me. I can hear them now. Like hyenas . . . Bertie!'

'Hullo?'

'Do you remember that kids' school we went to before Eton?'

'Quite. It was there I won my Scripture prize.'

'Never mind about your Scripture prize. I'm not talking about your Scripture prize. Do you recollect the Bosher incident?'

I did, indeed. It was one of the high spots of my youth.

'Major-General Sir Wilfred Bosher came to distribute the prizes at that school,' proceeded Gussie in a dull, toneless voice. 'He dropped a book. He stooped to pick it up. And, as he stooped, his trousers split up the back.'

'How we roared!'

Gussie's face twisted.

'We did, little swine that we were. Instead of remaining silent and exhibiting a decent sympathy for a gallant officer at a peculiarly embarrassing moment, we howled and yelled with mirth. I loudest of any. That is what will happen to me this afternoon, Bertie. It will be a judgment on me for laughing like that at Major-General Sir Wilfred Bosher.'

'No, no, Gussie, old man. Your trousers won't split.'

'How do you know they won't? Better men than I have split their trousers. General Bosher was a DSO, with a fine record of service on the north-western frontier of India, and his trousers split. I shall be a mockery and a scorn. I know it. And you, fully cognizant of what I am in for, come babbling about good news. What news could possibly be good to me at this moment except the information that bubonic plague had broken out among the scholars of Market Snodsbury Grammar School, and that they were all confined to their beds with spots?'

The moment had come for me to speak. I laid a hand gently on his shoulder. He brushed it off. I laid it on again. He brushed it off once more. I was endeavouring to lay it on for the third time, when he moved aside and desired, with a certain petulance, to be informed if I thought I was a ruddy osteopath.

I found his manner trying, but one has to make allowances. I was telling myself that I should be seeing a very different Gussie after lunch.

'When I said I had good news, old man, I meant about Madeline Bassett.'

The febrile gleam died out of his eyes, to be replaced by a look of infinite sadness.

'You can't have good news about her. I've dished myself there completely.'

'Not at all. I am convinced that if you take another whack at her, all will be well.'

And, keeping it snappy, I related what had passed between the Bassett and myself on the previous night.

'So all you have to do is play a return date, and you cannot fail to swing the voting. You are her dream man.'

He shook his head.

'No.'

'What?'

'No use.'

'What do you mean?'

'Not a bit of good trying.'

'But I tell you she said in so many words – '

'It doesn't make any difference. She may have loved me once. Last night will have killed all that.'

'Of course it won't.'

'It will. She despises me now.'

'Not a bit of it. She knows you simply got cold feet.'

'And I should get cold feet if I tried again. It's no good, Bertie. I'm hopeless, and there's an end of it. Fate made me the sort of chap who can't say "boo" to a goose.'

'It isn't a question of saying "boo" to a goose. The point doesn't arise at all. It is simply a matter of – '

'I know, I know. But it's no good. I can't do it. The whole thing is off. I am not going to risk a repetition of last night's fiasco. You talk in a light way of taking another whack at her, but you don't know what it means. You have not been through the experience of starting to ask the girl you love to marry you and then suddenly finding yourself talking about the plumlike external gills of the newly born newt. It's not a thing you can do twice. No, I accept my destiny. It's all over. And now, Bertie, like a good chap, shove off. I want to compose my speech. I can't compose my speech with you mucking around. If you are going to continue to muck around, at least give me a couple of stories. The little hell hounds are sure to expect a story or two.'

'Do you know the one about – '

'No good. I don't want any of your off-colour stuff from the Drones's smoking-room. I need something clean. Something that will be a help to them in their after-lives. Not that I care a damn about their after-lives, except that I hope they'll all choke.'

'I heard a story the other day. I can't quite remember it, but it was about a chap who snored and disturbed the neighbours, and it ended, "It was his adenoids that adenoid them."'

He made a weary gesture.

'You expect me to work that in, do you, into a speech to be delivered to an audience of boys, every one of whom is probably riddled with adenoids? Damn it, they'd rush the platform. Leave me, Bertie. Push off. That's all I ask you to do. Push off . . . Ladies and gentlemen,' said Gussie, in a low, soliloquizing sort of way, 'I do not propose to detain this auspicious occasion long – '

It was a thoughtful Wooster who walked away and left him at it. More than ever I was congratulating myself on having had the sterling good sense to make all my arrangements so that I could press a button and set things moving at an instant's notice.

Until now, you see, I had rather entertained a sort of hope that when I had revealed to him the Bassett's mental attitude, Nature would have done the rest, bracing him up to such an extent that artificial stimulants would not be required. Because, naturally, a chap doesn't want to have to sprint about country houses lugging jugs of orange juice, unless it is absolutely essential.

But now I saw that I must carry on as planned. The total absence of pep, ginger, and the right spirit which the man had displayed during these conversational exchanges convinced me that the strongest measures would be necessary. Immediately upon leaving him, therefore, I proceeded to the pantry, waited till the butler had removed himself elsewhere, and nipped in and secured the vital jug. A few moments later, after a wary passage of the stairs, I was in my room. And the first thing I saw there was Jeeves, fooling about with trousers.

He gave the jug a look which – wrongly, as it was to turn out – I diagnosed as censorious. I drew myself up a bit. I intended to have no rot from the fellow.

'Yes, Jeeves?'

'Sir?'

'You have the air of one about to make a remark, Jeeves.'

'Oh, no, sir. I note that you are in possession of Mr Fink-Nottle's orange juice. I was merely about to observe that in my opinion it would be injudicious to add spirit to it.'

'That is a remark, Jeeves, and it is precisely – '

'Because I have already attended to the matter, sir.'

'What?'

'Yes, sir. I decided, after all, to acquiesce in your wishes.'

I stared at the man, astounded. I was deeply moved. Well, I mean, wouldn't any chap who had been going about thinking that the old feudal spirit was dead and then suddenly found it wasn't have been deeply moved?

'Jeeves,' I said, 'I am touched.'

'Thank you, sir.'

'Touched and gratified.'

'Thank you very much, sir.'

'But what caused this change of heart?'

'I chanced to encounter Mr Fink-Nottle in the garden, sir, while you were still in bed, and we had a brief conversation.'

'And you came away feeling that he needed a bracer?'

'Very much so, sir. His attitude struck me as defeatist.'

I nodded.

'I felt the same. "Defeatist" sums it up to a nicety. Did you tell him his attitude struck you as defeatist?'

'Yes, sir.'

'But it didn't do any good?'

'No, sir.'

'Very well, then, Jeeves. We must act. How much gin did you put in the jug?'

'A liberal tumblerful, sir.'

'Would that be a normal dose for an adult defeatist, do you think?'

'I fancy it should prove adequate, sir.'

'I wonder. We must not spoil the ship for a ha'p'orth of tar. I think I'll add just another fluid ounce or so.'

'I would not advocate it, sir. In the case of Lord Brancaster's parrot – '

'You are falling into your old error, Jeeves, of thinking that Gussie is a parrot. Fight against this. I shall add the oz.'

'Very good, sir.'

'And, by the way, Jeeves, Mr Fink-Nottle is in the market for bright, clean stories to use in his speech. Do you know any?'

'I know a story about two Irishmen, sir.'

'Pat and Mike?'

'Yes, sir.'

'Who were walking along Broadway?'

'Yes, sir.'

'Just what he wants. Any more?'

'No, sir.'

'Well, every little helps. You had better go and tell it to him.'

'Very good, sir.'

He passed from the room, and I unscrewed the flask and tilted into the jug a generous modicum of its contents. And scarcely had I done so, when there came to my ears the sound of footsteps without. I had only just time to shove the jug behind the photograph of Uncle Tom on the mantelpiece before the door opened and in came Gussie, curveting like a circus horse.

'What-ho, Bertie,' he said. 'What-ho, what-ho, what-ho, and again what-ho. What a beautiful world this is, Bertie. One of the nicest I ever met.'

I stared at him, speechless. We Woosters are as quick as lightning, and I saw at once that something had happened.

I mean to say, I told you about him walking round in circles. I recorded what passed between us on the lawn. And if I portrayed the scene with anything like adequate skill, the picture you will have retained of this Fink-Nottle will have been that of a nervous wreck, sagging at the knees, green about the gills, and picking feverishly at the lapels of his coat in an ecstasy of craven fear. In a word, defeatist. Gussie, during that interview, had, in fine, exhibited all the earmarks of one licked to a custard.

Vastly different was the Gussie who stood before me now. Self-confidence seemed to ooze from the fellow's every pore. His face was flushed, there was a jovial light in his eyes, the lips were parted in a swashbuckling smile. And when with a genial hand he sloshed me on the back before I could sidestep, it was as if I had been kicked by a mule.

'Well, Bertie,' he proceeded, as blithely as a linnet without a thing on his mind, 'you will be glad to hear that you were right. Your theory has been tested and proved correct. I feel like a fighting cock.'

My brain ceased to reel. I saw all.

'Have you been having a drink?'

'I have. As you advised. Unpleasant stuff. Like medicine. Burns your throat, too, and makes one as thirsty as the dickens. How anyone can mop it up, as you do, for pleasure, beats me. Still, I would be the last to deny that it tunes up the system. I could bite a tiger.'

'What did you have?'

'Whisky. At least, that was the label on the decanter, and I have no reason to suppose that a woman like your aunt – staunch, true-blue, British – would deliberately deceive the public. If she labels her decanters Whisky, then I consider that we know where we are.'

'A whisky and soda, eh? You couldn't have done better.'

'Soda?' said Gussie thoughtfully. 'I knew there was something I had forgotten.'

'Didn't you put any soda in it?'

'It never occurred to me. I just nipped into the dining-room and drank out of the decanter.'

'How much?'

'Oh, about ten swallows. Twelve, maybe. Or fourteen. Say sixteen medium-sized gulps. Gosh, I'm thirsty.'

He moved over to the washstand and drank deeply out of the water bottle. I cast a covert glance at Uncle Tom's photograph behind his back. For the first time since it had come into my life, I was glad that it was so large. It hid its secret well. If Gussie had caught sight of that jug of orange juice, he would unquestionably have been on to it like a knife.

'Well, I'm glad you're feeling braced,' I said.

He moved buoyantly from the washstand, and endeavoured to slosh me on the back again. Foiled by my nimble footwork, he staggered to the bed and sat down upon it.

'Braced? Did I say I could bite a tiger?'

'You did.'

'Make it two tigers. I could chew holes in a steel door. What an ass you must have thought me out there in the garden. I see now you were laughing in your sleeve.'

'No, no.'

'Yes,' insisted Gussie. 'That very sleeve,' he said, pointing. 'And

I don't blame you. I can't imagine why I made all that fuss about a potty job like distributing prizes at a rotten little country grammar school. Can you imagine, Bertie?'

'No.'

'Exactly. Nor can I imagine. There's simply nothing to it. I just shin up on the platform, drop a few gracious words, hand the little blighters their prizes, and hop down again, admired by all. Not a suggestion of split trousers from start to finish. I mean, why should anybody split his trousers? I can't imagine. Can you imagine?'

'No.'

'Nor can I imagine. I shall be a riot. I know just the sort of stuff that's needed – simple, manly, optimistic stuff straight from the shoulder. This shoulder,' said Gussie, tapping. 'Why I was so nervous this morning I can't imagine. For anything simpler than distributing a few footling books to a bunch of grimy-faced kids I can't imagine. Still, for some reason I can't imagine, I was feeling a little nervous, but now I feel fine, Bertie – fine, fine, fine – and I say this to you as an old friend. Because that's what you are, old man, when all the smoke has cleared away – an old friend. I don't think I've ever met an older friend. How long have you been an old friend of mine, Bertie?'

'Oh, years and years.'

'Imagine! Though, of course, there must have been a time when you were a new friend . . . Hallo, the luncheon gong. Come on, old friend.'

And, rising from the bed like a performing flea, he made for the door.

I followed rather pensively. What had occurred was, of course, so much velvet, as you might say. I mean, I had wanted a braced Fink-Nottle – indeed, all my plans had had a braced Fink-Nottle as their end and aim – but I found myself wondering a little whether the Fink-Nottle now sliding down the banister wasn't, perhaps, a shade too braced. His demeanour seemed to me that of a man who might quite easily throw bread about at lunch.

Fortunately, however, the settled gloom of those round him exercised a restraining effect upon him at the table. It would have needed a far more plastered man to have been rollicking at such a gathering. I had told the Bassett that there were aching hearts in Brinkley Court, and it now looked probable that there would shortly be aching tummies. Anatole, I learned, had retired to his bed with a fit of the vapours, and the meal now before us had been cooked by the kitchen maid – as C3 a performer as ever wielded a skillet.

This, coming on top of their other troubles, induced in the company a pretty unanimous silence – a solemn stillness, as you might say – which even Gussie did not seem prepared to break. Except, therefore, for one short snatch of song on his part, nothing untoward marked the occasion, and presently we rose, with instructions from Aunt Dahlia to put on festal raiment and be at Market Snodsbury not later than 3.30. This leaving me ample time to smoke a gasper or two in a shady bower beside the lake, I did so, repairing to my room round about the hour of three.

Jeeves was on the job, adding the final polish to the old topper, and I was about to apprise him of the latest developments in the matter of Gussie, when he forestalled me by observing that the latter had only just concluded an agreeable visit to the Wooster bedchamber.

'I found Mr Fink-Nottle seated here when I arrived to lay out your clothes, sir.'

'Indeed, Jeeves? Gussie was in here, was he?'

'Yes, sir. He left only a few moments ago. He is driving to the school with Mr and Mrs Travers in the large car.'

'Did you give him your story of the two Irishmen?'

'Yes, sir. He laughed heartily.'

'Good. Had you any other contributions for him?'

'I ventured to suggest that he might mention to the young gentlemen that education is a drawing out, not a putting in. The late Lord Brancaster was much addicted to presenting prizes at schools, and he invariably employed this dictum.'

'And how did he react to that?'

'He laughed heartily, sir.'

'This surprised you, no doubt? This practically incessant merriment, I mean.'

'Yes, sir.'

'You thought it odd in one who, when you last saw him, was well up in Group A of the defeatists.'

'Yes, sir.'

'There is a ready explanation, Jeeves. Since you last saw him, Gussie has been on a bender. He's as tight as an owl.'

'Indeed, sir?'

'Absolutely. His nerve cracked under the strain, and he sneaked into the dining-room and started mopping the stuff up like a vacuum cleaner. Whisky would seem to be what he filled the radiator with. I gather that he used up most of the decanter. Golly, Jeeves, it's lucky he didn't get at that laced orange juice on top of that, what?'

'Extremely, sir.'

I eyed the jug. Uncle Tom's photograph had fallen into the fender, and it was standing there right out in the open, where Gussie couldn't have helped seeing it. Mercifully, it was empty now.

'It was a most prudent act on your part, if I may say so, sir, to dispose of the orange juice.'

I stared at the man.

'What? Didn't you?'

'No, sir.'

'Jeeves, let us get this clear. Was it not you who threw away that o.j.?'

'No, sir. I assumed, when I entered the room and found the pitcher empty, that you had done so.'

We looked at each other, awed. Two minds with but a single thought.

'I very much fear, sir – '

'So do I, Jeeves.'

'It would seem almost certain – '

'Quite certain. Weigh the facts. Sift the evidence. The jug was standing on the mantelpiece, for all eyes to behold. Gussie had been complaining of thirst. You found him in here, laughing heartily. I think that there can be little doubt, Jeeves, that the entire contents of that jug are at this moment reposing on top of the existing cargo in that already brilliantly lit man's interior. Disturbing, Jeeves.'

'Most disturbing, sir.'

'Let us face the position, forcing ourselves to be calm. You inserted in that jug – shall we say a tumblerful of the right stuff?'

'Fully a tumblerful, sir.'

'And I added of my plenty about the same amount.'

'Yes, sir.'

'And in two shakes of a duck's tail Gussie, with all that lapping about inside him, will be distributing the prizes at Market Snodsbury Grammar School before an audience of all that is fairest and most refined in the county.'

'Yes, sir.'

'It seems to me, Jeeves, that the ceremony may be one fraught with considerable interest.'

'Yes, sir.'

'What, in your opinion, will the harvest be?'

'One finds it difficult to hazard a conjecture, sir.'

'You mean imagination boggles?'

'Yes, sir.'

I inspected my imagination. He was right. It boggled.

17

'And yet, Jeeves,' I said, twiddling a thoughtful steering wheel, 'there is always the bright side.'

Some twenty minutes had elapsed, and, having picked the honest fellow up outside the front door, I was driving in the two-seater to the picturesque town of Market Snodsbury. Since we had parted – he to go to his lair and fetch his hat, I to remain in my room and complete the formal costume – I had been doing some close thinking.

The results of this I now proceeded to hand on to him.

'However dark the prospect may be, Jeeves, however murkily the storm clouds may seem to gather, a keen eye can usually discern the bluebird. It is bad, no doubt, that Gussie should be going, some ten minutes from now, to distribute prizes in a state of advanced intoxication, but we must never forget that these things cut both ways.'

'You imply, sir – '

'Precisely. I am thinking of him in his capacity of wooer. All this ought to have put him in rare shape for offering his hand in marriage. I shall be vastly surprised if it won't turn him into a sort of caveman. Have you ever seen James Cagney in the movies?'

'Yes, sir.'

'Something on those lines.'

I heard him cough, and sniped him with a sideways glance. He was wearing that informative look of his.

'Then you have not heard, sir?'

'Eh?'

'You are not aware that a marriage has been arranged and will shortly take place between Mr Fink-Nottle and Miss Bassett?'

'What?'

'Yes, sir.'

'When did this happen?'

'Shortly after Mr Fink-Nottle had left your room, sir.'

'Ah! In the post-orange-juice era?'

'Yes, sir.'

'But are you sure of your facts? How do you know?'

'My informant was Mr Fink-Nottle himself, sir. He appeared anxious to confide in me. His story was somewhat incoherent, but I had no difficulty in apprehending its substance. Prefacing his remarks with the statement that this was a beautiful world, he laughed heartily and said that he had become formally engaged.'

'No details?'

'No, sir.'

'But one can picture the scene.'

'Yes, sir.'

'I mean, imagination doesn't boggle.'

'No, sir.'

And it didn't. I could see exactly what must have happened. Insert a liberal dose of mixed spirits in a normally abstemious man, and he becomes a force. He does not stand around, twiddling his fingers and stammering. He acts. I had no doubt that Gussie must have reached for the Bassett and clasped her to him like a stevedore handling a sack of coals. And one could readily envisage the effect of that sort of thing on a girl of romantic mind.

'Well, well, well, Jeeves.'

'Yes, sir.'

'This is splendid news.'

'Yes, sir.'

'You see now how right I was.'

'Yes, sir.'

'It must have been rather an eye-opener for you, watching me handle this case.'

'Yes, sir.'

'The simple, direct method never fails.'

'No, sir.'

'Whereas the elaborate does.'

'Yes, sir.'

'Right ho, Jeeves.'

We had arrived at the main entrance of Market Snodsbury Grammar School. I parked the car, and went in, well content. True, the Tuppy-Angela problem still remained unsolved and Aunt Dahlia's five hundred quid seemed as far off as ever, but it was gratifying to feel that good old Gussie's troubles were over, at any rate.

The Grammar School at Market Snodsbury had, I understood, been built somewhere in the year 1416, and, as with so many of these ancient foundations, there still seemed to brood over its Great

Hall, where the afternoon's festivities were to take place, not a little of the fug of the centuries. It was the hottest day of the summer, and though somebody had opened a tentative window or two, the atmosphere remained distinctive and individual.

In this hall the youth of Market Snodsbury had been eating its daily lunch for a matter of five hundred years, and the flavour lingered. The air was sort of heavy and languorous, if you know what I mean, with the scent of Young England and boiled beef and carrots.

Aunt Dahlia, who was sitting with a bevy of the local nibs in the second row, sighted me as I entered and waved to me to join her, but I was too smart for that. I wedged myself in among the standees at the back, leaning up against a chap who from the aroma, might have been a corn chandler or something of that order. The essence of strategy on these occasions is to be as near the door as possible.

The hall was gaily decorated with flags and coloured paper, and the eye was further refreshed by the spectacle of a mixed drove of boys, parents, and what not, the former running a good deal to shiny faces and Eton collars, the latter stressing the black-satin note rather when female, and looking as if their coats were too tight, if male. And presently there was some applause – sporadic, Jeeves has since told me it was – and I saw Gussie being steered by a bearded bloke in a gown to a seat in the middle of the platform.

And I confess that as I beheld him and felt that there but for the grace of God went Bertram Wooster, a shudder ran through the frame. It all reminded me so vividly of the time I had addressed that girls' school.

Of course, looking at it dispassionately, you may say that for horror and peril there is no comparison between an almost human audience like the one before me and a mob of small girls with pigtails down their backs, and this, I concede, is true. Nevertheless, the spectacle was enough to make me feel like a fellow watching a pal going over Niagara Falls in a barrel, and the thought of what I had escaped caused everything for a moment to go black and swim before my eyes.

When I was able to see clearly once more, I perceived that Gussie was now seated. He had his hands on his knees, with his elbows out at right angles, like a negro minstrel of the old school about to ask Mr Bones why a chicken crosses the road, and he was staring before him with a smile so fixed and pebble-beached that I should have thought that anybody could have guessed that there sat one in whom the old familiar juice was splashing up against the back of the front teeth.

In fact, I saw Aunt Dahlia, who, having assisted at so many

hunting dinners in her time, is second to none as a judge of the symptoms, give a start and gaze long and earnestly. And she was just saying something to Uncle Tom on her left when the bearded bloke stepped to the footlights and started making a speech. From the fact that he spoke as if he had a hot potato in his mouth without getting the raspberry from the lads in the ringside seats, I deduced that he must be the headmaster.

With his arrival in the spotlight, a sort of perspiring resignation seemed to settle on the audience. Personally, I snuggled up against the chandler and let my attention wander. The speech was on the subject of the doings of the school during the past term, and this part of a prize giving is always apt rather to fail to grip the visiting stranger. I mean, you know how it is. You're told that J. B. Brewster has won an Exhibition for Classics at Cat's, Cambridge, and you feel that it's one of those stories where you can't see how funny it is unless you really know the fellow. And the same applies to G. Bullett being awarded the Lady Jane Wix Scholarship at the Birmingham College of Veterinary Science.

In fact, I and the corn chandler, who was looking a bit fagged I thought, as if he had had a hard morning chandling the corn, were beginning to doze lightly when things suddenly brisked up, bringing Gussie into the picture for the first time.

'Today,' said the bearded bloke, 'we are all happy to welcome as the guest of the afternoon Mr Fitz-Wattle – '

At the beginning of the address, Gussie had subsided into a sort of daydream, with his mouth hanging open. About halfway through, faint signs of life had begun to show. And for the last few minutes he had been trying to cross one leg over the other and failing and having another shot and failing again. But only now did he exhibit any real animation. He sat up with a jerk.

'Fink-Nottle,' he said, opening his eyes.

'Fitz-Nottle.'

'Fink-Nottle.'

'I should say Fink-Nottle.'

'Of course you should, you silly ass,' said Gussie genially. 'All right, get on with it.'

And closing his eyes, he began trying to cross his legs again.

I could see that this little spot of friction had rattled the bearded bloke a bit. He stood for a moment fumbling at the fungus with a hesitating hand. But they make these headmasters of tough stuff. The weakness passed. He came back nicely and carried on.

'We are all happy, I say, to welcome as the guest of the afternoon

Mr Fink-Nottle, who has kindly consented to award the prizes. This task, as you know, is one that should have devolved upon that well-beloved and vigorous member of our board of governors, the Rev. William Plomer, and we are all, I am sure, very sorry that illness at the last moment should have prevented him from being here today. But, if I may borrow a familiar metaphor from the – if I may employ a homely metaphor familiar to you all – what we lose on the swings we gain on the roundabouts.'

He paused, and beamed rather freely, to show that this was comedy. I could have told the man it was no use. Not a ripple. The corn chandler leaned against me and muttered 'Whoddidesay?' but that was all.

It's always a nasty jar to wait for the laugh and find that the gag hasn't got across. The bearded bloke was visibly discomposed. At that, however, I think he would have got by, had he not, at this juncture, unfortunately stirred Gussie up again.

'In other words, though deprived of Mr Plomer, we have with us this afternoon Mr Fink-Nottle. I am sure that Mr Fink-Nottle's name is one that needs no introduction to you. It is, I venture to assert, a name that is familiar to us all.'

'Not to you,' said Gussie.

And the next moment I saw what Jeeves had meant when he had described him as laughing heartily. 'Heartily' was absolutely the *mot juste*. It sounded like a gas explosion.

'You didn't seem to know it so dashed well, what, what?' said Gussie. And, reminded apparently by the word 'what' of the word 'Wattle', he repeated the latter some sixteen times with a rising inflection.

'Wattle, Wattle, Wattle,' he concluded. 'Right-ho. Push on.'

But the bearded bloke had shot his bolt. He stood there, licked at last; and, watching him closely, I could see that he was now at the crossroads. I could spot what he was thinking as clearly as if he had confided it to my personal ear. He wanted to sit down and call it a day, I mean, but the thought that gave him pause was that, if he did, he must then either uncork Gussie or take the Fink-Nottle speech as read and get straight on to the actual prize giving.

It was a dashed tricky thing, of course, to have to decide on the spur of the moment. I was reading in the paper the other day about those birds who are trying to split the atom, the nub being that they haven't the foggiest as to what will happen if they do. It may be all right. On the other hand, it may not be all right. And pretty silly a chap would feel, no doubt, if, having split the atom, he suddenly found the house going up in smoke and himself torn limb from limb.

So with the bearded bloke. Whether he was abreast of the inside facts in Gussie's case, I don't know, but it was obvious to him by this time that he had run into something pretty hot. Trial gallops had shown that Gussie had his own way of doing things. Those interruptions had been enough to prove to the perspicacious that here, seated on the platform at the big binge of the season, was one who, if pushed forward to make a speech, might let himself go in a rather epoch-making manner.

On the other hand, chain him up and put a green-baize cloth over him, and where were you? The proceedings would be over about half an hour too soon.

It was, as I say, a difficult problem to have to solve, and, left to himself, I don't know what conclusion he would have come to. Personally, I think he would have played it safe. As it happened, however, the thing was taken out of his hands, for at this moment, Gussie, having stretched his arms and yawned a bit, switched on that pebble-beached smile again and tacked down to the edge of the platform.

'Speech,' he said affably.

He then stood with his thumbs in the armholes of his waistcoat, waiting for the applause to die down.

It was some time before this happened, for he had got a very fine hand indeed. I suppose it wasn't often that the boys of Market Snodsbury Grammar School came across a man public-spirited enough to call their headmaster a silly ass, and they showed their appreciation in no uncertain manner. Gussie may have been one over the eight, but as far as the majority of those present were concerned he was sitting on top of the world.

'Boys,' said Gussie, 'I mean ladies and gentlemen and boys, I do not detain you long, but I suppose on this occasion to feel compelled to say a few auspicious words. Ladies – and boys and gentlemen – we have all listened with interest to the remarks of our friend here who forgot to shave this morning – I don't know his name, but then he didn't know mine – Fitz-Wattle, I mean, absolutely absurd – which squares things up a bit – and we are all sorry that the Reverend What-ever-he-was-called should be dying of adenoids, but after all, here today, gone tomorrow, and all flesh is as grass, and what not, but that wasn't what I wanted to say. What I wanted to say was this – and I say it confidently – without fear of contradiction – I say, in short, I am happy to be here on this auspicious occasion and I take much pleasure in kindly awarding the prizes, consisting of the handsome books you see laid out on that table. As Shakespeare says, there are sermons in books, stones in the running brooks, or, rather, the other way about, and there you have it in a nutshell.'

It went well, and I wasn't surprised. I couldn't quite follow some of it, but anybody could see that it was real ripe stuff, and I was amazed that even the course of treatment he had been taking could have rendered so normally tongue-tied a dumb brick as Gussie capable of it.

It just shows, what any Member of Parliament will tell you, that if you want real oratory, the preliminary noggin is essential. Unless pie-eyed, you cannot hope to grip.

'Gentlemen,' said Gussie, 'I mean ladies and gentlemen and, of course, boys, what a beautiful world this is. A beautiful world, full of happiness on every side. Let me tell you a little story. Two Irishmen, Pat and Mike, were walking along Broadway, and one said to the other, "Begorrah, the race is not always to the swift," and the other replied, "Faith and begob, education is a drawing out, not a putting in."'

I must say it seemed to me the rottenest story I had ever heard, and I was surprised that Jeeves should have considered it worthwhile shoving into a speech. However, when I taxed him with this later, he said that Gussie had altered the plot a good deal, and I dare say that accounts for it.

At any rate, that was the *conte* as Gussie told it, and when I say that it got a very fair laugh, you will understand what a popular favourite he had become with the multitude. There might be a bearded bloke or so on the platform and a small section in the second row who were wishing the speaker would conclude his remarks and resume his seat, but the audience as a whole was for him solidly.

There was applause, and a voice cried: 'Hear, hear!'

'Yes,' said Gussie, 'it is a beautiful world. The sky is blue, the birds are singing, there is optimism everywhere. And why not, boys and ladies and gentlemen? I'm happy, you're happy, we're all happy, even the meanest Irishman that walks along Broadway. Though, as I say, there were two of them – Pat and Mike, one drawing out, the other putting in. I should like you boys, taking the time from me, to give three cheers for this beautiful world. All together now.'

Presently the dust settled down and the plaster stopped falling from the ceiling, and he went on.

'People who say it isn't a beautiful world don't know what they are talking about. Driving here in the car today to award the kind prizes, I was reluctantly compelled to tick off my host on this very point. Old Tom Travers. You will see him sitting there in the second row next to the large lady in beige.'

He pointed helpfully, and the hundred or so Market Snodsburyians who craned their necks in the direction indicated were able to observe Uncle Tom blushing prettily.

'I ticked him off properly, the poor fish. He expressed the opinion that the world was in a deplorable state. I said, "Don't talk rot, old Tom Travers." "I am not accustomed to talk rot," he said. "Then, for a beginner," I said, "you do it dashed well." And I think you will admit, boys and ladies and gentlemen, that that was telling him.'

The audience seemed to agree with him. The point went big. The voice that had said, 'Hear, hear' said 'Hear, hear' again, and my corn chandler hammered the floor vigorously with a large-size walking stick.

'Well, boys,' resumed Gussie, having shot his cuffs and smirked horribly, 'this is the end of the summer term, and many of you, no doubt, are leaving the school. And I don't blame you, because there's a frost in here you could cut with a knife. You are going out into the great world. Soon many of you will be walking along Broadway. And what I want to impress upon you is that, however much you may suffer from adenoids, you must all use every effort to prevent yourselves becoming pessimists and talking rot like old Tom Travers. There in the second row. The fellow with a face rather like a walnut.'

He paused to allow those wishing to do so to refresh themselves with another look at Uncle Tom, and I found myself musing in some little perplexity. Long association with the members of the Drones has put me pretty well in touch with the various ways in which an overdose of the blushful Hippocrene can take the individual, but I had never seen anyone react quite as Gussie was doing.

There was a snap about his work which I had never witnessed before, even in Barmy Fotheringay-Phipps on New Year's Eve.

Jeeves, when I discussed the matter with him later, said it was something to do with inhibitions, if I caught the word correctly, and the suppression of, I think he said, the ego. What he meant, I gathered, was that, owing to the fact that Gussie had just completed a five-year-stretch of blameless seclusion among the newts, all the goofiness which ought to have been spread out thin over those five years and had been bottled up during that period came to the surface on this occasion in a lump – or, if you prefer to put it that way, like a tidal wave.

There may be something in this. Jeeves generally knows.

Anyway, be that as it may, I was dashed glad I had had the shrewdness to keep out of that second row. It might be unworthy of the prestige of a Wooster to squash in among the proletariat in the standing-room-only section, but at least, I felt, I was out of the danger zone. So thoroughly had Gussie got it up his nose by now that it seemed to me that had he sighted me he might have become personal about even an old school friend.

'If there's one thing in the world I can't stand,' proceeded Gussie, 'it's a pessimist. Be optimists, boys. You all know the difference between an optimist and a pessimist. An optimist is a man who – well, take the case of two Irishmen walking along Broadway. One is an optimist and one is a pessimist, just as one's name is Pat and the other's Mike ... Why, hullo, Bertie; I didn't know you were here.'

Too late, I endeavoured to go to earth behind the chandler, only to discover that there was no chandler there. Some appointment, suddenly remembered – possibly a promise to his wife that he would be home to tea – had caused him to ooze away while my attention was elsewhere, leaving me right out in the open.

Between me and Gussie, who was now pointing in an offensive manner, there was nothing but a sea of interested faces looking up at me.

'Now, there,' boomed Gussie, continuing to point, 'is an instance of what I mean. Boys and ladies and gentlemen, take a good look at that object standing up there at the back – morning-coat, trousers as worn, quiet grey tie, and carnation in buttonhole – you can't miss him. Bertie Wooster, that is, and as foul a pessimist as ever bit a tiger. I tell you I despise that man. And why do I despise him? Because, boys and ladies and gentlemen, he is a pessimist. His attitude is defeatist. When I told him I was going to address you this afternoon, he tried to dissuade me. And do you know why he tried to dissuade me? Because he said my trousers would split up the back.'

The cheers that greeted this were the loudest yet. Anything about splitting trousers went straight to the simple hearts of the young scholars of Market Snodsbury Grammar School. Two in the row in front of me turned purple, and a small lad with freckles seated beside them asked me for my autograph.

'Let me tell you a story about Bertie Wooster.'

A Wooster can stand a good deal, but he cannot stand having his name bandied in a public place. Picking my feet up softly, I was in the very process of executing a quiet sneak for the door, when I perceived that the bearded bloke had at last decided to apply the closure.

Why he hadn't done so before is beyond me. Spellbound, I take it. And, of course, when a chap is going like a breeze with the public, as Gussie had been, it's not so dashed easy to chip in. However, the prospect of hearing another of Gussie's anecdotes seemed to have done the trick. Rising rather as I had risen from my bench at the beginning of that painful scene with Tuppy in the twilight, he made a leap for the table, snatched up a book and came bearing down on the speaker.

He touched Gussie on the arm, and Gussie, turning sharply and seeing a large bloke with a beard apparently about to bean him with a book, sprang back in an attitude of self-defence.

'Perhaps, as time is getting on, Mr Fink-Nottle, we had better – '

'Oh, ah,' said Gussie, getting the trend. He relaxed. 'The prizes, eh? Of course, yes. Right ho. Yes, might as well be shoving along with it. What's this one?'

'Spelling and dictation – P. K. Purvis,' announced the bearded bloke.

'Spelling and dictation – P. K. Purvis,' echoed Gussie, as if he were calling coals. 'Forward, P. K. Purvis.'

Now that the whistle had been blown on his speech, it seemed to me that there was no longer any need for the strategic retreat which I had been planning. I had no wish to tear myself away unless I had to. I mean, I had told Jeeves that this binge would be fraught with interest, and it was fraught with interest. There was a fascination about Gussie's methods which gripped and made one reluctant to pass the thing up provided personal innuendos were steered clear of. I decided, accordingly, to remain, and presently there was a musical squeaking and P. K. Purvis climbed the platform.

The spelling-and-dictation champ was about three foot six in his squeaking shoes, with a pink face and sandy hair. Gussie patted his hair. He seemed to have taken an immediate fancy to the lad.

'You P. K. Purvis?'

'Sir, yes, sir.'

'It's a beautiful world, P. K. Purvis.'

'Sir, yes, sir.'

'Ah, you've noticed it, have you? Good. You married, by any chance?'

'Sir, no, sir.'

'Get married, P. K. Purvis,' said Gussie earnestly. 'It's the only life . . . Well, here's your book. Looks rather bilge to me from a glance at the title page, but, such as it is, here you are.'

P. K. Purvis squeaked off amidst sporadic applause, but one could not fail to note that the sporadic was followed by a rather strained silence. It was evident that Gussie was striking something of a new note in Market Snodsbury scholastic circles. Looks were exchanged between parent and parent. The bearded bloke had the air of one who has drained the bitter cup. As for Aunt Dahlia, her demeanour now told only too clearly that her last doubts had been resolved and her verdict was in. I saw her whisper to the Bassett, who sat on her right, and the Bassett nodded sadly and looked like a fairy about to shed a tear and add another star to the Milky Way.

Gussie, after the departure of P. K. Purvis, had fallen into a sort of daydream and was standing with his mouth open and his hands in his pockets. Becoming abruptly aware that a fat kid in knickerbockers was at his elbow, he started violently.

'Hullo!' he said, visibly shaken. 'Who are you?'

'This,' said the bearded bloke, 'Is R. V. Smethurst.'

'What's he doing here?' asked Gussie suspiciously.

'You are presenting him with the drawing prize, Mr Fink-Nottle.'

This apparently struck Gussie as a reasonable explanation. His face cleared.

'That's right, too,' he said . . . 'Well, here it is, cocky. You off?' he said, as the kid prepared to withdraw.

'Sir, yes, sir.'

'Wait, R. V. Smethurst. Not so fast. Before you go, there is a question I wish to ask you.'

But the bearded bloke's aim now seemed to be to rush the ceremonies a bit. He hustled R. V. Smethurst off stage rather like a chucker-out in a pub regretfully ejecting an old and respected customer, and started paging G. G. Simmons. A moment later the latter was up and coming, and conceive my emotion when it was announced that the subject on which he had clicked was Scripture knowledge. One of us, I mean to say.

G. G. Simmons was an unpleasant, perky-looking stripling, mostly front teeth and spectacles, but I gave him a big hand. We Scripture-knowledge sharks stick together.

Gussie, I was sorry to see, didn't like him. There was in his manner, as he regarded G. G. Simmons, none of the chumminess which had marked it during his interview with P. K. Purvis or, in a somewhat lesser degree, with R. V. Smethurst. He was cold and distant.

'Well, G. G. Simmons.'

'Sir, yes, sir.'

'What do you mean – sir, yes, sir? Dashed silly thing to say. So you've won the Scripture-knowledge prize, have you?'

'Sir, yes, sir.'

'Yes,' said Gussie, 'you look just the sort of little tick who would. And yet,' he said, pausing and eyeing the child keenly, 'how are we to know that this has all been open and above board? Let me test you, G. G. Simmons. What was What's-His-Name – the chap who begat Thingummy? can you answer me that, Simmons?'

'Sir, no, sir.'

Gussie turned to the bearded bloke.

'Fishy,' he said. 'Very fishy. This boy appears to totally lacking in Scripture knowledge.'

The bearded bloke passed a hand across his forehead.

'I can assure you, Mr Fink-Nottle, that every care was taken to ensure a correct marking and that Simmons outdistanced his competitors by a wide margin.'

'Well, if you say so,' said Gussie doubtfully. 'All right, G. G. Simmons, take your prize.'

'Sir, thank you, sir.'

'But let me tell you that there's nothing to stick on side about in winning a prize for Scripture knowledge. Bertie Wooster – '

I don't know when I've had a nastier shock. I had been going on the assumption that, now that they had stopped him making his speech, Gussie's fangs had been drawn, as you might say. To duck my head down and resume my edging toward the door was with me the work of a moment.

'Bertie Wooster won the Scripture-knowledge prize at a kids' school we were at together, and you know what he's like. But, of course, Bertie frankly cheated. He succeeded in scrounging that Scripture-knowledge trophy over the heads of better men by means of some of the rawest and most brazen swindling methods ever witnessed even at a school where such things were common. If that man's pockets, as he entered the examination room, were not stuffed to bursting point with lists of the kings of Judah – '

I heard no more. A moment later I was out in God's air, fumbling with a fevered foot at the self-starter of the old car.

The engine raced. The clutch slid into position. I tooted and drove off.

My ganglions were still vibrating as I ran the car into the stables of Brinkley Court, and it was a much shaken Bertram who tottered up to his room to change into something loose. Having donned flannels, I lay down on the bed for a bit, and I suppose I must have dozed off, for the next thing I remember is finding Jeeves at my side.

I sat up. 'My tea, Jeeves?'

'No, sir. It is nearly dinnertime.'

The mists cleared away.

'I must have been asleep.'

'Yes, sir.'

'Nature taking its toll of the exhausted frame.'

'Yes, sir.'

'And enough to make it.'

'Yes, sir.'

'And now it's nearly dinnertime, you say? All right. I am in no mood for dinner, but I suppose you had better lay out the clothes.'

'It will not be necessary, sir. The company will not be dressing tonight. A cold collation has been set out in the dining-room.'

'Why's that?'

'It was Mrs Travers's wish that this should be done in order to minimize the work for the staff, who are attending a dance at Sir Percival Stretchley-Budd's residence tonight.'

'Of course, yes. I remember. My cousin Angela told me. Tonight's the night, what? You going, Jeeves?'

'No, sir. I am not very fond of this form of entertainment in the rural districts, sir.'

'I know what you mean. These country binges are all the same. A piano, one fiddle, and a floor like sandpaper. Is Anatole going? Angela hinted not.'

'Miss Angela was correct, sir. Monsieur Anatole is in bed.'

'Temperamental blighters, these Frenchmen.'

'Yes, sir.'

There was a pause.

'Well, Jeeves,' I said, 'it was certainly one of those afternoons, what?'

'Yes, sir.'

'I cannot recall one more packed with incident. And I left before the finish.'

'Yes, sir. I observed your departure.'

'You couldn't blame me for withdrawing.'

'No, sir. Mr Fink-Nottle had undoubtedly become embarrassingly personal.'

'Was there much more of it after I went?'

'No, sir. The proceedings terminated very shortly. Mr Fink-Nottle's remarks with reference to Master G. G. Simmons brought about an early closure.'

'But he had finished his remarks about G. G. Simmons.'

'Only temporarily, sir. He resumed them immediately after your departure. If you recollect, sir, he had already proclaimed himself suspicious of Master Simmons's bona fides, and he now proceeded to deliver a violent verbal attack upon the young gentleman, asserting that it was impossible for him to have won the Scripture-knowledge prize without systematic cheating on an impressive scale. He went so far as to suggest that Master Simmons was well known to the police.'

'Golly, Jeeves!'

'Yes, sir. The words did create a considerable sensation. The reaction of those present to this accusation I should describe as mixed. The young students appeared pleased and applauded vigorously, but Master Simmons's mother rose from her seat and addressed Mr Fink-Nottle in terms of strong protest.'

'Did Gussie seem taken aback? Did he recede from his position?'

'No, sir. He said that he could see it all now, and hinted at a guilty liaison between Master Simmons's mother and the headmaster, accusing the latter of having cooked the marks, as his expression was, in order to gain favour with the former.'

'You don't mean that?'

'Yes, sir.'

'Egad, Jeeves! And then – '

'They sang the national anthem, sir.'

'Surely not?'

'Yes, sir.'

'At a moment like that?'

'Yes, sir.'

'Well, you were there and you know, of course, but I should have thought the last thing Gussie and this woman would have done in the circs would have been to start singing duets.'

'You misunderstand me, sir. It was the entire company who sang. The headmaster turned to the organist and said something to him in a low tone. Upon which the latter began to play the national anthem, and the proceedings terminated.'

'I see. About time, too.'

'Yes, sir. Mrs Simmons's attitude had become unquestionably menacing.'

I pondered. What I had heard was, of course, of a nature to excite pity and terror, not to mention alarm and despondency, and it would be paltering with the truth to say that I was pleased about it. On the other hand, it was all over now, and it seemed to me that the thing to do was not to mourn over the past but to fix the mind on the bright future. I mean to say, Gussie might have lowered the existing Worcestershire record for goofiness and definitely forfeited all chance of becoming Market Snodsbury's favourite son, but you couldn't get away from the fact that he had proposed to Madeline Bassett, and you had to admit that she had accepted him.

I put this to Jeeves.

'A frightful exhibition,' I said, 'and one which will very possibly ring down history's pages. But we must not forget, Jeeves, that Gussie, though now doubtless looked upon in the neighbourhood as the world's worst freak, is all right otherwise.'

'No, sir.'

I did not quite get this.

'When you say "No, sir", do you mean "Yes, sir"?'

'No, sir. I mean "No, sir".'

'He is not all right otherwise?'

'No, sir.'

'But he's betrothed.'

'No longer, sir. Miss Bassett has severed the engagement.'

'You don't mean that?'

'Yes, sir.'

I wonder if you have noticed a rather peculiar thing about this chronicle. I allude to the fact that at one time or another practically everybody playing a part in it has had occasion to bury his or her face in his or her hands. I have participated in some pretty glutinous affairs in my time, but I think that never before or since have I been mixed up with such a solid body of brow clutchers.

Uncle Tom did it, if you remember. So did Gussie. So did Tuppy. So, probably, though I have no data, did Anatole, and I wouldn't put it past the Bassett. And Aunt Dahlia, I have no doubt, would have done it, too, but for the risk of disarranging the carefully fixed coiffure.

Well, what I am trying to say is that at this juncture I did it myself. Up went the hands and down went the head, and in another jiffy I was clutching as energetically as the best of them.

And it was while I was still massaging the coconut and wondering what the next move was that something barged up against the door like the delivery of a ton of coals.

'I think this may very possibly be Mr Fink-Nottle himself, sir,' said Jeeves.

His intuition, however, had led him astray. It was not Gussie but Tuppy. He came in and stood breathing asthmatically. It was plain that he was deeply stirred.

18

I eyed him narrowly. I didn't like his looks. Mark you, I don't say I ever had, much, because Nature, when planning this sterling fellow, shoved in a lot more lower jaw than was absolutely necessary and made the eyes a bit too keen and piercing for one who was neither an Empire builder nor a traffic policeman. But on the present occasion, in addition to offending the aesthetic sense, this Glossop seemed to me to be wearing a distinct air of menace, and I found myself wishing that Jeeves wasn't always so dashed tactful.

I mean, it's all very well to remove yourself like an eel sliding into mud when the employer has a visitor, but there are moments – and it looked to me as if this was going to be one of them – when the truer tact is to stick around and stand ready to lend a hand in the free-for-all.

For Jeeves was no longer with us. I hadn't seen him go, and I hadn't heard him go, but he had gone. As far as the eye could reach, one noted nobody but Tuppy. And in Tuppy's demeanour, as I say, there was a certain something that tended to disquiet. He looked to me very much like a man who had come to reopen that matter of my tickling Angela's ankles.

However, his opening remark told me that I had been alarming myself unduly. It was of a pacific nature, and came as a great relief.

'Bertie,' he said, 'I owe you an apology. I have come to make it.'

My relief on hearing these words, containing as they did no reference of any sort to tickled ankles, was, as I say, great. But I don't think it was any greater than my surprise. Months had passed since that painful episode at the Drones, and until now he hadn't given a sign of remorse and contrition. Indeed, word had reached me through private sources that he frequently told the story at dinners and other gatherings and, when doing so, laughed his silly head off.

I found it hard to understand, accordingly, what could have caused him to abase himself at this later date. Presumably he had been given the elbow by his better self, but why?

Still, there it was.

'My dear chap,' I said, gentlemanly to the gills, 'don't mention it.'

'What's the sense of saying, "Don't mention it"? I have mentioned it.'

'I mean, don't mention it any more. Don't give the matter another thought. We all of us forget ourselves sometimes and do things which, in our calmer moments, we regret. No doubt you were a bit tight at the time.'

'What the devil do you think you're talking about?'

I didn't like his tone. Brusque.

'Correct me if I am wrong,' I said, with a certain stiffness, 'but I assumed that you were apologizing for your foul conduct in looping back the last ring that night in the Drones, causing me to plunge into the swimming b. in the full soup and fish.'

'Ass! Not that, at all.'

'Then what?'

'This Bassett business.'

'What Bassett business?'

'Bertie,' said Tuppy, 'when you told me last night that you were in love with Madeline Bassett, I gave you the impression that I believed you, but I didn't. The thing seemed too incredible. However, since then I have made inquiries, and the facts appear to square with your statement. I have now come to apologize for doubting you.'

'Made inquiries?'

'I asked her if you had proposed to her, and she said, yes, you had.'

'Tuppy! You didn't?'

'I did.'

'Have you no delicacy, no proper feeling?'

'No.'

'Oh? Well, right ho, of course, but I think you ought to have.'

'Delicacy be dashed. I wanted to be certain that it was not you who stole Angela from me. I now know it wasn't.'

So long as he knew that, I didn't so much mind him having no delicacy.

'Ah,' I said. 'Well, that's fine. Hold that thought.'

'I have found out who it was.'

'What?'

He stood brooding for a moment. His eyes were smouldering with a dull fire. His jaw stuck out like the back of Jeeves's head.

'Bertie,' he said, 'do you remember what I swore I would do to the chap who stole Angela from me?'

'As nearly as I recall, you planned to pull him inside out – '

'– and make him swallow himself. Correct. The programme still holds good.'

'But, Tuppy, I keep assuring you, as a competent eyewitness, that nobody snitched Angela from you during that Cannes trip.'

'No. But they did after she got back.'

'What?'

'Don't keep saying, "What?" You heard.'

'But she hasn't seen anybody since she got back.'

'Oh, no? How about that newt bloke?'

'Gussie?'

'Precisely. The serpent Fink-Nottle.'

This seemed to me absolute gibbering.

'But Gussie loves the Bassett.'

'You can't all love this blighted Bassett. What astonishes me is that anyone can do it. He loves Angela, I tell you. And she loves him.'

'But Angela handed you your hat before Gussie ever got here.'

'No, she didn't. Couple of hours after.'

'He couldn't have fallen in love with her in a couple of hours.'

'Why not? I fell in love with her in a couple of minutes. I worshipped her immediately we met, the pop-eyed little excrescence.'

'But, dash it – '

'Don't argue, Bertie. The facts are all docketed. She loves this newt-nuzzling blister.'

'Quite absurd, laddie – quite absurd.'

'Oh?' He ground a heel into the carpet – a thing I've often read about, but had never seen done before. 'Then perhaps you will explain how it is that she happens to come to be engaged to him?'

You could have knocked me down with a f.

'Engaged to him?'

'She told me herself.'

'She was kidding you.'

'She was not kidding me. Shortly after the conclusion of this afternoon's binge at Market Snodsbury Grammar School he asked her to marry him, and she appears to have right-hoed without a murmur.'

'There must be some mistake.'

'There was. The snake Fink-Nottle made it, and by now I bet he realizes it. I've been chasing him since 5.30.'

'Chasing him?'

'All over the place. I want to pull his head off.'

'I see. Quite.'

'You haven't seen him, by any chance?'

'No.'

'Well, if you do, say goodbye to him quickly and put in your order for lilies . . . Oh, Jeeves.'

'Sir?'

I hadn't heard the door open, but the man was on the spot once more. My private belief, as I think I have mentioned before, is that Jeeves doesn't have to open doors. He's like one of those birds in India who bung their astral bodies about – the chaps, I mean, who having gone into thin air in Bombay, reassemble the parts and appear two minutes later in Calcutta. Only some such theory will account for the fact that he's not there one moment and is there the next. He just seems to float from Spot A to Spot B like some form of gas.

'Have you seen Mr Fink-Nottle, Jeeves?'

'No, sir.'

'I'm going to murder him.'

'Very good, sir.'

Tuppy withdrew, banging the door behind him, and I put Jeeves abreast.

'Jeeves,' I said, 'do you know what? Mr Fink-Nottle is engaged to my cousin Angela.'

'Indeed, sir?'

'Well, how about it? Do you grasp the psychology? Does it make sense? Only a few hours ago he was engaged to Miss Bassett.'

'Gentlemen who have been discarded by one young lady are often apt to attach themselves without delay to another, sir. It is what is known as a gesture.'

I began to grasp.

'I see what you mean. Defiant stuff.'

'Yes, sir.'

'A sort of "Oh, right ho, please yourself, but if you don't want me, there are plenty who do."'

'Precisely, sir. My cousin George – '

'Never mind about your cousin George, Jeeves.'

'Very good, sir.'

'Keep him for the long winter evenings, what?'

'Just as you wish, sir.'

'And, anyway, I bet your cousin George wasn't a shrinking, non-goose-boo-ing jellyfish like Gussie. That is what astounds me, Jeeves – that it should be Gussie who has been putting in all this heavy gesture-making stuff.'

'You must remember, sir, that Mr Fink-Nottle is in a somewhat inflamed cerebral condition.'

'That's true. A bit above par at the moment, as it were?'

'Exactly, sir.'

'Well, I'll tell you one thing – he'll be in a jolly sight more inflamed cerebral condition if Tuppy gets hold of him . . . What's the time?'

'Just on eight o'clock, sir.'

'Then Tuppy has been chasing him for two hours and a half. We must save the unfortunate blighter, Jeeves.'

'Yes, sir.'

'A human life is a human life, what?'

'Exceedingly true, sir.'

'The first thing, then, is to find him. After that we can discuss plans and schemes. Go forth, Jeeves, and scour the neighbourhood.'

'It will not be necessary, sir. If you will glance behind you, you will see Mr Fink-Nottle coming out from beneath your bed.'

And, by Jove, he was absolutely right.

There was Gussie, emerging as stated. He was covered with fluff and looked like a tortoise popping forth for a bit of a breather.

'Gussie!' I said.

'Jeeves,' said Gussie.

'Sir?' said Jeeves.

'Is that door locked, Jeeves?'

'No, sir, but I will attend to the matter immediately.'

Gussie sat down on the bed, and I thought for a moment that he was going to be in the mode by burying his face in his hands. However, he merely brushed a dead spider from his brow.

'Have you locked the door, Jeeves?'

'Yes, sir.'

'Because you can never tell that that ghastly Glossop may not take it into his head to come – '

The word 'back' froze on his lips. He hadn't got any further than a b-ish sound, when the handle of the door began to twist and rattle. He sprang from the bed, and for an instant stood looking exactly like a picture my Aunt Agatha has in her dining-room – *The Stag at Bay* – Landseer. Then he made a dive for the cupboard and was inside it before one really got on to it that he had started leaping. I have seen fellows late for the 9.15 move less nippily.

I shot a glance at Jeeves. He allowed his right eyebrow to flicker slightly, which is as near as he ever gets to a display of the emotions.

'Hullo?' I yipped.

'Let me in, blast you!' responded Tuppy's voice from without. 'Who locked this door?'

I consulted Jeeves once more in the language of the eyebrow. He raised one of his. I raised one of mine. He raised his other. I raised my other. Then we both raised both. Finally, there seeming no other policy to pursue, I flung wide the gates and Tuppy came shooting in.

'Now what?' I said, as nonchalantly as I could manage.

'Why was the door locked?' demanded Tuppy.

I was in pretty good eyebrow-raising form by now, so I gave him a touch of it.

'Is one to have no privacy, Glossop?' I said coldly. 'I instructed Jeeves to lock the door because I was about to disrobe.'

'A likely story!' said Tuppy, and I'm not sure he didn't add 'Forsooth!' 'You needn't try to make me believe that you're afraid people are going to run excursion trains to see you in your underwear. You locked that door because you've got the snake Fink-Nottle concealed in here. I suspected it the moment I'd left, and I decided to come back and investigate. I'm going to search this room from end to end. I believe he's in that cupboard . . . What's in this cupboard?'

'Just clothes,' I said, having another stab at the nonchalant, though extremely dubious as to whether it would come off. 'The usual wardrobe of the English gentleman paying a country-house visit.'

'You're lying!'

Well, I wouldn't have been if he had only waited a minute before speaking, because the words were hardly out of his mouth before Gussie was out of the cupboard. I have commented on the speed with which he had gone in. It was as nothing to the speed with which he emerged. There was a sort of whir and blur, and he was no longer with us.

I think Tuppy was surprised. In fact, I'm sure he was. Despite the confidence with which he had stated his view that the cupboard contained Fink-Nottles, it plainly disconcerted him to have the chap fizzing out at him like this. He gargled sharply, and jumped back about five feet. The next moment, however, he had recovered his poise and was galloping down the corridor in pursuit. It only needed Aunt Dahlia after them, shouting 'Yoicks!' or whatever is customary on these occasions, to complete the resemblance to a brisk run with the Quorn.

I sank into a handy chair. I am not a man whom it is easy to discourage, but it seemed to me that things had at last begun to get too complex for Bertram.

'Jeeves,' I said, 'all this is a bit thick.'

'Yes, sir.'

'The head rather swims.'

'Yes, sir.'

'I think you had better leave me, Jeeves. I shall need to devote the very closest thought to the situation which has arisen.'

'Very good, sir.'

The door closed. I lit a cigarette and began to ponder.

19

Most chaps in my position, I imagine, would have pondered all the rest of the evening without getting a bite, but we Woosters have an uncanny knack of going straight to the heart of things, and I don't suppose it was much more than ten minutes after I had started pondering before I saw what had to be done.

What was needed to straighten matters out, I perceived, was a heart-to-heart talk with Angela. She had caused all the trouble by her mutton-headed behaviour in saying 'Yes' instead of 'No' when Gussie, in the grip of mixed drinks and cerebral excitement, had suggested teaming up. She must obviously be properly ticked off and made to return him to store. A quarter of an hour later, I had tracked her down to the summerhouse in which she was taking a cooler and was seating myself by her side.

'Angela,' I said, and if my voice was stern, well, whose wouldn't have been, 'this is all perfect drivel.'

She seemed to come out of a reverie. She looked at me inquiringly.

'I'm sorry, Bertie, I didn't hear. What were you talking drivel about?'

'I was not talking drivel.'

'Oh, sorry, I thought you said you were.'

'Is it likely that I would come out here in order to talk drivel?'

'Very likely.'

I thought it best to haul off and approach the matter from another angle.

'I've just been seeing Tuppy.'

'Oh?'

'And Gussie Fink-Nottle.'

'Oh, yes?'

'It appears that you have gone and got engaged to the latter.'

'Quite right.'

'Well, that's what I meant when I said it was all perfect drivel. You can't possibly love a chap like Gussie.'

'Why not?'

'You simply can't.'

Well, I mean to say, of course she couldn't. Nobody could love a freak like Gussie except a similar freak like the Bassett. The shot wasn't on the board. A splendid chap, of course, in many ways – courteous, amiable, and just the fellow to tell you what to do till the doctor came, if you had a sick newt on your hands – but quite obviously not of Mendelssohn's March timber. I have no doubt that you could have flung bricks by the hour in England's most densely populated districts without endangering the safety of a single girl capable of becoming Mrs Augustus Fink-Nottle without an anaesthetic.

I put this to her, and she was forced to admit the justice of it.

'All right, then. Perhaps I don't.'

'Then what,' I said keenly, 'did you want to go and get engaged to him for, you unreasonable young fathead?'

'I thought it would be fun.'

'Fun!'

'And so it has been. I've had a lot of fun out of it. You should have seen Tuppy's face when I told him.'

A sudden bright light shone upon me.

'Ha! A gesture!'

'What?'

'You got engaged to Gussie just to score off Tuppy?'

'I did.'

'Well, then, that was what I was saying. It was a gesture.'

'Yes, I suppose you could call it that.'

'And I'll tell you something else I'll call it – viz. a dashed low trick. I'm surprised at you, young Angela.'

'I don't see why.'

I curled the lip about half an inch. 'Being a female, you wouldn't. You gentler sexes are like that. You pull off the rawest stuff without a pang. You pride yourselves on it. Look at Jael, the wife of Heber.'

'Where did you ever hear of Jael, the wife of Heber?'

'Possibly you are not aware that I once won a Scripture-knowledge prize at school?'

'Oh, yes. I remember Augustus mentioning it in his speech.'

'Quite,' I said, a little hurriedly. I had no wish to be reminded of Augustus's speech. 'Well, as I say, look at Jael, the wife of Heber. Dug spikes into the guest's coconut while he was asleep, and then went swanking about the place like a Girl Guide. No wonder they say, "Oh, woman, woman!"'

'Who?'

'The chaps who do. Coo, what a sex! But you aren't proposing to keep this up, of course?'

'Keep what up?'

'This rot of being engaged to Gussie.'

'I certainly am.'

'Just to make Tuppy look silly.'

'Do you think he looks silly?'

'I do.'

'So he ought to.'

I began to get the idea that I wasn't making real headway. I remember when I won that Scripture-knowledge prize, having to go into the facts about Balaam's ass. I can't quite recall what they were, but I still retain a sort of general impression of something digging its feet in and putting its ears back and refusing to co-operate; and it seemed to me that this was what Angela was doing now. She and Balaam's ass were, so to speak, sisters under the skin. There's a word beginning with r – 're' something – 'recal' something – No, it's gone. But what I am driving at is that this is what Angela was showing herself.

'Silly young geezer,' I said.

She pinkened.

'I'm not a silly young geezer.'

'You are a silly young geezer. And, what's more, you know it.'

'I don't know anything of the kind.'

'Here you are, wrecking Tuppy's life, wrecking Gussie's life, all for the sake of a cheap score.'

'Well, it's no business of yours.'

I sat on this promptly:

'No business of mine when I see two lives I used to go to school with wrecked? Ha! Besides, you know you're potty about Tuppy.'

'I'm not!'

'Is that so? If I had a quid for every time I've seen you gaze at him with the love-light in your eyes – '

She gazed at me, but without the love-light.

'Oh, for goodness' sake, go away and boil your head, Bertie!'

I drew myself up.

'That,' I replied, with dignity, 'is just what I am going to go away and boil. At least, I mean, I shall now leave you. I have said my say.'

'Good.'

'But permit me to add – '

'I won't.'

'Very good,' I said coldly. 'In that case, tinkerty tonk.'

And I meant it to sting.

'Moody' and 'discouraged' were about the two adjectives you would have selected to describe me as I left the summerhouse. It would be idle to deny that I had expected better results from this little chat.

I was surprised at Angela. Odd how you never realize that every girl is at heart a vicious specimen until something goes wrong with her love affair. This cousin and I had been meeting freely since the days when I wore sailor suits and she hadn't any front teeth, yet only now was I beginning to get onto her hidden depths. A simple, jolly, kindly young pimple she had always struck me as – the sort you could more or less rely on not to hurt a fly. But here she was now laughing heartlessly – at least, I seemed to remember hearing her laugh heartlessly – like something cold and callous out of a sophisticated talkie, and fairly spitting on her hands in her determination to bring Tuppy's grey hairs in sorrow to the grave.

I've said it before, and I'll say it again – girls are rummy. Old Pop Kipling never said a truer word than when he made that crack about the f. of the s. being more d. than the m.

It seemed to me in the circs that there was but one thing to do – that is head for the dining-room and take a slash at the cold collation of which Jeeves had spoken. I felt in urgent need of sustenance, for the recent interview had pulled me down a bit. There is no gainsaying the fact that this naked-emotion stuff reduces a chap's vitality and puts him in the vein for a good whack at the beef and ham.

To the dining-room, accordingly, I repaired, and had barely crossed the threshold when I perceived Aunt Dahlia at the sideboard, tucking into salmon mayonnaise.

The spectacle drew from me a quick 'Oh, ah,' for I was somewhat embarrassed. The last time this relative and I had enjoyed a *tête-à-tête*, it will be remembered, she had sketched out plans for drowning me in the kitchen-garden pond, and I was not quite sure what my present standing with her was.

I was relieved to find her in genial mood. Nothing could have exceeded the cordiality with which she waved her fork.

'Hallo, Bertie, you old ass,' was her very matey greeting. 'I thought I shouldn't find you far away from the food. Try some of this salmon. Excellent.'

'Anatole's?' I queried.

'No. He's still in bed. But the kitchen maid has struck an inspired streak. It suddenly seems to have come home to her that she isn't catering for a covey of buzzards in the Sahara Desert, and she has put out something quite fit for human consumption. There is good in the girl, after all, and I hope she enjoys herself at the dance.'

I ladled out a portion of salmon, and we fell into pleasant conversation, chatting of this servants' ball at the Stretchley-Budds and speculating idly, I recall, as to what Seppings, the butler, would look like doing the rumba.

It was not till I had cleaned up the first platter and was embarking on a second that the subject of Gussie came up. Considering what had passed at Market Snodsbury that afternoon, it was one which I had been expecting her to touch on earlier. When she did touch on it, I could see that she had not yet been informed of Angela's engagement.

'I say, Bertie,' she said, meditatively chewing fruit salad, 'this Spink-Bottle.'

'Nottle.'

'Bottle,' insisted the aunt firmly. 'After that exhibition of his this afternoon, Bottle, and nothing but Bottle, is how I shall always think of him. However, what I was going to say was that, if you see him, I wish you would tell him that he has made an old woman very, very happy. Except for the time when the curate tripped over a loose shoelace and fell down the pulpit steps, I don't think I have ever had a more wonderful moment than when good old Bottle suddenly started ticking Tom off from the platform. In fact, I thought his whole performance in the most perfect taste.'

I could not but demur.

'Those references to myself – '

'Those were what I liked next best. I thought they were fine. Is it true that you cheated when you won that Scripture-knowledge prize?'

'Certainly not. My victory was the outcome of the most strenuous and unremitting efforts.'

'And how about this pessimism we hear of? Are you a pessimist, Bertie?'

I could have told her that what was occurring in this house was rapidly making me one, but I said no, I wasn't.

'That's right. Never be a pessimist. Everything is for the best in this best of all possible worlds. It's a long lane that has no turning. It's always darkest before the dawn. Have patience and all will come right. The sun will shine, although the day's a grey one ... Try some of this salad.'

I followed her advice, but even as I plied the spoon my thoughts were elsewhere. I was perplexed. It may have been the fact that I had recently been hobnobbing with so many bowed-down hearts that made this cheeriness of hers seem so bizarre, but bizarre was certainly what I found it.

'I thought you might have been a trifle peeved,' I said.

'Peeved?'

'By Gussie's manoeuvres on the platform this afternoon. I confess that I had rather expected the tapping foot and the drawn brow.'

'Nonsense. What was there to be peeved about? I took the whole thing as a great compliment, proud to feel that any drink from my cellars could have produced such a majestic jag. It restores one's faith in post-war whisky. Besides, I couldn't be peeved at anything tonight. I am like a little child clapping its hands and dancing in the sunshine. For though it has been some time getting a move on, Bertie, the sun has at last broken through the clouds. Ring out those joy bells. Anatole has withdrawn his notice.'

'What? Oh, very hearty congratulations.'

'Thanks. Yes, I worked on him like a beaver after I got back this afternoon, and finally, vowing he would ne'er consent, he consented. He stays on, praises be, and the way I look at it now is that God's in His heaven and all's right with – '

She broke off. The door had opened, and we were plus a butler.

'Hullo, Seppings,' said Aunt Dahlia. 'I thought you had gone.'

'Not yet, madam.'

'Well, I hope you will all have a good time.'

'Thank you, madam.'

'Was there something you wanted to see me about?'

'Yes, madam. It is with reference to Monsieur Anatole. Is it by your wish, madam, that Mr Fink-Nottle is making faces at Monsieur Anatole through the skylight of his bedroom?'

20

There was one of those long silences. Pregnant, I believe, is what they're generally called. Aunt looked at butler. Butler looked at aunt. I looked at both of them. An eerie stillness seemed to envelop the room like a linseed poultice. I happened to be biting on a slice of apple in my fruit salad at the moment, and it sounded as if Carnera had jumped off the top of the Eiffel Tower on to a cucumber frame.

Aunt Dahlia steadied herself against the sideboard, and spoke in a low, husky voice:

'Faces?'

'Yes, madam.'

'Through the skylight?'

'Yes, madam.'

'You mean he's sitting on the roof?'

'Yes, madam. It has upset Monsieur Anatole very much.'

I suppose it was that word 'upset' that touched Aunt Dahlia off. Experience had taught her what happened when Anatole got upset. I had always known her as a woman who was quite active on her pins, but I had never suspected her of being capable of the magnificent burst of speed which she now showed. Pausing merely to get a rich hunting-field expletive off her chest, she was out of the room and making for the stairs before I could swallow a sliver of – I think – banana. And feeling, as I had felt when I got that telegram of hers about Angela and Tuppy, that my place was by her side, I put down my plate and hastened after her, Seppings following at a loping gallop.

I say that my place was by her side, but it was not so dashed easy to get there, for she was setting a cracking pace. At the top of the first flight she must have led by a matter of half a dozen lengths, and was still shaking off my challenge when she rounded into the second. At the next landing, however, the gruelling going appeared to tell on her, for she slackened off a trifle and showed symptoms of roaring, and by the time we were in the straight we were running practically neck and neck. Our entry into Anatole's room was as close a finish as you could have wished to see.

Result:
1. *Aunt Dahlia.*
2. *Bertram.*
3. *Seppings.*
Won by a short head. Half a staircase separated second and third.

The first thing that met the eye on entering was Anatole. This wizard of the cooking stove is a tubby little man with a moustache of the outsize or soup-strainer type, and you can generally take a line through it as to the state of his emotions. When all is well, it turns up at the ends like a sergeant-major's. When the soul is bruised, it droops.

It was drooping now, striking a sinister note. And if any shadow of doubt had remained as to how he was feeling, the way he was carrying on would have dispelled it. He was standing by the bed in pink pyjamas, waving his fists at the skylight. Through the glass, Gussie was staring down. His eyes were bulging and his mouth was open, giving him so striking a resemblance to some rare fish in an aquarium that one's primary impulse was to offer him an ant's egg.

Watching this fist-waving cook and this goggling guest, I must say that my sympathies were completely with the former. I considered him thoroughly justified in waving all the fists he wanted to.

Review the facts, I mean to say. There he had been, lying in bed, thinking idly of whatever French cooks do think about when in bed, and he had suddenly become aware of that frightful face at the window. A thing to jar the most phlegmatic. I know I should hate to be lying in bed and have Gussie popping up like that. A chap's bedroom – you can't get away from it – is his castle, and he has every right to look askance if gargoyles come glaring in at him.

While I stood musing thus, Aunt Dahlia, in her practical way, was coming straight to the point:

'What's all this?'

Anatole did a sort of Swedish exercise, starting at the base of the spine, carrying on through the shoulder blades and finishing up among the back hair.

Then he told her.

In the chats I have had with this wonder man, I have always found his English fluent, but a bit on the mixed side. If you remember, he was with Mrs Bingo Little for a time before coming to Brinkley, and no doubt he picked up a good deal from Bingo. Before that, he had been a couple of years with an American family at Nice and had studied under their chauffeur, one of the Maloneys of Brooklyn. So, what with Bingo and what with Maloney, he is, as I say, fluent but a bit mixed.

He spoke, in part, as follows:

'Hot dog! You ask me what is it? Listen. Make some attention a little. Me, I have hit the hay, but I do not sleep so good, and presently I wake and up I look, and there is one who makes faces against me through the dashed window. Is that a pretty affair? Is that convenient? If you think I like it, you jolly well mistake yourself. I am so mad as a wet hen. And why not? I am somebody, isn't it? This is a bedroom, what-what, not a house for some apes? Then for what do blighters sit on my window so cool as a few cucumbers, making some faces?'

'Quite,' I said. Dashed reasonable, was my verdict.

He threw another look up at Gussie, and did Exercise 2 – the one where you clutch the moustache, give it a tug and then start catching flies.

'Wait yet a little. I am not finish. I say I see this type on my window, making a few faces. But what then? Does he buzz off when I shout a cry, and leave me peaceable? Not on your life. He remain planted there, not giving any damns, and sit regarding me like a cat watching a duck. He make faces against me and again he make faces against me, and the more I command that he should get to hell out of here, the more he do not get to hell out of here. He cry something towards me, and I demand what is his desire, but he do not explain. Oh, no, that arrives never. He does but shrug his head. What damn silliness! Is this amusing for me? You think I like it? I am not content with such folly. I think the poor mutt's loony. *Je me fiche de ce type infect. C'est idiot de faire comme ça l'oiseau . . . Allez-vous-en, louffier . . .* Tell the boob to go away. He is mad as some March hatters.'

I must say I thought he was making out a jolly good case, and evidently Aunt Dahlia felt the same. She laid a quivering hand on his shoulder.

'I will, Monsieur Anatole, I will,' she said, and I couldn't have believed that robust voice capable of sinking to such an absolute coo. More like a turtle dove calling to its mate than anything else. 'It's quite all right.'

She had said the wrong thing. He did Exercise 3.

'All right? *Nom d'un nom d'un nom!* The hell you say it's all right!

Of what use to pull stuff like that? Wait one half-moment. Not yet quite so quick, my old sport. It is by no means all right. See yet again a little. It is some very different dishes of fish. I can take a few smooths with a rough, it is true, but I do not find it agreeable when one play larks against me on my windows. That cannot do. A nice thing, no. I am a serious man. I do not wish a few larks on my windows. I enjoy larks on my windows worse as any. It is very little all right. If such rannygazoo is to arrive, I do not remain any longer in this house no more. I buzz off and do not stay planted.'

Sinister words, I had to admit, and I was not surprised that Aunt Dahlia, hearing them, should have uttered a cry like the wail of a master of hounds seeing a fox shot. Anatole had begun to wave his fists again at Gussie, and she now joined him. Seppings, who was puffing respectfully in the background, didn't actually wave his fists, but he gave Gussie a pretty austere look. It was plain to the thoughtful observer that this Fink-Nottle, in getting on to that skylight, had done a mistaken thing. He couldn't have been more unpopular in the home of G. G. Simmons.

'Go away, you crazy loon!' cried Aunt Dahlia, in that ringing voice of hers which had once caused nervous members of the Quorn to lose stirrups and take tosses from the saddle.

Gussie's reply was to waggle his eyebrows. I could read the message he was trying to convey.

'I think he means,' I said – reasonable old Bertram, always trying to throw oil on the troubled w. – 'that if he does he will fall down the side of the house and break his neck.'

'Well, why not?' said Aunt Dahlia.

I could see her point, of course, but it seemed to me that there might be a nearer solution. This skylight happened to be the only window in the house which Uncle Tom had not festooned with his bally bars. I suppose he felt that if a burglar had the nerve to climb up as far as this, he deserved what was coming to him.

'If you opened the skylight, he could jump in.'

The idea got across.

'Seppings, how does this skylight open?'

'With a pole, madam.'

'Then get a pole. Get two poles. Ten.'

And presently Gussie was mixing with the company. Like one of those chaps you read about in the papers, the wretched man seemed deeply conscious of his position.

I must say Aunt Dahlia's bearing and demeanour did nothing to assist toward a restored composure. Of the amiability which she had exhibited when discussing this unhappy chump's activities with me over the fruit salad, no trace remained, and I was not surprised that speech more or less froze on the Fink-Nottle lips. It isn't often that Aunt Dahlia, normally as genial a bird as ever encouraged a gaggle of hounds to get their noses down to it, lets her angry passions rise, but when she does, strong men climb trees and pull them up after them.

'Well?' she said.

In answer to this, all that Gussie could produce was a sort of strangled hiccough.

'Well?'

Aunt Dahlia's face grew darker. Hunting, if indulged in regularly over a period of years, is a pastime that seldom fails to lend a fairly deepish tinge to the patient's complexion, and her best friends could not have denied that even at normal times the relative's map tended a little toward the crushed strawberry. But never had I seen it take on so pronounced a richness as now. She looked like a tomato struggling for self-expression.

'Well?'

Gussie tried hard. And for a moment it seemed as if something was going to come through. But in the end it turned out nothing more than a sort of death-rattle.

'Oh, take him away, Bertie, and put ice on his head,' said Aunt Dahlia, giving the thing up. And she turned to tackle what looked like the rather man's-size job of soothing Anatole, who was now carrying on a muttered conversation with himself in a rapid sort of way.

Seeming to feel that the situation was one to which he could not do justice in Bingo-cum-Maloney Anglo-American, he had fallen back on his native tongue. Words like '*marmiton de Domange*,' '*pignouf*,' '*hurluberlu*,' and '*roustisseur*' were fluttering from him like bats out of a barn. Lost on me, of course, because, though I sweated a bit at the Gallic language during that Cannes visit, I'm still more or less in the Esker-vous-avez stage. I regretted this, for they sounded good.

I assisted Gussie down the stairs. A cooler thinker than Aunt Dahlia, I had already guessed the hidden springs and motives which had led him to the roof. Where she had seen only a cockeyed reveller indulging himself in a drunken prank or whimsy, I had spotted the hunted fawn.

'Was Tuppy after you?' I asked sympathetically.

What I believe is called a *frisson* shook him.

'He nearly got me on the top landing. I shinned out through a passage window and scrambled along a sort of ledge.'

'That baffled him, what?'

'Yes. But then I found I had stuck. The roof sloped down in all directions. I couldn't go back. I had to go on, crawling along this ledge. And then I found myself looking down the skylight. Who was that chap?'

'That was Anatole, Aunt Dahlia's chef.'

'French?'

'To the core.'

'That explains why I couldn't make him understand. What asses these Frenchmen are. They don't seem able to grasp the simplest thing. You'd have thought if a chap saw a chap on a skylight, the chap would realize the chap wanted to be let in. But no, he just stood there.'

'Waving a few fists.'

'Yes. Silly idiot. Still, here I am.'

'Here you are, yes – for the moment.'

'Eh?'

'I was thinking that Tuppy is probably lurking somewhere.'

He leaped like a lamb in springtime.

'What shall I do?'

I considered this.

'Sneak back to your room and barricade the door. That is the manly policy.'

'Suppose that's where he's lurking?'

'In that case, move elsewhere.'

But on arrival at the room, it transpired that Tuppy, if anywhere, was infesting some other portion of the house. Gussie shot in, and I heard the key turn. And feeling that there was no more that I could do in that quarter, I returned to the dining-room for further fruit salad and a quiet think. And I had barely filled my plate when the door opened and Aunt Dahlia came in. She sank into a chair, looking a bit shopworn.

'Give me a drink, Bertie.'

'What sort?'

'Any sort, so long as it's strong.'

Approach Bertram Wooster along these lines, and you catch him at his best. St Bernard dogs doing the square thing by Alpine travellers could not have bustled about more assiduously. I filled the order, and for some moments nothing was to be heard but the sloshing sound of an aunt restoring her tissues.

'Shove it down, Aunt Dahlia,' I said sympathetically. 'These things take it out of one, don't they? You've had a toughish time, no doubt, soothing Anatole,' I proceeded, helping myself to anchovy paste on toast. 'Everything pretty smooth now, I trust?'

She gazed at me in a long, lingering sort of way, her brow wrinkled as if in thought.

'Attila,' she said at length. 'That's the name. Attila, the Hun.'

'Eh?'

'I was trying to think who you reminded me of. Somebody who went about strewing ruin and desolation and breaking up homes which, until he came along, had been happy and peaceful. Attila is the man. It's amazing,' she said, drinking me in once more. 'To look at you, one would think you were just an ordinary sort of amiable idiot – certifiable, perhaps, but quite harmless. Yet, in reality, you are a worse scourge than the Black Death. I tell you, Bertie, when I contemplate you I seem to come up against all the underlying sorrow and horror of life with such a thud that I feel as if I had walked into a lamp post.'

Pained and surprised, I would have spoken, but the stuff I had thought was anchovy paste had turned out to be something far more gooey and adhesive. It seemed to wrap itself round the tongue and impede utterance like a gag. And while I was still endeavouring to clear the vocal cords for action, she went on:

'Do you realize what you started when you sent that Spink-Bottle man down here? As regards his getting blotto and turning the prize-giving ceremonies at Market Snodsbury Grammar School into a sort of two-reel comic film, I will say nothing, for frankly I enjoyed it. But when he comes leering at Anatole through skylights, just after I had with infinite pains and tact induced him to withdraw his notice, and makes him so temperamental that he won't hear of staying on after tomorrow – '

The paste stuff gave way. I was able to speak:

'What?'

'Yes, Anatole goes tomorrow, and I suppose poor old Tom will have indigestion for the rest of his life. And that is not all. I have just seen Angela, and she tells me she is engaged to this Bottle.'

'Temporarily, yes,' I had to admit.

'Temporarily be blowed. She's definitely engaged to him and talks with a sort of hideous coolness of getting married in October. So there it is. If the prophet Job were to walk into the room at this moment, I could sit swapping hard-luck stories with him till bedtime. Not that Job was in my class.'

'He had boils.'

'Well, what are boils?'

'Dashed painful, I understand.'

'Nonsense. I'd take all the boils on the market in exchange for my troubles. Can't you realize the position? I've lost the best cook in England. My husband, poor soul, will probably die of dyspepsia. And my only daughter, for whom I had dreamed such a wonderful future, is engaged to be married to an inebriated newt fancier. And you talk about boils!'

I corrected her on a small point:

'I don't absolutely talk about boils. I merely mentioned that Job had them. Yes, I agree with you, Aunt Dahlia, that things are not looking too oojah-cum-spiff at the moment, but be of good cheer. A Wooster is seldom baffled for more than the nonce.'

'You rather expect to be coming along shortly with another of your schemes?'

'At any minute.'

She sighed resignedly.

'I thought as much. Well, it needed but this. I don't see how things could possibly be worse than they are, but no doubt you will succeed in making them so. Your genius and insight will find the way. Carry on, Bertie. Yes, carry on. I am past caring now. I shall even find a faint interest in seeing into what darker and profounder abysses of hell you can plunge this home. Go to it, lad . . . What's that stuff you're eating?'

'I find it a little difficult to classify. Some sort of paste on toast. Rather like glue flavoured with beef extract.'

'Gimme,' said Aunt Dahlia listlessly.

'Be careful how you chew,' I advised. 'It sticketh closer than a brother . . . Yes, Jeeves?'

The man had materialized on the carpet. Absolutely noiseless, as usual.

'A note for you, sir.'

'A note for me, Jeeves?'

'A note for you, sir.'

'From whom, Jeeves?'

'From Miss Bassett, sir.'

'From whom, Jeeves?'

'From Miss Bassett, sir.'

'From Miss Bassett, Jeeves?'

'From Miss Bassett, sir.'

At this point, Aunt Dahlia, who had taken one nibble at her whatever-it-was-on-toast and laid it down, begged us – a little fretfully, I thought – for heaven's sake to cut out the cross-talk vaudeville stuff, as she had enough to bear already without having to listen to us doing our imitation of the Two Macs. Always willing to oblige, I dismissed Jeeves with a nod, and he flickered for a moment and was gone. Many a spectre would have been less slippy.

'But what,' I mused, toying with the envelope, 'can this female be writing to me about?'

'Why not open the damn thing and see?'

'A very excellent idea,' I said, and did so.

'And if you are interested in my movements,' proceeded Aunt Dahlia, heading for the door, 'I propose to go to my room, do some Yogi deep breathing, and try to forget.'

'Quite,' I said absently, skimming p. 1. And then, as I turned over, a sharp howl broke from my lips, causing Aunt Dahlia to shy like a startled mustang.

'Don't do it!' she exclaimed, quivering in every limb.

'Yes, but dash it – '

'What a pest you are, you miserable object,' she sighed. 'I remember years ago, when you were in your cradle, being left alone with you one day and you nearly swallowed your rubber comforter and started turning purple. And I, ass that I was, took it out and saved your life. Let me tell you, young Bertie, it will go very hard with you if you ever swallow a rubber comforter again when only I am by to aid.'

'But, dash it!' I cried. 'Do you know what's happened? Madeline Bassett says she's going to marry me!'

'I hope it keeps fine for you,' said the relative, and passed from the room looking like something out of an Edgar Allan Poe story.

21

I don't suppose I was looking so dashed unlike something out of an Edgar Allan Poe story myself, for, as you can readily imagine, the news item which I have just recorded had got in amongst me properly. If the Bassett, in the belief that the Wooster heart had long been hers and was waiting ready to be scooped in on demand, had decided to take up her option, I should, as a man of honour and sensibility, have no choice but to come across and kick in. The matter was obviously not one that could be straightened out with a curt *nolle prosequi*. All the evidence, therefore, seemed to point to the fact that the doom had come upon me and, what was more, had come to stay.

And yet, though it would be idle to pretend that my grip on the situation was quite the grip I would have liked it to be, I did not despair of arriving at a solution. A lesser man, caught in this awful snare, would no doubt have thrown in the towel at once and ceased to struggle; but the whole point about the Woosters is that they are not lesser men.

By way of a start, I read the note again. Not that I had any hope that a second perusal would enable me to place a different construction on its contents, but it helped to fill in while the brain was limbering up. I then, to assist thought, had another go at the fruit salad, and in addition ate a slice of sponge cake. And it was as I passed on to the cheese that the machinery started working. I saw what had to be done.

To the question which had been exercising the mind – viz., can Bertram cope? – I was now able to reply with a confident 'Absolutely.'

The great wheeze on these occasions of dirty work at the cross-roads is not to lose your head but to keep cool and try to find the ringleaders. Once find the ringleaders, and you know where you are.

The ringleader here was plainly the Bassett. It was she who had started the whole imbroglio by chucking Gussie, and it was clear that before anything could be done to solve and clarify, she must be induced to revise her views and take him on again. This would put Angela back into circulation, and that would cause Tuppy to simmer down a bit, and then we could begin to get somewhere.

I decided that as soon as I had had another morsel of cheese I would seek this Bassett out and be pretty eloquent.

And at this moment in she came. I might have foreseen that she would be turning up shortly. I mean to say, hearts may ache, but if they know that there is a cold collation set out in the dining-room, they are pretty sure to come popping in sooner or later.

Her eyes, as she entered the room, were fixed on the salmon mayonnaise, and she would no doubt have made a bee-line for it and started getting hers, had I not, in the emotion of seeing her, dropped a glass of the best with which I was endeavouring to bring about a calmer frame of mind. The noise caused her to turn, and for an instant embarrassment supervened. A slight flush mantled the cheek, and the eyes popped a bit.

'Oh!' she said.

I have always found that there is nothing that helps to ease you over one of these awkward moments like a spot of stage business. Find something to do with your hands, and it's half the battle. I grabbed a plate and hastened forward.

'A touch of salmon?'

'Thank you.'

'With a suspicion of salad?'

'If you please.'

'And to drink? Name the poison.'

'I think I would like a little orange juice.'

She gave a gulp. Not at the orange juice, I don't mean, because she hadn't got it yet, but at all the tender associations those two words provoked. It was as if someone had mentioned spaghetti to the relict of an Italian organ-grinder. Her face flushed a deeper shade, she registered anguish, and I saw that it was no longer within the sphere of practical politics to try to confine the conversation to neutral topics like cold boiled salmon.

So did she, I imagine, for when I, as a preliminary to getting down to brass tacks, said 'Er,' she said 'Er,' too, simultaneously, the brace of 'Ers' clashing in mid-air.

'I'm sorry.'

'I beg your pardon.'

'You were saying – '

'You were saying – '

'No, please go on.'

'Oh, right ho.'

I straightened the tie, my habit when in this girl's society, and had at it:

'With reference to yours of even date – '

She flushed again, and took a rather strained forkful of salmon.

'You got my note?'

'Yes, I got your note.'

'I gave it to Jeeves to give it to you.'

'Yes, he gave it to me. That's how I got it.'

There was another silence. And as she was plainly shrinking from talking turkey, I was reluctantly compelled to do so. I mean, somebody had got to. Too dashed silly, a male and female in our position simply standing eating salmon and cheese at one another without a word.

'Yes, I got it all right.'

'I see. You got it.'

'Yes, I got it. I've just been reading it. And what I was rather wanting to ask you, if we happened to run into each other, was – well, what about it?'

'What about it?'

'That's what I say: What about it?'

'But it was quite clear.'

'Oh, quite. Perfectly clear. Very well expressed and all that. But – I mean – Well, I mean, deeply sensible of the honour, and so forth – but – Well, dash it!'

She had polished off her salmon, and now put the plate down.

'Fruit salad?'

'No thank you.'

'Spot of pie?'

'No, thanks.'

'One of those glue things on toast?'

'No, thank you.'

She took a cheese straw. I found a cold egg which I had overlooked. Then I said 'I mean to say' just as she said 'I think I know', and there was another collision.

'I beg your pardon.'

'I'm sorry.'

'Do go on.'

'No, you go on.'

I waved my cold egg courteously, to indicate that she had the floor, and she started again:

'I think I know what you are trying to say. You are surprised.'

'Yes.'

'You are thinking of – '

'Exactly.'

'– Mr Fink-Nottle.'

'The very man.'

'You find what I have done hard to understand.'

'Absolutely.'

'I don't wonder.'

'I do.'

'And yet it is quite simple.'

She took another cheese straw. She seemed to like cheese straws.

'Quite simple, really. I want to make you happy.'

'Dashed decent of you.'

'I am going to devote the rest of my life to making you happy.'

'A very matey scheme.'

'I can at least do that. But – may I be quite frank with you, Bertie?'

'Oh, rather.'

'Then I must tell you this. I am fond of you. I will marry you. I will do my best to make you a good wife. But my affection for you can never be the flamelike passion I felt for Augustus.'

'Just the very point I was working round to. There, as you say, is the snag. Why not chuck the whole idea of hitching up with me? Wash it out altogether. I mean, if you love old Gussie – '

'No longer.'

'Oh, come.'

'No. What happened this afternoon has killed my love. A smear of ugliness has been drawn across a thing of beauty, and I can never feel towards him as I did.'

I saw what she meant, of course. Gussie had bunged his heart at her feet; she had picked it up, and, almost immediately after doing so, had discovered that he had been stewed to the eyebrows all the tine. The shock must have been severe. No girl likes to feel that a chap has got to be thoroughly plastered before he can ask her to marry him. It wounds the pride.

Nevertheless, I persevered.

'But have you considered,' I said, 'that you may have got a wrong line on Gussie's performance this afternoon? Admitted that all the evidence points to a more sinister theory, what price him simply having got a touch of the sun? Chaps do get touches of the sun, you know, especially when the weather's hot.'

She looked at me, and I saw that she was putting in a bit of the old drenched-irises stuff.

'It was like you to say that, Bertie. I respect you for it.'

'Oh, no.'

'Yes. You have a splendid, chivalrous soul.'

'Not a bit.'

'Yes, you have. You remind me of Cyrano.'

'Who?'

'Cyrano de Bergerac.'

'The chap with the nose?'

'Yes.'

I can't say I was any too pleased. I felt the old beak furtively. It was a bit on the prominent side, perhaps, but, dash it, not in the Cyrano class. It began to look as if the next thing this girl would do would be to compare me to Schnozzle Durante.

'He loved, but pleaded another's cause.'

'Oh, I see what you mean now.'

'I like you for that, Bertie. It was fine of you – fine and big. But it is no use. There are things which kill love. I can never forget Augustus, but my love for him is dead. I will be your wife.'

Well, one has to be civil.

'Right ho,' I said. 'Thanks awfully.'

Then the dialogue sort of poofed out once more, and we stood eating cheese straws and cold eggs respectively in silence. There seemed to exist some little uncertainty as to what the next move was.

Fortunately, before embarrassment could do much more supervening, Angela came in, and this broke up the meeting. The Bassett announced our engagement, and Angela kissed her and said she hoped she would be very, very happy, and the Bassett kissed her and said she hoped she would be very, very happy with Gussie, and Angela said she was sure she would, because Augustus was such a dear, and the Bassett kissed her again, and Angela kissed her again, and, in a word, the whole thing got so bally feminine that I was glad to edge away.

I would have been glad to do so, of course, in any case, for if ever there was a moment when it was up to Bertram to think, and think hard, this moment was that moment.

It was, it seemed to me, the end. Not even on the occasion, some years earlier, when I had inadvertently become betrothed to Tuppy's frightful cousin Honoria, had I experienced a deeper sense of being waist high in the gumbo and about to sink without trace. I wandered out into the garden, smoking a tortured gasper, with the iron well embedded in the soul. And I had fallen into a sort of trance, trying to picture what it would be like having the Bassett on the premises for the rest of my life and at the same time, if you follow me, trying not to picture what it would be like, when I charged into something which might have been a tree, but was not – being, in point of fact, Jeeves.

'I beg your pardon, sir,' he said. 'I should have moved to one side.'

I did not reply. I stood looking at him in silence. For the sight of him had opened up a new line of thought.

This Jeeves, now, I reflected. I had formed the opinion that he had lost his grip and was no longer the force he had been, but was it not possible, I asked myself, that I might be mistaken? Start him off exploring avenues and might he not discover one through which I would be enabled to sneak off to safety, leaving no hard feelings behind? I found myself answering that it was quite on the cards that he might.

After all, his head still bulged out at the back as of old. One noted in the eyes the same intelligent glitter.

Mind you, after what had passed between us in the matter of that white mess jacket with the brass buttons, I was not prepared absolutely to hand over to the man. I would, of course, merely take him into consultation. But, recalling some of his earlier triumphs – the Sipperley Case, the Episode of My Aunt Agatha and the Dog McIntosh, and the smoothly handled Affair of Uncle George and the Barmaid's Niece were a few that sprang to my mind – I felt justified at least in offering him the opportunity of coming to the aid of the young master in his hour of peril.

But before proceeding further there was one thing that had got to be understood between us, and understood clearly.

'Jeeves,' I said, 'a word with you.'

'Sir?'

'I am up against it a bit, Jeeves.'

'I am sorry to hear that, sir. Can I be of any assistance?'

'Quite possibly you can, if you have not lost your grip. Tell me frankly, Jeeves, are you in pretty good shape mentally?'

'Yes, sir.'

'Still eating plenty of fish?'

'Yes, sir.'

'Then it may be all right. But there is just one point before I begin. In the past, when you have contrived to extricate self or some pal from some little difficulty, you have frequently shown a disposition to take advantage of my gratitude to gain some private end. Those purple socks, for instance. Also the plus fours and the Old Etonian spats. Choosing your moment with subtle cunning, you came to me when I was weakened by relief and got me to get rid of them. And what I am saying now is that if you are successful on the present occasion there must be no rot of that description about that mess jacket of mine.'

'Very good, sir.'

'You will not come to me when all is over and ask me to jettison the jacket?'

'Certainly not, sir.'

'On that understanding then, I will carry on. Jeeves, I'm engaged.'

'I hope you will be very happy, sir.'

'Don't be an ass. I'm engaged to Miss Bassett.'

'Indeed, sir? I was not aware – '

'Nor was I. It came as a complete surprise. However, there it is. The official intimation was in that note you brought me.'

'Odd, sir.'

'What is?'

'Odd, sir, that the contents of that note should have been as you describe. It seemed to me that Miss Bassett, when she handed me the communication, was far from being in a happy frame of mind.'

'She is far from being in a happy frame of mind. You don't suppose she really wants to marry me, do you? Pshaw, Jeeves! Can't you see that this is simply another of those bally gestures which are rapidly rendering Brinkley Court a hell for man and beast? Dash all gestures, is my view.'

'Yes, sir.'

'Well, what's to be done?'

'You feel that Miss Bassett, despite what has occurred, still retains a fondness for Mr Fink-Nottle, sir?'

'She's pining for him.'

'In that case, sir, surely the best plan would be to bring about a reconciliation between them.'

'How? You see. You stand silent and twiddle the fingers. You are stumped.'

'No, sir. If I twiddled my fingers, it was merely to assist thought.'

'Then continue twiddling.'

'It will not be necessary, sir.'

'You don't mean you've got a bite already?'

'Yes, sir.'

'You astound me, Jeeves. Let's have it.'

'The device which I have in mind is one that I have already mentioned to you, sir.'

'When did you ever mention any device to me?'

'If you will throw your mind back to the evening of our arrival, sir. You were good enough to inquire of me if I had any plan to put forward with a view to bringing Miss Angela and Mr Glossop together, and I ventured to suggest – '

'Good Lord! Not the old fire-alarm thing?'

'Precisely, sir.'

'You're still sticking to that?'

'Yes, sir.'

It shows how much the ghastly blow I had received had shaken me when I say that, instead of dismissing the proposal with a curt 'Tchah!' or anything like that, I found myself speculating as to whether there might not be something in it, after all.

When he had first mooted this fire-alarm scheme of his, I had sat upon it, if you remember, with the maximum of promptitude and vigour. 'Rotten' was the adjective I had employed to describe it, and you may recall that I mused a bit sadly, considering the idea conclusive proof of the general breakdown of a once fine mind. But now it somehow began to look as if it might have possibilities. The fact of the matter was that I had about reached the stage where I was prepared to try anything once, however goofy.

'Just run through that wheeze again, Jeeves,' I said thoughtfully. 'I remember thinking it cuckoo, but it may be that I missed some of the finer shades.'

'Your criticism of it at the time, sir, was that it was too elaborate, but I do not think it is so in reality. As I see it, sir, the occupants of the house, hearing the fire bell ring, will suppose that a conflagration has broken out.'

I nodded. One could follow the train of thought.

'Yes, that seems reasonable.'

'Whereupon Mr Glossop will hasten to save Miss Angela, while Mr Fink-Nottle performs the same office for Miss Bassett.'

'Is that based on psychology?'

'Yes, sir. Possibly you may recollect that it was an axiom of the late Sir Arthur Conan Doyle's fictional detective, Sherlock Holmes, that the instinct of everyone, upon an alarm of fire, is to save the object dearest to them.'

'It seems to me that there is a grave danger of seeing Tuppy come out carrying a steak-and-kidney pie, but resume, Jeeves, resume. You think that this would clean everything up?'

'The relations of the two young couples could scarcely continue distant after such an occurrence, sir.'

'Perhaps you're right. But, dash it, if we go ringing fire bells in the night watches, shan't we scare half the domestic staff into fits? There is one of the housemaids – Jane, I believe – who already skips like the high hills if I so much as come on her unexpectedly round a corner.'

'A neurotic girl, sir, I agree. I have noticed her. But by acting promptly we should avoid such a contingency. The entire staff, with the exception of Monsieur Anatole, will be at the ball at Kingham Manor tonight.'

'Of course. That just shows the condition this thing has reduced me to. Forget my own name next. Well, then, let's just try to envisage. Bong goes the bell. Gussie rushes and grabs the Bassett . . . Wait. Why shouldn't she simply walk downstairs?'

'You are overlooking the effect of sudden alarm on the feminine temperament, sir.'

'That's true.'

'Miss Bassett's impulse, I would imagine, sir, would be to leap from her window.'

'Well, that's worse. We don't want her spread out in a sort of *purée* on the lawn. It seems to me that the flaw in this scheme of yours, Jeeves, is that it's going to litter the garden with mangled corpses.'

'No, sir. You will recall that Mr Travers's fear of burglars has caused him to have stout bars fixed to all the windows.'

'Of course, yes. Well, it sounds all right,' I said, though still a bit doubtfully. 'Quite possibly it may come off. But I have a feeling that it will slip up somewhere. However, I am in no position to cavil at even a 100 to 1 shot. I will adopt this policy of yours, Jeeves, though, as I say, with misgivings. At what hour would you suggest bonging the bell?'

'Not before midnight, sir.'

'That is to say, some time after midnight.'

'Yes, sir.'

'Right ho, then. At 12.30 on the dot, I will bong.'

'Very good, sir.'

22

I don't know why it is, but there's something about the rural districts after dark that always has a rummy effect on me. In London I can stay out till all hours and come home with the milk without a tremor, but put me in the garden of a country house after the strength of the company has gone to roost and the place is shut up, and a sort of goose-fleshy feeling steals over me. The night wind stirs the tree tops, twigs crack, bushes rustle, and before I know where I am, the morale has gone phut and I'm expecting the family ghost to come sneaking up behind me, making groaning noises.

Dashed unpleasant, the whole thing, and if you think it improves matters to know that you are shortly about to ring the loudest fire bell in England and start an all-hands-to-the-pumps panic in that quiet, darkened house, you err.

I knew all about the Brinkley Court fire bell. The dickens of a row it makes. Uncle Tom, in addition to not liking burglars, is a bloke who has always objected to the idea of being cooked in his sleep, so when he bought the place he saw to it that the fire bell should be something that might give you heart failure, but which you couldn't possibly mistake for the drowsy chirping of a sparrow in the ivy.

When I was a kid and spent my holidays at Brinkley, we used to have fire drills after closing time, and many is the night I've had it jerk me out of the dreamless like the Last Trump.

I confess that the recollection of what this bell could do when it buckled down to it gave me pause as I stood that night at 12.30 p.m. prompt beside the outhouse where it was located. The sight of the rope against the whitewashed wall and the thought of the bloodsome uproar which was about to smash the peace of the night into hash served to deepen that rummy feeling to which I have alluded.

Moreover, now that I had had time to meditate upon it, I was more than ever defeatist about this scheme of Jeeves's.

Jeeves seemed to take it for granted that Gussie and Tuppy, faced with a hideous fate, would have no thought beyond saving the Bassett and Angela.

I could not bring myself to share his sunny confidence.

I mean to say, I know how moments when they're faced with a hideous fate affect chaps. I remember Freddie Widgeon, one of the most chivalrous birds in the Drones, telling me how there was an alarm of fire once at a seaside hotel where he was staying and, so far from rushing about saving women, he was down the escape within ten seconds of the kick-off, his mind concerned with but one thing – viz., the personal well-being of F. Widgeon.

As far as any idea of doing the delicately nurtured a bit of good went, he tells me, he was prepared to stand underneath and catch them in blankets, but no more.

Why, then, should this not be so with Augustus Fink-Nottle and Hildebrand Glossop?

Such were my thoughts as I stood toying with the rope, and I believe I should have turned the whole thing up, had it not been that at this juncture there floated into my mind a picture of the Bassett hearing that bell for the first time. Coming as a wholly new experience, it would probably startle her into a decline.

And so agreeable was this reflection that I waited no longer, but seized the rope, braced the feet and snapped into it.

Well, as I say, I hadn't been expecting that bell to hush things up to any great extent. Nor did it. The last time I had heard it, I had been in my room on the other side of the house, and even so it had hoiked me out of bed as if something had exploded under me. Standing close to it like this, I got the full force and meaning of the thing, and I've never heard anything like it in my puff.

I rather enjoy a bit of noise, as a general rule. I remember Catsmeat Potter-Pirbright bringing a police rattle into the Drones one night and loosing it off behind my chair, and I just lay back and closed my eyes with a pleasant smile, like someone in a box at the opera. And the same applies to the time when my Aunt Agatha's son, young Thos., put a match to the parcel of Guy Fawkes' Day fireworks to see what would happen.

But the Brinkley Court fire bell was too much for me. I gave about half a dozen tugs, and then, feeling that enough was enough, sauntered round to the front lawn to ascertain what solid results had been achieved.

Brinkley Court had given of its best. A glance told me that we were playing to capacity. The eye, roving to and fro, noted here Uncle Tom in a purple dressing gown, there Aunt Dahlia in the old blue and yellow. It also fell upon Anatole, Tuppy, Gussie, Angela, the Bassett and Jeeves, in the order named. There they all were, present and correct.

But – and this was what caused me immediate concern – I could detect no sign whatever that there had been any rescue work going on.

What I had been hoping, of course, was to see Tuppy bending solicitously over Angela in one corner, while Gussie fanned the Bassett with a towel in the other. Instead of which, the Bassett was one of the group which included Aunt Dahlia and Uncle Tom and seemed to be busy trying to make Anatole see the bright side, while Angela and Gussie were, respectively, leaning against the sundial with a peeved look and sitting on the grass rubbing a barked shin. Tuppy was walking up and down the path, all by himself.

A disturbing picture, you will admit. It was with a rather imperious gesture that I summoned Jeeves to my side.

'Well, Jeeves?'

'Sir?'

I eyed him sternly. 'Sir?' forsooth!

'It's no good saying "Sir?" Jeeves. Look round you. See for yourself. Your scheme has proved a bust.'

'Certainly it would appear that matters have not arranged themselves quite as we anticipated, sir.'

'We?'

'As I had anticipated, sir.'

'That's more like it. Didn't I tell you it would be a flop?'

'I remember that you did seem dubious, sir.'

'Dubious is no word for it, Jeeves. I hadn't a scrap of faith in the idea from the start. When you first mooted it, I said it was rotten, and I was right. I'm not blaming you, Jeeves. It is not your fault that you have sprained your brain. But after this – forgive me if I hurt your feelings, Jeeves – I shall know better than to allow you to handle any but the simplest and most elementary problems. It is best to be candid about this, don't you think? Kindest to be frank and straightforward?'

'Certainly, sir.'

'I mean, the surgeon's knife, what?'

'Precisely, sir.'

'I consider – '

'If you will pardon me for interrupting you, sir, I fancy Mrs Travers is endeavouring to attract your attention.'

And at this moment a ringing 'Hoy!' which could have proceeded only from the relative in question, assured me that his view was correct.

'Just step this way a moment, Attila, if you don't mind,' boomed that well-known – and under certain conditions, well-loved – voice, and I moved over.

I was not feeling unmixedly at my ease. For the first time it was beginning to steal upon me that I had not prepared a really good story in support of my questionable behaviour in ringing fire bells at such an hour, and I have known Aunt Dahlia to express herself with a hearty freedom upon far smaller provocation.

She exhibited, however, no signs of violence. More a sort of frozen calm, if you know what I mean. You could see that she was a woman who had suffered.

'Well, Bertie, dear,' she said, 'here we all are.'

'Quite,' I replied guardedly.

'Nobody missing, is there?'

'I don't think so.'

'Splendid. So much healthier for us out in the open like this than frowsting in bed. I had just dropped off when you did your bell-ringing act. For it was you, my sweet child, who rang that bell, was it not?'

'I did ring the bell, yes.'

'Any particular reason, or just a whim?'

'I thought there was a fire.'

'What gave you that impression, dear?'

'I thought I saw flames.'

'Where, darling? Tell Aunt Dahlia.'

'In one of the windows.'

'I see. So we have all been dragged out of bed and scared rigid because you have been seeing things.'

Here Uncle Tom made a noise like a cork coming out of a bottle, and Anatole, whose moustache had hit a new low, said something about 'some apes' and, if I am not mistaken, a '*rogommier*' – whatever that is.

'I admit I was mistaken. I am sorry.'

'Don't apologize, ducky. Can't you see how pleased we all are? What were you doing out here, anyway?'

'Just taking a stroll.'

'I see. And are you proposing to continue your stroll?'

'No, I think I'll go in now.'

'That's fine. Because I was thinking of going in, too, and I don't believe I could sleep knowing you were out here giving rein to that powerful imagination of yours. The next thing that would happen would be that you would think you saw a pink elephant sitting on the drawing-room windowsill and start throwing bricks at it . . . Well, come on, Tom, the entertainment seems to be over . . . But wait. The newt king wishes a word with us . . . Yes, Mr Fink-Nottle?'

Gussie, as he joined our little group, seemed upset about something.

'I say!'

'Say on, Augustus.'

'I say, what are we going to do?'

'Speaking for myself, I intend to return to bed.'

'But the door's shut.'

'What door?'

'The front door. Somebody must have shut it.'

'Then I shall open it.'

'But it won't open.'

'Then I shall try another door.'

'But all the other doors are shut.'

'What? Who shut them?'

'I don't know.'

I advanced a theory:

'The wind?'

Aunt Dahlia's eyes met mine.

'Don't try me too high,' she begged. 'Not now, precious.' And, indeed, even as I spoke, it did strike me that the night was pretty still.

Uncle Tom said we must get in through a window. Aunt Dahlia sighed a bit.

'How? Could Lloyd George do it, could Winston do it, could Baldwin do it? No. Not since you had those bars of yours put on.'

'Well, well, well. God bless my soul, ring the bell, then.'

'The fire bell?'

'The door bell.'

'To what end, Thomas? There's nobody in the house. The servants are all at Kingham.'

'But, confound it all, we can't stop out here all night.'

'Can't we? You just watch us. There is nothing – literally nothing – which a country house party can't do with Attila here operating on the premises. Seppings presumably took the back-door key with him. We must just amuse ourselves till he comes back.'

Tuppy made a suggestion:

'Why not take out one of the cars and drive over to Kingham and get the key from Seppings?'

It went well. No question about that. For the first time, a smile lit up Aunt Dahlia's drawn face. Uncle Tom grunted approvingly.

Anatole said something in Provençal that sounded complimentary. And I thought I detected even on Angela's map a slight softening.

'A very excellent idea,' said Aunt Dahlia. 'One of the best. Nip round to the garage at once.'

After Tuppy had gone, some extremely flattering things were said about his intelligence and resource, and there was a disposition to draw rather invidious comparisons between him and Bertram. Painful for me, of course, but the ordeal didn't last long, for it couldn't have been more than five minutes before he was with us again.

Tuppy seemed perturbed.

'I say, it's all off.'

'Why?'

'The garage is locked.'

'Unlock it.'

'I haven't the key.'

'Shout, then, and wake Waterbury.'

'Who's Waterbury?'

'The chauffeur, ass. He sleeps over the garage.'

'But he's gone to the dance at Kingham.'

It was the final wallop. Until this moment, Aunt Dahlia had been able to preserve her frozen calm. The dam now burst. The years rolled away from her, and she was once more the Dahlia Wooster of the old yoicks-and-tantivy days – the emotional, free-speaking girl who had so often risen in her stirrups to yell derogatory personalities at people who were heading hounds.

'Curse all dancing chauffeurs! What on earth does a chauffeur want to dance for? I mistrusted that man from the start. Something told me he was a dancer. Well, this finishes it. We're out here till breakfast-time. If those blasted servants come back before eight o'clock, I shall be vastly surprised. You won't get Seppings away from a dance till you throw him out. I know him. The jazz'll go to his head, and he'll stand clapping and demanding encores till his hands blister. Damn all dancing butlers! What is Brinkley Court? A respectable English country house or a crimson dancing school? One might as well be living in the middle of the Russian Ballet. Well, all right. If we must stay out here, we must. We shall all be frozen stiff, except' – here she directed at me not one of her friendliest glances – 'Except dear old Attila, who is, I observe, well and warmly clad. We will resign ourselves to the prospect of freezing to death like the Babes in the Wood, merely expressing a dying wish that our old pal Attila will see that we are covered with leaves. No doubt he will also toll that fire bell of his as a mark of respect – And what might you want, my good man?'

She broke off, and stood glaring at Jeeves. During the latter portion of her address, he had been standing by in a respectful manner, endeavouring to catch the speaker's eye.

'If I might make a suggestion, madam.'

I am not saying that in the course of our long association I have always found myself able to view Jeeves with approval. There are aspects of his character which have frequently caused coldnesses to arise between us. He is one of those fellows who, if you give them a thingummy, take a what-d'you-call-it. His work is often raw, and he has been known to allude to me as 'mentally negligible'. More than once, as I have shown, it has been my painful task to squelch in him a tendency to get uppish and treat the young master as a serf or peon.

These are grave defects.

But one thing I have never failed to hand the man. He is magnetic. There is about him something that seems to soothe and hypnotize. To the best of my knowledge, he has never encountered a charging rhinoceros, but should this contingency occur, I have no doubt that the animal, meeting his eye, would check itself in midstride, roll over and lie purring with its legs in the air.

At any rate he calmed down Aunt Dahlia, the nearest thing to a charging rhinoceros, in under five seconds. He just stood there looking respectful, and though I didn't time the thing – not having a stopwatch on me – I should say it wasn't more than three seconds and a quarter before her whole manner underwent an astounding change for the better. She melted before one's eyes.

'Jeeves! You haven't got an idea?'

'Yes, madam.'

'That great brain of yours has really clicked as ever in the hour of need?'

'Yes, madam.'

'Jeeves,' said Aunt Dahlia in a shaking voice, 'I am sorry I spoke so abruptly. I was not myself. I might have known that you would not come simply trying to make conversation. Tell us this idea of yours, Jeeves. Join our little group of thinkers and let us hear what you have to say. Make yourself at home, Jeeves, and give us the good word. Can you really get us out of this mess?'

'Yes, madam, if one of the gentlemen would be willing to ride a bicycle.'

'A bicycle?'

'There is a bicycle in the gardener's shed in the kitchen garden, madam. Possibly one of the gentlemen might feel disposed to ride over to Kingham Manor and procure the back-door key from Mr Seppings.'

'Splendid, Jeeves!'

'Thank you, madam.'

'Wonderful!'

'Thank you, madam.'

'Attila!' said Aunt Dahlia, turning and speaking in a quiet, authoritative manner.

I had been expecting it. From the very moment those ill-judged words had passed the fellow's lips, I had had a presentiment that a determined effort would be made to elect me as the goat, and I braced myself to resist and obstruct.

And as I was about to do so, while I was in the very act of summoning up all my eloquence to protest that I didn't know how to ride a bike and couldn't possibly learn in the brief time at my disposal, I'm dashed if the man didn't go and nip me in the bud.

'Yes, madam, Mr Wooster would perform the task admirably. He is an expert cyclist. He has often boasted to me of his triumphs on the wheel.'

I hadn't. I hadn't done anything of the sort. It's simply monstrous how one's words get twisted. All I had ever done was to mention to him – casually, just as an interesting item of information, one day in New York when we were watching the six-day bicycle race – that at the age of fourteen, while spending my holidays with a vicar of sorts who had been told off to teach me Latin, I had won the Choir Boys' Handicap at the local school treat.

A different thing from boasting of one's triumphs on the wheel.

I mean, he was a man of the world and must have known that the form of school treats is never of the hottest. And, if I'm not mistaken, I had specifically told him that on the occasion referred to I had received half a lap start and that Willie Punting, the odds-on favourite to whom the race was expected to be a gift, had been forced to retire, owing to having pinched his elder brother's machine without asking the elder brother, and the elder brother coming along just as the pistol went and giving him one on the side of the head and taking it away from him, thus rendering him a scratched-at-the-post non-starter. Yet, from the way he talked, you would have thought I was one of those chaps in sweaters with medals all over them, whose photographs bob up from time to time in the illustrated press on the occasion of their having ridden from Hyde Park Corner to Glasgow in three seconds under the hour, or whatever it is.

And as if this were not bad enough, Tuppy had to shove his oar in.

'That's right,' said Tuppy. 'Bertie has always been a great cyclist. I remember at Oxford he used to take all his clothes off on bump-supper nights and ride around the quad, singing comic songs. Jolly fast he used to go too.'

'Then he can go jolly fast now,' said Aunt Dahlia with animation. 'He can't go too fast for me. He may also sing comic songs, if he likes . . . And if you wish to take your clothes off, Bertie, my lamb, by all means do so. But whether clothed or in the nude, whether singing comic songs or not singing comic songs, get a move on.'

I found speech:

'But I haven't ridden for years.'

'Then it's high time you began again.'

'I've probably forgotten how to ride.'

'You'll soon get the knack after you've taken a toss or two. Trial and error. The only way.'

'But it's miles to Kingham.'

'So the sooner you're off, the better.'

'But – '

'Bertie, dear.'

'But, dash it – '

'Bertie, darling.'

'Yes, but dash it – '

'Bertie, my sweet.'

And so it was arranged. Presently I was moving sombrely off through the darkness, Jeeves at my side, Aunt Dahlia calling after me something about trying to imagine myself the man who brought the good news from Ghent to Aix. The first I had heard of the chap.

'So, Jeeves,' I said, as we reached the shed, and my voice was cold and bitter, 'this is what your great scheme has accomplished! Tuppy, Angela, Gussie and the Bassett not on speaking terms, and self faced with an eight-mile ride – '

'Nine, I believe, sir.'

'– a nine-mile ride, and another nine-mile ride back.'

'I am sorry, sir.'

'No good being sorry now. Where is this foul boneshaker?'

'I will bring it out, sir.'

He did so. I eyed it sourly.

'Where's the lamp?'

'I fear there is no lamp, sir.'

'No lamp?'

'No, sir.'

'But I may come a fearful stinker without a lamp. Suppose I barge into something?'

I broke off and eyed him frigidly.

'You smile, Jeeves. The thought amuses you?'

'I beg your pardon, sir. I was thinking of a tale my Uncle Cyril used to tell me as a child. An absurd little story, sir, though I confess that I have always found it droll. According to my Uncle Cyril, two men named Nicholls and Jackson set out to ride to Brighton on a tandem bicycle, and were so unfortunate as to come into collision with a brewer's van. And when the rescue party arrived on the scene of the accident, it was discovered that they had been hurled together with such force that it was impossible to sort them out at all adequately. The keenest eye could not discern which portion of the fragments was Nicholls and which Jackson. So they collected as much as they could, and called it Nixon. I remember laughing very much at that story when I was a child, sir.'

I had to pause a moment to master my feelings.

'You did, eh?'

'Yes, sir.'

'You thought it funny?'

'Yes, sir.'

'And your Uncle Cyril thought it funny?'

'Yes, sir.'

'Golly, what a family! Next time you meet your Uncle Cyril, Jeeves, you can tell him from me that his sense of humour is morbid and unpleasant.'

'He is dead, sir.'

'Thank heaven for that . . . Well, give me the blasted machine.'

'Very good, sir.'

'Are the tyres inflated?'

'Yes, sir.'

'The nuts firm, the brakes in order, the sprockets running true with the differential gear?'

'Yes, sir.'

'Right ho, Jeeves.'

In Tuppy's statement that, when at the University of Oxford, I had been known to ride a bicycle in the nude about the quadrangle of our mutual college, there had been, I cannot deny, a certain amount of substance. Correct, however, though his facts were, so far as they went, he had not told all. What he had omitted to mention was that I had invariably been well oiled at the time, and when in that condition a chap is capable of feats at which in cooler moments his reason would rebel.

Stimulated by the juice, I believe, men have even been known to ride alligators.

As I started now to pedal out into the great world, I was icily sober, and the old skill, in consequence, had deserted me entirely. I found myself wobbling badly, and all the stories I had ever heard of nasty bicycle accidents came back to me with a rush, headed by Jeeves's Uncle Cyril's cheery little anecdote about Nicholls and Jackson.

Pounding wearily through the darkness, I found myself at a loss to fathom the mentality of men like Jeeves's Uncle Cyril. What on earth he could see funny in a disaster which had apparently involved the complete extinction of a human creature – or, at any rate, of half a human creature and half another human creature – was more than I could understand. To me, the thing was one of the most poignant tragedies that had ever been brought to my attention, and I have no doubt that I should have continued to brood over it for quite a time, had my thoughts not been diverted by the sudden necessity of zigzagging sharply in order to avoid a pig in the fairway.

For a moment it looked like being real Nicholls-and-Jackson stuff, but, fortunately, a quick zig on my part, coinciding with an adroit zag on the part of the pig, enabled me to win through, and I continued to ride safe, but with the heart fluttering like a captive bird.

The effect of this narrow squeak upon me was to shake the nerve to the utmost. The fact that pigs were abroad in the night seemed to bring home to me the perilous nature of my enterprise. It set me thinking of all the other things that could happen to a man out and about on a velocipede without a lamp after lighting-up time. In particular, I recalled the statement of a pal of mine that in certain sections of the rural districts goats were accustomed to stray across the road to the extent of their chains, thereby forming about as sound a booby trap as one could well wish.

He mentioned, I remember, the case of a friend of his whose machine got entangled with a goat chain and who was dragged seven miles – like skijoring in Switzerland – so that he was never the same man again. And there was one chap who ran into an elephant, left over from a travelling circus.

Indeed, taking it for all in all, it seemed to me that, with the possible exception of being bitten by sharks, there was virtually no front-page disaster that could not happen to a fellow, once he had allowed his dear ones to override his better judgment and shove him out into the great unknown on a push-bike, and I am not ashamed to confess that, taking it by and large, the amount of quailing I did from this point on was pretty considerable.

However, in respect to goats and elephants, I must say things panned out unexpectedly well.

Oddly enough, I encountered neither. But when you have said that you have said everything, for in every other way the conditions could scarcely have been fouler.

Apart from the ceaseless anxiety of having to keep an eye skinned for elephants, I found myself much depressed by barking dogs, and once I received a most unpleasant shock when, alighting to consult a signpost, I saw sitting on top of it an owl that looked exactly like my Aunt Agatha. So agitated, indeed, had my frame of mind become by this time that I thought at first it was Aunt Agatha, and only when reason and reflection told me how alien to her habits it would be to climb signposts and sit on them, could I pull myself together and overcome the weakness.

In short, what with all this mental disturbance added to the more purely physical anguish in the billowy portions and the calves and ankles, the Bertram Wooster who eventually toppled off at the door of Kingham Manor was a very different Bertram from the gay and insouciant *boulevardier* of Bond Street and Piccadilly.

Even to one unaware of the inside facts, it would have been evident that Kingham Manor was throwing its weight about a bit tonight. Lights shone in the windows, music was in the air, and as I drew nearer my ear detected the sibilant shuffling of the feet of butlers, footmen, chauffeurs, parlourmaids, housemaids, tweenies and, I have no doubt, cooks, who were busily treading the measure. I suppose you couldn't sum it up much better than by saying that there was a sound of revelry by night.

The orgy was taking place in one of the ground-floor rooms which had french windows opening on to the drive, and it was to these french windows that I now made my way. An orchestra was playing something with a good deal of zip to it, and under happier conditions I dare say my feet would have started twitching in time to the melody. But I had sterner work before me than to stand hoofing it by myself on gravel drives.

I wanted that back-door key, and I wanted it instanter.

Scanning the throng within, I found it difficult for a while to spot Seppings. Presently, however, he hove in view, doing fearfully lissom things in midfloor. I 'Hi-Seppings!'-ed a couple of times, but his mind was too much on his job to be diverted, and it was only when the swirl of the dance had brought him within prodding distance of my forefinger that a quick one to the lower ribs enabled me to claim his attention.

The unexpected buffet caused him to trip over his partner's feet, and it was with marked austerity that he turned. As he recognized Bertram, however, coldness melted, to be replaced by astonishment.

'Mr Wooster!'

I was in no mood for bandying words.

'Less of the "Mr Wooster" and more back-door keys,' I said curtly. 'Give me the key of the back door, Seppings.'

He did not seem to grasp the gist.

'The key of the back door, sir?'

'Precisely. The Brinkley Court back-door key.'

'But it is at the Court, sir.'

I clicked the tongue, annoyed.

'Don't be frivolous, my dear old butler,' I said. 'I haven't ridden nine miles on a push-bike to listen to you trying to be funny. You've got it in your trousers pocket.'

'No, sir. I left it with Mr Jeeves.'

'You did – what?'

'Yes, sir. Before I came away. Mr Jeeves said that he wished to walk in the garden before retiring for the night. He was to place the key on the kitchen windowsill.'

I stared at the man dumbly. His eye was clear, his hand steady. He had none of the appearance of a butler who has had a couple.

'You mean that all this while the key has been in Jeeves's possession?'

'Yes, sir.'

I could speak no more. Emotion had overmastered my voice. I was at a loss and not abreast; but of one thing, it seemed to me, there could be no doubt. For some reason, not to be fathomed now, but most certainly to be gone well into as soon as I had pushed this infernal sewing-machine of mine over those nine miles of lonely country road and got within striking distance of him, Jeeves had been doing the dirty. Knowing that at any given moment he could have solved the whole situation, he had kept Aunt Dahlia and others roosting out on the front lawn *en déshabille* and, worse still, had stood calmly by and watched his young employer set out on a wholly unnecessary eighteen-mile bicycle ride.

I could scarcely believe such a thing of him. Of his Uncle Cyril, yes. With that distorted sense of humour of his, Uncle Cyril might quite conceivably have been capable of such conduct. But that it should be Jeeves –

I leaped into the saddle and, stifling the cry of agony which rose to the lips as the bruised person touched the hard leather, set out on the homeward journey.

23

I remember Jeeves saying on one occasion – I forget how the subject had arisen – he may simply have thrown the observation out, as he does sometimes, for me to take or leave – that hell hath no fury like a woman scorned. And until tonight I had always felt that there was a lot in it. I had never scorned a woman myself, but Pongo Twistleton once scorned an aunt of his, flatly refusing to meet her son Gerald at Paddington and give him lunch and see him off to school at Waterloo, and he never heard the end of it. Letters were written, he tells me, which had to be seen to be believed. Also two very strong telegrams and a bitter picture postcard with a view of the Little Chilbury War Memorial on it.

Until tonight, therefore, as I say, I had never questioned the accuracy of the statement. Scorned women first and the rest nowhere, was how it had always seemed to me.

But tonight I revised my views. If you want to know what hell can really do in the way of furies, look for the chap who has been hornswoggled into taking a long and unnecessary bicycle ride in the dark without a lamp.

Mark that word 'unnecessary'. That was the part of it that really jabbed the iron into the soul. I mean, if it was a case of riding to the doctor's to save the child with croup, or going off to the local pub to fetch supplies in the event of the cellar having run dry, no-one would leap to the handlebars more readily than I. Young Lochinvar, absolutely. But this business of being put through it merely to gratify one's personal attendant's diseased sense of the amusing was a bit too thick, and I chafed from start to finish.

So, what I mean to say, although the providence which watches over good men saw to it that I was enabled to complete the homeward journey unscathed except in the billowy portions, removing from my path all goats, elephants, and even owls that looked like my Aunt Agatha, it was a frowning and jaundiced Bertram who finally came to anchor at the Brinkley Court front door. And when I saw a dark figure emerging from the porch to meet me, I prepared to let myself go and uncork all that was fizzing in the mind.

'Jeeves!' I said.

'It is I, Bertie.'

The voice which spoke sounded like warm treacle, and even if I had not recognized it immediately as that of the Bassett, I should have known that it did not proceed from the man I was yearning to confront. For this figure before me was wearing a simple tweed dress and had employed my first name in its remarks. And Jeeves, whatever his moral defects, would never go about in skirts calling me Bertie.

The last person, of course, whom I would have wished to meet after a long evening in the saddle, but I vouchsafed a courteous 'What ho!'

There was a pause, during which I massaged the calves. Mine, of course, I mean.

'You got in, then?' I said, in allusion to the change of costume.

'Oh, yes. About a quarter of an hour after you left Jeeves went searching about and found the back-door key on the kitchen windowsill.'

'Ha!'

'What?'

'Nothing.'

'I thought you said something.'

'No, nothing.'

And I continued to do so. For at this juncture, as had so often happened when this girl and I were closeted, the conversation once more went blue on us. The night breeze whispered, but not the Bassett. A bird twittered, but not so much as a chirp escaped Bertram. It was perfectly amazing, the way her mere presence seemed to wipe speech from my lips – and mine, for that matter, from hers. It began to look as if our married life together would be rather like twenty years among the Trappist monks.

'Seen Jeeves anywhere?' I asked, eventually coming through.

'Yes, in the dining-room.'

'The dining-room?'

'Waiting on everybody. They are having eggs and bacon and champagne . . . What did you say?'

I had said nothing – merely snorted. There was something about the thought of these people carelessly revelling at a time when, for all they knew, I was probably being dragged about the countryside by goats or chewed by elephants, that struck home at me like a poisoned dart. It was the sort of thing you read about as having happened just before the French Revolution – the haughty nobles in their castles callously digging in and quaffing while the unfortunate blighters outside were suffering frightful privations.

The voice of the Bassett cut in on these mordant reflections:

'Bertie.'

'Hallo!'

Silence.

'Hallo!' I said again.

No response. Whole thing rather like one of those telephone conversations where you sit at your end of the wire saying: 'Hallo! Hallo!' unaware that the party of the second part has gone off to tea.

Eventually, however, she came to the surface again:

'Bertie, I have something to say to you.'

'What?'

'I have something to say to you.'

'I know. I said "What?"'

'Oh, I thought you didn't hear what I said.'

'Yes, I heard what you said, all right, but not what you were going to say.'

'Oh, I see.'

'Right ho.'

So that was straightened out. Nevertheless, instead of proceeding she took time off once more. She stood twisting the fingers and scratching the gravel with her foot. When finally she spoke, it was to deliver an impressive boost:

'Bertie, do you read Tennyson?'

'Not if I can help.'

'You remind me so much of those Knights of the Round Table in the *Idylls of the King*.'

Of course I had heard of them – Lancelot, Galahad and all that lot, but I didn't see where the resemblance came in. It seemed to me that she must be thinking of a couple of other fellows.

'How do you mean?'

'You have such a great heart, such a fine soul. You are so generous, so unselfish, so chivalrous. I have always felt that about you – that you are one of the few really chivalrous men I have ever met.'

Well, dashed difficult, of course, to know what to say when someone is giving you the old oil on a scale like that. I muttered an 'Oh, yes?' or something on those lines, and rubbed the billowy portions in some embarrassment. And there was another silence, broken only by a sharp howl as I rubbed a bit too hard.

'Bertie.'

'Hallo?'

I heard her give a sort of gulp.

'Bertie, will you be chivalrous now?'

'Rather. Only too pleased. How do you mean?'

'I am going to try you to the utmost. I am going to test you as few men have ever been tested. I am going – '

I didn't like the sound of this.

'Well,' I said doubtfully, 'always glad to oblige, you know, but I've just had the dickens of a bicycle ride, and I'm a bit stiff and sore, especially in the – as I say, a bit stiff and sore. If it's anything to be fetched from upstairs – '

'No, no, you don't understand.'

'I don't, quite, no.'

'Oh, it's so difficult . . . How can I say it? . . . Can't you guess?'

'No. I'm dashed if I can.'

'Bertie – let me go!'

'But I haven't got hold of you.'

'Release me!'

'Re – '

And then I suddenly got it. I suppose it was fatigue that had made me so slow to apprehend the nub.

'What?'

I staggered, and the left pedal came up and caught me on the shin. But such was the ecstasy in the soul that I didn't utter a cry.

'Release you?'

'Yes.' I didn't want any confusion on the point.

'You mean you want to call it all off? You're going to hitch up with Gussie, after all?'

'Only if you are fine and big enough to consent.'

'Oh, I am.'

'I gave you my promise.'

'Dash promises.'

'Then you really – '

'Absolutely.'

'Oh, Bertie!'

She seemed to sway like a sapling. It is saplings that sway, I believe.

'A very parfait knight!' I heard her murmur, and there not being much to say after that, I excused myself on the ground that I had got about two pecks of dust down my back and would like to go and get my maid to put me into something loose.

'You go back to Gussie,' I said, 'and tell him that all is well.'

She gave a sort of hiccup and, darting forward, kissed me on the forehead. Unpleasant, of course, but, as Anatole would say, I can take a few smooths with a rough. The next moment she was legging it for the dining-room, while I, having bunged the bicycle into a bush, made for the stairs.

I need not dwell upon my buckedness. It can be readily imagined. Talk about chaps with the noose round their necks and the hangman about to let her go and somebody galloping up on a foaming horse, waving the reprieve – not in it. Absolutely not in it at all. I don't know that I can give you a better idea of the state of my feelings than by saying that as I started to cross the hall I was conscious of so profound a benevolence toward all created things that I found myself thinking kindly thoughts even of Jeeves.

I was about to mount the stairs when a sudden 'What ho!' from my rear caused me to turn. Tuppy was standing in the hall. He had apparently been down to the cellar for reinforcements, for there were a couple of bottles under his arm.

'Hullo, Bertie,' he said. 'You back?' He laughed amusedly. 'You look like the Wreck of the Hesperus. Get run over by a steamroller or something?'

At any other time I might have found his coarse badinage hard to bear. But such was my uplifted mood that I waved it aside and slipped him the good news.

'Tuppy, old man, the Bassett's going to marry Gussie Fink-Nottle.'

'Tough luck on both of them, what?'

'But don't you understand? Don't you see what this means? It means that Angela is once more out of pawn, and you have only to play your cards properly – '

He bellowed rollickingly. I saw now that he was in the pink. As a matter of fact, I had noticed something of the sort directly I met him, but had attributed it to alcoholic stimulant.

'Good Lord! You're right behind the times, Bertie. Only to be expected, of course, if you will go riding bicycles half the night. Angela and I made it up hours ago.'

'What?'

'Certainly. Nothing but a passing tiff. All you need in these matters is a little give and take, a bit of reasonableness on both sides. We got together and talked things over. She withdrew my double chin. I conceded her shark. Perfectly simple. All done in a couple of minutes.'

'But – '

'Sorry, Bertie. Can't stop chatting with you all night. There is a rather impressive beano in progress in the dining-room, and they are waiting for supplies.'

Endorsement was given to this statement by a sudden shout from the apartment named. I recognized – as who would not – Aunt Dahlia's voice:

'Glossop!'

'Hallo?'

'Hurry up with that stuff.'

'Coming, coming.'

'Well, come, then. Yoicks! Hard for-rard!'

'Tallyho, not to mention tantivy. Your aunt,' said Tuppy, 'is a bit above herself. I don't know all the facts of the case, but it appears that Anatole gave notice and has now consented to stay on, and also your uncle has given her a cheque for that paper of hers. I didn't get the details, but she is much braced. See you later. I must rush.'

To say that Bertram was now definitely nonplussed would be but to state the simple truth. I could make nothing of this. I had left Brinkley Court a stricken home, with hearts bleeding wherever you looked, and I had returned to find it a sort of earthly paradise. It baffled me.

I bathed bewilderedly. The toy duck was still in the soap dish, but I was too preoccupied to give it a thought. Still at a loss, I returned to my room, and there was Jeeves. And it is proof of my fogged condish that my first words to him were words not of reproach and stern recrimination but of inquiry:

'I say, Jeeves!'

'Good evening, sir. I was informed that you had returned. I trust you had an enjoyable ride.'

At any other moment, a crack like that would have woken the fiend in Bertram Wooster. I barely noticed it. I was intent on getting to the bottom of this mystery.

'But I say, Jeeves, what?'

'Sir?'

'What does all this mean?'

'You refer, sir – '

'Of course I refer. You know what I'm talking about. What has been happening here since I left? The place is positively stiff with happy endings.'

'Yes, sir. I am glad to say that my efforts have been rewarded.'

'What do you mean, your efforts? You aren't going to try to make out that that rotten fire-bell scheme of yours had anything to do with it?'

'Yes, sir.'

'Don't be an ass, Jeeves. It flopped.'

'Not altogether, sir. I fear, sir, that I was not entirely frank with regard to my suggestion of ringing the fire bell. I had not really anticipated that it would in itself produce the desired results. I had intended it merely as a preliminary to what I might describe as the real business of the evening.'

'You gibber, Jeeves.'

'No, sir. It was essential that the ladies and gentlemen should be brought from the house, in order that, once out of doors, I could ensure that they remained there for the necessary period of time.'

'How do you mean?'

'My plan was based on psychology, sir.'

'How?'

'It is a recognized fact, sir, that there is nothing that so satisfactorily unites individuals who have been so unfortunate as to quarrel amongst themselves as a strong mutual dislike for some definite person. In my own family, if I may give a homely illustration, it was a generally accepted axiom that in times of domestic disagreement it was necessary only to invite my Aunt Annie for a visit to heal all breaches between the other members of the household. In the mutual animosity excited by Aunt Annie, those who had become estranged were reconciled almost immediately. Remembering this, it occurred to me that were you, sir, to be established as the person responsible for the ladies and gentlemen being forced to spend the night in the garden, everybody would take so strong a dislike to you that in this common sympathy they would sooner or later come together.'

I would have spoken, but he continued:

'And such proved to be the case. All, as you see, sir, is now well. After your departure on the bicycle, the various estranged parties agreed so heartily in their abuse of you that the ice, if I may use the expression, was broken, and it was not long before Mr Glossop was walking beneath the trees with Miss Angela, telling her anecdotes of your career at the university in exchange for hers regarding your childhood; while Mr Fink-Nottle, leaning against the sun-dial, held Miss Bassett enthralled with stories of your schooldays. Mrs Travers, meanwhile, was telling Monsieur Anatole – '

I found speech.

'Oh?' I said. 'I see. And now, I suppose, as the result of this dashed psychology of yours, Aunt Dahlia is so sore with me that it will be years before I can dare to show my face here again – years, Jeeves, during which, night after night, Anatole will be cooking those dinners of his – '

'No, sir. It was to prevent any such contingency that I suggested that you should bicycle to Kingham Manor. When I informed the ladies and gentlemen that I had found the key, and it was borne in upon them that you were having that long ride for nothing, their animosity vanished immediately, to be replaced by cordial amusement. There was much laughter.'

'There was, eh?'

'Yes, sir. I fear you may possibly have to submit to a certain amount of good-natured chaff, but nothing more. All, if I may say so, is forgiven, sir.'

'Oh?'

'Yes, sir.'

I mused awhile.

'You certainly seem to have fixed things.'

'Yes, sir.'

'Tuppy and Angela are once more betrothed. Also Gussie and the Bassett. Uncle Tom appears to have coughed up that money for *Milady's Boudoir*. And Anatole is staying on.'

'Yes, sir.'

'I suppose you might say that all's well that ends well.'

'Very apt, sir.'

I mused again.

'All the same, your methods are a bit rough, Jeeves.'

'One cannot make an omelette without breaking eggs, sir.'

I started.

'Omelette! Do you think you could get me one?'

'Certainly, sir.'

'Together with half a bot. of something?'

'Undoubtedly, sir.'

'Do so, Jeeves, and with all speed.'

I climbed into bed and sank back against the pillows. I must say that my generous wrath had ebbed a bit. I was aching the whole length of my body, particularly toward the middle, but against this you had to set the fact that I was no longer engaged to Madeline Bassett. In a good cause one is prepared to suffer. Yes, looking at the thing from every angle, I saw that Jeeves had done well, and it was with an approving beam that I welcomed him as he returned with the needful.

He did not check up with this beam. A bit grave, he seemed

to me to be looking, and I probed the matter with a kindly query:

'Something on our mind, Jeeves?'

'Yes, sir. I should have mentioned it earlier, but in the evening's disturbance it escaped my memory. I fear I have been remiss, sir.'

'Yes, Jeeves?' I said, champing contentedly.

'In the matter of your mess jacket, sir.'

A nameless fear shot through me, causing me to swallow a mouthful of omelette the wrong way.

'I am sorry to say, sir, that while I was ironing it this afternoon I was careless enough to leave the hot instrument upon it. I very much fear that it will be impossible for you to wear it again, sir.'

One of those old pregnant silences filled the room.

'I am extremely sorry, sir.'

For a moment, I confess, that generous wrath of mine came bounding back, hitching up its muscles and snorting a bit through the nose, but, as we say on the Riviera, *à quoi sert-il?* There was nothing to be gained by g. w. now.

We Woosters can bite the bullet. I nodded moodily and speared another slab of omelette.

'Right ho, Jeeves.'

'Very good, sir.'

JOY IN THE MORNING

Preface

The world of which I have been writing ever since I was so high, the world of the Drones Club and the lads who congregate there was always a small world – one of the smallest I ever met, as Bertie Wooster would say. It was bounded on the east by St. James's Street, on the west by Hyde Park Corner, by Oxford Street on the north and by Piccadilly on the south. And now it is not even small, it is non-existent. It has gone with the wind and is one with Nineveh and Tyre. In a word, it has had it.

This is pointed out to me every time a new book of mine dealing with the Drones Club of Jeeves and Bertie is published in England. 'Edwardian!' the critics hiss at me. (It is not easy to hiss the word Edwardian, containing as it does no sibilant, but they manage it.) And I shuffle my feet and blush a good deal and say, 'Yes, I suppose you're right'. After all, I tell myself, there has been no generic term for the type of young man who figures in my stories since he used to be called a knut in the pre-first-war days, which certainly seems to suggest that the species has died out like the macaronis of the Regency and the whiskered mashers of the Victorian age.

But sometimes I am in more defiant mood. Mine, I protest, are historical novels. Nobody objects when an author writes the sort of things that begin, 'More skilled though I am at wielding the broadsword than the pen, I will set down for all to read the tale of how I, plain John Blunt, did follow my dear liege to the wars when Harry, yclept the Fifth, sat on our English throne'.

Then why am I not to be allowed to set down for all to read the tale of how the Hon. J. Blunt got fined five pounds by the beak at Bosher Street Police Court for disorderly conduct on Boat Race Night? Unfair discrimination is the phrase that springs to the lips.

I suppose one thing that makes these drones of mine seem creatures of a dead past is that with the exception of Oofy Prosser, the club millionaire, they are genial and good tempered, friends of all the world. In these days when everbody hates everybody else, anyone who is not snarling at something – or at everything – is an anachronism. The Edwardian knut was never an angry young man. He would get a little cross, perhaps, if his man Meadowes sent him out some morning with odd spats on, but his normal outlook on life was sunny. He was a humble, kindly soul, who knew he was a silly ass but hoped you wouldn't mind. He liked everybody, and most people liked him. Portrayed on the stage by George Grossmith and G. P. Huntley, he was a lovable figure, warming the hearts of all. You might disapprove of him not being a world's worker, but you could not help being fond of him.

Though, as a matter of fact, many of the members of my Drones Club *are* world's workers. Freddie Threepwood is a vice-president at Donaldson's Dog Joy Inc. of Long Island City, U.S.A., and sells as smart a dog-biscuit as the best of them. Bingo Little edits *Wee Tots*, the popular journal for the nursery and the home, Catsmeat Potter-Pirbright has played the juvenile in a number of West End comedies, generally coming on early in Act One with a cheery 'Tennis, anyone?', and even Bertie Wooster once wrote an article on 'What the Well-Dressed Man is Wearing' for his Aunt Dahlia's weekly, *Milady's Boudoir*.

Two things caused the decline of the drone or knut, the first of which was that hard times hit younger sons. Most knuts were younger sons, and in the reign of good King Edward the position of the younger son in aristocratic families was . . . what's the word, Jeeves? Anomolous? You're sure? Right ho, anomolous. Thank you, Jeeves. Putting it another way, he was a trifle on the superfluous side, his standing about that of the litter of kittens which the household cat deposits in the drawer where you keep your clean shirts.

What generally happened was this. An Earl, let us say, begat an heir. So far, so good. One can always do with an heir. But then – these Earls never know when to stop – he absent-mindedly, as it were, begat a second son and this time was not any too pleased about the state of affairs. It was difficult to see how to fit him in. But there he was, requiring his calories just the same as if he had been first in succession. It made the Earl feel that he was up against something hard to handle.

'Can't let Algy starve,' he said to himself, and forked out a monthly allowance. And so there came into being a group of ornamental young men whom the ravens fed. Like the lilies of the field, they toiled not neither did they spin but lived quite contentedly on the paternal dole. Their wants were few. Provided they could secure the services of a tailor who was prepared to accept charm of manner as a substitute for ready cash – and it was extraordinary how full London was of altruistic tailors in the early nineteen hundreds – they asked for little more. In short, so long as the ravens continued to do their stuff, they were in that blissful condition known as sitting pretty.

Then the economic factor reared its ugly head. Income tax and super-tax shot up like rocketing pheasants, and the Earl found himself doing some constructive thinking. A bright idea occurred to him and the more he turned it over in his mind, the better he liked it.

'*Why* can't I?' he said to his Countess as they sat one night trying to balance the budget.

'Why can't you what?' said the Countess.

'Let Algy starve.'

'Algy who?'

'Our Algy.'

'You mean our second son, the Hon. Algernon Blair Worthington ffinch-ffinch?'

'That's right. He's getting into my ribs to the tune of a cool thousand a year because I felt I couldn't let him starve. The point I'm making is why *not* let the young blighter starve?'

'It's a thought,' the Countess agreed. 'Yes, a very sound scheme. We all eat too much these days, anyway.'

So the ravens were retired from active duty, and Algy, faced with the prospect of not getting his three square meals a day unless he worked for them, hurried out and found a job, with the result that as of even date any poor hack like myself who, wishing to turn an honest penny, writes stories about him and all the other Algys, Freddies, Claudes and Berties, automatically becomes Edwardian.

The second thing that led to the elimination of the knut was the passing of the spat. In the brave old days spats were the hallmark of the young-feller-me-lad-about-town, the foundation stone on which his whole policy was based, and it is sad to reflect that a generation has arisen which does not know what spats were. I once wrote a book called *Young Men in Spats*. I could not use that title today.

Spatterdashes was, I believe, their full name, and they were made of white cloth and buttoned round the ankles, partly no doubt to protect the socks from getting dashed with spatter but principally because they lent a sort of gay *diablerie* to the wearer's appearance. The monocle might or might not be worn, according to taste, but spats, like the tightly rolled umbrella, were obligatory. I was never myself by knut standards really dressy as a young man (*circa* 1905), for a certain anaemia of the exchequer compelled me to go about my social duties in my brother's cast-off frock coat and trousers, neither of which fitted me, and a top hat bequeathed to me by an uncle with head some sizes larger than mine, but my umbrella was always rolled tight as a drum and though spats cost money I had mine all right. There they were, white and gleaming, fascinating the passers-by and causing seedy strangers who hoped for largesse to address me as 'Captain' and sometimes even as 'M'lord'. Many a butler at the turn of the century, opening the door to me and wincing visibly at the sight of my topper, would lower his eyes, see the spats and give a little sigh of relief, as much as to say, 'Not quite what we are accustomed to at the northern end, perhaps, but unexceptionable to the south'.

Naturally, if you cut off a fellow's allowance, he cannot afford spats, and without spats he is a spent force. Deprived of these indispensable adjuncts, the knut threw in the towel and called it a day.

But I have not altogether lost hope of a sensational revival of knuttery. Already one sees signs of a coming renaissance. To take but one instance, the butler is creeping back. Extinct, it seemed, only a few short years ago, he is now repeatedly seen in his old haunts like some shy bird which, driven from its native marshes by alarums and excursions, stiffens the sinews, summons up the blood and decides to give the old home another try. True, he wants a bit more than in the golden age, but pay his price and he will buttle. In hundreds of homes there is buttling going on just as of yore. Who can say that ere long spats and knuts and all the old bung-ho-ing will not be flourishing again?

When that happens, I shall look my critics in the eye and say, 'Edwardian? Where do you get that "Edwardian" stuff? I write of life as it is lived today.'

P.G. Wodehouse

1

After the thing was over, when peril had ceased to loom and happy endings had been distributed in heaping handfuls and we were driving home with our hats on the side of our heads, having shaken the dust of Steeple Bumpleigh from our tyres, I confessed to Jeeves that there had been moments during the recent proceedings when Bertram Wooster, though no weakling, had come very near to despair.

'Within a toucher, Jeeves.'

'Unquestionably affairs had developed a certain menacing trend, sir.'

'I saw no ray of hope. It looked to me as if the bluebird had thrown in the towel and formally ceased to function. And yet here we are, all boomps-a-daisy. Makes one think a bit, that.'

'Yes, sir.'

'There's an expression on the tip of my tongue which seems to me to sum the whole thing up. Or, rather, when I say an expression, I mean a saying. A wheeze. A gag. What I believe, is called a saw. Something about Joy doing something.'

'Joy cometh in the mornings, sir?'

'That's the baby. Not one of your things, is it?'

'No, sir.'

'Well, it's dashed good,' I said.

And I still think that there can be no neater way of putting in a nutshell the outcome of the super-sticky affair of Nobby Hopwood, Stilton Cheesewright, Florence Craye, my Uncle Percy, J. Chichester Clam, Edwin the Boy Scout and old Boko Fittleworth – or, as my biographers will probably call it, the Steeple Bumpleigh Horror.

Even before the events occurred which I am about to relate, the above hamlet had come high up on my list of places to be steered sedulously clear of. I don't know if you have ever seen one of those old maps where they mark a spot with a cross and put 'Here be dragons' or 'Keep ye eye skinned for hippogriffs', but I had always felt that some such kindly warning might well have been given to pedestrians and traffic with regard to this Steeple Bumpleigh.

A picturesque settlement, yes. None more so in all Hampshire. It lay embowered, as I believe the expression is, in the midst of smiling fields and leafy woods, hard by a willow-fringed river, and you couldn't have thrown a brick in it without hitting a honeysuckle-covered cottage or beaning an apple-cheeked villager. But you remember what the fellow said – it's not a bally bit of use every prospect pleasing if man is vile, and the catch about Steeple Bumpleigh was that it contained Bumpleigh Hall, which in its turn contained my Aunt Agatha and her second husband.

And when I tell you that this second h. was none other than Percival, Lord Worplesdon, and that he had with him his daughter Florence and his son Edwin, the latter as pestilential a stripling as ever wore khaki shorts and went spooring or whatever it is that these Boy Scouts do, you will understand why I had always declined my old pal Boko Fittleworth's invitations to visit him at the bijou residence he maintained in those parts.

I had also had to be similarly firm with Jeeves, who had repeatedly hinted his wish that I should take a cottage there for the summer months. There was, it appeared, admirable fishing in the river, and he is a man who dearly loves to flick the baited hook. 'No, Jeeves,' I had been compelled to say, 'much though it pains me to put a stopper on your simple pleasures, I cannot take the risk of running into that gang of pluguglies. Safety first.' And he had replied, 'Very good, sir,' and there the matter had rested.

But all the while, unsuspected by Bertram, the shadow of Steeple Bumpleigh was creeping nearer and nearer, and came a day when it tore off its whiskers and pounced.

Oddly enough, the morning on which this major disaster occurred was one that found me completely, even exuberantly, in the pink. No inkling of the soup into which I was to be plunged came to mar my perfect *bien être*. I had slept well, shaved well and shower-bathed well, and it was with a merry cry that I greeted Jeeves as he brought in the coffee and kippers.

'Odd's boddikins, Jeeves,' I said, 'I am in rare fettle this a.m. Talk about exulting in my youth! I feel up and doing, with a heart for any fate, as Tennyson says.'

'Longfellow, sir.'

'Or, if you prefer it, Longfellow. I am in no mood to split hairs. Well, what's the news?'

'Miss Hopwood called while you were still asleep, sir.'

'No, really? I wish I'd seen her.'

'The young lady was desirous of entering your room and rousing you with a wet sponge, but I dissuaded her. I considered it best that your repose should not be disturbed.'

I applauded this watch-dog spirit, showing as it did both the kindly heart and the feudal outlook, but continued to tut-tut a bit at having missed the young pipsqueak, with whom my relations had always been of the matiest. This Zenobia ('Nobby') Hopwood was old Worplesdon's ward, as I believe it is called. A pal of his, just before he stopped ticking over some years previously, had left him in charge of his daughter. I don't know how these things are arranged – no doubt documents have to be drawn up and dotted lines signed on – but, whatever the procedure, the upshot was as I have stated. When all the smoke had cleared away, my Uncle Percy was Nobby's guardian.

'Young Nobby, eh? When did she blow into the great city?' I asked. For, on becoming Uncle Percy's ward, she had of course joined the strength at his Steeple Bumpleigh lair, and it was only rarely nowadays that she came to London.

'Last night, sir.'

'Making a long stay?'

'Only until tomorrow, sir.'

'Hardly worthwhile sweating up just for a day, I should have thought.'

'I understand that she came because her ladyship desired her company, sir.'

I quailed a bit.

'You don't mean Aunt Agatha's in London?'

'Merely passing through, sir,' replied the honest fellow, calming my apprehensions. 'Her ladyship is on her way to minister to Master Thomas, who has contracted mumps at his school.'

His allusion was to the old relative's son by her first marriage, one of our vilest citizens. Many good judges rank him even higher in England's Rogue Gallery than her step-son Edwin. I was rejoiced to learn that he had got mumps, and toyed for a moment with a hope that Aunt Agatha would catch them from him.

'And what had Nobby to say for herself?'

'She was regretting that she saw so little of you nowadays, sir.'

'Quite mutual, the agony, Jeeves. There are few better eggs than this Hopwood.'

'She expressed a hope that you might shortly see your way to visiting Steeple Bumpleigh.'

I shook the head.

'Out of the q., Jeeves.'

'The young lady tells me the fish are biting well there just now.'

'No, Jeeves. I'm sorry. Not even if they bite like serpents do I go near Steeple Bumpleigh.'

'Very good, sir.'

He spoke sombrely, and I endeavoured to ease the strain by asking for another cup of coffee.

'Was Nobby alone?'

'No, sir. There was a gentleman with her, who spoke as if he were acquainted with you. Miss Hopwood addressed him as Stilton.'

'Big chap?'

'Noticeably well developed, sir.'

'With a head like a pumpkin?'

'Yes, sir. There was a certain resemblance to the vegetable.'

'It must have been a companion of my earlier years named G. D'Arcy Cheesewright. In our whimsical way we used to call him Stilton. I haven't seen him for ages. He lives in the country some-where, and to hobnob with Bertram Wooster it is imperative that you stick around the metropolis. Odd, him knowing Nobby.'

'I gathered from the young lady's remarks that Mr Cheesewright is also a resident of Steeple Bumpleigh, sir.'

'Really? It's a small world, Jeeves.'

'Yes, sir.'

'I don't know when I've seen a smaller,' I said, and would have gone more deeply into the subject, but at this juncture the telephone tinkled out a summons, and he shimmered off to answer it. Through the door, which he had chanced to leave ajar, the ear detected a good deal of Yes-my-lord-ing and Very-good-my-lord-ing, seeming to indicate that he had hooked one of the old nobility.

'Who was it?' I asked, as he filtered in again.

'Lord Worplesdon, sir.'

It seems almost incredible to me, looking back, that I should have received this news item with nothing more than a mildly surprised 'Oh, ah?' Amazing, I mean, that I shouldn't have spotted the sinister way in which what you might call the Steeple Bumpleigh note had begun to intrude itself like some creeping fog or miasma, and trembled in every limb, asking myself what this portended. But so it was. The significance of the thing failed to penetrate and, as I say, I oh-ahed with merely a faint spot of surprise.

'The call was for me, sir. His lordship wishes me to go to his office immediately.'

'He wants to see you?'

'Such was the impression I gathered, sir.'

'Did he say why?'

'No, sir. Merely that the matter was of considerable urgency.'

I mused, thoughtfully champing a kipper. It seemed to me that there could be but one solution.

'Do you know what I think, Jeeves? He's in a spot of some kind and needs your counsel.'

'It may be so sir.'

'I'll bet it's so. He must know all about your outstanding gifts. You can't go on as you have gone on so long, dishing out aid and comfort to all and sundry, without acquiring a certain reputation, if only in the family circle. Grab your hat and race along. I shall be all agog to learn the inside story. What sort of a day is it?'

'Extremely clement, sir.'

'Sunshine and all that?'

'Yes, sir.'

'I thought as much. That must by why I'm feeling so dashed fit. Then I think I'll take myself for an airing. Tell me,' I said, for I was a trifle remorseful at having had to adopt that firm attitude about going to Steeple Bumpleigh and wished to bring back into his life the joy which my refusal to allow him to get in among the local fish had excluded from it, 'is there any little thing I can do for you while I'm out?'

'Sir?'

'Any little gift you would like, I mean?'

'It is extremely kind of you, sir.'

'Not at all, Jeeves. The sky is the limit. State your desire.'

'Well, sir, there has recently been published a new and authoritatively annotated edition of the works of the philosopher Spinoza. Since you are so generous, I would appreciate that very much.'

'You shall have it. It shall be delivered to your door in a plain van without delay. You're sure you've got the name right? Spinoza?'

'Yes, sir.'

'It doesn't sound probable, but no doubt you know best. Spinoza, eh? Is he the Book Society's Choice of the Month?'

'I believe not, sir.'

'Well, he's the only fellow I ever heard of who wasn't. Right ho. I'll see to it instanter.'

And presently, having assembled the hat, the gloves and the neatly rolled u., I sauntered forth.

As I made my way to the bookery, I found my thoughts turning once more, as you may readily imagine, to this highly suggestive business of old Worplesdon. The thing intrigued me. I found it difficult to envisage what possible sort of jam a man like that could have got himself into.

When, about eighteen months before, news had reached me through well-informed channels that my Aunt Agatha, for many years a widow, or derelict, as I believe it is called, was about to take another pop at matrimony, my first emotion, as was natural in the circumstances, had been a gentle pity for the unfortunate goop slated to step up the aisle with her – she, as you are aware, being my tough aunt, the one who eats broken bottles and conducts human sacrifices by the light of the full moon.

But when the details began to come in, and I discovered that the bimbo who had drawn the short straw was Lord Worplesdon, the shipping magnate, this tender commiseration became sensibly diminished. The thing, I felt, would be no walkover. Even if in the fullness of time she wore him down and at length succeeded in making him jump through hoops, she would know she had been in a fight.

For he was hot stuff, this Worplesdon. I had known him all my life. It was he who at the age of fifteen – when I was fifteen, I mean, of course – found me smoking one of his special cigars in the stable yard and chased me a mile across difficult country with a hunting crop. And though with advancing years our relations had naturally grown more formal, I had never been able to think of him without getting goose pimples. Given the choice between him and a hippogriff as a companion for a walking tour, I would have picked the hippogriff every time.

It was not easy to see how such a man of blood and iron could have been reduced to sending out SOS's for Jeeves, and I was reflecting on the possibility of compromising letters in the possession of gold-digging blondes, when I reached my destination and started to lodge my order.

'Good morning, good morning,' I said. 'I want a book.'

Of course, I ought to have known that it's silly to try to buy a book when you go to a book shop. It merely startles and bewilders the inmates. The moth-eaten old bird who had stepped forward to attend to me ran true to form.

'A book, sir?' he replied, with ill-concealed astonishment.

'Spinoza,' I replied, specifying.

This had him rocking back on his heels.

'Did you say Spinoza, sir?'

'Spinoza was what I said.'

He seemed to be feeling that if we talked this thing out long enough as man to man, we might eventually hit upon a formula.

'You do not mean *The Spinning Wheel?*'

'No.'

'It would not be *The Poisoned Pin?*'

'It would not.'

'Or *With Gun and Camera in Little Known Borneo?*' he queried, trying a long shot.

'Spinoza,' I repeated firmly. That was my story, and I intended to stick to it.

He sighed a bit, like one who feels that the situation has got beyond him.

'I will go and see if we have it in stock, sir. But possibly this may be what you are requiring. Said to be very clever.'

He pushed off, Spinoza-ing under his breath in a hopeless sort of way, leaving me clutching a thing called *Spindrift*.

It looked pretty foul. Its jacket showed a female with a green, oblong face sniffing at a purple lily, and I was just about to fling it from me and start a hunt for that 'Poisoned Pin' of which he had spoken, when I became aware of someone Good-gracious-Bertie-ing and, turning, found that the animal cries proceeded from a tall girl of commanding aspect who had oiled up behind me.

'Good gracious, Bertie! Is it really you?'

I emitted a sharp gurgle, and shied like a startled mustang. It was old Worplesdon's daughter, Florence Craye.

And I'll tell you why, on beholding her, I shied and gurgled as described. I mean, if there's one thing I bar, it's the sort of story where people stagger to and fro, clutching their foreheads and registering strong emotion, and not a word of explanation as to what it's all about till the detective sums up in the last chapter.

Briefly, then, the reason why this girl's popping up had got in amongst me in this fashion was that we had once been engaged to be married, and not so dashed long ago, either. And though it all came out all right in the end, the thing being broken off and self-saved from the scaffold at the eleventh hour, it had been an extraordinarily narrow squeak and the memory remained green. The mere mention of her name was still enough to make me call for a couple of quick ones, so you can readily appreciate my agitation at bumping into her like this absolutely in the flesh.

I swayed in the breeze, and found myself a bit stumped for the necessary dialogue.

'Oh, hullo,' I said.

Not good, of course, but the best I could do.

2

Scanning the roster of the females I've nearly got married to in my time, we find the names of some tough babies. The eye rests on that of Honoria Glossop, and a shudder passes through the frame. So it does when we turn to the B's and come upon Madeline Bassett. But, taking everything into consideration and weighing this and that, I have always been inclined to consider Florence Craye the top. In the face of admittedly stiff competition, it is to her that I would award the biscuit.

Honoria Glossop was hearty, yes. Her laugh was like a steam-riveting machine, and from a child she had been a confirmed back-slapper. Madeline Bassett was soppy, true. She had large, melting eyes and thought the stars were God's daisy chain. These are grave defects, but to do this revolting duo justice neither had tried to mould me, and that was what Florence Craye had done from the start, seeming to look on Bertram Wooster as a mere chunk of plasticine in the hands of the sculptor.

The root of the trouble was that she was one of those intellectual girls, steeped to the gills in serious purpose, who are unable to see a male soul without wanting to get behind it and shove. We had scarcely arranged the preliminaries before she was checking up on my reading, giving the bird to *Blood On The Bannisters*, which happened to be what I was studying at the moment, and substituting for it a thing called *Types of Ethical Theory*. Nor did she attempt to conceal the fact that this was a mere pipe opener and that there was worse to come.

Have you ever dipped into *Types of Ethical Theory*? The volume is still on my shelves. Let us open it and see what it has to offer. Yes, here we are.

Of the two antithetic terms in the Greek philosophy one only was real and self-subsisting; and that one was Ideal Thought as opposed to that which it has to penetrate and mould. The other, corresponding to our Nature, was in itself phenomenal, unreal, without any permanent footing, having no predicates that held true for two moments together; in short, redeemed from negation only by including in-dwelling realities appearing through.

Right. You will have got the idea, and will, I think, be able to understand why the sight of her made me give at the knees somewhat. Old wounds had been reopened.

None of the embarrassment which was causing the Wooster toes to curl up inside their neat suède shoes like the tendrils of some sensitive plant seemed to be affecting this chunk of the dead past. Her manner, as always, was brisk and aunt-like. Even at the time when I had fallen beneath the spell of that profile of hers, which was a considerable profile and tended to make a man commit himself to statements which he later regretted, I had always felt that she was like someone training on to be an aunt.

'And how are you, Bertie?'

'Oh, fine, thanks.'

'I have just run up to London to see my publisher. Fancy meeting you, and in a book shop, of all places. What are you buying? Some trash, I suppose?'

Her gaze, which had been resting on me in a rather critical and censorious way, as if she was wondering how she could ever have contemplated linking her lot to anything so sub-human, now transferred itself to the volume in my hand. She took it from me, her lip curling in faint disgust, as if she wished she had had a pair of tongs handy.

And then, as she looked at it, her whole aspect suddenly altered. She switched off the curling lip. She smiled a pleased smile. The eye softened. A blush mantled the features. She positively giggled.

'Oh, Bertie!'

The gist got past me. 'Oh, Bertie!' was a thing she had frequently said to me in the days when we had been affianced, but always with that sort of nasty ring in the voice which made you feel that she had been on the point of expressing her exasperation with something a good deal fruitier but had remembered her ancient lineage just in time. This current 'Oh, Bertie!' was quite different. Practically a coo. As it might have been one turtle dove addressing another turtle dove.

'Oh, *Bertie!*' she repeated. 'Well, of course, I must autograph it for you,' she said, and at the same moment all was suddenly made clear to me. I had missed it at first, because I had been concentrating on the girl with the green face, but I now perceived at the bottom of the jacket the words 'By Florence Craye'. They had been half hidden by a gummed-on label which said 'Book Society Choice Of The Month'. I saw all, and the thought of how near I had come to marrying a female novelist made everything go black for a bit.

She wrote in the book with a firm hand, thus dishing any prospect that the shop would take it back and putting me seven bob and a tanner down almost, as you might say, before the day had started. Then she said 'Well!' still with that turtle dove timbre in her voice.

'Fancy you buying *Spindrift!*'

Well, one has to say the civil thing, and it may be that in the agitation of the moment I overdid it a bit. I rather think that the impression I must have conveyed, when I assured her that I had made a bee-line for the beastly volume, was that I had been counting the minutes till I could get my hooks on it. At any rate, she came back with a gratified simper.

'I can't tell you how pleased I am. Not just because it's mine, but because I see that all the trouble I took training your mind was not wasted. You have grown to love good literature.'

It was at this point, as if he had entered on cue, that the moth-eaten bird returned and said they had not got old Pop Spinoza, but could get him for me. He seemed rather depressed about it all, but Florence's eyes lit up as if somebody had pressed a switch.

'Bertie! This is amazing! Do you really read Spinoza?'

It's extraordinary how one yields to that fatal temptation to swank. It undoes the best of us. Nothing, I mean, would have been simpler than to reply that she had got the data twisted and that the authoritatively annotated edition was a present for Jeeves. But, instead of doing the simple, manly, straightforward thing, I had to go and put on dog.

'Oh, rather,' I said, with an intellectual flick of the umbrella. 'When I have a leisure moment, you will generally find me curled up with Spinoza's latest.'

'*Well!*'

A simple word, but as she spoke it a shudder ran through me from brilliantined topknot to rubber shoe sole.

It was the look that accompanied the yip that caused this shudder. It was exactly the same sort of look that Madeline Bassett had given me, that time I went to Totleigh Towers to pinch old Bassett's cow-creamer and she thought I had come because I loved her so much that I couldn't stay away from her side. A frightful, tender, melting look that went through me like a red-hot bradawl through a pat of butter and filled me with a name-less fear.

I wished now I hadn't plugged Spinoza so heartily, and above all I wished I hadn't been caught in the act of apparently buying this blighted *Spindrift*. I saw that unwittingly I had been giving myself a terrific build-up, causing this girl to see Bertram Wooster with new eyes and to get hep to his hidden depths. It might quite well happen that she would review the position in the light of this fresh evidence and decide that she had made a mistake in breaking off her engagement to so rare a spirit. And once she got thinking along those lines, who knew what the harvest might be?

An imperious urge came upon me to be elsewhere, before I could make a chump of myself further.

'Well, I'm afraid I must be popping,' I said. 'Most important appointment. Frightfully jolly, seeing you again.'

'We ought to see each other more,' she replied, still with that melting look. 'We ought to have some long talks.'

'Oh, rather.'

'A developing mind is so fascinating. Why don't you ever come to the Hall?'

'Oh, well, one gets a bit chained to the metropolis, you know.'

'I should like to show you the reviews of *Spindrift*. They are wonderful. Edwin is pasting them in an album for me.'

'I'd love to see them some time. Later on, perhaps. Goodbye.'

'You're forgetting your book.'

'Oh, thanks. Well, toodle-oo,' I said, and fought my way out.

The appointment to which I had alluded was with the barman at the Bollinger. Seldom, if ever, had I felt in such sore need of a restorative. I headed for my destination like a hart streaking towards cooling streams, when heated in the chase, and was speedily in conference with the dispenser of life savers.

Ten minutes later, feeling considerably better, though still shaken, I was standing in the doorway, twirling my umbrella and wondering what to do next, when my eye was arrested by an odd spectacle.

A certain rumminess had begun to manifest itself across the way.

3

The Bollinger bar conducts its beneficent activities about halfway up Bond Street, and on the other side of the thoroughfare, immediately opposite, there stands a courteous and popular jeweller's, where I generally make my purchases when the question of investing in *bijouterie* arises. In fact, the day being so fine, I was rather thinking of looking in there now and buying a new cigarette-case.

It was outside this jeweller's that the odd spectacle was in progress. A bloke of furtive aspect was shimmering to and fro on the threshold of the emporium, his demeanour rather like that of the cat in the adage, which, according to Jeeves, and I suppose he knows, let 'I dare not' wait upon 'I would'. He seemed, that is to say, desirous of entering, but was experiencing some difficulty in making the grade. He would have a sudden dash at it, and then draw back and stand shooting quick glances right and left, as if fearing the scrutiny of the public eye. Over in New York, during the days of Prohibition, I have seen fellows doing the same sort of thing outside speakeasies.

He was a massive bloke, and there was something in his appearance that seemed familiar. Then, as I narrowed my gaze and scanned him more closely, memory did its stuff. That beefy frame . . . That pumpkin shaped head . . . The face that looked like a slab of pink dough . . . It was none other than my old friend, Stilton Cheesewright. And what he was doing, pirouetting outside jewellery bins, was more than I could understand.

I started across the road with the idea of instituting a probe or quiz, and at the same moment he seemed to summon up a sudden burst of resolution. As I paused to disentangle myself from a passing bus, he picked up his feet, tossed his head in a mettlesome sort of way, and was through the door like a man dashing into a railway-station buffet with only two minutes for a gin and tonic before his train goes.

When I entered the establishment, he was leaning over the counter, his gaze riveted on some species of merchandise which was being shown him by the gentlemanly assistant. To prod him in the hind-quarters with my umbrella was with me the work of an instant.

'Ahoy, there, Stilton!' I cried.

He spun round with a sort of guilty bound, like an adagio dancer surprised while watering the cat's milk.

'Oh, hullo,' he said.

There was a pause. At a moment like this, with old boyhood friends meeting again after long separation, I mean to say, you might have expected a good deal of animated what-ho-ing and an immediate picking up of the threads. Of this, however, there was a marked absence. The Auld Lang Syne spirit was strong in me, but not, or I was mistaken, equally strong in G. D'Arcy Cheesewright. I have met so many people in my time who have wished that Bertram was elsewhere that I have come to recognize the signs. And it was these signs that this former playmate was now exhibiting.

He drew me away from the counter, shielding it from my gaze with his person, like somebody trying to hide the body.

'I wish you wouldn't go spiking people in the backside with your beastly umbrella,' he said, and one sensed the querulous note. 'Gave me a nasty shock.'

I apologized gracefully, explaining that if you have an umbrella and are fortunate enough to catch an old acquaintance bending, you naturally do not let the opportunity slip, and endeavoured to set him at his ease with genial chit-chat. From the embarrassment he was displaying, I might have been some high official in the police force interrupting him in the middle of a smash and grab raid. His demeanour perplexed me.

'Well, well, well, Stilton,' I said. 'Quite a while since we met.'

'Yes,' he responded, his air that of a man who was a bit sorry it hadn't been longer.

'How's the boy?'

'Oh, all right. How are you?'

'Fine, thanks. As a matter of fact, I'm feeling unusually fizzy.'

'That's good.'

'I thought you'd be pleased.'

'Oh, I am. Well, goodbye, Bertie,' he said, shaking me by the hand. 'Nice to have seen you.'

I looked at him, amazed. Did he really imagine, I asked myself, that I was as easily got rid of as this? Why, experts have tried to get rid of Bertram Wooster and have been forced to admit defeat.

'I'm not leaving you yet,' I assured him.

'Aren't you?' he said, wistfully.

'No, no. Still here. Jeeves tells me you dropped in on me this morning.'

'Yes.'

'Accompanied by Nobby.'

'Yes.'

'You live at Steeple Bumpleigh, too, I hear.'

'Yes.'

'It's a small world.'

'Not so very.'

'Jeeves thinks it is.'

'Well, fairly small, perhaps,' he agreed, making a concession. 'You're sure I'm not keeping you, Bertie?'

'No, no.'

'I thought you might have some date somewhere.'

'Oh, no, not a thing.'

There was another pause. He hummed a few bars of a popular melody, but not rollickingly. He also shuffled his feet quite a bit.

'Been there long?'

'Where?'

'Steeple Bumpleigh.'

'Oh? No, not very long.'

'Like it?'

'Very much.'

'What do you do there?'

'Do?'

'Come, come, you know what I mean by "do". Boko Fittleworth, for instance, writes wholesome fiction for the masses there. My Uncle Percy relaxes there after the day's shipping magnateing. What is your racket?'

A rather odd look came into his map, and he fixed me with a cold and challenging eye, as if daring me to start something. I remembered having seen the same defiant glitter behind the spectacles of a man I met in a country hotel once, just before he told me his name was Snodgrass. It was as if this old companion of mine were on the brink of some shameful confession.

Then he seemed to think better of it.

'Oh, I mess about.'

'Mess about?'

'Yes. Just mess about. Doing this and that, you know.'

There seemed nothing to be gained by pursuing this line of inquiry. It was obvious that he did not intend to loosen up. I passed on, accordingly, to the point which had been puzzling me so much.

'Well, flitting lightly over that,' I said, 'why were you hovering?'

'Hovering?'

'Yes.'

'When?'

'Just now. Outside the shop.'

'I wasn't hovering.'

'You were distinctly hovering. You reminded me of a girl Jeeves was speaking about the other day, who stood with reluctant feet where the brook and river met. And when I follow you in, I find you buzz-buzzing into the ear of the assistant, plainly making some furtive purchase. What are you buying, Stilton?'

Fixed by my penetrating eye, he came clean. I suppose he saw that further concealment was useless.

'A ring,' he said, in a low, hoarse voice.

'What sort of a ring?' I asked, pressing him.

'An engagement ring,' he muttered, twisting his fingers and in other ways showing that he was fully conscious of his position.

'Are you engaged?'

'Yes.'

'Well, well, well!'

I laughed heartily, as is my custom on these occasions, but on his inquiring in a throaty growl rather like the snarl of the Rocky Mountains timber wolf what the devil I was cackling about, cheesed the mirth. I had always found Stilton intimidating, when stirred. In a weak moment at Oxford, misled by my advisers, I once tried to do a bit of rowing, and Stilton was the bird who coached us from the towing path. I could still recall some of the things he had said about my stomach, which - rightly or wrongly - he considered that I was sticking out. It would seem that when you are a Volga boatman, you aren't supposed to stick your stomach out.

'I always laugh when people tell me they are engaged,' I explained, more soberly.

It did not seem to mollify him - if 'mollify' is the word I want. He continued to glower.

'You have no objection to my being engaged?'

'No, no.'

'Why shouldn't I be engaged?'

'Oh, quite.'

'What do you mean by "Oh, quite"?'

I didn't quite know what I had meant by 'Oh, quite', unless possibly 'Oh, quite'. I explained this, trying to infuse into my manner a soothing what-is-it, for he appeared to be hotting up.

'I hope you will be very, very happy,' I said.

He thanked me, though not effusively.

'Nice girl, I expect?'

'Yes.'

The response was not what you would call lyrical, but we Woosters can read between the lines. His eyes were rolling in their sockets, and his face had taken on the colour and expression of a devout tomato. I could see that he loved like a thousand of bricks.

A thought struck me.

'It isn't Nobby?'

'No. She's engaged to Boko Fittleworth.'

'What!'

'Yes.'

'I never knew that. He might have told me. Nobby and Boko have hitched up, have they?'

'Yes.'

'Well, well, well! The laughing Love God has been properly up on his toes in and around Steeple Bumpleigh of late, what?'

'Yes.'

'Never an idle moment. Day and night shifts. Your betrothed, I take it, is a resident?'

'Yes. Her name's Craye. Florence Craye.'

'What!'

The word escaped my lips in a sort of yowl, and he started and gave me the raised eyebrow. I suppose it always perplexes the young Romeo to some extent, when fellows begin yowling on being informed of the loved one's identity.

'What's the matter?' he asked, a rather strained note in his voice.

Well, of course, that yowl of mine, as you may well imagine, had been one of ecstasy and relief. I mean, if Florence was all tied up with him, the peril I had been envisaging could be considered to have blown a fuse and ceased to impend. Spinoza or no Spinoza, I felt, this let Bertram out. But I couldn't very well tell him that.

'Oh, nothing,' I said.

'You seem to know her.'

'Oh, yes, we've met.'

'I've never heard her speak of you.'

'No?'

'No. Have you known her long?'

'A certain time.'

'Do you know her well?'

'Pretty well.'

'When you say "Pretty well", you mean – ?'

'Fairly well. Tolerably well.'

'How did you come to know her?'

I was conscious of a growing embarrassment. A little more of this, I felt, and he would elicit the fact that his betrothed had once been very near to Bertram - a dashed sight nearer, as we have seen, than Bertram had liked: and no recently engaged bimbo cares to discover that he was not the little woman's first choice. It sort of rubs the bloom off the thing. What he wants to feel is that she spent her time gazing out of the turret window in a yearning spirit till he came galloping up on the white horse.

I temporized, accordingly. I believe the word is 'temporized'. I should have to check up with Jeeves.

'Her ghastly father married my frightful aunt.'

'Is Lady Worplesdon your aunt?'

'And how!'

'You didn't know her before that?'

'Well, yes. Slightly.'

'I see.'

He was still giving me that searching look, like a G-man hob-nobbing with a suspect, and I am not ashamed to confess that I wiped a bead of persp. from the brow with the ferrule of my umbrella. That embarrassment, to which I have referred, was still up and doing – in fact, more so than ever.

I could see now what I had failed to spot before, that in thinking of him as a Romeo I had made an incorrect diagnosis. The bird whose name ought to have sprung to my mind was Othello. In this Cheesewright, it was plain, I had run up against one of those touchy lovers who go about the place in a suspicious and red-eyed spirit, eager to hammer the stuffing out of such of the citizenry as they suppose to be or to have been in any sense matey with the adored object. It would, in short, require but a sketchy outline of the facts relating to self and Florence to unleash the cave man within him.

'When I say "slightly",' I hastened to add, 'I mean, of course, that we were just acquaintances.'

'Just acquaintances, eh?'

'Just.'

'You simply happened to meet her once or twice?'

'That's right. You put it in a nutshell.'

'I see. The reason I ask is that it seemed to me, when I told you she was engaged to me, that your manner was peculiar – '

'It always is before lunch.'

'You started – '

'Touch of cramp.'

'And uttered an exclamation. As if the news had come as an unpleasant shock to you.'

'Oh, no.'

'You're sure it didn't?'

'Not a bit.'

'In fact, you were mere acquaintances?'

'Mere to the core.'

'Still, it's strange that she has never mentioned you.'

'Well, pip-pip,' I said, changing the subject, and withdrew.

4

It was a grave and thoughtful Bertram Wooster who started to amble back to the old flat. I was feeling a bit weak, too. During the recent scene I had run the gamut of the emotions, as I believe it is called, and that always takes it out of one.

My first reaction to Stilton's revelation had, as I have indicated, been relief, and of course I was still rolling the eyes up to Heaven in silent thankfulness a goodish bit. But it is seldom that the Woosters think only of self, and I now found the contemplation of the dreadful thing which had come upon this man filling me almost to the brim with pity and terror. It seemed to me that a Save Stilton Cheesewright movement ought to be got under way immediately. For though he wasn't what you would call absolutely one of my bosom pals, like Boko Fittleworth, one has one's human feelings. I remembered how the iron had entered into my gizzard when I was faced with the prospect of being led to the altar by Florence Craye.

One could see, of course, how the tragedy had occurred. It was the poor blister's pathetic desire to do his soul a bit of good that had landed him in this awful predicament. As is so often the case with these stolid, beefy birds, he had always had a yearning for higher things.

This whole business of jacking up the soul is one that varies according to what Jeeves calls the psychology of the individual, some being all for it, others not. You take me, for instance. I don't say I've got much of a soul, but, such as it is, I'm perfectly satisfied with the little chap. I don't want people fooling about with it. 'Leave it alone,' I say. 'Don't touch it. I like it the way it is.'

But with Stilton it was different. Buttonhole him and offer to give his soul a shot in the arm, and you found in him a receptive audience and a disciple ready to try anything once. Florence must have seemed to him just what the doctor ordered, and he had probably quite enjoyed thumbing the pages of *Types of Ethical Theory*, feeling, no doubt, that this was the stuff to give the troops.

But – and this was the reflection that furrowed the brow – how long would this last? I mean to say, he might be liking the set-up, but, as I saw it, the time would come when he would examine his soul, note how it had sprouted and say, 'Fine. That's enough to be going on with. Let's call it a day,' only to discover that he was inextricably entangled with a girl who had merely started. It was from this fate, which is sometimes called the bitter awakening, that I wanted to rescue him.

How to do it was, of course, a problem, and many chaps in my place would, I suppose, have been nonplussed. But my brain was working like a buzz-saw this morning, and the two snifters at the Bollinger had put a keen edge on it. By the time I was latch-keying my way into the flat I had placed my finger on the solution. The thing to do, I saw, was to write a strong note to Nobby Hopwood, outlining the situation and urging her to draw Stilton aside and make it quite clear to him what he was up against. Nobby, I reasoned, had known Florence since she was so high, and would consequently be in a position to assemble all the talking points.

Still, just in case she might have overlooked any of them, I carefully pointed out in my communication all Florence's defects, considered not only as a prospective bride but as a human being. I put my whole heart into the thing, and it was with an agreeable feeling of duty done and a kindly act accomplished that I took it round the corner and dropped it in the pillar box.

When I got back, I found Jeeves once more in residence. He had returned from his mission and was fooling about at some domestic task in the dining-room. I gave him a hail, and he floated in.

'Jeeves,' I said, 'you remember Mr Cheesewright, who called this morning?'

'Yes, sir.'

'I ran into him just now, buying an engagement ring. He is betrothed.'

'Indeed, sir?'

'Yes. And do you know who to? Lady F. Craye.'

'Indeed, sir?'

We exchanged a meaningful glance. Or, rather, two meaning glances, I giving him one and he giving me the other. There was no need for words. Jeeves is familiar with every detail of the Wooster-Craye imbroglio, having been constantly at my side right through that critical period in my affairs. As a matter of fact, as I have recorded elsewhere in the archives, it was he who got me out of the thing.

'And what's so poignant, Jeeves, if that's the word I want, is that he seems to like it.'

'Indeed, sir?'

'Yes. Rather pleased about it all than otherwise, it struck me. It reminded me of those lines in the poem – "See how the little how-does-it-go tum tumty tiddly push". Perhaps you remember the passage?'

'"Alas, regardless of their fate, the little victims play", sir.'

'Quite. Sad, Jeeves.'

'Yes, sir.'

'He must be saved from himself, of course, and fortunately I have the situation well in hand. I have taken all the necessary steps, and anticipate a happy and successful issue. And now,' I said, turning to the other matter on the agenda paper, 'tell me about Uncle Percy. You saw him?'

'Yes, sir.'

'Was he in the market for aid and counsel?'

'Yes, sir.'

'I knew I was right. What was it? Blackmail? Does he want you to pinch damaging correspondence from the peroxided? Has some quick-thinking adventuress got him in her toils?'

'Oh, no, sir. I am sure his lordship's private life is above reproach.'

I weighed this in the light of the known facts.

'I'm not so dashed sure about that. It depends what you call above reproach. He once chased me over a measured mile, showing great accuracy with the hunting crop. At a moment, too, when, being half-way through my first cigar, I was in urgent need of quiet and repose. To my mind, a man capable of that would be capable of anything. Well, if it wasn't blackmail, what was the trouble?'

'His lordship finds himself in a somewhat difficult position, sir.'

'What's biting him?'

He did not reply for a space. A wooden expression had crept into his features, and his eyes had taken on the look of cautious reserve which you see in those of parrots, when offered half a banana by a stranger of whose bona fides they are not convinced. It meant that he had come over all discreet, as he sometimes does, and I hastened to assure him that he might speak freely.

'You know me, Jeeves. The silent tomb.'

'The matter is highly confidential, sir. It should not be allowed to go further.'

'Wild horses shall not drag it from me. Not that I suppose they'll try.'

'Well, then, sir, his lordship informs me that he is in the process of concluding the final details of a business agreement of great delicacy and importance.'

'And he wanted you to vet the thing for snags?'

'Not precisely that, sir. But he desired my advice.'

'They all come to you, Jeeves, don't they - from the lowest to the highest?'

'It is kind of you to say so, sir.'

'Did he mention what the b. a. of great d. and i. was?'

'No, sir. But, of course, one has read the papers.'

'I haven't.'

'You do not study the financial pages, sir?'

'Never give them a glance.'

'They have been devoting considerable space of late to rumours of a merger or combination which is said to be impending between his lordship's Pink Funnel Line and an equally prominent shipping firm of the United States of America, sir. It is undoubtedly to this that his lordship was guardedly alluding.'

The information did not make me leap about to any extent.

'Going to team up, are they, these nautical tycoons?'

'So it is supposed, sir.'

'Well, God bless them.'

'Yes, sir.'

'I mean, why shouldn't they?'

'Exactly, sir.'

'Well, what's his difficulty?'

'A somewhat tense situation has arisen, sir. The negotiations would appear to have arrived at a point where it is essential that his lordship shall meet and confer with the gentleman conducting the pourparlers on behalf of the American organization. On the other hand, it is vital that he shall not be seen in the latter's society, for such a meeting would instantly be accepted in the City as conclusive proof that the fusion of interests was about to take place, with immediate reactions on the respective shares of the two concerns.'

I began to see daylight. There have been mornings after some rout or revel at the Drones, when this sort of thing would merely have caused the head to throb, but today, as I have said, I was feeling exceptionally bright.

'They would go up, you mean?'

'A sharp rise would be inevitable, sir.'

'And Uncle Percy views such a prospect with concern?'

'Yes, sir.'

'His idea being to collect a parcel cheap before the many-headed can horn in and spoil the market?'

'Precisely, sir. *Rem acu tetigisti.*'

'*Rem*—?'

'*Acu tetigisti*, sir. A Latin expression. Literally, it means "You have touched the matter with a needle", but a more idiomatic rendering would be – '

'Put my finger on the nub?'

'Exactly, sir.'

'Yes, I get it now. You have clarified the situation. Getting right down to it, these two old buzzards have got to foregather in secret and require a hideout.'

'Precisely, sir. And, of course, the movements of both gentlemen are being closely watched by representatives of the financial press.'

'I suppose this mystic sort of stuff goes on all the time in the world of commerce?'

'Yes, sir.'

'One understands and sympathizes.'

'Yes, sir.'

'Though one dislikes the idea of Uncle Percy getting any richer. Already he has the stuff in gobs. However bearing in mind the fact that he is an uncle by marriage, I suppose one ought to espouse his cause. Had you anything to suggest?'

'Yes, sir.'

'I bet you had.'

'It occurred to me that such a meeting might well take place unobserved, if the two parties were to arrange to come together beneath the roof of some remote country cottage.'

I mused.

'You mean a cottage in the country somewhere?'

'You have interpreted me exactly, sir.'

'I don't think much of that, Jeeves. You must be losing your grip.'

'Sir?'

'Well, to name but one objection, how can you go to the owner of a country cottage, whom you don't know from Adam, and ask him to let you and your pals plot in the parlour?'

'It would be necessary, of course, that the proprietor of the establishment should be no stranger to his lordship.'

'He would have to be somebody who knew Uncle Percy, you mean?'

'Precisely, sir.'

'But, Jeeves, my dear old soul, don't you see that that makes it still worse? Use the bean. In that case, the chap says to himself, "Hullo! Old Worplesdon having secret meetings with mystery men? Come, come, what's all this? I'll bet this means that the merger I've been reading about so much is going to come off." And he nips out and phones his broker to start buying those shares and to keep on buying till he's blue in the face. Thus wrecking all Uncle Percy's carefully laid plans and rendering him sicker than mud. You follow me, Jeeves?'

'Completely, sir. I had not overlooked that contingency. The occupant of the cottage would, of course, have to be some gentleman whom his lordship could trust.'

'Such as –?'

'Well, yourself, sir.'

'But – sorry to have to rub it in like this, but it's only kind to remove the scales from your eyes – I haven't got a cottage.'

'Yes, sir.'

'I don't get you, Jeeves.'

'His lordship is placing one of his own at your disposal, sir. He instructed me to say that he wishes you to proceed tomorrow to Steeple Bumpleigh – '

'Steeple Bumpleigh!'

' – where you will find a small but compact residence awaiting you, in perfect condition for immediate occupation. It is delightfully situated not far from the river – '

It needed no more than that word 'river' to tell me what had occurred. On his good mornings, I don't suppose there are more than a handful of men in the W.1 postal district of London swifter to spot oompus-boompus than Bertram Wooster, and this was one of my particularly good mornings. I saw the whole hideous plot.

'Jeeves,' I said, 'you have done the dirty on me.'

'I am sorry, sir. It seemed the only solution of his lordship's problem. I feel sure, sir, that when you see the residence in question, your prejudice against Steeple Bumpleigh will be overcome. I speak, of course, only from hearsay, but I understand from his lordship that it is replete with every modern convenience. It contains one large master's bedroom, a well appointed sitting-room, water both hot and cold – '

'The usual domestic offices?' I said. And I meant it to sting.

'Yes, sir. Furthermore, you will be quite adjacent to Mr Fittleworth.'

'And you will be quite adjacent to your fish.'

'Why, yes, sir. The point had not occurred to me, but now that you mention it that is certainly so. I should find a little fishing most enjoyable, if you could spare me from time to time while we are at Wee Nooke.'

'Did you say "Wee Nooke"?'

'Yes, sir.'

'Spelled, I'll warrant, with an "e"?'

'Yes, sir.'

I breathed heavily through the nostrils.

'Well, listen to me, Jeeves. The thing's off. You understand? Off. Spelled with an o and two f's. I'm dashed if I'm going to be made a – what's the word?'

'Sir?'

'Catspaw. Though why catspaw? I mean, what have cats got to do with it?'

'The expression derives from the old story of the cat, the monkey and the chestnuts, sir. It appears – '

'Skip it, Jeeves. This is no time for chewing the fat about the animal kingdom. And if it's the story about where the monkey puts the nuts, I know it and it's very vulgar. Getting back to the *res*, I absolutely, positively and totally refuse to go to Steeple Bumpleigh.'

'Well, of course, sir, it is perfectly open to you to adopt the attitude you indicate, but – '

He paused, massaging the chin. I saw his point.

'Uncle Percy would look askance, you mean?'

'Yes, sir.'

'And might report the matter to Aunt Agatha?'

'Precisely, sir. And her ladyship, when incensed, can be noticeably unpleasant.'

'*Rem acu tetigisti*,' I said, moodily. 'All right, start packing.'

5

It has been well said of Bertram Wooster by those who enjoy his close acquaintance that if there is one quality more than another that distinguishes him, it is his ability to keep the lip stiff and upper and make the best of things. Though crushed to earth, as the expression is, he rises again – not absolutely in mid-season form, perhaps, but perkier than you would expect and with an eye alert for silver linings.

Waking next morning to another day and thumbing the bell for the cup of tea, I found myself, though still viewing the future with concern, considerably less down among the wines and spirits than I had been yestreen. The flesh continued to creep briskly at the thought of entering the zone of influence of Uncle Percy and loved ones, but I was able to discern one reasonably brightish spot in the set up.

'You did say, Jeeves,' I said, touching on this as he entered with the steaming Bohea, 'that Aunt Agatha would not be at Steeple Bumpleigh to greet me on my arrival?'

'Yes, sir. Her ladyship expects to be absent for some little time.'

'If she's going to remain with young Thos till they've demumped him, it may well be that she will be away during the whole of my sojourn.'

'Quite conceivably, sir.'

'That is a substantial bit of goose.'

'Yes, sir. And I am happy to be able to indicate another. In the course of her visit yesterday, Miss Hopwood mentioned a fancy dress ball which, it appears, is to take place at East Wibley, the market town adjacent to Steeple Bumpleigh. You will enjoy that, sir.'

'I shall, indeed,' I assented, for as a dancer I out-Fred the nimblest Astaire, and fancy dress binges have always been my dish. 'When does it come to a head?'

'Tomorrow night, I understand, sir.'

'Well, I must say this has brightened the horizon considerably.

When I have breakfasted, I will go out and buy a costume. Sinbad the Sailor, don't you think?'

'That should prove most effective, sir.'

'Not forgetting the ginger whiskers that go with it.'

'Precisely, sir. They are of the essence.'

'If you've finished the packing, you can cram it into the small suitcase.'

'Very good, sir.'

'We'll drive down, of course.'

'Possibly it would be best, sir, if I were to make the journey by train.'

'A bit haughty, this exclusiveness, is it not, Jeeves?'

'I should have mentioned, sir, that Miss Hopwood rang up, hoping that you would be able to accommodate her in your car. Assuming that I should be falling in with your wishes in doing so, I took the responsibility of replying that you would be quite agreeable.'

'I see. Yes, that's all right.'

'Her ladyship has also telephoned.'

'Aunt Agatha?'

'Yes, sir.'

'No rot, I trust, about having changed her mind and decided not to rally round young Thos?'

'Oh, no, sir. It was merely to leave a message, saying that she wishes you to call in at Aspinall's in Bond Street before you leave, and secure a brooch which she purchased there yesterday.'

'She does, does she? Why me?' I asked, speaking with a touch of acerbity, for I rather resented this seeming inability on the relative's part to distinguish between a nephew and a district messenger boy.

'I understand that the trinket is a present for Lady Florence, sir, who is celebrating her birthday today. Her ladyship wishes you to convey it to its destination personally, realizing that, should she entrust it to the ordinary channels, the gift will be delayed in its arrival beyond the essential date.'

'You mean, if she posts it, it won't get there in time?'

'Precisely, sir.'

'I see. Yes, there's something in that.'

'Her ladyship appeared a little dubious as to your ability to carry through the commission without mishap – '

'Ho!'

' – but I assured her that it was well within your scope.'

'I should think so,' I said, piqued. I balanced a thoughtful lump of sugar on the teaspoon. 'So it's Lady Florence's birthday, is it?' I said, pondering. 'This opens up a social problem on which I should be glad to have your opinion. Ought I to weigh in with a present?'

'No, sir.'

'Not necessary, you think?'

'No, sir. Not after what has occurred.'

I was glad to hear him say so. I mean, while one wants on all occasions to do the *preux* thing, it is a tricky business, this bestowing of gifts, and apt to put ideas into a girl's head. Coming on top of *Spindrift* and Spinoza, the merest bottle of scent at this juncture might well have set such a seal upon my glamour as to cause the beasel to decide to return Stilton to store and make other arrangements.

'Well, I defer to your judgement, Jeeves. No present for La Craye, then.'

'No, sir.'

'But, while on this subject, we shall shortly have to be nosing round for one for La Hopwood.'

'Sir?'

'A wedding gift. She's gone and got engaged to Boko Fittleworth.'

'Indeed, sir? I am sure I wish the young lady and gentleman every happiness.'

'Well spoken, Jeeves. Me, too. The projected union, I may say at once, is one that has my complete approval. Which is not always the case when a pal puts the banns up.'

'No, sir.'

'Too often on such occasions one feels, as I feel so strongly with regard to poor old Stilton, that the kindly thing to do would be to seize the prospective bridegroom's trousers in one's teeth and draw him back from danger, as faithful dogs do to their masters on the edge of precipices on dark nights.'

'Yes, sir.'

'But in the present case I have no such misgivings. Each of the contracting parties, in my opinion, has picked a winner, and it is with a light heart that I shall purchase the necessary fish slice. I am even prepared, if desired, to be best man and make a speech at the wedding breakfast, and one cannot say more than that.'

'No, sir.'

'Right ho, Jeeves,' I said, flinging back the bedclothes and rising from the couch. 'Unchain the eggs and bacon. I will be with you in a moment.'

After I had broken the fast and smoked a soothing cigarette, I sallied forth, for I had a busy morning before me. I popped in at

246 Joy in the Morning

Aspinall's and pocketed the brooch, and thence repaired to the establishment of the Cohen Bros. in Covent Garden, well known among the cognoscenti as the Mecca for the discriminating seeker after fancy dress costumes. They were fortunately able to supply me with the required Sinbad, the last they had in stock, and a visit to a nearby theatrical wiggery put me in possession of an admirable set of ginger whiskers, thus giving me a full hand.

The car was at the door on my return, a suitcase of feminine aspect in its rumble. This seemed to indicate that Nobby had arrived, and as I had expected I found her in the sitting-room, sipping a refresher.

It having been some considerable time since we had foregathered, there ensued, of course, a certain period of leaping about and fraternizing. Then, having put away a refresher myself, I escorted her to the car and bunged her in. Jeeves, following my instructions, had placed the small suitcase with the Sinbad in it beneath the front seat, so that it should be under my personal eye, and we were thus all set. I trod on the self-starter and we began the journey, Jeeves standing on the pavement, seeing us off like an archbishop blessing pilgrims, his air that of one who would shortly be following by train with the heavy luggage.

Though sorry to be deprived of this right-hand man's society, for his conversation always tends to elevate and instruct, I was glad to get Nobby alone. I wanted to hear all about this pending merger with Boko. Each being a valued member of my entourage, the news that they were affianced had interested me strangely.

I am never much of a lad for chatting in traffic, and until I had eased the vehicle out of the congested districts I remained strong and silent, the lips tense, the eyes keen. But when we were bowling along the Portsmouth Road, with nothing to distract the attention, I got down to it.

6

'So you and Boko are planning to leap in among the orange blossoms?' I said. 'I had the news from Stilton yesterday, and was much stirred.'

'I hope you approve?'

'Thoroughly. Nice work, in my opinion. I think you're both on to a good thing, and would be well advised to push it along with the utmost energy. I have always considered you an extremely sound young potato.'

She thanked me for these kind words, and I assured her that the tribute was well deserved.

'As for Boko,' I proceeded, 'one of the best, of course. I could tell you things about Boko which would drive it well into your nut that you have picked a winner.'

'You don't have to.'

Her voice was soft and tender, like that of a hen crooning over its egg, and it was easy to see that, as far as she was concerned, Cupid's dart had done its stuff. I gave the wheel a twiddle, to avoid a casual dog, and went into my questionnaire. I always like to know all the facts on these occasions.

'When did you arrange this match?'

'About a week ago.'

'But you felt it coming on before that, I take it?'

'Oh, yes. Directly we met.'

'When was that?'

'At the end of May.'

'It was love at first sight, was it?'

'It was.'

'On his side, also?'

'On his side, also.'

Well, I could readily understand Boko falling in love at first sight with Nobby, of course, for she is a girl liberally endowed with oomph. But how she could have fallen in love at first sight with Boko beat me. The first sight of Boko reveals to the beholder an object with a face like an intellectual parrot. Furthermore, as is the case with so many of the younger literati, he dresses like a tramp cyclist, affecting turtleneck sweaters and grey flannel bags with a patch on the knee and conveying a sort of general suggestion of having been left out in the rain overnight in an ash can. The only occasion on which I have ever seen Jeeves really rattled was when he met Boko for the first time. He winced visibly and tottered off to the kitchen, no doubt to pull himself together with cooking sherry.

I mentioned this to Nobby, and she said she knew what I meant.

'You would think he was the sort of man who would have to grow on a girl – gradually, as it were – wouldn't you? But no. There was one startled moment when I wondered if I was seeing things, and then – bang – like a thunderbolt.'

'As quick as that, was it?'

'Yes.'

'And his reactions were similar?'

'Yes.'

'Well, here's something I don't understand. You say you met in May, and we are now in July. Why did he take such a dickens of a time wooing you?'

'He didn't exactly woo me.'

'How do you mean, not exactly? A man either woos or he does not woo. There can be no middle course.'

'There were reasons why he couldn't let himself go.'

'You speak in riddles, young Nobby. Still, as long as he got round to it eventually. And when are the bells going to ring out in the little village church?'

'I don't know if they ever are.'

'Eh?'

'Uncle Percy doesn't seem to think so.'

'What do you mean?'

'He disapproves of the match.'

'What!'

I was astounded. It seemed to me for an instant that she must be pulling the Wooster leg. Then, scrutinizing her closely, I noted that the lips were tight and the brow clouded. This young Hopwood is a blue-eyed little half portion with, normally, an animated dial. The dial to which I refer was now contorted with anguish, as if she had just swallowed a bad oyster.

'You don't mean that?'

'I do.'

'Egad!' I said.

For this was serious. Nobby, you see, was peculiarly situated. As often occurs, I believe, when Girl A becomes the ward of Bloke B, a clause had been inserted in the contract to the effect that there must be no rot about her marrying without the big chief's consent till she was twenty-one or forty-one or something. So if Uncle Percy really had an anti-Boko complex, he was in a position to bung a spanner into the works with no uncertain hand.

I couldn't get it.

'But why? The man must be cuckoo. Boko is one of our most eligible young bachelors. He makes pots of money with his pen. You see his stuff everywhere. That play he had on last year was a substantial hit. And they were saying at the Drones the other day that he's had an offer to go to Hollywood. Has he?'

'Yes.'

'Well, then.'

'Oh, I know all that. But what you're overlooking is the fact that Uncle Percy is the sort of man who is suspicious of writers. He doesn't believe in their solvency. He's been in business all his life, and he can't imagine anybody having any real money except a business man.'

'But he must know that Boko's dashed near being a celebrity. He's had his photograph in the *Tatler*.'

'Yes, but Uncle Percy has the idea that an author's success is here today and gone tomorrow. Boko may be doing all right now, but he feels that his earning capacity may go phut at any moment. I suppose he pictures himself having to draw him out of the bread line a year or two from now and support him and me and half a dozen little Boko's for the rest of our lives. And then, of course, he was prejudiced against the poor darling from the start.'

'Because of those trousers?'

'They may have helped perhaps.'

'The man's an ass. Boko's a writer. He must know that writers are allowed a wide latitude. Besides, though I wouldn't care to have Jeeves hear me say so, trousers aren't everything.'

'But the real reason was that he thought Boko was a butter-fly.'

I couldn't follow her. She had me fogged. Anything less like a butterfly than good old Boko I've never set eyes on.

'A butterfly?'

'Yes. Flitting from flower to flower and sipping.'

'And he doesn't like butterflies?'

'Not when they flit and sip.'

'What on earth has put the extraordinary idea into his head that Boko's a flitting sipper?'

'Well, you see, when he arrived in Steeple Bumpleigh, he was engaged to Florence.'

'What!'

'It was she who made him settle there. That was what I meant when I said that he couldn't woo me, as you call it, with any real abandon at first. Being engaged to Florence sort of hampered him.'

I was amazed. I nearly ran over a hen in my emotion.

'Engaged to Florence? He never told me.'

'You haven't seen him for some time.'

'No, that's true. Well, I'll be dashed. Did you know that I was once engaged to Florence?'

'Of course.'

'And now Stilton is.'

'Yes.'

'How absolutely extraordinary. It's like one of those great race movements you read about.'

'I suppose it's her profile that does it. She has a lovely profile.'

'Seen from the left.'

'Seen from the right, too.'

'Well, yes, in a measure, seen from the right, too. But would that account for it? I mean, in these busy days you can't spend your whole time dodging round a girl, trying to see her sideways. I still maintain that this tendency on the part of the populace to get engaged to Florence is inexplicable. And that made Uncle Percy a bit frosty to Boko?'

'Glacial.'

'I see. One understands his point of view, of course. He frowns on this in and out running. Florence yesterday, you today. I suppose he thinks you are just another of the flowers that Boko is flitting in on for sipping purposes.'

'I suppose so.'

'And, in addition, he doubts his earning capacity.'

'Yes.'

I pondered. If Uncle Percy really thought that Boko was a butterfly that might go broke at any moment, Love's young dream had unquestionably stubbed its toe. I mean, an oofy butterfly is bad enough. But it can at least pay the rent. I could well imagine a man of conservative views recoiling from one which might come asking for handouts for the rest of its life.

A thought occurred to me. With that Wooster knack of looking on the bright side, I saw that all was not yet lost.

'How old do you have to be before you can marry without Uncle Percy's kayo?'

'Twenty-one.'

'How old are you now?'

'Twenty.'

'Well, there you are, then. I knew that if we looked close enough we should find that the sun was still shining. You've only got to wait another year, and there you are.'

'Yes. But Boko leaves for Hollywood next month. I don't know how you feel about this dream man of mine, but to me, and I have studied his character with loving care, he doesn't seem the sort of person to be allowed to go to Hollywood without a wife at his side to distract his attention from the local fauna.'

Her outlook shocked me, causing me to put a bit of austere top-spin on my next crack.

'There can be no love where there is not perfect trust.'

'Who told you that?'

'Jeeves, I think. It sounds like one of his things.'

'Well, Jeeves is wrong. There jolly well can be love without perfect trust, and don't you forget it. I love Boko distractedly, but at the thought of him going to Hollywood without me I come over all faint. He wouldn't mean to let me down. I don't suppose he would even know he was doing it. But one morning I should get an apologetic cable saying that he couldn't quite explain how it had happened, but that he had inadvertently got married last night, and had I anything to suggest. It's his sweet, impulsive nature. He can't say No. I believe that's how he came to get engaged to Florence.'

I frowned meditatively. Now that she had outlined the position of affairs, I could see that the situation was a tricky one.

'Then what's the procedure?'

'I don't know.'

I frowned another meditative one.

'Something must be done.'

'But what?'

I had an idea. It is often like that with the Woosters. They appear baffled, and then suddenly – *bingo!* – an inspiration.

'Leave this to me,' I said.

What had crossed my mind was the thought that by establishing myself at Wee Nooke on his behalf, I was doing Uncle Percy a dashed good turn – so dashed that if he had a spark of gratitude in his composition he ought to be all over me. I could picture him clasping my hand and saying that thanks to me that merger had come off and was there any reward I cared to ask, for he could deny me nothing.

'What you need here,' I said, 'is the suave intervention of a polished man of the world, a silver-tongued orator who will draw Uncle Percy aside and plead your cause, softening his heart and making him take the big broad view. I'll attend to it.'

'You?'

'In person. Within the next day or two.'

'Oh, Bertie!'

'It will be a pleasure to put in a word for you. I anticipate notable results. I shall probably play on the old crumb as on a stringed instrument.'

She registered girlish joy.

'Bertie, you're a lamb!'

'Maybe you're right. A touch of the lamb, perhaps.'

'It's a wonderful idea. You see, you've known Boko so long.'

'Virtually from the egg.'

'You'll be able to think of all sorts of things to say about him. Did he ever save your life, when you were a boy?'

'Not that I remember.'

'You could say he did.'

'I doubt if it would go well. Uncle Percy was none too keen on me at that epoch. It would be more likely to strike a chord if I told him that Boko had repeatedly tried to assassinate me when I was a boy. However, leave it to me. I'll find words.'

All this while, of course, the old two-seater had been humming along towards Steeple Bumpleigh with the needle in the sixties, and at this point Nobby notified me that we were approaching our destination.

'Those chimneys through the trees are the Hall. You see that little lane to the left. You go down it, and you come to Boko's place. Yours is about half a mile beyond it, up another sort of side turning. You really will plead with Uncle Percy?'

'Like billy-o.'

'You won't weaken?'

'Not a chance.'

'Of course, it's just possible that you may not have to. You see, I thought that if Boko and Uncle Percy could really get together, Uncle Percy might learn to love him. So, though it wasn't easy, I arranged that Boko should give him lunch today. I hope everything has gone all right. A lot depends on how Boko behaved. I mean, up till now, whenever they have met, he has always been so stiff in his manner. I begged him with tears in my eyes to let himself go and be bright and genial, and he promised he would try. So I'm hoping for the best.'

'Me, too,' I said, and – if I remember correctly – patted her little hand. I then drove to the Hall and decanted her at its gates, assuring her that, even if Boko had failed to fascinate at the midday meal, I would see to it that everything came out all right. With a final cheery wave of the hand, I backed the car and headed for the lane of which she had spoken.

All this talking had, of course, left me with a well defined thirst, and it seemed to me, despite a householder's natural desire to take possession as soon as possible, that my first move had better be to stop off at Boko's and touch him for the needful. I assumed that the whitewashed cottage standing on the river bank must be the Bokeries, for Nobby had indicated that I had to pass it on my way to Wee Nooke.

I hove to alongside, accordingly, and noting that one of the windows at the side was open I approached it and whistled.

A hoarse shout from within and a small china ornament whizzing past my head informed me that my old friend was at home.

7

The passing of the china ornament, which had come within an ace of copping me on the napper, drew from my lips a sharp 'Oi!' and as if in answer to the cry Boko now appeared at the window. His hair was disordered and his face flushed, presumably with literary composition. In appearance, as I have indicated, this man of letters is a cross between a comedy juggler and a parrot that has been dragged through a hedge backwards, and you never catch him at his nattiest in the workshop. I took it that I had interrupted him at a difficult point in a chapter.

He had been glaring at me through horn-rimmed spectacles, but now, as he perceived who it was that stood without, the flame faded behind the lenses, to be replaced by a look of astonishment.

'Good Lord, Bertie! Is that you?'

I assured him that such was the case, and he apologized for having bunged china ornaments at me.

'Why did you imitate the note of the lesser screech owl?' he said, rebukingly. 'I thought you were young Edwin. He comes sneaking round here, trying to do me acts of kindness, and that is always how he announces his presence. I am never without a certain amount of ammunition handy on the desk. Where on earth did you spring from?'

'The metropolis. I've just arrived.'

'Well, you might have had the sense to send a wire. I'd have killed the fatted calf.'

I saw that he was under a misapprehension.

'I haven't come to stay with you. I'm hanging out at a cottage which they tell me is a little farther down the road.'

'Wee Nooke?'

'That's right.'

'Have you taken Wee Nooke?'

'Yes.'

'What made you suddenly decide to do that?'

I had foreseen that some explanation of my presence might be required, and was ready with my story. My lips being sealed, of course, on the real reason which had brought me to Steeple Bumpleigh, it was necessary to dissemble.

'Jeeves thought he would like to do a bit of fishing. And,' I added, making the thing more plausible, 'they tell me a fancy dress dance is breaking out in these parts tomorrow night. Well, you know me when I hear rumours of these entertainments. The war horse and the bugle. And now,' I said, licking the lips, 'how about a cooling drink? The journey has left me a little parched.'

I climbed through the window, and sank into a chair, while he went off to fetch the ingredients. Presently he returned with the jingling tray, and after we had done a bit of stag-at-eve-ing and exchanged some desultory remarks about this and that, I did the civil thing by congratulating him on his engagement.

'I was saying to Nobby, whom I drove down here in my car, how extraordinary it was that any girl should have fallen in love with you at first sight. I wouldn't have thought it could be done.'

'It came as quite a surprise to me, too. You could have knocked me down with a feather.'

'I don't wonder. Still, all sorts of unlikely people do seem to excite the spark of passion. Look at my Aunt Agatha.'

'Ah.'

'And Stilton.'

'You know about Stilton?'

'I ran into him in a jeweller's, buying the ring, and he told me of his fearful predicament.'

'Sooner him than me.'

'Just how I feel. Nobby thinks it's Florence's profile that does it.'

'Quite possibly.'

There was a silence, broken only by the musical sound of us having another go at the elixir. Then he heaved a sigh and said that life was rummy, to which I assented that in many respects it was very rummy.

'Take my case,' he said. 'Did Nobby tell you what the position was?'

'About Uncle Percy gumming the works, you mean? Oh, rather.'

'A nice bit of box fruit, what?'

'So it struck me. Decidedly. The heart bled.'

'Fancy having to get anyone's consent to your getting married in this enlightened age! The thing's an anachronism. Why, you can't use it as a motive for a story even in a woman's magazine nowadays. Doesn't your Aunt Dahlia run some sort of women's rag?'

'*Milady's Boudoir*. Sixpence weekly. I once contributed an article to it on What The Well-Dressed Man Is Wearing.'

'Well, I've never read *Milady's Boudoir*, but I have no doubt it is the lowest dregs of the publishing world. Yet if I were to submit a story to your aunt about a girl who couldn't marry a fellow without some blasted head of the family's consent, she would hoot at it. That is to say, I am not allowed to turn an honest penny by using this complication in my work, but it is jolly well allowed to come barging in and ruining my life. A pretty state of things!'

'What happens if you go ahead regardless?'

'I believe I get jugged. Or is that only when you marry a ward in Chancery without the Lord Chancellor hoisting the All Right flag?'

'You have me there. We could ask Jeeves.'

'Yes, Jeeves would know. Have you brought him?'

'He's following with the heavy luggage.'

'How is he these days?'

'Fine.'

'Brain all right?'

'Colossal.'

'Then he may be able to think of some way out of this mess.'

'We shan't need Jeeves. I am handling the whole thing. I'm going to get hold of Uncle Percy and plead your cause.'

'You?'

'Oddly enough, that's what Nobby said. In the same surprised tone.'

'But I thought the man scared you stiff.'

'He does. But I've been able to do him a good turn, and my drag with him is now substantial.'

'Well, that's fine,' he said, brightening. 'Snap into it, Bertie. But,' he added, coming unbrightened again, 'you've got a tough job.'

'Oh, I don't know.'

'I do. After what happened at lunch today.'

I was conscious of a sudden, quick concern.

'Your lunch with Uncle Percy?'

'That's the one.'

'Didn't it go well?'

'Not too well.'

'Nobby was anticipating that it would bring home the bacon.'

'Ha! God bless her optimistic little soul.'

I gave him one of my keen looks. There was a sombre expression on his map. The nose was wiggling in an overwrought way. It was easy to perceive that pain and anguish racked the brow.

'Tell me all,' I said.

He unshipped a heavy sigh.

'You know, Bertie, the whole idea was a mistake from the start. She should never have brought us together. And, if she had to bring us together, she ought not to have told me to be bright and genial. You know about her wanting me to be bright and genial?'

'Yes. She said you were inclined to be a bit stiff in your manner with Uncle Percy.'

'I am always stiff in my manner with elderly gentlemen who snort like foghorns when I appear and glare at me as if I were somebody from Moscow distributing Red propaganda. It's the sensitive, highly strung artist in me. Old Hardened Arteries does not like me.'

'So Nobby said. She thinks it's because he regards you as a butter-fly. My personal view is that it's those grey flannel bags of yours.'

'What's wrong with them?'

'The patch on the knee, principally. It creates a bad impression. Haven't you another pair?'

'Who do you think I am? Beau Brummel?'

I forbore to pursue the subject.

'Well, go on.'

'Where was I?'

'You were saying you made a bloomer in trying to be bright and genial.'

'Ah, yes. That's right. I did. And this is how it came about. You see, the first thing a man has to ask himself, when he is told to be bright and genial, is "How bright? How genial?" Shall he, that is to say, be just a medium ray of sunshine, or shall he go all out and shoot the works? I thought it over, and decided to bar nothing and be absolutely rollicking. And that, I see now, is where I went wrong.'

He paused, and remained for a space in thought. I could see that some painful memory was engaging his attention.

'I wonder, Bertie,' he said, coming to the surface at length, 'if you were present one day at the Drones when Freddie Widgeon sprang those Joke Goods on the lunchers there?'

'Joke Goods?'

'The things you see advertised in toy-shop catalogues as handy for breaking the ice and setting the table in a roar. You know. The Plate Lifter. The Dribble Glass. The Surprise Salt Shaker.'

'Oh, those?'

I laughed heartily. I remembered the occasion well. Catsmeat Potter-Pirbright was suffering from a hangover at the moment, and I shall not readily forget his emotion when he picked up his roll and it squeaked and a rubber mouse ran out of it. Strong men had to rally round with brandy.

And then I stopped laughing heartily. The frightful significance of his words hit me, and I started as if somebody had jabbed a red-hot skewer through the epidermis.

'You aren't telling me you worked those off on Uncle Percy?'

'Yes, Bertie. That is what I did.'

'Golly!'

'That about covers it.'

I groaned a hollow one. The heart had sunk. One has, of course, to make allowances for writers, all of them being more or less loony. Look at Shakespeare, for instance. Very unbalanced. Used to go about stealing ducks. Nevertheless, I couldn't help feeling that in springing Joke Goods on the guardian of the girl he loved Boko had carried an author's natural goofiness too far. Even Shakespeare might have hesitated to go to such lengths.

'But why?'

'I suppose the idea at the back of my mind was that I ought to show him my human side.'

'Did he take it big?'

'Pretty big.'

'He didn't like it?'

'No. I can answer that question without reservation. He did not like it.'

'Has he forbidden you the house?'

'You don't have to forbid people houses after looking at them as he looked at me over the Surprise Salt Shaker. The language of the eyes is enough. Do you know the Surprise Salt Shaker? You joggle it, and out comes a spider. The impression I received was that he was allergic to spiders.'

I rose. I had heard enough.

'I'll be pushing along,' I said, rather faintly.

'What's the hurry?'

'I ought to be going to Wee Nooke. Jeeves will be arriving at any moment with the luggage, and I shall have to get settled in.'

'I see. I would come with you, only I am in the act of composing a well-expressed letter of apology to my Lord Worplesdon. I had better finish it, though it may not be needed, if all you say about being in a position to plead with him is true. Plead well, Bertie.

Pitch it strong. Let the golden phrases come rolling out like honey. For, as I say, I don't think you've got an easy job on your hands. Eloquence beyond the ordinary will be required. And, by the way. Not a word to Nobby about that lunch. The facts will have to be broken to her gently and by degrees, if at all.'

My mood, as I set a course for Wee Nooke, was, as you may well suppose, a good deal less effervescent than it had been. The idea of pleading with Uncle Percy had lost practically all its fascination.

There rose before me a vision of this relative by marriage, as he would probably appear directly I mentioned Boko's name – the eyes glaring, the moustache bristling and the *tout ensemble* presenting a strong resemblance to a short-tempered tiger of the jungle which has just seen its peasant shin up a tree. And while it would be going too far, perhaps, to say that Bertram Wooster shuddered, a certain coolness of the feet unquestionably existed.

I was trying to hold the thought that, once that merger had gone through, joy would most likely reign so supreme that the old bounder would look even on Boko with the eye of kindliness, when there came the ting of a bicycle bell, and a voice called my name, Woostering with such vehemence that I immediately braked the car and glanced round. The sight I saw smote me like a blow.

Heaving alongside was Stilton Cheesewright, and on his face, as he alighted from his bicycle and confronted me, there was about as unpleasant a look as ever caught me in the eyeball. It was a look pregnant with amazement and hostility. A Gorblimey-what's-this-blighter-doing-here look. The sort of look, in fine, which the heroine of a pantomime gives the Demon King when he comes popping up out of a trap at her elbow. And I could follow what was passing in his mind as clearly as if it had been broadcast on a nation-wide hook-up.

All along, I had been far from comfortable when speculating as to what this Othello's reactions would be on discovering me in the neighbourhood. The way in which he had received the information that I was an old acquaintance of Florence's had shown that his thoughts had been given a morbid turn, causing him to view Bertram with suspicion, and I had been afraid that he was going to place an unfortunate construction on my sudden arrival in her vicinity. It was almost inevitable, I mean, that the thing should smack, in his view, far too strongly of Young Lochinvar coming out of the West. And, of course, my lips being sealed, I couldn't explain.

A delicate and embarrassing situation.

And yet, amazing though you will find the statement, what was

260 Joy in the Morning

causing me to goggle at him with saucer eyes was not this look that told me that my fears had been well founded, but the fact that the face attached to it was topped by a policeman's helmet. The burly frame, moreover, was clad in a policeman's uniform, and on the feet one noted the regulation official boots or beetle crushers which go to complete the panoply of the awful majesty of the Law.

In a word, Stilton Cheesewright had suddenly turned into a country copper, and I could make nothing of it.

8

I stared at the man.

'Stap my vitals, Stilton,' I cried, in uncontrollable astonishment. 'Why the fancy dress?'

He, too, had a question to ask.

'What the hell are you doing here, you bloodstained Wooster?'

I held up a hand. This was no time for side issues.

'Why are you got up like a policeman?'

'I am a policeman.'

'A policeman?'

'Yes.'

'When you say "policeman",' I queried, groping, 'do you mean "policeman"?'

'Yes.'

'You're a policeman?'

'Yes, blast you. Are you deaf? I'm a policeman.'

I grasped it now. He was a policeman. And, my mind flashing back to yesterday's encounter in the jewellery bin, I realized what had made his manner furtive and evasive when I had asked him what he did at Steeple Bumpleigh. He had shrunk from revealing the truth, fearing lest I might be funny at his expense – as, indeed, I would have been, extraordinarily funny. Even now, though the gravity of the situation forbade their utterance, I was thinking of at least three priceless cracks I could make.

'What about it? Why shouldn't I be a policeman?'

'Oh rather.'

'Half the men you know go into the police nowadays.'

I nodded. This was undoubtedly true. Since they started that College at Hendon, the Force has become congested with one's old buddies. I remember Barmy Fotheringay-Phipps describing to me with gestures his emotions on being pinched in Leicester Square one Boat-Race Night by his younger brother George. And much the same thing happened to Freddie Widgeon at Hurst Park in connection with his cousin Cyril.

'Yes,' I said, spotting a flaw, 'but in London.'

'Not necessarily.'

'With the idea of getting into Scotland Yard and rising to great heights in their profession.'

'That's what I'm going to do.'

'Get into Scotland Yard?'

'Yes.'

'Rise to great heights?'

'Yes.'

'Well, I shall watch your future progress with considerable interest,' I said.

But I spoke dubiously. At Eton, Stilton had been Captain of the Boats, and he had also rowed assiduously for Oxford. His entire formative years, therefore, as you might say, had been spent in dipping an oar into the water, giving it a shove and hauling it out again. Only a pretty dumb brick would fritter away his golden youth doing that sort of thing – which, in addition to being silly, is also the deuce of a sweat – and Stilton Cheesewright was a pretty dumb brick. A fine figure of a young fellow as far northwards as the neck, but above that solid concrete. I could not see him as a member of the Big Four. Far more likely that he would end up as one of those Scotland Yard bunglers who used, if you remember, always to be getting into Sherlock Holmes's hair.

However, I didn't say so. As a matter of fact, I didn't say anything, for I was too busy pondering on this new and unforeseen development. I was profoundly thankful that Jeeves had voted against my giving Florence a birthday present. Such a gift, if Stilton heard of it, would have led to his tearing me limb from limb or, at the best, summoning me for failing to abate a smoky chimney. You can't be too careful how you stir up policemen.

I had succeeded in sidetracking his question for a space, but I knew that the respite would be merely temporary. They train these cops to stick to the point. I was not surprised, therefore, when he now repeated it. I'm not saying I didn't wish he hadn't. All I'm saying is that I wasn't surprised.

'Well, to blazes with all that. You haven't told me what you are doing in Steeple Bumpleigh.'

I temporized.

'Oh, just making a passing sojourn,' I said nonchalantly, the old, careless Bertram Wooster.

'You mean you've come to stay?'

'For a while. Somewhere over yonder is my little nest. I hope you will frequently drop in, when off duty.'

'And what made you suddenly decide to come taking little nests in these parts?'

I went into my routine.

'Jeeves wanted to do a bit of fishing.'

'Oh?'

'Yes. He tells me it is admirable here. You find the hook, and the fish do the rest.'

For quite a while he had been staring at me in an unpleasant, boiled sort of way, the brows drawn, the eyes bulging in their sockets. The austerity of his gaze now became intensified. Except for the fact that he hadn't taken out a notebook and a stub of pencil, he might have been questioning some rat of the underworld as to where he had been on the night of June the twenty-fifth.

'I see. That is your statement, is it? Jeeves wanted to do a bit of fishing?'

'That's right.'

'Oh? Well, I'll tell you what you wanted to do, young blasted Wooster. A bit of snake in the grassing.'

I affected not to have grabbed the gist, though in reality I had got it nicely.

'Snake in the whatting?'

'Grassing.'

'I don't follow you.'

'Then I'll make it clearer. You've come here to sneak round Florence.'

'My dear chap!'

He ground a tooth or two. It was plain that he was in dangerous mood.

'I may as well tell you,' he resumed, 'that I was not at all satisfied with your evidence – with what you said when I saw you yesterday. You stated that you had known Florence – '

'Just one moment, Stilton. Sorry to interrupt, but do we bandy a woman's name?'

'Yes, we do, and ruddy well keep on bandying it.'

'Oh, right ho. I just wanted to know.'

'You stated that you had known Florence only slightly. "Pretty well" was the exact expression you used, and it seemed to me that your manner was suspicious. So when I got back, I saw her and questioned her about you. She confessed that you and she had once been engaged.'

I moistened the lips with the tip of the tongue. I am never at my best *tête à tête* with the constabulary. They always seem somehow to quell my manly spirit. It may be the helmet that does it, or possibly the boots. And, of course, when one of the *gendarmerie* is accusing you of trying to pinch his girl, the embarrassment deepens. At moment of going to press, with Stilton's eyes boring holes through me, I had begun to feel like Eugene Aram just before they put the gyves on his wrists. I don't know if you remember the passage? 'Ti-tum-ti-tum ti-tumty tum, ti-tumty tumty mist (I think it's mist), and Eugene Aram walked between, with gyves upon his wrist.'

I cleared the throat, and endeavoured to speak with a winning frankness.

'Why, yes. That's right. It all comes back to me. We were. Long ago.'

'Not so long ago.'

'Well, it seems like long ago.'

'Oh?'

'Yes.'

'Is that so?'

'Positively.'

'The whole thing's over, eh?'

'Definitely.'

'Nothing between you now?'

'Not a thing.'

'Then how do you account for the fact that she gives you a copy of her novel and writes "To Bertie, with love from Florence" in it?'

I tottered. And at the same time, I'm bound to confess, I found myself feeling a new respect for Stilton. At first, if you recollect, when he had spoken of rising to great heights at Scotland Yard, I had thought lightly of his chances. It seemed to me now that he must have the makings of a very hot detective indeed.

'You had the book with you when you came into that jeweller's shop. You left it on the counter, and I looked inside.'

I revised my views about his sleuthing powers. Not so hot, after all. Sherlock Holmes, if you remember, always said that it was a mistake for a detective to explain his methods.

'Well?'

I laughed lightly. At least, I tried to. As a matter of fact, the thing came out more like a death rattle.

'Oh, that was rather amusing.'

'All right. Go on. Make me laugh.'

'I was in the book shop, and she came in – '

'You had an assignation with her in a book shop?'

'No, no. Just an accidental meeting.'

'I see. And you've come down here to arrange another.'

'Good Lord, no.'

'Do you seriously expect me to believe that you aren't trying to steal her from me?'

'Nothing could be farther from my thoughts, old man.'

'Don't call me "old man".'

'Right ho, if you don't like it. The whole thing, officer, is one of those absurd misunderstandings. As I was starting to tell you, I was in this book shop – '

Here he interrupted me, damning the book shop with a good deal of heartiness.

'I'm not interested in the book shop. The point is that you have come down here to make a snake in the grass of yourself, and I'm not going to have it. I have just one thing to say to you, Wooster. Get out!'

'But – '

'Push off. Remove your beastly presence. Pop back to your London residence and stay there. And do it quick.'

'But I can't.'

'What do you mean?'

Well, as I said before, my lips were sealed. But the Woosters are swift thinkers.

'Old Boko,' I explained. 'I am acting for him in a rather delicate matter. As you possibly may know, my Uncle Percy is endeavouring to put the bee on his union with Nobby, and I have promised the young couple that I will plead for them. This will, of course, involve my remaining *in statu* – what is it?'

'Pah!'

'No, not pah. *Quo*. That's the word I'm trying to think of. You can't plead with an uncle by marriage unless you're *in statu quo*.'

It seemed to me a pretty good and reasonable explanation, and I was distressed, accordingly, to observe that he was sneering unpleasantly.

'I don't believe a word of it. You plead? What's the good of you pleading? As if anything you could say would have any weight with anybody. I repeat – clear out. Otherwise – '

He didn't mention what would happen otherwise, but the menacing way in which he hopped on his bicycle and pedalled off spoke louder than words. I don't think I have ever seen anyone pedal with a more sinister touch to the ankle work.

I was still looking after him, feeling a little weak, when from the opposite or Wee Nooke direction there came the ting of another bicycle bell and, swivelling round, I perceived Florence approaching. As perfect an instance of one damn' thing after another as I have ever experienced.

In sharp contradistinction to those of Stilton, her eyes were shining with a welcoming light. She hopped off as she reached the car, and flashed a bright smile at me.

'Oh, here you are, Bertie. I have just been putting a few flowers in Wee Nooke for you.'

I thanked her, but with a sinking heart. I hadn't liked that smile, and I didn't like the idea of her sweating about strewing flowers in my path. The note struck seemed to me altogether too matey. Then I reminded myself that if she was betrothed to Stilton there could be no real cause for alarm. After all, her father had married my aunt, which made us sort of cousins, and there was nothing necessarily sinister in a bit of cousinly bustling about. Blood, I mean to say, when you come right down to it, being thicker than water.

'Frightfully decent of you,' I said. 'I've just been having a chat with Stilton.'

'Stilton?'

'Your affianced.'

'Oh, D'Arcy? Why do you call him Stilton?'

'Boyish nickname. We were at school together.'

'Oh? Then perhaps you can tell me if he was always such a perfect imbecile as he is today.'

I didn't like this. It didn't seem the language of love.

'In what sense do you use the word "imbecile"?'

'I use it as the only possible description of a man who, with a wealthy uncle willing and anxious to do everything for him, deliberately elects to become a common constable.'

'Why did he?' I asked. 'Become a common constable, I mean.'

'He says that every man ought to stand on his own feet and earn a living.'

'Conscientious.'

'Rubbish.'

'You don't think it does him credit?'

'No, I don't. I think he's a perfect idiot.'

There was a pause. It was plain that his behaviour rankled, and it seemed to me what was required here was a strong boost for the young copper. For I need scarcely say that, now that I was face to face again with this girl, all thought of carrying on with the promotion of that Save Stilton Cheesewright campaign was farther from my mind than ever.

'I should have thought you would have been rather bucked about it all. As giving evidence of Soul, I mean.'

'Soul?'

'It shows he's got a great soul.'

'I should be extremely surprised to find that he has any soul above those great, clodhopping boots he wears. He is just pigheaded. I have reasoned with him over and over again. His uncle wants him to stand for Parliament and is prepared to pay all his expenses and to finance him generously for the rest of his life, but no, he just looks mulish and talks about earning his living. I am sick and tired of the whole thing, and I really don't know what I shall do about it. Well, goodbye, Bertie, I must be getting along,' she concluded abruptly, as if she found the subject too painful to dwell on, and was off – just at the very moment when I had remembered that it was her birthday and that I had a brooch in my pocket to deliver to her from Aunt Agatha.

I could have called her back, I suppose, but somehow didn't feel in the mood. Her words had left me shaking in every limb. The revelation of the flimsiness of the foundations on which the Florence-Stilton romance appeared to be founded had appalled me, and I had to remain *in statu quo* and smoke a couple of cigarettes before I felt strong enough to resume my journey.

Then, feeling a little better and trying to tell myself that this was just a passing tiff and that matters would speedily adjust themselves, I pushed on and in another couple of minutes was coming to anchor abaft Wee Nooke.

9

Wee Nooke proved to be a decentish little shack, situated in agreeable surroundings. A bit Ye Olde, but otherwise all right. It had a
thatched roof and a lot of those windows with small leaded panes,
and there was a rockery in the front garden. It looked, in short,
as I subsequently learned was the case, as if it had formerly been
inhabited by an elderly female of good family who kept cats.

I had walked in and deposited the small suitcase in the hall, when,
as I stood gazing about me and inhaling the fug which always seems
to linger about these antique interiors, I became aware that there
was more in this joint than met the eye. In a word, I suddenly found
myself speculating on the possibility of it not only being fuggy, but
haunted.

What started this train of thought was the fact that odd noises
were in progress somewhere near at hand, here a bang and there
a crash, suggesting the presence of a poltergeist or what not.

The sounds seemed to proceed from the other side of a door at
the end of the hall, and I was hastening thither to investigate, for I was
dashed if I was going to have poltergeists lounging about the place as
if it belonged to them, when I took a toss over a pail which had been
placed in the fairway. And I had just picked myself up, rubbing the
spot, when the door opened and there entered a small boy with a
face like a ferret. He was wearing the uniform of a Boy Scout, and
I had no difficulty, in spite of the fact that his features were liberally
encrusted with dirt, in identifying him as Florence's little brother
Edwin — the child at whom Boko Fittleworth was accustomed to
throw china ornaments.

'Oh, hullo, Bertie,' he said, grinning all over his loathsome face.

'Hullo, you frightful young squirt,' I responded civilly. 'What are
you doing here?'

'Tidying up.'

I touched on a point of absorbing interest.

'Was it you who left that bally pail there?'

'Where?'

'In the middle of the hall.'

'Coo! Yes, I remember now. I put it there to be out of the way.'

'I see. Well, you'll be amused to learn that I've nearly broken my leg.'

He started. A fanatic gleam came into his eyes. He looked like a boy confronted with an unexpected saucer of ice cream.

'I say! Have you really? This is a bit of bunce. I can give you first aid.'

'No, you jolly well can't.'

'But if you've bust your leg – '

'I haven't bust my leg.'

'You said you had.'

'A mere figure of speech.'

'Well, you may have sprained your ankle.'

'I haven't sprained my ankle.'

'I can do first aid for contusions.'

'I haven't any contusions. Stand back!' I cried, for I was prepared to defend myself with iron resolution.

There was a pause. His manner was that of one who finds the situation at a deadlock. My spirited attitude had plainly disconcerted him.

'Can't I bandage you?'

'You'll get a thick ear, if you try.'

'You may get gangrene.'

'I anticipate no such contingency.'

'You'll look silly if you get gangrene.'

'No, I shan't. I shall look fine.'

'I knew a chap who bumped his leg, and it turned black and had to be cut off at the knee.'

'You do seem to mix with the most extraordinary people.'

'I could turn the cold tap on it.'

'No, you couldn't.'

Again, that baffled air came into his demeanour. I had nonplussed him.

'Then I'll be getting back to the kitchen,' he said. 'I'm going to do the chimney. It needs a jolly good cleaning out. This place would have been in a fearful mess, if it hadn't been for me,' he added, with a smugness which jarred upon my sensibilities.

'How do you mean, if it hadn't been for you?' I riposted, in my keen way. 'I'll bet you've been spreading ruin and desolation on all sides.'

'I've been tidying up,' he said, with a touch of pique. 'Florence put some flowers for you in the sitting-room.'

'I know. She told me.'

'I fetched the water. Well, I'll go and do that chimney, shall I?'

'Do it, if it pleases you, till your eyes bubble,' I said, and dismissed him with a cold gesture.

Now, I don't know how you would have made a cold gesture – no doubt people's methods vary – but the way I did it was by raising the right arm in a sort of salute and allowing it to fall to my side. And, as it fell, I became aware of something missing. The coat pocket against which the wrist impinged should have contained a small, solid object – to wit, the package containing the brooch which Aunt Agatha had told me to convey to Florence for her birthday. And it didn't. The pocket was empty.

And at the same moment the kid Edwin said 'Coo!' and stooped, and came up holding the thing.

'Did you drop this?' he asked.

Any doubts that may have lingered in the child's mind as to my having broken my leg must have been dispelled by the spring I made. I flew through the air with the greatest of ease. A panther could not have moved more nippily. I wrenched the thing from his grasp, and once more pocketed it.

He seemed intrigued.

'What was it?'

'A brooch. Birthday present for Florence.'

'Shall I take it to her?'

'No, thanks.'

'I will, if you like.'

'No, thanks.'

'It would save you trouble.'

Had the circumstances been other than they were, I might have found this benevolence of his cloying – so much so, indeed, as to cause me to kick him in the pants. But he had rendered me so signal a service that I merely smiled warmly at the young blister, a thing I hadn't done for years.

'No, thanks,' I said. 'I don't let it out of my hands. I will run across and deliver it this evening. Well, well, young Edwin,' I continued affably, 'a smart piece of work, that. They train you sprouts to keep your eyes open. Tell me, how have you been all this while? All right? No colds, colics or other juvenile ailments? Splendid. I should hate to feel that you had been suffering in any way. It was decent of you to suggest putting my leg under the tap. Greatly appreciated. I wish I had a drink to offer you. You must come up and see me some time, when I am more settled.'

And on this cordial note our interview terminated. I tottered out into the garden, and for a space stood leaning on the front gate, for my spine was still feeling a bit jellified and I needed support.

I say my spine had become as jelly, and if you knew my Aunt Agatha you would agree that so it jolly well might.

This relative is a woman who, like Napoleon, if it was Napoleon, listens to no excuses for failure, however sound. If she gives you a brooch to take to a stepdaughter, and you lose it, it is no sort of use trying to tell her that the whole thing was an Act of God, caused by your tripping over unforeseen pails and having the object jerked out of your pocket. Pawn though you may have been in the hands of Fate, you get put through it just the same.

If I had not recovered this blighted trinket, I should never have heard the last of it. The thing would have marked an epoch. World-shaking events would have been referred to as having happened 'about the time Bertie lost that brooch' or 'just after Bertie made such an idiot of himself over Florence's birthday present'. Aunt Agatha is like an elephant – not so much to look at, for in appearance she resembles more a well-bred vulture, but because she never forgets.

Leaning on the gate, I found myself seething with kindly feelings towards young Edwin. I wondered how I could ever have gone so astray in my judgement as to consider him a ferret-faced little son of a what not. And I was just going to debate in my mind the idea of buying him some sort of a gift as a reward for his admirable behaviour, when there was a loud explosion and, turning, I saw that Wee Nooke had gone up in flames.

It gave me quite a start.

10

Well, everybody enjoys a good fire, of course, and for a while it was in a purely detached and appreciative spirit that I stood eyeing the holocaust. I felt that this was going to be value for money. Already the thatched roof was well ablaze, and it seemed probable that before long the whole edifice, being the museum piece it was, all dry rot and what not, would spit on its hands and really get down to it. And so, as I say, for about the space of two shakes of a duck's tail I stood watching it with quiet relish.

Then, putting a bit of a damper on the festivities, there came floating into my mind a rather disturbing thought – to wit, that the last I had seen of young Edwin, he had been seeping back into the kitchen. Presumably, therefore, he was still on the premises, and the conclusion to which one was forced was that, unless somebody took prompt steps through the proper channels, he was likely 'ere long to be rendered unfit for human consumption. This was followed by a second and still more disturbing thought that the only person in a position to do the necessary spot of fireman-save-my-child-ing was good old Wooster.

I mused. I suppose you would call me a fairly intrepid man, taken by and large, but I'm bound to admit I wasn't any too keen on the thing. Apart from anything else, my whole attitude towards the stripling who was faced with the prospect of being grilled on both sides had undergone another quick change.

When last heard from, if you remember, I had been thinking kindly thoughts of young Edwin and even going to the length of considering buying him some inexpensive present. But now I found myself once more viewing him with the eye of censure. I mean to say, it was perfectly obvious to the meanest intelligence that it was owing to some phonus-bolonus on his part that the conflagration had been unleashed, and I was conscious of a strong disposition to leave well alone.

It being, however, one of those situations where *noblesse* more or less *obliges*, I decided that I had better do the square thing, and I had torn off my coat and flung it from me and was preparing to plunge into the burning building, though still feeling that it was a bit thick having to get myself all charred up to gratify a kid who would be far better cooked to a cinder, when he emerged. His face was black, and he hadn't any eyebrows, but in other respects appeared reasonably bobbish. Indeed, he seemed entertained rather than alarmed by what had occurred.

'Coo!' he said, in a pleased sort of voice. 'Bit of a bust up, wasn't it?'

I eyed him sternly.

'What the dickens have you been playing at, you abysmal young louse?' I demanded. 'What was that explosion?'

'That was the kitchen chimney. It was full of soot, so I shoved some gunpowder up it. And I think I may have used too much. Because there was a terrific bang and everything sort of caught fire. Coo! It didn't half make me laugh.'

'Why didn't you pour water on the flames?'

'I did. Only it turned out to be paraffin.'

I clutched the brow. I was deeply moved. It had just come home to me that this blazing pyre was the joint which was supposed to be the Wooster G.H.Q., and the householder spirit had awoken in me. Every impulse urged me to give the little snurge six of the best with a bludgeon. But you can't very well slosh a child who has just lost his eyebrows. Besides, I hadn't a bludgeon.

'Well, you've properly messed things up,' I said.

'It didn't all work out quite the way I meant,' he admitted. 'But I wanted to do my last Friday's act of kindness.'

At these words, all was suddenly made plain to me. It was so long since I had seen the young poison sac that I had forgotten the kink in his psychology which made him such a menace to society.

This Edwin, I now recalled, was one of those thorough kids who spare no effort. He had the same serious outlook on life as his sister Florence. And when he joined the Boy Scouts, he did so, resolved not to shirk his responsibilities. The programme called for a daily act of kindness, and he went at it in a grave and earnest spirit. Unfortunately, what with one thing and another, he was always dropping behind schedule, and would then set such a clip to try and catch up with himself that any spot in which he happened to be functioning rapidly became a perfect hell for man and beast. It was so at the house in Shropshire where I had first met him, and it was evidently just the same now.

It was with a grave face and a thoughtful tooth chewing the

lower lip that I picked up my coat and donned it. A weaker man, contemplating the fact that he was trapped in a locality containing not only Florence Craye, Police Constable Cheesewright and Uncle Percy, but also Edwin doing acts of kindness, would probably have given at the knees. And I am not so sure I might not have done so myself, had not my mind been diverted by a frightful discovery, so ghastly that I uttered a hoarse cry and all thoughts of Florence, Stilton, Uncle Percy and Edwin were wiped from my mind.

I had just remembered that my suitcase with the Sindbad the Sailor costume in it was in the Wee Nooke front hall and the flames leaping ever nearer.

There was no hesitation, no vacillating about my movements now. When it had been a matter of risking my life to save Boy Scouts, I may have stood scratching the chin a bit, but this was different. I needed that Sindbad. Only by retrieving it would I be able to attend the fancy dress ball at East Wibley tomorrow night, the one bright spot in a dark and sticky future. Well, I suppose I could have popped up to London and got something else, but probably a mere Pierrot, and my whole heart was set on the Sindbad and the ginger whiskers.

Edwin was saying something about fire brigades, and I right-hoed absently. Then, snapping into it like a jack rabbit, I commended my soul to God, and plunged in.

Well, as it turned out, I needn't have worried. It is true that there was a certain amount of smoke in the hall, billowing hither and thither in murky clouds, but nothing to bother a man who had often sat to leeward of Catsmeat Potter-Pirbright when he was enjoying one of those cigars of his. In a few minutes, it was plain, the whole place would be a cheerful blaze, but for the nonce conditions were reasonably normal.

It is no story, in short, of a jolly-nearly-fried-to-a-crisp Bertram Wooster that I have to tell, but rather of a Bertram Wooster who just scooped up the old suitcase, whistled a gay air and breezed out without a mark on him. I may have coughed once or twice, but nothing more.

But though peril might have failed to get off the mark inside the house, it was very strong on the wing outside. The first thing I saw, as I emerged was Uncle Percy standing at the gate. And as Edwin had now vanished, presumably in search of fire brigades, I was alone with him in the great open spaces – a thing I've always absolutely barred being from the days of childhood.

'Oh, hullo, Uncle Percy,' I said. 'Good afternoon, good afternoon.'

A casual passer-by, hearing the words and noting the hearty voice in which they had been spoken, might have been deceived into supposing that Bertram was at his ease. Such, however, was far from being the case. Whether anyone was ever at his ease in the society of this old Gawd-help-us, I cannot say, but I definitely was not. The spine, and I do not attempt to conceal the fact, had become soluble in the last degree.

You may wonder at this, arguing that as I was not responsible for the disaster which had come upon us, I had nothing to fear. But a longish experience has taught me that on these occasions innocence pays no dividends. Pure as the driven snow though he may be, or even purer, it is the man on the spot who gets the brickbats.

My civil greeting elicited no response. He was staring past me at the little home, now beyond any possible doubt destined to be a total loss. Edwin might return with all the fire brigades in Hampshire, but nothing was going to prevent Wee Nooke winding up as a heap of ashes.

'What?' he said, speaking thickly, as if the soul were bruised, as I imagine to have been the case. 'What? What? What? What . . . ?'

I saw that, unless checked, this was going to take some time.

'There's been a fire,' I said.

'What do you mean?'

Well I didn't see how I could have put it much clearer.

'A fire,' I repeated, waving a hand in the direction of the burning edifice, as much as to tell him to take a glance for himself. 'How are you, Uncle Percy? You're looking fine.'

He wasn't, as a matter of fact, nor did this attempt to ease the strain by giving him the old oil have the desired effect. He directed at me a kind of frenzied glare, containing practically nil in the way of an uncle's love, and spoke in a sort of hollow, despairing voice.

'I might have known! My best friends would have warned me what would come of letting a lunatic like you loose in the place. I ought to have guessed that the first thing you would do – before so much as unpacking – would be to set the whole damned premises ablaze.'

'Not me,' I said, wishing to give credit where credit was due. 'Edwin.'

'Edwin? My son?'

'Yes, I know,' I said sympathetically. 'Too bad. Yes, he's your son, all right. He's been tidying up.'

'You can't start a fire by tidying up.'

'You can if you use gunpowder.'

'Gunpowder?'

'He appears to have touched off a keg or two in the kitchen chimney, to correct a disposition on its part to harbour soot.'

Well, I had naturally supposed, as anyone would have supposed, that this frank explanation would have set me right, causing him to dismiss me without a stain on my character, and that the rather personal note which had crept into his remarks would instantly have been switched off. What I had anticipated was that he would issue an apology for that crack of his about lunatics, which I would gracefully accept, and that we would then get together like two old buddies and shake our heads over the impulsiveness of the younger generation.

Not a bit of it, however. He continued to bend upon me the accusing gaze which I had disliked so much from the start.

'Why the devil did you give the boy gunpowder?'

I saw that he had still got the wrong angle.

'I didn't give the boy gunpowder.'

'Only a congenital idiot would give a boy gunpowder. There's not a man in England, except you, who wouldn't know what would happen if you gave a boy gunpowder. Do you realize what you have done? The sole reason for your coming here was that I should have a place where I could meet an old friend and discuss certain matters of interest, and now look at it. I ask you. Look at it.'

'Not too good,' I was forced to concede, as the roof fell in, sending up a shower of sparks and causing a genial glow to play about our cheeks.

'I suppose it never occurred to you to throw water on the flames?'

'It did to Edwin. Only he used paraffin.'

He started, staring at me incredulously.

'You tried to put the fire out with paraffin? You ought to be certified, and as soon as I collect a couple of doctors, I'll have it seen to.'

What was making this conversation so difficult was, as you have probably spotted, the apparent impossibility of getting the old ass to sort out the principals in the affair and assign to each his respective role. He was one of those men you meet sometimes who only listen to about two words of any observation addressed to them. I suppose he had got that way through presiding at board meetings and constantly chipping in and squelching shareholders in the middle of sentences.

Once more, I tried to drive it home to him that it was Edwin who had done all the what you might call heavy work, Bertram having been throughout merely an innocent bystander, but it didn't penetrate. He was left with the settled conviction that I and the child had got together, forming a quorum, and after touching off the place with gunpowder had nursed the conflagration along with careful injections of paraffin, each encouraging each, as you might say, on the principle that it is team-work that tells.

When he finally pushed off, instructing me to send Jeeves along to him the moment he arrived, he was reiterating the opinion that I ought not to be at large, and wishing – though here I definitely could not see eye to eye with him – that I was ten years younger, so that he could have got after me with that hunting-crop of his. He then withdrew, leaving me to my meditations.

These, as you may suppose, were not of the juiciest. However, they didn't last long, for I don't suppose I had been meditating more than about a couple of minutes when a wheezing, rattling sound made itself heard off-stage and there entered left upper centre a vehicle which could only have been a station taxi. There was luggage on it, and looking more closely I saw Jeeves protruding from the side window.

The weird old object – the cab, I mean, not Jeeves – came to a halt at the gate. Jeeves paid it off, the luggage was dumped by the roadside, and he was at liberty to get into conference with the young master, not an instant too soon for the latter. I had need of his sympathy, encouragement and advice. I also wanted to tick him off a bit for letting me in for all this.

11

'Jeeves,' I said, getting right down to it in the old Wooster way, 'here's a nice state of things!'

'Sir?'

'Hell's foundations have been quivering.'

'Indeed, sir?'

'The curse has come upon me. As I warned you it would, if I ever visited Steeple Bumpleigh. You have long been familiar with my views on this leper colony. Have I not repeatedly said that, what though the spicy breezes blow soft o'er Steeple Bumpleigh, the undersigned deemed it wisest to give it the complete miss-in-baulk?'

'Yes, sir.'

'Very well, Jeeves. Perhaps you will listen to me another time. However, let us flit lightly over the recriminations and confine ourselves to the facts. You notice our little home has been gutted?'

'Yes, sir. I was just observing it.'

'Edwin did that. There's a lad, Jeeves. There's a boy who makes you feel that what this country wants is somebody like King Herod. Started in with gunpowder and carried on with paraffin. Just cast your eye over those smouldering ruins. You would scarcely have thought it possible, would you, that one frail child in a sport shirt and khaki shorts could have accomplished such devastation. Yet he did it, Jeeves, and did it on his head. You understand what this means?'

'Yes, sir.'

'He has properly put the kybosh on the trysting-place of Uncle Percy and his nautical pal. You'll have to think again.'

'Yes, sir. His lordship is fully alive to the fact that in the existing circumstances a meeting at Wee Nooke will not be feasible.'

'You've seen him, then?'

'He was emerging from the lane, as I entered it, sir.'

'Did he tell you he wants you to go and hobnob with him at your earliest convenience?'

'Yes, sir. Indeed, he insists on my taking up my residence at the Hall.'

'So as to be handy, in case you have a sudden inspiration?'

'No doubt that was in his lordship's mind, sir.'

'Was I invited?'

'No, sir.'

Well, I hadn't expected to be. Nevertheless, I was conscious of a pang.

'We part, then, for the nonce, do we?'

'I fear so, sir.'

'You taking the high road, and self taking the low road, as it were?'

'Yes, sir.'

'I shall miss you, Jeeves.'

'Thank you, sir.'

'Who was the chap who was always beefing about losing gazelles?'

'The poet Moore, sir. He complained that he had never nursed a dear gazelle, to glad him with its soft black eye, but when it came to know him well and love him, it was sure to die.'

'It's the same with me. I am a gazelle short. You don't mind me alluding to you as a gazelle, Jeeves?'

'Not at all, sir.'

'Well, that's that, then. I suppose I had better go and stay with Boko.'

'I was about to suggest it, sir. I am sure Mr Fittleworth will be most happy to accommodate you.'

'I think so. I hope so. Only recently, he was speaking about killing fatted calves. But to return to Uncle Percy and the old salt from America, have you any ideas on the subject of bringing them together?'

'Not at the moment, sir.'

'Well, bend the bean to it, because it's important. You remember me telling you that Boko and young Nobby were betrothed?'

'Yes, sir.'

'She can't marry without Uncle Percy's consent.'

'Indeed, sir?'

'Not till she's twenty-one. Legal stuff. And here's the nub, Jeeves. I haven't time to give you the full details now, but Boko, the silly ass, has been making a silly ass of himself, with the result that he has – what's the word that means making somebody froth at the mouth and chew pieces out of the carpet?'

'"Alienate", sir, is, I think, the verb for which you are groping.'

'That's it. Alienate. Well, as I say, I've no time to give you the inside story now, but Boko has played the goat and alienated Uncle Percy, and not a smell of a guardian's blessing is the latter prepared to give him. So you see what I mean about this meeting. It is vital that it takes place at the earliest possible date.'

'In order that his lordship may be brought to a more amiable frame of mind?'

'Exactly. If that merger comes off, the milk of human kindness will slosh about in him like the rising tide, swamping all animosity. Or don't you think so?'

'Undoubtedly, in my opinion, sir.'

'That's what I felt. And that is why you found me moody just now, Jeeves. I had just concluded an unpleasant interview with Uncle Percy, in the course of which he came out openly as not one of my admirers, thinking – incorrectly – that I had played an impressive part in the recent spot of arson.'

'He wronged you, sir?'

'Completely. I had nothing to do with it. I was a mere cipher in the affair. Edwin attended to the whole thing. But that was what he thought, and he blinded and stiffed with a will.'

'Unfortunate, sir.'

'Most. Of course, for the actual vote of censure that was passed I care little. A few poohs and a tush about cover that. Bertram Wooster is not a man who minds a few harsh words. He laughs lightly and snaps the fingers. It is wholly immaterial to me what the old bounder thinks of me, and in any case he didn't say a tithe of the things Aunt Agatha would have got off in similar circumstances. But the point is that I had promised Nobby that I would plead for her loved one, and what was saddening me when you came along was the thought that my potentialities in that direction had become greatly diminished. As far as Uncle Percy is concerned, I am not the force I was. So push that meeting along.'

'I will certainly use every endeavour, sir. I fully appreciate the situation.'

'Right. Now, what else have I to tell you? Oh, yes. Stilton.'

'Mr Cheesewright?'

'Police Constable Cheesewright, Jeeves. Stilton turns out to be the village bluebottle.'

He seemed surprised, and I didn't wonder. To him, of course, on the occasion when they had met at the flat, Stilton had been a mere, ordinary, tweed-suited popper-in. I mean, no uniform, no helmet and not a suggestion of any regulation boots.

'A policeman, sir?'

'Yes, and a nasty, vindictive policeman, too. With him, also, I have been having an unpleasant interview. He resents my presence here.'

'I suppose a great many young gentlemen enter the Force nowadays, sir.'

'I wish one fewer had. It is a tricky business falling foul of the constabulary, Jeeves.'

'Yes, sir.'

'I shall have to employ ceaseless vigilance, so as to give him no loophole for exercising his official powers. No drunken revels at the village pub.'

'No, sir.'

'One false step, and he'll swoop down on me like the – who was it who came down like a wolf on the fold?'

'The Assyrian, sir.'

'That's right. Well, that is what I have been through since I saw you last. First Stilton, then Edwin, then the fire, and finally Uncle Percy – all in about half an hour. It just shows what Steeple Bumpleigh can do, when it starts setting about you. And, oh my gosh, I was forgetting. You know the brooch?'

'Sir?'

'Aunt Agatha's brooch.'

'Oh, yes, sir.'

'I lost it. Oh, it's all right. I found it again. But what I mean is, picture my embarrassment. My heart stood still.'

'I can readily imagine it, sir. But you have it safely now?'

'Oh, rather,' I said, dipping a hand into the pocket. 'Or, rather,' I went on, bringing it out again with ashen face and bulging eyes. 'Oh, rather not. Jeeves,' I said, 'you will scarcely credit this, but the bally thing has gone again!'

It occasionally happens, and I have had to tell him off for doing so, that this man receives announcements that the young master's world is rocking about him with a mere 'Most disturbing, sir.' But now it was plain that he recognized that the thing was too big for that. I don't think he paled, and he certainly didn't say 'Golly!' or anything of that nature, but he came as near as he ever does to what they call in the movies 'the quick take 'um'. There was concern in his eyes, and if it hadn't been that his views are rigid in the matter of the correct etiquette between employee and employer, I have an idea that he would have patted me on the shoulder.

'This is a serious disaster, sir.'

'You are informing me, Jeeves!'

'Her ladyship will be vexed.'

'I can picture her screaming with annoyance.'

'Can you think where you could have dropped it, sir?'

'That's just what I'm trying to do. Wait, Jeeves,' I said, closing my eyes. 'Let me brood.'

I brooded.

'Oh, my gosh!'

'Sir?'

'I've got it.'

'The brooch, sir?'

'No, Jeeves, not the brooch. I mean I've reconstructed the scene and have now spotted where I must have parted company with it. Here's the sequence. The place caught fire, and I suddenly remembered I had left the small suitcase in the hall. I need scarcely remind you of its contents. My Sindbad the Sailor costume.'

'Ah, yes, sir.'

'Don't say "Ah, yes", Jeeves. Just keep on listening. I suddenly remembered, I repeat, that I had left the small suitcase in the hall. Well, you know me. To think is to act. I was inside, gathering it up, without a moment's delay. This involved stooping. This stooping must have caused the thing to fall out of my pocket.'

'Then it would still be in the hall, sir.'

'Yes. And take a look at the hall!'

We both took a look at it. I shook my head. He shook his. Wee Nooke was burning lower now, but its interior was still something which only Shadrach, Meshach and Abednego could have entered with any genuine enjoyment.

'No hope of getting it, if it's there.'

'No, sir.'

'Then what's to be done?'

'May I brood, sir?'

'Certainly, Jeeves.'

'Thank you, sir.'

He passed into the silence, and I filled in the time by thinking of what Aunt Agatha was going to say. I did not look forward to getting in touch with her. In fact, it almost seemed as if another of my quick trips to America would be rendered necessary. About the only advantage of having an aunt like her is that it makes one travel, thus broadening the mind and enabling one to see new faces.

And I was just saying to myself 'Young man, go West', when, happening to glance at the thinker, I observed that his face was wearing the brainy expression which always signifies that there is a hot one coming along.

'Yes, Jeeves?'

'I think I have hit on quite a simple solution of your difficulty, sir.'

'Let me have it, Jeeves, and speedily.'

'What I would suggest, sir, is that I take the car, drive to London, call at the emporium where her ladyship made her purchase and procure another brooch in place of the one that is missing.'

I weighed this. It sounded promising. Hope began to burgeon.

'You mean, put on an understudy?'

'Yes, sir.'

'Delivering it to addressee as the original?'

'Precisely, sir.'

I went on weighing. And the more I did so, the fruitier the idea seemed.

'Yes, I see what you mean. The mechanism is much the same as that which you employed in the case of Aunt Agatha's dog McIntosh.'

'Not dissimilar, sir.'

'There we were in the position of being minus an Aberdeen terrier, when we should have been plus an Aberdeen terrier. You reasoned correctly that all members of this particular canine family look very much alike, and rang in a ringer with complete success.'

'Yes, sir.'

'Would the same system work with brooches?'

'I think so, sir.'

'Is one brooch just like another brooch?'

'Not invariably, sir. But a few words of inquiry will enable me to obtain a description of the lost trinket and to ascertain the price which her ladyship paid for it. I shall thus be enabled to return with something virtually indistinguishable from the original.'

I was convinced. It was as if a heavy weight had been removed from my soul. I have mentioned that a short while back he had seemed to be thinking of patting me on the shoulder. It was now all I could do to restrain myself from patting him on his.

'A winner, Jeeves!'

'Thank you, sir.'

'*Rem* – what is it again?'

'*Acu tetigisti*, sir.'

'I might have known that you would find the way.'

'I am gratified to feel that I enjoy your confidence, sir.'

'I have an account at Aspinall's, so you can tell them to chalk it up on the slate.'

'Very good, sir.'

'Buzz off instanter.'

'There is ample time, sir. I shall be able to reach London long before the establishment closes for the day. Before proceeding thither, I think it would be best for me to stop at Mr Fittleworth's residence, apprise him of what has occurred, deposit the luggage and warn him of your coming.'

'Is "warn" the word?'

'"Inform" I should have said, sir.'

'Well, don't cut it too fine. The sands are running out, remember. That brooch must be in recipient's hands tonight. What one aims at is to have it lying alongside her plate at the dinner-table.'

'I shall undoubtedly be able to reach Steeple Bumpleigh on my return journey at about the dinner hour, sir.'

'Right ho, Jeeves. I know I can rely on you to run to time. First stop, Boko's, then. I, meanwhile, will be nosing round here. There is just a chance that I may have dropped the thing somewhere in the open. I can't remember exactly how the sight of that fire affected me, but I have no doubt that I sprang up and down a bit – quite nimbly enough to jerk packages out of pockets.'

Of course, I didn't think so, really. My original theory that I had become unbrooched while picking up the suitcase persisted. But on these occasions the instinct is to turn every stone and leave no avenue unexplored.

I nosed round, accordingly, scanning the turf and even going so far as to feel about in the rockery. As I had forseen, no dice. It wasn't long before I gave it up and started to stroll along to Boko's. And I had just reached his gate, when there was a ting of a bicycle bell – I noted as a curious phenomenon that the denizens of Steeple Bumpleigh seemed to do practically nothing but ride about on bicycles, tinging bells – and I saw Nobby approaching.

I hastened to meet her, for she was just the girl I wanted to get in touch with. I was anxious to thresh out with her the whole topic of Stilton and his love life.

12

She dismounted with lissom grace, beaming welcomingly. Since I had last seen her, she had washed off the stains of travel and changed her frock and was looking spruce and dapper. Why she should have bothered to smarten herself up, when she was only going to meet a bird in patched grey flannel trousers and a turtle-neck sweater, I was at a loss to understand, but girls will, of course, be girls.

'Hullo, Bertie,' she said. 'Are you paying a neighbourly call on Boko?'

I replied that that was about what it amounted to, but added that first I required a few moments of her valuable time.

'Listen, Nobby,' I said.

She didn't, of course. I've never met a girl yet who did. Say 'Listen' to any member of the delicately nurtured sex, and she takes it as a cue to start talking herself. However, as the subject she introduced proved to be the very one I had been planning to ventilate, the desire to beat her brains out with a brick was not so pronounced as it would otherwise have been.

'What have you been doing to inflame Stilton, Bertie? I met him just now and asked if he had seen you, and he turned vermilion and gnashed every tooth in his head. I don't think I've ever seen a more incandescent copper.'

'He didn't explain?'

'No. He simply pedalled on furiously, as if he had been competing in a six-day bicycle race and had just realized he was dropping behind the leaders. What was the trouble?'

I tapped her on the arm with a grave forefinger.

'Nobby,' I said, 'there has been a bit of a mix-up. What's that word that begins with "con"?'

'Con?'

'I've heard Jeeves use it. There's a cat in it somewhere.'

'What on earth are you drivelling about?'

'Concatenation,' I said, getting it. 'Owing to an unfortunate con-catenation of circumstances, Stilton is viewing me with concern. He has got the idea rooted in his bean that I've come down here to try to steal Florence from him.'

'Have you?'

'My dear young blister,' I said, with some impatience, 'would anybody want to steal Florence? Do use your intelligence. But, as I say, this unfortunate concatenation has led him to suspect the worst.'

And in a few simple words I gave her the run of the scenario, featuring the Young Lochinvar aspect of the matter. When I had finished, she made one of those foolish remarks which do so much to confirm a man in his conviction that women as a sex should be suppressed.

'You should have told him you were guiltless of the charge.'

I tut-tutted impatiently.

'I did tell him I was guiltless of the charge, and a fat lot he believed me. He continued to hot up, finally reaching a condition of so much Fahrenheit that I was surprised he didn't run me in on the spot. In which connexion, you might have told me he was a cop.'

'I forgot to.'

'It would have spared me a very disconcerting shock. When I heard someone calling my name and looked round and saw him cycling towards me in the complete rig-out of a rural policeman, I nearly got the vapours.'

She laughed – a solo effort. Nothing in the prevailing circumstances made me feel like turning it into a duet.

'Poor old Stilton!'

'Yes, that's all very well, but – '

'I think it's rather sporting of him, wanting to earn his living, instead of sitting on the knee of that uncle of his and helping himself out of his pockets.'

'I dare say, but – '

'Florence doesn't. And it's rather funny, because it was she who turned his thoughts in that direction. She talked Socialism to him, and made him read Karl Marx. He's very impressionable.'

I agreed with her there. I had never forgotten the time at Oxford when somebody temporarily converted him to Buddhism. It led to a lot of unpleasantness with the authorities, I recall, he immediately starting to cut chapels and go and meditate beneath the nearest thing the neighbourhood could provide to a bo tree.

'She's furious now, and says he was a fool to take her literally.'

She paused, in order to laugh again, and I seized the opportunity to get a word in edgeways.

'Exactly. As you state, she is furious. And that's just the aspect of the matter that I want to discuss. I could put up with a green-eyed Stilton, a Stilton who turns vermilion and gnashes the molars at the mention of my name. I don't say it could ever be pleasant, going about knowing that the Force was gnashing its teeth at you, but one learns to take the rough with the smooth. The real trouble is that I believe Florence is weakening on him.'

'What makes you think that?'

'She's just been talking to me about him. She used the expression "pigheaded", and said she was sick and tired of the whole thing and really didn't know what she was going to do about it. Her whole attitude seemed to me that of a girl on the very verge of giving her heart-throb the raspberry and returning the ring and presents. You spot the frightful menace?'

'You mean that if she breaks it off with Stilton, she may consider taking you on again?'

'That's what I mean. The peril is appalling. Owing to another unfortunate concatenation of circumstances, my stock has recently gone up with her to a fearful extent, and anything may happen at any moment.'

And I briefly outlined the *Spindrift*-Spinoza affair. When I had concluded, a meditative look came into her face.

'Do you know, Bertie,' she said, 'I've often thought that, of all the multitude Florence has been engaged to, you were the one she really wanted?'

'Oh, my gosh!'

'It's your fault for being so fascinating.'

'I dare say, but too late to do anything about that now.'

'Still, I don't see what you've got to worry about. If she proposes to you, just blush a little and smile tremulously and say "I'm sorry – so, so sorry. You have paid me the greatest compliment a woman can pay a man. But it cannot be. So shall we be pals – just real pals?" That'll fix her.'

'It won't do anything of the sort. You know what Florence is like. Propose, forsooth! She'll just notify me that the engagement is on again, like a governess telling a young charge to eat his spinach. And if you think I've got the force of character to come back with a *nolle prosequi* – '

'With a what?'

'One of Jeeves's gags. It means roughly "Nuts to you!" If, I say, you think I'm capable of asserting myself and giving her the bird, you greatly overestimate the Wooster fortitude. She must be reconciled to Stilton. It is the only way. Listen, Nobby. I wrote you a letter yesterday, giving my views on Florence and urging you to employ every means in your power to open Stilton's eyes to what he was in for. Have you read it?'

'Every syllable. It gripped me tremendously. I never knew you had such a vivid prose style. It reminded me of Ernest Hemingway. You don't by any chance write under the name of Ernest Hemingway, do you?'

I shook the head.

'No. The only thing I've ever written was an article for *Milady's Boudoir* on What The Well-Dressed Man Is Wearing. It appeared under my own name. But what I want to say is, pay no attention to that letter. I am now wholeheartedly in favour of the match. The wish to save Stilton has left me. The chap I have my eye on for saving purposes is B. Wooster. When chatting with Florence, therefore, boost Stilton in every possible way. Make her see what a prize she has got. And if you have any influence with him, endeavour to persuade him to chuck all this policeman nonsense and stand for Parliament, as she wants him to.'

'I'd love to see Stilton in Parliament.'

'So would I, if it means healing this rift.'

'Wouldn't he be a scream!'

'Not necessarily. There are bigger fatheads than Stilton among our legislators – dozens of them. They would probably shove him in the Cabinet. So push it along, young Nobby.'

'I'll do what I can. But Stilton isn't the easiest person to persuade, once the trend of his mind has set in any direction. You remember the deaf adder?'

'What deaf adder?'

'The one that stopped its ear, and would not listen to the voice of the charmers, charming never so wisely. That's Stilton. However, as I say, I'll do what I can. And now let's go and rout Boko out. I'm dying to hear what happened at that lunch of his.'

'You haven't seen Uncle Percy, then?'

'Not yet. He was out. Why?'

'Oh, nothing. I was only thinking that, if you had, you would have got an eye-witness's report from him,' I said, and was conscious of a pang of pity for my old friend and a hope that by this time he would have succeeded in thinking up a reasonably good story to cover the binge in question.

The sound of a typewriter greeted us as we crossed the threshold, indicating that Boko was still at work on that letter to Uncle Percy. It ceased abruptly as Nobby yoo-hooed, and when we passed on into the sitting-room, he was hastily dropping a sheet of paper into the basket.

'Oh, hullo darling,' he said brightly. Watching him bound from his chair and fold Nobby in a close embrace, the casual observer would have supposed him to have had nothing on his mind except the hair which he had apparently not brushed for days. 'I was just roughing out a *morceau*.'

'Oh, angel, have we interrupted the flow?'

'Not at all, not a-tall.'

'I was so anxious to hear how the lunch went off.'

'Of course, of course. I'll tell you all about it. By the way, Bertie, Jeeves delivered your effects. They are in the spare room. Delighted to put you up, of course. Too bad about that fire.'

'What fire?' asked Nobby.

'Jeeves tells me that Edwin has succeeded in burning Wee Nooke to the ground. Correct, Bertie?'

'Quite correct. It was his last Friday's act of kindness.'

'What a shame!' said Nobby, with a womanly sympathy that well became her.

Boko, however, looked on the bright side.

'Personally,' he said, 'I consider that Bertie has got off lightly. He appears not to have been even singed. A burned house is a mere bagatelle. Generally, when Edwin is trying to catch up with his acts of kindness, human life is imperilled. The mind flits back to the time when he mended my egg boiler. Occasionally, when I am much occupied with a job of work, sparing no effort to give my public of my best, I rise early, before my housekeeper turns up in the morning. On these occasions, it is my practice to boil myself a refreshing egg, using one of those patent machines for the purpose. You know the sort of thing I mean. It rings an alarm, hopes you've slept well, pours water on the coffee, lights a flame underneath and gets action on the egg. Well, the day after Edwin had fixed some trifling flaw in the apparatus, the egg was scarcely in position when it flew at me like a bullet, catching me on the tip of the nose and knocking me base over apex. I bled for hours. So I maintain that if you got off with a mere fire that destroyed your house, you are sitting pretty.'

Nobby speculated as to the chances of somebody some day murdering Edwin, and we agreed that the hour must eventually produce the man.

'And now,' said Boko, still with that strange brightness which, knowing the facts, I could not but admire, 'you will want to hear all about the lunch. Well, it was a great success.'

'Darling!'

'Yes, a notable success. I think I have made an excellent start.'

'Were you bright?'

'Very bright.'

'And genial?'

'The word understates it.'

'Angel!' said Nobby, and kissed him about fifteen times in rapid succession.

'Yes,' said Boko, 'I think I have got him on the run. It is difficult to tell with a man like that, who conceals his emotions behind a poker face, but I believe he's weakening. And we never expected him to fall on my neck right away, did we? It was agreed that the lunch was merely to prepare the soil.'

'What did you talk about?'

'Oh, this and that. The subject of spiders, I remember, was one that came up.'

'Spiders?'

'He seemed interested in spiders.'

'I never knew that.'

'Just a side of his character which he hasn't happened to reveal to you, I suppose. And then, of course, after talking of this and that, we talked of that and this.'

'There weren't any awkward pauses?'

'I didn't notice any. No, he rather prattled on, as it were, especially towards the end.'

'Did you tell him what a lot of money you were making?'

'Oh, yes, I touched on that.'

'I hope you explained that you were a steady young fellow and were bound to go on making it? That's what worries him. He thinks you may blow up at any moment.'

'Like Wee Nooke.'

'You see, when he was a young man, just starting in the shipping business, Uncle Percy used to go about with rather a rackety set in London, and he knew a lot of writers who made quite a bit from time to time and spent it all in a couple of days and then had to live on what they could borrow. My darling father was one of them.'

This was news to me. I had never pictured Uncle Percy as a bird who had gone about with rackety sets as a young man. In fact, I had never pictured him as ever having been a young man at all. It's always the way. If an old buster has a bristling moustache, a solid, lucrative business and the manners of a bear aroused while hibernating, you do not probe into his past and ask yourself whether he, too, in his day may not have been one of the boys.

'I covered that point,' said Boko. 'It was one of the first I stressed. The modern author, I told him, is keen and hard-headed. He is out for the stuff, and when he gets it he salts it away.'

'That ought to have pleased him.'

'Oh, it did.'

'Then everything's fine.'

'Splendid.'

'All we need now is for Bertie to do his act.'

'Exactly. The future hinges on Bertie.'

'When he pleads – '

'Ah, I didn't mean quite that. I'm afraid you are not abreast of the quick rush and swirl of recent events. I doubt if it would be any good for Bertie to plead now. His name has become mud.'

'Mud?'

'"Mud", I think, is the *mot juste*, Bertie?'

I was obliged to concede that this was more or less so.

'Uncle Percy,' I explained, 'has got it into his head that I aided and encouraged Edwin in his fire-bug activities. This has put me back in the betting a good bit, considered as a pleader. I should find it difficult now to sway him like a reed.'

'Then where are we?' said Nobby, registering anguish.

Boko patted her encouragingly on the shoulder.

'We're all right. Don't you worry.'

'But if Bertie can't plead – '

'Ah, but you're forgetting how versatile he is. What you are over-looking is the scullery-window-breaking side of his nature. That is what is going to see us through. Brooding tensely over this business, I have had an idea, and it is a pippin. Suppose, I said to myself, I were to save the heavy's home from being looted by a midnight marauder, that would make him feel I had the right stuff in me, I fancy. He would say "Egad! A fine young fellow, this Fittleworth!" would he not?'

'I suppose so.'

'You speak doubtfully.'

'I was only thinking that there isn't much chance of that happening. There hasn't been a burglary in Steeple Bumpleigh for centuries. Stilton was complaining about it only the other day. He said the place gave an ambitious young copper no scope.'

'These things can be arranged.'

'How do you mean?'

'It only needs a little organization. There is going to be a burglary in Steeple Bumpleigh this very night. Bertie will attend to it.'

There was only one comment to make on this, and I made it.

'Hey!' I cried.

'Don't interrupt, Bertie,' said Boko reprovingly. 'It prevents one marshalling one's thoughts. Here in a nutshell is the scheme I have evolved. Somewhere in the small hours, Bertie and I make our way to the Hall. We approach the scullery window. He busts it. I raise the alarm. He pops off – '

'Ah!' I said. It was the first point he had mentioned of which I found myself approving.

' – while I stay on, to accept the plaudits of all and be fawned on. I don't see how it can fail. The one thing a sturdy householder of the Worplesdon type dislikes is having the house he is holding broken into, and anyone who nips such a venture in the bud creeps straight into his heart. Before the night is out, I expect to have him promising to dance at our wedding.'

'Darling! It's wonderful!'

It was Nobby who said that, not me. I was still chewing the lower lip in open concern. I should have remembered, I was telling myself, that that play of Boko's, to which I alluded earlier, had been one of those mystery thrillers, and that it was only natural that some such set-up as this should have occurred to his diseased mind.

I mean to say, you get a chap whose thoughts run persistently in the direction of screams in the night and lights going out and mysterious hands appearing through the wall and people rushing about shouting 'Here comes The Shadow!' and it is inevitable that that will be the sort of stuff he will dish out in an emergency. I resolved there and then that I would put in a firm *nolle prosequi*. Nobody is more anxious than Bertram Wooster to lend a helping hand to Love's young dream, but there are limits to what he is prepared to sign on for, and sharply defined limits, at that.

Nobby's joyous animation had died away a bit. Like me, she was chewing the lip.

'Yes, it's wonderful. But – '

'I don't like to hear that word "but".'

'I was only going to say, how do you explain?'

'Explain?'

'Your being there to raise alarms and be fawned on.'

'Perfectly simple. My love for you is the talk of Steeple Bumpleigh. What more natural than that I should have come to stand beneath your window, gazing up at it?'

'I see! And then you heard a noise – '

'A curious noise that sounded like the splintering of glass. And I popped round the house to investigate, and there was a bounder smashing the scullery window.'

'Of course!'

'I knew you would see it.'

'Then everything depends on Bertie.'

'Everything.'

'You don't think he'll object?'

'I wish you wouldn't say things like that. You'll hurt his feelings. You don't realize the sort of fellow Bertie is. His nerve is like chilled steel, and when it is a question of helping a pal, he sticks at nothing.'

Nobby drew a deep breath.

'He's wonderful, isn't he?'

'He stands alone.'

'I've always been devoted to Bertie. When I was a child, he once gave me threepennyworth of acid drops.'

'Generous to a fault. These splendid fellows always are.'

'How I admired him!'

'Me, too. I don't know a man I admire more.'

'Doesn't he remind you rather of Sir Galahad?'

'The name was on the tip of my tongue.'

'Of course, he wouldn't dream of not doing his bit.'

'Of course not. All settled, eh, Bertie?'

It's odd what a few kind words will do. Until now, I had, as I say, been all ready with the *nolle prosequi*, and had indeed opened my lips to shoot it across with all the emphasis at my disposal. But as I caught Nobby's eye, fixed on me in a devout sort of way, and at the same time was conscious of Boko shaking my hand and kneading my shoulder, something seemed to check me. I mean, there really didn't seem to be any way of *nolle prosequi*-ing without spoiling the spirit of the party.

'Oh, rather,' I said. 'Absolutely.'

But not blithely. Not with any real chirpiness.

13

No, not with any real chirpiness. And this shortage of c., I must confess, continued to make its presence felt right up to zero hour. All through the quiet evenfall, the frugal dinner and the long, weary waiting for midnight to strike on the village clock, I was conscious of a growing concern. And when the moment arrived and Boko and self passed through the silent gardens of Bumpleigh Hall on our way to start the doings, it was going stronger than ever.

Boko was in gay and effervescent mood, speaking from time to time in a low but enthusiastic voice of the beauties of Nature and drawing my attention in a cautious whisper to the agreeable niffiness of the flowers past which we flitted, but it was far different with Bertram. Bertram, and I do not attempt to conceal it, was not at his fizziest. His spine crawled, and his heart was bowed down with weight of woe. The word of a Wooster was pledged; I had placed my services at the disposal of the young couple and there was no question of my doing a quick sneak and edging out of the enterprise, but nothing was going to make me like it.

I think I have mentioned before my dislike for creeping about strange gardens in the dark. Too many painful episodes in my past have been connected with other people's gardens, notably the time when circumstances compelled me to slide out in the small hours and ring the fire bell at Brinkley Court and that other occasion when Roberta Wickham induced me against my better judgement to climb a tree and drop a flower pot through the roof of a green-house, in order to create a diversion which would enable her cousin Clementina, who was A.W.O.L. from her school, to ooze back into it unobserved.

Of all these experiences, the last named had been, to date, the most soul searing, because it had culminated in the sudden appearance of a policeman saying 'What's all this?' And it was the thought that there might quite possibly be a repetition of this routine, and the realization that if a policeman did come muscling in now it would be Stilton, that curdled the blood and made me feel a dry, fluttering feeling in the pit of the stomach, as if I had swallowed a heaping tablespoonful of butterflies.

So pronounced was this sensation that I found myself clutching Boko's arm in ill-concealed panic and drawing him beneath a passing tree.

'Boko,' I gurgled, 'what about Stilton? Have you considered the Stilton angle?'

'Eh?'

'Suppose he's on duty at night? Suppose he's prowling? Suppose he suddenly pops out at us, complete with whistle and notebook?'

'Nonsense.'

'It would be an awful thing to be pinched by a chap you were boys together with. And he would spring to the task. He's got it in for me.'

'Nonsense, nonsense,' said Boko, continuing debonair to the gills. 'You mustn't allow your thoughts to take this morbid trend, Bertie. These tremors are unworthy of you. Don't you worry about Stilton. You have only to look at him – that clear eye, those rosy cheeks – to know that he is a man who makes a point of getting his regular eight hours. Early to bed and early to rise, is his slogan. Stilton is tucked up between the sheets, sleeping like a little child, and won't start functioning again till his alarm clock explodes at seven-thirty.'

Well, that was all right, as far as it went. His reasoning was specious, and did much to reassure me. Stilton's cheeks unquestionably were rosy. But it was only for a moment that I was strengthened. After all, I reflected, Stilton was merely a part of the menace. Even leaving him out of it, there was the Uncle Percy-Aunt Agatha side of the business. You couldn't get away from it that these gardens and messuages whose privacy we were violating belonged to the former, and that the latter had a joint interest in them. I might, that is to say, be safe from the dragon, but what about the hippogriffs? That was the question I asked myself. What price the hippogriffs?

If anything were to go wrong, if this frightful binge on which I had embarked were in the slightest detail to slip a cog, what would be the upshot? I'll tell you what would jolly well be the upshot. Not only should I be placed in the position of having to explain to a slavering uncle, justly incensed at being deprived of his beauty sleep, why I was going about the place breaking his scullery windows, but the whole story would be told to Aunt Agatha on her return with a wealth of detail, and then what?

Far less serious offences on my part in the past had brought the old relative leaping after me with her hatchet, like a Red Indian on the warpath, howling for my blood.

I mentioned this to Boko as we fetched up at journey's end, and he patted me on the shoulder. Well meant, no doubt, and a kindly gesture, but one that accomplished little or nothing in the way of stiffening my morale.

'If you're copped,' said Boko, 'just pass it off.'

'Pass it off?'

'That's right. Nonchalantly. Got the treacle?'

I said I had got the treacle.

'And the paper?'

'Yes.'

'Then I'll take a stroll for ten minutes. That will give you eight minutes to screw your courage to the sticking-point, one minute to break window and one to make getaway.'

This treacle idea was Boko's. He had insisted upon it as an indispensable adjunct to the proceedings, claiming that it would lend the professional touch at which we were aiming. According to him, and he is a chap who has studied these things, the knowledgeable burglar's first act is to equip himself with treacle and brown paper. He glues the latter to the window by means of the former, and then hauls off and busts the glass with a sharp buffet of the fist.

What a way to earn a living! I suppose I must have used up quite three minutes of my ten in meditating on these hardy fellows and wondering what made them go in for such an exacting life work. Large profits, no doubt, and virtually no overhead, but think what they must have to spend on nerve specialists and rest cures. Some sort of tonic alone must form a heavy item of a burglar's expenses.

I could have gone on for quite a while musing along these lines, but was obliged to dismiss the subject from my mind, for time was passing and I might expect Boko's return at any minute. And I shrank from the prospect of having to explain to him that I had been frittering away in day-dreaming the moments which should have been earmarked for action.

Feeling, therefore, that if the thing was to be smacked into, 'twere well 'twere smacked into quickly, as Shakespeare says, I treacled the paper and attached it to the window. All that now remained to be done was to deliver the sharp buffet. And it was at this point that I suddenly came over all cat-in-the-adage-y. The chilliness of the feet became intensified, and I began to hover, as Stilton had done outside that jeweller's shop.

I had thought, while watching him on that occasion, that he

had accomplished what you might call the last word in backing and filling, but I now realized that he had merely scratched the surface. Compared with mine at this juncture, Stilton's hovering could scarcely be termed at all. I moved towards my objective and away from my objective, and some of the time I moved sideways. To an observer, had one been present, it might have seemed that I was trying out the intricate steps of some rhythmic dance.

Finally, however, stiffening the sinews and summoning up all the splendid Wooster courage, I made a quick forward movement and was in the act of raising my fist, when it was as if a stick of dynamite had been touched off beneath me. The hair rose in a solid mass, and every nerve in the body stood straight up, curling at the ends. There have been moments in his career, many of them, when Bertram Wooster has not felt at his ease, but this one was the top.

From somewhere above, a voice had spoken.

'Coo!' it said. 'Who's there?'

If it hadn't been for that 'Coo!' I might have supposed it the voice of Conscience. As it was, I was enabled to ticket it correctly as that of young blasted Edwin. Glued against the wall, as if I had been a bit of treacled paper, I could just see him leaning out of an adjacent window. And when I reflected that, after all I had gone through, I was now being set upon by Boy Scouts, I don't mind admitting that the iron entered into my soul. Very bitter, the whole thing.

After he had said 'Who's there?' he was silent for a space, as if pausing for a reply, though you would have thought even a cloth-headed kid like that would have known that it's hopeless to expect burglars to keep the conversation going.

'Who's that?' he said, at length.

I maintained a prudent reserve. He then said 'I can see you all right,' but in an uncertain voice which told me he was lying in his teeth. The one thing that was serving to buoy me up and still the fluttering heart-strings at this most unpleasant moment was the fact that it was a dark night, without a moon or any rot of that sort. Stars, yes. Moon, no. A lynx might have seen me, but only a lynx, and it would have had to be a pretty sharp-sighted lynx, at that.

My silence seemed to discourage him. These one-sided conversations always flag fairly quickly. He brooded over the scene a bit longer – Jeeves would have spotted a resemblance to the Blessed Damozel gazing out from the gold bar of heaven – then drew his head in, and I was alone at last.

Not, however, for long. A moment later, Boko hove alongside.

'All set?' he asked, in a hearty voice that seemed to boom

through the garden like a costermonger calling attention to his brussels sprouts, and I grabbed him feverishly, begging him to pipe down a bit.

'Not so loud!'

'What's the matter?'

'Edwin.'

'Edwin?'

'He just poked his foul head out of a window and wanted to know who was there.'

'Did you tell him?'

'No.'

'Excellent. Very wise move. He's probably gone to sleep again.'

'Boy Scouts never sleep.'

'Of course they do. In droves. Have you smashed the window?'

'No.'

'Why not?'

'Because of Edwin.'

He clicked his tongue, causing me to quiver from stem to stern. To me, a little nervous at the moment, as I have shown, it sounded like a mass meeting of Spanish dancers playing the castanets.

'You mustn't let yourself be diverted from the task in hand by trifles, Bertie. I can't help wondering if you're taking this thing with the proper seriousness. I may be wrong, but there seems to me something frivolous in your attitude. Do pull yourself together and try to remember what this means to Nobby and me.'

'But I can't smash windows, with Edwin lurking above.'

'Of course you can. I can't see your difficulty. Pay no attention whatever to Edwin. If he is on the alert, so much the better. It will all help when the moment comes for me to put on my act. His story will support mine. I'll give you another ten minutes, and then I really must insist on a little action. Got a cigarette?'

'No.'

'Then I shall simply have to go on smoking mine. That's what it amounts to,' said Boko, and breezed off.

Now, reading the above splash of dialogue, you will have noticed something. I don't know if you happen to know the meaning of the French expression *sang-froid*, but, if you do, you can scarcely have failed to observe to what an extraordinary extent the recent Fittleworth had been exhibiting this quality. While I trembled and twittered, he remained as cool and calm as a turbot on ice, and it now occurred to me that the reason for this might very possibly be that he was keeping on the move.

It helps on these occasions to be able to circulate freely instead of standing on point duty outside the scullery windows, and it was quite on the cards, I felt, that a short stroll might do something towards keying up my sagging nervous system. With this end in view, I wandered off round the house.

Any hope I may have entertained, however, that the vibrating ganglions would cease to quiver and the fluttering feeling in the pit of the stomach simmer down was shattered before I had gone a dozen yards. A dim figure suddenly loomed up before me in the darkness, causing me to leap perhaps five feet in the air and utter a sharp yip.

My composure was somewhat restored – not altogether, but somewhat – when the dim f. spoke, and I recognized Jeeves's voice.

14

'Good evening, sir,' he said.

'Good evening, Jeeves,' I responded.

'You gave me quite a start, sir.'

'Nothing to the one you gave me. I thought the top of my head had come off.'

'I am sorry to have been the cause of you experiencing any discomfort, sir. I was unable to herald my approach, the encounter being quite unforeseen. You are up late, sir.'

'Yes.'

'One could scarcely desire more delightful conditions for a nocturnal ramble.'

'That is your view, is it?'

'It is indeed, sir. I always feel that nothing is so soothing as a walk in a garden at night.'

'Ha!'

'The cool air. The scent of growing things. That is tobacco plant which you can smell, sir.'

'Is it?'

'The stars, sir.'

'Stars?'

'Yes sir.'

'What about them?'

'I was merely directing your attention to them, sir. Look how the floor of heaven is thick inlaid with patines of bright gold.'

'Jeeves – '

'There's not the smallest orb which thou beholdest, sir, but in his motion like an angel sings, still quiring to the young-eyed cherubims.'

'Jeeves – '

'Such harmony is in immortal souls. But whilst this muddy vesture of decay doth grossly close it in, we cannot hear it.'

'Jeeves – '

'Sir?'

'You couldn't possibly switch it off, could you?'

'Certainly, sir, if you wish it.'

'I'm not in the mood.'

'Very good, sir.'

'You know how one isn't, sometimes.'

'Yes, sir. I quite understand. I procured the brooch, sir.'

'Brooch?'

'The one which you wished me to purchase in place of the trinket lost in the fire, sir. Lady Florence's birthday present.'

'Oh, ah.' It will give you some rough indication of how what he had called this nocturnal ramble of mine had affected me, when I say that I had completely forgotten about the damn' thing. 'You got it, eh?'

'Yes, sir.'

'And handed it in?'

'Yes, sir.'

'Good. That's off my mind, then. And, believe me, Jeeves, the more I can get off my mind at this juncture, the better I shall like it, because it's already loaded down well above the Plimsoll mark.'

'I am sorry to hear that, sir.'

'Do you know why I'm prowling about this garden?'

'I was hoping that you might enlighten me, sir.'

'I will. This is no careless saunter on which you find me engaged, Jeeves, but an enterprise whose consequences may well stagger humanity.'

He listened attentively while I sketched out the events which had led up to the tragedy, interrupting only with a respectful intake of the breath as I spoke of Uncle Percy, Boko and the Joke Goods. It was plain that my story had gripped him.

'An eccentric young gentleman, Mr Fittleworth, sir,' was his comment, as I concluded.

'Loony to the eyebrows,' I agreed.

'The scheme which he had formulated is not, however, without its ingenuity. His lordship would undoubtedly be most grateful to anyone whom he supposed to have foiled a raid on the premises on this particular night. I happen to be aware that, despite her ladyship's repeated instructions to him to attend to the matter, he forgot to post the letter renewing his burglary insurance.'

'How do you know that?'

'I had the facts from his lordship in person, sir. Ascertaining that I was about to drive to London this afternoon, he gave me the communication to dispatch in the metropolitan area, so that it should reach its destination tomorrow morning by the first delivery. His emotion, as he urged me not to fail him and alluded to what her ladyship would say if she ever discovered his negligence, was very noticeable. He shook visibly.'

I was amazed.

'You don't mean he's scared of Aunt Agatha?'

'Intensely, sir.'

'A tough bird like him? Practically a bucko mate of a tramp steamer?'

'Even bucko mates stand in awe of the captains of their vessels, sir.'

'Well, you absolutely astound me. I should have thought that if ever there was a bimbo who was master in his own home, that bimbo was Percival, Lord Worplesdon.'

'I am inclined to doubt whether the gentleman exists who could be master in a home that contained her ladyship, sir.'

'Perhaps you're right.'

'Yes, sir.'

I breathed deeply. For the first time since Boko had outlined the night's programme, I was conscious of a relaxation of the strain. It would be paltering with the truth to say that even now Bertram Wooster looked forward with any actual relish to busting that scullery window, but it was stimulating to feel that the action was likely to produce solid results.

'Then you think this scheme of Boko's will drag home the gravy?'

'Quite conceivably, sir.'

'That's a comfort.'

'On the other hand – '

'Oh, golly, Jeeves. What's wrong now?'

'I was merely about to say that Mr Fittleworth has selected a somewhat unfortunate moment for his enterprise, sir. It tends to clash with his lordship's arrangements.'

'How do you mean?'

'By an unfortunate coincidence, his lordship will in a few moments from now be proceeding to the potting shed to confer with Mr Chichester Clam.'

'Chichester Clam?'

'Yes, sir.'

I shook the head.

'I think the strain to which I have been subject must have affected my hearing. You sound to me just as if you were saying Chichester Clam.'

'Yes, sir. Mr J. Chichester Clam, managing director of the Clam Line.'

'What on earth's a clam line?'

'The shipping line, sir, which, if you remember is on the eve of being merged with his lordship's Pink Funnel.'

I got it at last.

'You mean the chap Uncle Percy is trying to get together with? The ancient mariner from America?'

'Precisely, sir. Owing to the conflagration at Wee Nooke, it became necessary to think of some other spot where the two gentlemen could meet and discuss their business without fear of interruption.'

'And you chose the potting shed?'

'Yes, sir.'

'God bless you, Jeeves.'

'Thank you, sir.'

'Is this bird in the potting shed now?'

'I should be disposed to imagine so, sir. When I motored to London this afternoon, it was with instructions for his lordship to establish telephonic communication with Mr Clam at his hotel and urge him to hasten to Steeple Bumpleigh and be in the potting shed half an hour after midnight. The gentleman expressed complete understanding and agreement, and assured me that he would drive down in good time to keep the appointment.'

I could not repress a pang of gentle pity for this hand across the sea. Born and brought up in America, he would, of course, not have the slightest idea of the sort of place Steeple Bumpleigh was and what he was letting himself in for in going there. I couldn't, offhand, say what Steeple Bumpleigh was saving up for Chichester Clam, but obviously he was headed for a sticky evening.

I saw, too, what Jeeves meant about Boko having selected an unfortunate moment for his enterprise.

'Half an hour after midnight? It must be nearly that now.'

'Exactly that, sir.'

'Then Uncle Percy will be manifesting himself at any moment.'

'If I am not mistaken, sir, this would be his lordship whom you can hear approaching.'

And, sure enough, from somewhere to the nor'-nor'-east there came the sound of some solid object shuffling through the night.

I inhaled in quick concern.

'Egad, Jeeves!'

'Sir?'

' 'Tis he!'

'Yes, sir.'

I mused a moment.

'Well,' I said, though not liking the prospect and wishing that the civility could have been avoided, 'I suppose I'd better pass the time of day. What ho,' I continued, as he came abreast. 'What ho, what ho!'

I must say the results were not unpleasing – to a man, I mean, who, like myself, had twice tonight been forced to skip like the hills on finding himself unexpectedly addressed from the shadows. Watching the relative soar skywards with a wordless squeak, obviously startled out of a year's growth, I was conscious of a distinct sensation of getting a bit of my own back. I felt that, whatever might befall, I was at least that much to the good.

In introducing this uncle by marriage, I showed him to be a man who, in moments of keen emotion, had a tendency to say 'What?' and keep on saying it. He did so now.

'What? What? What? What? What?' he ejaculated, making five in all. 'What?' he added, bringing it up to the round half dozen.

'Lovely evening, Uncle Percy,' I said, hoping by the exercise of suavity to keep the conversation on an amicable plane. 'Jeeves and I were just talking about the stars. What was it you said about the stars, Jeeves?'

'I alluded to the fact that there was not the smallest orb which did not sing in its motion like an angel, still quiring to the young-eyed cherubims, sir.'

'That's right. Worth knowing, that, eh, Uncle Percy?'

During these exchanges, the relative had been going on saying 'What?' in a sort of strangled voice, as if still finding it a bit hard to cope with the pressure of events. He now came forward and peered at me, feasting the eyes as far as was possible in the uncertain light.

'You!' he said, with a kind of gasp, like some strong swimmer in his agony. 'What the devil are you doing here?'

'Just sauntering.'

'Then go and saunter somewhere else, damn it.'

The Woosters are quick to take a hint, and are generally able to spot when our presence is not desired. Reading between the lines, I could see that he was wishing me elsewhere.

'Right ho, Uncle Percy,' I said, still maintaining the old suavity, and was about to withdraw, when another of those voices which seemed to be so common in these parts spoke in my immediate rear, causing me to equal, if not to improve upon, the old relative's recent standing high jump.

'What's all this?' it said, and with what is sometimes called a sickening qualm I perceived that it was Stilton who had joined our little group. Boko had been completely wrong about the man. Rosy though his cheeks may have been, here was no eight-hour slumberer, who had to be brought to life by alarm clocks, but a vigilant guardian of the peace who was always up and doing, working while others slept.

Stilton was looking gruesomely official. His helmet gleamed in the starlight. His regulation boots had settled themselves solidly into the turf. I rather think he had got his notebook out.

'What's all this?' he repeated.

I suppose Uncle Percy was still feeling a bit edgy. Nothing else could have explained the crisp, mouth-filling expletive which now proceeded from him like a shot out of a gun. It sounded to me like something he must have picked up from one of the sea captains in his employment. These rugged mariners always have excellent vocabularies, and no doubt they frequently drop in at the office on their return from a voyage and teach them something new.

'What the devil do you mean, what's all this? And who the devil are you to come trespassing in my grounds, asking what's all this? What's all this yourself? What,' proceeded Uncle Percy, warming to his work, 'are you doing here, you great oaf? I suppose you're just sauntering, too? Good God! I try to enjoy a quiet stroll in my garden, and before I can so much as inhale a breath of air I find it crawling with nephews and policemen. I come out to be alone with Nature, and the first thing I know I can't move for the crowd. What is this place? Piccadilly Circus? Hampstead Heath on Bank Holiday? The spot chosen for the annual outing of the police force?'

I saw his point. Nothing is more annoying to a man who is seeking privacy than to discover that, without knowing it, he had thrown his grounds open to the public. In addition to which, of course, Chichester Clam was waiting for him in the potting shed.

The acerbity of his tone had not been lost on Stilton. Well, I mean to say, it couldn't very well have been. That expletive alone would have been enough to tell him that he was not a welcome visitor. I could see that he was piqued. His was in many ways a haughty spirit, and it was plain that he resented this brusqueness. From the fact that the top of his helmet moved sharply in the direction of the stars, I knew that he had drawn himself to his full height.

He found himself, however, in a somewhat embarrassing position. He could not come back with anything really snappy, Uncle Percy being a Justice of the Peace and, as such, able to put it across him like the dickens if he talked out of his turn. Besides being his future father-in-law. He was compelled, accordingly, to temper his resentment with a modicum of reserve and to take it out in stiffness of manner.

'I am sorry – '

'No use being sorry. Thing is not to do it, blast it.'

' – to intrude – '

'Then stop intruding.'

' – but I am here in the performance of my duty.'

'What do you mean? Never heard such nonsense.'

'I received a telephone call just now, desiring me to proceed to the Hall immediately.'

'Telephone call? Telephone call? What rot! At this time of night? Who telephoned you?'

I suppose that stiff, official manner is difficult to keep up. Quite a bit of a strain, probably. At any rate, Stilton now lapsed from it.

'Young ruddy Edwin,' he replied sullenly.

'My son Edwin?'

'Yes. He said he had seen a burglar in the grounds.'

A spasm seemed to pass through Uncle Percy. The word 'burglar' had plainly touched a chord. He spun round with passionate gesture.

'Jeeves!'

'M'lord?'

'Did you post that letter?'

'Yes, m'lord.'

'Phew!' said Uncle Percy, and mopped his brow.

He was still mopping it, when there came the sound of galloping feet and somebody started giving tongue in the darkness.

'Hi! Hi! Hi! Wake up, everybody. Turn out the guard. I've caught a burglar in the potting shed.'

The voice was Boko's, and with another pang of pity I realized that J. Chichester Clam's troubles had begun. He knew now what happened to people who came to Steeple Bumpleigh.

15

In the brief interval which elapsed before Boko sighted us and came to join our little circle, I fell to musing on this Clam and thinking how different he must be feeling all this from what he had been accustomed to.

Here, I mean to say, was one of those solid businessmen who are America's pride, whose lives are as regular and placid as that of a bug in a rug. On my visits to New York I had met dozens of them, so I could envisage without difficulty a typical Clam day.

Up in the morning bright and early in his Long Island home. The bath. The shave. The eggs. The cereal. The coffee. The drive to the station. The 8.15. The cigar. The *New York Times*. The arrival at the Pennsylvania terminus. The morning's work. The lunch. The afternoon's work. The cocktail. The 5.50. The drive from the station. The return home. The kiss for the wife and tots, the pat for the welcoming dog. The shower. The change into something loose. The well-earned dinner. The quiet evening. Bed.

That was the year in, year out routine of a man like Chichester Clam, Sundays and holidays excepted, and it was one ill calculated to fit him for the raw excitements and jungle conditions of Steeple Bumpleigh. Steeple Bumpleigh must have come upon him as a totally new experience, causing him to wonder what had hit him – like a man who, stooping to pluck a nosegay of wild flowers on a railway line, is unexpectedly struck in the small of the back by the Cornish Express. As he now sat in the potting shed, listening to Boko's view halloos, he was probably convinced that all this must be that Collapse of Civilization, of which he had no doubt so often spoken at the Union League Club.

In spite of the floor of heaven being thick inlaid with patines of bright gold, it was, as I have said, a darkish night, not easy to see things in. The visibility was, however, quite good enough to enable one to perceive that Boko was pretty pleased with himself. Indeed, it would not be overstating it to say that he had got it right up his nose. That this was so was borne in upon me by the fact that he started right away calling Uncle Percy 'my dear Worplesdon' – a thing which in his calmer moments he wouldn't have done on a bet.

'Ah, my dear Worplesdon,' he said, having peered into the relative's face and identified him, 'so you're up and about, are you? Capital, capital. Stilton, too? And Jeeves? And Bertie? Fine. Between the five of us, we ought to be well able to overpower the miscreant. I don't know if you were listening to what I was saying just now, but I've locked a burglar up in the potting shed.'

He spoke these words with the air of a man getting ready to receive the thanks of the nation, tapping Uncle Percy's chest the while as if to suggest that the latter was a lucky chap to have Boko Fittleworths working day and night in his interests. It did not surprise me to observe the relative's growing restiveness under the treatment.

'Will you stop prodding me, sir!' he cried, plainly stirred. 'What's all this nonsense about burglars?'

Boko seemed taken aback. One could see that he was feeling that this was not quite the tone.

'Nonsense, Worplesdon?'

'How do you know the fellow's a burglar?'

'My dear Worplesdon! Would anybody but a burglar be lurking in potting sheds at this time of night? But, if you still need convincing, let me tell you that I was passing the scullery window just now, and I noticed that it was covered with a piece of brown paper.'

'Brown paper?'

'Brown paper. Pretty sinister, eh?'

'Why?'

'My dear Worplesdon, it proves to the hilt the man's criminal intentions. You were possibly not aware of it, but when these fellows plan to enter a house and snaffle contents, they always stick a bit of brown paper on a window with treacle and then smash it with a blow of the fist. It's the regular procedure. The fragments of glass adhere to the paper, and they were thus enabled to climb in without mincing themselves to hash. Oh, no, my dear Worplesdon, there can be no doubt concerning the scoundrel's guilty purpose. I bottled him up in the nick of time. I heard something moving in the potting shed, peeped in, saw a dark form, and slammed the door and fastened it, thus laying him a dead stymie and foiling all his plans.'

This statement drew a word of professional approbation from the sleepless guardian of the law.

'Good work, Boko.'

'Thanks, Stilton.'

'You showed great presence of mind.'

'Nice of you to say so.'

'I'll go and pinch him.'

'Just what I was about to suggest.'

'Has he a gun?'

'I don't know. You'll soon find out.'

'I don't care if he has.'

'The right spirit.'

'I shall just make a quick spring – '

'That's the idea.'

' – and disarm him.'

'We will hope so. We will certainly hope so. Yes, let us hope for the best. Still, whatever happens, you will have the satisfaction of knowing that you have done your duty.'

Throughout these exchanges, starting at the words 'Good work' and continuing right through to the tab line 'done your duty', Uncle Percy had been exhibiting much of the frank perturbation of a cat on hot bricks. Nor could one blame him. He had invited J. Chichester Clam for a quiet talk in the potting shed, and the thought of constables making quick springs at him must have been a very bitter one. You can't conduct delicate business negotiations with that sort of thing going on. In his agony of spirit, he now began saying 'What?' again, leading Boko to apply that patronizing finger to his brisket once more.

'It's quite all right, my dear Worplesdon,' said Boko, tapping like a woodpecker. 'Have no concern about Stilton. He won't get hurt. At least, I don't think so. One may be wrong, of course. Anyway, he is paid to take these risks. Ah, Florence,' he added, addressing the daughter of the house, who had just come alongside in a dressing-gown, with her hair in curling pins.

It was plain that Florence was not her usual calm and equable self. When she spoke, one noted a testiness.

'Never mind the "Ah, Florence". What is going on out here? What is all this noise and disturbance? I was woken up by someone shouting.'

'Me,' said Boko, and even in the uncertain light I could see that he was smirking. I doubt if in all Hampshire that night you could have found a fellow more thoroughly satisfied with himself. He had got it firmly rooted in his mind that he was the popular hero, beloved of all – little knowing that Uncle Percy's favourite reading would have been his name on a tombstone. Rather saddening, the whole thing.

'Well, I wish you wouldn't. It is perfectly impossible to sleep, with people romping all over the garden.'

'Romping? I was catching a burglar.'

'Catching a burglar?'

'You never spoke a truer word. A great desperate brute of a midnight marauder, who may or may not be armed to the teeth. That question we shall be able to answer better after Stilton has got together with him.'

'But how did you catch a burglar?'

'Oh, it's just a knack.'

'I mean, what were you doing here at this time of night?'

It was as if Uncle Percy had been waiting for someone to come along and throw him just that cue.

'Exactly,' he cried, having snorted the snort of a lifetime. 'The very thing I want to know. The precise question I was about to ask myself. What the devil are you doing here? I am not aware that I invited you to infest my private grounds and go charging about them like a buffalo, making an appalling din and rendering peace and quiet impossible. You have a garden of your own, I believe? If you must behave like a buffalo, kindly go and do so there. And the idea of locking people in my potting shed! I never heard of anything so officious in my life.'

'Officious?'

'Yes, damned officious.'

Boko was patently stunned. One sensed that thoughts about birds biting the hand that fed them were racing through his mind. He stuttered a while before speaking.

'Well!' he said, as length, having ceased to imitate a motor bicycle. 'Well, I'm dashed! Well, I must say! Well, I'm blowed! Officious, eh? That is the attitude you take, is it? Ha! One desires no thanks, of course, for these little good turns one does people – at some slight inconvenience to oneself, one might perhaps mention – but I should have thought that in the circumstances one was entitled to expect at least decent civility. Jeeves!'

'Sir?'

'What did Shakespeare say about ingratitude?'

'"Blow, blow, thou winter wind", sir, "thou art not so unkind as man's ingratitude". He also alludes to the quality as "thou marble-hearted fiend".'

'And he wasn't so dashed far wrong! I brood over his house like a guardian angel, sacrificing my sleep and leisure to its interests. I sweat myself to the bone, catching burglars – '

Uncle Percy turned in again.

'Burglars, indeed! All silly nonsense. The man is probably some harmless wayfarer, who had taken refuge in my potting shed from the storm – '

'What storm?'

'Never mind what storm.'

'There isn't a storm.'

'All right, all right!'

'It's a lovely night. No suggestion of a storm.'

'All right, all *right*! We aren't talking about the weather. We're talking about this poor waif in my potting shed. I say he is probably just some harmless wayfarer, and I refuse to persecute the unfortunate fellow. What harm has he done? All the riff-raff for miles around have been using my garden as if it were their own, so why shouldn't he? This is Liberty Hall, damn it – or seems to be.'

'So you don't think he's a burglar?'

'No, I do not.'

'Worplesdon, you're a silly ass. How about the brown paper? What price the treacle?'

'Damn the treacle. Curse the brown paper. And how dare you call me a silly ass? Jeeves!'

'M'lord?'

'Here's ten shillings. Go and give it to the poor chap and let him go. Tell him to buy himself a warm bed and supper.'

'Very good, m'lord.'

Boko uttered a sharp, yapping sound, like a displeased hyena.

'And, Jeeves!' he said.

'Sir?'

'When he's got the warm bed, better tuck him up and see that he has a hot water bottle.'

'Very good, sir.'

'Ten shillings, eh? Supper, egad? Warm bed, forsooth? Well, this lets me out,' said Boko. 'I wash my hands of the whole affair. This is the last occasion on which you may expect my help when you have burglars in this loony bin. Next time they come flocking round, I shall pat them on the back and hold the ladder for them.'

He strode off into the darkness, full to the brim of dudgeon, and I can't say I was much surprised. The way things had panned out had been enough to induce dudgeon in the mildest of men, let alone a temperamental young author, accustomed to calling on his publishers and raising hell at the smallest provocation.

But though seeing his viewpoint, I mourned. In fact, I would go further, I groaned in spirit. The tender Wooster heart had been deeply touched by the non-smooth running of the course of the

Boko-Nobby true love, and I had hoped that tonight's rannygazoo would have culminated in a thorough sweetening of Uncle Percy and a consequent straightening out of the tangle.

Instead of which, this impulsive scrivener had gone and deposited himself lower down among the wines and spirits than ever. If the betting against his scooping in a guardian's consent had been about four to one up to this point, it could scarcely be estimated now at anything shorter than a hundred to eight – and even at that generous price I doubt if the punters would have invested.

I was just wondering whether it would be any use my putting in a soothing word, and feeling on the whole perhaps not, when there came to my ears a low whistle, which may or may not have been the note of the lesser screech owl, and I observed something indistinct but apparently feminine bobbing about behind a distant tree. Everything seeming to point to this being Nobby, I detached myself from the main body and oiled off in her direction.

My surmise was correct. It was Nobby, in a dressing-gown but not curling pins. Apparently, with her style of hair you don't use them. She was fizzing with excitement and the desire to learn the latest hot news.

'I didn't like to join the party,' she said, after the preliminary what-hoes had been exchanged. 'Uncle Percy would have sent me to bed. How's it coming along, Bertie?'

It wrenched the heart-strings to have to ladle out bad tidings to the eager young prune, but the painful task could not be avoided.

'Not too well,' I replied sombrely.

As I had foreseen, the statement got right in amongst her. She uttered a stricken yowl.

'Not too well?'

'No.'

'What went wrong?'

'It would be better to ask what went right. The enterprise was a flop from start to finish.'

She sharp-exclamationed, and I saw that she was giving me one of those unpleasant, suspicious looks.

'I suppose you fell down on your end of the thing?'

'Nothing of the kind. I did all that man could have done. But there was one of those unfortunate concatenations of circumstances, which led to what we had anticipated would be a nice little night's work for the two of us becoming a mob scene. We were just getting on with it most satisfactorily, when the gardens and messuages became a seething mass of Uncle Percies, Jeeveses, Stiltons, Florences and what not. It dished our aims completely. And I am sorry to say that Boko did not show himself at his best.'

'What do you mean?'

'He would keep calling Uncle Percy "my dear Worplesdon". You can't address a man like that as "my dear Worplesdon" for long without something cracking under the strain. Heated words ensued, quite a few being contributed by Boko. The scene, a most painful one, concluded with him calling Uncle Percy a silly ass, and turning on his heel and stalking off. I fear his standing with the above has hit a new low.'

She moaned softly, and I considered for a moment the idea of patting her head. Not much use, though, I felt on consideration, and gave it a miss.

'I did think I could have trusted Boko not to make an ass of himself just for once,' she murmured with a wild regret.

'I doubt if you can ever trust an author not to make an ass of himself,' I responded gravely.

'Golly, I'll tick him off for this! Which way did he go, when he turned on his heel?'

'Somewhere in that direction.'

'Wait till I find him!' she cried, baying like an under-sized blood-hound, and was gone with the wind.

It was perhaps a couple of ticks later, or three, that Jeeves came shimmering up.

'A disturbing evening, sir,' he said. 'I released Mr Clam.'

'Never mind about Clam. Clam leaves me cold. The chap I'm worrying about is Boko.'

'Ah, yes, sir.'

'Silly idiot, alienating Uncle Percy like that.'

'Yes, sir. It was a pity that the young gentleman's manner should not have been more conciliatory.'

'He's sunk, unless you can think of some way of healing the breach.'

'Yes, sir.'

'Get hold of him, Jeeves.'

'Yes, sir.'

'Confer with him.'

'Yes, sir.'

'Strain the bean to the utmost in order to hit upon some solution.'

'Very good, sir.'

'You will find him somewhere out there in the silent night. At least, it won't be so dashed silent, because Nobby will be telling him what she thinks of him. Circle around till you hear a raised soprano voice, and that will be the spot to head for.'

He popped off, as desired, and I started to do a bit of pacing to and fro, knitting the brows. I had been knitting them for about five minutes, when something loomed up in the offing and I saw that it was Boko, come to play a return date.

16

Boko was looking subdued and chastened, as if his soul had been passed through the wringer. He wore the unmistakable air of a man who has just been properly told where he gets off by the girl of his dreams and has not yet reassembled the stunned faculties.

'Hullo, Bertie,' he said, in a sort of hushed, saint-like voice.

'Pip-pip, Boko.'

'Some night!'

'Considerable.'

'You haven't a flask on you, have you?'

'No.'

'A pity. One should always carry a flask about in case of emergencies. Saint Bernard dogs do it in the Alps. Fifty million Saint Bernard dogs can't be wrong. I have just passed through a great emotional experience, Bertie.'

'Did Nobby find you?'

He gave a little shiver.

'I've just been chatting with her.'

'I had a sort of idea you had.'

'It shows in my appearance, does it? Yes, I suppose it would. It wasn't you who told her about those Joke Goods, was it?'

'Of course not.'

'Somebody did.'

'Uncle Percy, probably.'

'That's true. She would have asked him how the lunch came out. Yes, I imagine that was the authoritative source from which she had her information.'

'So she touched on the Joke Goods?'

'Oh, yes. Yes, she touched on them. Her conversation dealt partly with them and partly with what happened tonight. She was at no loss for words on either theme. You're absolutely sure you haven't a flask?'

'Quite, I'm afraid.'

'Ah, well,' said Boko, and relapsed into silence for a while, emerging from it to ask me in a wondering sort of voice where girls picked up these expressions.

'What expressions?'

'I couldn't repeat them, with gentlemen present. I suppose they learn them at their finishing schools.'

'She gave you beans, did she?'

'With no niggardly hand. It was an extraordinary feeling, standing there while she put me through it. One had a dazed sensation of something small and shrill whirling about one, seething with fury. Like being attacked by a Pekingese.'

'I've never been attacked by a Pekingese.'

'Well, ask the man who has. He'll tell you. Every moment, I was expecting to get a nasty nip in the ankle.'

'How did it all end?'

'Oh, I got away with my life. Still, what's life?'

'Life's all right.'

'Not if you've lost the girl you love.'

'Have you lost the girl you love?'

'That's what I'm trying to figure out. I can't make up my mind. It all depends what construction you place on the words "I never want to see or speak to you again in this world or the next, you miserable fathead".'

'Did she say that?'

'Among other things.'

I saw that the time had come to soothe and encourage.

'I wouldn't let that worry me, Boko.'

He seemed surprised.

'You wouldn't?'

'No. She didn't mean it?'

'Didn't mean it?'

'Of course not.'

'Just said it for something to say? Making conversation, as it were?'

'Well, I'll tell you, Boko. I've made a pretty deep study of the sex, observing them in all their moods, and the conclusion I've come to is that when they shoot their heads off in the manner described, little attention need be paid to the subject matter.'

'You would advise ignoring it?'

'Absolutely. Dismiss it from the mind.'

He was silent for a moment. When he spoke, it was on a note of hope.

'There's one thing, of course. She used to love me. As recently as this afternoon. Dearly. She said so. One's got to remember that.'

'She still does.'

'You really feel that, do you?'

'Of course.'

'In spite of calling me a miserable fathead?'

'Certainly. You are a miserable fathead.'

'That's true.'

'You can't go by what a girl says, when she's giving you the devil for making a chump of yourself. It's like Shakespeare. Sounds well, but doesn't mean anything.'

'Your view, then, is that the old affection still lingers?'

'Definitely. Dash it, man, if she could love you in spite of those grey flannel trousers of yours, it isn't likely that any mere acting of the goat on your part will have choked her off. Love is indestructible. Its holy flame burneth forever.'

'Who told you that?'

'Jeeves.'

'He ought to know.'

'He does. You can bank on Jeeves.'

'That's right. You can, can't you? You're a great comfort, Bertie.'

'I try to be, Boko.'

'You give me hope. You raise me from the depths.'

He had perked up considerably. He wasn't actually squaring his shoulders and sticking his chin out, but the morale had plainly stiffened. And I have an idea that in another minute or two he might have become almost jaunty, had there not cut through the night air at this juncture a feminine voice, calling his name.

'Boko!'

He shook like an aspen.

'Yes, darling?'

'Come here. I want you.'

'Coming, darling. Oh, my God!' I heard him whisper. 'An encore!'

He tottered off, and I was left to ponder over the trend of affairs.

I may say at once that I viewed the situation without concern. To Boko, who had actually been in the ring with the young geezer while she was exploding in all directions, it had naturally seemed that the end of the world had come and Judgement Day set in with unusual severity. But to me, the cool and level-headed bystander, the whole thing had been pure routine. One shrugged the shoulders and recognized it for what it was – viz. pure apple sauce.

Love's silken bonds are not broken just because the female half of the sketch takes umbrage at the loony behaviour of the male partner and slips it across him in a series of impassioned speeches. However devoutly a girl may worship the man of her choice, there always comes a time when she feels an irresistible urge to haul off and let him have it in the neck. I suppose if the young lovers I've known in my time were placed end to end – difficult to manage, of course, but what I mean is just suppose they were – they would reach half-way down Piccadilly. And I couldn't think of a single dashed one who hadn't been through what Boko had been through tonight.

Already, I felt, the second phase had probably set in, where the female lovebird weeps on the male lovebird's chest and says she's sorry she was cross. And that my surmise was correct was proved by Boko's demeanour, as he rejoined me some minutes later. Even in the dim light, you could see that he was feeling like a million dollars. He walked as if on air, and the whole soul had obviously expanded, like a bath sponge placed in water.

'Bertie.'

'Hullo?'

'Still there?'

'On the spot.'

'It's all right, Bertie.'

'She loves you still?'

'Yes.'

'Good.'

'She wept on my chest.'

'Fine.'

'And said she was sorry she had been cross. I said "There, there!" and everything is once more gas and gaiters.'

'Splendid.'

'I felt terrific.'

'I bet you did.'

'She withdrew the words "miserable fathead".'

'Good.'

'She said I was the tree on which the fruit of her life hung.'

'Fine.'

'And apparently it was all a mistake when she told me she never wanted to see or speak to me again in this world or the next. She does. Frequently.'

'Splendid.'

'I clasped her to me, and kissed her madly.'

'I bet you did.'

'Jeeves, who was present, was much affected.'

'Oh, Jeeves was there?'

'Yes. He and Nobby had been discussing plans and schemes.'

'For sweetening Uncle Percy?'

'Yes. For, of course, that still has to be done.'

I looked grave. Not much use, of course, in that light.

'It's going to be difficult – '

'Not a bit.'

' – after your not only addressing him as "my dear Worplesdon" but also calling him a silly ass.'

'Not a bit, Bertie, not a bit. Jeeves has come across with one of his ripest suggestions.'

'He has?'

'What a man!'

'Ah!'

'I often say there's nobody like Jeeves.'

'And well you may.'

'Have you ever noticed how his head sticks out at the back?'

'Often.'

'That's where the brain is. Packed away behind the ears.'

'Yes. What's his idea?'

'Briefly this. He thinks it would make an excellent impression and enable me to recover the lost ground, if I stuck up for old Worplesdon.'

'Stuck him up? I don't get that. With a gun, do you mean?'

'I didn't say "stuck up". Stuck up for.'

'Oh, stuck up for?'

'That's right. Stuck up for. In other words, he advises me to take the old boy's part – protect him, as it were.'

'Protect Uncle Percy?'

'Oh, I know it sounds bizarre. But Jeeves thinks it will work.'

'I still don't get it.'

'It's perfectly simple, really. Look here. Suppose some great blustering brute of a chap barges into old Worplesdon's study at ten sharp tomorrow morning and starts ballyragging him like the dickens, calling him every name under the sun and generally making himself thoroughly offensive. I'm waiting outside the study window, and at the psychological moment I stick my head in and in a quiet, reproving voice, say "Stop Bertie! – "'

'Bertie?'

'The chap's name is Bertie. But don't interrupt. I'll lose the thread. I stick my head in and say "Stop, Bertie! You are strangely forgetting yourself. I cannot stand by and listen to you abusing a man I admire and respect as highly as Lord Worplesdon. Lord Worplesdon and I may have had our differences – the fault was mine and I am heartily sorry for it – but I never deviated from the opinion that it is an honour to know him. And when I hear you calling him a – "'

I am pretty quick. Already, I had spotted the nature of the frightful scheme.

'You want me to go into Uncle Percy's lair and call him names?'

'At ten sharp. Most important, that. We shall have to synchronize to the second. Nobby tells me he always spends the morning in his study, no doubt writing stinkers to the captains of his ships.'

'And you bob up and tick me off for ticking him off?'

'That's the idea. It can hardly fail to show me in a sympathetic light, causing him to warm to me and feel that I'm a pretty good chap, after all. There he will be, I mean to say, cowering in his chair, while you stand over him, shaking your finger in his face – '

The vision conjured up by these words was so ghastly that I staggered and would have fallen, had I not clutched at a tree.

'You say Jeeves suggested that?'

'As I told you, just like a flash.'

'He might be tight.'

A stiffness crept into Boko's manner.

'I don't understand you, Bertie. I rank the scheme among his very subtlest efforts. It seems to me one of those simple stratagems, all the more effective for their simplicity, which can hardly drop a stitch. Coming in at the moment when you are intimidating old Worplesdon, and throwing the whole weight of my sympathy and support on his side, I shall – '

There are moments when we Woosters can be very firm – adamant is perhaps the word – and one of these is when we are asked to intimidate men like Uncle Percy.

'I'm sorry, Boko.'

'Sorry? Why?'

'Include me out.'

'What!'

'Nothing doing.'

He leaned forward, the better to stare incredulously into my face. The man seemed stunned.

'Bertie!'

'Yes, I know. But I repeat – nothing doing.'

'Nothing doing?'

'Nothing doing.'

A pleading note came into his voice, the same sort of note I've sometimes heard in Bingo Little's, when asking a bookie to take the broad, spacious view and wait for his money till Wednesday week.

'But, Bertie, you're fond of Nobby?'

'Of course.'

'Of course you are, or you would never have given her that threepennyworth of acid drops. And you don't, I take it, dispute the fact that you and I were at school together? Of course, you don't. When I thought I heard you say you wouldn't sit in, I must have misunderstood you.'

'You didn't.'

'I didn't?'

'No.'

'You refuse to do your bit?'

'I do.'

'You – I want to get this straight – you really decline to play your part – your simple, easy part – in this enterprise?'

'That's right.'

'This *is* Bertie Wooster speaking?'

'It is.'

'The Bertie Wooster I was at school with?'

'That's right.'

He drew in his breath with a sort of whistle.

'Well, if anybody had told me this would happen, I wouldn't have believed it. I would have laughed mockingly. Bertie Wooster let me down? No, no, I would have said – not Bertie, who was not only at school with me but is at this very moment bursting with my meat.'

This was a nasty one. I wasn't actually bursting with his meat, of course, because there hadn't been such a frightful lot of it, but I saw what it meant. For an instant, when he put it like that, I nearly weakened. Then I thought of Uncle Percy 'cowering in his chair' – cowering in his chair, my foot! – and was strong again.

'I'm sorry, Boko.'

'So am I, Bertie. Sorry and disappointed. Sick at heart is the expression that leaps to the lips. Well, I suppose I shall have to go and break the news to Nobby. Golly, how she'll cry!'

I could not repress a pang.

'I don't want to make Nobby cry.'

'You will, though. Gallons.'

He faded away into the darkness, sighing reproachfully, leaving me alone with the stars.

And I was just examining them and wondering what had given Jeeves the idea that they were quiring to the young-eyed cherubims – I couldn't see the slightest indication of such a thing myself – when they suddenly merged, as if they had been Uncle Percy and J. Chichester Clam, and became a jagged sheet of flame.

This was because a hidden hand, creeping up behind me unperceived, had given me the dickens of a slosh with what I assumed to be some blunt instrument. It caught me squarely on the back hair, bringing me to earth with a sharp 'Ouch!'

17

I sat up rubbing the occiput, and a squeaky voice spoke in my earhole. Eyeing me solicitously, or else gloating over his handiwork, I couldn't tell which, was young blighted Edwin.

'Coo!' he said. 'Is that you, Bertie?'

'Yes, it jolly well is,' I replied with a touch of not unnatural asperity. I mean, life's difficult enough without having Boy Scouts beaning one every other minute, and I was incensed. 'What's the idea? What do you mean, you repellent young boll weevil, by socking me with a dashed great club?'

'It wasn't a club. It was my Scout's stick. Sort of like a hockey stick. Very useful.'

'Comes in handy, does it?'

'Rather! Did it hurt?'

'You may take it as definitely official that it hurt like blazes.'

'Coo! I'm sorry. I mistook you for the burglar. There's one lurking in the grounds. I heard him underneath my window. I said "Who's there?" and he slunk off with horrid imprecations. I say, I'm not having much luck tonight. The last chap I mistook for the burglar turned out to be Father.'

'Father?'

'Yes. How was I to know it was him? I never thought he would be wandering about the garden in the middle of the night. I saw a shadowy form crouching down, as if about to spring, and I crept up behind it and – '

'You didn't biff him?'

'Yes. Rather a juicy one.'

I must say my heart leaped up, as Jeeves tells me his does when he beholds a rainbow in the sky. The thought of Uncle Percy stopping a hot one with the trouser seat was pretty stimulating. It had been coming to him for years. I had that sort of awed feeling one gets sometimes, when one has a close-up of the workings of Providence and realizes that nothing is put into this world without a purpose, not even Edwin, and that the meanest creatures have their uses.

'He was a bit shirty about it.'

'It annoyed him, eh?'

'He wanted to give me beans, but Florence wouldn't let him. She said, "Father, you are not to touch him. It was a pure misunderstanding." Florence is very fond of me.'

I raised my eyebrows. A girl, I felt, of strange, even morbid tastes.

'So all he did was to tell me to go to bed.'

'Then why aren't you in bed?'

'Bed? Coo! Not likely. How's your head?'

'Rotten.'

'Does it ache?'

'Of course it aches.'

'Have you got a contusion?'

'Yes, I have.'

'This is where I could give you first aid.'

'No, it isn't.'

'Don't you want first aid?'

'No, I don't. We have threshed all this out before, young Edwin. You know my views.'

'I don't ever seem able to get anyone to let me give them first aid,' he said wistfully. 'And what one needs is lots of practice. What are you doing here, Bertie?'

'Everybody asks me what I'm doing here,' I replied, with a touch of pique. 'Why shouldn't I be here? This place is related to me by ties of blood. If you really want to know, I came here for an after dinner saunter with Boko Fittleworth.'

'I haven't seen Boko.'

'A bit of luck for him.'

'D'Arcy Cheesewright's here.'

'I know.'

'I phoned him after I saw the burglar.'

'I know.'

'Did you know he was engaged to Florence?'

'Yes.'

'I'm not sure it's not off. They were having an awful row just now.'

He spoke lightly, throwing the statement out as if it had been some news item of merely negligible interest, and was probably surprised at the concern which I exhibited.

'What!'

'Yes.'

'An awful row?'

'Yes.'

'What about?'

'I don't know.'

'When you say an awful row, how awful a row do you mean?'

'Well, fairly awful.'

'High words?'

'Pretty high.'

My heart, which had leaped up as described at the bulletin about Uncle Percy's trouser seat, was now down in the basement again. The whole trend of my foreign policy, as I have made abundantly clear, being to promote cordial relations between these two, the information that they had been having even fairly high words was calculated to freeze the blood.

You see, what I was saying apropos to Nobby hauling up her slacks and coming the Pekingese on Boko – all that stuff, if you remember, about girls giving their loved one the devil just for the fun of the thing and to keep the pores open – didn't apply to serious minded females like Florence and the sort of chap Stilton was. It's all a question of what Jeeves calls the psychology of the individual. If Florence and Stilton had gone to the mat and started chewing pieces out of each other, the outlook was unsettled.

'How much of it did you hear?'

'Not much. Because that was when I saw something moving in the darkness and went and biffed it with my Scout's stick, and it turned out to be you.'

This, of course, put a slightly better complexion on things. My first impression had been that he had had a ringside seat all through the conflict. If he had only heard the opening exchanges, it might be that matters had not proceeded too far. Cooler thoughts might have prevailed after his departure, causing the contestants to cheese it before the breach became irreparable. It often happens like that with girls and men of high spirit. They start off with a whoop and a holler, and then, their better selves prevailing, pipe down.

I mentioned this to Edwin, and he seemed to think that there might be something in it. But I noticed that he appeared distrait and not really interested, and after a pause of a few moments, during which I hoped for the best and he twiddled his Scout's stick, he revealed why this was so. He was worrying about a point of procedure.

'I say, Bertie,' he said, 'you know that slosh I gave you.'

I assured him that I had not forgotten it.

'I meant well, you know.'

'That's a comfort.'

'Still, of course, I did sock you, didn't I?'

'You did.'

'You can't get away from that.'

'No.'

'Then here's what I'm wondering. Have I wiped out the act of kindness I did you this afternoon?'

'When you tidied up Wee Nooke?'

'No, I'm afraid that doesn't count, because it didn't work out right. I meant finding that brooch.'

I had to watch my step rather sedulously here. I mean to say, the brooch he had found and the brooch Jeeves had delivered to Florence were supposed to be one and the same brooch, and he must never learn from my lips that I had lost the dashed thing again after he had found it that time in the hall.

'Oh, that?' I said. 'Yes, that was a Grade A act of kindness.'

'I know. But do you think it still counts?'

'Oh, rather.'

'In spite of my socking you?'

'Unquestionably.'

'Coo! Then I'm all square up to last Thursday.'

'You mean last Friday.'

'Thursday.'

'Friday.'

'Thursday.'

'Friday, you fatheaded young faulty reasoner,' I said, with some heat, for his inability to keep the score correctly was annoying me as much as that 'We are seven' stuff must have annoyed the poet – I forget his name – who got talking figures with another child. 'Listen. Your last Friday's act of kindness would have been the tidying up of Wee Nooke. Right. But owing to the unfortunate sequel that has to be scratched off the list. You admit that, don't you? Well, that makes the finding of the brooch your last Friday's act of kindness. Perfectly simple, if you'll only use the little grey cells a bit.'

'Yes, but you haven't got it right.'

'I have got it right. Listen – '

'I mean, you're talking about the first time I found the brooch. What I'm talking about is the second time. That counts as well.'

I couldn't follow him.

'How do you mean, the second time? You didn't find it twice.'

'Yes, I did. The first time was when you dropped it in the hall, you remember. Then I went off to clean the kitchen chimney. Then there was that explosion, and I came out, and you were standing on the lawn in your shirt sleeves. You had taken off your coat and chucked it away.'

'Oh my gosh!'

What with the stress of this and that, I had completely forgotten that coat sequence. It all came back to me now, and a cold hand seemed to clutch my heart. I could see where he was heading.

'I suppose the brooch must have fallen out of your pocket, because when you had gone into the house I saw it lying there. And I thought it would be an act of kindness if I saved you the trouble by taking it to Florence.'

I gazed at him dully. With a lack-lustre eye is, I believe, the expression.

'So you took it to Florence?'

'Yes.'

'Saying it was a present from me?'

'Yes.'

'Did she seem pleased?'

'Frightfully. Coo!'

He vanished abruptly, like an eel going into mud, and I was aware of the approach of someone breathing heavily.

It did not need the child's impulsive dash into the shadows to tell me that this stertorous newcomer was Florence.

18

Florence was obviously in the grip of some powerful emotion. She quivered gently, as if in the early stages of palsy, and her face, as far as I could gather from the sketchy view I was able to obtain of it, was pale and set, like the white of a hard-boiled egg.

'D'Arcy Cheesewright,' she said, getting right off the mark without so much as a preliminary "What ho, there", 'is an obstinate, mulish, pigheaded, overbearing, unimaginative, tyrannical jack in office!'

Her words froze me to the core. I was conscious of a sense of frightful peril. Owing to young Edwin's infernal officiousness, this pancake had been in receipt only a few hours earlier of a handsome diamond brooch, ostensibly a present from Bertram W., and now, right on top of it, she had had a falling out with Stilton, so substantial that it took her six distinct adjectives to describe him. When a girl uses six derogatory adjectives in her attempt to paint the portrait of the loved one, it means something. One may indicate a merely temporary tiff. Six is big stuff.

I didn't like the way things were shaping. I didn't like it at all. It seemed to me that what she must be saying to herself was 'Look here upon this picture and on this', as it were. I mean to say, on the one hand, a suave, knightly donor of expensive brooches; on the other, an obstinate, mulish, pigheaded, overbearing, unimaginative, tyrannical jack in office. If you were a girl, which would you prefer to link your lot with? Exactly.

I felt that I must spare no effort to plead Stilton's cause, to induce her to overlook whatever it was he had done to make her go about breathing like an asthma patient and scattering adjectives all over the place. The time had come for me to be eloquent and persuasive as never before, pouring oil on the troubled waters with a liberal hand, emptying the jug if necessary.

'Oh, dash it!' I cried.

'What do you mean by "Oh, dash it"?'

'Just. "Oh, dash it!" Sort of protest, if you follow me.'

'You do not agree with me?'

'I think you've misjudged him.'

'I have not.'

'Splendid fellow, Stilton.'

'He is nothing of the kind.'

'Wouldn't you say he was the sort of chap who has made England what it is?'

'No.'

'No?'

'I said no.'

'Yes, that's right. So you did.'

'He is a mere uncouth Cossack.'

A cossack, I knew, was one of those things clergymen wear, and I wondered why she thought Stilton was like one. An inquiry into this would have been fraught with interest, but before I could institute it she had continued.

'He has been abominably rude, not only to me but to Father. Just because Father would not allow him to arrest the man in the potting shed.'

A bright light shone upon me. Her words had made clear the root of the trouble. I had, if you remember, edged away from the Stilton-Florence-Uncle Percy group just after the last named had put the presidential veto on the able young officer's scheme of pinching J. Chichester Clam, and had, accordingly, not been there to hear Stilton's comments. These, it was now evident, must have been on the fruity side. Stilton, as I have indicated, is a man of strong passions – one who, when annoyed, does not mince his words.

My mind went back to that time at Oxford, when I had gone in for rowing and had drawn him as a coach. If what he had said to Uncle Percy had been even remotely in the same class as his remarks on that occasion with reference to my stomach, I could see that relations must inevitably have got pretty strained, and my heart sank as I visualized the scene.

'He said Father was shackling the police and that it was men like him, grossly lacking in any sense of civic duty, who were the cause of the ever-growing crime wave. He said that Father was a menace to the community and would be directly responsible if half the population of Steeple Bumpleigh were murdered in their beds.'

'You don't think he spoke laughingly?'

'No, I do not think he spoke laughingly.'

'With a twinkle in his eye, I mean.'

'There was not the slightest suggestion of any twinkle in his eye.'

'You might have missed it. It's a dark night.'

'Please do not be utterly absurd, Bertie. I have sufficient intelligence, I hope, to be able to recognize a vile exhibition of bad temper when I see it. His tone was most offensive. "And you", he said, looking at Father as if he were some sort of insect, "call yourself a Justice of the Peace. Faugh!"'

'Fore? Like at golf?'

'F-a-u-g-h.'

'Oh, ah.'

I was beginning to be almost sorry for Uncle Percy, as far as it is possible to be sorry for a man like that. I mean, there was no getting away from it that it hadn't been a big evening for the poor old bloke. First, Boko with his 'My dear Worplesdon'; then Edwin with his hockey stick; and now Stilton with his 'Faughs'. One of those nights you look back to with a shudder.

'His behaviour was a revelation to me. It laid bare a brutal, inhuman side of his character, of the existence of which I had never till then had a suspicion. There was something positively horrible in the fury he exhibited, when he realized that he was not to be allowed to arrest the man. He was like some malignant wild beast deprived of its prey.'

It was plain that Stilton's stock was in or approaching the cellar, and I did what I could to stop the slump.

'Still, it showed zeal, what?'

'Tchah!'

'And zeal, after all, when you come right down to it, is what he draws his weekly envelope for.'

'Don't talk to me about zeal. It was revolting. And when I said that Father was quite right, he turned on me like a tiger.'

Although by this time, as you may well imagine, I was rocking on my base and becoming more and more a prey to alarm and despondency, I couldn't help admiring Stilton for his intrepid courage. Circumstances had so arranged themselves as to extract most of the stuffing from what had been a closeish boyhood friendship, but I had to respect a man capable of turning on Florence like a tiger. I would hardly have thought Attila the Hun could have done it, even if at the peak of his form.

All the time, I wished he hadn't. Oh, I was saying to myself, that the voice of Prudence had whispered in his ear. It was so vital to my interests that the mutual love of these two should continue unimpaired, and already much of the gilt, I feared, must have been rubbed off the gingerbread of their romance. Love is a sensitive plant, which needs cherishing and fostering. This cannot be done by turning on girls like tigers.

'I told him that modern enlightened thought held that imprisonment merely brutalizes the criminal.'

'And what did he say to that?'

'"Oh yes?"'

'Ah, he agreed with you.'

'He did nothing of the kind He spoke in a most unpleasant, sneering voice. "It does, does it?" he said. And I said "Yes, it does." He then said something about modern enlightened thought which I cannot repeat.'

I wondered what this had been. Evidently something red hot, for it was clear that it still rankled like a boil on the back of the neck. Her fists, I saw, were clenched, and she had started to tap her foot on the ground – sure indications that the soul is fed to the eye teeth. Florence is one of those girls who look on modern enlightened thought as a sort of personal buddy, and receive with an ill grace cracks at its expense.

I groaned in spirit. The way things were shaping, I was expecting her to say next that she had broken off the engagement.

And that was just what she did say.

'Of course, I broke off the engagement instantly.'

In spite of the fact that, as I say, I had practically known it was coming, I skipped like the high hills.

'You broke off the engagement?'

'Yes.'

'Oh, I say, you shouldn't have done that.'

'Why not?'

'Sterling chap like Stilton.'

'He is nothing of the kind.'

'You ought to forget those cruel words he spoke. You should make allowances.'

'I don't understand you.'

'Well, look at it from the poor old buster's point of view. Stilton, you must bear in mind, entered the police force hoping for rapid advancement.'

'Well?'

'Well, of course, the men up top don't advance a young rozzer rapidly unless he comes through with something so spectacular as to make them draw in their breath with an awed "Lord love a duck!" For weeks, months perhaps, he had been chafing like a caged eagle at the frightful law-abidingness of this place, hoping vainly for even a collarless dog or a decent drunk and disorderly that he could get his teeth into, and the sudden arrival of a burglar must have seemed to him manna from heaven. Here, he must have said to himself, was where at last he made his presence felt. And just as he was hitching up his sleeves and preparing to take his big opportunity, Uncle Percy goes and puts him on the leash. It was enough to upset any cop. Naturally he forgot himself and spoke with a generous strength. But he never means what he says in moments of heat. You should have heard him once at Oxford, talking to me about sticking out my stomach while toiling at the oar. You would have thought he loathed my stomach and its contents. Yet only a few hours later we were dining *vis-à-vis* at the Clarendon – clear soup, turbot and a saddle of mutton, I remember – and he was amiability itself. You'll find it's just the same now. I'll bet remorse is already gnawing him, and nobody is sorrier than he for having said nasty things about modern enlightened thought. He loves you devotedly. This is official. I happen to know. So what I would suggest is that you go to him and tell him that all is forgotten and forgiven. Only thus can you avoid making a bloomer, the memory of which will haunt you through the years. If you give Stilton the bum's rush, you'll kick yourself practically incessantly for the rest of your life. The whitest man I know.'

I paused, partly for breath and partly because I felt I had said enough. I stood there, waiting for her reply, wishing I had a throat lozenge to suck.

Well, I don't know what reaction I had expected on her part – possibly the drooping of the head and the silent tear, as the truth of my words filtered through her system; possibly some verbal statement to the effect that I had spoken a mouthful. What I had definitely not expected was that she would kiss me, and with a heartiness that nearly dropped me in my tracks.

'Bertie, you are extraordinary!' She laughed, a thing I couldn't have done, if handsomely paid. 'So quixotic. It is what I love in you. Nobody hearing you would dream that it is your dearest wish to marry me yourself.'

I tried to utter, but could not. The tongue had got all tangled up with the uvula, and the brain seemed paralysed. I was feeling the same stunned feeling which, I imagine, Chichester Clam must have felt as the door of the potting shed slammed and he heard Boko starting to yodel without – a nightmare sensation of being but a helpless pawn in the hands of Fate.

She passed an arm through mine, and began to explain, like a governess instructing a backward pupil in the rudiments of simple arithmetic.

'Do you think I have not understood? My dear Bertie, I am not blind. When I broke off our engagement, I naturally supposed that you would forget – or perhaps that you would be angry and resentful and think hard, bitter thoughts of me. Tonight, I realized how wrong I had been. It was that brooch you gave me that opened my eyes to your real feelings. There was no need for you to have given me a birthday present at all, unless you wanted me to know that you still cared. And to give me one so absurdly expensive ... Of course, I knew at once what you were trying to tell me. It all fitted in so clearly with the other things you had said. About your reading Spinoza, for instance. You had lost me, as you thought, but you still went on studying good literature for my sake. And I found you in the bookshop buying my novel. I can't tell you how it touched me. And as the result of that chance meeting you could not keep yourself from coming to Steeple Bumpleigh, so that you might be near me once more. And tonight, you crept out, to stand beneath my window in the starlight ... No, let us have no more misunderstandings. I am thankful that I should have seen the meaning of your shy overtures in time, and that I should have had the real D'Arcy Cheesewright revealed to me before it was too late. I will be your wife, Bertie.'

There didn't seem much to say to this except 'Oh, thanks.' I said it, and the interview terminated. She kissed me again, expressed her preference for a quiet wedding, with just a few relations and intimate friends, and beetled off.

19

It was not immediately that I, too, departed. The hour was late, and my bed awaited me *chez* Boko, but for a considerable time I remained rooted to the spot, staring dazedly into the darkness. Winged creatures of the night came bumping into the old face and bumping off again, while others used the back stretches of my neck as a skating rink, but I did not even raise a hand to interfere with their revels. This awful thing that had come upon me had practically turned me into a pillar of salt. I doubt if the moth, or whatever it was that was doing Swedish exercises in and around my left ear, had the remotest notion that it had parked itself on the person of a once vivacious young clubman. A tree, it probably thought, or possibly even the living rock.

Presently, however, life returned to the rigid limbs, and I started to plod my weary way down the drive and out of the gate, eventually reaching Boko's door. It was open, and I heaved myself through. There was a light along the passage, and heading for it I won through to the sitting-room.

Boko was in an armchair, with his feet on the mantelpiece and his hand clasping a glass. The sight of another glass and a syphon and decanter drew me to the table like a magnet. The sloshing of the liquid seemed to rouse mine host from a reverie, causing him for the first time to become aware of my presence.

'Help yourself,' he said.

'Thanks, old man.'

'Though I'm surprised you have the heart to drink, after what has occurred tonight.'

He spoke coldly, and there was a distinct aloofness in his manner as he reached out and refilled his glass. He eyed me for a moment as if I had been a caterpillar in some salad of which he was about to partake, and resumed.

'I saw Nobby.'

'Oh, yes?'

'As I anticipated, she cried buckets.'

'I'm sorry.'

'So you should be. Yours was the hand that wrenched those pearly drops from her eyes.'

'Oh, dash it!'

'It's no good saying "Oh, dash it!" You have a conscience, I presume? Then it must have informed you that you were directly responsible for the downpour. Well, well, if anybody had told me that Bertie Wooster would let me down – '

'You said that before.'

'And I shall go on saying it. Even unto seventy times seven. One doesn't dismiss a thing like that with a single careless comment. When your whole faith in human nature has been shattered, you are entitled to repeat yourself a bit.'

He laughed a short, mirthless laugh, very rasping and hard on the ears. Then, as if dismissing an unpleasant subject for the time being, he drained his snootful and turned to the matter of my belated return, saying that he had expected me back hours ago.

'When I took you for an after dinner stroll, I didn't think you were going to stay out practically till the arrival of the morning milk. You will have to change these dissolute city ways, if you wish to fit in with the life of a decent English village.'

'I am a bit later than I had anticipated.'

'What kept you?'

'Well, for one thing, I was being biffed over the nut by Edwin with a hockey stick. That took time.'

'What?'

'Yes.'

'He socked you with a hockey stick?'

'Right on the bean.'

'Ah!' said Boko, and seemed to brighten quite a good deal. 'Fine little chap, Edwin. Good stuff in that boy. Got nice ideas.'

The circs being what they were, this absence of the sympathetic note distressed me, filling me with what I have heard Jeeves describe as thoughts that lie too deep for tears. A man in my position wants his friends to rally round him.

'Don't gibe and scoff,' I begged. 'I want sympathy, Boko – sympathy and advice. Do you know what?'

'What?'

'I'm engaged to Florence.'

'What, again? What's become of Stilton?'

'I will tell you the whole ghastly story.'

I suppose the poignant note in my voice stirred his better nature, for he listened gravely and with evidences of human feeling as I related my tragedy. When I had concluded, he shivered and reached out for the decanter, his whole aspect that of a man who needed one quick.

'There but for the grace of God,' he said, in a low voice, 'goes George Webster Fittleworth!'

I pointed out that he was missing the nub.

'Yes, that's all very well, Boko, and I am sure you have my heartiest congratulations, but the basic fact with which we have to deal is that there actually does go Bertram Wooster. Have you nothing to suggest?'

'Is any man safe?' he continued, still musing. 'I did think that the black spot had finally passed into Stilton's possession.'

'So did I.'

'It's a shame it hasn't, because he really loves that girl, Bertie. No doubt you have been feeling a decent pity for Stilton, but I assure you it was wasted. He loves her. And when a man with a head as fat as that loves, it is for ever. You and I would say that it was impossible that anyone should really want to marry this frightful girl, but it is a fact. Did she make you read *Types of Ethical Theory?*'

'Yes.'

'Me, too. It was that that first awoke me to a sense of my peril. But when she slipped it to Stilton, he ate it alive. I don't suppose he understood a word of it, but I repeat, he ate it alive. Theirs would have been an ideal match. Too bad it has blown a fuse. Of course, if Stilton would resign from the Force, a way could readily be paved to an understanding. It's that that is at the root of the trouble.'

Once more, I saw that the nub had eluded him.

'It's not Stilton I'm worrying about, Boko, old man, it's me. I view Stilton with a benevolent eye, and would be glad to see him happily mated, but the really vital question is Where does Bertram get off? How do we extricate poor old Wooster?'

'You really want to be extricated?'

'My dear chap!'

'She would be a good influence in your life, remember. Steadying. Educative.'

'Would you torture me, Boko?'

'Well, how did you extricate yourself, when you were engaged to her last time?'

'It's a long story.'

'Then for goodness' sake don't start it now. All I meant was, could the same technique be employed in the present crisis?'

'I'm afraid not. There was something she wanted me to do for her, and I failed to do it and she gave me the air. These circs could not arise again.'

'I see. Well, it's a pity you can't use the method I did. The Fittleworth System. Simple but efficacious. That would solve all your difficulties.'

'Why can't I use it?'

'Because you don't know what it is.'

'You could tell me.'

He shook his head.

'No, Bertie, not after the extraordinary attitude you have seen fit to take up with regard to my proposals for sweetening your Uncle Percy. The Fittleworth Method – tried and tested, I may say, and proved infallible – can be imparted only to the deserving. It is not a secret I would care to share with any except real friends who are as true as steel.'

'I'm as true as steel, Boko.'

'No, Bertie, you are not as true as steel, or anything like it. You may have shown that by your behaviour tonight. A real eye-opener it has been, causing me to revise my estimate of your friendship from the bottom up. Of course, if you were to reconsider your refusal to chip in on this scheme of Jeeves's and consent, after all, to play your allotted part, I should be delighted to . . . But what's the use of talking about it? You have declined, and that's that. I know your iron will. When you come to a decision, it stays come to.'

I didn't know so much about that. It is true, of course, that I have a will of iron, but it can be switched off if the circumstances seem to demand it. The strong man always knows when to yield and make concessions. I have frequently found myself doing so in my relation with Jeeves.

'You absolutely guarantee this secret method?' I asked earnestly.

'I can only tell you that it produced immediate and gratifying results in my own case. One moment, I was engaged to Florence; the next, I wasn't. As quick as that. It was more like magic than anything I can think of.'

'And you'll tell it me, if I promise to tick Uncle Percy off?'

'I'll tell it you *after* you've ticked him off.'

'Why not now?'

'Just a whim. It's not that I don't trust you, Bertie. It's not that I think that, having learned the Fittleworth secret, you would change your mind about carrying out your end of the contract. But it would be a temptation, and I don't want your pure soul to be sullied by it.'

'But you'll tell me without fail after I've done the deed?'

'Without fail.'

I pondered. It was a fearful choice to have to make. But I did not hesitate long.

'All right, Boko. I'll do it.'

He tapped me affectionately on the chest. It was odd how tonight's events had brought out the chest-tapper in him.

'Splendid fellow!' he said. 'I thought you would. Now, you pop off to bed, so as to get a good night's rest and rise alert and refreshed. I will sit up and rough out a few things for you to say to the old boy. It's no good your trusting to the inspiration of the moment. You must have your material all written out and studied. I doubt, too, if, left to yourself, you would be able to think of anything really adequate. This is one of the occasions when you need the literary touch.'

20

It was but a troubled slumber that I enjoyed that night, much disturbed by dreams of Uncle Percy chasing me with his hunting-crop. Waking next morning, I found that though the heart was leaden, the weather conditions were of the best and brightest. The sun shone, the sky was blue, and in the trees outside my window the ear detected the twittering of a covey or platoon of the local fowls of the air.

But though all Nature smiled, there was, as I have indicated, no disposition on the part of Bertram to follow its example. I got no kick from the shining sun, no uplift from the azure firmament, as it is sometimes called: while as for the twittering birds their heartiness in the circumstances seemed overdone and in dubious taste. When you're faced with the sort of ordeal I was faced with, there is but little satisfaction to be derived from the thought that you've got a nice day for it.

My watch showed me that the hour was considerably less advanced than my customary one for springing from between the sheets, and it is possible that, had the burden on the soul been lighter, I might have turned over and got another forty minutes. But the realization of what dark deeds must be done 'ere this day's sun should have set – or, for the matter of that, 'ere this day's lunch should have been eaten – forbade sleep. I rose, accordingly, and assembling sponge and towel was about to proceed to the bathroom for a bit of torso sluicing, when my eye was caught by a piece of paper protruding from beneath the door. I picked it up, and found it to be the material which Boko had sat up on the previous night composing for my benefit – the few things, if you remember, which he wanted me to say to Uncle Percy. And as my eye flitted over it, the persp. started out on my brow and I sank back on the bed, appalled. It was as if I had scooped in a snake.

I think that in an earlier chronicle I related how, when a growing boy at my private school, I once sneaked down at dead of night to the study of the headmaster, the Rev. Aubrey Upjohn, in order to pinch a few mixed biscuits from the store which I had been informed that he maintained in the cupboard there; and how, having got well ahead with the work in hand, I discovered that their proprietor was also among those present, seated at his desk regarding my activities with a frosty eye.

The reason I bring this up again is that on the occasion to which I allude, after a brief pause – on my side, of embarrassment, on his of working up steam – the Rev. Aubrey had started to give a sort of character sketch of the young Wooster, which until now I had always looked upon as the last word in scholarly invective. It was the kind of thing a minor prophet of the Old Testament might have thrown together on one of his bilious mornings, and, as I say, I considered it to have set up a mark at which other orators would shoot in vain. I had been wrong. This screed of Boko's left it nowhere. Boko began where the Rev. Aubrey Upjohn left off.

Typewritten, with single spaces, I suppose the stuff ran to about six hundred words, and of all those six hundred words I don't think there were more than half a dozen which I could have brought myself to say to a man of Uncle Percy's calibre, unless primed to the back teeth with the raw spirit. And Boko, you will recall, was expecting me to deliver my harangue at ten o'clock in the morning.

To shoot out of my room into his, bubbling over with expostulations and what not, was with me the work of an instant. But the eloquent outburst which I had been planning was rendered null and void by the fact that he was not there, and an inquiry of an aged female whom I found messing about in the kitchen elicited the information that he had gone for a swim in the river. Repairing thither, I perceived him splashing about in mid-stream with many a merry cry.

But once more I was obliged to choke back the burning words. A second glance, revealing a pink, porpoise-like object at his side, told me that he was accompanied by Stilton. It was to Steeple Bumpleigh's zealous police constable that the merry cries were addressed, and I deemed it wisest to leave my presence unrevealed. It seemed to me that a chat with Stilton at this particular juncture could be fraught with neither pleasure nor profit.

I pushed along the bank, therefore, pondering deeply, and I hadn't gone far when there came to my ears the swish of a fishing line, and there was Jeeves, harrying the finny denizens like nobody's business. I might have known that his first act on finding himself established in Steeple Bumpleigh would have been to head for the fluid and cast a fly or two.

As it was to this fly-caster that I owed my present hideous predicament, you will not be surprised to learn that my manner, as I came abreast, was on the distant side.

'Ah, Jeeves,' I said.

'Good morning, sir,' he responded. 'A lovely day.'

'Lovely for some of us, perhaps, Jeeves,' I said coolly, 'but not for the Last of the Woosters, who, thanks to you, is faced by a binge beside which all former binges fade into insignificance.'

'Sir?'

'It's no good saying "Sir?" You know perfectly well what I mean. Entirely through your instrumentality, I shall shortly be telling Uncle Percy things about himself which will do something to his knotted and combined locks which at the moment has slipped my memory.'

'Make his knotted and combined locks to part and each particular hair to stand on end like quills upon the fretful porpentine, sir.'

'Porpentine?'

'Yes, sir.'

'That can't be right. There isn't such a thing. However, let that pass. The point is that you have let me in for the ghastly task of ticking Uncle Percy off, and I want to know what you did it for. Was it kind, Jeeves? Was it feudal?'

He registered surprise. Mild surprise, of course. He never goes as far as the other sort. One eyebrow flickered a little, and the tip of the nose moved slightly.

'You are alluding to the suggestion I offered Mr Fittleworth, sir?'

'That is the suggestion I am alluding to, Jeeves.'

'But surely, sir, if you have decided to fall in with the scheme, it was entirely your kind heart that led you to do so? It would have been optional for you to have declined to lend your assistance.'

'Ha!'

'Sir?'

'I said "Ha!" Jeeves. And I meant "Ha!" Do you know what happened last night?'

'So much happened last night, sir.'

'True. Among other things, I got properly biffed over the coconut by young Edwin with his Scout's stick, he thinking I was a burglar.'

'Indeed, sir?'

'We then fell into conversation, and he informed me that he had found the brooch which we assumed to have perished in the flames and had delivered it to Lady Florence, telling her it was a birthday present from me.'

'Indeed sir,'

'It just turned the scale. She had a frightful row with Stilton, gave him the air for saying derogatory things about modern enlightened thought, and is now betrothed once more to the toad beneath the harrow whom you see before you.'

I thought he was going to say 'Indeed, sir?' again, in which case I might easily have forgotten all the decencies of civilized life and dotted him one. At the last moment, however, he checked the utterance and merely pursed his lips in a grave and sympathetic manner. A vast improvement.

'And the reason I consented to sit in on this scheme of yours was that Boko confided to me last night that he had a simple infallible remedy for getting out of being engaged to this specific girl, and he won't tell me what it is till I have interviewed Uncle Percy.'

'I see, sir.'

'I must learn it at all costs. It's no use my trying the Stilton method and saying nasty things about modern enlightened thought, because I couldn't think of any. It is the Boko way or nothing. You don't happen to know what it was that made Lady Florence sever her relations with him, do you?'

'No, sir. Indeed, it is news to me that Mr Fittleworth was affianced to her ladyship.'

'Oh, yes. He was affianced to her, all right. Post-Wooster, but pre-Stilton. And something occurred, an imbroglio of some description, took place, and the thing was instantly broken off. Just like magic, he said. I gathered that it was something he did. But what could it have been?'

'I fear I am unable to hazard a conjecture, sir. Would you wish me to institute inquiries among the domestic staff at the Hall?'

'An excellent idea, Jeeves.'

'It is possible that some member of that unit may have become cognisant of the facts.'

'The thing was probably the talk of the Housekeeper's Room for days. Sound the butler. Question the cook.'

'Very good, sir.'

'Or try Lady Florence's personal maid. Somebody is sure to know. There's not much that domestic staffs don't become cognisant of.'

'No, sir. One has usually found them well informed.'

'And bear in mind that speed is essential. If you can hand me the data before I see Uncle Percy – that is to say, any time up to ten o'clock, for which hour the kick-off is slated – I shall be in a position to edge out of giving him that straight talk, at the thought of which I don't mind telling you that the flesh creeps. As for the happiness of Boko and soulmate, I am all for giving that a boost, of course, but I feel that it can be done by other and less drastic methods. So lose no time, Jeeves, in instituting those inquiries.'

'Very good, sir.'

'Be at the main gate of the Hall from half-past nine onwards. I shall be arriving about then, and shall expect your report. Try not to fail me, Jeeves. Now is the time for all good men to come to the aid of the party. If I could show you that list Boko drafted out of the things he wants me to say – I unfortunately left it in my room, where it fell from my nerveless fingers – your knotted and combined locks would part all right, believe me. You're sure it's porpentine?'

'Yes, sir.'

'Very odd. But I suppose half the time Shakespeare just shoved down anything that came into his head.'

Having been *en route* for the bathroom at the moment when I buzzed off to seek audience of Boko, I was still, of course, in the ordinary slumberwear of the English gentleman, plus a dressing-gown, and it was some little time, accordingly, after I had returned to the house, before I showed up in the dining-salon. I found Boko there, getting outside a breakfast egg. I asked him if he knew what a porpentine was, and he said to hell with all porpentines and had I got that sheet of instructions all right and, if so, what did I think of it.

To this, my reply was that I certainly had jolly well got it and that it had frozen me to the marrow. No human power, I added, would induce me to pass on to Uncle Percy even a skeleton outline of the document's frightful contents.

'Frightful contents.'

'That was what I said.'

He seemed wounded, and murmured something about the artist and destructive criticism.

'I thought it was particularly good stuff. Crisp, terse and telling. The subject inspired me, and I was under the impression that I had given of my best. Still, if you feel that I stressed the personal note a bit too much, you can modify it here and there, if you like – preserving the substance, of course.'

'As a matter of fact,' I said, thinking it best to prepare him, 'you mustn't be surprised, Boko, if at the last moment I change my plans and decide to give the whole thing a miss.'

'What!'

'I am toying with the idea.'

'Well, I'm blowed! Is this – ?'

'Yes, it is.'

'You don't know what I was going to say.'

'Yes, I do. You were going to say "Is this Bertie Wooster speaking?"'

'Quite right. I was. Well, is it?'

'Yes.'

His table talk then took on a rather acid tone, touching disparagingly on so-called friends who, supposed by him hitherto to be staunch and true, turned out to his disappointment to be lily-livered poltroons lacking even the meagre courage of a rabbit.

'Where are the boys of the bulldog breed? That's what I want to know,' he concluded, plainly chagrined. 'Well, you understand clearly what this means. Fail me, and not an inkling of the Fittleworth secret do you get.'

I smiled subtly, and helped myself to a slice of ham. He little knew, I felt.

'I shall watch you walking up the aisle with Florence Craye, and not stir a finger to save you. In fact, you will hear a voice singing "Oh, perfect love" rather louder than the rest of the congregation, and it will be mine. Reconsider, Bertie. That is what I advise.'

'Well, of course,' I said, 'I don't say I will back out of the assignment. I only say I may.'

This calmed him somewhat, and he softened – saying that he was sure that when the hour struck, my better self would prevail. And a bit later, we parted with mutual good wishes.

For it had been arranged that we should proceed to the Hall separately. In his case, Boko felt, not without some reason, that there was need for stealth, lest he be fallen upon and slung out. He proposed, therefore, to circle round the outskirts till he found a gap in the hedge and then approach the study by a circuitous route, keeping well in the shelter of the bushes and not letting a twig snap beneath his feet.

I set out by myself, accordingly, and arriving at the main entrance found Jeeves waiting for me in the drive. It needed but a glance to inform me that the man had good tidings. I can always tell. He doesn't exactly smile on these occasions, because he never does, but the lips twitch slightly at the corners and the eye is benevolent.

I gave tongue eagerly.

'Well, Jeeves?'

'I have the data you require, sir.'

'Splendid fellow! You saw the butler! You probed the cook?'

'Actually, it was from the boy who cleans the knives and boots that I secured the information, sir. A young fellow of the name of Erbut.'

'How did he come to be our special correspondent?'

'It appears that he was actually an eyewitness of the scene, sir, sheltered in the obscurity of a neighbouring bush, where he had been enjoying a surreptitious cigarette. From this point of vantage he was enabled to view the entire proceedings.'

'And what were they? Tell me all, Jeeves, omitting no detail, however slight.'

'Well, sir, the first thing that attracted the lad's attention was the approach of Master Edwin.'

'He comes into it, does he?'

'Yes, sir. His role, as you will see, is an important one. Master Edwin, Erbut reports, was advancing through the undergrowth, his gaze fixed upon the ground. He seemed to be tracking something.'

'Spooring, no doubt. It is a practice to which these Scouts are much addicted.'

'So I understand, sir. His movements, Erbut noted, were being observed with a sisterly indulgence by Lady Florence, who was cutting flowers in an adjacent border.'

'She was watching him, eh?'

'Yes, sir. Simultaneously, Mr Fittleworth appeared, following the young gentleman.'

'Spooring the spoorer?'

'Yes, sir. Erbut describes his manner as keen and purposeful. That, at least, was his meaning, though the actual phrasing of his statement was different. These knives and boots boys seldom express themselves well.'

'I've often noticed it. Rotten vocabularies. Go on, Jeeves. I'm all agog. Boko, you say, was trailing Edwin. Why?'

'That was what Erbut appears to have asked himself, sir.'

'He was mystified?'

'Yes, sir.'

'I don't blame him. I'm mystified myself. I gather, of course, that the plot thickens, but I'm dashed if I can see where it's heading.'

'It was not long before Mr Fittleworth's motives were abundantly clear, sir. As Master Edwin approached the flower bed, he suddenly accelerated his movements – '

'Edwin did?'

'No, sir. Mr Fittleworth. He bounded forward at the young gentle-man, and taking advantage of the fact that the latter, in the course of his spooring, had just adopted a stooping posture, proceeded to deliver a forceful kick upon his person – '

'Golly, Jeeves!'

' – causing him to fly through the air and fall at Lady Florence's feet. Her ladyship, horrified and incensed, rebuked Mr Fittleworth sharply, demanding an immediate explanation of this wanton assault. The latter endeavoured to justify his action by accusing Master Edwin of having tampered with his patent egg boiler, so disorganizing the mechanism that a new-laid egg had flown from its base and struck him on the tip of the nose. Her ladyship, however, was unable to see her way to accepting this as a palliation of what had occurred, and shortly afterwards announced that the betrothal was at an end.'

I drew in the breath. The scales had fallen from my eyes. I saw all. So that was the Fittleworth remedy – booting young Edwin! No wonder Boko had spoken of it as simple and efficacious. All you needed was a good stout shoe and a sister's love.

I heard Jeeves cough.

'If you will glance to your left, sir,' he said, 'you will observe that Master Edwin has just entered the drive and is stooping over some object on the ground that appears to have engaged his attention.'

21

I got the gist. The significance of his words was not lost upon me. The grave, encouraging look with which he had accompanied the news bulletin would alone have been enough to enable me to sense the underlying message he was trying to convey. It was the sort of look a Roman father might have given his son, when handing him shield and spear and pushing him off to battle, and it ought, I suppose, to have stirred me like a bugle.

Nevertheless, I found myself hesitating. After that sock on the head he had given me on the previous night, the thought of kicking young Edwin was one that presented many attractions, of course, and there was no question but that the child had been asking for some such little personal attention for years. But there's something rather embarrassing about doing that sort of thing in cold blood. Difficult, I felt, to lead up to it neatly in the course of conversation. ('Hello, Edwin. How are you? Lovely day.' *Biff.* You see what I mean. Not easy.)

In Boko's case, of course, the whole set-up had been entirely different, for he had been in the grip of the berserk fury which comes upon a man when he is hit on the tip of the nose with new-laid eggs. This had enabled him, so to speak, to get a running start.

And so I fingered the chin dubiously.

'Yes,' I said. 'Yes, there he is, Jeeves – and, as you say, stooping. But do you really advise – '

'I do, sir.'

'What, now?'

'Yes, sir. There is a tide in the affairs of men which, taken at the flood, leads on to fortune. Omitted, all the voyage of their life is bound in shallows and in miseries.'

'Oh, rather. Quite. No argument about that. But – '

'If what you are trying to say, sir, is that it is of the essence that Lady Florence be present, to observe the proceedings as she did in the case of Mr Fittleworth, I fully concur. I would suggest that I go and inform her ladyship that you are waiting on the drive and would be glad of a word with her.'

I still hesitated. It was one of those cases where you approve the broad, general principle of an idea, but can't help being in a bit of a twitter at the prospect of putting it into practical effect. I explained this to Jeeves, and he said that much the same thing had bothered Hamlet.

'Your irresolution is quite understandable, sir. Between the acting of a dreadful thing and the first motion, all the interim is like a phantasma or a hideous dream. The genius and the mortal instruments are then in council; and that state of man, like to a little kingdom, suffers then the nature of an insurrection.'

'Absolutely,' I said. He puts these things well.

'If it would assist you to stiffen the sinews and summon up the blood, sir, may I remind you that it is very nearly ten o'clock, and that only the promptest action along the lines I have indicated can enable you to avoid appearing in his lordship's study at that hour.'

He had found the talking-point. I hesitated no longer.

'You're right, Jeeves. How long do you think it will be necessary to detail young Edwin in conversation before you can bring Lady Florence on stage?'

'Not more than a few minutes, sir. I happen to know that her ladyship is at the moment in her private apartment, engaged upon literary work. There will be but a brief interval before she appears.'

'Then tally ho!'

'Very good, sir.'

He flickered off upon his mission, while I, having summoned up the blood a bit and stiffened the sinews as far as was possible at such short notice, squared the shoulders and headed for where Edwin was squatting. The weather continued uniformly fine. The sun shone, and a blackbird, I remember, was singing in an adjoining thicket. No reason why it shouldn't have been, of course. I mention the fact merely to stress the general peace and tranquillity of everything. And I must say it did strike me as a passing thought that the sort of setting a job like this really needed was a blasted heath at midnight, with a cold wind whistling in the bushes and three witches doing their stuff at the cauldron.

However, one can't have everything, and I doubt if an observer would have noted any diffidence in Bertram's bearing as he advanced upon his prey. Bertram, I rather fancy he would have thought, was in pretty good form.

I hove to at the stripling's side.

'Hullo, young Edwin,' I said.

His gaze had been riveted on the ground, but at the sound of the familiar voice a couple of pink-rimmed eyes came swivelling round in my direction. He looked up at me like a ferret about to pass the time of day with another ferret.

'Hullo, Bertie. I say, Bertie, I did another act of kindness this morning.'

'Oh, yes?'

'I finished pasting the notices of Florence's novel in her album. That puts me all right up to last Wednesday.'

'Good work. You're catching up. And what do you think you're doing now?'

'I'm studying ants. Do you know anything about ants, Bertie?'

'Only from meeting them at picnics.'

'I've been reading up about them. Very interesting.'

'Vastly, I shouldn't wonder.'

I was glad the topic had been introduced, for it promised to be one that would carry us along nicely until Florence's arrival on the scene. It was obvious that the young squirt was bulging with information about these industrious little creatures and asked nothing better than to be allowed to impart it.

'Did you know that ants can talk?'

'Talk?'

'In a sort of way. To other ants, of course. They do it by tapping their heads on a leaf. How's your head this morning, Bertie? I nearly forgot to ask.'

'Still on the tender side.'

'I thought it would be. Coo! That was funny last night, wasn't it? I laughed for hours, when I got to bed.'

He emitted a ringing guffaw, and at the raucous sound any spark of compunction that might have been lingering in my bosom was quenched. A boy to whom the raising of a lump the size of a golf ball on the Wooster bean was a subject for heartless mirth deserved all that boot toe could do to him. For the first time, I found myself contemplating the task before me with real fire and enthusiasm – almost, as you might say, in a missionary spirit. I mean, I felt what a world of good a swift kick in the pants would do to this child. It might prove to be the turning-point in his life.

'You laughed, did you?'

'Rather!'

'Ha!' I said, and ground a few teeth.

The maddening thing was, of course, that though I was now keyed

up to give of my best, and though the position he had assumed for
this ant-studying session of his was the exact position demanded
by the run of the scenario, I was debarred from getting action.
You might have compared me to a greyhound on the leash. Until
Florence came along, I could not fulfil myself. As Jeeves had said,
her presence was of the essence. I scanned the horizon for a sight
of her, like a shipwrecked mariner hoping for a sail, but she did not
appear, and in the meantime we went on talking about ants, Edwin
saying that they were members of the Hymenoptera family and self
replying, 'Well, well. Quite the nibs, eh?'

'They are characterized by unusual distinctness of the three
regions of the body – head, thorax and abdomen – and by the
stack or petiole of the abdomen having one or two scales or nodes,
so that the abdomen moves very freely on the truck or thorax.'

'You wouldn't fool me?'

'The female, after laying her eggs, feeds the larvae with food
regurgitated from her stomach.'

'Try to keep it clean, my lad.'

'Both males and females are winged.'

'And why not?'

'But the female pulls off its wings and runs about without them.'

'I question that. I doubt if even an ant would be such an ass.'

'It's quite true. It says so in the book. Have you ever seen
ants fight?'

'Not that I remember.'

'They rise on their hind legs and curve the abdomen.'

And, to my consternation and chagrin, whether because it was
his intention to illustrate or because he found his squatting position
cramping to the limbs, this was just what he did himself. He rose on
his hind legs, and stood facing me, curving the abdomen – at the
exact moment when I perceived Florence emerging from the house
and walking briskly in our direction.

It was a crisis at which a less resourceful man might have supposed
that all was lost. But the Woosters are quick thinkers.

'Hullo!' I said.

'What's the matter?'

'Have you dropped sixpence?'

'No.'

'Somebody has. Look.'

'Where?'

'Under that bush,' I said, and pointed to a shrub of sorts on the
edge of the drive.

As you probably conjecture, in saying this I was descending to subterfuge, and anybody knowing Bertram Wooster and his rigid principles might have supposed that such wilful tampering with the truth would have caused the blush of shame to mantle his cheek. Not so, however. If there was a flush to be noted, it was the flush of excitement and triumph.

For my subtle appeal to the young blister's cupidity had not failed to achieve its end. Already, he was down on all fours, and if I had posed him with my own hands I could not have obtained better results. His bulging shorts seemed to smile up at me in a sort of inviting, welcoming way.

As Jeeves had rightly said, there is a tide in the affairs of men which, taken at the flood, leads on to fortune. I drew back the leg, and let him have it just where the pants were tightest.

It was a superb effort. Considering that I hadn't kicked anyone since the distant days of school, you might have thought that the machinery would have got rusty. But no. All the old skill still lingered. My timing was perfect, and so was my follow through. He disappeared into the bush, travelling as if out of a gun, and as he did so Florence's voice spoke.

'Ah!' she said.

There was no mistaking the emotion that animated the ejaculation. It was stiff with it. But with a dazed sensation of something having gone wrong I realized that it was not the emotion I had anticipated. Horror was completely absent, nor had there come through anything in the nature of indignation and sisterly resentment. Astounding as it may seem, joy was the predominating note. One might go further and say ecstasy. Her 'Ah!' in short, had been practically equivalent to 'Whoopee!' and I could make nothing of it.

'Thank you, Bertie!' she said. 'It was just what I was going to do myself. Edwin, come here!'

Down in the forest something stirred. It was the prudent child wriggling his way through the bush in a diametrically opposite direction. There came the sound of a faint and distant 'Coo!' and he was gone, leaving not a wrack behind.

Florence was gazing at me, a cordial and congratulatory light in her eyes, a happy smile playing about her lips.

'Thank you, Bertie!' she said again, once more with that wealth of emotion in her voice. 'I would like to skin him! I have just been looking at my album of press clippings, and he has gone and pasted in half the reviews of *Spindrift* wrong side up. I believe he did it on purpose. It's a pity I couldn't catch him, but there it is. I can't tell you how grateful I am, Bertie, for what you did. What gave you the idea?'

'Oh, it just came to me.'

'I understand. A sort of sudden inspiration. The central theme of *Spindrift* came like that. Jeeves says you want to speak to me. Is it something very important?'

'Oh, no. Not important.'

'Then we will keep it till later. I must go back now and see if there isn't some way of floating those clippings off with hot water.'

She hurried away, turning as she entered the house to wave a loving hand, and I was left alone to submit the situation to the analysis it demanded.

I don't know anything that seems to jar the back teeth like having a sure thing come unstuck, and it was with a dull sensation of having been hit in the stomach by a medicine ball, as once happened to me during a voyage to America, that I stood contemplating the future. Not even the fact that in the recent scene this girl had shown a warm, human side to her nature, which I had not suspected that she possessed, could reconcile me to what I was now so unavoidably in for. A Florence capable of wanting to skin Edwin was better, of course, than a Florence susceptible of no such emotion, but no, I couldn't bring myself to like the shape of things to come.

How long I stood brooding there before I became aware of the squeaking that was going on at my side, I cannot say. Quite a time it must have been. For when at length I came out of my reverie, to find that Nobby was endeavouring to attract my attention, I saw that her manner was impatient, like that of one who has been trying to hobnob with a deaf mute and is finding the one-sided conversation weighing upon the spirits.

'Bertie!'

'Oh, sorry. I was musing.'

'Well, stop musing. You'll be late.'

'Late?'

'For Uncle Percy. In the study.'

I have mentioned earlier in this narrative that I am a pretty good silver-lining spotter, and that if there is a bright side to any cataclysm or disaster I seldom fail to put my finger on it sooner or later. Her words reminded me that there was one attached to the present catastrophe. Murky the future might be, what with all those wedding bells and what not which now seemed so inescapable, but at least I was in a position to save something out of the wreck. I could at any rate give Uncle Percy the go-by.

'Oh, that?' I said. 'That's off.'

'Off?'

'My reward for sitting in on the scheme,' I explained, 'was to have been the learning of the Fittleworth secret process for getting out of being engaged to Florence. I have learned it, and it is a wash-out. I, therefore, hand in my portfolio.'

'You mean you won't help us?'

'In some other way, to be decided on later, certainly. But not by inflaming Uncle Percy.'

'Oh, Bertie!'

'And it's no good saying, "Oh, Bertie!"'

She looked at me with bulging eyes, and it seemed for an instant as if those pearly drops, of which Boko had spoken so eloquently, were about to start functioning once more. But there was good stuff in the Hopwoods. The dam did not burst.

'But I don't understand.'

I explained in some detail what had occurred.

'Boko,' I concluded, 'claimed that this secret remedy of his was infallible. It is not. So unless he has something else to suggest – '

'But he has. I mean, I have.'

'You?'

'You want Florence to break off the engagement?'

'I do.'

'Well, go and talk to Uncle Percy, and I'll show her that letter you wrote me, saying what you thought of her. That'll work it.'

I started. In fact, I leaped about a foot.

'Golly!'

'Don't you agree?'

'Well, I'm dashed!'

I don't know when I've been so affected. I had forgotten all about that letter, but now, as its burning phrases came back to me, hope, which I had thought dead, threw off the winding sheet and resumed business at the old stand. The Fittleworth method might have failed, but there was no question that the Hopwood remedy would bring home the bacon.

'Nobby!'

'Think on your feet!'

'You promise you'll show Florence that letter?'

'Faithfully. If you will give Uncle Percy the treatment.'

'Is Boko at his post?'

'Sure to be by now.'

'Then out of my way! Here we go!'

And, moving as if on wings, I flitted to the house, plunged across the threshold, shot down the passage that led to the relative's sanctum and dived in.

22

Uncle Percy's study, to which this was of course my first visit, proved to be what they call on the stage a 'rich interior', liberally equipped with desks, chairs, tables, carpets and all the usual fixings. Books covered one side of it, and on the opposite wall there hung a large picture showing nymphs, or something similar, sporting with what, from the look of them and the way they were behaving, I took to be fauns. One also noted a terrestrial globe, some bowls of flowers, a stuffed trout, a cigar humidor, and a bust which might have been that of the late Mr Gladstone.

In short, practically the only thing you could think of that could have been in the room, but wasn't, was Uncle Percy. He was not seated in the chair behind the desk, nor was he pacing the carpet, twiddling the globe, sniffing the flowers, reading the books, admiring the stuffed trout or taking a gander at the nymphs and fauns. Not a glimpse of him met the eye, and this total absence of uncles, so different from what I had been led to expect, brought me up with a bit of a turn.

It's a rummy feeling, when you've got yourself all braced for the fray and suddenly discover that the fray hasn't turned up. Rather like treading on the last stair when it isn't there. I stood chewing the lip in some perplexity, wondering what to do for the best.

The scent of a robust cigar, still lingering in the air, showed that he must have been on the spot quite recently, and the open french windows suggested that he had popped out into the garden, there possibly to wrestle with the problems which were weighing on his mind – notably, no doubt, that of how the dickens life at Steeple Bumpleigh being what it was, he was to obtain an uninterrupted five minutes with Chichester Clam. And what I was debating within myself was whether to follow him or to remain in *status quo* till he came back.

Much depended, of course, on how long he was going to be. I mean, it wasn't as if the mood of fiery resolution in which I had hurled myself across the threshold was a thing which would last indefinitely.

Already, the temperature of the feet had become sensibly lowered, and I was conscious of an emptiness behind the diaphragm and a disposition to gulp. Postpone the fixture for even another minute or two, and the evil would spread to such an extent that the relative, when he eventually showed up, would find a Bertram out of whom all the sawdust had trickled – a Wooster capable of nothing better than a mild 'Yes, Uncle Percy', and 'No, Uncle Percy'.

Looking at it from every angle, therefore, it seemed that it would be best to go and tackle him in the great open spaces, where Boko by this time was presumably lurking. And I had reached the french windows, and was about to pass through, though with little or no relish for what lay before me, when my attention was arrested by the sound of raised voices. They came from a certain distance, and the actual wording of the dialogue escaped the eardrum, but from the fact that they were addressing each other as 'My dear Worplesdon' and 'You blot', I divined that they belonged – respectively – to Boko and the seigneur of Bumpleigh Hall.

A moment later, my conjecture was proved correct. A little procession came into view, crossing the strip of lawn outside the study. Heading it was Boko, looking less debonair than I have sometimes seen him. Following him came a man of gardeneresque appearance, armed with a pitchfork and accompanied by a dog of uncertain breed. The rear was brought up by Uncle Percy, waving a cigar menacingly like the angel expelling Adam from the Garden of Eden.

It was he who seemed to be doing most of the talking. From time to time, Boko would look around, as if about to say something, but whatever eloquence he may have been intending was checked by the expression on the face of the dog, which was that of one fit for treasons, stratagems and spoils, and the fact that the pitchfork to which I have alluded was almost touching the seat of his trousers.

Half-way across the lawn, Uncle Percy detached himself from the convoy and came stumping rapidly towards me, puffing emotionally at his cigar. Boko and his new friends continued in the direction of the drive.

After the painful shock, inevitable on seeing an old friend given the push from enclosed premises, my first thought, as you may have surmised, had been that there was nothing to keep me. The whole essence of the scheme to which I had consented to lend my services had been that Boko should be within earshot while I was making my observations to Uncle Percy, and nothing was clearer than that by the time the latter reached his sanctum he would have drifted away like thistledown.

I shot off, accordingly, not standing upon the order of my going but going at once, as the fellow said, and was making good progress when, as I approached the door, I suddenly observed that there hung over it a striking portrait of Aunt Agatha, from the waist upwards. In making my entrance, I had, of course, missed this, but there it had been all the time, and now it caught my eye and halted me in my tracks as if I had run into a lamp-post.

It was the work of one of those artists who reveal the soul of the sitter, and it had revealed so much of Aunt Agatha's soul that for all practical purposes it might have been that danger to traffic in person. Indeed, I came within an ace of saying 'Oh, hullo!' at the same moment when I could have sworn it said 'Bertie!' in that compelling voice which had so often rung in my ears and caused me to curl up in a ball in the hope that a meek subservience would enable me to get off lightly.

The weakness was, of course, merely a temporary one. A moment later, Bertram was himself again. But the pause had been long enough to allow Uncle Percy to come clumping into the room, and escape was now impossible. I remained, therefore, and stood shooting my cuffs, trusting that the action would induce fortitude. It does sometimes.

Uncle Percy appeared to be soliloquizing.

'I trod on him! *Trod* on him! There he was, nestling in the grass, and I trod on him! It's not enough that the fellow comes roaming my grounds uninvited at all hours of the night. He comes also by day, and reclines in my personal grass. No keeping him out, apparently. He oozes into the place like oil.'

Here, for the first time, he seemed to become aware of a nephew's presence.

'Bertie!'

'Oh, hullo, Uncle Percy.'

'My dear fellow! Just the chap I wanted to see.'

To say that I was surprised at this remark would be to portray my emotions but feebly. It absolutely knocked me endways.

I mean, consider the facts. Man and boy, I had known this old buzzard a matter of fifteen years, and not once during that period had he even hinted that my society held any attraction for him. In fact, on most of the occasions when we had foregathered, he had rather gone out of his way to indicate that the reverse was the case. I have already alluded to the episode of the hunting-crop, and there had been other similar passages through the course of the years.

I have, I think, made it sufficiently clear that few harder eggs ever stepped out of the saucepan than this Percival, Lord Worplesdon.

Rugged sea captains, accustomed to facing gales in the Western Ocean without a tremor, quivered like blancmanges when hauled up before him in his office and asked why the devil they had – or had not – ported the helm or spliced the mainbrace during their latest voyage in his service. In disposition akin to a more than ordinarily short-tempered snapping turtle, he resembled in appearance a malevolent Aubrey Smith, and usually, when one encountered him, gave the impression of being just about to foam at the mouth.

Yet now he was gazing at me in a manner which, when you came to look closely and got past the bristling moustache, revealed itself as not only part human, but actually kindly. From the pain in the neck generally induced by the sight of Bertram Wooster he appeared to be absolutely free.

'Who, me?' I said, weakly, my amazement such that I was compelled to support myself against the terrestrial globe.

'Yes, you. The very fellow. Have a drink, Bertie.'

I said something about it being a bit early, but he pooh-poohed the suggestion.

'It's never too early to have a drink, if you've been wading ankle deep in blasted Fittleworths. I was taking a stroll with my cigar, my mind deeply occupied with vital personal problems, and my foot came down on something squashy, and there the frightful chap was, reclining in the lush grass by the lake as if he had been a dashed field-mouse or something. If I had had a weak heart, it might have been the end of me.'

I couldn't help mourning for Boko. I could picture what must have occurred. Making his way snakily towards the study window, he had heard Uncle Percy's approach and had taken cover, little knowing that a moment later the latter's number eleven foot was about to descend upon what – from the fact that the other had described it as squashy – must have been some tender portion of his anatomy. A nasty jar for the poor chap. A nasty jar for Uncle Percy, too, of course. In fact, one of those situations where the heart bleeds for both the party of the first part and the party of the second part.

'Fittleworth!' He shot an accusing glance at me. 'Friend of yours, isn't he?'

'Oh, bosom.'

'You would do well to choose your friends more carefully,' he said, with the first lapse from that strange benevolence of his which he had yet shown.

I suppose this was really the moment for embarking upon an impassioned defence of Boko, stressing his admirable qualities.

Not being able to think of any, however, I remained silent, and he carried on.

'But never mind him. My gardening staff is seeing him off the premises, with strict orders to jab him in the seat of his pants with a pitchfork if he dares to offer the slightest resistance. I venture to think that these grounds will see less of him in the future. And, by George, that is what Bumpleigh Hall wants, to make it an earthly Paradise – fewer and better Fittleworths. Have a cigar, Bertie.'

'I don't think so, thanks.'

'Nonsense. I can't understand this in and out policy of yours with regard to my cigars. When I don't want you to smoke them, you do – remember that hunting-crop, eh, ha, ha? – and when I do want you to smoke them, you don't. All silly nonsense. Put this in your face, you young rascal,' he said, producing from the humidor something that looked like a torpedo, 'and let's have no more of this "I don't think so, thanks". I want you to be all relaxed and comfortable, because I have something very important to consult you about. Ah, bring it here, Maple.'

On the cue 'It's never too early to have a drink', I should have mentioned, he had pressed the bell, causing the butler to appear and book instruction. The latter had now re-entered with a half-bot from the oldest bin, and it was while genially uncorking this that the relative resumed his remarks.

'Yes, never mind Fittleworth,' he repeated, handing me a foaming goblet. 'Let us dismiss him from our thoughts. I have other things to talk out. First and foremost . . . Cheerio, Bertie.'

'Cheerio,' I said, faintly.

'Success to crime.'

'Skin off your nose,' I responded, still on the dazed side.

'Mud in your eye,' said this extraordinary changeling. 'First and foremost,' he proceeded, passing a rapid glassful down the hatch, 'I wish to express my appreciation of your spectacularly admirable conduct on the drive just now. I met Edwin out there, and he told me you had kicked him. A thing I've been wanting to do for years, but never had the nerve.'

Here he rose from his chair with outstretched hand, shook mine warmly and reseated himself.

'Thinking over some of our recent meetings, Bertie,' he said – I don't say softly, because he couldn't speak softly, but as softly as a chap who found it so difficult to speak softly could speak, 'I fancy you may have run away with the idea that I was a bad-tempered, cross-grained old fellow. I believe I spoke harshly to you last night.

You must overlook it. You must make allowances. You can't judge a man with a son like Edwin by the same standards as men who haven't got a son like Edwin. Did you happen to hear that he got me squarely with that infernal Scout's stick of his last night?'

'Me, too.'

'Right on the – '

'He got me on the head.'

'Thinking I was a burglar, or some such nonsense. And when I wanted to take steps, Florence wouldn't let me. You can imagine how I felt when I learned that you had kicked him. I wish I had seen it. Still, I gathered enough from his story to tell me that you behaved with notable gallantry and resource, and I don't mind admitting, my boy, that the thing has completely revolutionized my opinion of you. For years I have been looking on you as a mere lackadaisical, spiritless young man about town. I see now how wrong I was. You have shown yourself to be possessed of the highest executive qualities, and I have decided that you are the chap to advise me in the crisis which has arisen in my affairs. I am in a painful dilemma, Bertie. It is absolutely essential that ... But perhaps you have heard about it from Jeeves?'

'He did give me a sort of outline.'

'Chichester Clam?'

'Yes.'

'My vital need for meeting him in secret session?'

'Yes.'

'That clears the ground then. Never mind why it is so urgent for me to meet Chichester Clam in secret session. So long as you understand that it is, that is all that matters. He was the man in the potting shed last night.'

'Yes.'

'You know that, do you? It was Jeeves's suggestion, and a very good one, too. In fact, if it hadn't been for that revolting Fittleworth ... But don't let me get on to the subject of Fittleworth. I want to keep calm. Yes, Clam was in the potting shed. Curious fellow.'

'Oh, yes?'

'Most curious. I wonder how I can describe him to you. Ever seen a fawn?'

'Like the chaps in that picture?'

'No, not that sort of faun. I mean the animal. The timid fawn that shivers and shakes and at the slightest suspicion of danger starts like a ... like a fawn. That's Clam. Not to look at, I don't mean. He's stouter than the average fawn, and he wears horn-rimmed spectacles, which, of course, fawns don't. I'm referring to his character and disposition. You agree with me?'

I reminded him that, owing to the fact that I had never had the pleasure of making his acquaintance, Clam's psychology was a sealed book to me.

'That's true. I was forgetting. Well, that's what he's like. A fawn. Nervous. Quivering. Gets the wind up at the slightest provocation. Came out of that potting shed, I understand, shaking like a leaf and saying "Never again!" Yes, every drop of his manly courage had evaporated, and any scheme which we may devise for a future meeting will have to be a good one, a foolproof one, a scheme which even he can see involves him in no peril. Odd, this neurotic tendency in the American businessman. Can you account for it? No? I can. Too much coffee.'

'Coffee?'

'That and the New Deal. Over in America, it appears, life for the businessman is one long series of large cups of coffee, punctuated with shocks from the New Deal. He drinks a quart of coffee, and gets a nasty surprise from the New Deal. To pull himself together, he drinks another quart of coffee, and along comes another nasty surprise from the New Deal. He staggers off, calling feebly for more coffee, and . . . Well, you see what I mean. Vicious circle. No nervous system could stand it. Chichester Clam's nerves are in ruins. He wants to take the next boat to New York. Knows he will be wrecking the business deal of a lifetime by doing so, but says he doesn't care, just so long as he gets God's broad, deep Atlantic Ocean in between him and the English potting shed. A most extraordinary prejudice he seems to have taken against potting sheds, so keep steadily in your mind the fact that whatever you may have to suggest must be totally free from anything in the nature of a potting-shed angle. What have you to suggest, Bertie?'

To this, of course, there was but one reply.

'I think we'd better consult Jeeves.'

'I have consulted Jeeves, and he says he's baffled.'

I shot out an aghastish puff of smoke. The thing seemed incredible.

'Jeeves says he's baffled?'

'Told me so himself. That's why I've come to you. Fresh mind.'

'When did he say that?'

'Last night.'

I saw that all was not lost.

'Ah, but he's had a refreshing sleep since then, and you know how a spot of sleep picks you up. And, by Jove, Uncle Percy, I'll tell you something I've just remembered. Early this morning I came upon him fishing in the river.'

'What of it?'

'The fact is tremendously significant. I didn't actually question him on the subject, but a man of his calibre would be bound to have caught a few. No doubt, he had them for breakfast. In which case, his faculties will have been greatly stimulated. Probably by now he's at the top of his form again, with his brain humming like a dynamo.'

It was plain that the relative found himself infected by my enthusiasm. In obvious excitement, he put the wrong end of his cigar in his mouth, singeing his moustache at the corner.

'I never thought of that,' he said, having cursed a bit.

'That often happens with Jeeves.'

'Is that so?'

'Most of his major triumphs have been accomplished on fish.'

'You don't say?'

'Absolutely. The phosphorus, you know.'

'Of course.'

'Even a single sardine will sometimes do the trick. Can you lay your hand on him?'

'I'll ring for Maple. Oh, Maple,' he said, as the butler fetched up at journey's end, 'send Jeeves to me.'

'Very good, m'lord.'

'And another half-bottle, I think, don't you Bertie?'

'Just as you say, Uncle Percy.'

'It would be rash not to have it. You have no conception how it shakes a man, bringing his foot down on what he thinks is solid ground and finding it's Fittleworth. Another of the same, Maple.'

'Very good, m'lord.'

During the stage wait, which was not of long duration, the old relative filled in with some *ad lib* stuff about Boko, mostly about how much he disliked his face. Then the door opened again to admit a procession headed by the half-bottle on a salver. This was followed by Maple, who in his turn was followed by Jeeves. Maple withdrew, and Uncle Percy got down to it.

'Jeeves.'

'M'lord?'

'Did you catch any fish this morning?'

'Two, m'lord.'

'Have 'em for breakfast?'

'Yes, m'lord.'

'Splendid. Capital. Excellent. Then come along. Hark for'rard.'

'M'lord?'

'I was telling his lordship how fish always gingered up your thought processes,' I explained. 'He is rather expecting that you may now have something constructive to suggest in re another meeting with Chichester Clam.'

'I am sorry, sir. I have used every endeavour to hit upon a solution of the problem confronting his lordship, but I regret to say that my efforts have not been crowned with success.'

'A wash-out, he says,' I construed, for Uncle Percy's benefit.

Uncle Percy said he had hoped for better things. Jeeves said he had, too.

'Any good offering you a glass of bubbly? Might buck you up.'

'I fear not, m'lord. Alcohol has a sedative rather than a stimulating effect on me.'

'In that case, nothing to be done, I suppose. All right, Jeeves. Thanks.'

A fairly sombre silence fell upon the room for some moments, after the man's departure. I gave the terrestrial globe a twirl. Uncle Percy stared at the stuffed trout.

'Well, that's that, what?' I said, at length.

'Eh?'

'I mean, if Jeeves is baffled, hope would appear to be more or less dead.'

To my surprise, he did not agree with me. His eye flashed fire. I had underestimated the fighting spirit of these blokes who have made large fortunes in the shipping business. You may depress them for a while, but you can't keep them down.

'Nonsense, nonsense. Nothing of the kind. Jeeves isn't the only man in this house with a head on his shoulders. Anyone who could conceive the idea of kicking Edwin and carry it out as brilliantly as you did is not to be beaten by a simple problem like this. I am relying on you, Bertie. Chichester Clam – how to meet him? Don't give it up. Think again.'

'Shall I go and brood a bit on the drive?'

'Brood wherever you like, all over the grounds.'

'Right ho,' I said, and took a meditative departure.

I had scarcely closed the door and started to push along the passage, when Nobby appeared, as if out of a trap.

23

She came leaping towards me, like Lady Macbeth coming to get first-hand news from the guest-room.

'Well?' she said, getting her hooks on my arm with girlish animation. 'I'm nearly expiring with excitement and suspense, Bertie. Did everything go off all right? I listened at the door for a bit, but it was so difficult to hear what was going on. All that came through was Uncle Percy's voice rumbling like thunder, and occasionally a bleat from you.'

I would have denied, and with some warmth, this charge that I had bleated, but she gave me no opportunity to speak.

'And what puzzled me was that, according to the programme, it should have been your voice rumbling like thunder and an occasional bleat from Uncle Percy. And I couldn't hear Boko at all. He might just as well not have been there.'

I winced. It seemed to be my constant task to have to dash the cup of joy from this young geezer's lips, and I didn't like it any more than I had the first time. However, I forced myself to give her the works.

'Boko wasn't there.'

'Not there?'

'No.'

'But the whole point – '

'I know. But he was unavoidably detained by a gardener with a pitchfork and a dog which seemed to me to have a dash of the wolf-hound in him.'

And in a few sympathetic words I related how the light of her life had become less than the dust beneath Uncle Percy's gent's Oxfords and had been slung off the premises with all his music still within him.

A hard, set look came into her face.

'So Boko's made an ass of himself *again*?'

'I wouldn't call it actually making an ass of himself this time. More accurate, don't you think, to chalk him up as the helpless prey of destiny?'

'He could have rolled out of the way.'

'Not very easily. Uncle Percy's foot covers a wide area.'

She seemed to see the justice of this. Her map softened, and she asked if the poor darling had been hurt.

I weighed this.

'His physical injuries, I imagine, were slight. He seemed to be navigating under his own steam. Spiritually, he did not appear to be doing so well.'

'Poor lamb! He's so sensitive. What would you say his standing was now with Uncle Percy?'

'Lowish.'

'This has put the lid on things, you think?'

'To some extent, yes. But,' I said, glad to be able to drop a word of comfort, 'there is just a chance that, wind and weather permitting, the sun will 'ere long peep through the clouds. All depends on how the Wooster brain responds to the spurring it is going to get in the next half-hour or so.'

'What do you mean?'

'Rummy things have been happening, Nobby. You will recall how I tried the Fittleworth patent process for getting out of being engaged to Florence.'

'By kicking Edwin?'

'By, as you say, kicking Edwin. It has produced a bountiful harvest.'

'But you told me it hadn't worked.'

'Not in the way I had anticipated. But there has been an amazing by-product. Uncle Percy, informed of my activities, is all over me. For years, apparently, he has wanted to kick the young gumboil himself, but Florence has always stayed his foot.'

'I never knew that.'

'No doubt he has worn the mask. But the yearning was there, and it reached fever-point last night, when Edwin, sneaking up behind him, let him have it in the pants with his Scout's stick. So you can understand how he felt on learning that I had rushed in where he had feared to tread. It revolutionized his whole outlook. He shook my hand, gave me a cigar, pressed drink on me, and I am now his trusted friend and adviser. He thinks the world of me.'

'Yes, but – '

'You spoke?'

'I was only going to say that that's splendid and wonderful and marvellous, and I hope you will be very, very happy, but what I want is for him to think the world of Boko.'

'I am coming to that. Does the old relative ever speak to you of his affairs?'

'Only to tell me not to come bothering him now, because he's busy.'

'Then you wouldn't have heard of an American tycoon named J. Chichester Clam, with whom he has got to have a secret meeting in order to complete an important deal. Mysterious commercial stuff. He has asked me to think out some way of arranging this meeting. If I do, you will be on velvet.'

'How do you make that out?'

'Well, dash it, already I am practically Uncle Percy's ewe lamb. That will make me still ewer. He will be able to deny me nothing. I shall be in a position to melt his heart – '

'Oh, golly, yes. I see now.'

' – and get you and Boko fixed up. Then you show Florence that letter of mine, and that will get me fixed up.'

'But, Bertie, this is stupendous.'

'Yes, the prospects are of the rosiest, provided – '

'Provided what?'

'Well, provided I can think of a way of arranging this secret meet-ing, which at the moment of going to press I'm absolutely dashed if I can.'

'There are millions of ways.'

'Name three.'

'Why, you could . . . No, I see what you mean . . . It is difficult. I know. Ask Jeeves.'

'We have asked Jeeves. He says he's baffled.'

'Baffled? Jeeves?'

'I know. It came as a great shock to me. Chap was full of fish, too.'

'Then what are you going to do?'

'I told Uncle Percy I would brood.'

'Perhaps Boko would have something to suggest.'

Here, I was obliged to be firm.

'I bet he would,' I said, 'and I bet it would be something which would land us so deeply in the soup that it would require a dredging outfit to get us out again. I love Boko like a brother, but what I always feel about the dear old bird is that it's wisest not to stir him.'

She agreed with this, admitting that if there was a way of making things worse than they were Boko would unquestionably find it.

'I'm going to see him,' she said suddenly, after taking time out for a few moments in order to knit the brow.

'Boko?'

'Jeeves. I don't believe all this stuff about him being baffled.'

'He said he was.'

'I don't care. I don't believe it. Have you ever known Jeeves to be baffled?'

'Very seldom.'

'Well, then,' she said, and legged it for the staff quarters, leaving me to pass from the hall – I rather think with bowed head – and move out into the open. Here for a space I pondered.

How long I pondered, I cannot say. When the bean is tensely occupied, it is difficult to keep tab on the passage of time. I am unable to state, therefore, whether it was ten minutes later or more like twenty when I emerged from a profound reverie to discover that Jeeves was in my midst. I had had no inkling of his approach, but then one very often hasn't. He has away of suddenly materializing at one's side like one of those Indian blokes who shoot their astral bodies to and fro, going into thin air in Rangoon and re-assembling the parts in Calcutta. I think it's done with mirrors.

Nobby was also there, looking pretty dashed pleased with herself.

'I told you so,' she said.

'Eh?'

'About Jeeves being baffled. I knew there must be some mistake. He isn't baffled at all.'

I stared at the man, astonished. True, he was looking in rare intellectual form, what with his head sticking out at the back and all the acumen gleaming from his eyes, but he had stated so definitely to Uncle Percy and self that he had been laid a stymie.

'Not baffled?'

'No. He was only fooling. He's got a terrific idea.'

'How much does he know of recent developments?'

'I've just been bringing him up to date.'

'You have been apprised of the failure of the Fittleworth system, Jeeves?'

'Yes, sir. And also of your *rapprochement* with his lordship.'

'My what with his lordship?'

'*Rapprochement*, sir. A French expression. I confess that I experienced no little surprise on finding you on such excellent terms, but Miss Hopwood's explanation has rendered everything perfectly clear.'

'And you really have a scheme for bringing Uncle Percy and Clam together?'

'Yes, sir. I must confess that in our recent interview I intentionally misled his lordship. Realizing how vital it was to the interests of Mr Fittleworth and Miss Hopwood that you should be in a position to use your influence on their behalf, I thought it better that the suggestion should appear to emanate from you.'

'So that you can become more than ever the ewe lamb,' explained Nobby.

I nodded. His meaning had not escaped me. If you analysed it, it was the old Bacon and Shakespeare gag. Bacon, as you no doubt remember, wrote Shakespeare's stuff for him and then, possibly because he owed the latter money or it may be from sheer good nature, allowed him to take the credit for it. I mentioned this to Jeeves, and he said that perhaps an even closer parallel was that of Cyrano de Bergerac.

'The nature of the scheme which I have evolved, I should begin by saying, sir, renders the laying of it before his lordship a matter of some little delicacy, and it may be that a certain finesse will be required to induce him to fall in with it.'

'One of those schemes, is it?'

'Yes, sir. So, if I might make the suggestion, I think it would be best if you were to leave the matter in my hands.'

'You mean, let you sell it to him?'

'Precisely, sir. I would, of course, stress the fact that you were its originator and myself merely the go-between or emissary.'

'Just as you feel, Jeeves. You know best. And what is this scheme?'

'Briefly this, sir. I see no reason why his lordship and Mr Clam should not meet in perfect secrecy and safety at the fancy dress dance which is to take place tonight at the East Wibley Town Hall.'

I was absolutely staggered. I had clean forgotten that those East Wibley doings were scheduled for tonight. Which, when you reflect how keenly I had been looking forward to them, will give you some idea of the extent to which the fierce rush of life at Steeple Bumpleigh had disorganized my faculties.

'Isn't that a ball of fire?' said Nobby, enthusiastically.

I could not wholly subscribe to this.

'I spot a fatal flaw.'

'What do you mean, a flaw?'

'Well, try this on your pianola. Where, at such short notice, can Uncle Percy procure a costume? He can't go without one. Fancy dress, I take it, is obligatory. In other words, we come up against the snag the Wedding Guest ran into.'

'Which Wedding Guest? The one who beat his breast?'

'No, the chap in the parable, who was invited to a wedding but, having omitted to dress the part, got slung out on his ear like – '

I had been about to say 'like Boko from the precincts of Bumpleigh Hall', but refrained, fearing lest it might wound. But even without the addition my remorselessly logical words struck home.

'Oh, golly! I had forgotten about the upholstery. How do you get round that, Jeeves?'

'Quite simply, miss. I fear it will be necessary for you to lend his lordship your Sindbad the Sailor costume, sir.'

I uttered a stricken cry, like a cat to whom the suggestion has been made that she part with her new-born kitten.

'My God, Jeeves!'

'I fear so, sir.'

'But, dash it, that means I won't be able to attend the function.'

'I fear not, sir.'

'Well, why do you want to attend the rotten function?' demanded Nobby.

I gnawed the lower lip.

'You feel that this is absolutely essential, Jeeves? Think well.'

'Quite essential, sir. It may be a little difficult to persuade his lordship to take part in a frivolous affair of this nature, owing to his fear of what her ladyship would say, should she learn of it, and I am relying on the ginger whiskers which go with the costume to turn the scale. In placing the proposition before his lordship, I shall lay great stress on the completeness of the disguise which these will afford, preventing recognition by any acquaintance whom he may chance to encounter in the course of the festivities.'

I nodded. He was right. I decided to make the great sacrifice. The Woosters are seldom deaf to the voice of Reason, even if it involves draining the bitter cup.

'True, Jeeves. The keenest eye could not pierce those whiskers.'

'No, sir.'

'So be it, then. I will donate the costume.'

'Thank you, sir. Then I will be seeing his lordship immediately.'

'Heaven speed your efforts, Jeeves.'

'Thank you, sir.'

'Same here, Jeeves.'

'Thank you, miss.'

He shimmered off, and I turned to Nobby, with a sigh, saying that this was a blow and I would not attempt to conceal it. And once more she asked me why I was so keen on attending what she described as a footling country dance.

'Well, for one thing, I had set my heart on knocking East Wibley's eye out with that Sindbad. You've never seen me as Sindbad the Sailor, have you, Nobby?'

'No.'

'You haven't lived. But,' I proceeded, 'there is another angle, and I wish it had floated into my mind before Jeeves popped off, because I should like his views on it. If Uncle Percy meets Chichester Clam at this orgy and all goes well, he will, of course, be in malleable mood. But the point is, do these malleable moods last? By the following morning, may he not have simmered down? In order to strike while the iron is hot, both I and Boko ought to be there – I to seize the psychological moment for approaching Uncle Percy on your behalf and Boko to carry on from where I leave off.'

She saw what I meant.

'Yes, that wants thinking out.'

'If you don't mind, I'll pace up and down a bit.'

I did so, and was still hard at it, when Nobby's voice hailed me, and I saw that Jeeves had returned from his mission. Joining them at my best speed, I found him looking modestly triumphant.

'His lordship has consented, sir.'

'God. But – '

'I am to proceed to London without delay, in order to see Mr Clam and secure his co-operation.'

'Quite. But – '

'Meanwhile, Miss Hopwood has drawn my attention to the point which you have raised, sir, and I am in cordial agreement with your view that both yourself and Mr Fittleworth should be present at the dance. What I would suggest, sir, is that Mr Fittleworth drives me to the metropolis in his car, starting as soon as possible in order that we may return in good time. While I am interviewing Mr Clam, Mr Fittleworth can be purchasing the necessary costumes. I think this meets your difficulty, sir?'

I brooded for a moment. The scheme did, as he had said, meet my difficulty. The only thing that was bothering me was whether an essentially delicate matter like the selection of fancy dress costumes could be left safely in the hands of a bird like Boko. He was the sort of chap who might quite easily come back with a couple of Pierrots.

'Wouldn't it be better if I drove you to London?'

'No, sir. I think that you should remain, in order to keep his lordship's courage screwed to the sticking-place. His acceptance of the scheme was not obtained without considerable trouble. He would agree, and then he would glance at the portrait of her ladyship which hangs above the study door and demur once more. Left to himself, without constant exhortation and encouragement, I fear he might yet change his mind.'

I saw what he meant.

'Something in that, Jeeves. A bit jumpy, is he?'

'Extremely so, sir.'

I could not blame the old bird. I have already described my own emotions on catching the eye of that portrait of Aunt Agatha.

'Right ho, Jeeves.'

'Very good, sir. I would recommend constant allusions to the efficacy of the whiskers. As I had anticipated, it was they that turned the scale. Would Mr Fittleworth be at his residence now, miss? Then I will proceed thither at once.'

24

Jeeves's prediction that Uncle Percy would require constant exhortation and encouragement, to prevent him issuing an eleventh hour *nolle prosequi* and ducking out of the assignment he had undertaken, was abundantly fulfilled, and I must say I found the task of holding his hand and shooting pep into him a bit wearing. As the long day wore on, I began to understand why prize-fighters' managers, burdened with the job of bringing their men to the scratch, are always fairly careworn birds, with lined faces and dark circles under the eyes.

I could not but feel that it was ironical that the old relative should have spoken disparagingly of fawns as a class, sneering at their timidity in that rather lofty and superior manner, for he himself could have walked straight into a gathering of these animals, and no questions asked. There were moments, as he sat gazing at that portrait of Aunt Agatha over the study door, when he would have made even an unusually jumpy fawn look like Dangerous Dan McGrew.

Take it for all in all, therefore, it was a relief when, towards the quiet evenfall, the telephone rang and the following dialogue took place.

Uncle Percy: What? What? What-what-what? What? What? . . . Oh, Hullo, Clam.
Clam (off stage): Quack, quack, quack, quack, quack, quack, quack, quack (about a minute and a half of this, in all).
Uncle Percy: Fine, good. Splendid. I'll look out for you, then.

'Clam,' he said, replacing the receiver. 'Says he's heart and soul in favour of the scheme, and is coming to the ball as Edward the Confessor.'

I nodded understandingly. I thought Clam's choice was good.

'A bearded bozo, was he not, this Edward?' I asked.

'To the eyebrows,' said Uncle Percy. 'Those were the days when the world was a solid mass of beavers. I shall keep my eye open for something that looks like a burst horsehair sofa, and that will be Clam.'

'Then you've really definitely and finally decided to attend the binge?'

'With bells on, my dear boy, with bells on. You might not think it, to look at me now, but there was a time when no Covent Garden ball was complete without me. I used to have the girls flocking round me like flies about a honey-pot. Between ourselves, it was owing to the fact that I got thrown out of a Covent Garden ball and taken to Vine Street Police Station in the company of a girl who, if memory serves me aright, was named Tottie that I escaped – that I had the misfortune not to marry your aunt thirty years earlier than I did.'

'Really?'

'I assure you. We had just got engaged at the time, and she broke it off within three minutes of reading my press notices in the evening papers. I was too late, of course, for the morning sheets, but the midday specials of the evening ones did me proud, and she was a little upset about it all. That is why I am so particularly anxious that no hint of tonight's doings shall reach her ears. Your aunt is a wonderful woman, Bertie . . . can't think what I should do without her . . . but – well, you know how it is.'

I said I knew how it was.

'So I trust that all will be well and that she will never learn of the dark deeds which have been done in her absence. I think I have the mechanics of the thing fairly well planned out. I shall sneak down the back stairs, muffled to the eyes in an overcoat, and tool over to East Wibley on my old push bicycle. It's only half a dozen miles. No flaws in that?'

'None that I can spot.'

'Of course, if Florence saw me – '

'She won't.'

'Or Edwin.'

'Not a chance.'

'Or Maple.'

I was distressed to note this resurgence of the old fawn complex just when everything had seemed hotsy-totsy, and addressed myself without delay to the task of putting a stopper on it. And eventually I succeeded. By the time I had finished pointing out that nothing was more unlikely than that Florence should be roaming the back stairs at such an hour, that Edwin was bound to take a day or two off from his spooring after the treatment I had administered that morning, and that Maple, if encountered, could readily be squared with a couple of quid, he bucked up enormously, and I left him trying out dance steps on the study floor.

Well, of course, you can't ginger up an uncle by marriage from shortly after breakfast to about five in the afternoon without paying the toll a bit. All this exhortation and encouragement had, as you may well imagine, taken it out of me not a little, inducing a limpness of the limbs and a sort of general feeling of stickiness. I don't say I was perspiring at every pore, but I felt in need of a thorough rinse: and, the river being at my very door, this was easy to obtain. A quarter of an hour later, I might have been observed breasting the waves, clad in a bathing suit from Boko's store.

In fact, I was observed, and by none other than G. D'Arcy Cheesewright. Doing the Australian crawl back to the bank after a refreshing plunge and holding on to a bush while I brushed the moisture from my eyes, I glanced up and saw him standing above me.

It was an embarrassing moment. I don't know when you feel less at ease than when encountering a bloke to whose *fiancée* you have just got engaged.

'Oh, hullo, Stilton,' I said. 'Coming in?'

'Not while you are polluting the water.'

'I'm just coming out.'

'Then I'll let it run a bit and perhaps it will be all right.'

His words alone would have been enough to inform a man of my quick intelligence that he was not unmixedly pro-Bertram, and as I climbed out and slid into the bath robe he gave me a look which drove the thing home. I have already, in another place, described at some length these looks of his, and I may say that this one was fully up to the sample he had given me outside Wee Nooke on the previous day.

However, if there is a chance that suavity will erase a situation, the Woosters always give it a buzz.

'Nice day,' I said. 'Pretty country, this.'

'Ruined by the people you meet.'

'Trippers, you mean?'

'No, I don't mean trippers. I refer to snakes in the grass.'

It would be absurd to say that his attitude was encouraging, but I persevered.

'Talking of grass,' I said, 'Boko was in that of Bumpleigh Hall this morning, and Uncle Percy trod on him.'

'I wish he had broken your neck.'

'I wasn't there.'

'I thought you said your uncle trod on you.'

'You don't listen, Stilton. I said he trod on Boko.'

'Oh Boko? Good Lord!' he cried, with honest heat. 'With a fellow like you around, he treads on Boko! What on earth was the use of treading on Boko?'

There was a pause, during which he tried to catch my eye and I tried to avoid his. Stilton's eye, even in repose, is nothing to write home about, being the sort of hard blue and rather bulging. In moments of emotion, it tends to protrude even farther, like that of an irascible snail, the general effect being rather displeasing.

Presently, he spoke again.

'I've just seen Florence.'

My embarrassment increased. I had been hoping that the topic might have been avoided. But Stilton is one of those rugged, forthright chaps who don't avoid topics.

'Oh, yes?' I said. 'Florence, eh?'

'She says she's going to marry you.'

I was liking this less and less.

'Oh, yes,' I said. 'Yes, I believe there is some idea of a union.'

'What do you mean, some idea? It's all fixed for September.'

'September?' I quavered, trembling from head to foot a bit. I hadn't had a notion that the curse was slated to come upon me so dashed quick.

'So she says,' he responded moodily. 'I'd like to break your neck. But I can't, because I'm in uniform.'

'Yes, there's that. One doesn't want one of these unpleasant police scandals does one?'

There was another pause. He was looking at me in a sort of yearning way.

'Gosh!' he murmured, almost dreamily. 'I wish there was something I could pinch you for!'

'Come, come, Stilton. Is this the tone?'

'I'd love to see you cowering in the dock, with me giving evidence against you.'

He was silent for a space, and I could see that he was still gloating over the vision he had conjured up. Then he asked me rather abruptly if I had finished with the river, and I said I had.

'Then in about five minutes or so I might take a chance and go in,' he said.

It was, as you may well imagine, in pretty fairly melancholy mood that I donned the bath robe and made my way back to the house. There's always something about the going phut of an old friendship that tends to lower the spirits. It was many years since this Cheesewright and I had started what I believe is known as plucking the gowans fine, and there had been a time when we had plucked them rather assiduously. But his attitude at the recent get-together had made it plain that the close season for gowans had now set in, and, as I say, it rather saddened me.

Shoving on the shirt and bags with an unshed tear in the eye, I trickled along to the sitting-room to see if Boko had returned from his mission to London. I found him sitting in an armchair with Nobby on his lap, seeming in admirable spirits.

'Come in, Bertie, come in,' he cried jovially. 'Jeeves is in the kitchen, brewing a dish of tea. You will join us in a cup?'

Inclining my head in assent to this suggestion, I addressed Nobby on a point of pre-eminent interest.

'Nobby,' I said, 'I have just seen Stilton, and he informs me that Florence has fixed the nuptials for a shockingly early date – viz. September. It is vital, therefore, that you lose no time in showing her that letter of mine.'

'If everything goes all right tonight, she will be skimming through it tomorrow morning over her early cup of tea.'

Relieved, I turned to Boko.

'Did you get the costumes?'

'Of course I got the costumes. What the dickens do you think I sweated up to London for? Two in all, one for self and one for you, the finest the Bros. Cohen could supply. Mine is a Cavalier. A rather sex-appealy wig goes with it. Yours – '

'Yes, what about mine?'

He hesitated a moment.

'You'll like yours. It's a Pierrot.'

I uttered a cry of chagrin. Boko, like all my circle, is well acquainted with my views on going to fancy dress dances as a Pierrot. I consider it roughly equivalent to shooting a sitting bird.

'Oh, is it?' I said, speaking with quiet firmness. 'Well, I'm jolly well going to have the Cavalier.'

'You can't, Bertie, old man. It wouldn't fit you. It was built for a shortish, squarish reveller like me. You are tall and slim and elegant. "Elegant" is the word?' he said, putting it up to Nobby.

'Just the word,' she assented.

'Another good adjective would be "willowy". Or "sylphlike". Gosh, I wish I had a figure like yours, Bertie. You don't know what you've got.'

'Yes, I do,' I riposted, coldly ignoring the salve. 'I've got a ruddy Pierrot costume. A Wooster going to fancy dress ball as a Pierrot!' I said, and laughed shortly.

Boko shot Nobby off his knee and rose and began patting my shoulder. I suppose he could see that I was in dangerous mood.

'You need have no qualms about appearing in this Pierrot, Bertie,' he said soothingly. 'Where you have gone astray is in supposing that it is an ordinary Pierrot. Far from it. I doubt if, strictly speaking, you could call it a Pierrot at all. For one thing, it is mauve in colour. For another . . . But I'll show it to you, and I'll bet you go dancing about the house, clapping your hands.'

He reached for the suitcase which lay in the foreground, opened it, pulled out its contents and stared at them, aghast. So did I. So did Nobby. We all stared at them, aghast.

They consisted of what appeared to be a football suit. There was a pair of blue shorts, a pair of purple stockings and a crimson jersey.

Across the chest of the jersey, in large white letters, ran the legend 'BORSTAL ROVERS'.

25

It was some moments before any of us broke what I believe is called the pregnant silence. Then Nobby spoke.

'Do either of you see what I see?' she asked, in a sort of hushed, awed voice.

My own was dull and toneless.

'If what you see is a gent's footballing outfit,' I replied, 'that is what is impressing itself on the Wooster retina.'

'With "Borstal Rovers" written across the jersey?'

'Right across the jersey.'

'In large white letters?'

'In very large white letters. I am waiting,' I said, coldly, 'for an explanation, Fittleworth.'

Nobby uttered a passionate cry.

'I can give the explanation. Boko has gone and made an ass of himself *again*!'

Cringing beneath her flaming eye, the wretched man broke into a storm of protest.

'I haven't! I swear I haven't, darling!'

'Come, come, Boko,' I said, sternly. I had no wish to grind the man into the dust, but he had the wages of sin coming to him. 'A Cavalier costume and a mauve – if your story is to be credited – Pierrot have changed, while in your custody, into a football kit belonging apparently to an athlete who turns out for the Borstal Rovers, though I wouldn't have said offhand that there was such a team. Someone has blundered, and all the evidence points to you.'

Boko had tottered to a chair, and was sitting in it with his head in his hands. He emitted a sudden yip.

'Catsmeat!' he cried. 'I see it all. It was that chump, Catsmeat. Before starting to return here,' he proceeded, looking up and looking quickly down again as his eye collided with Nobby's, 'I stopped in at the Drones to get one for the road. Catsmeat Potter-Pirbright was there. We fell into conversation, and it turned out that he, too, was going to a fancy dress binge tonight. We chatted for a while of this and that, and then he looked at his watch and found that he had only just time to catch his train, and buzzed off. What happened is obvious. Rendered cockeyed by haste, he took my suitcase in mistake for his own. And if you're going to make out that that was my fault,' said Boko, speaking now with some spirit, 'then all I can say is that there's no justice in the world and that it's a fat lot of use being as innocent as the driven snow.'

This appeal to our better feelings was not without its effect. Nobby flung herself into his arms, cooing over him to a considerable extent, and even I was compelled to admit that he had been more sinned against than sinning.

'Still, it's all right,' said Boko, now definitely chirpy once more. 'Catsmeat and I are about the same build, so I can wear this number. I would prefer, of course, not to have to flaunt myself before East Wibley as a member of the Borstal Rovers, but one realizes that this is not a time when one can pick and choose. Yes, I can take it.'

I mentioned a point which he appeared to have overlooked.

'And how about me? I've got to be there, too, to pave the way for you with Uncle Percy. A lot of solid talking will be required before it will be any use you approaching him. If I'm not at this East Wibley orgy, you might just as well stay at home.'

My words, as I had anticipated, produced a marked sensation. Nobby gave a sort of distraught hiccough, like a bull-pup choking on a rubber bone, and Boko confessed with a moody oath that he hadn't thought of that.

'Think of it now,' I said. 'Or, better,' I went on, as the door opened, 'ask Jeeves what his views on the matter are. You will probably have something to suggest, eh, Jeeves?'

'Sir?'

'A snag has arisen in our path, an Act of God having left us a costume short,' I explained, 'and we are frankly baffled.'

He placed the tea-tray on the table, and listened with respectful interest while we laid the facts before him.

'Might I take a short walk, sir,' he said, when we had finished, 'and think the problem over?'

'Certainly, Jeeves,' I replied, concealing a slight pang of disappointment, for I had hoped that he might have come across with an immediate solution. 'By all means take a short walk. You will find us here on your return.'

He oiled off, and we settled down to an informal debate, in which the note of hope was conspicuous by its a. It could scarcely escape the attention of three keen minds like ours that what looked like dishing us was the matter of time. It was now well past five o'clock, which rendered out of the question the idea of another quick dash to the metropolis and a second visit to the establishment of the Bros. Cohen. Zealous though they are in their self-chosen task of supplying the populace with clothing, there comes a moment when these merchants call it a day and put up the shutters. Not even by exceeding the speed limit all the way could a driver, starting from Steeple Bumpleigh now, reach the emporium in time to do business. Long 'ere he could arrive, the Bros. and their corps of assistants would have retired to their various residences and be relaxing over good books.

As for the chance of securing anything in the nature of a costume in Steeple Bumpleigh, that, it seemed to us, could be ruled out altogether. At the beginning of this chronicle, I gave a brief description of this hamlet, showing it to be rich in honeysuckle-covered cottages and apple-cheeked villagers, but that let it out. It had only one shop that so ably conducted by Mrs Greenlees opposite the Jubilee watering-trough: and this, after it had supplied you with string, pink sweets, sides of bacon, tinned goods and *Old Moore's Almanac*, was a spent force.

Taking it for all in all, accordingly, the situation seemed pretty bleak. When I tell you that the best suggestion was the one advanced by Boko, that I should strip to a loincloth and smear myself with boot polish and go to the dance as a Zulu chief, you will see how little constructive progress had been made by the time the door opened and Jeeves was once more in our midst.

There is something about the mere sight of this number-nine-size-hatted man that seldom fails to jerk the beholder from despondency's depths in times of travail. Although Reason told us that he couldn't possibly have formulated a scheme for dragging home the gravy, we hailed him eagerly.

'Well?' I said.

'Well?' said Boko.

'Well?' said Nobby.

'Any luck, Jeeves?' I asked.

He inclined the coconut.

'Yes, sir. I am happy to say that I have been successful in finding a solution to the problem confronting you.'

'Gosh!' cried Nobby, stunned to the core.

'Egad!' cried Boko, the same.

'Well, I'm blowed!' I ejaculated, ibid. 'You have? I wouldn't have thought it possible. Would you, Boko?'

'I certainly wouldn't.'

'Or you, Nobby?'

'Not in a million years.'

'Well, there it is. That's Jeeves. Where others merely smite the brow and clutch the hair, he acts. Napoleon was the same.'

Boko shook his head. 'You can't class Napoleon with Jeeves.'

'Like putting up a fairish selling-plater against a classic yearling,' agreed Nobby.

'Napoleon had his moments,' I urged.

'On a very limited scale compared with Jeeves,' said Boko. 'I have nothing against Napoleon, but I cannot see him sauntering out into Steeple Bumpleigh at half-past five in the afternoon and coming back ten minutes later with a costume for a fancy dress ball. And this, you say, is what you have accomplished, Jeeves?'

'Yes, sir.'

'Well, I don't know how you feel about it, Bertie,' said Boko, 'but to me the thing looks like a ruddy miracle. Where is this costume, Jeeves?'

'I have placed it on the bed in Mr Wooster's room, sir.'

'But where on earth did you get it?'

'I found it, sir.'

'Found it? Just lying around, do you mean?'

'Yes, sir. On the bank of the river.'

I don't know why it was, unless possibly because we Woosters are a bit quicker than other men, but at these words a sudden, horrible suspicion shot through me like a dose of salts, numbing the nerve centres and turning the blood to ice.

'Jeeves,' I faltered, 'this thing . . . this what-you-may-call-it . . . this costume of which you speak . . . what is it?'

'A policeman's uniform, sir.'

I collapsed into a chair as if the lower limbs had been mown off with a scythe. The s. had been well founded.

'It has occurred to me since that it may possibly have been the property of Mr Cheesewright, sir. I observed him disporting himself in the water not far away.'

I rose from the chair. It wasn't an easy thing to do, but I managed it.

'Jeeves,' I said, or perhaps it would be *mot juster* to say I thundered, 'you will go and restore that dashed uniform to its bally owner instanter!'

Boko and Nobby, who had been slapping each other's backs in the foreground, halted in mid-slap and stared at me, Boko as if he couldn't believe his ears, Nobby as if she couldn't believe hers.

'Restore it?' cried Nobby.

'To its bally owner?' gasped Boko. 'I simply fail to follow you, Bertie.'

'Me, too,' said Nobby. 'If you had been an Israelite in the wilderness, you wouldn't have passed up your plateful of manna, would you?'

'Exactly,' said Boko. 'Here, at the eleventh hour, just when the total downfall of all our hopes and dreams seemed to stare us in the eyeball because we were unable to lay our hooks on a fancy dress costume, an admirable costume has been sent from Heaven, as you might say, and you appear to be suggesting that we shall give it the go-by. You can't realize what you are saying. Reflect, Bertie. Consider.'

I preserved my iron front.

'That uniform,' I said, 'goes back to its proprietor by special messenger at the earliest possible date. My dear Boko, my good Nobby, have you the slightest conception of the bitterly anti-Wooster sentiments which prevail in Stilton's bosom? The man specifically stated to me not half an hour ago that his dearest wish was to catch Bertram bending. Let him discover that I have been pinching his uniform, and I can hope for no mercy. Three months in the second division will be the best I can expect.'

Nobby started to say something about three months soon passing, but Boko shushed her.

'Why on earth should he discover anything of the sort?' he said. 'You aren't proposing to parade Steeple Bumpleigh day in and day out in this uniform. You're only going to wear it tonight.'

I corrected this view.

'I am not going to wear it tonight.'

'Oh, aren't you?' cried Nobby. 'Well, then, I'm jolly well not going to show that letter of yours to Florence.'

'Good girl,' said Boko. 'Well spoken, young light of my life. Laugh that off, Bertie.'

I made no endeavour to do so. Her words had chilled the spine. I don't suppose there is a man living who is swifter than Bertram Wooster to perceive when someone has got him by the short hairs, and it was clear to me that this was what had happened now. However fearful the perils that confronted me if I accepted Jeeves's loathsome gift, they must be faced.

A moment's struggle for utterance, and I bowed the onion and right-hoed.

'Splendid fellow!' said Boko. 'I knew you would see the light.'

'Bertie's always so reasonable,' said Nobby.

'Clear-thinking chap. Very level-headed,' agreed Boko. 'Then we're all set, eh? You come to the ball – of which in such a costume you can scarcely fail to be the belle – and you lurk till you have ascertained that old Worplesdon has had a satisfactory conference with Clam. If all has gone well, you buttonhole him and give me a build up. As soon as he is in melting mood, you give me the high sign, and I carry on from there, while you come home and turn in with an easy mind. I doubt if the whole thing – your part of it – will take more than half an hour. And now I think I had better be stepping along and taking Stilton a raincoat. No doubt he has a spare uniform at his residence, but one would like to get him there without causing comment. We can't have chaps roaming the countryside in the nude. All right for the Riviera, no doubt, but thank God we have a stricter code in Steeple Bumpleigh.'

He pushed off, taking Nobby with him, and I turned to Jeeves, who during these exchanges had been standing completely motionless, looking like a stuffed owl, his habit on occasions when he is among those present but has not been invited to join in the chit-chat.

'Jeeves,' I said.

'Sir?' he responded, coming to life in a deferential sort of way.

I did not mince my words.

'Well, Jeeves,' I said, and my face was hard and cold, 'you appreciate the set-up, I trust? Thanks to you, I am as properly up against it as I can remember being in the course of a not uneventful career. My position, as I see it, is roughly that of one who has removed a favourite cub from the custody of a rather more than usually short-tempered tigress, and is obliged to carry it on his person in the animal's immediate neighbourhood. I am not a weak man, Jeeves, but when I think of what will happen if Stilton cops me while I am draped in that uniform, it makes my knotted and combined locks . . . what was that gag of yours?'

'Part, sir, and each particular hair – '

'Stand on end, wasn't it?'

'Yes, sir. Like quills upon the fretful porpentine.'

'That's right. And that brings me back to it. What the dickens is a porpentine?'

'A porcupine, sir.'

'Oh, a *porcupine*? Why didn't you say that at first? It's been worrying me all day. Well, that, as I say, is the posish, Jeeves, and it is you who have brought it about.'

'I acted from the best motives, sir. It seemed to me that at all costs it was essential that you take part in tonight's festivities.'

I saw his point. If there's one thing the Woosters are, it's fair-minded. We writhe, but we are just.

'Yes,' I assented with a moody nod, 'I suppose you meant well. And no doubt, in a sense, you did the right and judicious thing. But you can't get away from it that mine is a fearful predicament. One false step, and Stilton will be on the back of my neck, shouting for Justices of the Peace to come and sentence me to a long spell in the cooler. And, apart from that, has it occurred to you that this Cheesewright is about forty inches more round the chest and eight inches more round the head than me? Clad in his uniform, and especially wearing his helmet, I shall look like a Keystone Kop. Why, dash it, I'd rather go to this binge as the meanest Pierrot. Still, I suppose my bally preferences don't count.'

'I fear not, sir. For know, rash youth – if you will pardon me, sir – the expression is Mr Bernard Shaw's, not my own . . . For know, rash youth, that in this star crost world Fate drives us all to find our chiefest good in what we can and not in what we would.'

Again, I saw his point.

'Quite,' I responded. 'Yes, I suppose the bullet must be bitten. Right ho, Jeeves,' I said, summoning to my aid all the splendid Wooster fortitude, 'lead me to it.'

26

It had been Boko's idea that he and I should make the journey to East Wibley in his car, he at the wheel, I at his side, so that if there were any minor details to be settled which we had overlooked, we could get them ironed out before arrival, thus achieving a perfect preparedness and avoiding any chance of last minute stymies.

To this suggestion, though admitting its basic soundness, I demurred. In fact, when I say I demurred, I ought to put it stronger. I more or less recoiled in horror. I had been Boko's passenger on a previous occasion, and it was not an experience one would wish to repeat. Put an author in the driver's seat of a car, and his natural goofiness seems to become intensified. Not only did Boko persistently overtake on blind corners, but he did it with a dreamy, faraway look in his eyes, telling one the plot of his next novel the while and not infrequently removing both hands from the wheel in order to drive home some dramatic point with gestures.

Another reason why I preferred to travel in the Wooster two-seater was that I was naturally anxious to get home and out of that uniform as speedily as possible. And, of course, it would be necessary, if all went well, for Boko to linger on and talk turkey to Uncle Percy.

My qualms regarding spending the evening in Stilton's plumage had in no way diminished with the passage of time. I still viewed the ordeal with concern.

Boko, returning from his errand of mercy to the zealous officer, had reported that the latter had seemed a bit upset about it all and inclined to suspect me of being the motivating force behind the outrage. To this, Boko had rather cleverly replied by saying that it was far more likely to have been young Edwin who had done the horrid deed. There comes a moment, he had pointed out, in the life of every Boy Scout when he suddenly feels fed up with doing acts of kindness and allows his human side to get uppermost. On such occasions, the sight of a policeman's uniform lying on the river bank would, he maintained, call to such a Scout like deep calling to deep and prove practically irresistible. He told me he thought he had lulled Stilton's suspicions, all right.

This, of course, was all very well, as far as it went, but I could not conceal it from myself that if Stilton were to see me wearing the uniform, his suspicions would pretty damn' soon come unlulled. He might or might not have what it takes to make a man a master-mind of Scotland Yard, but he unquestionably had sufficient intelligence, should such a contingency occur, to put two and two together, as the expression is. I mean to say, a policeman who has had his uniform pinched and later in the day comes on someone swathed in it is practically bound to fall into a certain train of thought.

'No, Boko,' I said. 'I proceed to the tryst under my own steam, and I come away the moment I have completed my share in the proceedings, driving like the wind.'

And so it was arranged.

Well, of course, it being so essential for me to get to the scene of operations in good time, you might have known what would happen. At about the half-way mark, the old two-seater suddenly faded out, coming to a placid standstill in prettily wooded country miles from anywhere. And as I don't know the first thing about fixing a car, my talents being limited to twisting the wheel and tooting the tooter, I had to wait there till the United States Marines arrived.

These took the shape – at about a quarter to twelve – of a kindly bird in a lorry who, on being hailed, put everything right with a careless twiddle of the fingers so rapidly that he had occasion to spit only twice from start to finish. I thanked him, flung him a purse of gold and proceeded on my way, fetching up at journey's end just as the local clocks were striking midnight.

The interior of the East Wibley Town Hall presented a gay and fairylike appearance. Coloured lanterns hung from the roof, there was a good deal of smilax here and there, and on all sides the eye detected fair women and brave men. One of the latter, a footballer in the striking colours of the Borstal Rovers, detached himself from the throng and arrested my progress, full of recriminations.

'Bertie, you outstanding louse,' said Boko, for it was he, 'where the devil have you been? I was expecting you hours ago.'

I explained the reasons for my delay, and he said peevishly that I was just the sort of chap whose car would break down when every moment was precious, adding that it was a lucky thing that it hadn't been me they sent to bring the good news from Aix to Ghent, because, if it had been, Ghent would have got it first in the Sunday papers.

'It's going to be touch and go, Bertie,' he proceeded. 'A wholly unforeseen situation has arisen. Old Worplesdon has gone to earth in the bar and is lowering the stuff by the pailful.'

'But that's fine,' I said. 'The significance of his actions has probably escaped you, but I can read between the lines. It means that he has seen Clam and that everything is satisfactorily fixed up.'

He clicked his tongue impatiently.

'Of course it does. But the frightful danger is that at any moment he may pass completely out, and then where are we?'

I saw what he meant, and it was as if a hand of ice had been placed on my heart. No wonder he had used the words, 'frightful danger'. The peril was hideous. Our whole plan of strategy called for an Uncle Percy in whom the neap tide of the milk of human kindness was at its height. A blind and speechless Uncle P., stacked up against the wall in a corner of the bar like an umbrella in an umbrella stand, would defeat all our aims.

'Go to him without a second's delay,' said Boko, urgently. 'Pray Heaven it may not be too late!'

The words had scarcely left his lips before I was skimming barwards like a greyhound released from the slips. And it was with profound relief that I saw that I was in time. Uncle Percy had not passed out. He was still up and doing, playing the genial host to a platoon of friends and admirers who had plainly come to look on him in the light of a public drinking fountain.

I was just starting to head in his direction, when the band struck up another tune and his pals swallowed theirs quick and streamed out, leaving the old relative leaning back in his chair with his feet on the table. I lost no time in stepping up and fraternizing.

'What ho, Uncle Percy,' I said.

'Ah, Bertie,' he replied. He shut one eye and scrutinized me narrowly. 'I am right,' he queried, 'in supposing that that is Bertram Wooster rattling about inside that helmet?'

'It is,' I replied shortly. The uniform and helmet were proving even roomier than I had feared they would be, and I was about fed up with them. The almost universal merriment which had greeted me, as I passed through the crowd of revellers, had been hard to bear. The Woosters are not accustomed to getting the horse's laugh when they lend their presence to fancy dress dances.

'It doesn't fit. It's too large. You should change your hatter, or your armourer, or whatever it is. Still, be that as it may, tiddly-om-pom-pom. Sit down and have some of this disgusting champagne, Bertie. I'll join you.'

I thought it best to speak the word in season.

'Haven't you had enough, Uncle Percy?'

He weighed this.

'If what you mean by that question is, am I stinko,' he replied, 'in a broad, general sense you are right. I *am* stinko. But everything is relative, Bertie . . . You, for instance, are my relative, and I am your relative . . . and the point I want to make is that I am not one bit as stinko as I'm going to be later on. This is a night for unstinted rejoicing, my dear boy, and if you think I am not going to rejoice – and unstintedly, at that – then I reply "Watch me!" That is all I say. Watch me!'

The spectacle of an uncle, even if only an uncle by marriage, going down for the third time in a sea of dance champagne can never be an agreeable one. But though I mourned as a nephew, I'm bound to say I found myself pretty bucked in my capacity of ambassador for Boko. Pie-eyed, even plastered, this man might be, but there was no mistaking his geniality. It was like something out of Dickens, and I saw that he was going to be clay in my hands.

'I've seen Clam,' he proceeded.

'You have?'

'With the naked eye. And I refuse to believe that Edward the Confessor really looked like that. Nobody presenting such an obscene appearance as J. Chichester Clam could possibly have held the throne of England for five minutes. Lynching parties would have been organized, knights sent out to cope with the nuisance with battle-axes.'

'Is everything all right?'

'Everything's fine, except that I am beginning to see two of you. And one was ample.'

'I mean, you've had your conference?'

'Oh, our conference? Yes, we had that, and I don't mind telling you, if you can hear me from inside that helmet, that I put it all over him. When he looks at that agreement we sketched out on the back of the wine list – an agreement, I may mention, legally witnessed by the chap behind the bar and impossible to get out of – he'll realize that he's practically given me his bally shipping line. That is why I say – and with all the emphasis at my disposal – tiddly-om-pom-pom. Fill your glass, Bertie. Don't spare the vitriol.'

I felt that the word of praise would not be amiss. However mellowed a man may be, it never hurts to mellow him a bit more by giving him the old oil.

'Smooth work, Uncle Percy.'

'You may well say so, my boy.'

'There can't be many fellows about with brains like yours.'

'There aren't.'

'Very creditable to you, the whole thing. I mean, considering your condition.'

'You allude to my being tight? Quite, quite. But I wasn't tight when I was dealing with Clam. Though my shoes were. I seem,' he said, his lips contorted by a spasm of pain, 'to have come out in a pair of shoes about eleven sizes too small, and they're nipping me like nobody's business. I'm going to look for a quiet spot where I can take them off for a bit.'

I drew my breath in sharply. I had seen the way. I suppose this is how great generals win battles, by suddenly spotting the right course to pursue and immediately pulling up their socks and snapping into it.

You see, what I had been alive to all along had been the danger that this man, as soon as I switched the conversation to the subject of Boko, would turn on his heel and stalk off, leaving me flat. Catch him with his shoes off, and this problem would not arise. An uncle by marriage with only socks on finds it dashed difficult to turn on his heel, especially if he's sitting in a car. And it was into a car that I proposed to decant this Percy.

'What you want,' I said, 'is to go and sit in a car.'

'I haven't got a car. I tooled over on my push bike, and a hell of a sweat it was, taxing the unaccustomed calf muscles like billy-o.'

'I'll find a car.'

'Not that rotten little two-seater of yours, I trust? I shall require space. I want to stretch my legs out and relax. The calves are still throbbing.'

'No, this is a bigger, better car altogether. The property of a friend of mine.'

'Will he object to my taking my shoes off?'

'Not a bit.'

'Excellent. Lead the way, then, my boy. Before starting, however, I had better procure another quart of this gooseberry cider and take it along.'

'If you think it advisable.'

'Not merely advisable. Imperative. One doesn't want to lose a moment.'

I had no difficulty in spotting Boko's car. It was a thing about the size of a young tank, which he had bought second-hand in his less oofy days and refused to part with because its admirable solidity served him so well in the give and take of traffic. He told me once that it brushed ordinary sports models aside like flies, and that his money would be on it even in the event of a collision with an omnibus.

I ushered the old relative into its cavernous depths, and he removed the shoes. Not till he was safely reclining on his spine, twiddling his toes out of the window, so that the cool night air could play on them, did I start to bring up the big item on the agenda paper.

'So you slipped it across Clam, did you, Uncle Percy?' I said. 'Splendid. Capital. And after accomplishing so notable a business triumph you are, I take it, feeling pretty benevolent towards your fellow men?'

'I love them all,' he said handsomely. 'I look on the entire human species with a kindly and indulgent eye.'

'Well, that's fine.'

'Always excepting, of course, the foe of that species, the hellhound Fittleworth.'

This wasn't so good.

'Would you make exceptions, Uncle Percy? On a night like this?'

'Oh this or any other night, and also by day. Fittleworth! Invites me to lunch – '

'I know. He told me.'

' – and wantonly causes spiders to emerge from the salt cellar.'

'I know. But – '

'Roams my grounds, officiously locking my business associates in potting sheds – '

'I know. Quite. But – '

'And, to top it all off, lurks in my grass like a ruddy grasshopper, so that I can't stir a step without treading on him. When I reflect that I have not dissected Fittleworth, limb by limb, and danced on his remains, my moderation astounds me. Don't talk to me about Fittleworth.'

'But that's just what I want to talk about. I want to plead his cause. You are aware, Uncle Percy,' I said, bunging a bit of a tremolo into the old voice, 'that he loves young Nobby.'

'So I have been informed, dash his cheek.'

'It would be an ideal match. You and he may not always have seen eye to eye in such matters as spiders in salt cellars, but you can't get away from it that he is one of the hottest of England's younger littérateurs. He earns more per annum than a Cabinet Minister.'

'He ought to be ashamed of himself, if he didn't. Have you ever met a Cabinet Minister? I know dozens, and not one of them that wouldn't be grossly overpaid at thirty shillings a week.'

'He could support Nobby in the style to which she is accustomed.'

'No, he couldn't. Ask me why not.'

'Why not?'

'Because I'm jolly well not going to let him.'

'But he loves, Uncle Percy.'

'Has he got an Uncle Percy?'

I saw that unless prompt steps were taken, we should be getting muddled.

'When I say He loves, Uncle Percy,' I explained, 'I don't mean he loves, verb transitive, Uncle Percy, accusative. I mean he loves, comma, Uncle Percy, exclamation mark.'

Even while uttering the words, I had had a fear lest I might be making the thing a shade too complex for one in the relative's condition. And so it proved.

'Bertie,' he said, gravely, 'I should have watched you more carefully. You're tighter than I am.'

'No, no.'

'Then just go over that observation of yours again slowly. I would be the last man to dispute that my faculties are a little blurred, but – '

'I only said, that he loved, and shoved in an "Uncle Percy" at the end of my remarks.'

'Addressing me, you mean?'

'Yes.'

'In the vocative, as it were?'

'That's right.'

'Now we've got it straight. And where does it get us? Just where we were before. You say he loves my ward, Zenobia. I reply, "All right, let him, and I hope he has a fine day for it. But I'm dashed if he's going to marry her." I take my position as guardian of that girl pretty seriously. You might say I regard it as a sacred trust. When confiding her to my care, I remember, her poor old father, as fine a fellow as ever stepped, though too fond of pink gin, clasped my hand and said, "Watch her like a hawk, Percy, old boy, or she'll go marrying some bally blot on the landscape." And I said, "Roddy, old man" – his name was Roderick – "just slip a clause in the lease, saying that she's got to get my consent first, and you need have no further uneasiness." And what happens? First thing you know, up pops probably the worst blot any landscape was ever afflicted with. But he finds me ready, my boy. He finds me ready and prepared. There is my authority in black and white, and I intend to exercise it.'

'But her father wasn't thinking of a chap like Boko.'

'There are limits to every man's imagination.'

'Boko's a frightfully good egg.'

'He is nothing of the kind. Good egg, forsooth! Tell me a single thing this Fittleworth has ever done that entitles him to consideration and respect.'

I thought for a moment. And when the Woosters think for a moment, they generally spear something good.

'It may be news to you,' I said, 'that he once kicked Edwin.'

This got home. His mouth opened, and his feet twitched, as if stirred by a passing zephyr.

'Is this true?'

'Ask Florence. Ask the knives and boots boy.'

'Well, I'm dashed.'

He sat for a while, deep in thought. I could see that revelation had made a deep impression.

'I confess,' he said at length, raising the bottle to his lips and swallowing about a third of its contents, 'that what you tell me causes me to look on the fellow with a somewhat kindlier eye. Yes, to some extent, I admit, it has modified my views regarding him. It just shows that there is good in all of us.'

'Then on consideration – '

He shook his head.

'No, Bertie, I cannot consent to this match. Look at it from my point of view. The fellow lives at my very doors. Give him an excuse like being married to my ward, and he would always be popping in. Every time I took a stroll in my garden, I should be watching my step in case he happened to be hiding in the grass. Every time he came to lunch, my eyes would be riveted on the salt cellar. No nervous system could stand it.'

I saw the talking point.

'But you haven't heard the latest, Uncle Percy. Boko leaves next month for Hollywood. Do you realize that America is three thousand miles away, and that Hollywood is three thousand miles on the other side of America?'

He started.

'Is it?'

'Absolutely.'

He sat for a moment twiddling his fingers.

'I make that six thousand miles.'

'That's right.'

'Six thousand miles,' he said, rolling the words round his tongue. 'Why, this alters everything. You think Zenobia loves him?'

'Devotedly.'

'Odd. Strange. And his financial position is as sound as you suggest?'

'Sounder. Editors scream like frightened children when his agent looks in to talk terms for a new contract.'

'And about Hollywood. You're sure your fingers are right? Six thousand miles?'

'A bit more, if anything.'

'Well, then, really, dash it, in that case – '

I saw that the iron was hot, and that the moment had come for Boko to strike it.

'I'll send him to you,' I said, 'and you can have a talk and rough out the arrangements. No need for you to move. This is his car. By Jove, Uncle Percy, you'll be thankful for this later on, when you realize what a bit of a goose you're handing two young hearts in springtime.'

'Tiddly-om-pom-pom,' said the relative, waving a cordial toe and once more applying his lips to the bot.

I did not let the g. grow under the feet. Hastening back to the ballroom, I sorted Boko out from the revellers, and sent him off with many a hearty 'Tails up' and 'God speed'. Then, unleashing the two-seater, I drove home, thankful that a sticky bit of business had been safely concluded.

My first act, on reaching journey's end, was, of course, to tear off the uniform. Having crept to the river bank and consigned it to the dark waters, which might or might not eventually cast it up some distant shore whence it would be returned to its owner, I whizzed back to my room and darted into bed.

It was not immediately that the tired eyelids closed in sleep, for some hidden hand had placed a hedgehog between the sheets – practically, you might say, a fretful porpentine. Assuming this to be Boko's handiwork, I was strongly inclined to transfer it to his couch. Reflecting, however, that while this would teach him a much needed lesson it would be a bit tough on the porpentine, I took the latter out into the garden and loosed it into the grass.

Then, the day's work done, I turned in and soon sank into a dreamless slumber.

27

The sun was high in the heavens, or fairly high, when I awoke next morning. From behind the closed door of Boko's sleeping apartment there proceeded a rhythmic sound like the sawing of wood, indicating that he had not yet sprung from his bed. I would have liked to waken him and ask if all was well, but refrained. No doubt, I felt, he had returned at a late hour and needed an extra bit of what I have heard Jeeves call tired Nature's sweet restorer. I donned the bathing suit and bath robe, and started off for the river, and I hadn't more than shoved my nose outside the garden gate when along came Nobby on her bicycle.

It would have been plain even to the most casual observer that Nobby was in the pink. Her eyes were shining like twin stars as the expression is, and she greeted me with one of the heartiest pip-pips that ever proceeded from female throat.

'Hullo, Bertie,' she cried. 'I say, Bertie, isn't everything super-colossal!'

'I think so,' I replied. 'I hope so. I left Uncle Percy in malleable mood, and Boko was just going to confer with him. All should have gone well.'

'Then you haven't heard? Didn't Boko tell you?'

'I haven't seen him yet. Our waking moments have not synchronized. When he got back, I was asleep, and when I got up, he was asleep.'

'Oh, I see. Well, he came round in the small hours and threw gravel at my window and made his report. Everything went like a breeze.'

'It did?'

'According to Boko, the thing was a love feast. Uncle Percy sent him back to the bar for another bottle of champagne, and they split it like a couple of sailors on shore leave.'

'And he's given his consent?'

'Definitely, Boko says. He's so grateful to you for all you have done, Bertie. So am I. I could kiss you.'

'Just as you wish,' I assented civilly, and she did so. Then she legged it for the house, and I proceeded on my way to the river.

My mood, as I clove its crystal waters was, as you may imagine, pretty uplifted. Nobby's story had left no room for doubt that happy endings had come popping up like rabbits. I had forgotten to ask her when she was going to show that letter to Florence, but no doubt this would be done in the course of the morning, releasing me from my honourable obligations. And, as for her and Boko, it was well within the bounds of possibility that before nightfall they would be united in the bonds of holy wedlock. Boko had made no secret of the fact that for many a day past he had had the licence tucked away in the drawer of his desk, ready to do its stuff the moment the starter's pistol went.

In addition to this, Stilton's uniform was floating on its way to the sea, and absolutely nothing to prove that it and Bertram had ever been in any way connected. It was just possible that some inkling of the truth might come to the promising young copper, causing him to regard me, when we next met, with sullen suspicion and even to go as far as to grind his teeth: but as for his assembling a telling weight of evidence which would land me in the dock and subsequently in the lowest dungeon beneath the castle moat, not a hope.

It was, accordingly, with no uncertain feeling that this was the maddest, merriest day of all the glad new year that I returned to the house, where genial smells from the dining-room greeted the nostrils and caused me to dress like a streak. Entering the food zone a few moments later, I found Boko restoring his tissues, with Nobby sitting on the end of the table, drinking in his every word.

'Ah, Bertie,' said Boko. 'Good morning, Bertie. Now you're here, I'd better start again.'

He did so, and for some minutes held me spellbound. Even though I had heard the outline of the plot from Nobby and so knew how it all came out in the end, I hung upon his lips from start to finish.

'You didn't get his consent in writing?' I asked, as he concluded.

'Well, no,' he admitted. 'It never occurred to me. But if what is in your mind is that he may try to back out of it, don't worry. You have no conception, Bertie, literally no conception of the chumminess which exists between us. Hands were shaken, and backs slapped. He was all over me like a bedspread. Well, to give you some idea, he said he wished he had a son like me.'

'Well, considering he's got a son like Edwin, that isn't saying much.'

'Don't be a wet blanket, Bertie. Don't try to cast a gloom on this wonderful morning. Another thing he said was that he hoped I would be very successful in Hollywood and would remain working there for many years – in fact, indefinitely. One sees what he meant, of course. Like others, he has long chafed at the rottenness of motion pictures and is relying on me to raise the standard.'

'You will, angel,' said Nobby.

'You betcher,' said Boko, swilling coffee.

The meal proceeded on its pleasant course. A less kindly man than Bertram Wooster might have struck a jarring note by bringing up the matter of that porpentine in my bed, but I refrained from this. Instead, I asked what became of Uncle Percy at the close of the proceedings.

'I suppose he pushed home on his push bike,' said Boko. 'What did you do with Stilton's uniform?'

I explained that I had committed it to the deep, and he said I could not have made a wiser move. And he was just starting to be dashed funny about my last night's outer crust, when I stopped him with an imperious gesture.

Out of the corner of my eye, I had seen something large and blue turning in at the garden gate. A moment later, there came the sound of feet crunching on gravel, and the *timbre* and volume of the noise was such that only regulation official boots could have caused it. I was not surprised when in due season the torso and helmeted head of Stilton were framed in the open window. And more profoundly than ever I congratulated myself on the shrewdness and foresight which had led me to bung that uniform into the river.

'Ah, Stilton,' I said, and, what is more, I said it airily. The keenest ear could not have detected that the conscience was not as clean as a whistle. One prefers, of course, on all occasions to be stainless and above reproach, but, failing that, the next best thing is unquestionably to have got rid of the body.

Boko, who is always a perfect host, bade the newcomer a cheery good morning, and asked him to keep his mouth open and he would throw a sardine into it. But apparently the latter had already breakfasted, for he declined the invitation with a petulant jerk of the head.

'Ho!' he said.

Touching for a moment on this matter of policemen and the word 'Ho'. I have an idea that the first thing they teach the young recruit on joining the Force is how to utter this ejaculation. I've never met a rozzer yet who didn't say it, and they all say it in just the same way. Inevitably one is led to assume a course of schooling.

'So there you are, you blasted Wooster!'

Speculating, as I had done from time to time since the previous evening, on the probable demeanour of this painstaking young officer when next he should catch sight of me, I had never anticipated that it would be elfin. I had budgeted for the dark frown, the flushed face and the hard and bulging eye. And there they all were, precisely as foreshadowed, and they found me ready to cope with them.

I preserved my aplomb.

'Yes, here I am,' I responded, buttering a nonchalant slice of toast. 'Where else would I be, my dear Stilton? This, thanks to Boko's princely hospitality, is where I am living.'

'Ho!' said Stilton. 'Well, you won't be living here much longer, because you're bally well coming along with me.'

Boko looked at me, and raised his eyebrows. I looked at Boko, and raised my eyebrows. Nobby looked at us both, and raised her eyebrows. Then we looked at Stilton, and all raised our eyebrows. It was one of those big eyebrow-raising mornings.

'Coming along with you? Surely, Stilton,' said Boko, 'you do not use that expression in a technical sense?'

'Yes I do.'

'You have come to arrest Bertie?'

'Yes, I have,'

'What for?'

'Pinching my uniform.'

Nobby turned to me in girlish astonishment.

'Have you been pinching Stilton's uniform, Bertie?'

'Certainly not.'

'How lucky.'

'Extremely fortunate.'

'Because I suppose you could get about three months for a thing like that.'

'Besides the shame of it all,' I pointed out. 'If I ever feel the temptation to commit this rash act, I must fight against it. Not that I imagine I shall.'

'Pretty unlikely,' Nobby agreed. 'I mean, what on earth would you want a policeman's uniform for?'

'Exactly,' I said. 'You have touched the matter with a needle.'

'Done what?'

'One of Jeeves's gags,' I explained. '*Rem* something. Latin stuff.'

Boko, who had been frowning thoughtfully, went more deeply into the matter.

'I believe I know what's on Stilton's mind,' he said. 'I don't think I told you, but yesterday, while he was bathing, somebody snitched his uniform, which he had left lying on the bank. Did I mention it?'

'Not to my recollection,' said Nobby.

'Nor to mine,' I said, shaking the bean.

'Odd,' said Boko. 'I suppose it slipped my mind.'

'Things do,' said Nobby.

'Frequently,' I agreed.

'Well, that's what happened, and one can't blame him for wanting to bring the criminal to justice. But why he has got this extraordinary idea that it was Bertie who was responsible for the foul outrage is more than I can understand. I told you yesterday, Stilton, that the hidden hand was almost certainly young Edwin's.'

'Yes, and I've just been tackling him about it. He denies it categorically.'

'And you accept his word?'

'Yes, I do. He has an alibi.'

'Well, you perfect chump,' cried Nobby, 'don't you know that that dishes him? Haven't you ever read any detective stories? Ask Lord Peter Wimsey what an alibi amounts to.'

'Or Monsieur Poirot,' I suggested.

'Yes. Or Reggie Fortune, or Inspector French, or Nero Wolfe. I can't understand a man of your intelligence falling for that alibi stuff.'

'Incredible,' I said. 'The oldest trick in the game.'

'Trot along and bust it, is my advice, Stilton,' said Boko.

One might have expected a cop to wilt beneath all this, but it speedily became plain that the Cheesewrights were made of sterner stuff.

'If you want to know why I accept young Edwin's alibi,' said Stilton, allowing his eyes to bulge a bit farther from the parent sockets, 'it's because it's supported by the vicar, the vicar's wife, the curate, the curate's sister, the doctor, the doctor's aunt, a scoutmaster, fifteen assorted tradesmen and forty-seven Boy Scouts. It appears that the doctor was giving a lecture on First Aid in the village hall yesterday evening, and Edwin was the chap who went on the platform and was illustrated on. At the moment when my uniform was pinched, he was lying on a table, swathed in bandages, showing what you have to do to a bloke with a fractured thigh bone.'

This, I admit, spiked our guns to no little extent. Nobby did say that it might have been an accomplice cunningly disguised to look like Edwin, but you could see that it was simply a suggestion.

'Yes,' said Boko, at length, 'that does seem to let Edwin out. But

I still don't see where you get this extraordinary idea that Bertie is the culprit.'

'I'll tell you that, too,' said Stilton, plainly resolved to keep nothing from us. 'Edwin, questioned, had an amazing story to relate. He stated that, going to accused's bedroom later in the evening to put a hedgehog in his bed – '

'Ha!' I exclaimed, and gave Boko a penitent look, remorseful that even in thought I should have wronged my kind host.

'– he saw the uniform there. And I met a chap this morning who had been an extra waiter at the fancy dress ball at East Wibley last night, and he informs me that there was a loathsome-looking object taking part in the festivities, dressed in a policeman's uniform six sizes too large for him. I am ready to step along, Wooster, if you are.'

It seemed to me a fair cop, as I believe the expression is, and I saw nothing to be gained by postponing the inevitable. I rose, and wiped the lips with the napkin, like a French aristocrat informed that the tumbrel is at the door.

Boko's hat, however, was still in the ring.

'Just a minute, Stilton,' he said. 'Not so fast, officer. Have you a warrant?'

The question seemed to discompose Stilton.

'Why, I . . . Er, no.'

'Must have a warrant,' said Boko. 'You can't make a summary arrest on a serious charge like this.'

The momentary weakness passed. Stilton was himself again.

'I don't believe it,' he said stoutly. 'I think you're talking through your hat. Still, I'll go to the station and ask the sergeant.'

He vanished, and Boko became brisk and efficient.

'You'll have to leg it, Bertie,' he said, 'and without a second's delay. Get your car, drive to London and go abroad. They won't be watching the ports yet. Better look in on the Cohen Bros. *en route* and buy a false moustache.'

It isn't often that I would care to allow this borderline case's counsel to rule my actions, but on this occasion it seemed to me that his advice was good. I had been thinking along the same lines myself. Oh, as a matter of fact, I had just been saying to myself at that very moment, for the wings of a dove. Briefly requesting him to get hold of Jeeves and tell him to follow with the personal effects, I streaked for the garage.

And I was just about to fling wide the gates, when there suddenly came from the other side of the door the sound of a hoarse voice, and I paused, astounded. Unless the ears had deceived me, there was a human soul inside the edifice.

It spoke again, and what enabled me to get abreast and identify the thorax from which it proceeded was the fact that one caught the name 'Fittleworth', preceded by a number of qualifying adjectives of a rugged and rather Elizabethan nature. In a flash, I got the whole set-up.

Driving away from the East Wibley Town Hall at the conclusion of the recent festivities, Boko must inadvertently have taken Uncle Percy with him. He had sped homewards with a song on his lips, and all unknown to him, overlooked while getting a spot of tired Nature's sweet restorer in the back of the car, the old relative had come along for the ride.

28

I drew in the breath with a startled whoosh, and for some moments stood rooted to the s., the brow furrowed, the eyes bulging. To say that this thing had come upon me like a sock behind the ear from a stuffed eelskin would be in no wise to overstate the facts. As I stood there with my ear against the door, listening to what was filtering through the woodwork, it is not too much to say that melancholy marked me for its own.

Consider the posish, I mean. The one thing that was of the essence was that Boko should keep this man a thing of sweetness and light, and it was absurd to suppose that this could be done by locking him up all night in garages in the costume of Sindbad the Sailor. A man of generous spirit, like Uncle Percy, inevitably chafes at such treatment.

He was chafing now. I could hear him. The tone of his observations left no room for misunderstanding. They were not the obiter dicts of one who, when released, would laugh heartily at the amusing little misunderstanding, but rather of a man whose earnest endeavour it would be to skin the person responsible for his incarceration.

Indeed, it was upon this very point that he had now begun to touch. And not only was he resolved to skin Boko. He stressed in unmistakable terms his intention of doing it lingeringly and with a blunt knife. In short, it was abundantly clear that, however beautiful might have been the friendship which had been started overnight between his host and himself, it had now taken a bad toss and definitely come unstuck.

I found myself frankly unable to cope with the situation. It was one of those which seemed to call imperiously for a word or two of advice from Jeeves. And I was just regretting that he was not there, when a gentle cough in my rear told me that he was. It was as if some sort of telepathy, if that's the word I want, had warned him that the young master had lost his grip and could do with twopennyworth of feudal assistance.

'Jeeves!' I cried, and clutched him by the coat sleeve, like a lost child hooking on to its mother. When I had finished pouring my tale into his receptive ear, it was plain that he had not failed to grasp the nub.

'Most disturbing, sir,' he said.

'Most,' I responded.

I refrained from wounding him with any word of censure and rebuke, but I could not feel, as I have so frequently felt before, that a spot of leaping about and eyeball-rolling would have been more in keeping with the gravity of the situation. If Jeeves has a fault, as I think I have already mentioned, it is that he is too prone merely to tut at times when you would prefer to see his knotted and combined locks do a bit of parting.

'His lordship, you gather, sir, is incensed?'

I could answer that one.

'Yes, Jeeves. His remarks, as far as I was able to catch them, were unquestionably those of a man a good deal steamed up. What is the Death of the Thousand Cuts?'

'It is a penal sentence in vogue in Chinese police courts for minor offences. Roughly equivalent to our fourteen days with the option of a fine. Why do you ask, sir?'

'Uncle Percy happened to mention it in passing. It's one of the things he is planning to do to Boko when they get together. Good Lord, Jeeves!' I exclaimed.

'Sir?'

The reason I had exclaimed as above was that this mention of police courts and penal sentences had suddenly reminded me of my own position. For a brief space, the mind, occupied with this business of uncles in garages, had slid away from the fact that I was a fugitive from a chain gang.

'You haven't heard the latest. Stilton. He has found out about that uniform and has gone off to get warrants and things.'

'Indeed, sir?'

'Yes. Young Edwin, creeping into my room last night in order to insinuate a hedgehog into my bed, saw the thing lying there, and went and squealed to Stilton, the degraded little copper's nark. Only by making an immediate getaway can I hope to escape undergoing the utmost rigours of the Law. You see the frightful dilemma I'm on the horns of. My car's in the garage. To get it, I shall have to open the door. And opening the door involves having Uncle Percy come popping out like a cork out of a bottle.'

'You shrink from an encounter with his lordship, sir?'

'Yes, Jeeves. I shrink from an encounter with his lordship. Oh, I know what you are going to say. You are about to point out that it was Boko who lodged him in the coop, not me.'

'Precisely, sir. You are not armed so strong in honesty that his lordship's displeasure will pass by you as the idle wind, which you respect not.'

'I dare say. But have you ever removed a wounded puma from a trap?'

'No, sir. I have not had that experience.'

'Well, anyone will tell you that on such occasions the animal does not pause to pick and choose. It just goes baldheaded for the nearest innocent bystander in sight.'

'I appreciate your point, sir. It might be better if you were to return to the house and allow me to extricate his lordship.'

His nobility stunned me.

'Would you, Jeeves?'

'Certainly, sir.'

'Pretty white of you.'

'Not at all, sir.'

'You could turn the key, shout "All clear", and then run like a rabbit.'

'I would prefer to linger on the scene, sir, in the hope of doing something to smooth his lordship's wounded feelings.'

'With honeyed words, you mean?'

'Precisely, sir.'

I drew a deep breath.

'You wouldn't consider at least climbing a tree?'

'No, sir.'

I drew another one.

'Well, all right, if you say so. You know best. Carry on, then, Jeeves.'

'Very good, sir. I will bring your car to the front door, so that you will be enabled to make an immediate start. I will follow later in the day with the suitcases.'

It was some slight consolation to me in this dark hour to reflect, as I tooled back to the house, that the news I was bearing would, if he were still eating sardines, cause those sardines to turn to ashes in Boko's mouth. I am not a vindictive man, but I was feeling in no amiable frame of mind towards this literary screwball. I mean, it's all very well for a chap to plead that he's an author and expect on the strength of that to get away with conduct which would qualify the ordinary man for a one-way ticket to Colney Hatch, but even an author, I felt – and I think with justice – ought to have had the sense to glance through his car before he locked it up for the night, to make sure there weren't any shipping magnates dozing in the back seat.

As it happened, he was past the sardines phase. He was lolling in his chair in quiet enjoyment of the after-breakfast pipe, while Nobby, at his side, did the crossword puzzle in the morning paper. At the sight of Bertram, both expressed surprise.

'Why, hullo!' said Nobby.

'Haven't you gone yet?' said Boko.

'No, I haven't,' I replied, and laughed a hard, mirthless one.

It caused Boko to frown disapprovingly.

'What's the idea of coming here and trilling with laughter?' he asked austerely. 'You must try to get it into your head, my lad, that this is not the time for that sort of thing. Don't you realize your position? Unless you're across the Channel by nightfall, you haven't a hope. Where's your car?'

'In the garage.'

'Then get it out of the garage.'

'I can't,' I said, letting him have it right in the gizzard. 'Uncle Percy's there.'

And in a few crisp words I slipped him the lowdown.

I had anticipated that my statement would get in amongst him a bit, and this expectation was fulfilled. Man and boy, I have seen a good many lower jaws fall, but never one that shot down with such a sudden swoop as his. It was surprising that the thing didn't come off its hinges.

'But how was he in my car? He can't have been in my car. Why didn't I notice him?'

This, of course, was susceptible of a ready explanation.

'Because you're a fathead.'

Nobby, who since the initial spilling of the beans had been sitting bolt upright in her chair with gleaming eyes, making little gulping noises and chewing the lower lip with pearly teeth, endorsed this.

'Fathead,' she concurred, speaking in a strange, strangled voice, 'is right. Of all – '

Preoccupied though Boko was, there must have penetrated to his consciousness some inkling of what the harvest would be, were she permitted to get going and really start hauling up her slacks. He strove to head her off with a tortured gesture.

'Just a minute, darling.'

'Of all the – '

'Yes, yes.'

'Of all the gibbering – '

'Quite, quite. But half a second, angel. Bertie and I are threshing out an important point. Let me just try to envisage what happened after you left last night. Bertie. Here is the sequence, as I recall it. I had my talk with old Worplesdon, and, as I told you, secured a guardian's blessing: and then – yes, then I went back to the ballroom to tread the measure for a while.'

'Of all the gibbering, half-witted – '

'Exactly, exactly. But don't interrupt the flow of my thoughts, precious. I'm trying to get this thing straight. I danced, a saraband or two, and then looked in at the bar for a moment. I wanted to get a snootful and muse over my happiness. And I was doing this, when it suddenly occurred to me that Nobby was probably tossing sleeplessly on her pillow, dying to hear how everything had come out, and I felt that I must get home immediately and go and bung gravel at her window. I raced back to the car, accordingly, sprang to the wheel and drove off. I see now why I didn't notice old Worplesdon. Obviously, the man by that time had passed out and was lying on the floor. Well, dash it, a chap in my frame of mind, all joy and ecstasy and excitement, with his soul full to the brim of tender thoughts of the girl he loved, couldn't be expected to go over the floor of his car with a magnifying-glass, on the chance that there might be Worplesdons there. Naturally, not observing him, I assumed that he had gone off on his push bike. Would you have had me borrow a couple of bloodhounds and search the *tonneau* from end to end? I'm sure you understand everything now, darling, and will be the first to withdraw the adjective "gibbering". Oh, I am not angry,' said Boko, 'in fact, not even surprised that in the heat of the moment you should have spoken as you did. Just so long as you realize that I am innocent, blameless . . . '

At this juncture there was a confused noise without, and Uncle Percy crossed the threshold, moving well. A moment later, Jeeves shimmered in his wake.

Having become so accustomed during our hobnobbings of the previous day to seeing this uncle by marriage in genial and comradely mood, I had almost forgotten how like the Assyrian swooping down on the fold he could look, when deeply stirred. And that he was so now rather leaped to the eye. The ginger whiskers which go with the costume of Sindbad the Sailor obscured his countenance to a great extent, rendering it difficult to note the full play of expression on the features, but one was able to observe his eyes, and that was enough to be going on with. Fixed on Boko with an unwinking glare, they had the effect of causing that unhappy purveyor of wholesome literature for the masses to recoil at least a dozen feet. And he would undoubtedly have gone farther, had he not fetched up against the wall.

Jeeves had spoke of his intention of trying to smooth the ruffled Worplesdon feelings with honeyed words. Whether he hadn't been allowed to get one in edgeways, or whether he had tried a few and they hadn't been honeyed enough, I was not in a position to say. But the fact was patent that the above feelings were still as ruffled as dammit, and that Hampshire contained at this moment no hotter-under-the-collar shipping magnate.

Proof of this was given by his opening speech, which consisted of the word 'What', repeated over and over again as if fired from a machine-gun. It was always this uncle's practice, as I have mentioned, to what-what-what rather freely in moments of emotion, and he did not deviate from it on this occasion.

'What?' he said, in part, continuing to focus the eye on Boko. 'What-what-what-what-what-what-what-what?'

Here he paused, as if for a reply, and I think Boko did the wrong thing by asking him if he would like a sardine. The question, seeming to touch an exposed nerve, caused a sheet of flame to shoot from his eyes.

'Sardine?' he said, with a bitter intonation. 'Sardine? Sardine? Sardine?'

'You'll feel better, when you've had some breakfast,' said Nobby, pulling a quick ministering-angel-thou.

Uncle Percy opposed this view.

'I shall not. The only thing that can make me feel better is to thrash that pie-faced young wart-hog Fittleworth within an inch of his life. Bertie, get me a horsewhip.'

I pursed the lips dubiously.

'I don't believe we have one,' I said. 'Are there any horsewhips on the premises, Boko?'

'No, no horsewhips,' the latter responded, now trying to get through the wall.

Uncle Percy snorted.

'What a house! Jeeves.'

'M'lord?'

'Go over to the Hall and bring me my horsewhip with the ivory handle.'

'Yes, m'lord.'

'I think it's in my study. If not, hunt about for it.'

'Very good, m'lord. No doubt her ladyship will be able to inform me of the instrument's whereabouts.'

He spoke so casually that it was perhaps three seconds by the stop-watch before Uncle Percy got the gist. When he did, he started, like one jabbed in the fleshy parts with a sudden bradawl.

'Her . . . what?'

'Her ladyship, m'lord.'

'Her ladyship?'

'Yes, m'lord.'

Uncle Percy had crumpled like a wet sock. He sank into a chair, and clutched the marmalade jar, as if for support. His eyes popped out of his head, and waved about on their stalks.

'But her ladyship – '

' – returned unexpectedly late last night, m'lord.'

29

I don't know if the name of Lot's wife is familiar to you, and if you were told about her rather remarkable finish. I may not have got the facts right, but the story, as I heard it, was that she was advised not to look round at something or other or she would turn into a pillar of salt, so, naturally imagining that they were simply pulling her leg, she looked round, and – *bing* – a pillar of salt. And the reason I mention this now is that the very same thing seemed to have happened to Uncle Percy. Crouching there with his fingers riveted to the marmalade jar, he appeared to have turned into a pillar of salt. If it hadn't been that the ginger whiskers were quivering gently, you would have said that life had ceased to animate the rigid limbs.

'It appears that Master Thomas is now out of danger, m'lord, and no longer has need of her ladyship's ministrations.'

The whiskers continued to quiver, and I didn't blame them. I knew just how the old relative must be feeling, for, as I have already indicated, he had made no secret when chatting with me of his apprehensions concerning the shape of things to come, should Aunt Agatha ever learn that he had been attending fancy dress dances in her absence.

The poignant drama of it all had not escaped Nobby, either.

'Golly, Uncle Percy,' she said, a womanly pity in her voice that became her well, 'this is a bit awkward, is it not? You'll have to devote a minute or two, when you see her, to explaining why you were out all night, won't you?'

Her words had the effect of bringing the unhappy man out of his trance or coma as if she had touched off a stick of dynamite under him. He moved, he stirred, he seemed to feel the rush of life along his keel.

'Jeeves,' he said hoarsely.

'M'lord?'

'Jeeves.'

'M'lord?'

Uncle Percy shoved out his tongue about an inch, moistening the lips with the tip of it. It was plain that he was finding it no easy matter to get speech over the larynx.

'Her ladyship, Jeeves . . . Tell me . . . Is she . . . Has she . . . Is she by any chance aware of my absence?'

'Yes, m'lord. She was apprised of it by the head housemaid. I left them in conference. "You tell me his lordship's bed *has not been slept in?*" her ladyship was saying. Her agitation was most pronounced.'

I caught Uncle Percy's eye. It had swivelled round at me with a dumb, pleading look in it, as if saying that suggestions would be welcomed.

'How would it be,' I said – well, one had to say something, 'if you told her the truth?'

'The truth?' he repeated dazedly, and you could see he thought the idea a novel one.

'That you went to the ball to confer with Clam.'

He shook his head.

'I could never convince your aunt that I had gone to a fancy dress ball from purely business motives. Women are so prone to think the worst.'

'Something in that.'

'And it's no good trying to make them see reason, because they talk so damn' quick. No,' said Uncle Percy, 'this is the end. I can only set my teeth and take my medicine like an English gentleman.'

'Unless, of course, Jeeves has something to suggest.'

This perked him up for an instant. Then the drawn, haggard look came back into his face, and he shook the lemon again, slowly and despondently.

'Impossible. The situation is beyond Jeeves.'

'No situation is beyond Jeeves,' I said, with quiet rebuke. 'In fact,' I went on, scrutinizing the man closely, 'I believe something is fermenting now inside that spacious bean. Am I wrong, Jeeves, in supposing that I can see the light of inspiration in your eye?'

'No, sir. You are quite correct. I think that I may perhaps be able to offer a satisfactory solution of his lordship's difficulty.'

Uncle Percy inhaled sharply. An awed look came into the unoccupied areas of his face. I heard him murmur something under his breath about fish.

'You mean that, Jeeves?'

'Yes, m'lord.'

'Then let us have it,' I said, feeling rather like some impresario of performing fleas who watches the star member of his troupe advance to the footlights. 'What is this solution of which you speak?'

'Well, sir, it occurred to me that as his lordship has, as I under-stand, given his consent to the union of Mr Fittleworth and Miss Hopwood – '

Uncle Percy uttered an animal cry.

'I haven't! Or, if I did, I've withdrawn it.'

'Very good, m'lord. In that case, I have nothing to suggest.'

There was a silence. One could sense the struggle proceeding in Uncle Percy's bosom. I saw him look at Boko, and quiver. Then a strong shudder passed through the frame, and I knew he was recalling what Jeeves had said about Aunt Agatha's agitation being most pronounced. When Aunt Agatha's agitation is pronounced, she has a way of drawing her eyebrows together and making her nose look like an eagle's beak. Strong men have quailed at the spectacle, repeatedly.

'May as well hear what you've got to say, I suppose,' he said, at length.

'Quite,' I agreed. 'No harm in having a – what, Jeeves?'

'Academic discussion, sir.'

'Thank you, Jeeves.'

'Not at all, sir.'

'Carry on, then.'

'Very good, sir. It merely occurred to me that, had his lordship consented to the union, nothing would have been more natural than that he should have visited Mr Fittleworth at his house for the purpose of talking the matter over and making arrangements for the wedding. Immersed in this absorbing subject, his lordship would quite understandably have lost count of time – '

I yipped intelligently. I had got the set-up.

'And when he looked at his watch and found how late it was – '

'Precisely, sir. When his lordship looked at his watch and found how late it was, Mr Fittleworth hospitably suggested that he should pass the remainder of the night beneath his roof. His lordship agreed that this would be the most convenient course, and so it was arranged.'

I looked at Uncle Percy, confidently expecting the salvo of applause, and was amazed to find him shaking the bean once more.

'It wouldn't work,' he said.

'Why on earth not? It's a pip.'

He kept on oscillating the lozenge.

'No, Bertie, the scheme is not practical. Your aunt, my dear boy, is a suspicious woman. She probes beneath the surface and asks questions. And the first one she would ask on this occasion would be, why, merely in order to discuss wedding arrangements with my ward's future husband, did I dress up as Sindbad the Sailor? You can see for yourself how awkward that question would be, and how difficult to answer.'

The point was well taken.

'A snag, Jeeves. Can you get round it?'

'Quite easily, sir. Before returning to the Hall, his lordship could borrow a suit of clothes from you, sir.'

'Off course he could. Clad in the herring-bone tweed which is in the cupboard in my bedroom, Uncle Percy, you could look Aunt Agatha in the eye without a tremor.'

I dare say you have frequently, when strolling in your garden, seen a parched flower beneath a refreshing downpour. It was of such a flower that Uncle Percy now irresistibly reminded me. He seemed to swell and burgeon, as it were, and the strained eyes lost that resemblance to the underside of a dead fish which had been so noticeable since the beginning of this sequence.

'Good Lord!' he exclaimed. 'You're quite right. So I could. Jeeves,' he went on, emotionally, 'you must have that brain of yours pickled and presented to some national museum.'

'Very good, m'lord.'

'When you've done with it, of course. Come on, Bertie, action, action! Ho for the herring-bone tweed!'

'This way, Uncle Percy,' I said, and we started for the door, to find our path barred by Boko. He was looking a bit green about the gills, but firm and resolute.

'Just a minute,' said Boko. 'Not so jolly fast, if you don't mind. How about that guardian's blessing? Do I cop?'

'Of course you do, old bird,' I said soothingly. 'That's all budgeted for in the estimates, Uncle Percy?'

'Eh? What?'

'The guardian's b. You're dishing that out?'

Once more there was that silent struggle. Then he nodded sombrely.

'It seems unavoidable.'

'It is unavoidable.'

'Then I won't try to avoid it.'

'Okay, Boko, you're all set.'

'Good,' said Boko. 'I'll just have that in writing, if you don't mind, my dear Worplesdon. I don't want to carp or criticize, but there's been a lot of in-and-out running about this business to present date, and one would welcome a few words in black and white. You will find pen and ink on the table in the corner. Sing out, my dear Worplesdon, if the nib doesn't suit you, and I will provide you with another.'

Uncle Percy went to the table in the corner, and took pen in hand. It would be too much to say that his demeanour, as he did so, was rollicking. I fancy that up to this moment he had been entertaining a faint hope that, if his luck held, he might somehow derive the benefits from Jeeves's scheme without having to sit in on its drawbacks. However, as I say, he took pen in hand and, having scribbled for a minute or so, handed the result to Boko, who read it through and handed it to Nobby, who read it through and tucked it away with a satisfied 'Okay-doke' in some safe deposit in the recesses of her costume.

She had scarcely done so, when heavy, official footsteps sounded without, and Stilton came clumping in.

You will scarcely believe me, but it is a fact that I had been so tensely gripped by the drama of the last quarter of an hour that the Stilton angle had been completely expunged from my mind, and it was only now, as I watched him heave to, that the thought of the Wooster personal peril came back to me. The first thing he did on entering the room was to give me one of those looks of his, and it chilled my insides like a quart of ice cream.

I had a shot at an airy 'Ah, there you are, Stilton', but my heart was not in it, and it elicited no response except a short 'Ho!' Having got off this 'Ho!' which, as I have explained, was in the nature of a sort of signature tune, he addressed himself to Boko.

'You were right about that warrant,' he said. 'The sergeant says I've got to have one. I've brought it along. It has to be signed by a Justice of the Peace.' Here, for the first time, he appeared to become aware of Uncle Percy's identity, which, of course, had been shrouded from him by the whiskers. 'Why, hullo, Lord Worplesdon,' he said, 'you're just the man I was looking for. If you will shove your name on the dotted line, we can go ahead. So you went to that fancy dress ball last night?' he said, giving him the eye.

I think he had merely intended to be chatty and to show a kindly interest, as it were, in the relative's affairs, but he had said the wrong thing. Uncle Percy stiffened haughtily.

'What do you mean, I went to the fancy dress ball last night? I did nothing of the kind, and I shall be glad if you will refrain from making loose statements of that description. Went to the fancy dress ball, indeed! What fancy dress ball? Where? It is news to me that there has been a fancy dress ball.'

His generous indignation seemed to take Stilton aback.

'Oh, sorry,' he said. 'I just thought ... The costume, I mean.'

'And what about the costume? If my ward and her future husband are planning an evening of amateur theatricals and asked me as a personal favour to put on the costume of Sindbad the Sailor, to see if I was the type for the part, is it so singular that I should good-humouredly have acceded to their wishes? And is it any business of yours? Does it entitle you to jump to idiotic conclusions about fancy dress balls? Have I got to explain every simple little action of mine to every flatfooted copper who comes along and can't keep his infernal nose out of my business?'

These were not easy questions to answer, and the best Stilton could do was to shuffle his feet and say 'Oh, ah.'

'Well, anyway,' he said, after a rather painful pause, changing the subject and getting back to the *res*, 'would you mind signing this warrant?'

'Warrant? What warrant? What's it all about? What's all this nonsense about warrants?'

There was a sound in the background like a distant sheep coughing gently on a mountainside. Jeeves sailing into action.

'If I might explain, your lordship. It appears that in the course of yesterday afternoon the officer's uniform was purloined as he bathed in the river. He accuses Mr Wooster of the crime.'

'Mr Wooster? Bertie? My nephew?'

'Yes, m'lord. To me, a most bizarre theory. One seeks in vain for a motive which could plausibly have led Mr Wooster to perpetrate such an outrage. The constable, I understand, alleges that Mr Wooster desired the uniform in order to be able to attend the fancy dress ball.'

This seemed to interest Uncle Percy.

'There really was a fancy dress ball, was there?'

'Yes, m'lord. At the neighbouring town of East Wibley.'

'Odd. I never heard about it.'

'A very minor affair, m'lord, I gather. Not at all the sort of entertainment in which a gentleman of Mr Wooster's position would condescend to participate.'

'Of course not. I wouldn't have gone to it myself. Just one of those potty little country affairs, eh?'

'Precisely, m'lord. Nobody, knowing Mr Wooster, would suppose for a moment that he would waste his sweetness on such desert air.'

'Eh?'

'A quotation, m'lord. The poet Gray.'

'Ah. But you say the officer sticks to it that he did?'

'Yes, m'lord. It is fortunate, therefore, that your lordship passed the night in this house, and so is able to testify that Mr Wooster never left the premises.'

'Dashed fortunate. Settles the whole thing.'

I never know, when I am telling a story where a couple of fellows are talking and a third fellow is trying to shove his oar in, whether to interpolate the last named's gulps and gurgles in the run of the dialogue or to wait till it's all over and then chalk up these gulps and gurgles to their utterer's score. I think it works out smoother the second way, and that is why, in recording the above exchanges, I have left out Stilton's attempts to chip in. All through this Jeeves-Worplesdon exchange of ideas he had been trying to catch the Speaker's eye, only to be 'Tchah'-ed and 'Be quiet, officer'-ed by Uncle Percy. A lull in the conversation having occurred at the word 'thing', he was now able to speak his piece.

'I tell you the accused Wooster did pinch my uniform!' he cried, his eyes bulging more than ever and his cheeks a pretty scarlet.

'It was seen on his bed by the witness Edwin.'

Things were going so well that I felt equal to raising the eyebrows and coming through with a light, amused laugh.

'Edwin, Uncle Percy! One smiles, does one not?'

The relative backed me up nobly.

'Smiles? Certainly one smiles. Like the dickens. Are you trying to tell me,' he said, letting Stilton have the eye in no uncertain measure, 'that this preposterous accusation of yours is based on the unsupported word of my son Edwin? I can scarcely credit it. Can you, Jeeves?'

'Most extraordinary, m'lord. But possibly the officer is not aware that Mr Wooster inflicted a personal assault upon Master Edwin yesterday, and so does not realize how biased any statement on the part of the young gentleman regarding Mr Wooster must inevitably be.'

'Don't make excuses for him. The man's a fool. And I should like to say,' said Uncle Percy, swelling like a balloon and starting to give Stilton the strong remarks from the bench, 'that we have had in my opinion far too much of late of these wild and irresponsible accusations on the part of the police. A deplorable spirit is creeping into the Force, and as long as I remain a Justice of the Peace I shall omit no word or act to express my strongest disapproval of it. I shall stamp it out, root and branch, and see to it that the liberty of the subject is not placed in jeopardy by officers of the Law who so far forget their – yes, dash it, their sacred obligations as to being trumped-up charges right and left in a selfish desire to secure promotion. I have nothing further to add except to express my profound regret that you should have been subjected to this monstrous persecution, Bertie.'

'Quite all right, Uncle Percy.'

'It is not all right. It is outrageous. I advise you in future, officer, to be careful, very careful. And as for that warrant of yours, you can take it and stick it . . . However, that is neither here nor there.'

It was good stuff. Indeed, I can't remember ever having heard better, except once, when I was a stripling and Aunt Agatha was ticking me off for breaking a valuable china vase with my catapult. I confidently expected Stilton to cower beneath it like a worm in a thunderstorm. But he didn't. It was plain that he burned, not with shame and remorse but with the baffled fury of the man who, while not quite abreast of the run of the scenario, realizes that dirty work is afoot at the crossroads and that something swift is being slipped across him.

'Ho!' he said, and paused for a moment to wrestle with his feelings. Then, with generous emotion: 'It's a bally conspiracy,' he cried. 'It's a lowdown, hornswoggling plot to defeat the ends of justice. For the last time, Lord Worplesdon, will you sign this warrant?'

Nothing could have been more dignified than Uncle Percy's demeanour. He drew himself up, and his voice was quiet and cold.

'I have already indicated what you can do with that warrant. I think, officer, that it would be well if you were to go and sleep it off. For the kindest interpretation which I can place upon your extraordinary behaviour is that you are intoxicated. Bertie, show the constable the door.'

I showed Stilton the door, and he took a sort of dazed look at it, as if it was the first time he had seen the bally thing. Then he navigated slowly through, and disappeared, not even pausing to say 'Ho' over his shoulder. The impression I received was that his haughty spirit was at last crushed. Presently we heard the sound of his violin cases tramping away down the garden path.

'And now, my boy,' said Uncle Percy, as the last echoes died away, 'for the herring-bone tweed. Also a bath and a shave and a cup of strong black coffee with perhaps the merest suspicion of brandy in it. And perhaps it would be as well, when I am ready to start for the Hall, if you were to accompany me, to add your testimony to mine regarding my spending last night under this roof. You will not falter, will you? You will support my statement, will you not, in a strong resonant voice, carrying conviction in every syllable? Nothing on these occasions creates so unfortunate an impression as the pause for thought, the hesitating utterance, the nervous twiddling of the fingers. Above all things, remember not to stand on one leg. Right, my boy. Let us go.'

I escorted him to my room, dug out the suit, showed him the bathroom and left him to it. When I got back to the dining-room, Boko had gone, but Nobby was still there, chatting with Jeeves. She greeted me warmly.

'Boko's gone to fetch his car,' she said. 'We're going to run up to London and get married. Wonderful how everything has come out, isn't it? I thought Uncle Percy was terrific.'

'Most impressive,' I agreed.

'And what words that tongue could utter could give even a sketchy idea of how one feels about you, Jeeves.'

'I am deeply gratified, miss, if I have been able to give satisfaction.'

'I've said it before, and I'll say it again – there's nobody like you.'

'Thank you very much, miss.'

I think this might have gone on for some time, for Nobby was plainly filled to the back teeth with girlish enthusiasm, but at this point I interrupted. I would be the last man ever to deprive Jeeves of his meed of praise, but I had a question of compelling interest to put.

'Have you shown Florence that letter of mine, Nobby?' I asked.

A sudden cloud came over her eager map, and she made a clicking noise.

'I knew there was something I had forgotten. Oh, Bertie, I'm so sorry.'

'Sorry?' I said, filled with a nameless fear.

'I've been meaning to tell you. When I got up this morning, I couldn't find that letter anywhere, and I was looking for it, when Edwin came along and told me he had done an act of kindness last night by tidying my room. I think he must have destroyed the letter. He generally does destroy all correspondence when he tidies rooms. I'm most awfully sorry, but I expect you'll find some other way of coping with Florence. Ask Jeeves. He's sure to think of something. Ah,' she said, as a booming voice came from the great open spaces, 'there's Boko calling me. Goodbye, Bertie. Goodbye, Jeeves. I must rush.'

She was gone with the wind, and I turned to Jeeves with a pale, set face.

'Yes, sir.'

'Can you think of a course to pursue?'

'No, sir.'

'You are baffled?'

'For the moment, sir, unquestionably. I fear that Miss Hopwood overestimated my potentialities.'

'Come, come, Jeeves. It is not like you to be a . . . what's the word . . . it's on the tip of my tongue.'

'Defeatist, sir?'

'That's right. It is not like you to be a defeatist. Don't give it up. Go and brood in the kitchen. There may be some fish there. Did you notice any, when you were there yesterday?'

'Only a tin of anchovy paste, sir.'

My heart sank a bit. Anchovy paste is a slender reed on which to lean in a major crisis. Still, it was fish within the meaning of the act, and no doubt contained its quota of phosphorus.

'Go and wade into it.'

'Very good, sir.'

'Don't spare the stuff. Dig it out with a spoon,' I said, and dismissed him with a moody gesture.

Moody was the word which would have described my aspect, as a few moments later I left the house and proceeded to the garden, feeling in need of a bit of air. I had kept up a brave front, but I had little real hope that anchovy paste would bring home the bacon. As I stood at the garden gate, staring sombrely before me, I was at a pretty low ebb.

I mean to say, I had been banking everything on that letter. I had counted on it to destroy the Wooster glamour in Florence's eyes. And, lacking it, I couldn't see how she was going to be persuaded that I was not a king among men. Not for the first time, I found myself musing bitterly on young Edwin, the *fons et origo* – a Latin expression – of all my troubles.

And I was just regretting that we were not in China, where it would have been a simple matter to frame up something against the child, thus putting him in line for the Death of the Thousand Cuts, when my reverie was interrupted by the ting of a bicycle bell, and Stilton came wheeling up.

After what had passed, of course, it was not agreeable to be closeted with this vindictive copper, and I am not ashamed to say that I backed a pace. In fact, I would probably have gone on backing, had he not reached out a hand like a ham and grabbed me by the slack of my coat.

'Stand still, you blasted object,' he said. 'I have something to say to you.'

'You couldn't write?'

'No, I could not write. Don't wriggle. Listen.'

I could see that the man was wrestling with some strong emotion, and could only hope that it was not homicidal. The eyes were glittering, and the face flushed.

'Listen,' he said again. 'You know that engagement of yours?'

'To Florence?'

'To Florence. It's off.'

'Off?'

'Off,' said Stilton

A sharp exclamation passed my lips. I clutched at the gate for support. The sun, which a moment before had gone behind a cloud, suddenly came shooting out like a rabbit and started shining like the dickens. On every side, it seemed to me, birds began to tottle their songs of joy. It will give you some rough indication of my feelings when I tell you that not only did all Nature become beautiful, but even for an instant Stilton.

Through a sort of pink mist, I heard myself asking faintly what he meant. The question caused him to frown with some impatience.

'You can understand words of one syllable, can't you? I tell you your engagement is off. Florence is going to marry me. I met her, as I came away from this pest house, and had it out with her. After that revolting exhibition of fraud and skulduggery in there, I had decided to resign from the Force, and I told her so. It removed the only barrier there had ever been between us. Questioned, she broke down and came clean, admitting that she had always loved me, and had got engaged to you merely to score off me for something I had said about modern enlightened thought. I withdrew the remark, and she fell into my arms. She seemed not to like the idea of breaking the news to you, so I said I would do it. "And if young blasted Wooster has anything to say", I told her, "I will twist his head off and ram it down his throat." Have you anything to say, Wooster?'

I paused for a moment to listen to the tootling birds. Then I raised the map, and allowed the beaming sun to play on it.

'Not a thing,' I assured him.

'You realize the position? She has returned you to store. No ruddy wedding bells for you.'

'Quite.'

'Good. You will be leaving here fairly soon, I take it?'

'Almost at once.'

'Good,' said Stilton, and sprang on his bicycle as if it had been a mettlesome charger.

Nor did I linger. I did the distance from the gate to the kitchen in about three seconds flat. From the window of the bathroom, as I passed, there came the voice of Uncle Percy as he sluiced the frame. He was singing some gay air. A sea chanty, probably, which he had learned from Clam or one of the captains in his employment.

Jeeves was pacing the kitchen floor, deep in thought. He looked round, as I entered, and his manner was apologetic.

'It appears, sir, I regret to say, that there is no anchovy paste. It was finished yesterday.'

I didn't actually slap him on the back, but I gave him the dickens of a beaming smile.

'Never mind the anchovy paste, Jeeves. It will not be required. I've just seen Stilton. A reconciliation has taken place between him and Lady Florence, and they are once more headed for the altar rails. So, there being nothing to keep us in Steeple Bumpleigh, let's go.'

'Very good sir. The car is at the door.'

I paused.

'Oh, but, dash it, we can't.'

'Sir?'

'I've just remembered I promised Uncle Percy to go to the Hall with him and help him cope with Aunt Agatha.'

'Her ladyship is not at the Hall, sir.'

'What! But you said she was.'

'Yes, sir. I fear I was guilty of subterfuge. I regretted the necessity, but it seemed to me essential in the best interests of all concerned.'

I goggled at the man.

'Egad, Jeeves!'

'Yes, sir.'

Faintly from the distance there came the sound of Uncle Percy working through his chanty.

'How would it be,' I suggested, 'to zoom off immediately, without waiting to pack?'

'I was about to suggest such a course myself, sir.'

'It would enable one to avoid tedious explanations.'

'Precisely, sir.'

'Then shift ho, Jeeves,' I said.

It was as we were about half-way between Steeple Bumpleigh and the old metrop, that I mentioned that there was an expression on the tip of my tongue which seemed to me to sum up the nub of the recent proceedings.

Or, rather, when I say an expression, I mean a saying. A wheeze. A gag. What I believe is called a saw. Something about Joy . . .

But we went into all that before, didn't we?

Carry on, Jeeves

To
Bernard le Strange

1

JEEVES TAKES CHARGE

Now, touching this business of old Jeeves – my man, you know – how do we stand? Lots of people think I'm much too dependent on him. My Aunt Agatha, in fact, has even gone so far as to call him my keeper. Well, what I say is: Why not? The man's a genius. From the collar upwards he stands alone. I gave up trying to run my own affairs within a week of his coming to me. That was about half a dozen years ago, directly after the rather rummy business of Florence Craye, my Uncle Willoughby's book, and Edwin, the Boy Scout.

The thing really began when I got back to Easeby, my uncle's place in Shropshire. I was spending a week or so there, as I generally did in the summer; and I had to break my visit to come back to London to get a new valet. I had found Meadowes, the fellow I had taken to Easeby with me, sneaking my silk socks, a thing no bloke of spirit could stick at any price. It transpiring, moreover, that he had looted a lot of other things here and there about the place, I was reluctantly compelled to hand the misguided blighter the mitten and go to London to ask the registry office to dig up another specimen for my approval. They sent me Jeeves.

I shall always remember the morning he came. It so happened that the night before I had been present at a rather cheery little supper, and I was feeling pretty rocky. On top of this I was trying to read a book Florence Craye had given me. She had been one of the house-party at Easeby, and two or three days before I left we had got engaged. I was due back at the end of the week, and I knew she would expect me to have finished the book by then. You see, she was particularly keen on boosting me up a bit nearer her own plane of intellect. She was a girl with a wonderful profile, but steeped to the gills in serious purpose. I can't give you a better idea of the way things stood than by telling you that the book she'd given me to read was called *Types of Ethical Theory*, and that when I opened it at random I struck a page beginning:

The postulate or common understanding involved in speech is certainly co-extensive, in the obligation it carries, with the social organism of which language is the instrument, and the ends of which it is an effort to subserve.

All perfectly true, no doubt; but not the sort of thing to spring on a lad with a morning head.

I was doing my best to skim through this bright little volume when the bell rang. I crawled off the sofa and opened the door. A kind of darkish sort of respectful Johnnie stood without.

'I was sent by the agency, sir,' he said. 'I was given to understand that you require a valet.'

I'd have preferred an undertaker; but I told him to stagger in, and he floated noiselessly through the doorway like a healing zephyr. That impressed me from the start. Meadowes had had flat feet and used to clump. This fellow didn't seem to have any feet at all. He just streamed in. He had a grave, sympathetic face, as if he, too, knew what it was to sup with the lads.

'Excuse me, sir,' he said gently.

Then he seemed to flicker, and wasn't there any longer. I heard him moving about in the kitchen, and presently he came back with a glass on a tray.

'If you would drink this, sir,' he said, with a kind of bedside manner, rather like the royal doctor shooting the bracer into the sick prince. 'It is a little preparation of my own invention. It is the Worcester Sauce that gives it its colour. The raw egg makes it nutritious. The red pepper gives it its bite. Gentlemen have told me they have found it extremely invigorating after a late evening.'

I would have clutched at anything that looked like a lifeline that morning. I swallowed the stuff. For a moment I felt as if somebody had touched off a bomb inside the old bean and was strolling down my throat with a lighted torch, and then everything seemed suddenly to get all right. The sun shone in through the window; birds twittered in the tree-tops; and, generally speaking, hope dawned once more.

'You're engaged!' I said, as soon as I could say anything.

I perceived clearly that this cove was one of the world's workers, the sort no home should be without.

'Thank you, sir. My name is Jeeves.'

'You can start in at once?'

'Immediately, sir.'

'Because I'm due down at Easeby, in Shropshire, the day after tomorrow.'

'Very good, sir.' He looked past me at the mantelpiece. 'That is an excellent likeness of Lady Florence Craye, sir. It is two years since I saw her ladyship. I was at one time in Lord Worplesdon's employment. I tendered my resignation because I could not see eye to eye with his lordship in his desire to dine in dress trousers, a flannel shirt, and a shooting coat.'

He couldn't tell me anything I didn't know about the old boy's eccentricity. This Lord Worplesdon was Florence's father. He was the old buster who, a few years later, came down to breakfast one morning, lifted the first cover he saw, said 'Eggs! Eggs! Eggs! Damn all eggs!' in an overwrought sort of voice, and instantly legged it for France, never to return to the bosom of his family. This, mind you, being a bit of luck for the bosom of the family, for old Worplesdon had the worst temper in the county.

I had known the family ever since I was a kid, and from boyhood up this old boy had put the fear of death into me. Time, the great healer, could never remove from my memory the occasion when he found me – then a stripling of fifteen – smoking one of his special cigars in the stables. He got after me with a hunting-crop just at the moment when I was beginning to realize that what I wanted most on earth was solitude and repose, and chased me more than a mile across difficult country. If there was a flaw, so to speak, in the pure joy of being engaged to Florence, it was the fact that she rather took after her father, and one was never certain when she might erupt. She had a wonderful profile, though.

'Lady Florence and I are engaged, Jeeves,' I said.

'Indeed, sir?'

You know, there was a kind of rummy something about his manner. Perfectly all right and all that, but not what you'd call chirpy. It somehow gave me the impression that he wasn't keen on Florence. Well, of course, it wasn't my business. I supposed that while he had been valeting old Worplesdon she must have trodden on his toes in some way. Florence was a dear girl, and, seen sideways, most awfully good-looking; but if she had a fault it was a tendency to be a bit imperious with the domestic staff.

At this point in the proceedings there was another ring at the front door. Jeeves shimmered out and came back with a telegram. I opened it. It ran:

Return immediately. Extremely urgent. Catch first train. Florence.

'Rum!' I said.

'Sir?'

'Oh, nothing!'

It shows how little I knew Jeeves in those days that I didn't go a bit deeper into the matter with him. Nowadays I would never dream of reading a rummy communication without asking him what he thought of it. And this one was devilish odd. What I mean is, Florence knew I was going back to Easeby the day after tomorrow, anyway; so why the hurry call? Something must have happened, of course; but I couldn't see what on earth it could be.

'Jeeves,' I said, 'we shall be going down to Easeby this afternoon. Can you manage it?'

'Certainly, sir.'

'You can get your packing done and all that?'

'Without any difficulty, sir. Which suit will you wear for the journey?'

'This one.'

I had on a rather sprightly young check that morning, to which I was a good deal attached; I fancied it, in fact, more than a little. It was perhaps rather sudden till you got used to it, but, nevertheless, an extremely sound effort, which many lads at the club and elsewhere had admired unrestrainedly.

'Very good, sir.'

Again there was that kind of rummy something in his manner. It was the way he said it, don't you know. He didn't like the suit. I pulled myself together to assert myself. Something seemed to tell me that, unless I was jolly careful and nipped this lad in the bud, he would be starting to boss me. He had the aspect of a distinctly resolute blighter.

Well, I wasn't going to have any of that sort of thing, by Jove! I'd seen so many cases of fellows who had become perfect slaves to their valets. I remember poor old Aubrey Fothergill telling me – with absolute tears in his eyes, poor chap! – one night at the club, that he had been compelled to give up a favourite pair of brown shoes simply because Meekyn, his man, disapproved of them. You have to keep these fellows in their place, don't you know. You have to work the good old iron-hand-in-the-velvet-glove wheeze. If you give them a what's-its-name, they take a thingummy.

'Don't you like this suit, Jeeves?' I said coldly.

'Oh, yes, sir.'

'Well, what don't you like about it?'

'It is a very nice suit, sir.'

'Well, what's wrong with it? Out with it, dash it!'

'If I might make the suggestion, sir, a simple brown or blue, with a hint of some quiet twill – '

'What absolute rot!'

'Very good, sir.'

'Perfectly blithering, my dear man!'

'As you say, sir.'

I felt as if I had stepped on the place where the last stair ought to have been, but wasn't. I felt defiant, if you know what I mean, and there didn't seem anything to defy.

'All right, then,' I said.

'Yes, sir.'

And then he went away to collect his kit, while I started in again on *Types of Ethical Theory* and took a stab at a chapter headed 'Idiopsychological Ethics'.

Most of the way down in the train that afternoon, I was wondering what could be up at the other end. I simply couldn't see what could have happened. Easeby wasn't one of those country houses you read about in the society novels, where young girls are lured on to play baccarat and then skinned to the bone of their jewellery, and so on. The house-party I had left had consisted entirely of law-abiding birds like myself.

Besides, my uncle wouldn't have let anything of that kind go on in his house. He was a rather stiff, precise sort of old boy, who liked a quiet life. He was just finishing a history of the family or something, which he had been working on for the last year, and didn't stir much from the library. He was rather a good instance of what they say about its being a good scheme for a fellow to sow his wild oats. I'd been told that in his youth Uncle Willoughby had been a bit of a bounder. You would never have thought it to look at him now.

When I got to the house, Oakshott, the butler, told me that Florence was in her room, watching her maid pack. Apparently there was a dance on at a house about twenty miles away that night, and she was motoring over with some of the Easeby lot and would be away some nights. Oakshott said she had told him to tell her the moment I arrived; so I trickled into the smoking-room and waited, and presently in she came. A glance showed me that she was perturbed, and even peeved. Her eyes had a goggly look, and altogether she appeared considerably pipped.

'Darling!' I said, and attempted the good old embrace; but she side-stepped like a bantam-weight.

'Don't!'

'What's the matter?'

'Everything's the matter! Bertie, you remember asking me, when you left, to make myself pleasant to your uncle?'

'Yes.'

The idea being, of course, that as at that time I was more or less dependent on Uncle Willoughby I couldn't very well marry without his approval. And though I knew he wouldn't have any objection to Florence, having known her father since they were at Oxford together, I hadn't wanted to take any chances; so I had told her to make an effort to fascinate the old boy.

'You told me it would please him particularly if I asked him to read me some of his history of the family.'

'Wasn't he pleased.'

'He was delighted. He finished writing the thing yesterday afternoon, and read me nearly all of it last night. I have never had such a shock in my life. The book is an outrage. It is impossible. It is horrible!'

'But, dash it, the family weren't so bad as all that.'

'It is not a history of the family at all. Your uncle has written his reminiscences! He calls them "Recollections of a Long Life"!'

I began to understand. As I say, Uncle Willoughby had been somewhat on the tabasco side as a young man, and it began to look as if he might have turned out something pretty fruity if he had started recollecting his long life.

'If half of what he has written is true,' said Florence, 'your uncle's youth must have been perfectly appalling. The moment we began to read he plunged straight into a most scandalous story of how he and my father were thrown out of a music-hall in 1887!'

'Why?'

'I decline to tell you why.'

It must have been something pretty bad. It took a lot to make them chuck people out of music-halls in 1887.

'Your uncle specifically states that father had drunk a quart and a half of champagne before beginning the evening,' she went on. 'The book is full of stories like that. There is a dreadful one about Lord Emsworth.'

'Lord Emsworth? Not the one we know? Not the one at Blandings?'

A most respectable old Johnnie, don't you know. Doesn't do a thing nowadays but dig in the garden with a spud.

'The very same. That is what makes the book so unspeakable. It is full of stories about people one knows who are the essence of propriety today, but who seem to have behaved, when they were in London in the eighties, in a manner that would not have been tolerated in the fo'c'sle of a whaler. Your uncle seems to remember everything disgraceful that happend to anybody when he was in his early twenties. There is a story about Sir Stanley Gervase-Gervase at Rosherville Gardens which is ghastly in its perfection of detail. It seems that Sir Stanley – but I can't tell you!'

'Have a dash!'

'No!'

'Oh, well, I shouldn't worry. No publisher will print the book if it's as bad as all that.'

'On the contrary, your uncle told me that all negotiations are settled with Riggs and Ballinger, and he's sending off the manuscript tomorrow for immediate publication. They make a special thing of that sort of book. They published Lady Carnaby's *Memories of Eighty Interesting Years*.'

'I read 'em!'

'Well, then, when I tell you that Lady Carnaby's Memories are simply not to be compared with your uncle's Recollections, you will understand my state of mind. And Father appears in nearly every story in the book! I am horrified at the things he did when he was a young man!'

'What's to be done?'

'The manuscript must be intercepted before it reaches Riggs and Ballinger, and destroyed!'

I sat up.

This sounded rather sporting.

'How are you going to do it?' I inquired.

'How can I do it? Didn't I tell you the parcel goes off tomorrow? I am going to the Murgatroyds' dance tonight and shall not be back till Monday. You must do it. That is why I telegraphed to you.'

'What!'

She gave me a look.

'Do you mean to say you refuse to help me, Bertie?'

'No; but – I say!'

'It's quite simple.'

'But even if I – What I mean is – Of course, anything I can do – but – if you know what I mean –'

'You say you want to marry me, Bertie?'

'Yes, of course; but still –'

For a moment she looked exactly like her old father.

'I will never marry you if those Recollections are published.'

'But, Florence, old thing!'

'I mean it. You may look on it as a test, Bertie. If you have the resource and courage to carry this thing through, I will take it as evidence that you are not the vapid and shiftless person most people think you. If you fail, I shall know that your Aunt Agatha was right when she called you a spineless invertebrate and advised me strongly not to marry you. It will be perfectly simple for you to intercept the manuscript, Bertie. It only requires a little resolution.'

'But suppose Uncle Willoughby catches me at it? He'd cut me off with a bob.'

'If you care more for your uncle's money than for me – '

'No, no! Rather not!'

'Very well, then. The parcel containing the manuscript will, of course, be placed on the hall table tomorrow for Oakshott to take to the village with the letters. All you have to do is to take it away and destroy it. Then your uncle will think it has been lost in the post.'

It sounded thin to me.

'Hasn't he got a copy of it?'

'No; it has not been typed. He is sending the manuscript just as he wrote it.'

'But he could write it over again.'

'As if he would have the energy!'

'But – '

'If you are going to do nothing but make absurd objections, Bertie – '

'I was only pointing things out.'

'Well, don't! Once and for all, will you do me this quite simple act of kindness?'

The way she put it gave me an idea.

'Why not get Edwin to do it? Keep it in the family, kind of, don't you know. Besides, it would be a boon to the kid.'

A jolly bright idea it seemed to me. Edwin was her young brother, who was spending his holidays at Easeby. He was a ferret-faced kid, whom I had disliked since birth. As a matter of fact, talking of Recollections and Memories, it was young blighted Edwin who, nine years before, had led his father to where I was smoking his cigar and caused all the unpleasantness. He was fourteen now and had just joined the Boy Scouts. He was one of those thorough kids, and took his responsibilities pretty seriously. He was always in a sort of fever because he was dropping behind schedule with his daily acts of kindness. However hard he tried, he'd fall behind; and then you would find him prowling about the house, setting such a clip to try and catch up with himself that Easeby was rapidly becoming a perfect hell for man and beast.

The idea didn't seem to strike Florence.

'I shall do nothing of the kind, Bertie. I wonder you can't appreciate the compliment I am paying you – trusting you like this.'

'Oh, I see that all right, but what I mean is, Edwin would do it so much better than I would. These Boy Scouts are up to all sorts of dodges. They spoor, don't you know, and take cover and creep about, and what not.'

'Bertie, will you or will you not do this perfectly trivial thing for me? If not, say so now, and let us end this farce of pretending that you care a snap of the fingers for me.'

'Dear old soul, I love you devotedly!'

'Then will you or will you not – '

'Oh, all right,' I said. 'All right! All right!'

And then I tottered forth to think it over. I met Jeeves in the passage just outside.

'I beg your pardon, sir. I was endeavouring to find you.'

'What's the matter?'

'I felt that I should tell you, sir, that somebody had been putting black polish on your brown walking shoes.'

'What! Who? Why?'

'I could not say, sir.'

'Can anything be done with them?'

'Nothing, sir.'

'Damn!'

'Very good, sir.'

I've often wondered since then how these murderer fellows manage to keep in shape while they're contemplating their next effort. I had a much simpler sort of job on hand, and the thought of it rattled me to such an extent in the night watches that I was a perfect wreck next day. Dark circles under the eyes – I give you my word! I had to call on Jeeves to rally round with one of those life-savers of his.

From breakfast on I felt like a bag-snatcher at a railway station. I had to hang about waiting for the parcel to be put on the hall table, and it wasn't put. Uncle Willoughby was a fixture in the library, adding the finishing touches to the great work, I supposed, and the more I thought the thing over the less I liked it. The chances against my pulling it off seemed about three to two, and the thought of what would happen if I didn't gave me cold shivers down the spine. Uncle Willoughby was a pretty mild sort of old boy, as a rule, but I've known him to cut up rough, and, by Jove, he was scheduled to extend himself if he caught me trying to get away with his life work.

It wasn't till nearly four that he toddled out of the library with the parcel under his arm, put it on the table, and toddled off again. I was hiding a bit to the south-east at the moment, behind a suit of armour.

I bounded out and legged it for the table. Then I nipped upstairs to hide the swag. I charged in like a mustang and nearly stubbed my toe on young blighted Edwin, the Boy Scout. He was standing at the chest of drawers, confound him, messing about with my ties.

'Hallo!' he said.

'What are you doing here?'

'I'm tidying your room. It's my last Saturday's act of kindness.'

'Last Saturday's.'

'I'm five days behind. I was six till last night, but I polished your shoes.'

'Was it you – '

'Yes. Did you see them? I just happened to think of it. I was in here, looking round. Mr Berkeley had this room while you were away. He left this morning. I thought perhaps he might have left something in it that I could have sent on. I've often done acts of kindness that way.'

'You must be a comfort to one and all!'

It became more and more apparent to me that this infernal kid must somehow be turned out eftsoons or right speedily. I had hidden the parcel behind my back, and I didn't think he had seen it; but I wanted to get at that chest of drawers quick, before anyone else came along.

'I shouldn't bother about tidying the room,' I said.

'I like tidying it. It's not a bit of trouble – really.'

'But it's quite tidy now.'

'Not so tidy as I shall make it.'

This was getting perfectly rotten. I didn't want to murder the kid, and yet there didn't seem any other way of shifting him. I pressed down the mental accelerator. The old lemon throbbed fiercely. I got an idea.

'There's something much kinder than that which you could do,' I said. 'You see that box of cigars? Take it down to the smoking-room and snip off the ends for me. That would save me no end of trouble. Stagger along, laddie.'

He seemed a bit doubtful; but he staggered. I shoved the parcel into a drawer, locked it, trousered the key, and felt better. I might be a chump, but, dash it, I could out-general a mere kid with a face like a ferret. I went downstairs again. Just as I was passing the smoking-room door out curveted Edwin. It seemed to me that if he wanted to do a real act of kindness he would commit suicide.

'I'm snipping them,' he said.

'Snip on! Snip on!'

'Do you like them snipped much, or only a bit?'
'Medium.'
'All right. I'll be getting on, then.'
'I should.'
And we parted.

Fellows who know all about that sort of thing – detectives, and so on – will tell you that the most difficult thing in the world is to get rid of the body. I remember, as a kid, having to learn by heart a poem about a bird by the name of Eugene Aram, who had the deuce of a job in this respect. All I can recall of the actual poetry is the bit that goes:

> Tum-tum, tum-tum, tum-tumty-tum,
> I slew him, tum-tum tum!

But I recollect that the poor blighter spent much of his valuable time dumping the corpse into ponds and burying it, and what not, only to have it pop out at him again. It was about an hour after I had shoved the parcel into the drawer when I realized that I had let myself in for just the same sort of thing.

Florence had talked in an airy sort of way about destroying the manuscript; but when one came down to it, how the deuce can a chap destroy a great chunky mass of paper in somebody else's house in the middle of summer? I couldn't ask to have a fire in my bedroom, with the thermometer in the eighties. And if I didn't burn the thing, how else could I get rid of it? Fellows on the battlefield eat dispatches to keep them from falling into the hands of the enemy, but it would have taken me a year to eat Uncle Willoughby's Recollections.

I'm bound to say the problem absolutely baffled me. The only thing seemed to be to leave the parcel in the drawer and hope for the best.

I don't know whether you have ever experienced it, but it's a dashed unpleasant thing having a crime on one's conscience. Towards the end of the day the mere sight of the drawer began to depress me. I found myself getting all on edge; and once when Uncle Willoughby trickled silently into the smoking-room when I was alone there and spoke to me before I knew he was there, I broke the record for the sitting high jump.

I was wondering all the time when Uncle Willoughby would sit up and take notice. I didn't think he would have time to suspect that anything had gone wrong till Saturday morning, when he would be expecting, of course, to get the acknowledgement of the manuscript from the publishers. But early on Friday evening he came out of the library as I was passing and asked me to step in. He was looking considerably rattled.

'Bertie,' he said – he always spoke in a precise sort of pompous kind of way – 'an exceedingly disturbing thing has happened. As you know, I dispatched the manuscript of my book to Messrs Riggs and Ballinger, the publishers, yesterday afternoon. It should have reached them by the first post this morning. Why I should have been uneasy I cannot say, but my mind was not altogether at rest respecting the safety of the parcel. I therefore telephoned to Messrs Riggs and Ballinger a few moments back to make inquiries. To my consternation they informed me that they were not yet in receipt of my manuscript.'

'Very rum!'

'I recollect distinctly placing it myself on the hall table in good time to be taken to the village. But here is a sinister thing. I have spoken to Oakshott, who took the rest of the letters to the post office, and he cannot recall seeing it there. He is, indeed, unswerving in his assertions that when he went to the hall to collect the letters there was no parcel among them.'

'Sounds funny!'

'Bertie, shall I tell you what I suspect?'

'What's that?'

'The suspicion will no doubt sound to you incredible, but it alone seems to fit the facts as we know them. I incline to the belief that the parcel has been stolen.'

'Oh, I say! Surely not!'

'Wait! Hear me out. Though I have said nothing to you before, or to anyone else, concerning the matter, the fact remains that during the past few weeks a number of objects – some valuable, others not – have disappeared in this house. The conclusion to which one is irresistibly impelled is that we have a kleptomaniac in our midst. It is a peculiarity of kleptomania, as you are no doubt aware, that the subject is unable to differentiate between the intrinsic values of objects. He will purloin an old coat as readily as a diamond ring, or a tobacco pipe costing but a few shillings with the same eagerness as a purse of gold. The fact that this manuscript of mine could be of no possible value to any outside person convinces me that – '

'But, Uncle, one moment; I know all about those things that were stolen. It was Meadowes, my man, who pinched them. I caught him snaffling my silk socks. Right in the act, by Jove!'

He was tremendously impressed.

'You amaze me, Bertie! Send for the man at once and question him.'

'But he isn't here. You see, directly I found that he was a sock-sneaker I gave him the boot. That's why I went to London – to get a new man.'

'Then, if the man Meadowes is no longer in the house it could not be he who purloined my manuscript. The whole thing is inexplicable.'

After which we brooded for a bit. Uncle Willoughby pottered about the room, registering baffledness, while I sat sucking at a cigarette, feeling rather like a chappie I'd once read about in a book, who murdered another cove and hid the body under the dining-room table, and then had to be the life and soul of a dinner party, with it there all the time. My guilty secret oppressed me to such an extent that after a while I couldn't stick it any longer. I lit another cigarette and started for a stroll in the grounds, by way of cooling off.

It was one of those still evenings you get in the summer, when you can hear a snail clear its throat a mile away. The sun was sinking over the hills and the gnats were fooling about all over the place, and everything smelled rather topping - what with the falling dew and so on – and I was just beginning to feel a little soothed by the peace of it all when suddenly I heard my name spoken.

'It's about Bertie.'

It was the loathsome voice of young blighted Edwin! For a moment I couldn't locate it. Then I realized that it came from the library. My stroll had taken me within a few yards of the open window.

I had often wondered how those Johnnies in books did it – I mean the fellows with whom it was the work of a moment to do about a dozen things that ought to have taken them about ten minutes. But, as a matter of fact, it was the work of a moment with me to chuck away my cigarette, swear a bit, leap about ten yards, dive into a bush that stood near the library window, and stand there with my ears flapping. I was as certain as I've ever been of anything that all sorts of rotten things were in the offing.

'About Bertie?' I heard Uncle Willoughby say.

'About Bertie and your parcel. I heard you talking to him just now. I believe he's got it.'

When I tell you that just as I heard these frightful words a fairly substantial beetle of sorts dropped from the bush down the back of my neck, and I couldn't even stir to squash the same, you will understand that I felt pretty rotten. Everything seemed against me.

'What do you mean, boy? I was discussing the disappearance of my manuscript with Bertie only a moment back, and he professed himself as perplexed by the mystery as myself.'

'Well, I was in his room yesterday afternoon, doing him an act of kindness, and he came in with a parcel. I could see it, though he tried to keep it behind his back. And then he asked me to go to the smoking-room and snip some cigars for him; and about two minutes afterwards he came down – and he wasn't carrying anything. So it must be in his room.'

I understand they deliberately teach these dashed Boy Scouts to cultivate their powers of observation and deduction and what not. Devilish thoughtless and inconsiderate of them, I call it. Look at the trouble it causes.

'It sounds incredible,' said Uncle Willoughby, thereby bucking me up a trifle.

'Shall I go and look in his room?' asked young blighted Edwin. 'I'm sure the parcel's there.'

'But what could be his motive for perpetrating this extraordinary theft?'

'Perhaps he's a – what you said just now.'

'A kleptomaniac? Impossible!'

'It might have been Bertie who took all those things from the very start,' suggested the little brute hopefully. 'He may be like Raffles.'

'Raffles?'

'He's a chap in a book who went about pinching things.'

'I cannot believe that Bertie would – ah – go about pinching things.'

'Well, I'm sure he's got the parcel. I'll tell you what you might do. You might say that Mr Berkeley wired that he had left something here. He had Bertie's room, you know. You might say you wanted to look for it.'

'That would be possible. I – '

I didn't wait to hear any more. Things were getting too hot. I sneaked softly out of my bush and raced for the front door. I sprinted up to my room and made for the drawer where I had put the parcel. And then I found I hadn't the key. It wasn't for the deuce of a time that I recollected I had shifted it to my evening trousers the night before and must have forgotten to take it out again.

Where the dickens were my evening things? I had looked all over the place before I remembered that Jeeves must have taken them away to brush. To leap at the bell and ring it was, with me, the work of a moment. I had just rung it when there was a footstep outside, and in came Uncle Willoughby.

'Oh, Bertie,' he said, without a blush, 'I have – ah – received a telegram from Berkeley, who occupied this room in your absence, asking me to forward him his – er – his cigarette-case, which, it would appear, he inadvertently omitted to take with him when he left the house. I cannot find it downstairs; and it has, therefore, occurred to me that he may have left it in this room. I will – er – just take a look round.'

It was one of the most disgusting spectacles I've ever seen – this white-haired old man, who should have been thinking of the hereafter, standing there lying like an actor.

'I haven't seen it anywhere,' I said.

'Nevertheless, I will search. I must – ah – spare no effort.'

'I should have seen it if it had been here – what?'

'It may have escaped your notice. It is – er – possibly in one of the drawers.'

He began to nose about. He pulled out drawer after drawer, pottering round like an old bloodhound, and babbling from time to time about Berkeley and his cigarette-case in a way that struck me as perfectly ghastly. I just stood there, losing weight every moment.

Then he came to the drawer where the parcel was.

'This appears to be locked,' he said, rattling the handle.

'Yes; I shouldn't bother about that one. It – it's – er – locked, and all that sort of thing.'

'You have not the key?'

A soft, respectful voice spoke behind me.

'I fancy, sir, that this must be the key you require. It was in the pocket of your evening trousers.'

It was Jeeves. He had shimmered in, carrying my evening things, and was standing there holding out the key. I could have massacred the man.

'Thank you,' said my uncle.

'Not at all, sir.'

The next moment Uncle Willoughby had opened the drawer. I shut my eyes.

'No,' said Uncle Willoughby, 'there is nothing here. The drawer is empty. Thank you, Bertie. I hope I have not disturbed you. I fancy – er – Berkeley must have taken his case with him after all.'

When he had gone I shut the door carefully. Then I turned to Jeeves. The man was putting my evening things out on a chair.

'Er – Jeeves!'

'Sir?'

'Oh, nothing.'

It was deuced difficult to know how to begin.

'Er – Jeeves!'

'Sir?'

'Did you – Was there – Have you by chance – '

'I removed the parcel this morning, sir.'

'Oh – ah – why?'

'I considered it more prudent, sir.'

I mused for a while.

'Of course, I suppose all this seems tolerably rummy to you, Jeeves?'

'Not at all, sir. I chanced to overhear you and Lady Florence speaking of the matter the other evening, sir.'

'Did you, by Jove?'

'Yes, sir.'

'Well – er – Jeeves, I think that, on the whole, if you were to – as it were – freeze on to that parcel until we get back to London – '

'Exactly, sir.'

'And then we might – er – so to speak – chuck it away somewhere – what?'

'Precisely, sir.'

'I'll leave it in your hands.'

'Entirely, sir.'

'You know, Jeeves, you're by way of being rather a topper.'

'I endeavour to give satisfaction, sir.'

'One in a million, by Jove!'

'It is very kind of you to say so, sir.'

'Well, that's about all, then, I think.'

'Very good, sir.'

Florence came back on Monday. I didn't see her till we were all having tea in the hall. It wasn't till the crowd had cleared away a bit that we got a chance of having a word together.

'Well, Bertie?' she said.

'It's all right.'

'You have destroyed the manuscript?'

'Not exactly; but – '

'What do you mean?'

'I mean I haven't absolutely – '

'Bertie, your manner is furtive!'

'It's all right. It's this way – '

And I was just going to explain how things stood when out of the library came leaping Uncle Willoughby, looking as braced as a two-year-old. The old boy was a changed man.

'A most remarkable thing, Bertie! I have just been speaking with Mr Riggs on the telephone, and he tells me he received my manuscript by the first post this morning. I cannot imagine what can have caused the delay. Our postal facilities are extremely inadequate in the rural districts. I shall write to headquarters about it. It is insufferable if valuable parcels are to be delayed in this fashion.'

I happened to be looking at Florence's profile at the moment, and at this juncture she swung round and gave me a look that went right through me like a knife. Uncle Willoughby meandered back to the library, and there was a silence that you could have dug bits out of with a spoon.

'I can't understand it,' I said at last. 'I can't understand it, by Jove!'

'I can. I can understand it perfectly, Bertie. Your heart failed you. Rather than risk offending your uncle you – '

'No, no! Absolutely!'

'You preferred to lose me rather than risk losing the money. Perhaps you did not think I meant what I said. I meant every word. Our engagement is ended.'

'But – I say!'

'Not another word!'

'But, Florence, old thing!'

'I do not wish to hear any more. I see now that your Aunt Agatha was perfectly right. I consider that I have had a very lucky escape. There was a time when I thought that, with patience, you might be moulded into something worth while. I see now that you are impossible!'

And she popped off, leaving me to pick up the pieces. When I had collected the debris to some extent I went to my room and rang for Jeeves. He came in looking as if nothing had happened or was ever going to happen. He was the calmest thing in captivity.

'Jeeves!' I yelled. 'Jeeves, that parcel has arrived in London!'

'Yes, sir?'

'Did you send it?'

'Yes, sir. I acted for the best, sir. I think that both you and Lady Florence overestimate the danger of people being offended at being mentioned in Sir Willoughby's Recollections. It has been my experience, sir, that the normal person enjoys seeing his or her name in print, irrespective of what is said about them. I have an aunt, sir, who a few years ago was a martyr to swollen limbs. She tried Walkinshaw's Supreme Ointment and obtained considerable relief – so much so that she sent them an unsolicited testimonial. Her pride at seeing her photograph in the daily papers in connexion with descriptions of her lower limbs before taking, which were nothing less than revolting, was so intense that it led me to believe that publicity, of whatever sort, is what nearly everybody desires. Moreover, if you have ever studied psychology, sir, you will know that respectable old gentlemen are by no means averse to having it advertised that they were extremely wild in their youth. I have an uncle – '

I cursed his aunts and his uncles and him and all the rest of the family.

'Do you know that Lady Florence has broken off her engagement with me?'

'Indeed, sir?'

Not a bit of sympathy! I might have been telling him it was a fine day.

'You're sacked!'

'Very good, sir.'

He coughed gently.

'As I am no longer in your employment, sir, I can speak freely without appearing to take a liberty. In my opinion you and Lady Florence were quite unsuitably matched. Her ladyship is of a highly determined and arbitrary temperament, quite opposed to your own. I was in Lord Worplesdon's service for nearly a year, during which time I had ample opportunities of studying her ladyship. The opinion of the servants' hall was far from favourable to her. Her ladyship's temper caused a good deal of adverse comment among us. It was at times quite impossible. You would not have been happy, sir!'

'Get out!'

'I think you would also have found her educational methods a little trying, sir. I have glanced at the book her ladyship gave you – it has been lying on your table since our arrival – and it is, in my opinion, quite unsuitable. You would not have enjoyed it. And I have it from her ladyship's own maid, who happened to overhear a conversation between her ladyship and one of the gentlemen staying here – Mr Maxwell, who is employed in an editorial capacity by one of the reviews – that it was her intention to start you almost immediately upon Nietzsche. You would not enjoy Nietzsche, sir. He is fundamentally unsound.'

'Get out!'

'Very good, sir.'

It's rummy how sleeping on a thing often makes you feel quite different about it. It's happened to me over and over again. Somehow or other, when I woke next morning the old heart didn't feel half so broken as it had done. It was a perfectly topping day, and there was something about the way the sun came in at the window and the row the birds were kicking up in the ivy that made me half wonder whether Jeeves wasn't right. After all, though she had a wonderful profile, was it such a catch being engaged to Florence Craye as the casual observer might imagine? Wasn't there something in what Jeeves had said about her character? I began to realize that my ideal wife was something quite different, something a lot more clinging and drooping and prattling, and what not.

I had got as far as this in thinking the thing out when that *Types of Ethical Theory* caught my eye. I opened it, and I give you my honest word this was what hit me:

Of the two antithetic terms in the Greek philosophy one only was real and self-subsisting; and that one was Ideal Thought as opposed to that which it has to penetrate and mould. The other, corresponding to our Nature, was in itself phenomenal, unreal, without any permanent footing, having no predicates that held true for two moments together; in short, redeemed from negation only by including indwelling realities appearing through.

Well – I mean to say – what? And Nietzsche, from all accounts, a lot worse than that!

'Jeeves,' I said, when he came in with my morning tea, 'I've been thinking it over. You're engaged again.'

'Thank you, sir.'

I sucked down a cheerful mouthful. A great respect for this bloke's judgement began to soak through me.

'Oh, Jeeves,' I said; 'about that check suit.'

'Yes, sir?'

'Is it really a frost?'

'A trifle too bizarre, sir, in my opinion.'

'But lots of fellows have asked me who my tailor is.'

'Doubtless in order to avoid him, sir.'

'He's supposed to be one of the best men in London.'

'I am saying nothing against his moral character, sir.'

I hesitated a bit. I had a feeling that I was passing into this chappie's clutches, and that if I gave in now I should become just like poor old Aubrey Fothergill, unable to call my soul my own. On the other hand, this was obviously a cove of rare intelligence, and it would be a comfort in a lot of ways to have him doing the thinking for me. I made up my mind.

'All right, Jeeves,' I said. 'You know! Give the bally thing away to somebody!'

He looked down at me like a father gazing tenderly at the wayward child.

'Thank you, sir. I gave it to the under-gardener last night. A little more tea, sir?'

2

THE ARTISTIC CAREER
OF CORKY

You will notice, as you flit through these reminiscences of mine, that from time to time the scene of action is laid in and around the city of New York; and it is just possible that this may occasion the puzzled look and the start of surprise. 'What,' it is possible that you may ask yourselves, 'is Bertram doing so far from his beloved native land?'

Well, it's a fairly longish story; but, reefing it down a bit and turning it for the nonce into a two-reeler, what happened was that my Aunt Agatha on one occasion sent me over to America to try to stop young Gussie, my cousin, marrying a girl on the vaudeville stage, and I got the whole thing so mixed up that I decided it would be a sound scheme to stop on in New York for a bit instead of going back and having long, cosy chats with her about the affair.

So I sent Jeeves out to find a decent flat, and settled down for a spell of exile.

I'm bound to say New York's a most sprightly place to be exiled in. Everybody was awfully good to me, and there seemed to be plenty of things going on so, take it for all in all, I didn't undergo any frightful hardships. Blokes introduced me to other blokes, and so on and so forth, and it wasn't long before I knew squads of the right sort, some who rolled in the stuff in houses up by the Park, and others who lived with the gas turned down mostly around Washington Square – artists and writers and so forth. Brainy coves.

Corky, the bird I am about to treat of, was one of the artists. A portrait-painter, he called himself, but as a matter of fact his score up to date had been nil. You see, the catch about portrait-painting – I've looked into the thing a bit – is that you can't start painting portraits till people come along and ask you to, and they won't come and ask you to until you've painted a lot first. This makes it kind of difficult, not to say tough, for the ambitious youngster.

Corky managed to get along by drawing an occasional picture for the comic papers – he had rather a gift for funny stuff when he got a good idea – and doing bedsteads and chairs and things for the advertisements. His principal source of income, however, was derived from biting the ear of a rich uncle – one Alexander Worple, who was in the jute business. I'm a bit foggy as to what jute is, but it's apparently something the populace is pretty keen on, for Mr Worple had made quite an indecently large stack of it.

Now, a great many fellows think that having a rich uncle is a pretty soft snap; but, according to Corky, such is not the case. Corky's uncle was a robust sort of cove, who looked like living for ever. He was fifty-one, and it seemed as if he might go to par. It was not this, however, that distressed poor Corky, for he was not bigoted and had no objection to the man going on living. What Corky kicked at was the way the above Worple used to harry him.

Corky's uncle, you see, didn't want him to be an artist. He didn't think he had any talent in that direction. He was always urging him to chuck Art and go into the jute business and start at the bottom and work his way up. And what Corky said was that, while he didn't know what they did at the bottom of a jute business, instinct told him that it was something too beastly for words. Corky, moreover, believed in his future as an artist. Some day, he said, he was going to make a hit. Meanwhile, by using the utmost tact and persuasiveness, he was inducing his uncle to cough up very grudgingly a small quarterly allowance.

He wouldn't have got this if his uncle hadn't had a hobby. Mr Worple was peculiar in this respect. As a rule, from what I've observed, the American captain of industry doesn't do anything out of business hours. When he has put the cat out and locked up the office for the night, he just relapses into a state of coma from which he emerges only to start being a captain of industry again. But Mr Worple in his spare time was what is known as an ornithologist. He had written a book called *American Birds*, and was writing another, to be called *More American Birds*. When he had finished that, the presumption was that he would begin a third, and keep on till the supply of American birds gave out. Corky used to go to him about once every three months and let him talk about American birds. Apparently you could do what you liked with old Worple if you gave him his head first on his pet subject, so these little chats used to make Corky's allowance all right for the time being. But it was pretty rotten for the poor chap. There was the frightful suspense, you see, and, apart from that, birds, except when broiled and in the society of a cold bottle, bored him stiff.

To complete the character-study of Mr Worple, he was a man of extremely uncertain temper, and his general tendency was to think that Corky was a poor chump and that whatever step he took in any direction on his own account was just another proof of his innate idiocy. I should imagine Jeeves feels very much the same about me.

So when Corky trickled into my apartment one afternoon, shooing a girl in front of him, and said, 'Bertie, I want you to meet my fiancée, Miss Singer,' the aspect of the matter which hit me first was precisely the one which he had come to consult me about. The very first words I spoke were, 'Corky, how about your uncle?'

The poor chap gave one of those mirthless laughs. He was looking anxious and worried, like a man who has done the murder all right but can't think what the deuce to do with the body.

'We're so scared, Mr Wooster,' said the girl. 'We were hoping that you might suggest a way of breaking it to him.'

Muriel Singer was one of those very quiet, appealing girls who have a way of looking at you with their big eyes as if they thought you were the greatest thing on earth and wondered that you hadn't got on to it yet yourself. She sat there in a sort of shrinking way, looking at me as if she were saying to herself, 'Oh, I do hope this great strong man isn't going to hurt me.' She gave a fellow a protective kind of feeling, made him want to stroke her hand and say, 'There, there, little one!' or words to that effect. She made me feel that there was nothing I wouldn't do for her. She was rather like one of those innocent-tasting American drinks which creep imperceptibly into your system so that, before you know what you're doing, you're starting out to reform the world by force if necessary and pausing on your way to tell the large man in the corner that, if he looks at you like that, you will knock his head off. What I mean is, she made me feel alert and dashing, like a knight-errant or something of that kind. I felt that I was with her in this thing to the limit.

'I don't see why your uncle shouldn't be most awfully bucked,' I said to Corky. 'He will think Miss Singer the ideal wife for you.'

Corky declined to cheer up.

'You don't know him. Even if he did like Muriel, he wouldn't admit it. That's the sort of pig-headed ass he is. It would be a matter of principle with him to kick. All he would consider would be that I had gone and taken an important step without asking his advice, and he would raise Cain automatically. He's always done it.'

I strained the old bean to meet this emergency.

'You want to work it so that he makes Miss Singer's acquaintance without knowing that you know her. Then you come along – '

'But how can I work it that way?'

I saw his point. That was the catch.

'There's only one thing to do,' I said.

'What's that?'

'Leave it to Jeeves.'

And I rang the bell.

'Sir? said Jeeves, kind of manifesting himself. One of the rummy things about Jeeves is that, unless you watch like a hawk, you very seldom see him come into a room. He's like one of those weird birds in India who dissolve themselves into thin air and nip through space in a sort of disembodied way and assemble the parts again just where they want them. I've got a cousin who's what they call a Theosophist, and he says he's often nearly worked the thing himself, but couldn't quite bring it off, probably owing to having fed in his boyhood on the flesh of animals slain in anger and pie.

The moment I saw the man standing there, registering respectful attention, a weight seemed to roll off my mind. I felt like a lost child who spots his father in the offing.

'Jeeves,' I said, 'we want your advice.'

'Very good, sir.'

I boiled down Corky's painful case into a few well-chosen words.

'So you see what it amounts to, Jeeves. We want you to suggest some way by which Mr Worple can make Miss Singer's acquaintance without getting on to the fact that Mr Corcoran already knows her. Understand?'

'Perfectly, sir.'

'Well, try to think of something.'

'I have thought of something already, sir.'

'You have!'

'The scheme I would suggest cannot fail of success, but it has what may seem to you a drawback, sir, in that it requires a certain financial outlay.'

'He means,' I translated to Corky, 'that he has got a pippin of an idea, but it's going to cost a bit.'

Naturally the poor chap's face dropped, for this seemed to dish the whole thing. But I was still under the influence of the girl's melting gaze, and I saw that this was where I started in as the knight-errant.

'You can count on me for all that sort of thing, Corky,' I said. 'Only too glad. Carry on, Jeeves.'

'I would suggest, sir, that Mr Corcoran take advantage of Mr Worple's attachment to ornithology.'

'How on earth did you know that he was fond of birds?'

'It is the way these New York apartments are constructed, sir. Quite unlike our London houses. The partitions between the rooms are of the flimsiest nature. With no wish to overhear, I have sometimes heard Mr Corcoran expressing himself with a generous strength on the subject I have mentioned.'

'Oh! Well?'

'Why should not the young lady write a small volume, to be entitled – let us say – *The Children's Book of American Birds* and dedicate it to Mr Worple? A limited edition could be published at Your expense, sir, and a great deal of the book would, of course, be given over to eulogistic remarks concerning Mr Worple's own larger treatise on the same subject. I should recommend the dispatching of a presentation copy to Mr Worple, immediately on publication, accompanied by a letter in which the young lady asks to be allowed to make the acquaintance of one to whom she owes so much. This would, I fancy, produce the desired result, but as I say, the expense involved would be considerable.'

I felt like the proprietor of a performing dog on the vaudeville stage when the tyke has just pulled off his trick without a hitch. I had betted on Jeeves all along, and I had known that he wouldn't let me down. It beats me sometimes why a man with his genius is satisfied to hang around pressing my clothes and what not. If I had half Jeeves's brain I should have a stab at being Prime Minister or something.

'Jeeves,' I said, 'that is absolutely ripping! One of your very best efforts.'

'Thank you, sir.'

The girl made an objection.

'But I'm sure I couldn't write a book about anything. I can't even write good letters.'

'Muriel's talents,' said Corky, with a little cough, 'lie more in the direction of the drama, Bertie. I didn't mention it before, but one of our reasons for being a trifle nervous as to how Uncle Alexander will receive the news is that Muriel is in the chorus of that show *Choose Your Exit* at the Manhattan. It's absurdly unreasonable, but we both feel that the fact might increase Uncle Alexander's natural tendency to kick like a steer.'

I saw what he meant. I don't know why it is – one of these psychology sharps could explain it, I suppose – but uncles and aunts, as a class, are always dead against the drama, legitimate or otherwise. They don't seem able to stick it at any price.

But Jeeves had a solution, of course.

'I fancy it would be a simple matter, sir, to find some impecunious author who would be glad to do the actual composition of the volume for a small fee. It is only necessary that the young lady's name should appear on the title page.'

'That's true,' said Corky. 'Sam Patterson would do it for a hundred dollars. He writes a novelette, three short stories, and ten thousand words of a serial for one of the all-fiction magazines under different names every month. A little thing like this would be nothing to him. I'll get after him right away.'

'Fine!'

'Will that be all, sir?' said Jeeves. 'Very good, sir. Thank you, sir.'

I always used to think that publishers has to be devilish intelligent fellows, loaded down with the grey matter; but I've got their number now. All a publisher has to do is to write cheques at intervals, while a lot of deserving and industrious chappies rally round and do the real work. I know, because I have been one myself. I simply sat tight in the old flat with a fountain-pen, and in due season a topping, shiny book came along.

I happened to be down at Corky's place when the first copies of *The Children's Book of American Birds* bobbed up. Muriel Singer was there, and we were talking of things in general when there was a bang at the door and the parcel was delivered.

It was certainly some book. It had a red cover with a fowl of some species on it, and underneath the girl's name in gold letters. I opened a copy at random.

'Often of a spring morning,' it said at the top of page twenty-one, 'as you wander through the fields, you will hear the sweet-toned, carelessly-flowing warble of the purple finch linnet. When you are older you must read all about him in Mr Alexander Worple's wonderful book, *American Birds*.'

You see. A boost for the uncle right away. And only a few pages later there he was in the limelight again in connexion with the yellow-billed cuckoo. It was great stuff. The more I read, the more I admired the chap who had written it and Jeeves's genius in putting us on to the wheeze. I didn't see how the uncle could fail to drop. You can't call a chap the world's greatest authority on the yellow-billed cuckoo without rousing a certain disposition towards chumminess in him.

'It's a cert!' I said.

'An absolute cinch!' said Corky.

And a day or two later he meandered up the Avenue to my flat to tell me that all was well. The uncle had written Muriel a letter so dripping with the milk of human kindness that if he hadn't known

Mr Worple's handwriting Corky would have refused to believe him the author of it. Any time it suited Miss Singer to call, said the uncle, he would be delighted to make her acquaintance.

Shortly after this I had to go out of town. Divers sound sportsmen had invited me to pay visits to their country places, and it wasn't for several months that I settled down in the city again. I had been wondering a lot, of course, about Corky, whether it all turned out right, and so forth, and my first evening in New York, happening to pop into a quiet sort of little restaurant which I go to when I don't feel inclined for the bright lights, I found Muriel Singer there, sitting by herself at a table near the door. Corky, I took it, was out telephoning. I went up and passed the time of day.

'Well, well, well, what?' I said.

'Why, Mr Wooster! How do you do?'

'Corky around?'

'I beg your pardon?'

'You're waiting for Corky, aren't you?'

'Oh, I didn't understand. No, I'm not waiting for him.'

It seemed to me that there was a sort of something in her voice, a kind of thingummy, you know.

'I say, you haven't had a row with Corky, have you?'

'A row.'

'A spat, don't you know – little misunderstanding – faults on both sides – er – and all that sort of thing.'

'Why, whatever makes you think that?'

'Oh, well, as it were, what? What I mean is – I thought you usually dined with him before you went to the theatre.'

'I've left the stage now.'

Suddenly the whole thing dawned on me. I had forgotten what a long time I had been away.

'Why, of course, I see now! You're married!'

'Yes.'

'How perfectly topping! I wish you all kinds of happiness.'

'Thank you so much. Oh, Alexander,' she said, looking past me, 'this is a friend of mine – Mr Wooster.'

I spun round. A bloke with a lot of stiff grey hair and a red sort of healthy face was standing there. Rather a formidable Johnnie, he looked, though peaceful at the moment.

'I want you to meet my husband, Mr Wooster. Mr Wooster is a friend of Bruce's, Alexander.'

The old boy grasped my hand warmly, and that was all that

kept me from hitting the floor in a heap. The place was rocking. Absolutely.

'So you know my nephew, Mr Wooster?' I heard him say. 'I wish you would try to knock a little sense into him and make him quit this playing at painting. But I have an idea that he is steadying down. I noticed it first that night he came to dinner with us, my dear, to be introduced to you. He seemed altogether quieter and more serious. Something seemed to have sobered him. Perhaps you will give us the pleasure of your company at dinner tonight, Mr Wooster? Or have you dined?'

I said I had. What I needed then was air, not dinner. I felt that I wanted to get into the open and think this thing out.

When I reached my flat I heard Jeeves moving about in his lair. I called him.

'Jeeves,' I said, 'now is the time for all good men to come to the aid of the party. A stiff b-and-s first of all, and then I've a bit of news for you.'

He came back with a tray and a long glass.

'Better have one yourself, Jeeves. You'll need it.'

'Later on, perhaps, thank you, sir.'

'All right. Please yourself. But you're going to get a shock. You remember my friend, Mr Corcoran?'

'Yes, sir.'

'And the girl who was to slide gracefully into his uncle's esteem by writing the book on birds?'

'Perfectly, sir.'

'Well, she's slid. She's married the uncle.'

He took it without blinking. You can't rattle Jeeves.

'That was always a development to be feared, sir.'

'You don't mean to tell me that you were expecting it?'

'It crossed my mind as a possibility.'

'Did it, by Jove! Well, I think you might have warned us!'

'I hardly liked to take the liberty, sir.'

Of course, as I saw after I had had a bite to eat and was in a calmer frame of mind, what had happened wasn't my fault, if you came down to it. I couldn't be expected to foresee that the scheme, in itself a cracker-jack, would skid into the ditch as it had done; but all the same I'm bound to admit that I didn't relish the idea of meeting Corky again until time, the great healer, had been able to get in a bit of soothing work. I cut Washington Square out absolutely for the next few months. I gave it the complete miss-in-baulk. And then, just when

I was beginning to think I might safely pop down in that direction and gather up the dropped threads, so to speak, time, instead of working the healing wheeze, went and pulled the most awful bone and put the lid on it. Opening the paper one morning, I read that Mrs Alexander Worple had presented her husband with a son and heir.

I was so dashed sorry for poor old Corky that I hadn't the heart to touch my breakfast. I was bowled over. Absolutely. It was the limit.

I hardly knew what to do. I wanted, of course, to rush down to Washington Square and grip the poor blighter silently by the hand; and then, thinking it over, I hadn't the nerve. Absent treatment seemd the touch. I gave it him in waves.

But after a month or so I began to hesitate again. It struck me that it was playing it a bit low-down on the poor chap, avoiding him like this just when he probably wanted his pals to surge round him most. I pictured him sitting in his lonely studio with no company but his bitter thoughts, and the pathos of it got me to such an extent that I bounded straight into a taxi and told the driver to go all out for the studio.

I rushed in, and there was Corky, hunched up at the easel, painting away, while on the model throne sat a severe-looking female of middle age, holding a baby.

A fellow has to be ready for that sort of thing.

'Oh, ah!' I said, and started to back out.

Corky looked over his shoulder.

'Hallo, Bertie. Don't go. We're just finishing for the day. That will be all this afternoon,' he said to the nurse, who got up with the baby and decanted it into a perambulator which was standing in the fairway.

'At the same hour tomorrow, Mr Corcoran?'

'Yes, please.'

'Good afternoon.'

'Good afternoon.'

Corky stood there, looking at the door, and then he turned to me and began to get it off his chest. Fortunately, he seemed to take it for granted that I knew all about what had happened, so it wasn't as awkward as it might have been.

'It's my uncle's idea,' he said. 'Muriel doesn't know about it yet. The portrait's to be a surprise for her on her birthday. The nurse takes the kid out ostensibly to get a breather, and they beat it down here. If you want an instance of the irony of fate, Bertie, get acquainted with this. Here's the first commission I have ever had to paint a portrait, and the sitter is that human poached egg that has butted in and bounced me out of my inheritance. Can you beat it! I call it rubbing the thing in to expect me to spend my afternoons gazing into the ugly face of a little brat who to all intents and purposes has hit me behind the ear with a black-jack and swiped all I possess. I can't refuse to paint the portrait, because if I did my uncle would stop my allowance; yet every time I look up and catch that kid's vacant eye, I suffer agonies. I tell you, Bertie, sometimes when he gives me a patronizing glance and then turns away and is sick, as if it revolted him to look at me, I come within an ace of occupying the entire front page of the evening papers as the latest murder sensation. There are moments when I can almost see the headlines: "Promising Young Artist Beans Baby With Axe".'

I patted his shoulder silently. My sympathy for the poor old scout was too deep for words.

I kept away from the studio for some time after that, because it didn't seem right of me to intrude on the poor chappie's sorrow. Besides, I'm bound to say that nurse intimidated me. She reminded me so infernally of Aunt Agatha. She was the same gimlet-eyed type.

But one afternoon Corky called me on the phone.

'Bertie!'

'Hallo?'

'Are you doing anything this afternoon?'

'Nothing special.'

'You couldn't come down here, could you?'

'What's the trouble? Anything up?'

'I've finished the portrait.'

'Good boy! Stout work!'

'Yes.' His voice sounded rather doubtful. 'The fact is, Bertie, it doesn't look quite right to me. There's something about it – My uncle's coming in half an hour to inspect it, and – I don't know why it is, but I kind of feel I'd like your moral support!'

I began to see that I was letting myself in for something. The sympathetic cooperation of Jeeves seemed to me to be indicated.

'You think he'll cut up rough?'

'He may.'

I threw my mind back to the red-faced chappie I had met at the restaurant, and tried to picture him cutting up rough. It was only too easy. I spoke to Corky firmly on the telephone.

'I'll come,' I said.

'Good!'

'But only if I may bring Jeeves.'

'Why Jeeves? What's Jeeves got to do with it? Who wants Jeeves? Jeeves is the fool who suggested the scheme that has led – '

'Listen, Corky, old top! If you think I am going to face that uncle of yours without Jeeves's support, you're mistaken. I'd sooner go into a den of wild beasts and bite a lion on the back of the neck.'

'Oh, all right,' said Corky. Not cordially, but he said it; so I rang for Jeeves, and explained the situation.

'Very good, sir,' said Jeeves.

We found Corky near the door, looking at the picture with one hand up in a defensive sort of way, as if he thought it might swing on him.

'Stand right where you are, Bertie,' he said, without moving. 'Now, tell me honestly, how does it strike you?'

The light from the big window fell right on the picture. I took a good look at it. Then I shifted a bit nearer and took another look. Then I went back to where I had been at first, because it hadn't seemed quite so bad from there.

'Well?' said Corky anxiously.

I hesitated a bit.

'Of course, old man, I only saw the kid once, and then only for a moment, but – but it *was* an ugly sort of kid, wasn't it, if I remember rightly?'

'As ugly as that?'

I looked again, and honesty compelled me to be frank.

'I don't see how it could have been, old chap.'

Poor old Corky ran his fingers through his hair in a temperamental sort of way. He groaned.

'You're quite right, Bertie. Something's gone wrong with the darned thing. My private impression is that, without knowing it, I've worked that stunt that Sargent used to pull – painting the soul of the sitter. I've got through the mere outward appearance, and have put the child's soul on canvas.'

'But could a child of that age have a soul like that? I don't see how he could have managed it in the time. What do you think, Jeeves?'

'I doubt it, sir.'

'It – it sort of leers at you, doesn't it?'

'You've noticed that, too?' said Corky.

'I don't see how one could help noticing.'

'All I tried to do was to give the little brute a cheerful expression. But, as it has worked out, he looks positively dissipated.'

'Just what I was going to suggest, old man. He looks as if he were in the middle of a colossal spree, and enjoying every minute of it. Don't you think so, Jeeves?'

'He has a decidedly inebriated air, sir.'

Corky was starting to say something, when the door opened and the uncle came in.

For about three seconds all was joy, jollity and goodwill. The old boy shook hands with me, slapped Corky on the back, said he didn't think he had ever seen such a fine day, and whacked his leg with his stick. Jeeves had projected himself into the background, and he didn't notice him.

'Well, Bruce, my boy; so the portrait is really finished, is it – really finished? Well, bring it out. Let's have a look at it. This will be a wonderful surprise for your aunt. Where is it? Let's – '

And then he got it – suddenly, when he wasn't set for the punch; and he rocked back on his heels.

'Oosh!' he exclaimed. And for perhaps a minute there was one of the scaliest silences I've ever run up against.

'Is this a practical joke?' he said at last, in a way that set about sixteen draughts cutting through the room at once.

I thought it was up to me to rally round old Corky.

'You want to stand a bit farther away from it,' I said.

'You're perfectly right!' he snorted. 'I do! I want to stand so far away from it that I can't see the thing with a telescope!' He turned on Corky like an untamed tiger of the jungle who has just located a chunk of meat. 'And this – this – is what you have been wasting your time and my money for all these years! A painter! I wouldn't let you paint a house of mine. I gave you this commission, thinking that you were a competent worker, and this – this – this extract from a comic supplement is the result!' He swung towards the door, lashing his tail and growling to himself. 'This ends it. If you wish to continue this foolery of pretending to be an artist because you want an excuse for idleness, please yourself. But let me tell you this. Unless you report at my office on Monday morning, prepared to abandon all this idiocy and start in at the bottom of the business to work your way up, as you should have done half a dozen years ago, not another cent – not another cent – not another – Boosh!'

Then the door closed and he was no longer with us. And I crawled out of the bomb-proof shelter.

'Corky, old top!' I whispered faintly.

Corky was standing staring at the picture. His face was set. There was a hunted look in his eye.

'Well, that finishes it!' he muttered brokenly.

'What are you going to do?'

'Do? What can I do? I can't stick on here if he cuts off supplies. You heard what he said. I shall have to go to the office on Monday.'

I couldn't think of a thing to say. I knew exactly how he felt about the office. I don't know when I've been so infernally uncomfortable. It was like hanging round trying to make conversation to a pal who's just been sentenced to twenty years in quod.

And then a soothing voice broke the silence.

'If I might make a suggestion, sir!'

It was Jeeves. He had slid from the shadows and was gazing gravely at the picture. Upon my word, I can't give you a better idea of the shattering effect of Corky's Uncle Alexander when in action than by saying that he had absolutely made me forget for the moment that Jeeves was there.

'I wonder if I have ever happened to mention to you, sir, a Mr Digby Thistleton, with whom I was once in service? Perhaps you have met him? He was a financier. He is now Lord Bridgworth. It was a favourite saying of his that there is always a way. The first time I heard him use the expression was after the failure of a patent depilatory which he promoted.'

'Jeeves,' I said, 'what on earth are you talking about?'

'I mentioned Mr Thistleton, sir, because his was in some respects a parallel case to the present one. His depilatory failed, but he did not despair. He put it on the market again under the name of Hair-o, guaranteed to produce a full crop of hair in a few months. It was advertised, if you remember, sir, by a humorous picture of a billiard ball, before and after taking, and made such a substantial fortune that Mr Thistleton was soon afterwards elevated to the peerage for services to his Party. It seems to me that, if Mr Corcoran looks into the matter, he will find, like Mr Thistleton, that there is always a way. Mr Worple himself suggested the solution of the difficulty. In the heat of the moment he compared the portrait to an extract from a coloured comic supplement. I consider the suggestion a very valuable one, sir. Mr Corcoran's portrait may not have pleased Mr Worple as a likeness of his only child, but I have no doubt that editors would gladly consider it as a foundation for a series of humorous drawings. If Mr Corcoran will allow me to make the suggestion, his talent has always been for the humorous. There is something about this picture – something bold and vigorous, which arrests the attention. I feel sure it would be highly popular.'

Corky was glaring at the picture, and making a sort of dry, sucking noise with his mouth. He seemed completely over-wrought.

And then suddenly he began to laugh in a wild way.

'Corky, old man!' I said, massaging him tenderly. I feared the poor blighter was hysterical.

He began to stagger about all over the floor.

'He's right! The man's absolutely right! Jeeves, you're a life-saver. You've hit on the greatest idea of the age. Report at the office on Monday! Start at the bottom of the business! I'll buy the business if I feel like it. I know the man who runs the comic section of the *Sunday Star*. He'll eat this thing. He was telling me only the other day how hard it was to get a good new series. He'll give me anything I ask for a real winner like this. I've got a gold mine. Where's my hat? I've got an income for life! Where's that confounded hat? Lend me a fiver, Bertie. I want to take a taxi down to Park Row!'

Jeeves smiled paternally. Or, rather, he had a kind of paternal muscular spasm about the mouth, which is the nearest he ever gets to smiling.

'If I might make the suggestion, Mr Corcoran – for a title of the series which you have in mind – "The Adventures of Baby Blobbs".'

Corky and I looked at the picture, then at each other in an awed way. Jeeves was right. There could be no other title.

'Jeeves,' I said. It was a few weeks later, and I had just finished looking at the comic section of the *Sunday Star*. 'I'm an optimist. I always have been. The older I get, the more I agree with Shakespeare and those poet Johnnies about it always being darkest before the dawn and there's a silver lining and what you lose on the swings you make up on the roundabouts. Look at Mr Corcoran, for instance. There was a fellow, one would have said, clear up to the eyebrows in the soup. To all appearances he had got it right in the neck. Yet look at him now. Have you seen these pictures?'

'I took the liberty of glancing at them before bringing them to you, sir. Extremely diverting.'

'They have made a big hit, you know.'

'I anticipated it, sir.'

I leaned back against the pillows.

'You know, Jeeves, you're a genius. You ought to be drawing a commission on these things.'

'I have nothing to complain of in that respect, sir. Mr Corcoran has been most generous. I am putting out the brown suit, sir.'

'No, I think I'll wear the blue with the faint red stripe.'

'Not the blue with the faint red stripe, sir.'
'But I rather fancy myself in it.'
'Not the blue with the faint red stripe, sir.'
'Oh, all right, have it your own way.'
'Very good, sir. Thank you, sir.'

3

JEEVES AND THE UNBIDDEN GUEST

I'm not absolutely certain of my facts, but I rather fancy it's Shakespeare – or, if not, it's some equally brainy bird – who says that it's always just when a fellow is feeling particularly braced with things in general that Fate sneaks up behind him with the bit of lead piping. And what I'm driving at is that the man is perfectly right. Take, for instance, the business of Lady Malvern and her son Wilmot. That was one of the scaliest affairs I was ever mixed up with, and a moment before they came into my life I was just thinking how thoroughly all right everything was.

I was still in New York when the thing started, and it was about the time of year when New York is at its best. It was one of those topping mornings, and I had just climbed out from under the cold shower, feeling like a million dollars. As a matter of fact, what was bucking me up more than anything was the fact that the day before I had asserted myself with Jeeves – absolutely asserted myself, don't you know. You see, the way things had been going on I was rapidly becoming a dashed serf. The man had jolly well oppressed me. I didn't so much mind when he made me give up one of my new suits, because Jeeves's judgement about suits is sound and can generally be relied upon.

But I as near as a toucher rebelled when he wouldn't let me wear a pair of cloth-topped boots which I loved like a couple of brothers. And, finally, when he tried to tread on me like a worm in the matter of a hat, I put the Wooster foot down and showed him in no uncertain manner who was who.

It's a long story, and I haven't time to tell you now, but the nub of the thing was that he wanted me to wear the White House Wonder – as worn by President Coolidge – when I had set my heart on the Broadway Special, much patronized by the Younger Set; and the end of the matter was that, after a rather painful scene, I bought the Broadway Special. So that's how things were on this particular morning, and I was feeling pretty manly and independent.

Well, I was in the bathroom, wondering what there was going to be for breakfast while I massaged the spine with a rough towel and sang slightly, when there was a tap at the door. I stopped singing and opened the door an inch.

'What ho, without there!' I said.

'Lady Malvern has called, sir.'

'Eh?'

'Lady Malvern, sir. She is waiting in the sitting-room.'

'Pull yourself together, Jeeves, my man,' I said rather severely, for I bar practical jokes before breakfast. 'You know perfectly well there's no-one waiting for me in the sitting-room. How could there be when it's barely ten o'clock yet?'

'I gathered from her ladyship, sir, that she had landed from an ocean liner at an early hour this morning.'

This made the thing a bit more plausible. I remembered that when I had arrived in America about a year before, the proceedings had begun at some ghastly hour like six, and that I had been shot out on to a foreign shore considerably before eight.

'Who the deuce is Lady Malvern, Jeeves?'

'Her ladyship did not confide in me, sir.'

'Is she alone?'

'Her ladyship is accompanied by a Lord Pershore, sir. I fancy that his lordship would be her ladyship's son.'

'Oh, well, put out rich raiment of sorts, and I'll be dressing.'

'Our heather-mixture lounge is in readiness, sir.'

'Then lead me to it.'

While I was dressing I kept trying to think who on earth Lady Malvern could be. It wasn't till I had climbed through the top of my shirt and was reaching out for the studs that I remembered.

'I've placed her, Jeeves. She's a pal of my Aunt Agatha.'

'Indeed, sir?'

'Yes. I met her at lunch one Sunday before I left London. A very vicious specimen. Writes books. She wrote a book on social conditions in India when she came back from the Durbar.'

'Yes, sir? Pardon me, sir, but not that tie.'

'Eh?'

'Not that tie with the heather-mixture lounge, sir.'

It was a shock to me. I thought I had quelled the fellow. It was rather a solemn moment. What I mean is, if I weakened now, all my good work the night before would be thrown away. I braced myself.

'What's wrong with this tie? I've seen you give it a nasty look before. Speak out like a man! What's the matter with it?'

'Too ornate, sir.'

'Nonsense! A cheerful pink. Nothing more.'

'Unsuitable, sir.'

'Jeeves, this is the tie I wear!'

'Very good, sir.'

Dashed unpleasant. I could see that the man was wounded. But I was firm. I tied the tie, got into the coat and waistcoat, and went into the sitting-room.

'Hullo-ullo-ullo!' I said. 'What?'

'Ah! How do you do, Mr Wooster? You have never met my son Wilmot, I think? Motty, darling, this is Mr Wooster.'

Lady Malvern was a hearty, happy, healthy, overpowering sort of dashed female, not so very tall but making up for it by measuring about six feet from the O.P. to the Prompt Side. She fitted into my biggest armchair as if it had been built round her by someone who knew they were wearing arm-chairs tight about the hips that season. She had bright, bulging eyes and a lot of yellow hair, and when she spoke she showed about fifty-seven front teeth. She was one of those women who kind of numb a fellow's faculties. She made me feel as if I were ten years old and had been brought into the drawing-room in my Sunday clothes to say how-d'you-do. Altogether by no means the sort of thing a chappie would wish to find in his sitting-room before breakfast.

Motty, the son, was about twenty-three, tall and thin and meek-looking. He had the same yellow hair as his mother, but he wore it plastered down and parted in the middle. His eyes bulged, too, but they weren't bright. They were a dull grey with pink rims. His chin gave up the struggle about half-way down, and he didn't appear to have any eyelashes. A mild, furtive, sheepish sort of blighter, in short.

'Awfully glad to see you,' I said, though this was far from the case, for already I was beginning to have a sort of feeling that dirty work was threatening in the offing. 'So you've popped over, eh? Making a long stay in America?'

'About a month. Your aunt gave me your address and told me to be sure to call on you.'

I was glad to hear this, for it seemed to indicate that Aunt Agatha was beginning to come round a bit. As I believe I told you before, there had been some slight unpleasantness between us, arising from the occasion when she had sent me over to New York to disentangle my cousin Gussie from the clutches of a girl on the music-hall stage. When I tell you that by the time I had finished my operations Gussie had not only married the girl but had gone on the Halls himself and was doing well, you'll understand that relations were a trifle strained between aunt and nephew.

I simply hadn't dared to go back and face her, and it was a relief to find that time had healed the wound enough to make her tell her pals to call on me. What I mean is, much as I liked America, I didn't want to have England barred to me for the rest of my natural; and, believe me, England is a jolly sight too small for anyone to live in with Aunt Agatha, if she's really on the war-path. So I was braced at hearing these words and smiled genially on the assemblage.

'Your aunt said that you would do anything that was in your power to be of assistance to us.'

'Rather! Oh, rather. Absolutely.'

'Thank you so much. I want you to put dear Motty up for a little while.'

I didn't get this for a moment.

'Put him up! For my clubs?'

'No, no! Darling Motty is essentially a home bird. Aren't you, Motty, darling?'

Motty, who was sucking the knob of his stick, uncorked himself.

'Yes, Mother,' he said, and corked himself up again.

'I should not like him to belong to clubs. I mean put him up here. Have him to live with you while I am away.'

These frightful words trickled out of her like honey. The woman simply didn't seem to understand the ghastly nature of her proposal. I gave Motty the swift east-to-west. He was sitting with his mouth nuzzling the stick, blinking at the wall. The thought of having this planted on me for an indefinite period appalled me. Absolutely appalled me, don't you know. I was just starting to say that the shot wasn't on the board at any price, and that the first sign Motty gave of trying to nestle into my little home I would yell for the police, when she went on, rolling placidly over me, as it were.

There was something about this woman that sapped one's will-power.

'I am leaving New York by the midday train, as I have to pay a visit to Sing-Sing prison. I am extremely interested in prison conditions in America. After that I work my way gradually across to the coast, visiting the points of interest on the journey. You see, Mr Wooster, I am in America principally on business. No doubt you read my book, *India and the Indians*? My publishers are anxious for me to write a companion volume on the United States. I shall not be able to spend more than a month in the country, as I have to get back for the season, but a month should be ample. I was less than a month in India, and my dear friend Sir Roger Cremorne wrote his *America from Within* after a stay of only two weeks. I should love to take Motty with me, but the poor boy gets so sick when he travels by train. I shall have to pick him up on my return.'

From where I sat I could see Jeeves in the dining-room, laying the breakfast table. I wished I could have had a minute with him alone. I felt certain that he would have been able to think of some way of putting a stop to this woman.

'It will be such a relief to know that Motty is safe with you, Mr Wooster. I know what the temptations of a great city are. Hitherto dear Motty has been sheltered from them. He has lived quietly with me in the country. I know that you will look after him carefully, Mr Wooster. He will give very little trouble.' She talked about the poor blighter as if he wasn't there. Not that Motty seemed to mind. He had stopped chewing his walking-stick and was sitting there with his mouth open. 'He is a vegetarian and a teetotaller and is devoted to reading. Give him a nice book and he will be quite contented.' She got up. 'Thank you so much, Mr Wooster. I don't know what I should have done without your help. Come, Motty. We have just time to see a few of the sights before my train goes. But I shall have to rely on you for most of my information about New York, darling. Be sure to keep your eyes open and take notes of your impressions. It will be such a help. Goodbye, Mr Wooster. I will send Motty back early in the afternoon.'

They went out, and I howled for Jeeves.

'Jeeves!'

'Sir?'

'What's to be done? You heard it all, didn't you? You were in the dining-room most of the time. That pill is coming to stay here.'

'Pill, sir?'

'The excrescence.'

'I beg your pardon, sir?'

I looked at Jeeves sharply. This sort of thing wasn't like him. Then I understood. The man was really upset about that tie. He was trying to get his own back.

'Lord Pershore will be staying here from tonight, Jeeves,' I said coldly.

'Very good, sir. Breakfast is ready, sir.'

I could have sobbed into the bacon and eggs. That there wasn't any sympathy to be got out of Jeeves was what put the lid on it. For a moment I almost weakened and told him to destroy the hat and tie if he didn't like them, but I pulled myself together again. I was dashed if I was going to let Jeeves treat me like a bally one-man chain-gang.

But, what with brooding on Jeeves and brooding on Motty, I was in a pretty reduced sort of state. The more I examined the situation, the more blighted it became. There was nothing I could do. If I slung Motty out, he would report to his mother, and she would pass it on to Aunt Agatha, and I didn't like to think what would happen then. Sooner or later I should be wanting to go back to England, and I didn't want to get there and find Aunt Agatha waiting on the quay for me with a stuffed eelskin. There was absolutely nothing for it but to put the fellow up and make the best of it.

About midday Motty's luggage arrived, and soon afterwards a large parcel of what I took to be nice books. I brightened up a little when I saw it. It was one of those massive parcels and looked as if it had enough in it to keep him busy for a year. I felt a trifle more cheerful, and I got my Broadway Special and stuck it on my head, and gave the pink tie a twist, and reeled out to take a bite of lunch with one or two of the lads at a neighbouring hostelry; and what with excellent browsing and sluicing and cheery conversation and what not, the afternoon passed quite happily. By dinner time I had almost forgotten Motty's existence.

I dined at the club and looked in at a show afterwards, and it wasn't till fairly late that I got back to the flat. There were no signs of Motty, and I took it that he had gone to bed.

It seemed rummy to me, though, that the parcel of nice books was still there with the string and paper on it. It looked as if Motty, after seeing Mother off at the station, had decided to call it a day.

Jeeves came in with the nightly whisky and soda. I could tell by the chappie's manner that he was still upset.

'Lord Pershore gone to bed, Jeeves?' I asked, with reserved hauteur and what not.

'No sir. His lordship has not yet returned.'

'Not returned? What do you mean?'

'His lordship came in shortly after six-thirty, and, having dressed, went out again.'

At this moment there was a noise outside the front door, a sort of scrabbling noise, as if somebody were trying to paw his way through the woodwork. Then a sort of thud.

'Better go and see what that is, Jeeves.'

'Very good, sir.'

He went out and came back again.

'If you would not mind stepping this way, sir, I think we might be able to carry him in.'

'Carry him in?'

'His lordship is lying on the mat, sir.'

I went to the front door. The man was right. There was Motty huddled up outside on the floor. He was moaning a bit.

'He's had some sort of dashed fit,' I said. I took another look. 'Jeeves! Someone's been feeding him meat!'

'Sir?'

'He's a vegetarian, you know. He must have been digging into a steak or something. Call up a doctor!'

'I hardly think it will be necessary, sir. If you would take his lordship's legs, while I – '

'Great Scott, Jeeves! You don't think – he can't be – '

'I am inclined to think so, sir.'

And, by Jove, he was right! Once on the right track, you couldn't mistake it. Motty was under the surface. Completely sozzled.

It was the deuce of a shock.

'You never can tell, Jeeves!'

'Very seldom, sir.'

'Remove the eye of authority and where are you?'

'Precisely, sir.'

'Where is my wandering boy tonight and all that sort of thing, what?'

'It would seem so, sir.'

'Well, we had better bring him in, eh?'

'Yes, sir.'

So we lugged him in, and Jeeves put him to bed, and I lit a cigarette and sat down to think the thing over. I had a kind of foreboding. It seemed to me that I had let myself in for something pretty rocky.

Next morning, after I had sucked down a thoughtful cup of tea, I went into Motty's room to investigate. I expected to find the fellow a wreck, but there he was, sitting up in bed, quite chirpy, reading *Gingery Stories*.

'What ho!' I said.

'What ho!' said Motty.

'What ho! What ho!'

'What ho! What ho! What ho!'

After that it seemed rather difficult to go on with the conversation.

'How are you feeling this morning?' I asked.

'Topping!' replied Motty, blithely and with abandon. 'I say, you know, that fellow of yours – Jeeves, you know – is a corker. I had a most frightful headache when I woke up, and he brought me a sort of rummy dark drink, and it put me right again at once. Said it was his own invention. I must see more of that lad. He seems to me distinctly one of the ones.'

I couldn't believe that this was the same blighter who had sat and sucked his stick the day before.

'You ate something that disagreed with you last night, didn't you?' I said, by way of giving him a chance to slide out of it if he wanted to. But he wouldn't have it at any price.

'No!' he replied firmly. 'I didn't do anything of the kind. I drank too much. Much too much. Lots and lots too much. And, what's more, I'm going to do it again. I'm going to do it every night. If ever you see me sober, old top,' he said, with a kind of holy exaltation, 'tap me on the shoulder and say, "Tut! tut!" and I'll apologize and remedy the defect.'

'But I say, you know, what about me?'

'What about you?'

'Well, I'm, so to speak, as it were, kind of responsible for you. What I mean to say is, if you go doing this sort of thing I'm apt to get in the soup somewhat.'

'I can't help your troubles,' said Motty firmly. 'Listen to me, old thing: this is the first time in my life that I've had a real chance to yield to the temptations of a great city. What's the use of a great city having temptations if fellows don't yield to them? Makes it so bally discouraging for the great city. Besides, Mother told me to keep my eyes open and collect impressions.'

I sat on the edge of the bed. I felt dizzy.

'I know just how you feel, old dear,' said Motty consolingly. 'And, if my principles would permit it, I would simmer down for your sake. But duty first! This is the first time I've been let out alone, and I mean to make the most of it. We're only young once. Why interfere with life's morning? Young man, rejoice in thy youth! Tra-la! What ho!'

Put like that, it did seem reasonable.

'All my bally life, dear boy,' Motty went on, 'I've been cooped up in the ancestral home at Much Middlefold, in Shropshire, and till you've been cooped up in Much Middlefold you don't know what cooping is. The only time we get any excitement is when one of the choir-boys is caught sucking chocolate during the sermon. When that happens, we talk about it for days. I've got a month of New York, and I mean to store up a few happy memories for the long winter evenings. This is my only chance to collect a past, and I'm going to do it. Now tell me, old sport, as man to man, how does one get in touch with that very decent bird Jeeves? Does one ring a bell or shout a bit? I should like to discuss the subject of a good stiff b-and-s with him.'

I had had a sort of vague idea, don't you know, that if I stuck close to Motty and went about the place with him, I might act as a bit of a damper on the gaiety. What I mean is, I thought that if, when he was being the life and soul of the party, he were to catch my reproving eye he might ease up a trifle on the revelry. So the next night I took him along to supper with me. It was the last time. I'm a quiet, peaceful sort of bloke who has lived all his life in London, and I can't stand the pace these swift sportsmen from the rural districts set. What I mean to say is, I'm all for rational enjoyment and so forth, but I think a chappie makes himself conspicuous when he throws soft-boiled eggs at the electric fan. And decent mirth and all that sort of thing are all right, but I do bar dancing on tables and having to dash all over the place dodging waiters, managers, and chuckers-out, just when you want to sit still and digest.

Directly I managed to tear myself away that night and get home, I made up my mind that this was jolly well the last time that I went about with Motty. The only time I met him late at night after that was once when I passed the door of a fairly low-down sort of restaurant and had to step aside to dodge him as he sailed through the air *en route* for the opposite pavement, with a muscular looking sort of fellow peering out after him with a kind of gloomy satisfaction.

In a way, I couldn't help sympathizing with the chap. He had about four weeks to have the good time that ought to have been spread over about ten years, and I didn't wonder at his wanting to be pretty busy. I should have been just the same in his place. Still, there was no denying that it was a bit thick. If it hadn't been for the thought of Lady Malvern and Aunt Agatha in the background, I should have regarded Motty's rapid work with an indulgent smile. But I couldn't get rid of the feeling that, sooner or later, I was the lad who was scheduled to get it behind the ear. And what with brooding on this prospect, and sitting up in the old flat waiting for the familiar footstep, and putting it to bed when it got there, and stealing into the sick-chamber next morning to contemplate the wreckage, I was beginning to lose weight. Absolutely becoming the good old shadow, I give you my honest word. Starting at sudden noises and what not.

And no sympathy from Jeeves. That was what cut me to the quick.

The man was still thoroughly pipped about the hat and tie, and simply wouldn't rally round. One morning I wanted comforting so much that I sank the pride of the Woosters and appealed to the fellow direct.

'Jeeves,' I said, 'this is getting a bit thick!'

'Sir?'

'You know what I mean. This lad seems to have chucked all the principles of a well-spent boyhood. He has got it up his nose!'

'Yes, sir.'

'Well, I shall get blamed, don't you know. You know what my Aunt Agatha is.'

'Yes, sir.'

'Very well, then.'

I waited a moment, but he wouldn't unbend.

'Jeeves,' I said, 'haven't you any scheme up your sleeve for coping with this blighter?'

'No, sir.'

And he shimmered off to his lair. Obstinate devil! So dashed absurd, don't you know. It wasn't as if there was anything wrong with that Broadway Special hat. It was a remarkably priceless effort, and much admired by the lads. But, just because he preferred the White House Wonder, he left me flat.

It was shortly after this that young Motty got the idea of bringing pals back in the small hours to continue the gay revels in the home. This was where I began to crack under the strain. You see, the part of town where I was living wasn't the right place for that sort of thing. I knew lots of chappies down Washington Square way who started the evening at about two a.m. – artists and writers and so forth who frolicked considerably till checked by the arrival of the morning milk. That was all right. They like that sort of thing down there. The neighbours can't get to sleep unless there's someone dancing Hawaiian dances over their heads. But on Fifty-seventh Street the atmosphere wasn't right, and when Motty turned up at three in the morning with a collection of hearty lads, who only stopped singing their college song when they started singing 'The Old Oaken Bucket', there was a marked peevishness among the old settlers in the flats. The management was extremely terse over the telephone at breakfast-time, and took a lot of soothing.

The next night I came home early, after a lonely dinner at a place which I'd chosen because there didn't seem any chance of meeting Motty there. The sitting-room was quite dark, and I was just moving to switch on the light, when there was a sort of explosion and something collared hold of my trouser-leg. Living with Motty had reduced me to such an extent that I was simply unable to cope with this thing. I jumped backward with a loud yell of anguish, and tumbled out into the hall just as Jeeves came out of his den to see what the matter was.

'Did you call, sir?'

'Jeeves! There's something in there that grabs you by the leg!'

'That would be Rollo, sir.'

'Eh?'

'I would have warned you of his presence, but I did not hear you come in. His temper is a little uncertain at present, as he had not yet settled down.'

'Who the deuce is Rollo?'

'His lordship's bull-terrier, sir. His lordship won him in a raffle, and tied him to the leg of the table. If you will allow me, sir, I will go in and switch on the light.'

There really is nobody like Jeeves. He walked straight into the sitting-room, the biggest feat since Daniel and the lions' den, without a quiver. What's more, his magnetism or whatever they call it was such that the dashed animal, instead of pinning him by the leg, calmed down as if he had had a bromide, and rolled over on his back with all his paws in the air. If Jeeves had been his rich uncle he couldn't have been more chummy. Yet directly he caught sight of me again, he got all worked up and seemed to have only one idea in life – to start chewing me where he had left off.

'Rollo is not used to you yet, sir,' said Jeeves, regarding the bally quadruped in an admiring sort of way. 'He is an excellent watch-dog.'

I don't want a watch-dog to keep me out of my rooms.'

'No, sir.'

'Well, what am I to do?'

'No doubt in time the animal will learn to discriminate, sir. He will learn to distinguish your peculiar scent.'

'What do you mean – my peculiar scent? Correct the impression that I intend to hang about in the hall while life slips by, in the hope that one of these days that dashed animal will decide that I smell all right.' I thought for a bit. 'Jeeves!'

'Sir?'

'I'm going away – tomorrow morning by the first train. I shall go and stop with Mr Todd in the country.'

'Do you wish me to accompany you, sir?'

'No.'

'Very good, sir.'

'I don't know when I shall be back. Forward my letters.'
'Yes, sir.'

As a matter of fact, I was back within the week, Rocky Todd, the pal I went to stay with, is a rummy sort of a chap who lives all alone in the wilds of Long Island, and likes it; but a little of that sort of thing goes a long way with me. Dear old Rocky is one of the best, but after a few days in his cottage in the woods, miles away from anywhere, New York, even with Motty on the premises, began to look pretty good to me. The days down on Long Island have forty-eight hours in them; you can't go to sleep at night because of the bellowing of the crickets; and you have to walk two miles for a drink and six for an evening paper. I thanked Rocky for his kind hospitality, and caught the only train they have down in those parts. It landed me in New York about dinner-time. I went straight to the old flat. Jeeves came out of his lair. I looked round cautiously for Rollo.

'Where's that dog, Jeeves? Have you got him tied up?'

'The animal is no longer here, sir. His lordship gave him to the porter, who sold him. His lordship took a prejudice against the animal on account of being bitten by him in the calf of the leg.'

I don't think I've ever been so bucked by a bit of news. I felt I had misjudged Rollo. Evidently, when you got to know him better, he had a lot of good in him.

'Fine!' I said. 'Is Lord Pershore in, Jeeves?'

'No, sir.'

'Do you expect him back to dinner?'

'No, sir.'

'Where is he?'

'In prison, sir.'

'In prison!'

'Yes, sir.'

'You don't mean – in prison?'

'Yes, sir.'

I lowered myself into a chair.

'Why?' I said.

'He assaulted a constable, sir.'

'Lord Pershore assaulted a constable!'

'Yes, sir.'

I digested this.

'But, Jeeves, I say! This is frightful!'

'Sir?'

'What will Lady Malvern say when she finds out?'

'I do not fancy that her ladyship will find out, sir.'

'But she'll come back and want to know where he is.'

'I rather fancy, sir, that his lordship's bit of time will have run out by then.'

'But supposing it hasn't?'

'In that event, sir, it may be judicious to prevaricate a little.'

'How?'

'If I might make the suggestion, sir, I should inform her ladyship that his lordship has left for a short visit to Boston.'

'Why Boston?'

'Very interesting and respectable centre, sir.'

'Jeeves, I believe you've hit it.'

'I fancy so, sir.'

'Why, this is really the best thing that could have happened. If this hadn't turned up to prevent him, young Motty would have been in a sanatorium by the time Lady Malvern got back.'

'Exactly, sir.'

The more I looked at it in that way, the sounder this prison wheeze seemed to me. There was no doubt in the world that prison was just what the doctor ordered for Motty. It was the only thing that could have pulled him up. I was sorry for the poor blighter, but after all, I reflected, a fellow who had lived all his life with Lady Malvern, in a small village in the interior of Shropshire, wouldn't have much to kick at in a prison. Altogether, I began to feel absolutely braced again. Life became like what the poet Johnnie says – one grand, sweet song. Things went on so comfortably and peacefully for a couple of weeks that I give you my word that I'd almost forgotten such a person as Motty existed. The only flaw in the scheme of things was that Jeeves was still pained and distant. It wasn't anything he said, or did, mind you, but there was a rummy something about him all the time. Once when I was tying the pink tie I caught sight of him in the looking-glass. There was a kind of grieved look in his eyes.

And then Lady Malvern came back, a good bit ahead of schedule. I hadn't been expecting her for days. I'd forgotten how time had been slipping along. She turned up one morning while I was still in bed sipping tea and thinking of this and that. Jeeves flowed in with the announcement that he had just loosed her into the sitting-room. I draped a few garments round me and went in.

There she was, sitting in the same arm chair, looking as massive as ever. The only difference was that she didn't uncover the teeth as she had done the first time.

'Good morning,' I said. 'So you've got back, what?'

'I have got back.'

There was something sort of bleak about her tone, rather as if she had swallowed an east wind. This I took to be due to the fact that she probably hadn't breakfasted. It's only after a bit of breakfast that I'm able to regard the world with that sunny cheeriness which makes a fellow the universal favourite. I'm never much of a lad till I've engulfed an egg or two and a beaker of coffee.

'I suppose you haven't breakfasted?'

'I have not yet breakfasted.'

'Won't you have an egg or something? Or a sausage or something? Or something?'

'No, thank you.'

She spoke as if she belonged to an anti-sausage society or a league for the suppression of eggs. There was a bit of a silence.

'I called on you last night,' she said, 'but you were out.'

'Awfully sorry. Had a pleasant trip?'

'Extremely, thank you.'

'See everything? Niagara Falls, Yellowstone Park, and the jolly old Grand Canyon, and what not?'

'I saw a great deal.'

There was another slight *frappé* silence. Jeeves floated silently into the dining-room and began to lay the breakfast-table.

'I hope Wilmot was not in your way, Mr Wooster?'

I had been wondering when she was going to mention Motty.

'Rather not! Great pals. Hit it off splendidly.'

'You were his constant companion, then?'

'Absolutely. We were always together. Saw all the sights, don't you know. We'd take in the Museum of Art in the morning, and have a bit of lunch at some good vegetarian place, and then toddle along to a sacred concert in the afternoon, and home to an early dinner. We usually played dominoes after dinner. And then the early bed and the refreshing sleep. We had a great time. I was awfully sorry when he went away to Boston.'

'Oh! Wilmot is in Boston?'

'Yes. I ought to have let you know, but of course we didn't know where you were. You were dodging all over the place like a snipe – I mean, don't you know, dodging all over the place, and we couldn't get at you. Yes, Motty went off to Boston.'

'You're sure he went to Boston?'

'Oh, absolutely.' I called out to Jeeves, who was now messing about in the next room with forks and so forth: 'Jeeves, Lord Pershore didn't change his mind about going to Boston, did he?'

'No, sir.'

'I thought I was right. Yes, Motty went to Boston.'

'Then how do you account, Mr Wooster, for the fact that when I went yesterday afternoon to Blackwell's Island prison, to secure material for my book, I saw poor, dear Wilmot there, dressed in a striped suit, seated beside a pile of stones with a hammer in his hands?'

I tried to think of something to say, but nothing came. A fellow has to be a lot broader about the forehead than I am to handle a jolt like this. I strained the old bean till it creaked, but between the collar and the hair parting nothing stirred. I was dumb. Which was lucky, because I wouldn't have had a chance to get any persiflage out of my system. Lady Malvern collared the conversation. She had been bottling it up, and now it came out with a rush.

'So this is how you have looked after my poor, dear boy, Mr Wooster! So this is how you have abused my trust! I left him in your charge, thinking that I could rely on you to shield him from evil. He came to you innocent, unversed in the ways of the world, confiding, unused to the temptations of a large city, and you led him astray!'

I hadn't any remarks to make. All I could think of was the picture of Aunt Agatha drinking all this in and reaching out to sharpen the hatchet against my return.

'You deliberately – '

Far away in the misty distance a soft voice spoke:

'If I might explain, your ladyship.'

Jeeves had projected himself in from the dining room and materialized on the rug. Lady Malvern tried to freeze him with a look, but you can't do that sort of thing to Jeeves. He is look-proof.

'I fancy, your ladyship, that you may have misunderstood Mr Wooster, and that he may have given you the impression that he was in New York when his lordship was – removed. When Mr Wooster informed your ladyship that his lordship had gone to Boston, he was relying on the version I had given him of his lordship's movements. Mr Wooster was away, visiting a friend in the country, at the time, and knew nothing of the matter till your ladyship informed him.'

Lady Malvern gave a kind of grunt. It didn't rattle Jeeves.

'I feared Mr Wooster might be disturbed if he knew the truth, as he is so attached to his lordship and has taken such pains to look after him, so I took the liberty of telling him that his lordship had gone away for a visit. It might have been hard for Mr Wooster to believe that his lordship had gone to prison voluntarily and from the best motives, but your ladyship, knowing him better, will readily understand.'

'What!' Lady Malvern goggled at him. 'Did you say that Lord Pershore went to prison voluntarily?'

'If I might explain, your ladyship. I think that your ladyship's parting words made a deep impression on his lordship. I have frequently heard him speak to Mr Wooster of his desire to do something to follow your ladyship's instructions and collect material for your ladyship's book on America. Mr Wooster will bear me out when I say that his lordship was frequently extremely depressed at the thought that he was doing so little to help.'

'Absolutely, by Jove! Quite pipped about it!' I said.

'The idea of making a personal examination into the prison system of the country – from within – occurred to his lordship very suddenly one night. He embraced it eagerly. There was no restraining him.'

Lady Malvern looked at Jeeves, then at me, then at Jeeves again. I could see her struggling with the thing.

'Surely, your ladyship,' said Jeeves, 'it is more reasonable to suppose that a gentleman of his lordship's character went to prison of his own volition that that he committed some breach of the law which necessitated his arrest?'

Lady Malvern blinked. Then she got up.

'Mr Wooster,' she said, 'I apologize. I have done you an injustice. I should have known Wilmot better. I should have had more faith in his pure, fine spirit.'

'Absolutely!' I said.

'Your breakfast is ready, sir,' said Jeeves.

I sat down and dallied in a dazed sort of way with a poached egg.

'Jeeves,' I said, 'you are certainly a life-saver.'

'Thank you, sir.'

'Nothing would have convinced my Aunt Agatha that I hadn't lured that blighter into riotous living.'

'I fancy you are right, sir.'

I champed my egg for a bit. I was most awfully moved, don't you know, by the way Jeeves had rallied round. Something seemed to tell me that this was an occasion that called for rich rewards. For a moment I hesitated. Then I made up my mind.

'Jeeves!'

'Sir?'

'That pink tie.'

'Yes, sir?'

'Burn it.'

'Thank you, sir.'

'And, Jeeves.'

'Yes, sir?'

'Take a taxi and get me that White House Wonder hat, as worn by President Coolidge.'

'Thank you very much, sir.'

I felt most awfully braced. I felt as if the clouds had rolled away and all was as it used to be. I felt like one of those chappies in the novels who calls off the fight with his wife in the last chapter and decides to forget and forgive. I felt I wanted to do all sorts of other things to show Jeeves that I appreciated him.

'Jeeves,' I said, 'it isn't enough. Is there anything else you would like?'

'Yes, sir. If I may make the suggestion – fifty dollars.'

'Fifty dollars?'

'It will enable me to pay a debt of honour, sir. I owe it to His Lordship.'

'You owe Lord Pershore fifty dollars?'

'Yes, sir. I happened to meet him in the street the night His Lordship was arrested. I had been thinking a good deal about the most suitable method of inducing him to abandon his mode of living, sir. His lordship was a little over-excited at the time, and I fancy that he mistook me for a friend of his. At any rate, when I took the liberty of wagering him fifty dollars that he would not punch a passing policeman in the eye, he accepted the bet very cordially and won it.'

I produced my pocket-book and counted out a hundred.

'Take this, Jeeves,' I said; 'fifty isn't enough. Do you know, Jeeves, you're – well, you absolutely stand alone!'

'I endeavour to give satisfaction, sir,' said Jeeves.

4

JEEVES AND THE HARD-BOILED EGG

Sometimes of a morning, as I've sat in bed sucking down the early cup of tea and watched Jeeves flitting about the room and putting out the raiment for the day, I've wondered what the deuce I should do if the fellow ever took it into his head to leave me. It's not so bad when I'm in New York, but in London the anxiety is frightful. There used to be all sorts of attempts on the part of low blighters to sneak him away from me. Young Reggie Foljambe to my certain knowledge offered him double what I was giving him, and Alistair Bingham-Reeves, who's got a valet who had been known to press his trousers sideways, used to look at him, when he came to see me, with a kind of glittering, hungry eye which disturbed me deucedly. Bally pirates!

The thing, you see, is that Jeeves is so dashed competent. You can spot it even in the way he shoves studs into a shirt.

I rely on him absolutely in every crisis, and he never lets me down. And, what's more, he can always be counted on to extend himself on behalf of any pal of mine who happens to be to all appearances knee-deep in the bouillon. Take the rather rummy case, for instance, of dear old Bicky and his uncle, the hard-boiled egg.

It happened after I had been in America for a few months. I got back to the flat latish one night, and when Jeeves brought me the final drink he said:

'Mr Bickersteth called to see you this evening, sir, while you were out.'

'Oh?' I said.

'Twice, sir. He appeared a trifle agitated.'

'What, pipped?'

'He gave that impression, sir.'

I sipped the whisky. I was sorry if Bicky was in trouble, but, as a matter of fact, I was rather glad to have something I could discuss freely with Jeeves just then, because things had been a bit strained between us for some time, and it had been rather difficult to hit on anything to talk about that wasn't apt to take a personal turn. You see, I had decided – rightly or wrongly – to grow a moustache, and this had cut Jeeves to the quick. He couldn't stick the thing at any price, and I had been living ever since in an atmosphere of bally disapproval till I was getting jolly well fed up with it. What I mean is, while there's no doubt that in certain matters of dress Jeeves's judgement is absolutely sound and should be followed, it seemed to me that it was getting a bit too thick if he was going to edit my face as well as my costume. No one can call me an unreasonable chappie, and many's the time I've given in like a lamb when Jeeves has voted against one of my pet suits or ties; but when it comes to a valet's staking out a claim on your upper lip you've simply got to have a bit of the good old bulldog pluck and defy the blighter.

'He said that he would call again later, sir.'

'Something must be up, Jeeves.'

'Yes, sir.'

I gave the moustache a thoughtful twirl. It seemed to hurt Jeeves a good deal, so I chucked it.

'I see by the papers, sir, that Mr Bickersteth's uncle is arriving on the *Carmantic*.'

'Yes?'

'His Grace the Duke of Chiswick, sir.'

This was news to me, that Bicky's uncle was a duke. Rum, how little one knows about one's pals. I had met Bicky for the first time at a species of beano or jamboree down in Washington Square, not long after my arrival in New York. I suppose I was a bit homesick at the time, and I rather took to Bicky when I found that he was an Englishman and had, in fact, been up at Oxford with me. Besides, he was a frightful chump, so we naturally drifted together; and while we were taking a quiet snort in a corner that wasn't all cluttered up with artists and sculptors, he furthermore endeared himself to me by a most extraordinarily gifted imitation of a bull-terrier chasing a cat up a tree. But, though we had subsequently become extremely pally, all I really knew about him was that he was generally hard up, and had an uncle who relieved the strain a bit from time to time by sending him monthly remittances.

'If the Duke of Chiswick is his uncle,' I said, 'why hasn't he a title? Why isn't he Lord What-Not?'

'Mr Bickersteth is the son of His Grace's late sister, sir, who married Captain Rollo Bickersteth of the Coldstream Guards.'

Jeeves knows everything.

'Is Mr Bickersteth's father dead too?'

'Yes, sir.'

'Leave any money?'

'No, sir.'

I began to understand why poor old Bicky was always more or less on the rocks. To the casual and irreflective observer it may sound a pretty good wheeze having a duke for an uncle, but the trouble about old Chiswick was that, though an extremely wealthy old buster, owning half London and about five counties up north, he was notoriously the most prudent spender in England. He was what Americans call a hard-boiled egg. If Bicky's people hadn't left him anything and he depended on what he could prise out of the old duke, he was in a pretty bad way. Not that that explained why he was hunting me like this, because he was a chap who never borrowed money. He said he wanted to keep his pals, so never bit anyone's ear on principle.

At this juncture the door-bell rang. Jeeves floated out to answer it.

'Yes, sir. Mr Wooster has just returned,' I heard him say. And Bicky came beetling in, looking pretty sorry for himself.

'Hallo, Bicky,' I said. 'Jeeves told me you had been trying to get me. What's the trouble, Bicky?'

'I'm in a hole, Bertie. I want your advice.'

'Say on, old lad.'

'My uncle's turning up tomorrow, Bertie.'

'So Jeeves told me.'

'The Duke of Chiswick, you know.'

'So Jeeves told me.'

Bicky seemed a bit surprised.

'Jeeves seems to know everything.'

'Rather rummily, that's exactly what I was thinking just now myself.'

'Well, I wish,' said Bicky, gloomily, 'that he knew a way to get me out of the hole I'm in.'

'Mr Bickersteth is in a hole, Jeeves,' I said, 'and wants you to rally round.'

'Very good, sir.'

Bicky looked a bit doubtful.

'Well, of course, you know, Bertie, this thing is by way of being a bit private and all that.'

'I shouldn't worry about that, old top. I bet Jeeves knows all about it already. Don't you, Jeeves?'

'Yes, sir.'

'Eh?' said Bicky, rattled.

'I am open to correction, sir, but is not your dilemma due to the fact that you are at a loss to explain to His Grace why you are in New York instead of in Colorado?'

Bicky rocked like a jelly in a high wind.

'How the deuce do you know anything about it?'

'I chanced to meet His Grace's butler before we left England. He informed me that he happened to overhear His Grace speaking to you on the matter, sir, as he passed the library door.'

Bicky gave a hollow sort of laugh.

'Well, as everybody seems to know all about it, there's no need to try to keep it dark. The old boy turfed me out, Bertie, because he said I was a brainless nincompoop. The idea was that he would give me a remittance on condition that I dashed out to some blighted locality of the name of Colorado and learned farming or ranching, or whatever they call it, at some bally ranch or farm, or whatever it's called. I didn't fancy the idea a bit. I should have had to ride horses and pursue cows, and so forth. At the same time, don't you know, I had to have that remittance.'

'I get you absolutely, old thing.'

'Well, when I got to New York it looked a decent sort of place to me, so I thought it would be a pretty sound notion to stop here. So I cabled to my uncle telling him that I had dropped into a good business wheeze in the city and wanted to chuck the ranch idea. He wrote back that it was all right, and here I've been ever since. He thinks I'm doing well at something or other over here. I never dreamed, don't you know, that he would ever come out here. What on earth am I to do?'

'Jeeves,' I said, 'what on earth is Mr Bickersteth to do?'

'You see,' said Bicky, 'I had a wireless from him to say that he was coming to stay with me – to save hotel bills, I suppose. I've always given him the impression that I was living in pretty good style. I can't have him to stay at my boarding-house.'

'Thought of anything, Jeeves?' I said.

'To what extent, sir, if the question is not a delicate one, are you prepared to assist Mr Bickersteth?'

'I'll do anything I can for you, of course, Bicky, old man.'

'Then, if I might make the suggestion, sir, you might lend Mr Bickersteth – '

'No, by Jove!' said Bicky firmly. 'I never have touched you, Bertie, and I'm not going to start now. I may be a chump, but it's my boast that I don't owe a penny to a single soul – not counting tradesmen, of course.'

'I was about to suggest, sir, that you might lend Mr Bickersteth this flat. Mr Bickersteth could give His Grace the impression that he was the owner of it. With your permission I could convey the notion that I was in Mr Bickersteth's employment and not in yours. You would be residing here temporarily as Mr Bickersteth's guest. His Grace would occupy the second spare bedroom. I fancy that you would find this answer satisfactory, sir.'

Bicky had stopped rocking himself and was staring at Jeeves in an awed sort of way.

'I would advocate the dispatching of a wireless message to His Grace on board the vessel, notifying him of the change of address. Mr Bickersteth could meet His Grace at the dock and proceed directly here. Will that meet the situation, sir?'

'Absolutely.'

'Thank you, sir.'

Bicky followed him with his eye till the door closed.

'How does he do it, Bertie?' he said. 'I'll tell you what I think it is. I believe it's something to do with the shape of his head. Have you ever noticed his head, Bertie, old man? It sort of sticks out at the back!'

I hopped out of bed pretty early next morning, so as to be among those present when the old boy should arrive. I knew from experience that these ocean liners fetch up at the dock at a deucedly ungodly hour. It wasn't much after nine by the time I'd dressed and had my morning tea and was leaning out of the window, watching the street for Bicky and his uncle. It was one of those jolly, peaceful mornings that make a chappie wish he'd got a soul or something, and I was just brooding on life in general when I became aware of the dickens of a spat in progress down below. A taxi had driven up, and an old boy in a top hat had got out and was kicking up a frightful row about the fare. As far as I could make out, he was trying to get the cabby to switch from New York to London prices, and the cabby had apparently never heard of London before, and didn't seem to think a lot of it now. The old boy said that in London the trip would have set him back a shilling; and the cabby said he should worry. I called to Jeeves.

'The duke has arrived, Jeeves.'

'Yes, sir?'

'That'll be him at the door now.'

Jeeves made a long arm and opened the front door, and the old boy crawled in.

'How do you do, sir?' I said, bustling up and being the ray of sunshine. 'Your nephew went down to the dock to meet you, but you must have missed him. My name's Wooster, don't you know. Great pal of Bicky's, and all that sort of thing. I'm staying with him, you know. Would you like a cup of tea? Jeeves, bring a cup of tea.'

Old Chiswick had sunk into an arm chair and was looking about the room.

'Does this luxurious flat belong to my nephew Francis?'

'Absolutely.'

'It must be terribly expensive.'

'Pretty well, of course. Everything costs a lot over here, you know.'

He moaned. Jeeves filtered in with the tea. Old Chiswick took a stab at it to restore his tissues, and nodded.

'A terrible country, Mr Wooster! A terrible country. Nearly eight shillings for a short cab-drive. Iniquitous!' He took another look round the room. It seemed to fascinate him. 'Have you any idea how much my nephew pays for this flat, Mr Wooster?'

'About two hundred dollars a month, I believe.'

'What! Forty pounds a month!'

I began to see that, unless I made the thing a bit more plausible, the scheme might turn out a frost. I could guess what the old boy was thinking. He was trying to square all this prosperity with what he knew of poor old Bicky. And one had to admit that it took a lot of squaring, for dear old Bicky, though a stout fellow and absolutely unrivalled as an imitator of bull-terriers and cats, was in many ways one of the most pronounced fatheads that ever pulled on a suit of gents' underwear.

'I suppose it seems rummy to you,' I said, 'but the fact is New York often bucks fellows up and makes them show a flash of speed that you wouldn't have imagined them capable of. It sort of develops them. Something in the air, don't you know. I imagine that Bicky in the past, when you knew him, may have been something of a chump, but it's quite different now. Devilish efficient sort of bird, and looked on in commercial circles as quite the nib!'

'I am amazed! What is the nature of my nephew's business, Mr Wooster?'

'Oh, just business, don't you know. The same sort of thing Rockefeller and all these coves do, you know.' I slid for the door. 'Awfully sorry to leave you, but I've got to meet some of the lads elsewhere.'

Coming out of the lift I met Bicky bustling in from the street.

'Hallo, Bertie. I missed him. Has he turned up?'

'He's upstairs now, having some tea.'

'What does he think of it all?'

'He's absolutely rattled.'

'Ripping! I'll be toddling up, then. Toodle-oo, Bertie, old man. See you later.'

'Pip-pip, Bicky, dear boy.'

He trotted off, full of merriment and good cheer, and I went off to the club to sit in the window and watch the traffic coming up one way and going down the other.

It was latish in the evening when I looked in at the flat to dress for dinner.

'Where's everybody, Jeeves?' I said, finding no little feet pattering about the place. 'Gone out?'

'His Grace desired to see some of the sights of the city, sir. Mr Bickersteth is acting as his escort. I fancy their immediate objective was Grant's Tomb.'

'I suppose Mr Bickersteth is a bit bucked at the way things are going – what?'

'Sir?'

'I say, I take it that Mr Bickersteth is tolerably full of beans.'

'Not altogether, sir.'

'What's his trouble now?'

'The scheme which I took the liberty of suggesting to Mr Bickersteth and yourself has, unfortunately, not answered entirely satisfactorily, sir.'

'Surely the duke believes that Mr Bickersteth is doing well in business, and all that sort of thing?'

'Exactly, sir. With the result that he has decided to cancel Mr Bickersteth's monthly allowance, on the ground that, as Mr Bickersteth is doing so well on his own account, he no longer requires pecuniary assistance.'

'Great Scott, Jeeves! This is awful!'

'Somewhat disturbing, sir.'

'I never expected anything like this!'

'I confess I scarcely anticipated the contingency myself, sir.'

'I suppose it bowled the poor blighter over absolutely?'

'Mr Bickersteth appeared somewhat taken aback, sir.'

My heart bled for Bicky.

'We must do something, Jeeves.'

'Yes, sir.'

'Can you think of anything?'

'Not at the moment, sir.'

'There must be something we can do.'

'It was a maxim of one of my former employers, sir – as I believe I mentioned to you once before – the present Lord Bridgworth, that there is always a way. No doubt we shall be able to discover some solution of Mr Bickersteth's difficulty, sir.'

'Well, have a stab at it, Jeeves.'

'I will spare no pains, sir.'

I went and dressed sadly. It will show you pretty well how pipped I was when I tell you that I as near as a toucher put on a white tie with a dinner-jacket. I sallied out for a bit of food more to pass the time than because I wanted it. It seemed brutal to be wading into the bill of fare with poor old Bicky headed for the bread-line.

When I got back old Chiswick had gone to bed, but Bicky was there, hunched up in an arm chair, brooding pretty tensely, with a cigarette hanging out of the corner of his mouth and a more or less glassy stare in his eyes.

'This is a bit thick, old thing – what!' I said.

He picked up his glass and drained it feverishly, overlooking the fact that it hadn't anything in it.

'I'm done, Bertie!' he said.

He had another go at the glass. It didn't seem to do him any good.

'If only this had happened a week later, Bertie! My next month's money was due to roll in on Saturday. I could have worked a wheeze I've been reading about in the magazine advertisements. It seems that you can make a dashed amount of money if you can only collect a few dollars and start a chicken-farm. Jolly life, too, keeping hens!' He had begun to get quite worked up at the thought of it, but he slopped back in his chair at this juncture with a good deal of gloom. 'But, of course, it's no good,' he said, 'because I haven't the cash.'

'You've only to say the word, you know, Bicky, old top.'

'Thanks awfully, Bertie, but I'm not going to sponge on you.'

That's always the way in this world. The chappies you'd like to lend money to won't let you, whereas the chappies you don't want to lend it to will do everything except actually stand you on your head and lift the specie out of your pockets. As a lad who has always rolled tolerably freely in the right stuff, I've had lots of experience of the second class. Many's the time, back in London, I've hurried along Piccadilly and felt the hot breath of the toucher on the back of my neck and heard his sharp, excited yapping as he closed in on me. I've simply spent my life scattering largesse to blighters I didn't care a hang for; yet here was I now, dripping doubloons and pieces of eight and longing to hand them over, and Bicky, poor fish, absolutely on his uppers, not taking any at any price.

'Well, there's only one hope then.'

'What's that?'

'Jeeves.'

'Sir?'

There was Jeeves, standing behind me, full of zeal. In this matter of shimmering into rooms the man is rummy to a degree. You're sitting in the old arm chair, thinking of this and that, and then suddenly you look up, and there he is. He moves from point to point with as little uproar as a jelly-fish. The thing startled poor old Bicky considerably. He rose from his seat like a rocketing pheasant. I'm used to Jeeves now, but often in the days when he first came to me I've bitten my tongue freely on finding him unexpectedly in my midst.

'Did you call, sir?'

'Oh, there you are, Jeeves!'

'Precisely, sir.'

'Any ideas, Jeeves?'

'Why, yes, sir. Since we had our recent conversation I fancy I have found what may prove a solution. I do not wish to appear to be taking a liberty, sir, but I think that we have overlooked His Grace's potentialities as a source of revenue.'

Bicky laughed what I have sometimes seen described as a hollow, mocking laugh, a sort of bitter cackle from the back of the throat, rather like a gargle.

'I do not allude, sir,' explained Jeeves, 'to the possibility of inducing His Grace to part with money. I am taking the liberty of regarding His Grace in the light of an at present – if I may say so – useless property, which is capable of being developed.'

Bicky looked at me in a helpless kind of way. I'm bound to say I didn't get it myself.

'Couldn't you make it a bit easier, Jeeves?'

'In a nutshell, sir, what I mean is this: His Grace is, in a sense, a prominent personage. The inhabitants of this country, as no doubt you are aware, sir, are peculiarly addicted to shaking hands with prominent personages. It occurred to me that Mr Bickersteth or yourself might know of persons who would be willing to pay a small fee – let us say two dollars or three – for the privilege of an introduction, including handshake, to His Grace.'

Bicky didn't seem to think much of it.

'Do you mean to say that anyone would be mug enough to part with solid cash just to shake hands with my uncle?'

'I have an aunt, sir, who paid five shillings to a young fellow for bringing a moving-picture actor to tea at her house one Sunday. It gave her social standing among the neighbours.'

Bicky wavered.

'If you think it could be done – '

'I feel convinced of it, sir.'

'What do you think, Bertie?'

'I'm for it, old boy, absolutely. A very brainy wheeze.'

'Thank you, sir. Will there be anything further? Good night, sir.'

And he flitted out, leaving us to discuss details.

Until we started this business of floating old Chiswick as a money-making proposition I had never realized what a perfectly foul time those Stock Exchange fellows must have when the public isn't biting freely. Nowadays I read that bit they put in the financial reports about 'The market opened quietly' with a sympathetic eye, for, by Jove, it certainly opened quietly for us. You'd hardly believe how difficult it was to interest the public and make them take a flutter on the old boy. By the end of a week the only name we had on our list was a delicatessen-store keeper down in Bicky's part of the town, and as he wanted us to take it out in sliced ham instead of cash that didn't help much. There was a gleam of light when the brother of Bicky's pawnbroker offered ten dollars, money down, for an introduction to old Chiswick, but the deal fell through, owing to its turning out that the chap was an anarchist and intended to kick the old boy instead of shaking hands with him. At that, it took me the deuce of a time to persuade Bicky not to grab the cash and let things take their course. He seemed to regard the pawnbroker's brother rather as a sportsman and benefactor of his species than otherwise.

The whole thing, I'm inclined to think, would have been off if it hadn't been for Jeeves. There is no doubt that Jeeves is in a class of his own. In the matter of brain and resource I don't think I have ever met a chappie so supremely like mother made. He trickled into my room one morning with the good old cup of tea, and intimated that there was something doing.

'Might I speak to you with regard to that matter of His Grace, sir?'

'It's all off. We've decided to chuck it.'

'Sir?'

'It won't work. We can't get anybody to come.'

'I fancy I can arrange that aspect of the matter, sir.'

'Do you mean to say you've managed to get anybody?'

'Yes, sir. Eighty-seven gentlemen from Birdsburg, sir.'

I sat up in bed and spilt the tea.

'Birdsburg?'

'Birdsburg, Missouri, sir.'

'How did you get them?'

'I happened last night, sir, as you had intimated that you would be absent from home, to attend a theatrical performance, and entered into conversation between the acts with the occupant of the adjoining seat. I had observed that he was wearing a somewhat ornate decoration in his buttonhole, sir – a large blue button with the words "Boost for Birdsburg" upon it in red letters, scarcely a judicious addition to a gentleman's evening costume. To my surprise I noticed that the auditorium was full of persons similarly decorated. I ventured to inquire the explanation, and was informed that these gentlemen, forming a party of eighty-seven, are a convention from a town of the name of Birdsburg in the State of Missouri. Their visit, I gathered, was purely of a social and pleasurable nature, and my informant spoke at some length of the entertainments arranged for their stay in the city. It was when he related with a considerable amount of satisfaction and pride that a deputation of their number had been introduced to and had shaken hands with a well-known prize-fighter that it occurred to me to broach the subject of His Grace. To make a long story short, sir, I have arranged, subject to your approval, that the entire convention shall be presented to His Grace tomorrow afternoon.'

I was amazed.

'Eighty-seven, Jeeves! At how much a head?'

'I was obliged to agree to a reduction for quantity, sir. The terms finally arrived at were one hundred and fifty dollars for the party.'

I thought a bit.

'Payable in advance?'

'No, sir. I endeavoured to obtain payment in advance, but was not successful.'

'Well, anyway, when we get it I'll make it up to five hundred. Bicky'll never know. Do you suppose Mr Bickersteth would suspect anything, Jeeves, if I made it up to five hundred?'

'I fancy not, sir. Mr Bickersteth is an agreeable gentleman, but not bright.'

'All right, then. After breakfast run down to the bank and get me some money.'

'Yes, sir.'

'You know, you're a bit of a marvel, Jeeves.'

'Thank you, sir.'

'Right ho!'

'Very good, sir.'

When I took dear old Bicky aside in the course of the morning and told him what had happened he nearly broke down. He tottered into the sitting-room and buttonholed old Chiswick, who was reading the comic section of the morning paper with a kind of grim resolution.

'Uncle,' he said, 'are you doing anything special tomorrow afternoon? I mean to say, I've asked a few of my pals in to meet you, don't you know.'

The old boy cocked a speculative eye at him.

'There will be no reporters among them?'

'Reporters? Rather not. Why?'

'I refuse to be badgered by reporters. There were a number of adhesive young men who endeavoured to elicit from me my views on America while the boat was approaching the dock. I will not be subjected to this persecution again.'

'That'll be absolutely all right, Uncle. There won't be a newspaper man in the place.'

'In that case I shall be glad to make the acquaintance of your friends.'

'You'll shake hands with them, and so forth?'

'I shall naturally order my behaviour according to the accepted rules of civilized intercourse.'

Bicky thanked him heartily and came off to lunch with me at the club, where he babbled freely of hens, incubators, and other rotten things.

After mature consideration we had decided to unleash the Birdsburg contingent on the old boy ten at a time. Jeeves brought his theatre pal round to see us, and we arranged the whole thing with him. A very decent chappie, but rather inclined to collar the conversation and turn it in the direction of his home-town's new water-supply system. We settled that, as an hour was about all he would be likely to stand, each gang should consider itself entitled to seven minutes of the duke's society by Jeeves's stop-watch, and that when their time was up Jeeves should slide into the room and cough meaningly. Then we parted with what I believe are called mutual expressions of goodwill, the Birdsburg chappie extending a cordial invitation to us all to pop out some day and take a look at the new water-supply system, for which we thanked him.

Next day the deputation rolled in. The first shift consisted of the cove we had met and nine others almost exactly like him in

every respect. They all looked deuced keen and business-like, as
if from youth up they had been working in the office and catching
the boss's eye and what not. They shook hands with the old boy with
a good deal of apparent satisfaction – all except one chappie, who
seemed to be brooding about something – and then they stood off
and became chatty.

'What message have you for Birdsburg, duke?' asked our pal.

The old boy seemed a bit rattled.

'I have never been to Birdsburg.'

The chappie seemed pained.

'You should pay it a visit,' he said. 'The most rapidly growing city
in the country. Boost for Birdsburg!'

'Boost for Birdsburg!' said the other chappies reverently.

The chappie who had been brooding suddenly gave tongue.

'Say!'

He was a stout sort of well-fed cove with one of those determined
chins and a cold eye.

The assemblage looked at him.

'As a matter of business,' said the chappie – 'mind you, I'm not
questioning anybody's good faith, but, as a matter of strict business
– I think this gentleman here ought to put himself on record before
witnesses as stating that he really is a duke.'

'What do you mean, sir?' cried the old boy, getting purple.

'No offence, simply business. I'm not saying anything, mind you,
but there's one thing that seems kind of funny to me. This gentleman
here says his name's Mr Bickersteth, as I understand it. Well, if you're
the Duke of Chiswick, why isn't he Lord Percy Something? I've read
English novels, and I know all about it.'

'This is monstrous!'

'Now don't get hot under the collar. I'm only asking. I've a right to
know. You're going to take our money, so it's only fair that we should
see that we get our money's worth.'

The water-supply cove chipped in:

'You're quite right, Simms. I overlooked that when making the
agreement. You see, gentlemen, as business men we've a right to
reasonable guarantees of good faith. We are paying Mr Bickersteth
here a hundred and fifty dollars for this reception, and we naturally
want to know – '

Old Chiswick gave Bicky a searching look; then he turned to the
water-supply chappie. He was frightfully calm.

'I can assure you that I know nothing of this,' he said quite politely.
'I should be grateful if you would explain.'

'Well, we arranged with Mr Bickersteth that eighty-seven citizens of Birdsburg should have the privilege of meeting and shaking hands with you for a financial consideration mutually arranged, and what my friend Simms here means – and I'm with him – is that we have only Mr Bickersteth's word for it – and he is a stranger to us – that you are the Duke of Chiswick at all.'

Old Chiswick gulped.

'Allow me to assure you, sir,' he said in a rummy kind of voice, 'that I am the Duke of Chiswick.'

'Then that's all right,' said the chappie heartily. 'That was all we wanted to know. Let the thing go on.'

'I am sorry to say,' said old Chiswick, 'that it cannot go on. I am feeling a little tired. I fear I must ask to be excused.'

'But there are seventy-seven of the boys waiting round the corner at this moment, Duke, to be introduced to you.'

'I fear I must disappoint them.'

'But in that case the deal would have to be off.'

'That is a matter for you and my nephew to discuss.'

The chappie seemed troubled.

'You really won't meet the rest of them?'

'No!'

'Well, then, I guess we'll be going.'

They went out, and there was a pretty solid silence. Then old Chiswick turned to Bicky:

'Well?'

Bicky didn't seem to have anything to say.

'Was it true what that man said?'

'Yes, Uncle.'

'What do you mean by playing this trick?'

Bicky seemed pretty well knocked out, so I put in a word:

'I think you'd better explain the whole thing, Bicky, old top.'

Bicky's adam's apple jumped about a bit; then he started.

'You see, you had cut off my allowance, Uncle, and I wanted a bit of money to start a chicken farm. I mean to say it's an absolute cert if you once get a bit of capital. You buy a hen, and it lays an egg every day of the week, and you sell the egg, say, seven for twenty-five cents. Keep of hen costs nothing. Profit practically – '

'What is all this nonsense about hens? You led me to suppose you were a substantial business man.'

'Old Bicky rather exaggerated, sir,' I said, helping the chappie out. 'The fact is, the poor old lad is absolutely dependent on that remittance of yours, and when you cut it off, don't you know, he was pretty solidly in the soup, and had to think of some way of closing in on a bit of the ready pretty quick. That's why we thought of this hand-shaking scheme.'

Old Chiswick foamed at the mouth.

'So you have lied to me! You have deliberately deceived me as to your financial status!'

'Poor old Bicky didn't want to go to that ranch,' I explained. 'He doesn't like cows and horses, but he rather thinks he would be hot stuff among the hens. All he wants is a bit of capital. Don't you think it would be rather a wheeze if you were to – '

'After what has happened? After this – this deceit and foolery? Not a penny!'

'But – '

'Not a penny!'

There was a respectful cough in the background.

'If I might make a suggestion, sir?'

Jeeves was standing on the horizon, looking devilish brainy.

'Go ahead, Jeeves!' I said.

'I would merely suggest, sir, that if Mr Bickersteth is in need of a little ready money, and is at a loss to obtain it elsewhere, he might secure the sum he requires by describing the occurrences of this afternoon for the Sunday issue of one of the more spirited and enterprising newspapers.'

'By Jove!' I said.

'By George!' said Bicky.

'Great heavens!' said old Chiswick.

'Very good, sir,' said Jeeves.

Bicky turned to old Chiswick with a gleaming eye.

'Jeeves is right! I'll do it! The *Chronicle* would jump at it. They eat that sort of stuff.'

Old Chiswick gave a kind of moaning howl.

'I absolutely forbid you, Francis, to do this thing!'

'That's all very well,' said Bicky, wonderfully braced, 'but if I can't get the money any other way – '

'Wait! Er – wait, my boy! You are so impetuous! We might arrange something.'

'I won't go to that bally ranch.'

'No, no! No, no, my boy! I would not suggest it. I would not for a moment suggest it. I – I think – ' He seemed to have a bit of a struggle with himself. 'I – I think that, on the whole it would be best if you returned with me to England. I – I might – in fact, I think I see my way to doing – to – I might be able to utilize your services in some secretarial position.'

'I shouldn't mind that.'

'I should not be able to offer you a salary, but, as you know, in English political life the unpaid secretary is a recognized figure – '

'The only figure I'll recognize,' said Bicky firmly, 'is five hundred quid a year, paid quarterly.'

'My dear boy!'

'Absolutely!'

'But your recompense, my dear Francis, would consist in the unrivalled opportunities you would have, as my secretary, to gain experience, to accustom yourself to the intricacies of political life, to – in fact, you would be in an exceedingly advantageous position.'

'Five hundred a year!' said Bicky, rolling it round his tongue. 'Why, that would be nothing to what I could make if I started a chicken farm. It stands to reason. Suppose you have a dozen hens. Each of the hens has a dozen chickens. After a bit the chickens grow up and have a dozen chickens each themselves, and then they all start laying eggs! There's a fortune in it. You can get anything you like for eggs in America. Fellows keep them on ice for years and years, and don't sell them till they fetch about a dollar a whirl. You don't think I'm going to chuck a future like this for anything under five hundred o' goblins a year – what?'

A look of anguish passed over old Chiswick's face, then he seemed to be resigned to it. 'Very well, my boy,' he said.

'What ho!' said Bicky. 'All right, then.'

'Jeeves,' I said. Bicky had taken the old boy off to dinner to celebrate, and we were alone. 'Jeeves, this has been one of your best efforts.'

'Thank you, sir.'

'It beats me how you do it.'

'Yes, sir?'

'The only trouble is you haven't got much out of it yourself.'

'I fancy Mr Bickersteth intends – I judge from his remarks – to signify his appreciation of anything I have been fortunate enough to do to assist him, at some later date when he is in a more favourable position to do so.'

'It isn't enough, Jeeves!'

'Sir?'

It was a wrench, but I felt it was the only possible thing to be done.

'Bring my shaving things.'

A gleam of hope shone in the man's eye, mixed with doubt.

'You mean, sir?'

'And shave off my moustache.'

There was a moment's silence. I could see the fellow was deeply moved.

'Thank you very much indeed, sir,' he said, in a low voice.

5

THE AUNT AND THE SLUGGARD

Now that it's all over, I may as well admit that there was a time during the affair of Rockmetteller Todd when I thought that Jeeves was going to let me down. Silly of me, of course, knowing him as I do, but that is what I thought. It seemed to me that the man had the appearance of being baffled.

The Rocky Todd business broke loose early one morning in spring. I was in bed, restoring the physique with my usual nine hours of the dreamless, when the door flew open and somebody prodded me in the lower ribs and began to shake the bedclothes in an unpleasant manner. And after blinking a bit and generally pulling myself together, I located Rocky, and my first impression was that it must be some horrid dream.

Rocky, you see, lived down on Long Island somewhere, miles away from New York; and not only that, but he had told me himself more than once that he never got up before twelve, and seldom earlier than one. Constitutionally the laziest young devil in America, he had hit on a walk in life which enabled him to go the limit in that direction. He was a poet. At least, he wrote poems when he did anything; but most of his time, as far as I could make out, he spent in a sort of trance. He told me once that he could sit on a fence, watching a worm and wondering what on earth it was up to for hours at a stretch.

He had his scheme of life worked out to a fine point. About once a month he would take three days writing a few poems; the other three hundred and twenty-nine days of the year he rested. I didn't know there was enough money in poetry to support a chappie, even in the way in which Rocky lived; but it seems that, if you stick to exhortations to young men to lead the strenuous life and don't shove in any rhymes, American editors fight for the stuff. Rocky showed me one of his things once. It began:

Be!
Be!
   The past is dead,
   Tomorrow is not born.
   Be today!
Today!
   Be with every nerve,
   With every fibre,
   With every drop of your red blood!
Be!
Be!

There were three more verses, and the thing was printed opposite the frontispiece of a magazine with a sort of scroll round it, and a picture in the middle of a fairly nude chappie with bulging muscles giving the rising sun the glad eye. Rocky said they gave him a hundred dollars for it, and he stayed in bed till four in the afternoon for over a month.

As regarded the future he was pretty solid, owing to the fact that he had a moneyed aunt tucked away somewhere in Illinois. It's a curious thing how many of my pals seem to have aunts and uncles who are their main source of supply. There is Bicky for one, with his uncle the Duke of Chiswick; Corky, who, until things went wrong, looked to Alexander Worple, the bird specialist, for sustenance. And I shall be telling you a story shortly of a dear old friend of mine, Oliver Sipperley, who had an aunt in Yorkshire. These things cannot be mere coincidence. They must be meant. What I'm driving at is that Providence seems to look after the chumps of this world; and, personally, I'm all for it. I suppose the fact is that, having been snootered from infancy upwards by my own aunts, I like to see that it is possible for these relatives to have a better and a softer side.

However, this is more or less of a side-track. Coming back to Rocky, what I was saying was that he had this aunt in Illinois; and, as he had been named Rockmetteller after her (which in itself, you might say, entitled him to substantial compensation) and was her only nephew, his position looked pretty sound. He told me that when he did come into the money he meant to do no work at all, except perhaps an occasional poem recommending the young man with life opening out before him with all its splendid possibilities to light a pipe and shove his feet up on the mantelpiece.

And this was the man who was prodding me in the ribs in the grey dawn!

'Read this, Bertie!' babbled old Rocky.

I could just see that he was waving a letter or something equally foul in my face. 'Wake up and read this!'

I can't read before I've had my morning tea and a cigarette. I groped for the bell.

Jeeves came in, looking as fresh as a dewy violet. It's a mystery to me how he does it.

'Tea, Jeeves.'

'Very good, sir.'

I found that Rocky was surging round with his beastly letter again.

'What is it?' I said. 'What on earth's the matter?'

'Read it!'

'I can't. I haven't had my tea.'

'Well, listen then.'

'Who's it from?'

'My aunt.'

At this point I fell asleep again. I woke to hear him saying:

'So what on earth am I to do?'

Jeeves flowed in with the tray, like some silent stream meandering over its mossy bed; and I saw daylight.

'Read it again, Rocky, old top,' I said. 'I want Jeeves to hear it. Mr Todd's aunt has written him a rather rummy letter, Jeeves, and we want your advice.'

'Very good, sir.'

He stood in the middle of the room, registering devotion to the cause, and Rocky started again:

'My dear Rockmetteller,

'I have been thinking things over for a long while, and I have come to the conclusion that I have been very thoughtless to wait so long before doing what I have made up my mind to do now.'

'What do you make of that, Jeeves?'

'It seems a little obscure at present, sir, but no doubt it becomes clearer at a later point in the communication.'

'Proceed, old scout,' I said, champing my bread and butter.

'You know how all my life I have longed to visit New York and see for myself the wonderful gay life of which I have read so much. I fear that now it will be impossible for me to fulfil my dream. I am old and worn out. I seem to have no strength left in me.'

'Sad, Jeeves, what?'
'Extremely, sir.'
'Sad nothing!' said Rocky. 'It's sheer laziness. I went to see her last Christmas and she was bursting with health. Her doctor told me himself that there was nothing wrong with her whatever. But she will insist that she's a hopeless invalid, so he has to agree with her. She's got a fixed idea that the trip to New York would kill her; so, though it's been her ambition all her life to come here, she stays where she is.'
'Rather like the chappie whose heart was "in the Highlands a-chasing of the deer", Jeeves?'
'The cases are in some respects parallel, sir.'
'Carry on, Rocky, dear boy.'

'So I have decided that, if I cannot enjoy all the marvels of the city myself, I can at least enjoy them through you. I suddenly thought of this yesterday after reading a beautiful poem in the Sunday paper about a young man who had longed all his life for a certain thing and won it in the end only when he was too old to enjoy it. It was very sad, and it touched me.'

'A thing,' interpolated Rocky bitterly, 'that I've not been able to do in ten years.'

'As you know, you will have my money when I am gone; but until now I have never been able to see my way to giving you an allowance. I have now decided to do so – on one condition. I have written to a firm of lawyers in New York, giving them instructions to pay you quite a substantial sum each month. My one condition is that you live in New York and enjoy yourself as I have always wished to do. I want you to be my representative, to spend this money for me as I should do myself. I want you to plunge into the gay, prismatic life of New York. I want you to be the life and soul of brilliant supper parties.

'Above all, I want you – indeed, I insist on this – to write me letters at least once a week, giving me a full description of all you are doing and all that is going on in the city, so that I may enjoy at second-hand what my wretched health prevents my enjoying for myself. Remember that I shall expect full details, and that no detail is too trivial to interest.
Your affectionate Aunt,
    Isabel Rockmetteller.'

'What about it?' said Rocky.

'What about it?' I said.

'Yes. What on earth am I going to do?'

It was only then that I really got on to the extremely rummy attitude of the chappie, in view of the fact that a quite unexpected mess of good cash had suddenly descended on him from a blue sky. To my mind it was an occasion for the beaming smile and the joyous whoop; yet here the man was, looking and talking as if Fate had swung on his solar plexus. It amazed me.

'Aren't you bucked?' I said.

'Bucked!'

'If I were in your place I should be frightfully braced. I consider this pretty soft for you.'

He gave a kind of yelp, stared at me for a moment, and then began to talk of New York in a way that reminded me of Jimmy Mundy, the reformer bloke. Jimmy had just come to New York on a hit-the-trail campaign, and I had popped in at Madison Square Garden a couple of days before, for half an hour or so, to hear him. He had certainly told New York some pretty straight things about itself, having apparently taken a dislike to the place, but, by Jove, you know, dear old Rocky made him look like a publicity agent for the old metrop!

'Pretty soft!' he cried. 'To have to come and live in New York! To have to leave my little cottage and take a stuffy, smelly, overheated hole of an apartment in this Heaven-forsaken, festering Gehenna. To have to mix night after night with a mob who think that life is a sort of St Vitus's dance, and imagine that they're having a good time because they're making enough noise for six and drinking too much for ten. I loathe New York, Bertie. I wouldn't come near the place if I hadn't got to see editors occasionally. There's a blight on it. It's got moral delirium tremens. It's the limit. The very thought of staying more than a day in it makes me sick. And you call this thing pretty soft for me!'

I felt rather like Lot's friends must have done when they dropped in for a quiet chat and their genial host began to criticize the Cities of the Plain. I had no idea old Rocky could be so eloquent.

'It would kill me to have to live in New York,' he went on. 'To have to share the air with six million people! To have to wear stiff collars and decent clothes all the time! To – ' He started. 'Good Lord! I suppose I should have to dress for dinner in the evenings. What a ghastly notion!'

I was shocked, absolutely shocked.

'My dear chap!' I said, reproachfully.

'Do you dress for dinner every night, Bertie?'

'Jeeves,' I said coldly. 'How many suits of evening clothes have we?'

'We have three suits of full evening dress, sir; two dinner jackets – '

'Three.'

'For practical purposes two only, sir. If you remember, we cannot wear the third. We have also seven white waistcoats.'

'And shirts?'

'Four dozen, sir.'

'And white ties?'

'The first two shallow shelves in the chest of drawers are completely filled with our white ties, sir.'

I turned to Rocky.

'You see?'

The chappie writhed like an electric fan.

'I won't do it! I can't do it! I'll be hanged if I'll do it! How on earth can I dress up like that? Do you realize that most days I don't get out of my pyjamas till five in the afternoon, and then I just put on an old sweater?'

I saw Jeeves wince, poor chap. This sort of revelation shocked his finest feelings.

'Then, what are you going to do about it?' I said.

'That's what I want to know.'

'You might write and explain to your aunt.'

'I might – if I wanted her to get round to her lawyer's in two rapid leaps and cut me out of her will.'

I saw his point.

'What do you suggest, Jeeves?' I said.

Jeeves cleared his throat respectfully.

'The crux of the matter would appear to be, sir, that Mr Todd is obliged by the conditions under which the money is delivered into his possession to write Miss Rockmetteller long and detailed letters relating to his movements, and the only method by which this can be accomplished, if Mr Todd adheres to his expressed intention of remaining in the country, is for Mr Todd to induce some second party to gather the actual experiences which Miss Rockmetteller wishes reported to her, and to convey these to him in the shape of a careful report, on which it would be possible for him, with the aid of his imagination, to base the suggested correspondence.'

Having got which off the old diaphragm, Jeeves was silent. Rocky looked at me in a helpless sort of way. He hasn't been brought up on Jeeves as I have, and he isn't on to his curves.

'Could he put it a little clearer, Bertie?' he said. 'I thought at the start it was going to make sense, but it kind of flickered. What's the idea?'

'My dear old man, perfectly simple. I knew we could stand on Jeeves. All you've got to do is to get somebody to go round the town for you and take a few notes, and then you work the notes up into letters. That's it, isn't it, Jeeves?'

'Precisely, sir.'

The light of hope gleamed in Rocky's eyes. He looked at Jeeves in a startled way, dazed by the man's vast intellect.

'But who would do it?' he said. 'It would have to be a pretty smart sort of man, a man who would notice things.'

'Jeeves!' I said. 'Let Jeeves do it.'

'But would he?'

'You would do it, wouldn't you, Jeeves?'

For the first time in our long connexion I observed Jeeves almost smile. The corner of his mouth curved quite a quarter of an inch, and for a moment his eye ceased to look like a meditative fish's.

'I should be delighted to oblige, sir. As a matter of fact, I have already visited some of New York's places of interest on my evening out, and it would be most enjoyable to make a practice of the pursuit.'

'Fine! I know exactly what your aunt wants to hear about, Rocky. She wants an earful of cabaret stuff. The place you ought to go to first, Jeeves, is Reigelheimers's. It's on Forty-second Street. Anybody will show you the way.'

Jeeves shook his head.

'Pardon me, sir. People are no longer going to Reigelheimer's. The place at the moment is Frolics on the Roof.'

'You see?' I said to Rocky. 'Leave it to Jeeves. He knows.'

It isn't often that you find an entire group of your fellow-humans happy in this world; but our little circle was certainly an example of the fact that it can be done. We were all full of beans. Everything went absolutely right from the start.

Jeeves was happy, partly because he loves to exercise his giant brain, and partly because he was having a corking time among the bright lights. I saw him one night at the Midnight Revels. He was sitting at a table on the edge of the dancing floor, doing himself remarkably well with a fat cigar. His face wore an expression of austere benevolence, and he was making notes in a small book.

As for the rest of us, I was feeling pretty good, because I was fond of old Rocky and glad to be able to do him a good turn. Rocky was perfectly contented, because he was still able to sit on fences in his pyjamas and watch worms. And, as for the aunt, she seemed tickled to death. She was getting Broadway at pretty long range, but it seemed to be hitting her just right. I read one of her letters to Rocky, and it was full of life.

But then Rocky's letters, based on Jeeve's notes, were enough to buck anybody up. It was rummy when you came to think of it. There was I, loving the life, while the mere mention of it gave Rocky a tired feeling; yet here is a letter I wrote home to a pal of mine in London:

Dear Freddie,

Well, here I am in New York. It's not a bad place. I'm not having a bad time. Everything's not bad. The cabarets aren't bad. Don't know when I shall be back. How's everybody? Cheerio!

Yours,

Bertie.

P.S. – Seen old Ted lately?

Not that I cared about old Ted; but if I hadn't dragged him in I couldn't have got the confounded thing on to the second page.

Now here's old Rocky on exactly the same subject:

Dearest Aunt Isabel,

How can I ever thank you enough for giving me the opportunity to live in this astounding city! New York seems more wonderful every day.

Fifth Avenue is at its best, of course, just now. The dresses are magnificent!

Wads of stuff about the dresses. I didn't know Jeeves was such an authority.

I was out with some of the crowd at the Midnight Revels the other night. We took in a show first, after a little dinner at a new place on Forty-third Street. We were quite a gay party. Georgie Cohan looked in about midnight and got off a good story about Willie Collier. Fred Stone could only stay a minute, but Doug. Fairbanks did all sorts of stunts and made us roar. Ed. Wynn was there, and Laurette Taylor showed up with a party. The show at the Revels is quite good. I am enclosing a programme.

Last night a few of us went round to Frolics on the Roof –

And so on and so forth, yards of it. I suppose it's the artistic temperament or something. What I mean is, it's easier for a chappie who's used to writing poems and that sort of tosh to put a bit of a punch into a letter than it is for a fellow like me. Anyway, there's no doubt that Rocky's correspondence was hot stuff. I called Jeeves in and congratulated him.

'Jeeves, you're a wonder!'

'Thank you, sir.'

'How you notice everything at these places beats me. I couldn't tell you a thing about them, except that I've had a good time.'

'It's just a knack, sir.'

'Well, Mr Todd's letters ought to brace Miss Rockmetteller all right, what?'

'Undoubtedly, sir,' agreed Jeeves.

And, by Jove, they did! They certainly did, by George! What I mean to say is, I was sitting in the apartment one afternoon, about a month after the thing had started, smoking a cigarette and resting the old bean, when the door opened and the voice of Jeeves burst the silence like a bomb.

It wasn't that he spoke loud. He has one of those soft, soothing voices that slide through the atmosphere like the note of a far-off sheep. It was what he said that made me leap like a young gazelle.

'Miss Rockmetteller!'

And in came a large, solid female.

The situation floored me. I'm not denying it. Hamlet must have felt much as I did when his father's ghost bobbed up in the fairway. I'd come to look on Rocky's aunt as such a permanency at her own home that it didn't seem possible that she could really be here in New York. I stared at her. Then I looked at Jeeves. He was standing there in an attitude of dignified detachment, the chump, when, if ever he should have been rallying round the young master, it was now.

Rocky's aunt looked less like an invalid than anyone I've ever seen, except my Aunt Agatha. She had a good deal of Aunt Agatha about her, as a matter of fact. She looked as if she might be deucedly dangerous if put upon; and something seemed to tell me that she would certainly regard herself as put upon if she ever found out the game which poor old Rocky had been pulling on her.

'Good afternoon,' I managed to say.

'How do you do?' she said. 'Mr Cohan?'

'Er – no.'

'Mr Fred Stone?'

'Not absolutely. As a matter of fact, my name's Wooster – Bertie Wooster.'

She seemed disappointed. The fine old name of Wooster appeared to mean nothing in her life.

'Isn't Rockmetteller home?' she said. 'Where is he?'

She had me with the first shot. I couldn't think of anything to say. I couldn't tell her that Rocky was down in the country, watching worms.

There was the faintest flutter of sound in the background. It was the respectful cough with which Jeeves announces that he is about to speak without having been spoken to.

'If you remember, sir, Mr Todd went out in the automobile with a party earlier in the afternoon.'

'So he did, Jeeves; so he did,' I said, looking at my watch. 'Did he say when he would be back?'

'He gave me to understand, sir, that he would be somewhat late in returning.'

He vanished; and the aunt took the chair which I'd forgotten to offer her. She looked at me in rather a rummy way. It was a nasty look. It made me feel as if I were something the dog had brought in and intended to bury later on, when he had time. My own Aunt Agatha, back in England, has looked at me in exactly the same way many a time, and it never fails to make my spine curl.

'You seem very much at home here, young man. Are you a great friend of Rockmetteller's?'

'Oh, yes, rather!'

She frowned as if she had expected better things of old Rocky.

'Well, you need to be,' she said, 'the way you treat his flat as your own!'

I give you my word, this quite unforeseen slam simply robbed me of the power of speech. I'd been looking on myself in the light of the dashing host, and suddenly to be treated as an intruder jarred me. It wasn't, mark you, as if she had spoken in a way to suggest that she considered my presence in the place as an ordinary social call. She obviously looked on me as a cross between a burglar and the plumber's man come to fix the leak in the bathroom. It hurt her – my being there.

At this juncture, with the conversation showing every sign of being about to die in awful agonies, an idea came to me. Tea – the good old stand-by.

'Would you care for a cup of tea?' I said.

'Tea?'

She spoke as if she had never heard of the stuff.

'Nothing like a cup after a journey,' I said. 'Bucks you up! Puts a bit of zip into you. What I mean is, restores you, and so on, don't you know. I'll go and tell Jeeves.'

I tottered down the passage to Jeeves's lair. The man was reading the evening paper as if he hadn't a care in the world.

'Jeeves,' I said, 'we want some tea.'

'Very good, sir.'

'I say, Jeeves, this is a bit thick, what?'

I wanted sympathy, don't you know – sympathy and kindness. The old nerve centres had had the deuce of a shock.

'She's got the idea this place belongs to Mr Todd. What on earth put that into her head?'

Jeeves filled the kettle with a restrained dignity.

'No doubt because of Mr Todd's letters, sir,' he said. 'It was my suggestion, sir, if you remember, that they should be addressed from this apartment in order that Mr Todd should appear to possess a good central residence in the city.'

I remembered. We had thought it a brainy scheme at the time.

'Well, it's dashed awkward, you know, Jeeves. She looks on me as an intruder. By Jove! I suppose she thinks I'm someone who hangs about here, touching Mr Todd for free meals and borrowing his shirts.'

'Extremely probable, sir.'

'It's pretty rotten, you know.'

'Most disturbing, sir.'

'And there's another thing: What are we to do about Mr Todd? We've got to get him up here as soon as ever we can. When you have brought the tea you had better go out and send him a telegram, telling him to come up by the next train.'

'I have already done so, sir. I took the liberty of writing the message and dispatching it by the lift attendant.'

'By Jove, you think of everything, Jeeves!'

'Thank you, sir. A little buttered toast with the tea? Just so, sir. Thank you.'

I went back to the sitting-room. She hadn't moved an inch. She was still bolt upright on the edge of her chair, gripping her umbrella like a hammer-thrower. She gave me another of those looks as I came in. There was no doubt about it; for some reason she had taken a dislike to me. I suppose because I wasn't George M. Cohan. It was a bit hard on a chap.

'This is a surprise, what?' I said, after about five minutes' restful silence, trying to crank the conversation up again.

'What is a surprise?'

'Your coming here, don't you know, and so on.'

She raised her eyebrows and drank me in a bit more through her glasses.

'Why is it surprising that I should visit my only nephew?' she said.

'Oh, rather,' I said. 'Of course! Certainly. What I mean is – '

Jeeves projected himself into the room with the tea. I was jolly glad to see him. There's nothing like having a bit of business arranged for one when one isn't certain of one's lines. With the teapot to fool about with I felt happier.

'Tea, tea, tea – what! What!' I said.

It wasn't what I had meant to say. My idea had been to be a good deal more formal, and so on. Still, it covered the situation. I poured her out a cup. She sipped it and put the cup down with a shudder.

'Do you mean to say, young man,' she said, frostily, 'that you expect me to drink this stuff?'

'Rather! Bucks you up, you know.'

'What do you mean by the expression, "Bucks you up"?'

'Well, makes you full of beans, you know. Makes you fizz.'

'I don't understand a word you say. You're English, aren't you?'

I admitted it. She didn't say a word. And she did it in a way that made it worse than if she had spoken for hours. Somehow it was brought home to me that she didn't like Englishmen, and that if she had had to meet an Englishman I was the one she'd have chosen last.

Conversation languished once more after that.

Then I tried again. I was becoming more convinced every moment that you can't make a real lively *salon* with a couple of people, especially if one of them lets it go a word at a time.

'Are you comfortable at your hotel?' I said.

'At which hotel?'

'The hotel you're staying at.'

'I am not staying at an hotel.'

'Stopping with friends – what?'

'I am naturally stopping with my nephew.'

I didn't get it for the moment; then it hit me.

'What! Here?' I gurgled.

'Certainly! Where else should I go?'

The full horror of the situation rolled over me like a wave. I couldn't see what on earth I was to do. I couldn't explain that this wasn't Rocky's flat without giving the poor old chap away hopelessly, because she would then ask me where he did live, and then he would be right in the soup. I was trying to recover from the shock when she spoke again.

'Will you kindly tell my nephew's manservant to prepare my room? I wish to lie down.'

'Your nephew's manservant?'

'The man you call Jeeves. If Rockmetteller has gone for an automobile ride there is no need for you to wait for him. He will naturally wish to be alone with me when he returns.'

I found myself tottering out of the room. The thing was too much for me. I crept into Jeeves's den.

'Jeeves!' I whispered.

'Sir?'

'Mix me a b-and-s, Jeeves. I feel weak.'

'Very good, sir.'

'This is getting thicker every minute, Jeeves.'

'Sir?'

'She thinks you're Mr Todd's man. She thinks the whole place is his, and everything in it. I don't see what you're to do, except stay on and keep it up. We can't say anything or she'll get on to the whole thing, and I don't want to let Mr Todd down. By the way, Jeeves, she wants you to prepare her bed.'

He looked wounded.

'It is hardly my place, sir – '

'I know – I know. But do it as a personal favour to me. If you come to that, it's hardly my place to be flung out of the flat like this and have to go to an hotel, what?'

'Is it your intention to go to an hotel, sir? What will you do for clothes?'

'Good Lord! I hadn't thought of that. Can you put a few things in a bag when she isn't looking, and sneak them down to me at the St Aurea?'

'I will endeavour to do so, sir.'

'Well, I don't think there's anything more, is there? Tell Mr Todd where I am when he gets here.'

'Very good, sir.'

I looked round the place. The moment of parting had come. I felt sad. The whole thing reminded me of one of those melodramas where they drive chappies out of the old homestead into the snow.

'Goodbye, Jeeves,' I said.

'Goodbye, sir.'

And I staggered out.

You know, I rather think I agree with those poet-and-philosopher Johnnies who insist that a fellow ought to be devilish pleased if he has a bit of trouble. All that stuff about being refined by suffering, you know. Suffering does give a chap a sort of broader and more sympathetic outlook. It helps you to understand other people's misfortunes if you've been through the same thing yourself.

As I stood in my lonely bedroom at the hotel, trying to tie my white tie myself, it struck me for the first time that there must be whole squads of chappies in the world who had to get along without a man to look after them. I'd always thought of Jeeves as a kind of natural phenomenon; but, by Jove! of course, when you come to think of it, there must be quite a lot of fellows who have to press their own clothes themselves, and haven't got anybody to bring them tea in the morning, and so on. It was rather a solemn thought, don't you know. I mean to say, ever since then I've been able to appreciate the frightful privations the poor have to stick.

I got dressed somehow. Jeeves hadn't forgotten a thing in his packing. Everything was there, down to the final stud. I'm not sure this didn't make me feel worse. It kind of deepened the pathos. It was like what somebody or other wrote about the touch of a vanished hand.

I had a bit of dinner somewhere and went to a show of some kind; but nothing seemed to make any difference. I simply hadn't the heart to go on to supper anywhere. I just went straight up to bed. I don't know when I've felt so rotten. Somehow I found myself moving about the room softly, as if there had been a death in the family. If I had anybody to talk to I should have talked in a whisper; in fact, when the telephone-bell rang I answered in such a sad, hushed voice that the fellow at the other end of the wire said 'Hallo!' five times, thinking he hadn't got me.

It was Rocky. The poor old scout was deeply agitated.

'Bertie! Is that you, Bertie? Oh, gosh! I'm having a time!'

'Where are you speaking from?'

'The Midnight Revels. We've been here an hour, and I think we're a fixture for the night. I've told Aunt Isabel I've gone out to call up a friend to join us. She's glued to a chair, with this-is-the-life written all over her, taking it in through the pores. She loves it, and I'm nearly crazy.'

'Tell me all, old top,' I said.

'A little more of this,' he said, 'and I shall sneak quietly off to the river and end it all. Do you mean to say you go through this sort of thing every night, Bertie, and enjoy it? It's simply infernal! I was just snatching a wink of sleep behind the bill of fare just now when about a million yelling girls swooped down, with toy balloons. There are two orchestras here, each trying to see if it can't play louder than the other. I'm a mental and physical wreck. When your telegram arrived I was just lying down for a quiet pipe, with a sense of absolute peace stealing over me. I had to get dressed and sprint two miles to catch the train. It nearly gave me heart-failure; and on top of that I almost got brain fever inventing lies to tell Aunt Isabel. And then I had to cram myself into these confounded evening clothes of yours.'

I gave a sharp wail of agony. It hadn't struck me till then that Rocky was depending on my wardrobe to see him through.

'You'll ruin them!'

'I hope so,' said Rocky in the most unpleasant way. His troubles seemed to have had the worst effect on his character. 'I should like to get back at them somehow; they've given me a bad enough time. They're about three sizes too small, and something's apt to give at any moment. I wish to goodness it would, and give me a chance to breathe. I haven't breathed since half past seven. Thank Heaven, Jeeves managed to get out and buy me a collar that fitted, or I should be a strangled corpse by now! It was touch and go till the stud broke. Bertie, this is pure Hades! Aunt Isabel keeps on urging me to dance. How on earth can I dance when I don't know a soul to dance with? And how the deuce could I, even if I knew every girl in the place? It's taking big chances even to move in these trousers. I had to tell her I've hurt my ankle. She keeps asking me when Cohan and Stone are going to turn up; and it's simply a question of time before she discovers that Stone is sitting two tables away. Something's got to be done, Bertie! You've got to think up some way of getting me out of this mess. It was you who got me into it.'

'Me! What do you mean?'

'Well, Jeeves, then. It's all the same. It was you who suggested leaving it to Jeeves. It was those letters I wrote from his notes that did the mischief. I made them too good. My aunt's just been telling me about it. She says she had resigned herself to ending her life where she was, and then my letters began to arrive, describing the joys of New York; and they stimulated her to such an extent that she pulled herself together and made the trip. She seems to think she's had some miraculous kind of faith cure. I tell you I can't stand it, Bertie! It's got to end!'

'Can't Jeeves think of anything?'

'No. He just hangs round, saying: "Most disturbing, sir!" A fat lot of help that is!'

'Well, old lad,' I said, 'after all, it's far worse for me than it is for you. You've got a comfortable home and Jeeves. And you're saving a lot of money.'

'Saving money? What do you mean – saving money?'

'Why, the allowance your aunt was giving you. I suppose she's paying all the expenses now, isn't she?'

'Certainly she is: but she's stopped the allowance. She wrote the lawyers tonight. She says that, now she's in New York, there is no necessity for it to go on, as we shall always be together, and it's simpler for her to look after that end of it. I tell you, Bertie, I've examined the darned cloud with a microscope, and if it's got a silver lining it's some little dissembler!'

'But, Rocky, old top, it's too bally awful! You've no notion of what I'm going through in this beastly hotel, without Jeeves. I must get back to the flat.'

'Don't come near the flat!'

'But it's my own flat.'

'I can't help that. Aunt Isabel doesn't like you. She asked me what you did for a living. And when I told her you didn't do anything she said she thought as much, and that you were a typical specimen of a useless and decaying aristocracy. So if you think you have made a hit, forget it. Now I must be going back, or she'll be coming out here after me. Goodbye.'

Next morning Jeeves came round. It was all so home-like when he floated noiselessly into the room that I nearly broke down.

'Good morning, sir,' he said. 'I have brought a few more of your personal belongings.'

He began to unstrap the suitcase he was carrying.

'Did you have any trouble sneaking them away?'

'It was not easy, sir. I had to watch my chance. Miss Rockmetteller is a remarkably alert lady.'

'You know, Jeeves, say what you like – this *is* a bit thick, isn't it?'

'The situation is certainly one that has never before come under my notice, sir. I have brought the heather-mixture suit, as the climatic conditions are congenial. Tomorrow, if not prevented, I will endeavour to add the brown lounge with the faint green twill.'

'It can't go on – this sort of thing – Jeeves.'

'We must hope for the best, sir.'

'Can't you think of anything to do?'

'I have been giving the matter considerable thought, sir, but so far without success. I am placing three silk shirts – the dove-coloured, the light blue, and the mauve – in the first long drawer, sir.'

'You don't mean to say you can't think of anything, Jeeves?'

'For the moment, sir, no. You will find a dozen handkerchiefs and the tan socks in the upper drawer on the left.' He strapped the suit-case and put it on a chair. 'A curious lady, Miss Rockmetteller, sir.'

'You understate it, Jeeves.'

He gazed meditatively out of the window.

'In many ways, sir, Miss Rockmetteller reminds me of an aunt of mine who resides in the south-east portion of London. Their temperaments are much alike. My aunt has the same taste for the pleasures of the great city. It is a passion with her to ride in hansom cabs, sir. Whenever the family take their eyes off her she escapes from the house and spends the day riding about in cabs. On several occasions she has broken into the children's savings bank to secure the means to enable her to gratify this desire.'

'I love to have these little chats with you about your female relatives, Jeeves,' I said coldly, for I felt that the man had let me down, and I was fed up with him. 'But I don't see what all this has got to do with my trouble.'

'I beg your pardon, sir. I am leaving a small assortment of your neckties on the mantelpiece, sir, for you to select according to your preference. I should recommend the blue with the red domino pattern, sir.'

Then he streamed imperceptibly towards the door and flowed silently out.

I've often heard that fellows after some great shock or loss have a habit, after they've been on the floor for a while wondering what hit them, of picking themselves up and piecing themselves together, and sort of taking a whirl at beginning a new life. Time, the great healer, and Nature adjusting itself and so on and so forth. There's a lot in it. I know, because in my own case, after a day or two of what you might call prostration, I began to recover. The frightful loss of Jeeves made any thought of pleasure more or less a mockery, but at least I found that I was able to have a dash at enjoying life again. What I mean is, I braced up to the extent of going round the cabarets once more, so as to try to forget, if only for the moment.

New York's a small place when it comes to the part of it that wakes up just as the rest is going to bed, and it wasn't long before my tracks began to cross old Rocky's. I saw him once at Peale's, and again at Frolics on the Roof. There wasn't anybody with him either time except the aunt, and, though he was trying to look as if he had struck the ideal life, it wasn't difficult for me, knowing the circumstances, to see that beneath the mask the poor chap was suffering. My heart bled for the fellow. At least, what there was of it that wasn't bleeding for myself bled for him. He had the air of one who was about to crack under the strain.

It seemed to me that the aunt was looking slightly upset also. I took it that she was beginning to wonder when the celebrities were going to surge round, and what had suddenly become of all those wild, careless spirits Rocky used to mix with in his letters. I didn't blame her. I had only read a couple of his letters, but they certainly gave the impression that poor old Rocky was by way of being the hub of New York night life, and that, if by any chance he failed to show up at a cabaret, the management said, 'What's the use?' and put up the shutters.

The next two nights I didn't come across them, but the night after that I was sitting by myself at the Maison Pierre when somebody tapped me on the shoulder-blade, and I found Rocky standing beside me, with a sort of mixed expression of wistfulness and apoplexy on his face. How the man had contrived to wear my evening clothes so many times without disaster was a mystery to me. He confided later that early in the proceedings he had slit the waistcoat up the back and that that had helped a lot.

For a moment I had the idea that he had managed to get away from his aunt for the evening; but, looking past him, I saw that she was in again. She was at a table over by the wall, looking at me as if I were something the management ought to be complained to about.

'Bertie, old scout,' said Rocky, in a quiet, sort of crushed voice, 'we've always been pals, haven't we? I mean, you know I'd do you a good turn if you asked me.'

'My dear old lad,' I said. The man had moved me.

'Then, for Heaven's sake, come over and sit at our table for the rest of the evening.'

Well, you know, there are limits to the sacred claims of friendship.

'My dear chap,' I said, 'you know I'd do anything in reason; but – '

'You must come, Bertie. You've got to. Something's got to be done to divert her mind. She's brooding about something. She's been like that for the last two days. I think she's beginning to suspect. She can't understand why we never seem to meet anyone I know at these joints. A few nights ago I happened to run into two newspaper men I used to know fairly well. That kept me going for a while. I introduced them to Aunt Isabel as David Belasco and Jim Corbett, and it went well. But the effect has worn off now, and she's beginning to wonder again.

Something's got to be done, or she will find out everything, and if she does I'd take a nickel for my chance of getting a cent from her later on. So, for the love of Mike, come across to our table and help things along.'

I went along. One has to rally round a pal in distress. Aunt Isabel was sitting bolt upright, as usual. It certainly did seem as if she had lost a bit of the zest with which she had started out to explore Broadway. She looked as if she had been thinking a good deal about rather unpleasant things.

'You've met Bertie Wooster, Aunt Isabel?' said Rocky.

'I have.'

'Take a seat, Bertie.' said Rocky.

And so the merry party began. It was one of those jolly, happy, bread-crumbling parties where you cough twice before you speak, and then decide not to say it after all. After we had had an hour of this wild dissipation, Aunt Isabel said she wanted to go home. In the light of what Rocky had been telling me, this struck me as sinister. I had gathered that at the beginning of her visit she had had to be dragged home with ropes.

It must have hit Rocky the same way, for he gave me a pleading look.

'You'll come along, won't you, Bertie, and have a drink at the flat?'

I had a feeling that this wasn't in the contract, but there wasn't anything to be done. It seemed brutal to leave the poor chap alone with the woman, so I went along.

Right from the start, from the moment we stepped into the taxi, the feeling began to grow that something was about to break loose. A massive silence prevailed in the corner where the aunt sat, and, though Rocky, balancing himself on the little seat in front, did his best to supply dialogue, we weren't a chatty party.

I had a glimpse of Jeeves as we went into the flat, sitting in his lair, and I wished I could have called to him to rally round. Something told me that I was about to need him.

The stuff was on the table in the sitting-room. Rocky took up the decanter.

'Say when, Bertie.'

'Stop!' barked the aunt, and he dropped it.

I caught Rocky's eye as he stooped to pick up the ruins. It was the eye of one who sees it coming.

'Leave it there, Rockmetteller!' said Aunt Isabel; and Rocky left it there.

'The time has come to speak,' she said. 'I cannot stand idly by and see a young man going to perdition!'

Poor old Rocky gave a sort of gurgle, a kind of sound rather like the whisky had made running out of the decanter on to my carpet.

'Eh?' he said, blinking.

The aunt proceeded.

'The fault,' she said, 'was mine. I had not then seen the light. But now my eyes are open. I see the hideous mistake I have made. I shudder at the thought of the wrong I did you, Rockmetteller, by urging you into contact with this wicked city.'

I saw Rocky grope feebly for the table. His fingers touched it, and a look of relief came into the poor chappie's face. I understood his feelings.

'But when I wrote you that letter, Rockmetteller, instructing you to go to the city and live its life, I had not had the privilege of hearing Mr Mundy speak on the subject of New York.'

'Jimmy Mundy!' I cried.

You know how it is sometimes when everything seems all mixed up and you suddenly get a clue. When she mentioned Jimmy Mundy I began to understand more or less what had happened. I'd seen it happen before. I remember, back in England, the man I had before Jeeves sneaked off to a meeting on his evening out and came back and denounced me in front of a crowd of chappies I was giving a bit of supper to as a useless blot on the fabric of Society.

The aunt gave me a withering up and down.

'Yes; Jimmy Mundy!' she said. 'I am surprised at a man of your stamp having heard of him. There is no music, there are no drunken, dancing men, no shameless, flaunting women at his meetings; so for you they would have no attraction. But for others, less dead in sin, he has his message. He has come to save New York from itself; to force it – in his picturesque phrase – to hit the trail. It was three days ago, Rockmetteller, that I first heard him. It was an accident that took me to his meeting. How often in this life a mere accident may shape our whole future!

'You had been called away by that telephone message from Mr Belasco; so you could not take me to the Hippodrome, as we had arranged. I asked your manservant, Jeeves, to take me there. The man has very little intelligence. He seems to have misunderstood me. I am thankful that he did. He took me to what I subsequently learned was Madison Square Garden, where Mr Mundy is holding his meetings. He escorted me to a seat and then left me. And it was not till the meeting had begun that I discovered the mistake which had been made. My seat was in the middle of a row. I could not leave without inconveniencing a great many people, so I remained.'

She gulped.

'Rockmetteller, I have never been so thankful for anything else. Mr Mundy was wonderful! He was like some prophet of old, scouring the sins of the people. He leaped about in a frenzy of inspiration till I feared he would do himself an injury. Sometimes he expressed himself in a somewhat odd manner, but every word carried conviction. He showed me New York in its true colours. He showed me the vanity and wickedness of sitting in gilded haunts of vice, eating lobster when decent people should be in bed.

'He said that the tango and the fox-trot were devices of the devil to drag people down into the Bottomless Pit. He said that there was more sin in ten minutes with a negro banjo orchestra than in all the ancient revels of Nineveh and Babylon. And when he stood on one leg and pointed right at where I was sitting and shouted "This means you!" I could have sunk through the floor. I came away a changed woman. Surely you must have noticed the change in me, Rockmetteller? You must have seen that I was no longer the careless, thoughtless person who had urged you to dance in those places of wickedness?'

Rocky was holding on to the table as if it was his only friend.

'Yes,' he stammered; 'I – I thought something was wrong.'

'Wrong? Something was right! Everything was right! Rockmetteller, it is not too late for you to be saved. You have only sipped of the evil cup. You have not drained it. It will be hard at first, but you will find that you can do it if you fight with a stout heart against the glamour and fascination of this dreadful city. Won't you, for my sake, try, Rockmetteller? Won't you go to the country tomorrow and begin the struggle? Little by little, if you use your will – '

I can't help thinking it must have been that word 'will' that roused dear old Rocky like a trumpet call. It must have brought home to him the realization that a miracle had come off and saved him from being cut out of Aunt Isabel's. At any rate, as she said it he perked up, let go of the table, and faced her with gleaming eyes.

'Do you want me to go to the country, Aunt Isabel?'

'Yes.'

'To live in the country?'

'Yes, Rockmetteller.'

'Stay in the country all the time? Never come to New York?'

'Yes, Rockmetteller; I mean just that. It is the only way. Only there can you be safe from temptation. Will you do it, Rockmetteller? Will you – for my sake?'

Rocky grabbed the table again. He seemed to draw a lot of encouragement from that table.

'I will,' he said.

'Jeeves,' I said. It was next day, and I was back in the old flat, lying in the old armchair, with my feet upon the good old table. I had just come from seeing dear old Rocky off to his country cottage, and an hour before he had seen his aunt off to whatever hamlet it was that she was the curse of; so we were alone at last. 'Jeeves, there's no place like home – what?'

'Very true, sir.'

'The jolly old roof-tree, and all sort of thing – what?'

'Precisely, sir.'

I lit another cigarette.

'Jeeves.'

'Sir?'

'Do you know, at one point in the business I really thought you were baffled.'

'Indeed, sir?'

'When did you get the idea of taking Miss Rockmetteller to the meeting? It was pure genius!'

'Thank you, sir. It came to me a little suddenly, one morning when I was thinking of my aunt, sir.'

'Your aunt? The hansom cab one?'

'Yes, sir. I recollected that, whenever we observed one of her attacks coming on, we used to send for the clergyman of the parish. We always found that if he talked to her a while of higher things it diverted her mind from hansom cabs. It occurred to me that the same treatment might prove efficacious in the case of Miss Rockmetteller.'

I was stunned by the man's resource.

'It's brain,' I said; 'pure brain! What do you do to get like that, Jeeves? I believe you must eat a lot of fish, or something. Do you eat a lot of fish, Jeeves?'

'No, sir.'

'Oh, well, then, it's just a gift, I take it; and if you aren't born that way there's no use worrying.'

'Precisely, sir,' said Jeeves. 'If I might make the suggestion, sir, I should not continue to wear your present tie. The green shade gives you a slightly bilious air. I should strongly advocate the blue with the red domino pattern instead, sir.'

'All right, Jeeves,' I said humbly. 'You know!'

6

THE RUMMY AFFAIR OF OLD BIFFY

'Jeeves,' I said, emerging from the old tub, 'rally round.'

'Yes, sir.'

I beamed on the man with no little geniality. I was putting in a week or two in Paris at the moment, and there's something about Paris that always makes me feel fairly full of *espièglerie* and *joie de vivre*.

'Lay out our gent's medium-smart raiment, suitable for Bohemian revels,' I said. 'I am lunching with an artist bloke on the other side of the river.'

'Very good, sir.'

'And if anybody calls for me, Jeeves, say that I shall be back towards the quiet evenfall.'

'Yes, sir. Mr Biffen rang up on the telephone while you were in your bath.'

'Mr Biffen? Good heavens!'

Amazing how one's always running across fellows in foreign cities – coves, I mean, whom you haven't seen for ages and would have betted weren't anywhere in the neighbourhood. Paris was the last place where I should have expected to find old Biffy popping up. There was a time when he and I had been lads about town together, lunching and dining together practically every day; but some eighteen months back his old godmother had died and left him that place in Herefordshire, and he had retired there to wear gaiters and prod cows in the ribs and generally be the country gentleman and landed proprietor. Since then I had hardly seen him.

'Old Biffy in Paris? What's he doing here?'

'He did not confide in me, sir,' said Jeeves – a trifle frostily, I thought. It sounded somehow as if he didn't like Biffy. And yet they had always been matey enough in the old days.

'Where's he staying?'

'At the Hotel Avenida, Rue du Colisée, sir. He informed me that he was about to take a walk and would call this afternoon.'

'Well, if he comes when I'm out, tell him to wait. And now, Jeeves, *mes gants, mon chapeau, et le whangee de monsieur*. I must be popping.'

It was such a corking day and I had so much time in hand that near the Sorbonne I stopped my cab, deciding to walk the rest of the way. And I had hardly gone three steps and a half when there on the pavement before me stood old Biffy in person. If I had completed the last step I should have rammed him.

'Biffy!' I cried. 'Well, well, well!'

He peered at me in a blinking kind of way, rather like one of his Herefordshire cows prodded unexpectedly while lunching.

'Bertie!' he gurgled, in a devout sort of tone. 'Thank God!' He clutched my arm. 'Don't leave me, Bertie. I'm lost.'

'What do you mean, lost?'

'I came out for a walk and suddenly discovered after a mile or two that I didn't know where on earth I was. I've been wandering round in circles for hours.'

'Why didn't you ask the way?'

'I can't speak a word of French.'

'Well, why didn't you call a taxi?'

'I suddenly discovered I'd left all my money at my hotel.'

'You could have taken a cab and paid it when you got to the hotel.'

'Yes, but I suddenly discovered, dash it, that I'd forgotten its name.'

And there in a nutshell you have Charles Edward Biffen. As vague and woollen-headed a blighter as ever bit a sandwich. Goodness knows – and my Aunt Agatha will bear me out in this – I'm no master-mind myself; but compared with Biffy I'm one of the great thinkers of all time.

'I'd give a shilling,' said Biffy wistfully, 'to know the name of that hotel.'

'You can owe it me. Hotel Avenida, Rue du Colisée.'

'Bertie! This is uncanny. How the deuce did you know?'

'That was the address you left with Jeeves this morning.'

'So it was. I had forgotten.'

'Well, come along and have a drink and then I'll put you in a cab and send you home. I'm engaged for lunch, but I've plenty of time.'

We drifted to one of the eleven cafés which jostled each other along the street and I ordered restoratives.

'What on earth are you doing in Paris?' I asked.

'Bertie, old man,' said Biffy solemnly, 'I came here to try and forget.'

'Well, you've certainly succeeded.'

'You don't understand. The fact is, Bertie, old lad, my heart is broken. I'll tell you the whole story.'

'No, I say!' I protested. But he was off.

'Last year,' said Biffy, 'I buzzed over to Canada to do a bit of salmon fishing.'

I ordered another. If this was going to be a fish-story, I needed stimulants.

'On the liner going to New York I met a girl.' Biffy made a sort of curious gulping noise not unlike a bulldog trying to swallow half a cutlet in a hurry so as to be ready for the other half. 'Bertie, old man, I can't describe her. I simply can't describe her.'

This was all to the good.

'She was wonderful! We used to walk on the boat-deck after dinner. She was on the stage. At least, sort of.'

'How do you mean, sort of?'

'Well, she had posed for artists and been a mannequin in a big dressmaker's and all that sort of thing, don't you know. Anyway, she had saved up a few pounds and was on her way to see if she could get a job in New York. She told me all about herself. Her father ran a milk-walk in Clapham. Or it may have been Cricklewood. At least, it was either a milk-walk or a boot-shop.'

'Easily confused.'

'What I'm trying to make you understand,' said Biffy, 'is that she came of good, sturdy, respectable middle-class stock. Nothing flashy about her. The sort of wife any man might have been proud of.'

'Well, whose wife was she?'

'Nobody's. That's the whole point of the story. I wanted her to be mine, and I lost her.'

'Had a quarrel, you mean?'

'No, I don't mean we had a quarrel. I mean I literally lost her. The last I ever saw of her was in the Customs sheds at New York. We were behind a pile of trunks, and I had just asked her to be my wife, and she had just said she would and everything was perfectly splendid, when a most offensive blighter in a peaked cap came up to talk about some cigarettes which he had found at the bottom of my trunk and which I had forgotten to declare. It was getting pretty late by then, for we hadn't docked till about ten-thirty, so I told Mabel to go on to her hotel and I would come round next day and take her to lunch. And since then I haven't set eyes on her.'

'You mean she wasn't at the hotel?'

'Probably she was. But – '

'You don't mean you never turned up?'

'Bertie, old man,' said Biffy, in an overwrought kind of way, 'for Heaven's sake don't keep trying to tell me what I mean and what I don't mean! Let me tell this my own way, or I shall get all mixed up and have to go back to the beginning.'

'Tell it your own way,' I said hastily.

'Well, then, to put it in a word, Bertie, I forgot the name of the hotel. By the time I'd done half an hour's heavy explaining about those cigarettes my mind was a blank. I had an idea I had written the name down somewhere, but I couldn't have done, for it wasn't on any of the papers in my pocket. No, it was no good. She was gone.'

'Why didn't you make inquiries?'

'Well, the fact is, Bertie, I had forgotten her name.'

'Oh, no, dash it!' I said. This seemed a bit too thick even for Biffy. 'How could you forget her name? Besides, you told it me a moment ago. Muriel or something.'

'Mabel,' corrected Biffy coldly. 'It was her surname I'd forgotten. So I gave it up and went to Canada.'

'But half a second,' I said. 'You must have told her your name. I mean, if you couldn't trace her, she could trace you.'

'Exactly. That's what makes it all seem so infernally hopeless. She knows my name and where I live and everything, but I haven't heard a word from her. I suppose, when I didn't turn up at the hotel, she took it that that was my way of hinting delicately that I had changed my mind and wanted to call the thing off.'

'I suppose so,' I said. There didn't seem anything else to suppose. 'Well, the only thing to do is to whizz around and try to heal the wound, what? How about dinner tonight, winding up at the Abbaye or one of those places?'

Biffy shook his head.

'It wouldn't be any good. I've tried it. Besides, I'm leaving on the four o'clock train. I have a dinner engagement tomorrow with a man who's nibbling at that house of mine in Herefordshire.'

'Oh, are you trying to sell that place? I thought you liked it.'

'I did. But the idea of going on living in that great, lonely barn of a house after what has happened appals me, Bertie. So when Sir Roderick Glossop came along – '

'Sir Roderick Glossop! You don't mean the loony-doctor?'

'The great nerve specialist, yes. Why, do you know him?'

It was a warm day, but I shivered.

'I was engaged to his daughter for a week or two,' I said, in a hushed voice. The memory of that narrow squeak always made me feel faint.

'Has he a daughter?' said Biffy absently.

'He has. Let me tell you about – '

'Not just now, old man,' said Biffy, getting up. 'I ought to be going back to my hotel to see about my packing.'

Which, after I had listened to his story, struck me as pretty low-down. However, the longer you live, the more you realize that the good old sporting spirit of give-and-take has practically died out in our midst. So I boosted him into a cab and went off to lunch.

It can't have been more than ten days after this that I received a nasty shock while getting outside my morning tea and toast. The English papers had arrived, and Jeeves was just drifting out of the room after depositing *The Times* by my bedside, when, as I idly turned the pages in search of the sporting section, a paragraph leaped out and hit me squarely in the eyeball.

As follows:-

FORTHCOMING MARRIAGES
MR C.E. BIFFEN AND MISS GLOSSOP

The engagement is announced between Charles Edward, only son of the late Mr E.C. Biffen, and Mrs Biffen, of 11 Penslow Square, Mayfair, and Honoria Jane Louise, only daughter of Sir Roderick and Lady Glossop, of 6b Harley Street, W.

'Great Scott!' I exclaimed.

'Sir?' said Jeeves, turning at the door.

'Jeeves, you remember Miss Glossop?'

'Very vividly, sir.'

'She's engaged to Mr Biffen!'

'Indeed, sir?' said Jeeves. And, with not another word, he slid out. The blighter's calm amazed and shocked me. It seemed to indicate that there must be a horrible streak of callousness in him. I mean to say, it wasn't as if he didn't know Honoria Glossop.

I read the paragraph again. A peculiar feeling it gave me. I don't know if you have ever experienced the sensation of seeing the announcement of the engagement of a pal of yours to a girl whom you were only saved from marrying yourself by the skin of your teeth. It induces a sort of – well, it's difficult to describe it exactly; but I should imagine a fellow would feel much the same if he happened to be strolling through the jungle with a boyhood chum and met a tigress or a jaguar, or what not, and managed to shin up a tree and looked down and saw the friend of his youth vanishing into the undergrowth in the animal's slavering jaws. A sort of profound, prayerful relief, if you know what I mean, blended at the same time with a pang of pity. What I'm driving at is that, thankful as I was that I hadn't had to marry Honoria myself, I was sorry to see a real good chap like old Biffy copping it. I sucked down a spot of tea and began to brood over the business.

Of course, there are probably fellows in the world – tough, hardy blokes with strong chins and glittering eyes – who could get engaged to this Glossop menace and like it, but I knew perfectly well that Biffy was not one of them. Honoria, you see, is one of those robust, dynamic girls with the muscles of a welterweight and a laugh like a squadron of cavalry charging over a tin bridge. A beastly thing to have to face over the breakfast table. Brainy, moreover. The sort of girl who reduces you to pulp with sixteen sets of tennis and a few rounds of golf and then comes down to dinner as fresh as a daisy, expecting you to take an intelligent interest in Freud. If I had been engaged to her another week, her old father would have had one more patient on his books; and Biffy is much the same quiet sort of peaceful, inoffensive bird as me. I was shocked, I tell you, shocked.

And, as I was saying, the thing that shocked me most was Jeeves's frightful lack of proper emotion. The man happening to float in at this juncture, I gave him one more chance to show some human sympathy.

'You got the name correctly, didn't you, Jeeves?' I said. 'Mr Biffen is going to marry Honoria Glossop, the daughter of the old boy with the egg-like head and the eyebrows.'

'Yes, sir. Which suit would you wish me to lay out this morning?'

And this, mark you, from the man who, when I was engaged to the Glossop, strained every fibre in his brain to extricate me. It beat me. I couldn't understand it.

'The blue with the red twill,' I said coldly. My manner was marked, and I meant him to see that he had disappointed me sorely.

About a week later I went back to London, and scarcely had I got settled in the old flat when Biffy blew in. One glance was enough to tell me that the poisoned wound had begun to fester. The man did not look bright. No, there was no getting away from it, not bright. He had that kind of stunned, glassy expression which I used to see on my own face in the shaving-mirror during my brief engagement to the Glossop pestilence. However, if you don't want to be one of the What is Wrong With This Picture brigade, you must observe the conventions, so I shook his hand as warmly as I could.

'Well, well, old man,' I said. 'Congratulations.'

'Thanks,' said Biffy wanly, and there was rather a weighty silence.

'Bertie,' said Biffy, after the silence had lasted about three minutes.

'Hallo?'

'Is it really true – ?'

'What?'

'Oh, nothing,' said Biffy, and conversation languished again. After about a minute and a half he came to the surface once more.

'Bertie.'

'Still here, old thing. What is it?'

'I say, Bertie, is it really true that you were once engaged to Honoria?'

'It is.'

Biffy coughed.

'How did you get out – I mean, what was the nature of the tragedy that prevented the marriage?'

'Jeeves worked it. He thought out the entire scheme.'

'I think, before I go,' said Biffy, thoughtfully, 'I'll just step into the kitchen and have a word with Jeeves.'

I felt that the situation called for complete candour.

'Biffy, old egg,' I said, 'as man to man, do you want to oil out of this thing?'

'Bertie, old cork,' said Biffy earnestly, 'as one friend to another I do.'

'Then why the dickens did you ever get into it?'

'I don't know. Why did you?'

'I – well, it sort of happened.'

'And it sort of happened with me. You know how it is when your heart's broken. A kind of lethargy comes over you. You get absent-minded and cease to exercise proper precautions, and the first thing you know you're for it. I don't know how it happened, old man, but there it is. And what I want you to tell me is, what's the procedure?'

'You mean, how does a fellow edge out?'

'Exactly. I don't want to hurt anybody's feelings, Bertie, but I can't go through with this thing. The shot is not on the board. For about a day and a half I thought it might be all right, but now – You remember that laugh of hers?'

'I do.'

'Well, there's that, and then all this business of never letting a fellow alone – improving his mind and so forth – '

'I know. I know.'

'Very well, then. What do you recommend? What did you mean when you said that Jeeves worked a scheme?'

'Well, you see, old Sir Roderick, who's a loony-doctor and nothing but a loony-doctor, however much you may call him a nerve specialist, discovered that there was a modicum of insanity in my family. Nothing serious. Just one of my uncles. Used to keep rabbits in his bedroom. And the old boy came to lunch here to give me the once-over, and Jeeves arranged matters so that he went away firmly convinced that I was off my onion.'

'I see,' said Biffy thoughtfully. 'The trouble is there isn't any insanity in my family.'

'None?'

It seemed to me almost incredible that a fellow could be such a perfect chump as dear old Biffy without a bit of assistance.

'Not a loony on the list,' he said gloomily. 'It's just my luck. The old boy's coming to lunch with me tomorrow, no doubt to test me as he did you. And I never felt saner in my life.'

I thought for a moment. The idea of meeting Sir Roderick again gave me a cold shivery feeling; but when there is a chance of helping a pal we Woosters have no thought of self.

'Look here, Biffy,' I said, 'I'll tell you what. I'll roll up for that lunch. It may easily happen that when he finds you are a pal of mine he will forbid the banns right away and no more questions asked.'

'Something in that,' said Biffy, brightening. 'Awfully sporting of you, Bertie.'

'Oh, not at all,' I said. 'And meanwhile I'll consult Jeeves. Put the whole thing up to him and ask his advice. He's never failed me yet.'

Biffy pushed off, a good deal braced, and I went into the kitchen.

'Jeeves,' I said, 'I want your help once more. I've just been having a painful interview with Mr Biffen.'

'Indeed, sir?'

'It's like this,' I said, and told him the whole thing.

It was rummy, but I could feel him freezing from the start. As a rule, when I call Jeeves into conference on one of these little problems, he's all sympathy and bright ideas; but not today.

'I fear, sir,' he said, when I had finished, 'it is hardly my place to intervene in a private matter affecting – '

'Oh, come!'

'No, sir. It would be taking a liberty.'

'Jeeves,' I said, tackling the blighter squarely, 'what have you got against old Biffy?'

'I, sir?'

'Yes, you.'

'I assure you, sir!'

'Oh, well, if you don't want to chip in and save a fellow-creature, I suppose I can't make you. But let me tell you this. I am now going back to the sitting-room, and I am going to put in some very tense thinking. You'll look pretty silly when I come and tell you that I've got Mr Biffen out of the soup without your assistance. Extremely silly you'll look.'

'Yes, sir. Shall I bring you a whisky-and-soda, sir?'

'No. Coffee! Strong and black. And if anybody wants to see me, tell 'em that I'm busy and can't be disturbed.'

An hour later I rang the bell.

'Jeeves,' I said with hauteur.

'Yes, sir?'

'Kindly ring Mr Biffen up on the phone and say that Mr Wooster presents his compliments and that he has got it.'

I was feeling more than a little pleased with myself next morning as I strolled round to Biffy's. As a rule the bright ideas you get overnight have a trick of not seeming quite so frightfully fruity when you examine them by the light of day; but this one looked as good at breakfast as it had done before dinner. I examined it narrowly from every angle, and I didn't see how it could fail.

A few days before, my Aunt Emily's son Harold had celebrated his sixth birthday; and, being up against the necessity of weighing in with a present of some kind, I had happened to see in a shop in the Strand a rather sprightly little gadget, well calculated in my opinion to amuse the child and endear him to one and all. It was a bunch of flowers in a sort of holder ending in an ingenious bulb attachment which, when pressed, shot about a pint and a half of pure spring water into the face of anyone who was ass enough to sniff at it. It seemed to me just the thing to please the growing mind of a kid of six, and I had rolled round with it.

But when I got to the house I found Harold sitting in the midst of a mass of gifts so luxurious and costly that I simply hadn't the crust to contribute a thing that had set me back a mere elevenpence-ha'penny; so with rare presence of mind – for we Woosters can think quick on occasion – I wrenched my Uncle James's card off a toy aeroplane, substituted my own, and trousered the squirt, which I took away with me. It had been lying around in my flat ever since, and it seemed to me that the time had come to send it into action.

'Well?' said Biffy anxiously, as I curveted into his sitting-room.

The poor old bird was looking pretty green about the gills. I recognized the symptoms. I had felt much the same myself when waiting for Sir Roderick to turn up and lunch with me. How the deuce people who have anything wrong with their nerves can bring themselves to chat with that man, I can't imagine; and yet he has the largest practice in London. Scarcely a day passes without his having to sit on somebody's head and ring for the attendant to bring the strait-waistcoat: and his outlook on life has become so jaundiced through constant association with coves who are picking straws out of their hair that I was convinced that Biffy had merely got to press the bulb and nature would do the rest.

So I patted him on the shoulder and said: 'It's all right, old man!'

'What does Jeeves suggest?' asked Biffy eagerly.

'Jeeves doesn't suggest anything.'

'But you said it was all right.'

'Jeeves isn't the only thinker in the Wooster home, my lad. I have taken over your little problem, and I can tell you at once that I have the situation well in hand.'

'You?' said Biffy.

His tone was far from flattering. It suggested a lack of faith in my abilities, and my view was that an ounce of demonstration would be worth a ton of explanation. I shoved the bouquet at him.

'Are you fond of flowers, Biffy?' I said.

'Eh?'

'Smell these.'

Biffy extended the old beak in a careworn sort of way, and I pressed the bulb as per printed instructions on the label.

I do like getting my money's worth. Elevenpence-ha'penny the thing had cost me, and it would have been cheap at double. The advertisement on the outside of the box had said that its effects were 'indescribably ludicrous', and I can testify that it was no over-statement. Poor old Biffy leaped three feet in the air and smashed a small table.

'There!' I said.

The old egg was a trifle incoherent at first, but he found words fairly soon and began to express himself with a good deal of warmth.

'Calm yourself, laddie,' I said, as he paused for breath. 'It was no mere jest to pass an idle hour. It was a demonstration. Take this, Biffy, with an old friend's blessing, refill the bulb, shove it into Sir

Roderick's face, press firmly, and leave the rest to him. I'll guarantee that in something under three seconds the idea will have dawned on him that you are not required in his family.'

Biffy stared at me.

'Are you suggesting that I squirt Sir Roderick?'

'Absolutely. Squirt him good. Squirt as you have never squirted before.'

'But – '

He was still yammering at me in a feverish sort of way when there was a ring at the front-door bell.

'Good Lord!' cried Biffy, quivering like a jelly. 'There he is. Talk to him while I go and change my shirt.'

I had just time to refill the bulb and shove it beside Biffy's plate, when the door opened and Sir Roderick came in. I was picking up the fallen table at the moment, and he started talking brightly to my back.

'Good afternoon. I trust I am not – Mr Wooster!'

I'm bound to say I was not feeling entirely at my ease. There is something about the man that is calculated to strike terror into the stoutest heart. If ever there was a bloke at the very mention of whose name it would be excusable for people to tremble like aspens, that bloke is Sir Roderick Glossop. He has an enormous bald head, all the hair which ought to be on it seeming to have run into his eyebrows, and his eyes go through you like a couple of Death Rays.

'How are you, how are you, how are you?' I said, overcoming a slight desire to leap backwards out of the window. 'Long time since we met, what?'

'Nevertheless, I remember you most distinctly, Mr Wooster.'

'That's fine,' I said. 'Old Biffy asked me to come and join you in mangling a bit of lunch.'

He waggled the eyebrows at me.

'Are you a friend of Charles Biffen?'

'Oh, rather. Been friends for years and years.'

He drew in his breath sharply, and I could see that Biffy's stock had dropped several points. His eye fell on the floor, which was strewn with things that had tumbled off the upset table.

'Have you had an accident?'

'Nothing serious,' I explained. 'Old Biffy had some sort of fit or seizure just now and knocked over the table.'

'A fit!'

'Or seizure.'

'Is he subject to fits?'

I was about to answer, when Biffy hurried in. He had forgotten to brush his hair, which gave him a wild look, and I saw the old boy direct a keen glance at him. It seemed to me that what you might call the preliminary spade-work had been most satisfactorily attended to and that the success of the good old bulb could be in no doubt whatever.

Biffy's man came in with the nose-bags and we sat down to lunch.

It looked at first as though the meal was going to be one of those complete frosts which occur from time to time in the career of a constant luncher-out. Biffy, a very C-3 host, contributed nothing to the feast of reason and flow of soul beyond an occasional hiccup, and every time I started to pull a nifty, Sir Roderick swung round on me with such a piercing stare that it stopped me in my tracks. Fortunately, however, the second course consisted of a chicken fricassee of such outstanding excellence that the old boy, after wolfing a plateful, handed up his dinner-pail for a second instalment and became almost genial.

'I am here this afternoon, Charles,' he said, with what practically amounted to bonhomie, 'on what I might describe as a mission. Yes, a mission. This is most excellent chicken.'

'Glad you like it,' mumbled old Biffy.

'Singularly toothsome,' said Sir Roderick, pronging another half ounce. 'Yes, as I was saying, a mission. You young fellows nowadays are, I know, content to live in the centre of the most wonderful metropolis the world has seen, blind and indifferent to its many marvels. I should be prepared – were I a betting man, which I am not – to wager a considerable sum that you have never in your life visited even so historic a spot as Westminster Abbey. Am I right?'

Biffy gurgled something about always having meant to.

'Nor the Tower of London.'

'No, nor the Tower of London.'

'And there exists at this very moment, not twenty minutes by cab from Hyde Park Corner, the most supremely absorbing and educational collection of objects, both animate and inanimate, gathered from the four corners of the Empire, that has ever been assembled in England's history. I allude to the British Empire Exhibition now situated at Wembley.'

'A fellow told me one about Wembley yesterday,' I said, to help on the cheery flow of conversation. 'Stop me if you've heard it before. Chap goes up to deaf chap outside the Exhibition and says, "Is this Wembley?" "Hey?" says deaf chap. "Is this Wembley?" says chap. "Hey?" says deaf chap. "Is this Wembley?" says chap. "No, Thursday," says deaf chap. Ha, ha, I mean, what?'

The merry laughter froze on my lips. Sir Roderick sort of just waggled an eyebrow in my direction and I saw that it was back to the basket for Bertram. I never met a man who had such a knack of making a fellow feel like a waste-product.

'Have you yet paid a visit to Wembley, Charles?' he asked. 'No? Precisely as I suspected. Well, that is the mission on which I am here this afternoon. Honoria wishes me to take you to Wembley. She says it will broaden your mind, in which view I am at one with her. We will start immediately after luncheon.'

Biffy cast an imploring look at me.

'You'll come too, Bertie?'

There was such agony in his eyes that I only hesitated for a second. A pal is a pal. Besides, I felt that, if only the bulb fulfilled the high expectations I had formed of it, the merry expedition would be cancelled in no uncertain manner.

'Oh, rather,' I said.

'We must not trespass on Mr Wooster's good nature,' said Sir Roderick, looking pretty puff-faced.

'Oh, that's all right,' I said. 'I've been meaning to go to the good old Exhibish for a long time. I'll slip home and change my clothes and pick you up here in my car.'

There was a silence. Biffy seemed too relieved at the thought of not having to spend the afternoon alone with Sir Roderick to be capable of speech, and Sir Roderick was registering silent disapproval. And then he caught sight of the bouquet by Biffy's plate.

'Ah, flowers,' he said. 'Sweet peas, if I am not in error. A charming plant, pleasing alike to the eye and the nose.'

I caught Biffy's eye across the table. It was bulging, and a strange light shone in it.

'Are you fond of flowers, Sir Roderick?' he croaked.

'Extremely.'

'Smell these.'

Sir Roderick dipped his head and sniffed. Biffy's fingers closed slowly over the bulb. I shut my eyes and clutched the table.

'Very pleasant,' I heard Sir Roderick say. 'Very pleasant indeed.'

I opened my eyes, and there was Biffy leaning back in his chair with a ghastly look, and the bouquet on the cloth beside him. I realized what had happened. In that supreme crisis of his life, with his whole happiness depending on a mere pressure of the fingers, Biffy, the poor spineless fish, had lost his nerve. My closely reasoned scheme had gone phut.

Jeeves was fooling about with the geraniums in the sitting-room window-box when I got home.

'They make a very nice display, sir,' he said, cocking a paternal eye at the things.

'Don't talk to me about flowers,' I said. 'Jeeves, I know now how a general feels when he plans out some great scientific movement and his troops let him down at the eleventh hour.'

'Indeed, sir?'

'Yes,' I said, and told him what had happened.

He listened thoughtfully.

'A somewhat vacillating and changeable young gentleman, Mr Biffen,' was his comment when I had finished. 'Would you be requiring me for the remainder of the afternoon, sir?'

'No, I'm going to Wembley. I just came back to change and get the car. Produce some fairly durable garments which can stand getting squashed by the many-headed, Jeeves, and then phone to the garage.'

'Very good, sir. The grey cheviot lounge will, I fancy, be suitable. Would it be too much if I asked you to give me a seat in the car, sir? I had thought of going to Wembley myself this afternoon.'

'Eh? Oh, all right.'

'Thank you very much, sir.'

I got dressed, and we drove round to Biffy's flat. Biffy and Sir Roderick got in at the back and Jeeves climbed into the front seat next to me. Biffy looked so ill-attuned to an afternoon's pleasure that my heart bled for the blighter and I made one last attempt to appeal to Jeeves's better feelings.

'I must say, Jeeves,' I said, 'I'm dashed disappointed in you.'

'I am sorry to hear that, sir.'

'Well, I am. Dashed disappointed. I do think you might rally round. Did you see Mr Biffen's face?'

'Yes, sir.'

'Well, then.'

'If you will pardon my saying so, sir, Mr Biffen has surely only himself to thank if he has entered upon matrimonial obligations which do not please him.'

'You're talking absolute rot, Jeeves. You know as well as I do that Honoria Glossop is an Act of God. You might just as well blame a fellow for getting run over by a truck.'

'Yes, sir.'

'Absolutely yes. Besides, the poor ass wasn't in a condition to resist. He told me all about it. He had lost the only girl he had ever loved, and you know what a man's like when that happens to him.'

'How was that, sir?'

'Apparently he fell in love with some girl on the boat going over to New York, and they parted at the Customs sheds, arranging to meet next day at her hotel. Well, you know what Biffy's like. He forgets his own name half the time. He never made a note of the address, and it passed clean out of his mind. He went about in a sort of trance, and suddenly woke up to find that he was engaged to Honoria Glossop.'

'I did not know of this, sir.'

'I don't suppose anybody knows of it except me. He told me when I was in Paris.'

'I should have supposed it would have been feasible to make inquiries, sir.'

'That's what I said. But he had forgotten her name.'

'That sounds remarkable, sir.'

'I said that too. But it's a fact. All he remembered was that her Christian name was Mabel. Well, you can't go scouring New York for a girl named Mabel, what?'

'I appreciate the difficulty, sir.'

'Well, there it is, then.'

'I see, sir.'

We had got into a mob of vehicles outside the Exhibition by this time, and, some tricky driving being indicated, I had to suspend the conversation. We parked ourselves eventually and went in. Jeeves drifted away, and Sir Roderick took charge of the expedition. He headed for the Palace of Industry, with Biffy and myself trailing behind.

Well, you know, I have never been much of a lad for exhibitions. The citizenry in the mass always rather puts me off, and after I have been shuffling along with the multitude for a quarter of an hour or so I feel as if I were walking on hot bricks. About this particular binge, too, there seemed to me a lack of what you might call human interest. I mean to say, millions of people, no doubt, are so constituted that they scream with joy and excitement at the spectacle of a stuffed porcupine fish or a glass jar of seeds from Western Australia – but not Bertram. No; if you will take the word of one who would not deceive you, not Bertram. By the time we had tottered out of the Gold Coast village and were working towards the Palace of Machinery, everything pointed to my shortly executing a quiet sneak in the direction of that rather jolly Planters' Bar in the West Indian section. Sir Roderick had whizzed up past this at a high rate of speed, it touching no chord in him; but I had been able to observe that there was a sprightly sportsman behind the counter mixing things out of bottles and stirring them up with a stick in long glasses that seemed to have ice in them, and the urge came upon me to see more of this man. I was about to drop away from the main body and become a straggler, when something pawed at my coat sleeve. It was Biffy, and he had the air of one who has had about sufficient.

There are certain moments in life when words are not needed. I looked at Biffy, Biffy looked at me. A perfect understanding linked our two souls.

'?'

'!'

Three minutes later we had joined the Planters.

I have never been in the West Indies, but I am in a position to state that in certain of the fundamentals of life they are streets ahead of our European civilization. The man behind the counter, as kindly a bloke as I ever wish to meet, seemed to guess our requirements the moment we hove in view. Scarcely had our elbows touched the wood before he was leaping to and fro, bringing down a new bottle with each leap. A planter, apparently, does not consider he has had a drink unless it contains at least seven ingredients, and I'm not saying, mind you, that he isn't right. The man behind the bar told us the things were called Green Swizzles; and, if ever I marry and have a son, Green Swizzle Wooster is the name that will go down on the register, in memory of the day his father's life was saved at Wembley.

After the third, Biffy breathed a contented sigh.

'Where do you think Sir Roderick is?' he said.

'Biffy, old thing,' I replied frankly, 'I'm not worrying.'

'Bertie, old bird,' said Biffy, 'nor am I.'

He sighed again, and broke a long silence by asking the man for a straw.

'Bertie,' he said, 'I've just remembered something rather rummy. You know Jeeves?'

I said I knew Jeeves.

'Well, a rather rummy incident occurred as we were going into this place. Old Jeeves sidled up to me and said something rather rummy. You'll never guess what it was.'

'No, I don't believe I ever shall.'

'Jeeves said,' proceeded Biffy earnestly, 'and I am quoting his very words – Jeeves said, "Mr Biffen" – addressing me, you understand – '

'I understand.'

'"Mr Biffen," he said, "I strongly advise you to visit the – "'

'The what?' I asked as he paused.

'Bertie, old man,' said Biffy, deeply concerned, 'I've absolutely forgotten!'

I stared at the man.

'What I can't understand,' I said, 'is how you manage to run that Herefordshire place of yours for a day. How on earth do you remember to milk the cows and give the pigs their dinner?'

'Oh, that's all right. There are divers blokes about the places – hirelings and menials, you know – who look after that.'

'Ah!' I said. 'Well, that being so, let us have one more Green Swizzle, and then hey for the Amusement Park.'

When I indulged in those few rather bitter words about exhibitions, it must be distinctly understood that I was not alluding to what you might call the more earthy portion of these curious places. I yield to no man in my approval of those institutions where on payment of a shilling you are permitted to slide down a slippery runway sitting on a mat. I love the Jiggle-Joggle, and I am prepared to take on all and sundry at Skee Ball for money, stamps, or Brazil nuts.

But, joyous reveller as I am on these occasions, I was simply not in it with old Biffy. Whether it was the Green Swizzles or merely the relief of being parted from Sir Roderick, I don't know, but Biffy flung himself into the pastimes of the proletariat with a zest that was almost frightening. I could hardly drag him away from the Whip, and as for the Switchback, he looked like spending the rest of his life on it. I managed to remove him at last, and he was wandering through the crowd at my side with gleaming eyes, hesitating between having his fortune told and taking a whirl at the Wheel of Joy, when he suddenly grabbed my arm and uttered a sharp animal cry.

'Bertie!'

'Now what?'

He was pointing at a large sign over a building.

'Look! Palace of Beauty!'

I tried to choke him off. I was getting a bit weary by this time. Not so young as I was.

'You don't want to go in there,' I said. 'A fellow at the club was telling me about that. It's only a lot of girls. You don't want to see a lot of girls.'

'I do want to see a lot of girls,' said Biffy firmly. 'Dozens of girls, and the more unlike Honoria they are, the better. Besides, I've suddenly remembered that that's the place Jeeves told me to be sure and visit. It all comes back to me. "Mr Biffen," he said, "I strongly advise you to visit the Palace of Beauty." Now, what the man was driving at or what his motive was, I don't know; but I ask you, Bertie, is it wise, is it safe, is it judicious ever to ignore Jeeves's lightest word? We enter by the door on the left.'

I don't know if you know this Palace of Beauty place? It's a sort of aquarium full of the delicately-nurtured instead of fishes. You go in, and there is a kind of cage with a female goggling out at you through a sheet of plate glass. She's dressed in some weird kind of costume, and over the cage is written 'Helen of Troy'. You pass on to the next, and there's another one doing jiu-jitsu with a snake. Sub-title, 'Cleopatra'. You get the idea – Famous Women Through the Ages and all that. I can't say it fascinated me to any great extent. I maintain that a lovely woman loses a lot of her charm if you have to stare at her in a tank. Moreover, it gave me a rummy sort of feeling of having wandered into the wrong bedroom at a country house, and I was flying past at a fair rate of speed, anxious to get it over, when Biffy suddenly went off his rocker.

At least, it looked like that. He let out a piercing yell, grabbed my arm with a sudden clutch that felt like the bite of a crocodile, and stood there gibbering.

'Wuk!' ejaculated Biffy, or words to that general import.

A large and interested crowd had gathered round. I think they thought the girls were going to be fed or something. But Biffy paid no attention to them. He was pointing in a loony manner at one of the cages. I forget which it was, but the female inside wore a ruff, so it may have been Queen Elizabeth or Boadicea or someone of that period. She was a rather nice-looking girl, and she was staring at Biffy in much the same pop-eyed way as he was staring at her.

'Mabel!' yelled Biff, going off in my ear like a bomb.

I can't say I was feeling my chirpiest. Drama is all very well, but I hate getting mixed up in it in a public spot; and I had not realized before how dashed public this spot was. The crowd seemed to have doubled itself in the last five seconds, and, while most of them had their eye on Biffy, quite a goodish few were looking at me as if they thought I was an important principal in the scene and might be expected at any moment to give of my best in the way of wholesome entertainment for the masses.

Biffy was jumping about like a lamb in the springtime – and, what is more, a feeble-minded lamb.

'Bertie! It's her! It's she!' He looked about him wildly. 'Where the deuce is the stage-door?' he cried. 'Where's the manager? I want to see the house-manager immediately.'

And then he suddenly bounded forward and began hammering on the glass with his stick.

'I say, old lad!' I began, but he shook me off.

These fellows who live in the country are apt to go in for fairly sizable clubs instead of the light canes which your well-dressed man about town considers suitable for metropolitan use; and down in Herefordshire, apparently, something in the nature of a knobkerrie is *de rigueur.* Biffy's first slosh smashed the glass all to a hash. Three more cleared the way for him to go into the cage without cutting himself. And, before the crowd had time to realize what a wonderful bob's-worth it was getting in exchange for its entrance fee, he was inside, engaging the girl in earnest conversation. And at the same moment two large policemen rolled up.

You can't make policemen take the romantic view. Not a tear did these two blighters stop to brush away. They were inside the cage and out of it and marching Biffy through the crowd before you had time to blink. I hurried after them, to do what I could in the way of soothing Biffy's last moments, and the poor old lad turned a glowing face in my direction.

'Chiswick, 60873,' he bellowed in a voice charged with emotion. 'Write it down, Bertie, or I shall forget it. Chiswick, 60873. Her telephone number.'

And then he disappeared, accompanied by about eleven thousand sightseers, and a voice spoke at my elbow.

'Mr Wooster! What – what – what is the meaning of this?'

Sir Roderick, with bigger eyebrows than ever, was standing at my side.

'It's all right,' I said. 'Poor old Biffy's only gone off his crumpet.'

He tottered.

'What?'

'Had a sort of fit or seizure, you know.'

'Another!' Sir Roderick, drew a deep breath. 'And this is the man I was about to allow my daughter to marry!' I heard him mutter.

I tapped him in a kindly spirit on the shoulder. It took some doing, mark you, but I did it.

'If I were you,' I said, 'I should call that off. Scratch the fixture. Wash it out absolutely, is my advice.'

He gave me a nasty look.

'I do not require your advice, Mr Wooster! I had already arrived independently at the decision of which you speak. Mr Wooster, you are a friend of this man – a fact which should in itself have been sufficient warning to me. You will – unlike myself – be seeing him again. Kindly inform him, when you do see him, that he may consider his engagement at an end.'

'Right-ho,' I said, and hurried off after the crowd. It seemed to me that a little bailing-out might be in order.

It was about an our later that I shoved my way out to where I had parked the car. Jeeves was sitting in the front seat, brooding over the cosmos. He rose courteously as I approached.

'You are leaving, sir?'

'I am.'

'And Sir Roderick, sir?'

'Not coming. I am revealing no secrets, Jeeves, when I inform you that he and I have parted brass rags. Not on speaking terms now.'

'Indeed, sir? And Mr Biffen? Will you wait for him?'

'No. He's in prison.'

'Really, sir?'

'Yes. I tried to bail him out, but they decided on second thoughts to coop him up for the night.'

'What was his offence, sir?'

'You remember that girl of his I was telling you about? He found her in a tank at the Palace of Beauty and went after her by the quickest route, which was via a plate-glass window. He was then scooped up and borne off in irons by the constabulary.' I gazed sideways at him. It is difficult to bring off a penetrating glance out of the corner of your eye, but I managed it. 'Jeeves,' I said, 'there is more in this than the casual observer would suppose. You told Mr Biffen to go to the Palace of Beauty. Did you know the girl would be there?'

'Yes, sir.'

This was most remarkable and rummy to a degree.

'Dash it, do you know everything?'

'Oh, no, sir,' said Jeeves with an indulgent smile. Humouring the young master.

'Well, how did you know that?'

'I happen to be acquainted with the future Mrs Biffen, sir.'

'I see. Then you knew all about that business in New York?'

'Yes, sir. And it was for that reason that I was not altogether favourably disposed towards Mr Biffen when you were first kind enough to suggest that I might be able to offer some slight assistance. I mistakenly supposed that he had been trifling with the girl's affections, sir. But when you told me the true facts of the case I appreciated the injustice I had done to Mr Biffen and endeavoured to make amends.'

'Well, he certainly owes you a lot. He's crazy about her.'

'That is very gratifying, sir.'

'And she ought to be pretty grateful to you, too. Old Biffy's got fifteen thousand a year, not to mention more cows, pigs, hens, and ducks than he knows what to do with. A dashed useful bird to have in any family.'

'Yes, sir.'

'Tell me, Jeeves,' I said, 'how did you happen to know the girl in the first place?'

Jeeves looked dreamily out into the traffic.

'She is my niece, sir. If I might make a suggestion, sir, I should not jerk the steering wheel with quite such suddenness. We very nearly collided with that omnibus.'

7

WITHOUT THE OPTION

The evidence was all in. The machinery of the law had worked without a hitch. And the beak, having adjusted a pair of pince-nez which looked as though they were going to do a nosedive any moment, coughed like a pained sheep and slipped us the bad news. 'The prisoner, Wooster,' he said – and who can paint the shame and agony of Bertram at hearing himself so described? – 'will pay a fine of five pounds.'

'Oh, rather!' I said. 'Absolutely! Like a shot!'

I was dashed glad to get the thing settled at such a reasonable figure. I gazed across what they call the sea of faces till I picked up Jeeves, sitting at the back. Stout fellow, he had come to see the young master through his hour of trial.

'I say, Jeeves,' I sang out, 'have you got a fiver? I'm a bit short.'

'Silence!' bellowed some officious blighter.

'It's all right,' I said, 'just arranging the financial details. Got the stuff, Jeeves?'

'Yes, sir.'

'Good egg!'

'Are you a friend of the prisoner?' asked the beak.

'I am in Mr Wooster's employment, Your Worship, in the capacity of gentleman's personal gentleman.'

'Then pay the fine to the clerk.'

'Very good, Your Worship.'

The beak gave a coldish nod in my direction, as much as to say that they might now strike the fetters from my wrists; and having hitched up the pince-nez once more, proceeded to hand poor old Sippy one of the nastiest looks ever seen in Bosher Street Police Court.

'The case of the prisoner Leon Trotzky – which,' he said, giving Sippy the eye again, 'I am strongly inclined to think an assumed and fictitious name – is more serious. He has been convicted of a wanton and violent assault upon the police. The evidence of the officer has proved that the prisoner struck him in the abdomen, causing severe internal pain, and in other ways interfered with him in the execution of his duties. I am aware that on the night following the annual aquatic contest between the Universities of Oxford and Cambridge a certain licence is traditionally granted by the authorities, but aggravated acts of ruffianly hooliganism like that of the prisoner Trotzky cannot be overlooked or palliated. He will serve a sentence of thirty days in the Second Division without the option of a fine.'

'No, I say – here – hi – dash it all!' protested poor old Sippy.

'Silence!' bellowed the officious blighter.

'Next case,' said the beak. And that was that.

The whole affair was most unfortunate. Memory is a trifle blurred; but as far as I can piece together the facts, what happened was more or less this:

Abstemious cove though I am as a general thing there is one night in the year when, putting all other engagements aside, I am rather apt to let myself go a bit and renew my lost youth, as it were. The night to which I allude is the one following the annual aquatic contest between the Universities of Oxford and Cambridge; or, putting it another way, Boat-Race Night. Then, if ever, you will see Bertram under the influence. And on this occasion, I freely admit, I had been doing myself rather juicily, with the result that when I ran into old Sippy opposite the Empire I was in quite fairly bonhomous mood. This being so, it cut me to the quick to perceive that Sippy, generally the brightest of revellers, was far from being his usual sunny self. He had the air of a man with a secret sorrow.

'Bertie,' he said as we strolled along towards Piccadilly Circus, 'the heart bowed down by the weight of woe to weakest hope will cling.' Sippy is by way of being an author, though mainly dependent for the necessaries of life on subsidies from an old aunt who lives in the country, and his conversation often takes a literary turn. 'But the trouble is that I have no hope to cling to, weak or otherwise. I am up against it, Bertie.'

'In what way, laddie?'

'I've got to go tomorrow and spend three weeks with some absolutely dud – and I go further – some positively scaly friends of my Aunt Vera. She has fixed the thing up, and may a nephew's curse blister every bulb in her garden.'

'Who are these hounds of hell?' I asked.

'Some people named Pringle. I haven't seen them since I was ten, but I remember them at that time striking me as England's premier warts.'

'Tough luck. No wonder you've lost your morale.'

'The world,' said Sippy, 'is very grey. How can I shake off this awful depression?'

It was then that I got one of those bright ideas one does get round about 11.30 on Boat-Race Night.

'What you want, old man,' I said, 'is a policeman's helmet.'

'Do I, Bertie?'

'If I were you, I'd just step straight across the street and get that one over there.'

'But there's a policeman inside it. You can see him distinctly.'

'What does that matter?' I said. I simply couldn't follow his reasoning.

Sippy stood for a moment in thought.

'I believe you're absolutely right,' he said at last. 'Funny I never thought of it before. You really recommend me to get that helmet?'

'I do, indeed.'

'Then I will,' said Sippy, brightening up in the most remarkable manner.

So there you have the posish, and you can see why, as I left the dock a free man, remorse gnawed at my vitals. In his twenty-fifth year, with life opening out before him and all that sort of thing, Oliver Randolph Sipperley had become a jail-bird, and it was all my fault. It was I who had dragged that fine spirit down into the mire, so to speak, and the question now arose, What could I do to atone?

Obviously the first move must be to get in touch with Sippy and see if he had any last messages and what not. I pushed about a bit, making inquiries, and presently found myself in a little dark room with whitewashed walls and a wooden bench. Sippy was sitting on the bench with his head in his hands.

'How are you, old lad?' I asked in a hushed, bedside voice.

'I'm a ruined man,' said Sippy, looking like a poached egg.

'Oh, come,' I said, 'it's not so bad as all that. I mean to say, you had the swift intelligence to give a false name. There won't be anything about you in the papers.'

'I'm not worrying about the papers. What's bothering me is, how can I go and spend three weeks with the Pringles, starting today, when I've got to sit in a prison cell with a ball and chain on my ankle?'

'But you said you didn't want to go.'

'It isn't a question of wanting, fathead. I've got to go. If I don't my aunt will find out where I am. And if she finds out that I am doing thirty days, without the option, in the lowest dungeon beneath the castle moat – well, where shall I get off?'

I saw his point.

'This is not a thing we can settle for ourselves,' I said gravely. 'We must put our trust in a higher power. Jeeves is the man we must consult.'

And having collected a few of the necessary data, I shook his hand, patted him on the back and tooled off home to Jeeves.

'Jeeves,' I said, when I had climbed outside the pick-me-up which he had thoughtfully prepared against my coming, 'I've got something to tell you; something important; something that vitally affects one whom you have always regarded with – one whom you have always looked upon – one whom you have – well, to cut a long story short, as I'm not feeling quite myself – Mr Sipperley.'

'Yes, sir?'

'Jeeves, Mr Souperley is in the sip.'

'Sir?'

'I mean, Mr Sipperley is in the soup.'

'Indeed, sir?'

'And all owing to me. It was I who, in a moment of mistaken kindness, wishing only to cheer him up and give him something to occupy his mind, recommended him to pinch that policeman's helmet.'

'Is that so, sir?'

'Do you mind not intoning the responses, Jeeves?' I said. 'This is a most complicated story for a man with a headache to have to tell, and if you interrupt you'll make me lose the thread. As a favour to me, therefore, don't do it. Just nod every now and then to show that you're following me.'

I closed my eyes and marshalled the facts.

'To start with then, Jeeves, you may or may not know that Mr Sipperley is practically dependent on his Aunt Vera.'

'Would that be Miss Sipperley of the Paddock, Beckley-on-the-Moor in Yorkshire, sir?'

'Yes. Don't tell me you know her!'

'Not personally, sir. But I have a cousin residing in the village who has some slight acquaintance with Miss Sipperley. He has described her to me as an imperious and quick-tempered old lady ... But I beg your pardon, sir, I should have nodded.'

'Quite right, you should have nodded. Yes, Jeeves, you should have nodded. But it's too late now.'

I nodded myself. I hadn't had my eight hours the night before, and what you might call a lethargy was showing a tendency to steal over me from time to time.

'Yes, sir?' said Jeeves.

'Oh – ah – yes,' I said, giving myself a bit of a hitch up. 'Where had I got to?'

'You were saying that Mr Sipperley is practically dependent upon Miss Sipperley, sir.'

'Was I?'

'You were, sir.'

'You're perfectly right; so I was. Well, then, you can readily understand, Jeeves, that he has got to take jolly good care to keep in with her. You get that?'

Jeeves nodded.

'Now mark this closely: The other day she wrote to old Sippy, telling him to come down and sing at her village concert. It was equivalent to a royal command, if you see what I mean, so Sippy couldn't refuse in so many words. But he had sung at her village concert once before and had got the bird in no uncertain manner, so he wasn't playing any return dates. You follow so far, Jeeves?'

Jeeves nodded.

'So what did he do, Jeeves? He did what seemed to him at the moment a rather brainy thing. He told her that, though he would have been delighted to sing at her village concert, by a most unfortunate chance an editor had commissioned him to write a series of articles on the colleges of Cambridge and he was obliged to pop down there at once and would be away for quite three weeks. All clear up to now?'

Jeeves inclined the coco-nut.

'Whereupon, Jeeves, Miss Sipperley wrote back, saying that she quite realized that work must come before pleasure – pleasure being her loose way of describing the act of singing songs at the Beckley-on-the-Moor concert and getting the laugh from the local toughs; but that, if he was going to Cambridge, he must certainly stay with her friends, the Pringles, at their house just outside the town. And she dropped them a line telling them to expect him on the twenty-eighth, and they dropped another line saying right-ho, and the thing was settled. And now Mr Sipperley is in the jug, and what will be the ultimate outcome or upshot? Jeeves, it is a problem worthy of your great intellect. I rely on you.'

'I will do my best to justify your confidence, sir.'

'Carry on, then. And meanwhile pull down the blinds and bring a couple more cushions and heave that small chair this way so that I can put my feet up, and then go away and brood and let me hear from you in – say, a couple of hours, or maybe three.

And if anybody calls and wants to see me, inform them that I am dead.'

'Dead, sir?'

'Dead. You won't be so far wrong.'

It must have been well towards evening when I woke up with a crick in my neck but otherwise somewhat refreshed. I pressed the bell.

'I looked in twice, sir,' said Jeeves, 'but on each occasion you were asleep and I did not like to disturb you.'

'The right spirit, Jeeves . . . Well?'

'I have been giving close thought to the little problem which you indicated, sir, and I can see only one solution.'

'One is enough. What do you suggest?'

'That you go to Cambridge in Mr Sipperley's place, sir.'

I stared at the man. Certainly I was feeling a good deal better than I had been a few hours before; but I was far from being in a fit condition to have rot like this talked to me.

'Jeeves,' I said sternly, 'pull yourself together. This is mere babble from the sick-bed.'

'I fear I can suggest no other plan of action, sir, which will extricate Mr Sipperley from his dilemma.'

'But think! Reflect! Why, even I, in spite of having had a disturbed night and a most painful morning with the minions of the law, can see that the scheme is a loony one. To put the finger on only one leak in the thing, it isn't me these people want to see; it's Mr Sipperley. They don't know me from Adam.'

'So much the better, sir. For what I am suggesting is that you go to Cambridge, affecting actually to be Mr Sipperley.'

This was too much.

'Jeeves,' I said, and I'm not half sure there weren't tears in my eyes, 'surely you can see for yourself that this is pure banana oil. It is not like you to come into the presence of a sick man and gibber.'

'I think the plan I have suggested would be practicable, sir. While you were sleeping, I was able to have a few words with Mr Sipperley, and he informed me that Professor and Mrs Pringle have not set eyes upon him since he was a lad of ten.'

'No, that's true. He told me that. But even so, they would be sure to ask him questions about my aunt – or rather his aunt. Where would I be then?'

'Mr Sipperley was kind enough to give me a few facts respecting Miss Sipperley, sir, which I jotted down. With these, added to what my cousin has told me of the lady's habits, I think you would be in a position to answer any ordinary question.'

There is something dashed insidious about Jeeves. Time and again since we first came together he has stunned me with some apparently drivelling suggestion or scheme or ruse or plan of campaign, and after about five minutes has convinced me that it is not only sound but fruity. It took nearly a quarter of an hour to reason me into this particular one, it being considerably the weirdest to date; but he did it. I was holding out pretty firmly, when he suddenly clinched the thing.

'I would certainly suggest, sir,' he said, 'that you left London as soon as possible and remained hid for some little time in some retreat where you would not be likely to be found.'

'Eh? Why?'

'During the last hours Mrs Spenser has been on the telephone three times, sir, endeavouring to get into communication with you.'

'Aunt Agatha!' I cried, paling beneath my tan.

'Yes, sir. I gathered from her remarks that she had been reading in the evening paper a report of this morning's proceedings in the police court.'

I hopped from the chair like a jack rabbit of the prairie. If Aunt Agatha was out with her hatchet, a move was most certainly indicated.

'Jeeves,' I said, 'this is a time for deeds, not words. Pack – and that right speedily.'

'I have packed, sir.'

'Find out when there is a train for Cambridge.'

'There is one in forty minutes, sir.'

'Call a taxi.'

'A taxi is at the door, sir.'

'Good!' I said. 'Then lead me to it.'

The Maison Pringle was quite a bit of a way out of Cambridge, a mile or two down the Trumpington Road; and when I arrived everybody was dressing for dinner. So it wasn't till I had shoved on the evening raiment and got down to the drawing-room that I met the gang.

'Hullo-ullo!' I said, taking a deep breath and floating in.

I tried to speak in a clear and ringing voice, but I wasn't feeling my chirpiest. It is always a nervous job for a diffident and unassuming bloke to visit a strange house for the first time; and it doesn't make the thing any better when he goes there pretending to be another fellow. I was conscious of a rather pronounced sinking feeling, which the appearance of the Pringles did nothing to allay.

Sippy had described them as England's premier warts, and it

542 *Carry on, Jeeves*

looked to me as if he might be about right. Professor Pringle was a thinnish, baldish, dyspeptic-lookingish cove with an eye like a haddock, while Mrs Pringle's aspect was that of one who had had bad news round about the year 1900 and never really got over it. And I was just staggering under the impact of these two when I was introduced to a couple of ancient females with shawls all over them.

'No doubt you remember my mother?' said Professor Pringle mournfully, indicating Exhibit A.

'Oh – ah!' I said, achieving a bit of a beam.

'And my aunt,' sighed the Prof, as if things were getting worse and worse.

'Well, well, well!' I said, shooting another beam in the direction of Exhibit B.

'They were only saying this morning that they remembered you,' groaned the Prof, abandoning all hope.

There was a pause. The whole strength of the company gazed at me like a family group out of one of Edgar Allan Poe's less cheery yarns, and I felt my *joie de vivre* dying at the roots.

'I remember Oliver,' said Exhibit A. She heaved a sigh. 'He was such a pretty child. What a pity! What a pity!'

Tactful, of course, and calculated to put the guest completely at his ease.

'I remember Oliver,' said Exhibit B, looking at me in much the same way as the Bosher Street beak had looked at Sippy before putting on the black cap. 'Nasty little boy! He teased my cat.'

'Aunt Jane's memory is wonderful, considering that she will be eighty-seven next birthday,' whispered Mrs Pringle with mournful pride.

'What did you say?' asked the Exhibit suspiciously.

'I said your memory was wonderful.'

'Ah!' The dear old creature gave me another glare. I could see that no beautiful friendship was to be looked for by Bertram in this quarter. 'He chased my Tibby all over the garden, shooting arrows at her from a bow.'

At this moment a cat strolled out from under the sofa and made for me its tail up. Cats always do take to me, which made it all the sadder that I should be saddled with Sippy's criminal record. I stooped to tickle it under the ear, such being my invariable policy, and the Exhibit uttered a piercing cry.

'Stop him! Stop him!'

She leaped forward, moving uncommonly well for one of her years, and having scooped up the cat, stood eyeing me with bitter defiance, as if daring me to start anything. Most unpleasant.

'I like cats,' I said feebly.

It didn't go. The sympathy of the audience was not with me. And conversation was at what you might call a low ebb, when the door opened and a girl came in.

'My daughter Heloise,' said the Prof moodily, as if he hated to admit it.

I turned to mitt the female, and stood there with my hand out, gaping. I can't remember when I've had such a nasty shock.

I suppose everybody has had the experience of suddenly meeting somebody who reminded them frightfully of some fearful person. I mean to say, by way of an example, once when I was golfing in Scotland I saw a woman come into the hotel who was the living image of my Aunt Agatha. Probably a very decent sort, if I had only waited to see, but I didn't wait. I legged it that evening, utterly unable to stand the spectacle. And on another occasion I was driven out of a thoroughly festive night club because the head waiter reminded me of my Uncle Percy.

Well, Heloise Pringle, in the most ghastly way, resembled Honoria Glossop.

I think I may have told you before about this Glossop scourge. She was the daughter of Sir Roderick Glossop, the loony-doctor, and I had been engaged to her for about three weeks, much against my wishes, when the old boy most fortunately got the idea that I was off my rocker and put the bee on the proceedings. Since then the mere thought of her had been enough to make me start out of my sleep with a loud cry. And this girl was exactly like her.

'Er – how are you?' I said.

'How do you do?'

Her voice put the lid on it. It might have been Honoria herself talking. Honoria Glossop has a voice like a lion tamer making some authoritative announcement to one of the troupe, and so had this girl. I backed away convulsively and sprang into the air as my foot stubbed itself against something squashy. A sharp yowl rent the air, followed by an indignant cry, and I turned to see Aunt Jane, on all fours, trying to put things right with the cat, which had gone to earth under the sofa. She gave me a look, and I could see that her worst fears had been realized.

At this juncture dinner was announced – not before I was ready for it.

*

'Jeeves,' I said, when I got him alone that night, 'I am no faint heart, but I am inclined to think that this binge is going to prove a shade above the odds.'

'You are not enjoying your visit, sir?'

'I am not, Jeeves. Have you seen Miss Pringle?'

'Yes, sir, from a distance.'

'The best way to see her. Did you observe her keenly?'

'Yes, sir.'

'Did she remind you of anybody?'

'She appeared to me to bear a remarkable likeness to her cousin, Miss Glossop, sir.'

'Her cousin! You don't mean to say she's Honoria Glossop's cousin!'

'Yes, sir. Mrs Pringle was a Miss Blatherwick – the younger of two sisters, the elder of whom married Sir Roderick Glossop.'

'Great Scott! That accounts for the resemblance.'

'Yes, sir.'

'And what a resemblance, Jeeves! She even talks like Miss Glossop.'

'Indeed, sir? I have not yet heard Miss Pringle speak.'

'You have missed little. And what it amounts to, Jeeves, is that, though nothing will induce me to let old Sippy down, I can see that this visit is going to try me high. At a pinch, I could stand the Prof and wife. I could even make the effort of a lifetime and bear up against Aunt Jane. But to expect a man to mix daily with the girl Heloise – and to do it, what is more, on lemonade, which is all there was to drink at dinner – is to ask too much of him. What shall I do, Jeeves?'

'I think you should avoid Miss Pringle's society as much as possible.'

'The same great thought had occurred to me,' I said.

It is all very well, though, to talk airily about avoiding a female's society; but when you are living in the same house with her, and she doesn't want to avoid you, it takes a bit of doing. It is a peculiar thing in life that the people you most particularly want to edge away from always seem to cluster round like a poultice. I hadn't been twenty-four hours in the place before I perceived that I was going to see a lot of this pestilence.

She was one of those girls you're always meeting on the stairs and in passages. I couldn't go into a room without seeing her drift in a minute later. And if I walked in the garden she was sure to leap out at me from a laurel bush or the onion bed or something. By about the tenth day I had begun to feel absolutely haunted.

'Jeeves,' I said, 'I have begun to feel absolutely haunted.'

'Sir!'

'This woman dogs me. I never seem to get a moment to myself. Old Sippy was supposed to come here to make a study of the Cambridge colleges, and she took me round about fifty-seven this morning. This afternoon I went to sit in the garden, and she popped up through a trap and was in my midst. This evening she cornered me in the morning-room. It's getting so that, when I have a bath, I wouldn't be a bit surprised to find her nestling in the soap dish.'

'Extremely trying, sir.'

'Dashed so. Have you any remedy to suggest?'

'Not at the moment, sir. Miss Pringle does appear to be distinctly interested in you, sir. She was asking me questions this morning respecting your mode of life in London.'

'What?'

'Yes, sir.'

I stared at the man in horror. A ghastly thought had struck me. I quivered like an aspen.

At lunch that day a curious thing had happened. We had just finished mangling the cutlets and I was sitting back in my chair, taking a bit of an easy before being allotted my slab of boiled pudding, when, happening to look up, I caught the girl Heloise's eye fixed on me in what seemed to me a rather rummy manner. I didn't think much about it at the time, because boiled pudding is a thing you have to give your undivided attention to if you want to do yourself justice; but now, recalling the episode in the light of Jeeves's words, the full sinister meaning of the thing seemed to come home to me.

Even at the moment, something about that look had struck me as oddly familiar, and now I suddenly saw why. It had been the identical look which I had observed in the eye of Honoria Glossop in the days immediately preceding our engagement – the look of a tigress that has marked down its prey.

'Jeeves, do you know what I think?'

'Sir?'

I gulped slightly.

'Jeeves,' I said, 'listen attentively. I don't want to give the impression that I consider myself one of those deadly coves who exercise an irresistible fascination over one and all and can't meet a girl without wrecking her peace of mind in the first half-minute. As a matter of fact, it's rather the other way with me, for girls on entering my presence are most inclined to give me the raised eyebrow and the twitching upper lip. Nobody, therefore, can say that I am a man who's likely to take alarm unnecessarily. You admit that, don't you?'

'Yes, sir.'

'Nevertheless, Jeeves, it is a known scientific fact that there is a particular style of female that does seem strangely attracted to the sort of fellow I am.'

'Very true, sir.'

'I mean to say, I know perfectly well that I've got, roughly speaking, half the amount of brain a normal bloke ought to possess. And when a girl comes along who has about twice the regular allowance, she too often makes a bee-line for me with the love-light in her eyes. I don't know how to account for it, but it is so.'

'It may be Nature's provision for maintaining the balance of the species, sir.'

'Very possibly. Anyway, it has happened to me over and over again. It was what happened in the case of Honoria Glossop. She was notoriously one of the brainiest women of her year at Girton, and she just gathered me in like a bull pup swallowing a piece of steak.'

'Miss Pringle, I am informed, sir, was an even more brilliant scholar than Miss Glossop.'

'Well, there you are! Jeeves, she looks at me.'

'Yes, sir?'

'I keep meeting her on the stairs and in passages.'

'Indeed, sir?'

'She recommends me books to read, to improve my mind.'

'Highly suggestive, sir.'

'And at breakfast this morning, when I was eating a sausage, she told me I shouldn't, as modern medical science held that a four-inch sausage contained as many germs as a dead rat. The maternal touch, you understand; fussing over my health.'

'I think we may regard that, sir, as practically conclusive.'

I sank into a chair, thoroughly pipped.

'What's to be done, Jeeves?'

'We must think, sir.'

'You think. I haven't the machinery.'

'I will most certainly devote my very best attention to the matter, sir, and will endeavour to give satisfaction.'

Well, that was something. But I was ill at ease. Yes, there is no getting away from it, Bertram was ill at ease.

*

Next morning we visited sixty-three more Cambridge colleges, and after lunch I said I was going to my room to lie down. After staying there for half an hour to give the coast time to clear, I shoved a book and smoking materials in my pocket, and climbing out of a window, shinned down a convenient water-pipe into the garden. My objective was the summer-house, where it seemed to me that a man might put in a quiet hour or so without interruption.

It was extremely jolly in the garden. The sun was shining, the crocuses were all to the mustard and there wasn't a sign of Heloise Pringle anywhere. The cat was fooling about on the lawn, so I chirruped to it and it gave a low gargle and came trotting up. I had just got it in my arms and was scratching it under the ear when there was a loud shriek from above, and there was Aunt Jane half out of the window. Dashed disturbing.

'Oh, right-ho,' I said.

I dropped the cat, which galloped off into the bushes, and dismissing the idea of bunging a brick at the aged relative, went on my way, heading for the shrubbery. Once safely hidden there, I worked round till I got to the summer-house. And, believe me, I had hardly got my first cigarette nicely under way when a shadow fell on my book and there was young Sticketh-Closer-Than-a-Brother in person.

'So there you are,' she said.

She seated herself by my side, and with a sort of gruesome playfulness jerked the gasper out of the holder and heaved it through the door.

'You're always smoking,' she said, a lot too much like a lovingly chiding young bride for my comfort. 'I wish you wouldn't. It's so bad for you. And you ought not to be sitting out here without your light overcoat. You want someone to look after you.'

'I've got Jeeves.'

She frowned a bit.

'I don't like him,' she said.

'Eh? Why not?'

'I don't know. I wish you would get rid of him.'

My flesh absolutely crept. And I'll tell you why. One of the first things Honoria Glossop had done after we had become engaged was to tell me she didn't like Jeeves and wanted him shot out. The realization that this girl resembled Honoria not only in body but in blackness of soul made me go all faint.

'What are you reading?'

She picked up my book and frowned again. The thing was one I had brought down from the old flat in London, to glance at in the train – a fairly zippy effort in the detective line called *The Trail of Blood*. She turned the pages with a nasty sneer.

'I can't understand you liking nonsense of this –' She stopped suddenly. 'Good gracious!'

'What's the matter?'

'Do you know Bertie Wooster?'

And then I saw that my name was scrawled right across the title page, and my heart did three back somersaults.

'Oh – er – well that is to say – well, slightly.'

'He must be a perfect horror. I'm surprised that you can make a friend of him. Apart from anything else, the man is practically an imbecile. He was engaged to my Cousin Honoria at one time, and it was broken off because he was next door to insane. You should hear my Uncle Roderick talk about him!'

I wasn't keen.

'Do you see much of him?'

'A goodish bit.'

'I saw in the paper the other day that he was fined for making a disgraceful disturbance in the street.'

'Yes, I saw that.'

She gazed at me in a foul, motherly way.

'He can't be a good influence for you,' she said. 'I do wish you would drop him. Will you?'

'Well –' I began. And at this point old Cuthbert, the cat, having presumably found it a bit slow by himself in the bushes, wandered in with a matey expression on his face and jumped on my lap. I welcomed him with a good deal of cordiality. Though but a cat, he did make a sort of third at this party; and he afforded a good excuse for changing the conversation.

'Jolly birds, cats,' I said.

She wasn't having any.

'Will you drop Bertie Wooster?' she said, absolutely ignoring the cat *motif*.

'It would be so difficult.'

'Nonsense! It only needs a little will-power. The man surely can't be so interesting a companion as all that. Uncle Roderick says he is an invertebrate waster.'

I could have mentioned a few things that I thought Uncle Roderick was, but my lips were sealed, so to speak.

'You have changed a great deal since we last met,' said the Pringle disease reproachfully. She bent forward and began to scratch the cat under the other ear. 'Do you remember, when we were children together, you used to say that you would do anything for me?'

'Did I?'

'I remember once you cried because I was cross and wouldn't let you kiss me.'

I didn't believe it at the time, and I don't believe it now. Sippy is in many ways a good deal of a chump, but surely even at the age of ten he cannot have been such a priceless ass as that. I think the girl was lying, but that didn't make the position of affairs any better. I edged away a couple of inches and sat staring before me, the old brow beginning to get slightly bedewed.

And then suddenly – well, you know how it is, I mean. I suppose everyone has had that ghastly feeling at one time or another of being urged by some overwhelming force to do some absolutely blithering act. You get it every now and then when you're in a crowded theatre, and something seems to be egging you on to shout, 'Fire!' and see what happens. Or you're talking to someone and all at once you feel, 'Now, suppose I suddenly biffed this bird in the eye!'

Well, what I'm driving at is this: at this juncture, with her shoulder squashing against mine and her black hair tickling my nose, a perfectly loony impulse came sweeping over me to kiss her.

'No, really?' I croaked.

'Have you forgotten?'

She lifted the old onion and her eyes looked straight into mine. I could feel myself skidding. I shut my eyes. And then from the doorway there spoke the most beautiful voice I had ever heard in my life:

'Give me that cat!'

I opened my eyes. There was good old Aunt Jane, that queen of her sex, standing before me, glaring at me as if I were a vivisectionist and she had surprised me in the middle of an experiment. How this pearl among women had tracked me down I don't know, but there she stood, bless her dear, intelligent old soul, like the rescue party in the last reel of a motion picture.

I didn't wait. The spell was broken and I legged it. As I went, I heard that lovely voice again.

'He shot arrows at my Tibby from a bow,' said this most deserving and excellent octogenarian.

For the next few days all was peace. I saw comparatively little of Heloise. I found the strategic value of that water-pipe outside my window beyond praise. I seldom left the house now by any other route. It seemed to me that, if only the luck held like this, I might after all be able to stick this visit out for the full term of the sentence.

But meanwhile, as they say in the movies –

The whole family appeared to be present and correct as I came down to the drawing-room a couple of nights later. The Prof, Mrs Prof, the two Exhibits and the girl Heloise were scattered about at intervals. The cat slept on the rug, the canary in its cage. There was nothing, in short, to indicate that this was not just one of our ordinary evenings.

'Well, well, well!' I said cheerily. 'Hullo-ullo-ullo!'

I always like to make something in the nature of an entrance speech, it seeming to me to lend a chummy tone to the proceedings.

The girl Heloise looked at me reproachfully.

'Where have you been all day?' she asked.

'I went to my room after lunch.'

'You weren't there at five.'

'No. After putting in a spell of work on the good old colleges I went for a stroll. Fellow must have exercise if he means to keep fit.'

'*Mens sana in corpore sano*,' observed the Prof.

'I shouldn't wonder,' I said cordially.

At this point, when everything was going as sweet as a nut and I was feeling on top of my form, Mrs Pringle suddenly soaked me on the base of the skull with a sandbag. Not actually, I don't mean. No, no. I speak figuratively, as it were.

'Roderick is very late,' she said.

You may think it strange that the sound of that name should have sloshed into my nerve centres, like a half-brick. But, take it from me, to a man who has had any dealings with Sir Roderick Glossop there is only one Roderick in the world – and this is one too many.

'Roderick?' I gurgled.

'My brother-in-law, Sir Roderick Glossop, comes to Cambridge tonight,' said the Prof. 'He lectures at St Luke's tomorrow. He is coming here to dinner.'

And while I stood there, feeling like the hero when he discovers that he is trapped in the den of the Secret Nine, the door opened.

'Sir Roderick Glossop,' announced the maid or some such person, and in he came.

One of the things that gets this old crumb so generally disliked among the better element of the community is the fact that he has a head like the dome of St Paul's and eyebrows that want bobbing or shingling to reduce them to anything like reasonable size. It is a nasty experience to see this bald and bushy bloke advancing on you when you haven't prepared the strategic railways in your rear.

As he came into the room I backed behind a sofa and commended my soul to God. I didn't need to have my hand read to know that trouble was coming to me through a dark man.

He didn't spot me at first. He shook hands with the Prof and wife, kissed Heloise and waggled his head at the Exhibits.

'I fear I am somewhat late,' he said. 'A slight accident on the road, affecting what my chauffeur termed the – '

And then he saw me lurking on the outskirts and gave a startled grunt, as if I hurt him a good deal internally.

'This – ' began the Prof, waving in my direction.

'I am already acquainted with Mr Wooster.'

'This,' went on the Prof, 'is Miss Sipperley's nephew, Oliver. You remember Miss Sipperley?'

'What do you mean?' barked Sir Roderick. Having had so much to do with loonies has given him a rather sharp and authoritative manner on occasion. 'This is that wretched young man, Bertram Wooster. What is all this nonsense about Olivers and Sipperleys?'

The Prof was eyeing me with some natural surprise. So were the others. I beamed a bit weakly.

'Well, as a matter of fact – ' I said.

The Prof was wrestling with the situation. You could hear his brain buzzing.

'He said he was Oliver Sipperley,' he moaned.

'Come here!' bellowed Sir Roderick. 'Am I to understand that you have inflicted yourself on this household under the pretence of being the nephew of an old friend?'

It seemed a pretty accurate description of the facts.

'Well – er – yes,' I said.

Sir Roderick shot an eye at me. It entered the body somewhere about the top stud, roamed around inside for a bit and went out at the back.

'Insane! Quite insane, as I knew from the first moment I saw him.'

'What did he say?' asked Aunt Jane.

'Roderick says this young man is insane,' roared the Prof.

'Ah!' said Aunt Jane, nodding. 'I thought so. He climbs down water-pipes.'

'Does what?'

'I've seen him – ah, many a time!'

Sir Roderick snorted violently.

'He ought to be under proper restraint. It is abominable that a person in his mental condition should be permitted to roam the world at large. The next stage may quite easily be homicidal.'

It seemed to me that, even at the expense of giving old Sippy away, I must be cleared of this frightful charge. After all, Sippy's number was up anyway.

'Let me explain,' I said. 'Sippy asked me to come here.'

'What do you mean?'

'He couldn't come himself, because he was jugged for biffing a cop on Boat-Race Night.'

Well, it wasn't easy to make them get the hang of the story, and even when I'd done it it didn't seem to make them any chummier towards me. A certain coldness about expresses it, and when dinner was announced I counted myself out and pushed off rapidly to my room. I could have done with a bit of dinner, but the atmosphere didn't seem just right.

'Jeeves,' I said, having shot in and pressed the bell, 'we're sunk.'

'Sir?'

'Hell's foundations are quivering and the game is up.'

He listened attentively.

'The contingency was one always to have been anticipated as a possibility, sir. It only remains to take the obvious step.'

'What's that?'

'Go and see Miss Sipperley, sir.'

'What on earth for?'

'I think it would be judicious to apprise her of the facts yourself, sir, instead of allowing her to hear of them through the medium of a letter from Professor Pringle. That is to say, if you are still anxious to do all in your power to assist Mr Sipperley.'

'I can't let Sippy down. If you think it's any good – '

'We can but try it, sir. I have an idea, sir, that we may find Miss Sipperley disposed to look leniently upon Mr Sipperley's misdemeanour.'

'What makes you think that?'

'It is just a feeling that I have, sir.'

'Well, if you think it would be worth trying – How do we get there?'

'The distance is about a hundred and fifty miles, sir. Our best plane would be to hire a car.'

'Get it at once,' I said.

The idea of being a hundred and fifty miles away from Heloise

Pringle, not to mention Aunt Jane and Sir Roderick Glossop, sounded about as good to me as anything I had ever heard.

The Paddock, Beckley-on-the-Moor, was about a couple of parasangs from the village, and I set out for it next morning, after partaking of a hearty breakfast at the local inn, practically without a tremor. I suppose when a fellow has been through it as I had in the last two weeks his system becomes hardened. After all, I felt, whatever this aunt of Sippy's might be like, she wasn't Sir Roderick Glossop, so I was that much on velvet from the start.

The Paddock was one of those medium-sized houses with a goodish bit of very tidy garden and a carefully rolled gravel drive curving past a shrubbery that looked as if it had just come back from the dry cleaner – the sort of house you take one look at and say to yourself, 'Somebody's aunt lives there.' I pushed on up the drive, and as I turned the bend I observed in the middle distance a woman messing about by a flower-bed with a trowel in her hand. If this wasn't the female I was after, I was very much mistaken, so I halted, cleared the throat and gave tongue.

'Miss Sipperley?'

She had her back to me, and at the sound of my voice she executed a sort of leap or bound, not unlike a barefoot dancer who steps on a tin-tack halfway through the Vision of Salome. She came to earth and goggled at me in a rather goofy manner. A large, stout female with a reddish face.

'Hope I didn't startle you,' I said.

'Who are you?'

'My name's Wooster. I'm a pal of your nephew, Oliver.'

Her breathing had become more regular.

'Oh?' she said. 'When I heard your voice I thought you were someone else.'

'No, that's who I am. I came up here to tell you about Oliver.'

'What about him?'

I hesitated. Now that we were approaching what you might call the nub, or crux, of the situation, a good deal of my breezy confidence seemed to have slipped from me.

'Well, it's rather a painful tale, I must warn you.'

'Oliver isn't ill? He hasn't had an accident?'

She spoke anxiously, and I was pleased at this evidence of human feeling. I decided to shoot the works with no more delay.

'Oh, no, he isn't ill,' I said, 'and as regards having accidents, it depends on what you call an accident. He's in chokey.'

'In what?'

'In prison.'

'In prison!'

'It was entirely my fault. We were strolling along on Boat-Race Night and I advised him to pinch a policeman's helmet.'

'I don't understand.'

'Well, he seemed depressed, don't you know; and rightly or wrongly, I thought it might cheer him up if he stepped across the street and collared a policeman's helmet. He thought it a good idea, too, so he started doing it, and the man made a fuss and Oliver sloshed him.'

'Sloshed him?'

'Biffed him – smote him a blow – in the stomach.'

'My nephew Oliver hit a policeman in the stomach?'

'Absolutely in the stomach. And next morning the beak sent him to the bastille for thirty days without the option.'

I was looking at her a bit anxiously all this while to see how she was taking the thing, and at this moment her face seemed suddenly to split in half. For an instant she appeared to be all mouth, and then she was staggering about the grass, shouting with laughter and waving the trowel madly.

It seemed to me a bit of luck for her that Sir Roderick Glossop wasn't on the spot. He would have been sitting on her head and calling for the strait-waistcoat in the first half-minute.

'You aren't annoyed?' I said.

'Annoyed?' She chuckled happily. 'I've never heard of such a splendid thing in my life.'

I was pleased and relieved. I had hoped the news wouldn't upset her too much, but I had never expected it to go with such a roar as this.

'I'm proud of him,' she said.

'That's fine.'

'If every young man in England went about hitting policemen in the stomach, it would be a better country to live in.'

I couldn't follow her reasoning, but everything seemed to be all right; so after a few more cheery words I said goodbye and legged it.

'Jeeves,' I said when I got back to the inn, 'everything's fine. But I am far from understanding why.'

'What actually occurred when you met Miss Sipperley, sir?'

'I told her Sippy was in the jug for assaulting the police. Upon which she burst into hearty laughter, waved her trowel in a pleased manner and said she was proud of him.'

'I think I can explain her apparently eccentric behaviour, sir. I am informed that Miss Sipperley has had a good deal of annoyance at the hands of the local constable during the past two weeks. This has doubtless resulted in a prejudice on her part against the force as a whole.'

'Really? How was that?'

'The constable has been somewhat over-zealous in the performance of his duties, sir. On no fewer than three occasions in the last ten days he has served summonses upon Miss Sipperley – for exceeding the speed limit in her car; for allowing her dog to appear in public without a collar; and for failing to abate a smoking chimney. Being in the nature of an autocrat, if I may use the term, in the village, Miss Sipperley has been accustomed to do these things in the past with impunity, and the constable's unexpected zeal has made her somewhat ill-disposed to policemen as a class and consequently disposed to look upon such assaults as Mr Sipperley's in a kindly and broadminded spirit.'

I saw his point.

'What an amazing bit of luck, Jeeves!'

'Yes, sir.'

'Where did you hear all this?'

'My informant was the constable himself, sir. He is my cousin.'

I gaped at the man. I saw, so to speak, all.

'Good Lord, Jeeves! You didn't bribe him?'

'Oh, no, sir. But it was his birthday last week, and I gave him a little present. I have always been fond of Egbert, sir.'

'How much?'

'A matter of five pounds, sir.'

I felt in my pocket.

'Here you are,' I said. 'And another five for luck.'

'Thank you very much, sir.'

'Jeeves,' I said, 'you move in a mysterious way your wonders to perform. You don't mind if I sing a bit, do you?'

'Not at all, sir,' said Jeeves.

8

FIXING IT FOR FREDDIE

'Jeeves,' I said, looking in on him one afternoon on my return from the club, 'I don't want to interrupt you.'

'No, sir?'

'But I would like a word with you.'

'Yes, sir?'

He had been packing a few of the Wooster necessaries in the old kitbag against our approaching visit to the seaside, and he now rose and stood bursting with courteous zeal.

'Jeeves,' I said, 'a somewhat disturbing situation has arisen with regard to a pal of mine.'

'Indeed sir?'

'You know Mr Bullivant?'

'Yes, sir.'

'Well, I slid into the Drones this morning for a bite of lunch, and found him in a dark corner of the smoking-room looking like the last rose of summer. Naturally I was surprised. You know what a bright lad he is as a rule. The life and soul of every gathering he attends.'

'Yes, sir.'

'Quite the little lump of fun, in fact.'

'Precisely, sir.'

'Well, I made inquiries, and he told me that he had had a quarrel with the girl he's engaged to. You knew he was engaged to Miss Elizabeth Vickers?'

'Yes, sir. I recall reading the announcement in the *Morning Post*.'

'Well, he isn't any longer. What the row was about he didn't say, but the broad facts, Jeeves, are that she has scratched the fixture. She won't let him come near her, refuses to talk on the phone, and sends back his letters unopened.'

'Extremely trying, sir.'

'We ought to do something, Jeeves. But what?'

'It is somewhat difficult to make a suggestion, sir.'

'Well, what I'm going to do for a start is to take him down to Marvis Bay with me. I know these birds who have been handed their hat by the girl of their dreams, Jeeves. What they want is complete change of scene.'

'There is much in what you say, sir.'

'Yes. Change of scene is the thing. I heard of a man. Girl refused him. Man went abroad. Two months later girl wired him "Come back, Muriel." Man started to write out a reply; suddenly found that he couldn't remember girl's surname; so never answered at all, and lived happily ever after. It may well be, Jeeves, that after Freddie Bullivant has had a few weeks of Marvis Bay he will get completely over it.'

'Very possibly, sir.'

'And, if not, it's quite likely that, refreshed by sea air and good simple food, you will get a brainwave and think up some scheme for bringing these two misguided blighters together again.'

'I will do my best, sir.'

'I knew it, Jeeves, I knew it. Don't forget to put in plenty of socks.'

'No, sir.'

'Also of tennis shirts not a few.'

'Very good, sir.'

I left him to his packing, and a couple of days later we started off for Marvis Bay, where I had taken a cottage for July and August.

I don't know if you know Marvis Bay? It's in Dorsetshire; and, while not what you would call a fiercely exciting spot, has many good points. You spend the day there bathing and sitting on the sands, and in the evening you stroll out on the shore with the mosquitoes. At nine p.m. you rub ointment on the wounds and go to bed. It was a simple, healthy life, and it seemed to suit poor old Freddie absolutely. Once the moon was up and the breeze sighing in the trees, you couldn't drag him from that beach with ropes. He became quite a popular pet with the mosquitoes. They would hang round waiting for him to come out, and would give a miss to perfectly good strollers just so as to be in good condition for him.

It was during the day that I found Freddie, poor old chap, a trifle heavy as a guest. I suppose you can't blame a bloke whose heart is broken, but it required a good deal of fortitude to bear up against this gloom-crushed exhibit during the early days of our little holiday. When he wasn't chewing a pipe and scowling at the carpet, he was sitting at the piano, playing 'The Rosary' with one finger. He couldn't play anything except 'The Rosary', and he couldn't play much of that. However firmly and confidently he started off, somewhere around the third bar a fuse would blow out and he would have to start all over again.

He was playing it as usual one morning when I came in from bathing: and it seemed to me that he was extracting more hideous melancholy from it even than usual. Nor had my sense deceived me.

'Bertie,' he said in a hollow voice, skidding on the fourth crotchet from the left as you enter the second bar and producing a distressing sound like the death-rattle of a sand-eel. 'I've seen her!'

'Seen her?' I said. 'What, Elizabeth Vickers? How do you mean, you've seen her? She isn't down here.'

'Yes, she is. I suppose she's staying with relations or something. I was down at the post office, seeing if there were any letters, and we met in the doorway.'

'What happened?'

'She cut me dead.'

He started 'The Rosary' again, and stubbed his finger on a semi-quaver.

'Bertie,' he said, 'you ought never to have brought me here. I must go away.'

'Go away? Don't talk such rot. This is the best thing that could have happened. It's a most amazing bit of luck, her being down here. This is where you come out strong.'

'She cut me.'

'Never mind. Be a sportsman. Have another dash at her.'

'She looked clean through me.'

'Well, don't mind that. Stick at it. Now, having got her down here, what you want,' I said, 'is to place her under some obligation to you. What you want is to get her timidly thanking you. What you want – '

'What's she going to thank me timidly for?'

I thought for a while. Undoubtedly he had put his finger on the nub of the problem. For some moments I was at a loss, not to say nonplussed. Then I saw the way.

'What you want,' I said, 'is to look out for a chance and save her from drowning.'

'I can't swim.'

That was Freddie Bullivant all over. A dear old chap in a thousand ways, but no help to a fellow, if you know what I mean.

He cranked up the piano once more, and I legged it for the open.

I strolled out on the beach and began to think this thing over. I would have liked to consult Jeeves, of course, but Jeeves had disappeared for the morning. There was no doubt that it was hopeless expecting Freddie to do anything for himself in this crisis. I'm not saying that dear old Freddie hasn't got his strong qualities. He is good at polo, and I have heard him spoken of as a coming man at snooker-pool. But apart from this you couldn't call him a man of enterprise.

Well, I was rounding some rocks, thinking pretty tensely, when I caught sight of a blue dress, and there was the girl in person. I had never met her, but Freddie had sixteen photographs of her sprinkled round his bedroom, and I knew I couldn't be mistaken. She was sitting on the sand, helping a small, fat child to build a castle. On a chair close by was an elderly female reading a novel. I heard the girl call her 'aunt'. So getting the reasoning faculties to work, I deduced that the fat child must be her cousin. It struck me that if Freddie had been there he would probably have tried to work up some sentiment about the kid on the strength of it. I couldn't manage this. I don't think I ever saw a kid who made me feel less sentimental. He was one of those round, bulging kids.

After he had finished his castle he seemed to get bored with life and began to cry. The girl, who seemed to read him like a book, took him off to where a fellow was selling sweets at a stall. And I walked on.

Now, those who know me, if you ask them, will tell you that I'm a chump. My Aunt Agatha would testify to this effect. So would my Uncle Percy and many more of my nearest and – if you like to use the expression – dearest. Well, I don't mind. I admit it. I *am* a chump. But what I do say – and I should like to lay the greatest possible stress on this – is that every now and then, just when the populace has given up hope that I will ever show any real human intelligence – I get what it is idle to pretend is not an inspiration. And that's what happened now. I doubt if the idea that came to me at this juncture would have occurred to a single one of any dozen of the largest-brained blokes in history. Napoleon might have got it, but I'll bet Darwin and Shakespeare and Thomas Hardy wouldn't have thought of it in a thousand years.

It came to me on my return journey. I was walking back along the shore, exercising the old bean fiercely, when I saw the fat child meditatively smacking a jelly-fish with a spade. The girl wasn't with him. The aunt wasn't with him. In fact, there wasn't anybody else in sight. And the solution of the whole trouble between Freddie and his Elizabeth suddenly came to me in a flash.

From what I had seen of the two, the girl was evidently fond of this kid: and, anyhow, he was her cousin, so what I said to myself was this: If I kidnap this young heavyweight for a brief space of time: and if, when the girl has got frightfully anxious about where he can have got to, dear old Freddie suddenly appears leading the infant by the hand and telling a story to the effect that he found him wandering at large about the country and practically saved his life, the girl's gratitude is bound to make her chuck hostilities and be friends again.

So I gathered up the kid and made off with him.

Freddie, dear old chap, was rather slow at first in getting on to the fine points of the idea. When I appeared at the cottage, carrying the child, and dumped him down in the sitting-room, he showed no joy whatever. The child had started to bellow by this time, not thinking much of the thing, and Freddie seemed to find it rather trying.

'What the devil's all this?' he asked, regarding the little visitor with a good deal of loathing.

The kid loosed off a yell that made the windows rattle, and I saw that this was a time for strategy. I raced to the kitchen and fetched a pot of honey. It was the right idea. The kid stopped bellowing and began to smear his face with the stuff.

'Well?' said Freddie, when silence had set in.

I explained the scheme. After a while it began to strike him. The careworn look faded from his face, and for the first time since his arrival at Marvis Bay he smiled almost happily.

'There's something in this, Bertie.'

'It's the goods.'

'I think it will work,' said Freddie.

And, disentangling the child from the honey, he led him out.

'I expect Elizabeth will be on the beach somewhere,' he said.

What you might call a quiet happiness suffused me, if that's the word I want. I was very fond of old Freddie, and it was jolly to think that he was shortly about to click once more. I was leaning back in a chair on the veranda, smoking a peaceful cigarette, when down the road I saw the old boy returning, and, by George, the kid was still with him.

'Hallo!' I said. 'Couldn't you find her?'

I then perceived that Freddie was looking as if he had been kicked in the stomach.

'Yes, I found her,' he replied, with one of those bitter, mirthless laughs you read about.

'Well, then – ?'

He sank into a chair and groaned.

'This isn't her cousin, you idiot,' he said. 'He's no relation at all – just a kid she met on the beach. She had never seen him before in her life.'

'But she was helping him build a sand-castle.'

'I don't care. He's a perfect stranger.'

It seemed to me that, if the modern girl goes about building sand-castles with kids she has only known for five minutes and probably without a proper introduction at that, then all that has been written about her is perfectly true. Brazen is the word that seems to meet the case.

I said as much to Freddie, but he wasn't listening.

'Well, who is this ghastly child, then?' I said.

'I don't know. O Lord, I've had a time! Thank goodness you will probably spend the next few years of your life in Dartmoor for kidnapping. That's my only consolation. I'll come and jeer at you through the bars on visiting days.'

'Tell me all, old man,' I said.

He told me all. It took him a good long time to do it, for he broke off in the middle of nearly every sentence to call me names, but I gradually gathered what had happened. The girl Elizabeth had listened like an iceberg while he worked off the story he had prepared, and then – well, she didn't actually call him a liar in so many words, but she gave him to understand in a general sort of way that he was a worm and an outcast. And then he crawled off with the kid, licked to a splinter.

'And mind,' he concluded, 'this is your affair. I'm not mixed up in it at all. If you want to escape your sentence – or anyway get a portion of it remitted – you'd better go and find the child's parents and return him before the police come for you.'

'Who are his parents?'

'I don't know.'

'Where do they live?'

'I don't know.'

The kid didn't seem to know, either. A thoroughly vapid and uninformed infant. I got out of him the fact that he had a father, but that was as far as he went. It didn't seem ever to have occurred to him, chatting of an evening with the old man, to ask him his name and address. So, after a wasted ten minutes, out we went into the great world, more or less what you might call at random.

I give you my word that, until I started to tramp the place with this child, I never had a notion that it was such a difficult job restoring a son to his parents. How kidnappers ever get caught is a mystery to me. I searched Marvis Bay like a bloodhound, but nobody came forward to claim the infant. You would have thought, from the lack of interest in him, that he was stopping there all by himself in a cottage of his own. It wasn't till, by another inspiration, I thought to ask the sweet-stall man that I got on the track. The sweet-stall man, who seemed to have seen a lot of him, said that the child's name was Kegworthy, and that his parents lived at a place called Ocean Rest.

It then remained to find Ocean Rest. And eventually, after visiting Ocean View, Ocean Prospect, Ocean Breeze, Ocean Cottage, Ocean Bungalow, Ocean Nook and Ocean Homestead, I trailed it down.

I knocked at the door. Nobody answered. I knocked again. I could hear movements inside, but nobody appeared. I was just going to get to work with that knocker in such a way that it would filter through these people's heads that I wasn't standing there just for the fun of the thing, when a voice from somewhere above shouted 'Hi!'

I looked up and saw a round, pink face, with grey whiskers east and west of it, staring down at me from an upper window.

'Hi!' it shouted again. 'You can't come in.'

'I don't want to come in.'

'Because – Oh, is that Tootles?'

'My name is not Tootles. Are you Mr Kegworthy? I've brought back your son.'

'I see him. Peep-bo, Tootles, Dadda can see 'oo.'

The face disappeared with a jerk. I could hear voices. The face reappeared.

'Hi!'

I churned the gravel madly. This blighter was giving me the pip.

'Do you live here?' asked the face.

'I have taken a cottage here for a few weeks.'

'What's your name?'

'Wooster.'

'Fancy that! Do you spell it W-o-r-c-e-s-t-e-r or W-o-o-s-t-e-r?'

'W-o-o-'

'I ask because I once knew a Miss Wooster, spelled W-o- – '

I had had about enough of this spelling-bee.

'Will you open the door and take this child in?'

'I mustn't open the door. This Miss Wooster that I knew married a man named Spenser. Was she any relation?'

'She is my Aunt Agatha,' I replied, and I spoke with a good deal of bitterness, trying to suggest by my manner that he was exactly the sort of man, in my opinion, who would know my Aunt Agatha.

He beamed down at me.

'This is most fortunate. We were wondering what to do with

Tootles. You see, we have mumps here. My daughter Bootles has just developed mumps. Tootles must not be exposed to the risk of infection. We could not think what to do with him. It was most fortunate, your finding the dear child. He strayed from his nurse. I would hesitate to trust him to a stranger, but you are different. Any nephew of Mrs Spenser's has my complete confidence. You must take Tootles into your house. It will be an ideal arrangement. I have written to my brother in London to come and fetch him. He may be here in a few days.'

'May!'

'He is a busy man, of course; but he should certainly be here within a week. Till then Tootles can stop with you. It is an excellent plan. Very much obliged to you. Your wife will like Tootles.'

'I haven't got a wife!' I yelled; but the window had closed with a bang, as if the man with the whiskers had found a germ trying to escape and had headed it off just in time.

I breathed a deep breath and wiped the old forehead.

The window flew up again.

'Hi!'

A package weighing about a ton hit me on the head and burst like a bomb.

'Did you catch it?' said the face, reappearing. 'Dear me, you missed it. Never mind. You can get it at the grocer's. Ask for Bailey's Granulated Breakfast Chips. Tootles takes them for breakfast with a little milk. Not cream. Milk. Be sure to get Bailey's.'

'Yes, but –'

The face disappeared, and the window was banged down again. I lingered a while, but nothing else happened, so, taking Tootles by the hand, I walked slowly away.

And as we turned up the road we met Freddie's Elizabeth.

'Well, baby?' she said, sighting the kid. 'So Daddy found you again, did he? Your little son and I made great friends on the beach this morning,' she said to me.

This was the limit. Coming on top of that interview with the whiskered lunatic, it so utterly unnerved me that she had nodded goodbye and was half-way down the road before I caught up with my breath enough to deny the charge of being the infant's father.

I hadn't expected Freddie to sing with joy when he saw me looming up with child complete, but I did think he might have showed a little more manly fortitude, a little more of the old British bulldog spirit. He leaped up when we came in, glared at the kid and clutched his head. He didn't speak for a long time; but, to make up for it, when he began he did not leave off for a long time.

'Well,' he said, when he had finished the body of his remarks, 'say something! Heavens, man, why don't you say something?'

'If you give me a chance, I will,' I said, and shot the bad news.

'What are you going to do about it?' he asked. And it would be idle to deny that his manner was peevish.

'What can we do about it?'

'We? What do you mean, we? I'm not going to spend my time taking turns as a nursemaid to this excrescence. I'm going back to London.'

'Freddie!' I cried. 'Freddie, old man!' My voice shook. 'Would you desert a pal at a time like this?'

'Yes, I would.'

'Freddie,' I said, 'you've got to stand by me. You must. Do you realize that this child has to be undressed, and bathed, and dressed again? You wouldn't leave me to do all that single-handed?'

'Jeeves can help you.'

'No, sir,' said Jeeves, who had just rolled in with lunch. 'I must, I fear, disassociate myself completely from the matter.' He spoke respectfully, but firmly. 'I have had little or no experience with children.'

'Now's the time to start,' I urged.

'No, sir; I am sorry to say that I cannot involve myself in any way.'

'Then you must stand by me, Freddie.'

'I won't.'

'You must. Reflect, old man! We have been pals for years. Your mother likes me.'

'No, she doesn't.'

'Well, anyway, we were at school together and you owe me a tenner.'

'Oh, well,' he said in a resigned sort of voice.

'Besides, old thing,' I said, 'I did it all for your sake, you know.'

He looked at me in a curious way, and breathed rather hard for some moments.

'Bertie,' he said, 'one moment. I will stand a good deal, but I will not stand being expected to be grateful.'

Looking back at it, I can see that what saved me from Colney Hatch in this crisis was my bright idea in buying up most of the contents of the local sweet-shop. By serving out sweets to the kid practically incessantly we managed to get through the rest of that day pretty satisfactorily. At eight o'clock he fell asleep in a chair; and, having undressed him by unbuttoning every button in sight and, where there were no buttons, pulling till something gave, we carried him up to bed.

Freddie stood looking at the pile of clothes on the floor with a sort of careworn wrinkle between his eyes, and I knew what he was thinking. To get the kid undressed had been simple – a mere matter of muscle. But how were we to get him into his clothes again? I stirred the heap with my foot. There was a long linen arrangement which might have been anything. Also a strip of pink flannel which was like nothing on earth. All most unpleasant.

But in the morning I remembered that there were children in the next bungalow but one, and I went there before breakfast and borrowed their nurse. Women are wonderful, by Jove they are! This nurse had all the spare parts assembled and in the right places in about eight minutes, and there was the kid dressed and looking fit to go to a garden party at Buckingham Palace. I showered wealth upon her, and she promised to come in morning and evening. I sat down to breakfast almost cheerful again. It was the first bit of silver lining that had presented itself to date.

'And, after all,' I said, 'there's lots to be argued in favour of having a child about the place, if you know what I mean. Kind of cosy and domestic, what?'

Just then the kid upset the milk over Freddie's trousers, and when he had come back after changing he lacked sparkle.

It was shortly after breakfast that Jeeves asked if he could have a word in my ear.

Now, though in the anguish of recent events I had rather tended to forget what had been the original idea in bringing Freddie down to this place, I hadn't forgotten it altogether; and I'm bound to say that, as the days went by, I had found myself a little disappointed in Jeeves. The scheme had been, if you recall, that he should refresh himself with sea-air and simple food and, having thus got his brain into prime working order, evolve some means of bringing Freddie and his Elizabeth together again.

And what had happened? The man had eaten well and he had slept well, but not a step did he appear to have taken towards bringing about the happy ending. The only move that had been made in that direction had been made by me, alone and unaided; and, though I freely admit that it had turned out a good deal of a bloomer, still the fact remains

that I had shown zeal and enterprise. Consequently I received him
with a bit of hauteur when he blew in. Slightly cold. A trifle frosty.

'Yes, Jeeves?' I said. 'You wished to speak to me?'

'Yes, sir.'

'Say on, Jeeves,' I said.

'Thank you, sir. What I desired to say, sir, was this: I attended a
performance at the local cinema last night.'

I raised the eyebrows. I was surprised at the man. With life in the
home so frightfully tense and the young master up against it to such
a fearful extent, I disapproved of him coming toddling in and prattling
about his amusements.

'I hope you enjoyed yourself,' I said in rather a nasty manner.

'Yes sir, thank you. The management was presenting a super-super-
film in seven reels, dealing with life in the wilder and more feverish
strata of New York Society, featuring Bertha Blevitch, Orlando Murphy and Baby Bobbie. I found it most entertaining, sir.'

'That's good,' I said. 'And if you have a nice time this morning on
the sands with your spade and bucket, you will come and tell me all
about it, won't you? I have so little on my mind just now that it's a
treat to hear all about your happy holiday.'

Satirical, if you see what I mean. Sarcastic. Almost bitter, as a
matter of fact, if you come right down to it.

'The title of the film was *Tiny Hands*, sir. And the father and
mother of the character played by Baby Bobbie had unfortunately
drifted apart – '

'Too bad,' I said.

'Although at heart they loved each other still, sir.'

'Did they really? I'm glad you told me that.'

'And so matters went on, sir, till came a day when – '

'Jeeves,' I said, fixing him with a dashed unpleasant eye, 'what the
dickens do you think you're talking about? Do you suppose that, with
this infernal child landed on me and the peace of the home practically
shattered into a million bits, I want to hear – '

'I beg your pardon, sir. I would not have mentioned this cinema
performance were it not for the fact that it gave me an idea, sir.'

'An idea!'

'An idea that will, I fancy, sir, prove of value in straightening out the
matrimonial future of Mr Bullivant. To which end, if you recollect,
sir, you desired me to – '

I snorted with remorse.

'Jeeves,' I said, 'I wronged you.'

'Not at all, sir.'

'Yes, I did. I wronged you. I had a notion that you had given yourself up entirely to the pleasures of the seaside and had chucked that businesss altogether. I might have known better. Tell me all, Jeeves.'

He bowed in a gratified manner. I beamed. And, while we didn't actually fall on each other's necks, we gave each other to understand that all was well once more.

'In this super-super-film *Tiny Hands*, sir,' said Jeeves, 'the parents of the child had, as I say, drifted apart.'

'Drifted apart,' I said, nodding. 'Right! And then?'

'Came a day, sir, when their little child brought them together again.'

'How?'

'If I remember rightly, sir, he said, "Dadda, doesn't 'oo love Mummie no more?"'

'And then?'

'They exhibited a good deal of emotion. There was what I believe is termed a cut-back, showing scenes from their courtship and early married life and some glimpses of Lovers Through the Ages, and the picture concluded with a close-up of the pair in an embrace, with the child looking on with natural gratification and an organ playing "Hearts and Flowers" in the distance.'

'Proceed, Jeeves,' I said. 'You interest me strangely. I begin to grasp the idea. You mean – ?'

'I mean, sir, that, with this young gentleman on the premises, it might be possible to arrange a *dénouement* of a somewhat similar nature in regard to Mr Bullivant and Miss Vickers.'

'Aren't you overlooking the fact that this kid is no relation of Mr Bullivant and Miss Vickers?'

'Even with that handicap, sir, I fancy that good results might ensue. I think that, if it were possible to bring Mr Bullivant and Miss Vickers together for a short space of time in the presence of the child, sir, and if the child were to say something of a touching nature – '

'I follow you absolutely, Jeeves,' I cried with enthusiasm. 'It's big. This is the way I see it. We lay the scene in this room. Child, centre. Girl, l.c. Freddie up stage, playing the piano. No, that won't do. He can only play a little of "The Rosary" with one finger, so we'll have to cut out the soft music. But the rest's all right. Look here,' I said, 'this inkpot is Miss Vickers. This mug with "A Present from Marvis Bay" on it is the child. This penwiper is Mr Bullivant. Start with dialogue leading up to child's line. Child speaks line, let us say, "Boofer lady, does 'oo love Dadda?" Business of outstretched hands. Hold picture for a moment. Freddie crosses l. takes girl's hand. Business of swallowing lump in throat. Then big speech: "Ah, Elizabeth, has not this misunderstanding of ours gone on too long? See! A little child rebukes us!" And so on. I'm just giving you the general outline. Freddie must work up his own part. And we must get a good line for the child. "Boofer lady, does 'oo love Dadda?" isn't definite enough. We want something more – '

'If I might make a suggestion, sir – ?'

'Yes?'

'I would advocate the words "Kiss Freddie?" It is short, readily memorized, and has what I believe is technically termed the punch.'

'Genius, Jeeves!'

'Thank you very much, sir.'

'"Kiss Freddie!" it is, then. But, I say, Jeeves, how the deuce are we to get them together in here? Miss Vickers cuts Mr Bullivant. She wouldn't come within a mile of him.'

'It is awkward, sir.'

'It doesn't matter. We shall have to make it an exterior set instead of an interior. We can easily corner her on the beach somewhere, when we're ready. Meanwhile, we must get the kid word-perfect.'

'Yes, sir.'

'Right! First rehearsal for lines and business at eleven sharp tomorrow morning.'

Poor old Freddie was in such a gloomy frame of mind that I decided not to tell him the idea till we had finished coaching the child. He wasn't in the mood to have a thing like that hanging over him. So we concentrated on Tootles. And pretty early in the proceedings we saw that the only way to get Tootles worked up to the spirit of the thing was to introduce sweets of some sort as a sub-motive, so to speak.

'The chief difficulty, sir,' said Jeeves, at the end of the first rehearsal, 'is, as I envisage it, to establish in the young gentleman's mind a connexion between the words we desire him to say and the refreshment.'

'Exactly,' I said. 'Once the blighter has grasped the basic fact that these two words, clearly spoken, result automatically in chocolate nougat, we have got a success.'

I've often thought how interesting it must be to be one of those animal-trainer blokes – to stimulate the dawning intelligence and all that. Well, this was every bit as exciting. Some days success seemed to be staring us in the eyeball, and the kid got out the line as if he had been an old professional. And then he would go all to pieces again. And time was flying.

'We must hurry up, Jeeves,' I said. 'The kid's uncle may arrive any day now and take him away.'

'Exactly, sir.'

'And we have no understudy.'

'Very true, sir.'

'We must work! I must say this child is a bit discouraging at times. I should have thought a deaf-mute would have learned his part by now.'

I will say this for the kid, though: he was a trier. Failure didn't damp him. Whenever there was any kind of sweet in sight he had a dash at his line, and kept saying something till he had got what he was after. His chief fault was his uncertainty. Personally, I would have been prepared to risk opening in the act and was ready to start the public performance at the first opportunity, but Jeeves said no.

'I would not advocate undue haste, sir,' he said. 'As long as the young gentleman's memory refuses to act with any certainty, we are running grave risks of failure. Today, if you recollect, sir, he said "Kick Freddie!" That is not a speech to win a young lady's heart, sir.'

'No. And she might do it, too. You're right. We must postpone production.'

But, by Jove, we didn't! The curtain went up the very next afternoon.

It was nobody's fault – certainly not mine. It was just fate. Jeeves was out, and I was alone in the house with Freddie and the child. Freddie had just settled down at the piano, and I was leading the kid out of the place for a bit of exercise, when, just as we'd got onto the veranda, along came the girl Elizabeth on her way to the beach. And at the sight of her the kid set up a matey yell, and she stopped at the foot of the steps.

'Hallo, baby,' she said. 'Good morning,' she said to me. 'May I come up?'

She didn't wait for an answer. She just hopped on to the veranda. She seemed to be that sort of girl. She started fussing over the child. And six feet away, mind you, Freddie smiting the piano in the sitting-room. It was a dashed disturbing situation, take it from Bertram. At any minute Freddie might take it into his head to come out on the veranda, and I hadn't even begun to rehearse him in his part.

I tried to break up the scene.

'We were just going down to the beach.' I said.

'Yes?' said the girl. She listened for a moment. 'So you're having your piano tuned?' she said. 'My aunt has been trying to find a tuner for ours. Do you mind if I go in and tell this man to come on to us when he has finished here?'

I mopped the brow.

'Er – I shouldn't go in just now.' I said. 'Not just now, while he's working, if you don't mind. These fellows can't bear to be disturbed when they're at work. It's the artistic temperament. I'll tell him later.'

'Very well. Ask him to call at Pine Bungalow. Vickers is the name . . . Oh, he seems to have stopped. I suppose he will be out in a minute now. I'll wait.'

'Don't you think – shouldn't you be getting on to the beach?' I said.

She had started talking to the kid and didn't hear. She was feeling in her bag for something.

'The beach,' I babbled.

'See what I've got for you, baby,' said the girl. 'I thought I might meet you somewhere, so I bought some of your favourite sweets.'

And, by Jove, she held up in front of the kid's bulging eyes, a chunk of toffee about the size of the Albert Memorial!

That finished it. We had just been having a long rehearsal, and the kid was all worked up in his part. He got it right first time.

'Kiss Fweddie!' he shouted.

And the french windows opened and Freddie came out on to the veranda, for all the world as if he had been taking a cue.

'Kiss Fweddie!' shrieked the child.

Freddie looked at the girl, and the girl looked at him. I looked at the ground, and the kid looked at the toffee.

'Kiss Fweddie!' he yelled. 'Kiss Fweddie!'

'What does this mean?' said the girl, turning on me.

'You'd better give it to him,' I said. 'He'll go on till you do, you know.'

She gave the kid the toffee and he subsided. Freddie, poor ass, still stood there gaping, without a word.

'What does it mean?' said the girl again. Her face was pink, and her eyes were sparkling in the sort of way, don't you know, that makes a fellow feel as if he hadn't any bones in him, if you know what I mean. Yes, Bertram felt filleted. Did you ever tread on your partner's dress at a dance – I'm speaking now of the days when women wore dresses long enough to be trodden on – and hear it rip and see her smile at you like an angel and say, '*Please* don't apologize. It's nothing,' and then suddenly meet her clear blue eyes and feel as if you had stepped on the teeth of a rake and had the handle jump up and hit you in the face? Well, that's how Freddie's Elizabeth looked.

'*Well?*' she said, and her teeth gave a little click.

I gulped. Then I said it was nothing. Then I said it was nothing much. Then I said, 'Oh, well, it was this way.' And told her all about it. And all the while Idiot Freddie stood there gaping, without a word. Not one solitary yip had he let out of himself from the start.

And the girl didn't speak, either. She just stood listening.

And then she began to laugh. I never heard a girl laugh so much. She leaned against the side of the veranda and shrieked. And all the while Freddie, the World's Champion Dumb Brick, standing there, saying nothing.

Well, I finished my story and sidled to the steps. I had said all I had to say, and it seemed to me that about here the stage-direction 'exit cautiously' was written in my part. I gave poor old Freddie up in despair. If only he had said a word it might have been all right. But there he stood speechless.

Just out of sight of the house I met Jeeves, returning from his stroll.

'Jeeves,' I said, 'all is over. The thing's finished. Poor dear old Freddie has made a complete ass of himself and killed the whole show.'

'Indeed, sir? What has actually happened?'

I told him.

'He fluffed his lines,' I concluded. 'Just stood there saying nothing, when if ever there was a time for eloquence, this was it. He . . . Great Scott! Look!'

We had come back within view of the cottage, and there in front of it stood six children, a nurse, two loafers, another nurse, and the fellow from the grocer's. They were all staring. Down the road came galloping five more children, a dog, three men and a boy, all about to stare. And on our porch, as unconscious of the spectators as if they had been alone in the Sahara, stood Freddie and his Elizabeth, clasped in each other's arms.

'Great Scott!' I said.

'It would appear, sir,' said Jeeves, 'that everything has concluded most satisfactorily, after all.'

'Yes. Dear old Freddie may have been fluffy in his lines,' I said, 'but his business certainly seems to have gone with a bang.'

'Very true, sir,' said Jeeves.

9

CLUSTERING ROUND YOUNG BINGO

I blotted the last page of my manuscript and sank back, feeling more or less of a spent force. After incredible sweat of the old brow the thing seemed to be in pretty fair shape, and I was just reading through and debating whether to bung in another paragraph at the end, when there was a tap at the door and Jeeves appeared.

'Mrs Travers, sir, on the telephone.'

'Oh?' I said. Preoccupied, don't you know.

'Yes, sir. She presents her compliments and would be glad to know what progress you have made with the article which you are writing for her.'

'Jeeves, can I mention men's knee-length underclothing in a woman's paper?'

'No, sir.'

'Then tell her it's finished.'

'Very good, sir.'

'And, Jeeves, when you're through, come back. I want you to cast your eye over this effort and give it the O.K.'

My Aunt Dahlia, who runs a woman's paper called *Milady's Boudoir*, had recently backed me into a corner and made me promise to write her a few authoritative words for her 'Husbands and Brothers' page on 'What the Well-Dressed Man is Wearing'. I believe in encouraging aunts, when deserving; and, as there are many worse eggs than her knocking about the metrop I had consented blithely. But I give you my honest word that if I had had the foggiest notion of what I was letting myself in for, not even a nephew's devotion would have kept me from giving her the raspberry. A deuce of a job it had been, taxing the physique to the utmost. I don't wonder now that all these author blokes have bald heads and faces like birds who have suffered.

'Jeeves,' I said, when he came back, 'you don't read a paper called *Milady's Boudoir* by any chance, do you?'

'No, sir. The periodical has not come to my notice.'

'Well, spring sixpence on it next week, because this article will appear in it. Wooster on the well-dressed man, don't you know.'

'Indeed, sir?'

'Yes, indeed, Jeeves. I've rather extended myself over this little bijou. There's a bit about socks that I think you will like.'

He took the manuscript, brooded over it, and smiled a gentle, approving smile.

'The sock passage is quite in the proper vein, sir,' he said.

'Well expressed, what?'

'Extremely, sir.'

I watched him narrowly as he read on, and, as I was expecting, what you might call the love-light suddenly died out of his eyes. I braced myself for an unpleasant scene.

'Come to the bit about soft silk shirts for evening wear?' I asked carelessly.

'Yes, sir,' said Jeeves, in a low, cold voice, as if he had been bitten in the leg by a personal friend. 'And if I may be pardoned for saying so – '

'You don't like it?'

'No, sir. I do not. Soft silk shirts with evening costume are not worn, sir.'

'Jeeves,' I said, looking the blighter diametrically in the centre of the eyeball, 'they're dashed well going to be. I may as well tell you now that I have ordered a dozen of those shirtings from Peabody and Simms, and it's no good looking like that, because I am jolly well adamant.'

'If I might – '

'No, Jeeves,' I said, raising my hand, 'argument is useless. Nobody has a greater respect than I have for your judgement in socks, ties, and – I will go farther – in spats; but when it comes to evening shirts you nerve seems to fail you. You have no vision. You are prejudiced and reactionary. Hidebound is the word that suggests itself. It may interest you to learn that when I was at Le Touquet the Prince of Wales buzzed into the Casino one night with soft silk shirt complete.'

'His Royal Highness, sir, may permit himself a certain licence which in your own case – '

'No, Jeeves,' I said firmly, 'it's no use. When we Woosters are adamant, we are – well, adamant, if you know what I mean.'

'Very good, sir.'

I could see the man was wounded, and, of course, the whole episode had been extremely jarring and unpleasant; but these things have to be gone through. Is one a serf or isn't one? That's what it all boils down to. Having made my point, I changed the subject.

'Well, that's that,' I said. 'We now approach another topic. Do you know any housemaids, Jeeves?'

'Housemaids, sir?'

'Come, come, Jeeves, you know what housemaids are.'

'Are you requiring a housemaid, sir?'

'No, but Mr Little is. I met him at the club a couple of days ago, and he told me that Mrs Little is offering rich rewards to anybody who will find her one guaranteed to go light on the china.'

'Indeed, sir?'

'Yes. The one now in office apparently runs through the *objets d'art* like a typhoon, simoom, or sirocco. So if you know any – '

'I know a great many, sir. Some intimately, others mere acquaintances.'

'Well, start digging round among the old pals. And now the hat, the stick, and other necessaries. I must be getting along and handing in this article.'

The offices of *Milady's Boudoir* were in one of those rummy streets in the Covent Garden neighbourhood; and I had just got to the door, after wading through a deep top-dressing of old cabbages and tomatoes, when who should come out but Mrs Little. She greeted me with the warmth due to the old family friend, in spite of the fact that I hadn't been round to the house for a goodish while.

'Whatever are you doing in these parts, Bertie? I thought you never came east of Leicester Square.'

'I've come to deliver an article of sorts which my Aunt Dahlia asked me to write. She edits a species of journal up those stairs. *Milady's Boudoir*.'

'What a coincidence! I have just promised to write an article for her, too.'

'Don't you do it,' I said earnestly. 'You've simply no notion what a ghastly labour – Oh, but, of course, I was forgetting. You're used to it, what?'

Silly of me to have talked like that. Young Bingo Little, if you remember, had married the famous female novelist, Rosie M. Banks, author of some of the most pronounced and widely-read tripe ever put on the market. Naturally a mere article would be pie for her.

'No, I don't think it will give me much trouble,' she said. 'Your aunt has suggested a most delightful subject.'

'That's good. By the way, I spoke to my man Jeeves about getting you a housemaid. He knows all the hummers.'

'Thank you so much. Oh, are you doing anything tomorrow night?'

'Not a thing.'

'Then do come and dine with us. Your aunt is coming, and hopes to bring your uncle. I am looking forward to meeting him.'

'Thanks. Delighted.'

I meant it, too. The Little household may be weak on housemaids, but it is right there when it comes to cooks. Somewhere or other some time ago Bingo's missus managed to dig up a Frenchman of the most extraordinary vim and skill. A most amazing Johnnie who dishes a wicked *ragout*. Old Bingo has put on at least ten pounds in weight since this fellow Anatole arrived in the home.

'At eight, then.'

'Right. Thanks ever so much.'

She popped off, and I went upstairs to hand in my copy, as we boys of the Press call it. I found Aunt Dahlia immersed to the gills in papers of all descriptions.

I am not much of a lad for my relatives as a general thing, but I've always been very pally with Aunt Dahlia. She married my Uncle Thomas – between ourselves a bit of a squirt – the year Bluebottle won the Cambridgeshire; and they hadn't got halfway down the aisle before I was saying to myself, 'That woman is much too good for the old bird.' Aunt Dahlia is a large, genial soul, the sort you see in dozens on the hunting field. As a matter of fact, until she married Uncle Thomas, she put in most of her time on horseback; but he won't live in the country, so nowadays she expends her energy on this paper of hers.

She came to the surface as I entered, and flung a cheery look at my head.

'Hullo, Bertie! I say, have you really finished that article?'

'To the last comma.'

'Good boy! My gosh, I'll bet it's rotten.'

'On the contrary, it is extremely hot stuff, and most of it approved by Jeeves, what's more. The bit about soft silk shirts got in amongst him a trifle; but you can take it from me, Aunt Dahlia, that they are the latest yodel and will be much seen at first nights and other occasions where Society assembles.'

'Your man Jeeves,' said Aunt Dahlia, flinging the article into a basket and skewering a few loose pieces of paper on a sort of meat hook, 'is a washout, and you can tell him I said so.'

'Oh, come,' I said. 'He may not be sound on shirtings – '

'I'm not referring to that. As long as a week ago I asked him to get me a cook, and he hasn't found one yet.'

'Great Scott! Is Jeeves a domestic employment agency? Mrs Little wants him to find her a housemaid. I met her outside. She tells me she's doing something for you.'

'Yes, thank goodness. I'm relying on it to bump the circulation up a bit. I can't read her stuff myself, but women love it. Her name on the cover will mean a lot. And we need it.'

'Paper not doing well?'

'It's doing all right really, but it's got to be a slow job building up a circulation.'

'I suppose so.'

'I can get Tom to see that in his lucid moments,' said Aunt Dahlia, skewering a few more papers. 'But just at present the poor fathead has got one of his pessimistic spells. It's entirely due to that mechanic who calls herself a cook. A few more of her alleged dinners, and Tom will refuse to go on paying the printer's bills.'

'You don't mean that!'

'I do mean it. There was what she called a *ris de veau à la financière* last night which made him talk for three-quarters of an hour about good money going to waste and nothing to show for it.'

I quite understood, and I was dashed sorry for her. My Uncle Thomas is a cove who made a colossal pile of money out in the East, but in doing so put his digestion on the blink. This has made him a tricky proposition to handle. Many a time I've lunched with him and found him perfectly chirpy up to the fish, only to have him turn blue on me well before the cheese.

Who was that lad they used to try to make me read at Oxford? Ship – Shop – Schopenhauer. That's the name. A grouch of the most pronounced description. Well, Uncle Thomas, when his gastric juices have been giving him the elbow, can make Schopenhauer look like Pollyanna. And the worst of it is, from Aunt Dahlia's point of view, that on these occasions he always seems to think he's on the brink of ruin and wants to start to economize.

'Pretty tough,' I said. 'Well, anyway, he'll get one good dinner tomorrow night at the Littles'.'

'Can you guarantee that, Bertie?' asked Aunt Dahlia earnestly. 'I simply daren't risk unleashing him on anything at all wonky.'

'They've got a marvellous cook. I haven't been round there for some time, but unless he's lost his form of two months ago Uncle Thomas is going to have the treat of a lifetime.'

'It'll only make it all the worse for him, coming back to our steak-incinerator,' said Aunt Dahlia, a bit on the Schopenhauer side herself.

*

The little nest where Bingo and his bride had settled themselves was up in St John's Wood; one of those rather jolly houses with a bit of garden. When I got there on the following night, I found that I was the last to weigh in. Aunt Dahlia was chatting with Rosie in a corner, while Uncle Thomas, standing by the mantelpiece with Bingo, sucked down a cocktail in a frowning, suspicious sort of manner, rather like a chappie having a short snort before dining with the Borgias: as if he were saying to himself that, even if this particular cocktail wasn't poisoned, he was bound to cop it later on.

Well, I hadn't expected anything in the nature of beaming *joie de vivre* from Uncle Thomas, so I didn't pay much attention to him. What did surprise me was the extraordinary gloom of young Bingo. You may say what you like against Bingo, but nobody has ever found him a depressing host. Why, many a time in the days of his bachelorhood I've known him to start throwing bread before the soup course. Yet now he and Uncle Thomas were a pair. He looked haggard and careworn, like a Borgia who has suddenly remembered that he has forgotten to shove cyanide in the *consommé*, and the dinner gong due any moment.

And the mystery wasn't helped at all by the one remark he made to me before conversation became general. As he poured out my cocktail, he suddenly bent forward.

'Bertie,' he whispered, in a nasty, feverish manner. 'I want to see you. Life and death matter. Be in tomorrow morning.'

That was all. Immediately after that the starting-gun went and we toddled down to the festive. And from that moment, I'm bound to say, in the superior interests of the proceedings he rather faded out of my mind. For good old Anatole, braced presumably by the fact of there being guests, had absolutely surpassed himself.

I am not a man who speaks hastily on these matters. I weigh my words. And I say again that Anatole had surpassed himself. It was as good a dinner as I have ever absorbed, and it revived Uncle Thomas like a watered flower. As we sat down he was saying some things about the Government which they wouldn't have cared to hear. With the *consommé pâté d'Italie* he said but what could you expect nowadays? With the *paupiettes de sole à la princesse* he admitted rather decently that the Government couldn't be held responsible for the rotten weather, anyway. And shortly after the *caneton Aylesbury à la broche* he was practically giving the lads the benefit of his whole-hearted support.

And all the time young Bingo looking like an owl with a secret sorrow. Rummy!

I thought about it a good deal as I walked home, and I was hoping he wouldn't roll round with his hard-luck story too early in the morning. He had the air of one who intends to charge in at about six-thirty.

Jeeves was waiting up for me when I got back.

'A pleasant dinner, sir?' he said.

'Magnificent, Jeeves.'

'I am glad to hear that, sir. Mr George Travers rang up on the telephone shortly after you had left. He was extremely desirous that you should join him at Harrogate, sir. He leaves for that town by an early train tomorrow.'

My Uncle George is a festive old bird who has made a habit for years of doing himself a dashed sight too well, with the result that he's always got Harrogate or Buxton hanging over him like the sword of what's-his-name. And he hates going there alone.

'It can't be done,' I said. Uncle George is bad enough in London, and I wasn't going to let myself be cooped up with him in one of these cure-places.

'He was extremely urgent, sir.'

'No, Jeeves,' I said firmly. 'I am always anxious to oblige, but Uncle George – no, no! I mean to say, what?'

'Very good, sir,' said Jeeves.

It was a pleasure to hear the way he said it. Docile the man was becoming, absolutely docile. It just showed that I had been right in putting my foot down about those shirts.

When Bingo showed up next morning I had had breakfast and was all ready for him. Jeeves shot him into the presence, and he sat down on the bed.

'Good morning, Bertie,' said young Bingo.

'Good morning, old thing,' I replied courteously.

'Don't go, Jeeves,' said young Bingo hollowly. 'Wait.'

'Sir?'

'Remain. Stay. Cluster round. I shall need you.'

'Very good, sir.'

Bingo lit a cigarette and frowned bleakly at the wallpaper.

'Bertie,' he said, 'the most frightful calamity has occurred. Unless something is done, and done right speedily, my social prestige is doomed, my self-respect will be obliterated, my name will be mud, and I shall not dare to show my face in the West End of London again.'

'My aunt!' I cried, deeply impressed.

'Exactly,' said young Bingo, with a hollow laugh. 'You have put it in a nutshell. The whole trouble is due to your blasted aunt.'

'Which blasted aunt? Specify, old thing. I have so many.'

'Mrs Travers. The one who runs that infernal paper.'

'Oh, no, dash it, old man,' I protested. 'She's the only decent aunt I've got. Jeeves, you will bear me out in this?'

'Such has always been my impression, I must confess, sir.'

'Well, get rid of it, then,' said young Bingo. 'The woman is a menace to society, a home-wrecker, and a pest. Do you know what she's done? She's got Rosie to write an article for that rag of hers.'

'I know that.'

'Yes, but you don't know what it's about.'

'No. She told me Aunt Dahlia had given her a splendid idea for the thing.'

'It's about me!'

'You?'

'Yes, me! And do you know what it's called? It is called "How I Keep the Love of My Husband-Baby".'

'My what?'

'Husband-baby!'

'What's a husband-baby?'

'I am, apparently,' said young Bingo, with much bitterness. 'I am also, according to this article, a lot of other things which I have too much sense of decency to repeat even to an old friend. This beastly composition, in short, is one of those things they call "human interest stories"; one of those intimate revelations of married life over which the female public loves to gloat; all about Rosie and me and what she does when I come home cross, and so on. I tell you, Bertie, I am still blushing all over at the recollection of something she says in paragraph two.'

'What?'

'I decline to tell you. But you can take it from me that it's the edge. Nobody could be fonder of Rosie than I am, but – dear, sensible girl as she is in ordinary life – the moment she gets in front of a dictating machine she becomes absolutely maudlin. Bertie, that article must not appear!'

'But –'

'If it does I shall have to resign from my clubs, grow a beard, and become a hermit. I shall not be able to face the world.'

'Aren't you pitching it a bit strong, old lad?' I said. 'Jeeves, don't you think he's pitching it a bit strong?'

'Well, sir –'

'I am pitching it feebly,' said young Bingo earnestly. 'You haven't heard the thing. I have. Rosie shoved the cylinder on the dictating machine last night before dinner, and it was grisly to hear the instrument croaking out those awful sentences. If that article appears I shall be kidded to death by every pal I've got. Bertie,' he said, his voice sinking to a hoarse whisper, 'you have about as much imagination as a warthog, but surely even you can picture to yourself what Jimmy Bowles and Tuppy Rogers, to name only two, will say when they see me referred to in print as "half god, half prattling, mischievous child"?'

I jolly well could.

'She doesn't say that?' I gasped.

'She certainly does. And when I tell you that I selected that particular quotation because it's about the only one I can stand hearing spoken, you will realize what I'm up against.'

I picked at the coverlet. I had been a pal of Bingo's for many years, and we Woosters stand by our pals.

'Jeeves,' I said, 'you have heard?'

'Yes, sir.'

'The position is serious.'

'Yes, sir.'

'We must cluster round.'

'Yes, sir.'

'Does anything suggest itself to you?'

'Yes, sir.'

'What! You don't really mean that?'

'Yes, sir.'

'Bingo,' I said, 'the sun is still shining. Something suggests itself to Jeeves.'

'Jeeves,' said young Bingo, in a quivering voice, 'if you see me through this fearful crisis, ask of me what you will even unto half my kingdom.'

'The matter,' said Jeeves, 'fits in very nicely, sir, with another mission which was entrusted to me this morning.'

'What do you mean?'

'Mrs Travers rang me up on the telephone shortly before I brought you your tea, sir, and was most urgent that I should endeavour to persuade Mr Little's cook to leave Mr Little's service and join her staff. It appears that Mr Travers was fascinated by the man's ability, sir, and talked far into the night of his astonishing gifts.'

Young Bingo uttered a frightful cry of agony.

'What! Is that – that buzzard trying to pinch our cook?'

'Yes, sir.'

'After eating our bread and salt, dammit?'

'I fear, sir,' sighed Jeeves, 'that when it comes to a matter of cooks, ladies have but a rudimentary sense of morality.'

'Half a second, Bingo,' I said, as the fellow seemed about to plunge into something of an oration. 'How does this fit in with the other thing, Jeeves?'

'Well, sir, it has been my experience that no lady can ever forgive another lady for taking a really good cook away from her. I am convinced that, if I am able to accomplish the mission which Mrs Travers entrusted to me, an instant breach of cordial relations must inevitably ensue. Mrs Little will, I feel certain, be so aggrieved with Mrs Travers that she will decline to contribute to her paper. We shall therefore not only bring happiness to Mr Travers, but also suppress the article. Thus killing two birds with one stone, if I may use the expression, sir.'

'Certainly you may use the expression, Jeeves,' I said cordially. 'And I may add that in my opinion this is one of your best and ripest.'

'Yes, but I say, you know,' bleated young Bingo. 'I mean to say – old Anatole, I mean – what I'm driving at is that he's a cook in a million.'

'You poor chump, if he wasn't there would be no point in the scheme.'

'Yes, but what I mean – I shall miss him, you know. Miss him fearfully.'

'Good heavens!' I cried. 'Don't tell me that you are thinking of your tummy in a crisis like this?'

Bingo sighed heavily.

'Oh, all right,' he said. 'I suppose it's a case of the surgeon's knife. All right, Jeeves, you may carry on. Yes, carry on, Jeeves. Yes, yes, Jeeves, carry on. I'll look in tomorrow morning and hear what you have to report.'

And with bowed head young Bingo biffed off.

He was bright and early next morning. In fact, he turned up at such an indecent hour that Jeeves very properly refused to allow him to break in on my slumbers.

By the time I was awake and receiving, he and Jeeves had had a heart-to-heart chat in the kitchen; and when Bingo eventually crept into my room I could see by the look on his face that something had gone wrong.

'It's all off,' he said, slumping down on the bed.

'Off?'

'Yes; that cook-pinching business. Jeeves tells me he saw Anatole last night, and Anatole refused to leave.'

'But surely Aunt Dahlia had the sense to offer him more than he was getting with you?'

'The sky was the limit, as far as she was concerned. Nevertheless, he refused to skid. It seems he's in love with our parlourmaid.'

'But you haven't got a parlourmaid.'

'We have got a parlourmaid.'

'I've never seen her. A sort of bloke who looked like a provincial undertaker waited at the table the night before last.'

'That was the local greengrocer, who comes to help out when desired. The parlourmaid is away on her holiday – or was till last night. She returned about ten minutes before Jeeves made his call, and Anatole, I take it, was in such a state of elation and devotion and what not on seeing her again that the contents of the Mint wouldn't have bribed him to part from her.'

'But look here, Bingo,' I said, 'this is all rot. I see the solution right off. I'm surprised that a bloke of Jeeves's mentality overlooked it. Aunt Dahlia must engage the parlourmaid as well as Anatole. Then they won't be parted.'

'I thought of that, too. Naturally.'

'I bet you didn't.'

'I certainly did.'

'Well, what's wrong with the scheme?'

'It can't be worked. If your aunt engaged our parlourmaid she would have to sack her own, wouldn't she?'

'Well?'

'Well, if she sacks her parlourmaid, it will mean that the chauffeur will quit. He's in love with her.'

'With my aunt?'

'No, with the parlourmaid. And apparently he's the only chauffeur your uncle has ever found who drives carefully enough for him.'

I gave it up. I had never imagined before that life below stairs was so frightfully mixed up with what these coves call the sex complex. The personnel of domestic staffs seemed to pair off like characters in a musical comedy.

'Oh!' I said. 'Well, that being so, we do seem to be more or less stymied. That article will have to appear after all, what?'

'No, it won't.'

'Has Jeeves thought of another scheme?'

'No, but I have,' Bingo bent forward and patted my knee affectionately. 'Look here, Bertie,' he said, 'you and I were at school together. You'll admit that?'

'Yes, but – '

'And you're a fellow who never lets a pal down. That's well known, isn't it?'

'Yes, but listen – '

'You'll cluster round. Of course you will. As if,' said Bingo with a scornful laugh, 'I ever doubted it! You won't let an old school-friend down in his hour of need. Not you. Not Bertie Wooster. No, no!'

'Yes, but just one moment. What is this scheme of yours?'

Bingo massaged my shoulder soothingly.

'It's something right in your line, Bertie, old man; something that'll come as easy as pie to you. As a matter of fact, you've done very much the same thing before – that time you were telling me about when you pinched your uncle's Memoirs at Easeby. I suddenly remembered that, and it gave me the idea. It's – '

'Here! Listen!'

'It's all settled, Bertie. Nothing for you to worry about. Nothing whatever. I see now that we made a big mistake in ever trying to tackle this job in Jeeves's silly, roundabout way. Much better to charge straight ahead without any of that finesse and fooling about. And so – '

'Yes, but listen – '

'And so this afternoon I'm going to take Rosie to a matinée. I shall leave the window of her study open, and when we have got well away you will climb in, pinch the cylinder and pop off again. It's absurdly simple – '

'Yes, but half a second – '

'I know what you are going to say,' said Bingo, raising his hand. 'How are you to find the cylinder? That's what is bothering you, isn't it? Well, it will be quite easy. Not a chance of a mistake. The thing is in the top left-hand drawer of the desk, and the drawer will be left unlocked because Rosie's stenographer is to come round at four o'clock and type the article.'

'Now listen, Bingo,' I said. 'I'm frightfully sorry for you and all that, but I must firmly draw the line at burglary.'

'But, dash it, I'm only asking you to do what you did at Easeby.'

'No, you aren't. I was staying at Easeby. It was simply a case of having to lift a parcel off the hall table. I hadn't got to break into a house. I'm sorry, but I simply will not break into your beastly house on any consideration whatever.'

He gazed at me, astonished and hurt.

'Is this Bertie Wooster speaking?' he said in a low voice.

'Yes, it is!'

'But, Bertie,' he said gently, 'we agreed that you were at school
with me.'

'I don't care.'

'At school, Bertie. The dear old school.'

'I don't care. I will not – '

'Bertie!'

'I will not – '

'Bertie!'

'No!'

'Bertie!'

'Oh, all right,' I said.

'There,' said young Bingo, patting me on the shoulder, 'spoke the
true Bertram Wooster!'

I don't know if it has ever occurred to you, but to the thoughtful cove
there is something dashed reassuring in all the reports of burglaries
you read in the papers. I mean, if you're keen on Great Britain
maintaining her prestige and all that. I mean, there can't be much
wrong with the morale of a country whose sons go in to such a large
extent for housebreaking, because you can take it from me that the
job requires a nerve of the most cast-iron description. I suppose I was
walking up and down in front of that house for half an hour before I
could bring myself to dash in at the front gate and slide round to the
side where the study window was. And even then I stood for about ten
minutes cowering against the wall and listening for police-whistles.

Eventually, however, I braced myself up and got to business. The
study was on the ground floor and the window was nice and large,
and, what is more, wide open. I got the old knee over the sill, gave
a jerk which took an inch of skin off my ankle, and hopped down into
the room. And there I was, if you follow me.

I stood for a moment, listening. Everything seemed to be all right.
I was apparently alone in the world.

In fact, I was so much alone that the atmosphere seemed positively
creepy. You know how it is on these occasions. There was a clock
on the mantelpiece that ticked in a slow, shocked sort of way that
was dashed unpleasant. And over the clock a large portrait stared
at me with a good deal of dislike and suspicion. It was a portrait
of somebody's grandfather. Whether he was Rosie's or Bingo's I
didn't know, but he was certainly a grandfather. In fact, I wouldn't
be prepared to swear that he wasn't a great-grandfather. He was a
big, stout old buffer in a high collar that seemed to hurt his neck,
for he had drawn his chin back a goodish way and was looking

down his nose as much as to say, '*You* made me put this dam' thing on!'

Well, it was only a step to the desk, and nothing between me and it but a brown shaggy rug; so I avoided grandfather's eye and, summoning up the good old bulldog courage of the Woosters, moved forward and started to navigate the rug. And I had hardly taken a step when the south-east corner of it suddenly detached itself from the rest and sat up with a snuffle.

Well, I mean to say, to bear yourself fittingly in the face of an occurrence of this sort you want to be one of those strong, silent, phlegmatic birds who are ready for anything. This type of bloke, I imagine, would simply have cocked an eye at the rug, said to himself, 'Ah, a Pekingese dog, and quite a good one, too!' and started at once to make cordial overtures to the animal in order to win its sympathy and moral support. I suppose I must be one of the neurotic younger generation you read about in the papers nowadays, because it was pretty plain within half a second that I wasn't strong and I wasn't phlegmatic. This wouldn't have mattered so much, but I wasn't silent either. In the emotion of the moment I let out a sort of sharp yowl and leaped about four feet in a north-westerly direction. And there was a crash that sounded as though somebody had touched off a bomb.

What a female novelist wants with an occasional table in her study containing a vase, two framed photographs, a saucer, a lacquer box, and a jar of pot-pourri, I don't know; but that was what Bingo's Rosie had, and I caught it squarely with my right hip and knocked it endways. It seemed to me for a moment as if the whole world had dissolved into a kind of cataract of glass and china. A few years ago, when I legged it to America to elude my Aunt Agatha, who was out with her hatchet, I remember going to Niagara and listening to the Falls. They made much the same sort of row, but not so loud.

And at the same instant the dog began to bark.

It was a small dog – the sort of animal from which you would have expected a noise like a squeaking, slate-pencil; but it was simply baying. It had retired into a corner, and was leaning against the wall with bulging eyes; and every two seconds it chucked its head back in a kind of pained way and let out another terrific bellow.

Well, I know when I'm licked. I was sorry for Bingo and regretted the necessity of having to let him down; but the time had come, I felt, to shift. 'Outside for Bertram!' was the slogan, and I took a running leap at the window and scrambled through.

And there on the path, as if they had been waiting for me by appointment, stood a policeman and a parlourmaid.

It was an embarrassing moment.

'Oh – er – there you are!' I said. And there was what you might call a contemplative silence for a moment.

'I told you I heard something,' said the parlourmaid.

The policeman was regarding me in a boiled way.

'What's all this?' he asked.

I smiled in a sort of saint-like manner.

'It's a little hard to explain,' I said.

'Yes, it is!' said the policeman.

'I was just – er – having a look round, you know. Old friend of the family, you understand.'

'How did you get in?'

'Through the window. Being an old friend of the family, if you follow me.'

'Old friend of the family, are you?'

'Oh, very. Very. Very old. Oh, a very old friend of the family.'

'I've never seen him before,' said the parlourmaid.

I looked at the girl with positive loathing. How she could have inspired affection in anyone, even a French cook, beat me. Not that she was a bad-looking girl, mind you. Not at all. On another and happier occasion I might even have thought her rather pretty. But now she seemed one of the most unpleasant females I had ever encountered.

'No,' I said. 'You have never seen me before. But I'm an old friend of the family.'

'Then why didn't you ring at the front door?'

'I didn't want to give any trouble.'

'It's no trouble answering front doors, that being what you're paid for,' said the parlourmaid virtuously. 'I've never seen him before in my life,' she added, perfectly gratuitously. A horrid girl.

'Well, look here,' I said, with an inspiration, 'the undertaker knows me.'

'What undertaker?'

'The cove who was waiting at table when I dined here the night before last.'

'Did the undertaker wait at table on the sixteenth instant?' asked the policeman.

'Of course he didn't,' said the parlourmaid.

'Well, he looked like – By Jove, no. I remember now. He was the greengrocer.'

'On the sixteenth instant,' said the policeman – pompous ass! – 'did the greengrocer – ?'

'Yes, he did, if you want to know,' said the parlourmaid. She seemed disappointed and baffled, like a tigress that sees its prey being sneaked away from it. Then she brightened. 'But this fellow could easily have found that out by asking round about.'

A perfectly poisonous girl.

'What's your name?' asked the policeman.

'Well, I say, do you mind awfully if I don't give my name, because – '

'Suit yourself. You'll have to tell it to the magistrate.'

'Oh, no, I say, dash it!'

'I think you'd better come along.'

'But I say, really, you know, I am an old friend of the family. Why, by Jove, now I remember, there's a photograph of me in the drawing-room. Well, I mean, that shows you!'

'If there is,' said the policeman.

'I've never seen it,' said the parlourmaid.

I absolutely hated this girl.

'You would have seen it if you had done your dusting more conscientiously,' I said severely. And I meant it to sting, by Jove!

'It is not a parlourmaid's place to dust the drawing-room,' she sniffed haughtily.

'No,' I said bitterly. 'It seems to be a parlourmaid's place to lurk about and hang about and – er – waste her time fooling about in the garden with policemen who ought to be busy about their duties elsewhere.'

'It's a parlourmaid's place to open the front door to visitors. Them that don't come in through windows.'

I perceived that I was getting the loser's end of the thing. I tried to be conciliatory.

'My dear old parlourmaid,' I said, 'don't let us descend to vulgar wrangling. All I'm driving at is that there is a photograph of me in the drawing-room, cared for and dusted by whom I know not; and this photograph will, I think, prove to you that I am an old friend of the family. I fancy so, officer?'

'If it's there,' said the man in a grudging way.

'Oh, it's there all right. Oh, yes, it's there.'

'Well, we'll go to the drawing-room and see.'

'Spoken like a man, my dear old policeman,' I said.

The drawing-room was on the first floor, and the photograph was on the table by the fireplace. Only, if you understand me, it wasn't. What I mean is there was the fireplace, and there was the table by the fireplace, but, by Jove, not a sign of any photograph of me whatsoever.

A photograph of Bingo, yes. A photograph of Bingo's uncle, Lord Bittlesham, right. A photograph of Mrs Bingo, three-quarter face, with a tender smile on her lips, all present and correct. But of anything resembling Bertram Wooster, not a trace.

'Ho!' said the policeman.

'But, dash it, it was there the night before last.'

'Ho!' he said again. 'Ho! Ho!' As if he were starting a drinking-chorus in a comic opera, confound him.

Then I got what amounted to the brainwave of a lifetime.

'Who dusts these things?' I said, turning on the parlourmaid.

'I don't.'

'I didn't say you did. I said who did.'

'Mary. The housemaid, of course.'

'Exactly. As I suspected. As I foresaw. Mary, officer, is notoriously the worst smasher in London. There have been complaints about her on all sides. You see what has happened? The wretched girl has broken the glass of my photograph and, not being willing to come forward and admit it in an honest, manly way, has taken the thing off and concealed it somewhere.'

'Ho!' said the policeman, still working through the drinking-chorus.

'Well, ask her. Go down and ask her.'

'You go down and ask her,' said the policeman to the parlourmaid. 'If it's going to make him any happier.'

The parlourmaid left the room, casting a pestilential glance at me over her shoulder as she went. I'm not sure she didn't say 'Ho!' too. And then there was a bit of a lull. The policeman took up a position with a large beefy back against the door, and I wandered to and fro and hither and yonder.

'What are you playing at?' demanded the policeman.

'Just looking round. They may have moved the thing.'

'Ho!'

And then there was another bit of a lull. And suddenly I found myself by the window, and, by Jove, it was six inches open at the bottom. And the world beyond looked so bright and sunny and – Well, I don't claim that I am a particularly swift thinker, but once more something seemed to whisper 'Outside for Bertram!' I slid my fingers nonchalantly under the sash, gave a hefty heave, and up she came. And the next moment I was in a laurel bush, feeling like the cross which marks the spot where the accident occurred.

A large red face appeared in the window. I got up and skipped lightly to the gate.

'Hi!' shouted the policeman.

'Ho!' I replied, and went forth, moving well.

'This,' I said to myself, as I hailed a passing cab and sank back on the cushions, 'is the last time I try to do anything for young Bingo!'

These sentiments I expressed in no guarded language to Jeeves when I was back in the old flat with my feet on the mantelpiece, pushing down a soothing whisky-and.

'Never again, Jeeves!' I said. 'Never again!'

'Well, sir – '

'No, never again!'

'Well, sir – '

'What do you mean, "Well, sir"? What are you driving at?'

'Well, sir, Mr Little is an extremely persistent young gentleman, and yours, if I may say so, sir, is a yielding and obliging nature – '

'You don't think that young Bingo would have the immortal rind to try to get me into some other foul enterprise?'

'I should say that it was more than probable, sir.'

I removed the dogs swiftly from the mantelpiece, and jumped up, all of a twitter.

'Jeeves, what would you advise?'

'Well, sir, I think a little change of scene would be judicious.'

'Do a bolt?'

'Precisely, sir. If I might suggest it, sir, why not change your mind and join Mr George Travers at Harrogate?'

'Oh, I say, Jeeves!'

'You would be out of what I might describe as the danger zone there, sir.'

'Perhaps you're right, Jeeves,' I said thoughtfully. 'Yes, possibly you're right. How far is Harrogate from London?'

'Two hundred and six miles, sir.'

'Yes, I think you're right. Is there a train this afternoon?'

'Yes, sir. You could catch it quite easily.'

'All right, then. Bung a few necessaries in a bag.'

'I have already done so, sir.'

'Ho!' I said.

It's a rummy thing, but when you come down to it Jeeves is always right. He had tried to cheer me up at the station by saying that I would not find Harrogate unpleasant, and, by Jove, he was perfectly correct. What I had overlooked, when examining the project, was the fact that I should be in the middle of a bevy of blokes who were taking the cure and I shouldn't be taking it myself. You've no notion what a dashed cosy, satisfying feeling that gives a fellow.

I mean to say, there was old Uncle George, for instance. The medicine-man, having given him the once-over, had ordered him to abstain from all alcoholic liquids, and in addition to tool down the hill to the Royal Pump-Room each morning at eight-thirty and imbibe twelve ounces of warm crescent saline and magnesia. It doesn't sound much, put that way, but I gather from contemporary accounts that it's practically equivalent to getting outside a couple of little old last year's eggs beaten up in sea-water. And the thought of Uncle George, who had oppressed me sorely in my childhood, sucking down that stuff and having to hop out of bed at eight-fifteen to do so was extremely grateful and comforting of a morning.

At four in the afternoon he would toddle down the hill again and repeat the process, and at night we would dine together and I would loll back in my chair, sipping my wine, and listen to him telling me what the stuff had tasted like. In many ways the ideal existence.

I generally managed to fit it in with my engagements to go down and watch him tackle his afternoon dose, for we Woosters are as fond of a laugh as anyone. And it was while I was enjoying the performance in the middle of the second week that I heard my name spoken. And there was Aunt Dahlia.

'Hallo!' I said. 'What are you doing here?'

'I came down yesterday with Tom.'

'Is Tom taking the cure?' asked Uncle George, looking up hopefully from the hell-brew.

'Yes.'

'Are you taking the cure?'

'Yes.'

'Ah!' said Uncle George, looking happier than I had seen him for days. He swallowed the last drops, and then, the programme calling for a brisk walk before his massage, left us.

'I shouldn't have thought you would have been able to get away from the paper,' I said. 'I say,' I went on, struck by a pleasing idea. 'It hasn't bust up, has it?'

'Bust up? I should say not. A pal of mine is looking after it for me while I'm here. It's right on its feet now. Tom has given me a couple of thousand and says there's more if I want it, and I've been able to buy serial rights of Lady Bablockhythe's *Frank Recollections of a Long Life*. The hottest stuff, Bertie. Certain to double the circulation and send half the best-known people in London into hysterics for a year.'

'Oh!' I said. 'Then you're pretty well fixed, what? I mean, what with the Frank Recollections and that article of Mrs Little's.'

Aunt Dahlia was drinking something that smelled like a leak in the gas-pipe, and I thought for a moment that it was that that made her twist up her face. But I was wrong.

'Don't mention that woman to me, Bertie!' she said. 'One of the worst.'

'But I thought you were rather pally.'

'No longer. Will you credit it that she positively refuses to let me have that article – '

'What!'

'–purely and simply on account of some fancied grievance she thinks she has against me because her cook left her and came to me.'

I couldn't follow this at all.

'Anatole left her?' I said. 'But what about the parlourmaid?'

'Pull yourself together, Bertie. You're babbling. What do you mean?'

'Why, I understood – '

'I'll bet you never understood anything in your life.' She laid down her empty glass. 'Well, that's done!' she said with relief. 'Thank goodness, I'll be able to watch Tom drinking his in a few minutes. It's the only thing that enables me to bear up. Poor old chap, he does hate it so! But I cheer him by telling him it's going to put him in shape for Anatole's cooking. And that, Bertie, is something worth going into training for. A master of his art, that man. Sometimes I'm not altogether surprised that Mrs Little made such a fuss when he went. But, really, you know, she ought not to mix sentiment with business. She has no right to refuse to let me have that article just because of a private difference. Well, she jolly well can't use it anywhere else, because it was my idea and I have witnesses to prove it. If she tries to sell it to another paper, I'll sue her. And, talking of sewers, it's high time Tom was here to drink his sulphur-water.'

'But look here – '

'Oh, by the way, Bertie,' said Aunt Dahlia, 'I withdraw any harsh expressions I may have used about your man Jeeves. A most capable feller!'

'Jeeves?'

'Yes; he attended to the negotiations. And very well he did it, too. And he hasn't lost by it, you can bet. I saw to that. I'm grateful to him. Why, if Tom gives up a couple of thousand now, practically without a murmur, the imagination reels at what he'll do with Anatole cooking regularly for him. He'll be signing cheques in his sleep.'

I got up. Aunt Dahlia pleaded with me to stick around and watch Uncle Tom in action, claiming it to be a sight nobody should miss, but I couldn't wait. I rushed up the hill, left a farewell note for Uncle George, and caught the next train for London.

'Jeeves,' I said, when I had washed off the stains of travel, 'tell me frankly all about it. Be as frank as Lady Bablockhythe.'

'Sir?'

'Never mind, if you've not heard of her. Tell me how you worked this binge. The last I heard was that Anatole loved that parlourmaid – goodness knows why! – so much that he refused to leave her. Well, then?'

'I was somewhat baffled for a while, I must confess, sir. Then I was materially assisted by a fortunate discovery.'

'What was that?'

'I chanced to be chatting with Mrs Travers's housemaid, sir, and, remembering that Mrs Little was anxious to obtain a domestic of that description, I asked her if she would consent to leave Mrs Travers and go at an advanced wage to Mrs Little. To this she assented, and I saw Mrs Little and arranged the matter.'

'Well? What was the fortunate discovery?'

'That the girl, in a previous situation some little time back, had been a colleague of Anatole, sir. And Anatole, as is the too frequent practice of these Frenchmen, had made love to her. In fact, they were, so I understand it, sir, formally affianced until Anatole disappeared one morning, leaving no address, and passed out of the poor girl's life. You will readily appreciate that this discovery simplified matters considerably. The girl no longer had any affection for Anatole, but the prospect of being under the same roof with two young persons, both of whom he had led to assume – '

'Great Scott! Yes, I see! It was rather like putting in a ferret to start a rabbit.'

'The principle was much the same, sir. Anatole was out of the house and in Mrs Travers's service within half an hour of the receipt of the information that the young person was about to arrive. A volatile man, sir. Like so many of these Frenchmen.'

'Jeeves,' I said, 'this is genius of a high order.'

'It is very good of you to say so, sir.'

'What did Mr Little say about it?'

'He appeared gratified, sir.'

'To go into sordid figures, did he – '

'Yes, sir. Twenty pounds. Having been fortunate in his selections at Hurst Park on the previous Saturday.'

'My aunt told me that she – '

'Yes, sir. Most generous. Twenty-five pounds.'

'Good Lord, Jeeves! You've been coining the stuff!'

'I have added appreciably to my savings, yes, sir. Mrs Little was good enough to present me with ten pounds from finding her such a satisfactory housemaid. And then there was Mr Travers – '

'Uncle Thomas?'

'Yes, sir. He also behaved most handsomely, quite independently of Mrs Travers. Another twenty-five pounds. And Mr George Travers – '

'Don't tell me that Uncle George gave you something, too! What on earth for?'

'Well, really, sir, I do not quite understand myself. But I received a cheque for ten pounds from him. He seemed to be under the impression that I had been in some way responsible for your joining him at Harrogate, sir.'

I gaped at the fellow.

'Well, everybody seems to be doing it,' I said, 'so I suppose I had better make the thing unanimous. Here's a fiver.'

'Why, thank you, sir. This is extremely – '

'It won't seem much compared with these vast sums you've been acquiring.'

'Oh, I assure you, sir.'

'And I don't know why I'm giving it to you.'

'No, sir.'

'Still, there it is.'

'Thank you very much, sir.'

I got up.

'It's pretty late,' I said, 'but I think I'll dress and go out and have a bite somewhere. I feel like having a whirl of some kind after two weeks in Harrogate.'

'Yes, sir. I will unpack your clothes.'

'Oh, Jeeves,' I said, 'did Peabody and Simms send those soft silk shirts?'

'Yes, sir. I sent them back.'

'Sent them back?'

'Yes, sir.'

I eyed him for a moment. But I mean to say. I mean, what's the use?

'Oh, all right,' I said. 'Then lay out one of the gents' stiff-bosomed.'

'Very good, sir,' said Jeeves.

10

BERTIE CHANGES HIS MIND

It has happened so frequently in the past few years that young fellows starting in my profession have come to me for a word of advice, that I have found it convenient now to condense my system into a brief formula. 'Resource and Tact' – that is my motto. Tact, of course, has always been with me a *sine qua non*; while as for resource, I think I may say that I have usually contrived to show a certain modicum of what I might call *finesse* in handling those little *contretemps* which inevitably arise from time to time in the daily life of a gentleman's personal gentleman. I am reminded, by way of an instance, of the Episode of the School for Young Ladies near Brighton – an affair which, I think, may be said to have commenced one evening at the moment when I brought Mr Wooster his whisky and siphon and he addressed me with such remarkable petulance.

Not a little moody Mr Wooster had been for some days – far from his usual bright self. This I had attributed to the natural reaction from a slight attack of influenza from which he had been suffering; and, of course, took no notice, merely performing my duties as usual, until on the evening of which I speak he exhibited this remarkable petulance when I brought him his whisky and siphon.

'Oh, dash it, Jeeves!' he said, manifestly overwrought. 'I wish at least you'd put it on another table for a change.'

'Sir?' I said.

'Every night, dash it all,' proceeded Mr Wooster morosely, 'you come in at exactly the same old time with the same old tray and put it on the same old table. I'm fed up, I tell you. It's the bally monotony of it that makes it all seem so frightfully bally.'

I confess that his words filled me with a certain apprehension. I had heard gentlemen in whose employment I have been speak in very much the same way before, and it had almost invariably meant that they were contemplating matrimony. It disturbed me, therefore, I am free to admit, when Mr Wooster addressed me in this fashion. I had no desire to sever a connexion so pleasant in every respect as his and mine had been, and my experience is that when the wife comes in at the front door the valet of bachelor days goes out at the back.

'It's not your fault, of course,' went on Mr Wooster, regaining a certain degree of composure. 'I'm not blaming you. But, by Jove, I mean, you must acknowledge – I mean to say, I've been thinking pretty deeply these last few days, Jeeves, and I've come to the conclusion mine is an empty life. I'm lonely, Jeeves.'

'You have a great many friends, sir.'

'What's the good of friends?'

'Emerson,' I reminded him, 'says a friend may well be reckoned the masterpiece of Nature, sir.'

'Well, you can tell Emerson from me next time you see him that he's an ass.'

'Very good, sir.'

'What I want – Jeeves, have you seen that play called I-forget-its-dashed-name?'

'No, sir.'

'It's on at the What-d'you-call-it. I went last night. The hero's a chap who's buzzing along, you know, quite merry and bright, and suddenly a kid turns up and says she's his daughter. Left over from act one, you know – absolutely the first he'd heard of it. Well, of course, there's a bit of a fuss and they say to him "What-ho?" and he says, "Well, what about it?" and they say, "Well, *what* about it?" and he says, "Oh, all right, then, if that's the way you feel!" and he takes the kid and goes off with her out into the world together, you know. Well, what I'm driving at, Jeeves, is that I envied that chappie. Most awfully jolly little girl, you know, clinging to him trustingly and what not. Something to look after, if you know what I mean. Jeeves, I wish I had a daughter. I wonder what the procedure is?'

'Marriage is, I believe, considered the preliminary step, sir.'

'No, I mean about adopting a kid. You can adopt kids, you know, Jeeves. But what I want to know is how you start about it.'

'The process I should imagine, would be highly complicated and laborious, sir. It would cut into your spare time.'

'Well, I'll tell you what I could do, then. My sister will be back from India next week with her three little girls. I'll give up this flat and take a house and have them all to live with me. By Jove, Jeeves, I think that's rather a scheme, what? Prattle of childish voices, eh? Little feet pattering hither and thither, yes?'

I concealed my perturbation, but the effort to preserve my *sang-froid* tested my powers to the utmost. The course of action outlined by Mr Wooster meant the finish of our cosy bachelor establishment if it came into being as a practical proposition; and no doubt some men in my place would at this juncture have voiced their disapproval. I avoided this blunder.

'If you will pardon my saying so, sir,' I suggested, 'I think you are not quite yourself after your influenza. If I might express the opinion, what you require is a few days by the sea. Brighton is very handy, sir.'

'Are you suggesting that I'm talking through my hat?'

'By no means, sir. I merely advocate a short stay at Brighton as a physical recuperative.'

Mr Wooster considered.

'Well, I'm not sure you're not right,' he said at length. ' I *am* feeling more or less an onion. You might shove a few things in a suitcase and drive me down in the car tomorrow.'

'Very good, sir.'

'And when we get back I'll be in the pink and ready to tackle this pattering-feet wheeze.'

'Exactly, sir.'

Well, it was a respite, and I welcomed it. But I began to see that a crisis had arisen which would require adroit handling. Rarely had I observed Mr Wooster more set on a thing. Indeed, I could recall no such exhibition of determination on his part since the time when he had insisted, against my frank disapproval, on wearing purple socks. However, I had coped successfully with that outbreak, and I was by no means unsanguine that I should eventually be able to bring the present affair to a happy issue. Employers are like horses. They require managing. Some gentlemen's personal gentlemen have the knack of managing them, some have not. I, I am happy to say, have no cause for complaint.

For myself, I found our stay at Brighton highly enjoyable, and should have been willing to extend it, but Mr Wooster, still restless, wearied of the place by the end of two days, and on the third afternoon he instructed me to pack up and bring the car round to the hotel. We started back along the London road at about five on a fine summer's day, and had travelled perhaps two miles when I perceived in the road before us a young lady, gesticulating with no little animation. I applied the brake and brought the vehicle to a standstill.

'What,' inquired Mr Wooster, waking from a reverie, 'is the big thought at the back of this, Jeeves?'

'I observed a young lady endeavouring to attract our attention with signals a little way down the road, sir,' I explained. 'She is now making her way towards us.'

Mr Wooster peered.

'I see her. I expect she wants a lift, Jeeves.'

'That was the interpretation which I placed upon her actions, sir.'

'A jolly-looking kid,' said Mr Wooster. 'I wonder what she's doing, biffing about the high road.'

'She has the air to me, sir, of one who has been absenting herself without leave from her school, sir.'

'Hallo-allo-allo!' said Mr Wooster, as the child reached us. 'Do you want a lift?'

'Oh, I say, can you?' said the child, with marked pleasure.

'Where do you want to go?'

'There's a turning to the left about a mile farther on. If you'll put me down there, I'll walk the rest of the way. I say, thanks awfully. I've got a nail in my shoe.'

She climbed in at the back. A red-haired young person with a snub-nose and an extremely large grin. Her age, I should imagine, would be about twelve. She let down one of the spare seats, and knelt on it to facilitate conversation.

'I'm going to get into a frightful row,' she began. 'Miss Tomlinson will be perfectly furious.'

'No, really?' said Mr Wooster.

'It's a half-holiday, you know, and I sneaked away to Brighton, because I wanted to go on the pier and put pennies in the slot-machines. I thought I could get back in time so that nobody would notice I'd gone, but I got this nail in my shoe, and now there'll be a fearful row. Oh, well,' she said, with a philosophy which, I confess, I admired, 'it can't be helped. What's your car? A Sunbeam, isn't it? We've got a Wolseley at home.'

Mr Wooster was visibly perturbed. As I have indicated, he was at this time in a highly malleable frame of mind, tender-hearted to a degree where the young of the female sex was concerned. Her sad case touched him deeply.

'Oh, I say, this is rather rotten,' he observed. 'Isn't there anything to be done? I say, Jeeves, don't you think something could be done?'

'It was not my place to make the suggestion, sir,' I replied, 'but, as you yourself have brought the matter up, I fancy the trouble is susceptible of adjustment. I think it would be a legitimate subterfuge were you to inform the young lady's schoolmistress that you are an old friend of the young lady's father. In this case you could inform Miss Tomlinson that you had been passing the school and had seen the young lady at the gate and taken her for a drive. Miss Tomlinson's chagrin would no doubt in these circumstances be sensibly diminished if not altogether dispersed.'

'Well, you *are* a sportsman!' observed the young person, with considerable enthusiasm. And she proceeded to kiss me – in connexion with which I have only to say that I was sorry she had just been devouring some sticky species of sweetmeat.

'Jeeves, you've hit it!' said Mr Wooster. 'A sound, even fruity, scheme. I say, I suppose I'd better know your name and all that, if I'm a friend of your father's.'

'My name's Peggy Mainwaring, thanks awfully,' said the young person. 'And my father's Professor Mainwaring. He's written a lot of books. You'll be expected to know that.'

'Author of the well-known series of philosophical treatises, sir,' I ventured to interject. 'They have a great vogue, though, if the young lady will pardon my saying so, many of the Professor's opinions strike me personally as somewhat empirical. Shall I drive on to the school, sir?'

'Yes, carry on. I say, Jeeves, it's a rummy thing. Do you know, I've never been inside a girl's school in my life?'

'Indeed, sir?'

'Ought to be a dashed interesting experience, Jeeves, what?'

'I fancy that you may find it so, sir,' I said.

We drove on a matter of half a mile down a lane, and, directed by the young person, I turned in at the gates of a house of imposing dimensions, bringing the car to a halt at the front door. Mr Wooster and child entered, and presently a parlourmaid came out.

'You're to take the car round to the stables, please,' she said.

'Ah!' I said. 'Then everything is satisfactory, eh? Where has Mr Wooster gone?'

'Miss Peggy has taken him off to meet her friends. And cook says she hopes you'll step round to the kitchen later and have a cup of tea.'

'Inform her that I shall be delighted. Before I take the car to the stables, would it be possible for me to have a word with Miss Tomlinson?'

A moment later I was following her into the drawing-room.

Handsome but strong-minded – that was how I summed up Miss Tomlinson at first glance. In some ways she recalled to mind Mr Wooster's Aunt Agatha. She had the same penetrating gaze and that indefinable air of being reluctant to stand any nonsense.

'I fear I am possibly taking a liberty, madam,' I began, 'but I am hoping that you will allow me to say a word with respect to my employer. I fancy I am correct in supposing that Mr Wooster did not tell you a great deal about himself?'

'He told me nothing about himself, except that he was a friend of Professor Mainwaring.'

'He did not inform you, then, that he was *the* Mr Wooster?'

'*The* Mr Wooster?'

'Bertram Wooster, madam.'

I will say for Mr Wooster that, mentally negligible though he no doubt is, he has a name that suggests almost infinite possibilities. He sounds, if I may elucidate my meaning, like Someone – especially if you have just been informed that he is an intimate friend of so eminent a man as Professor Mainwaring. You might not, no doubt, be able to say offhand whether he was Bertram Wooster the novelist, or Bertram Wooster the founder of a new school of thought; but you would have an uneasy feeling that you were exposing you ignorance if you did not give the impression of familiarity with the name. Miss Tomlinson, as I had rather foreseen, nodded brightly.

'Oh, *Bertram* Wooster!' she said.

'He is an extremely retiring gentleman, madam, and would be the last to suggest it himself, but, knowing him as I do, I am sure that he would take it as a graceful compliment if you were to ask him to address the young ladies. He is an excellent extempore speaker.'

'A very good idea,' said Miss Tomlinson decidedly. 'I am very much obliged to you for suggesting it. I will certainly ask him to talk to the girls.'

'And should he make a pretence – through modesty – of not wishing – '

'I shall insist.'

'Thank you, madam. I am obliged. You will not mention my share in the matter? Mr Wooster might think I had exceeded my duties.'

I drove round to the stables and halted the car in the yard. As I got out, I looked at it somewhat intently. It was a good car, and appeared to be in excellent condition, but somehow I seemed to feel that something was going to go wrong with it – something serious – something that would not be able to be put right again for at least a couple of hours.

One gets these presentiments.

It may have been some half-hour later that Mr Wooster came into the stable-yard and I was leaning against the car enjoying a quiet cigarette.

'No, don't chuck it away, Jeeves,' he said, as I withdrew the cigarette from my mouth. 'As a matter of fact, I've come to touch you for a smoke. Got one to spare?'

'Only gaspers, I fear, sir.'

'They'll do,' responded Mr Wooster, with no little eagerness. I observed that his manner was a trifle fatigued and his eyes somewhat wild. 'It's a rummy thing, Jeeves, I seem to have lost my cigarette-case. Can't find it anywhere.'

'I am sorry to hear that, sir. It is not in the car.'

'No? Must have dropped it somewhere, then.' He drew at his gasper with relish. 'Jolly creatures, small girls, Jeeves,' he remarked, after a pause.

'Extremely so, sir.'

'Of course, I can imagine some fellows finding them a bit exhausting in – er – '

'*En masse*, sir?'

'That's the word. A bit exhausting *en masse*.'

'I must confess, sir, that that is how they used to strike me. In my younger days, at the outset of my career, sir, I was at one time page-boy in a school for young ladies.'

'No, really? I never knew that before. I say, Jeeves – er – did the – er – dear little souls *giggle* much in your day?'

'Practically without cessation, sir.'

'Makes a fellow feel a bit of an ass, what? I shouldn't wonder if they usedn't to stare at you from time to time, too, eh?'

'At the school where I was employed, sir, the young ladies had a regular game which they were accustomed to play when a male visitor arrived. They would stare fixedly at him and giggle, and there was a small prize for the one who made him blush first.'

'Oh, no, I say, Jeeves, not really?'

'Yes, sir. They derived real enjoyment from the pastime.'

'I'd no idea small girls were such demons.'

'More deadly than the male, sir.'

Mr Wooster passed a handkerchief over his brow.

'Well, we're going to have tea in a few minutes, Jeeves. I expect I shall feel better after tea.'

'We will hope so, sir.'

But I was by no means sanguine.

I had an agreeable tea in the kitchen. The buttered toast was good and the maids nice girls, though with little conversation. The parlourmaid, who joined us towards the end of the meal, after performing her duties in the school dining-room, reported that Mr Wooster was sticking it pluckily, but seemed feverish. I went back to the stable-yard, and I was just giving the car another look over when the young Mainwaring child appeared.

'Oh, I say,' she said, 'will you give this to Mr Wooster when you see him?' She held out Mr Wooster's cigarette-case. 'He must have dropped it somewhere. I say,' she proceeded, 'it's an awful lark. He's going to give a lecture to the school.'

'Indeed, miss?'

'We love it when there are lectures. We sit and stare at the poor dears, and try to make them dry up. There was a man last term who got hiccoughs. Do you think Mr Wooster will get hiccoughs?'

'We can but hope for the best, miss.'

'It would be such a lark, wouldn't it?'

'Highly enjoyable, miss.'

'Well, I must be getting back. I want to get a front seat.'

And she scampered off. An engaging child. Full of spirits.

She had hardly gone when there was an agitated noise, and round the corner came Mr Wooster. Perturbed. Deeply so.

'Jeeves!'

'Sir?'

'Start the car!'

'Sir?'

'I'm off!'

'Sir?'

Mr Wooster danced a few steps.

'Don't stand there saying "sir?" I tell you I'm off. Bally off! There's not a moment to waste. The situation's desperate. Dash it, Jeeves, do you know what's happened? The Tomlinson female has just sprung it on me that I'm expected to make a speech to the girls! Got to stand up there in front of the whole dashed collection and talk! I can just see myself! Get that car going, Jeeves, dash it all. A little speed, a little speed!'

'Impossible, I fear, sir. The car is out of order.'

Mr Wooster gaped at me. Very glassily he gaped.

'Out of order!'

'Yes, sir. Something is wrong. Trivial, perhaps, but possibly a matter of some little time to repair.' Mr Wooster being one of those easy going young gentlemen who will drive a car but never take the trouble to study its mechanism, I felt justified in becoming technical. 'I think it is the differential gear, sir. Either that or the exhaust.'

I am fond of Mr Wooster, and I admit I came very near to melting as I looked at his face. He was staring at me in a sort of dumb despair that would have touched anybody.

'Then I'm sunk! Or' – a slight gleam of hope flickered across his drawn features – 'do you think I could sneak out and leg it across country, Jeeves?'

'Too late, I fear, sir.' I indicated with a slight gesture the approaching figure of Miss Tomlinson, who was advancing with a serene determination in his immediate rear.

'Ah, there you are, Mr Wooster.'

He smiled a sickly smile.

'Yes – er – here I am!'

'We are all waiting for you in the large schoolroom.'

'But I say, look here,' said Mr Wooster, 'I – I don't know a bit what to talk about.'

'Why, anything, Mr Wooster. Anything that comes into your head. Be bright,' said Miss Tomlinson. 'Bright and amusing.'

'Oh, bright and amusing?'

'Possibly tell them a few entertaining stories. But, at the same time, do not neglect the graver note. Remember that my girls are on the threshold of life, and will be eager to hear something brave and helpful and stimulating – something which they can remember in after years. But, of course, you know the sort of thing, Mr Wooster. Come. The young people are waiting.'

I have spoken earlier of resource and the part it plays in the life of a gentleman's personal gentleman. It is a quality peculiarly necessary if one is to share in scenes not primarily designed for one's co-operation. So much that is interesting in life goes on apart behind closed doors that your gentleman's gentleman, if he is not to remain hopelessly behind the march of events, should exercise his wits in order to enable himself to be – if not a spectator – at least an auditor when there is anything of interest toward. I deprecate as vulgar and undignified the practice of listening at keyholes, but, without lowering myself to that, I have generally contrived to find a way.

In the present case it was simple. The large schoolroom was situated on the ground floor, with commodious french windows, which, as the weather was clement, remained open throughout the proceedings. By stationing myself behind a pillar on the porch or veranda which adjoined the room, I was enabled to see and hear all. It was an experience which I should be sorry to have missed. Mr Wooster, I may say at once, indubitably excelled himself.

Mr Wooster is a young gentleman with practically every desirable quality except one. I do not mean brains, for in an employer brains are not desirable. The quality to which I allude is hard to define, but perhaps I might call it the gift of dealing with the Unusual Situation. In the presence of the Unusual, Mr Wooster is too prone to smile weakly and allow his eyes to protrude. He lacks Presence. I have often wished that I had the power to bestow upon him some of the *savoir-faire* of a former employer of mine, Mr Montague-Todd, the well-known financier, now in the second year of his sentence. I have known men call upon Mr Todd with the express intention of horsewhipping him and go away half an hour later laughing heartily and smoking one of his cigars. To Mr Todd it would have been a child's play to speak a few impromptu words to a schoolroom full of young ladies; in fact, before he had finished he would probably have induced them to invest all their pocket-money in one of his numerous companies; but to Mr Wooster it was plainly an ordeal of the worst description. He gave one look at the young ladies, who were all staring at him in an extremely unwinking manner, then blinked and started to pick feebly at his coat-sleeve. His aspect reminded me of that of a bashful young man who, persuaded against his better judgement to go on the platform and assist a conjurer in his entertainment, suddenly discovers that rabbits and hard-boiled eggs are being taken out of the top of his head.

The proceedings opened with a short but graceful speech of introduction from Miss Tomlinson.

'Girls,' said Miss Tomlinson, 'some of you have already met Mr Wooster – Mr *Bertram* Wooster, and you all, I hope, know him by reputation.' Here, I regret to say, Mr Wooster gave a hideous, gurgling laugh, and, catching Miss Tomlinson's eye, turned a bright scarlet. Miss Tomlinson resumed: 'He has very kindly consented to say a few words to you before he leaves, and I am sure that you will all give him your very earnest attention. Now, please.'

She gave a spacious gesture with her right hand as she said the last two words, and Mr Wooster, apparently under the impression that they were addressed to him, cleared his throat and began to speak. But it appeared that her remark was directed to the young ladies, and was in the nature of a cue or signal, for she had no sooner spoken to them than the whole school rose to its feet in a body and burst into a species of chant, of which I am glad to say I remember the words, though the tune eludes me. The words ran as follows:

Many greetings to you!
Many greetings to you!
Many greetings, dear stranger,
Many greetings,
Many greetings,
Many greetings to you!
Many greetings to you!
To you!

Considerable latitude of choice was given to the singers in the matter of key, and there was little of what I might call co-operative effort.
Each child went on till she had reached the end, then stopped and
waited for the stragglers to come up. It was an unusual performance,
and I, personally, found it extremely exhilarating. It seemed to smite
Mr Wooster, however, like a blow. He recoiled a couple of steps and
flung up an arm defensively. Then the uproar died away, and an air
of expectancy fell upon the room. Miss Tomlinson directed a brightly
authoritative gaze upon Mr Wooster, and he blinked, gulped once or
twice, and tottered forward.

'Well, you know – ' he said.

Then it seemed to strike him that this opening lacked the proper
formal dignity.

'Ladies – '

A silvery peal of laughter from the front row stopped him again.

'Girls!' said Miss Tomlinson. She spoke in a low, soft voice, but
the effect was immediate. Perfect stillness instantly descended upon
all present. I am bound to say that, brief as my acquaintance with
Miss Tomlinson had been, I could recall few women I had admired
more. She had grip.

I fancy that Miss Tomlinson had gauged Mr Wooster's oratorical
capabilities pretty correctly by this time, and had come to the conclusion that little in the way of a stirring address was to be expected
from him.

'Perhaps,' she said, 'as it is getting late, and he has not very much
time to spare, Mr Wooster will just give you some little word of advice
which may be helpful to you in after-life, and then we will sing the
school song and disperse to our evening lessons.'

She looked at Mr Wooster. He passed a finger round the inside
of his collar.

'Advice? After-life? What? Well, I don't know – '

'Just some brief word of counsel, Mr Wooster,' said Miss Tomlinson
firmly.

'Oh, well – Well, yes – Well – ' It was painful to see Mr Wooster's brain endeavouring to work. 'Well, I'll tell you something that's often done *me* a bit of good, and it's a thing not many people know. My old Uncle Henry gave me the tip when I first came to London. "Never forget, my boy," he said, "that, if you stand outside Romano's in the Strand, you can see the clock on the wall of the Law Courts down in Fleet Street. Most people who don't know don't believe it's possible, because there are a couple of churches in the middle of the road, and you would think they would be in the way. But you can, and it's worth knowing. You can win a lot of money betting on it with fellows who haven't found it out." And, by Jove, he was perfectly right, and it's a thing to remember. Many a quid I – '

Miss Tomlinson gave a hard, dry cough, and he stopped in the middle of a sentence.

'Perhaps it will be better, Mr Wooster,' she said, in a cold, even voice, 'if you were to tell my girls some little story. What you say is, no doubt, extremely interesting, but perhaps a little – '

'Oh, ah, yes,' said Mr Wooster. 'Story? Story?' He appeared completely distraught, poor young gentleman. 'I wonder if you've heard the one about the stockbroker and the chorus-girl?'

'We will now sing the school song,' said Miss Tomlinson, rising like an iceberg.

I decided not to remain for the singing of the school song. It seemed probable to me that Mr Wooster would shortly be requiring the car, so I made my way back to the stable-yard, to be in readiness.

I had not long to wait. In a very few moments he appeared, tottering. Mr Wooster's is not one of those inscrutable faces which it is impossible to read. On the contrary, it is a limpid pool in which is mirrored each passing emotion. I could read it now like a book, and his first words were very much on the lines I had anticipated.

'Jeeves,' he said hoarsely, 'is that damned car mended yet?'

'Just this moment, sir. I have been working on it assiduously.'

'Then for heaven's sake, let's go!'

'But I understood that you were to address the young ladies, sir.'

'Oh, I've done that!' responded Mr Wooster, blinking twice with extraordinary rapidity. 'Yes, I've done that.'

'It was a success, I hope, sir?'

'Oh, yes. Oh, yes. Most extraordinarily successful. Went like a breeze. But – er – I think I may as well be going. No use outstaying one's welcome, what?'

'Assuredly not, sir.'

I had climbed into my seat and was about to start the engine, when voices made themselves heard; and at the first sound of them Mr Wooster sprang with almost incredible nimbleness into the tonneau, and when I glanced round he was on the floor covering himself with a rug. The last I saw of him was a pleading eye.

'Have you seen Mr Wooster, my man?'

Miss Tomlinson had entered the stable-yard, accompanied by a lady of, I should say, judging from her accent, French origin.

'No, madam.'

The French lady uttered some exclamation in her native tongue.

'Is anything wrong, madam?' I inquired.

Miss Tomlinson in normal mood was, I should be disposed to imagine, a lady who would not readily confide her troubles to the ear of a gentleman's gentleman, however sympathetic his aspect. That she did so now was sufficient indication of the depth to which she was stirred.

'Yes, there is! Mademoiselle has just found several of the girls smoking cigarettes in the shrubbery. When questioned, they stated that Mr Wooster had given them the horrid things.' She turned. 'He must be in the garden somewhere, or in the house. I think the man is out of his senses. Come, mademoiselle!'

It must have been about a minute later that Mr Wooster poked his head out of the rug like a tortoise.

'Jeeves!'

'Sir?'

'Get a move on! Start her up! Get going and *keep* going!'

I applied my foot to the self-starter.

'It would perhaps be safest to drive carefully until we are out of the school grounds, sir,' I said. 'I might run over one of the young ladies, sir.'

'Well, what's the objection to that?' demanded Mr Wooster with extraordinary bitterness.

'Or even Miss Tomlinson, sir.'

'Don't!' said Mr Wooster wistfully. 'You make my mouth water!'

'Jeeves,' said Mr Wooster, when I brought him his whisky and siphon one night about a week later, 'this is dashed jolly.'

'Sir?'

'Jolly. Cosy and pleasant, you know. I mean, looking at the clock and wondering if you're going to be late with the good old drinks, and then you coming in with the tray always on time, never a minute late, and shoving it down on the table and biffing off, and the next night coming in and shoving it down and biffing off, and the next night – I mean, gives you a sort of safe, restful feeling. Soothing! That's the word. Soothing!'

'Yes, sir. Oh, by the way, sir – '

'Well?'

'Have you succeeded in finding a suitable house yet, sir?'

'House? What do you mean, house?'

'I understood, sir, that it was your intention to give up the flat and take a house of sufficient size to enable you to have your sister, Mrs Scholfield, and her three young ladies to live with you.'

Mr Wooster shuddered strongly.

'That's off, Jeeves,' he said.

'Very good, sir,' I replied.

To be published February 2000
What Ho!
The best of P. G. Wodehouse
Introduced by Stephen Fry

Published to mark the 25th anniversary of his death, this is the first major selection of P. G. Wodehouse's work to appear for a generation. Introduced by Stephen Fry, it also includes previously unpublished work.

There are old favourites aplenty, but this selection provides the best overall celebration available in the pages of any book. The anthology has been compiled with enthusiastic support from the various P. G. Wodehouse societies around the world.

The P G Wodehouse Society (UK)

The P G Wodehouse Society (UK) was formed in 1997 and exists to promote the enjoyment of the works of the greatest humorist of the twentieth century.

The Society publishes a quarterly magazine, *Wooster Sauce*, which features articles, reviews, archive material and current news. It also publishes an occasional newsletter in the *By The Way* series which relates a single matter of Wodehousean interest. Members are rewarded in their second and subsequent years by receiving a specially produced text of a Wodehouse magazine story which has never been collected into one of his books.

A variety of Society events are arranged for members including regular meetings at a London club, a golf day, a cricket match, a Society dinner, and walks around Bertie Wooster's London. Meetings are also arranged in other parts of the country.

Membership enquiries   Membership of the Society is available to applicants from all parts of the world. The cost of a year's membership in 1999 was £15. Enquiries and requests for an application form should be addressed in writing to the Membership Secretary, Helen Murphy, at 16 Herbert Street, Plaistow, London E13 8BE, or write to the Editor of *Wooster Sauce*, Tony Ring, at 34 Longfield Road, Great Missenden, Bucks HP16 0EG.

You can visit their website at:
http://www.eclipse.co.uk/wodehouse